Wild Geese Calling

STEWART EDWARD WHITE

Wild Geese Calling

The Literary Guild of America, Inc.

NEW YORK   1940

PRINTED AT THE *Country Life Press*, GARDEN CITY, N. Y., U. S. A.

Foreword

LATTERLY a number of presumably well-meaning professional people have applied themselves to the job of "debunking" the pioneer. He is, say they, nothing but an escapist. He takes to the wilderness because he is unable to deal with civilization. So far from being the heroic figure of legend, he is basically nothing but a lazy bum.

The logic is perfect. To the professional mind civilized life is complex; wilderness life is simple. Simple things are easier to deal with than complex things. The man who avoids the difficult in favor of the easy is the lazy man, the inferior man. Q.E.D.

Many essays, and a few novels, have been comfortingly constructed on this logical framework. The only difficulty is that their authors know nothing at first hand of what they are talking about. Their facts are accurate, but the yardsticks of their evaluations do not apply. It is as though they tried to measure distance by the quart. Their criterion of judgment is their own world, the world they say these pioneers escaped from. They have only a theoretical conception of the world he escaped to. A personal venture might do them good. It would certainly modify their conception of what is "easy" and what

v

is "difficult"; and, I suspect, might—in their own case—reverse the direction of "escape"!

As a matter of fact these coddlers of their own inferiority complex —which is the basis of most wholesale debunking—do little more disservice to accurate estimation than the equally inexperienced glorifier, though the intentions of some of the latter are honorable. Reconstruction through imagination only is chancy at best. It is fatal to claim, even for heroes, deeds and endurances beyond the possibility of the human physical organism. One who has himself made hard marches knows it simply cannot be done. The inexperienced reader is miseducated—for a time—but subconsciously he is ripened thereby for the debunker. An excellent, and historically accurate, recent best-seller loses its solidity because its author, who has obviously never been really up against it in the wilderness, describes in detail an impossible endurance of privation and hardship. Even mild actual experience would have enabled him to gauge down to the possibilities.

They all miss the point. The pioneer movement is not a matter of surface characteristics. Fundamentally it is receptivity to a racial urge. The man who is attuned to that impulse must go. The man who is insulated from it must stay. Whether he is energetic or lazy; integrated or dissolute; able or inept has little to do with it. Those qualities will determine his career, but not the direction of it.

Contents

vii

CONTENTS

PART I
THE WOODS

CHAPTER I

BOY AND GIRL

IN THE remote hills of northern Scotland dwelt the clan of Murdock. Of it, one man, John, the generations bred to attunement, so that he, alone of all his people, felt and must respond to the first faint lift of the wave. Therefore, he took ship and sailed west, to better his condition, he thought and said, though his condition was well enough. He landed on the New England coast. There he hewed him a farm from the forest and married and prospered and in due time raised a family. He became a selectman, and afterwards an assemblyman in the legislature. He lived to a good old age, content with his establishment. This was in 1731.

To his numerous children he left a prosperous estate, but to one, Luke, he bequeathed, unknown to himself, also certain hormones, so that when, in the '70s, the rhythm again surged westward Luke was borne on it over the Alleghanies with Boone into the Dark and Bloody Ground, to better his condition, he said, though his condition, too, was well enough to satisfy his brothers.

From his broad acres and the mansion he had built in the foundation of what was to be an ancestral home, set out another Luke, his son, with his bride, in a covered wagon following Marcus Whitman toward Oregon; and to them, on the journey, and in the covered wagon, a son was born who was named Marcus in the leader's

3

honor. Luke did not follow Whitman all the way, however. In his case the wave spent itself near the Dalles, on the Columbia River; and there he took up land and raised a family. His wife died in the birth of the third boy John. When the latter had reached the age of twelve Luke was killed by a horse. He had bettered his condition precisely to the extent of three sod-and-wattle shacks, a well and windmill, a corral of greasewood, twenty horses and about six hundred cattle.

His personal accomplishment might have seemed small, but it was a far cry from the Highlands to the Dalles. And there was John.

John stayed with his two brothers on the ranch near the Dalles for three years after their father's death. Then he tied the roll of his slicker behind his cantle and rode away. He told the brothers he could not stand them any longer, bossing him around; but the impulse of his forthfaring was a deeper compulsion. Possibly the three felt this to be so, for at the last the parting was amicable. It was understood John's share in the patrimony would be intact for his return and claiming.

So he rode forth on his pinto, driving his remuda of four. His saddle, a rifle under his leg, a pair of slick-leather chaps, a pair of silver-inlaid spurs, a tall slender figure hard as steel wire, a contagious grin and a reckless flick of the eye were all his valuables. He had in addition a few perishables, such as his age of fifteen and the worn and bleached blue jeans he rode in and the modest blanket roll lashed athwart one of the spare horses.

He entertained no definite ideas, so he headed to the southeast, the ranch country of eastern Oregon. He got a job promptly enough, for he was well grown and strong, and men were scarce. He rode boundary and chopped wood and peeled potatoes occasionally, when Wong the cook was pressed, and shod horses and pitched alfalfa hay and strung wire fence and drove chuck wagon. To all these things he was accustomed. He made good at them and at the scores of other jobs that would naturally be shunted toward a willing and handy boy of fifteen. Jim Carston wanted to keep him and offered him man's wages to stay. But something stronger than his liking for

Jim Carston was lifting within him. He tied the roll of his slicker behind his cantle, waved his old Stetson, flashed his gay smile and rode away. He was richer by six months, by some added knowledge of how to do things, some friendly good wishes and a rather ancient forty-five-caliber frontier-model Colt revolver, astoundingly thrust upon him by Wong at the moment of departure. There was also the matter of a few dollars of wages.

For the next ten years John ranged the great basin between the Rockies and the Cascades, seeking, he told himself, to better his condition. He punched cattle as a cowboy; he peeled cayuses as a bronco buster; he acted as sportsmen's guide in the game country; he prospected with the desert rats, but half-heartedly, for this type of mania quickly wore thin for him; he took a look at the southern mines and shot deer for their commissary, which was well enough, for he liked hunting; he rode as express messenger atop a Concord coach with a sawed-off shotgun across his knees. He was good at all these things. But always, just as his condition looked well toward settled betterment, he rode on. Curiously enough the job that held him longest would seem to have the least adventurous appeal of the lot. In western Washington he stayed for almost a year on a wheat farm. Here was something new to him—and to the country, for that matter. Its owner had progressive ideas and a little capital, and he had brought in the first harvesting machinery. John discovered an enormous aptitude for machinery. It fascinated him. He loved to run it and figure it out and repair it, make it obey. But it could not hold him.

"Reckon I'm just a bum, a rolling stone," he laughed and rode away. Sometimes, on rare occasions, when he took more serious stock of himself, his conscience reproached him. Perhaps he *was* a bum, just a natural hobo. He would settle down. But deep within him he knew he would not settle down. He had to find something first.

In the spring of 1895 he imagined he had found it, or rather them, for the objects of his search must, it seemed, be two—a woman and a place in work that suited his whole desire. He had no ideals as to the one, or definite ideas as to the other, but he was certain he would know them when he saw them.

This proved to be the case. Riding early one morning into Siler's Bend, near the Deschutes, he came upon the woman, seated under a cottonwood tree outside the little settlement. This was Sarah Slocum, spinster and orphan: age twenty, schoolteacher, native of Borland, which is west of the Cascades, reduced to penury by the decease of her father after a disastrous law suit, lineal descendant of Joshua Slocum, trader, immigrant of '51, and therefore also possibly harboring in her life essence the genes and hormones of attunement to the racial urge of which we write. Of these statistics John Murdock remained ignorant until much later. More pressing matters claimed his enterprise; and so masterfully did he press them, and perhaps so predestined were they to fulfillment, that he and the schoolteacher rode out from Siler's Bend that very afternoon as man and wife.

"Where are we going?" she asked.

He waved his hand toward the west.

"A place I been saving. I always meant to camp there, but I never got around to it. Now I know why." The copper bronze of his face deepened. He stared straight ahead. "There's a river," he chose his words at first a little awkwardly, "it comes out from underground full growed. Worth seeing. There's a lot of big ferns and those wide-leaf things that sort of hide the hole it comes out from, and all of a sudden there she is, wide and cold and full growed, a regular river, just like that! It's in a pine park, pretty high up in the foothills, so it's cool. And there's a lot of green feed and flowers and those birds that sing sort of solemn and slow, like bells. Hi you, Sukey! Git back there!" He slapped his quirt against heavy leather in admonition of the single pack horse. "There's trout there, too," he added.

They came to the park late in the afternoon. The tall pines stood about it, consulting in whispers. Azaleas and rhododendrons bordered the meadow. The stream was wide and shallow, with small deep pools behind boulders and rims of bracken and saxifrage and tufts of them here and there in the current, like little islands. The horses must be unpacked and off-saddled and belled and hobbled. John did this and set the saddles in a row along a brown log, as though it were a horse's back, and threw across them the cinches and stirrups and then spread on top the coronas and the saddle blankets, after the cowboy's neat fashion; after which he took the ax and departed. He made no comments on these activities; nor did he offer any suggestions to Sarah; but this omission was only, the latter sensed, because he assumed she must know what to do. Except in theory this was not the case. She emptied the kyacks of their contents and surveyed the provisions and utensils. Then she gathered some dry sticks and fallen rubbish for a fire and began to arrange them at the base of a boulder. She looked up at the sound of John Murdock's laugh.

His back and shoulders were piled high with fir-balsam fronds. He looked like a walking green haystack.

"Aiming to smoke out a ground hog?" said John. He caught the expression in her eyes. "Reckon this is all new to you." Mysteriously the green haystack swung from his shoulders to the ground and stood upright. John stretched his arms. "This party is on me," said he. "You just sit and watch."

"I'm so useless," she lamented.

"Think so?" said John. That was all he said; but something in his manner of saying comforted her. She was content.

She arose to her feet.

"How in the world . . . ?" She was curious about the fir-balsam fronds and their inexplicable cohesion and uprightness. Then she saw just the tip of the ax handle protruding from the center of the mass.

"Just lay them crisscross across the blade and keep on piling them up," said John.

"But what holds them together? Why don't they fall off?" she marveled.

"They just hold themselves. They don't fall off." He was tickled at her amazement over this simple commonplace. "That's our bed. Where 'd you wish it?"

"I—I don't know." Curiously the little park seemed to fall very still. The faint sweet tinkle of the horse bell and the sigh of wind high in the trees were only an embroidery on the texture of waiting silence. She turned her head slowly and looked wide eyed into his face, as though she were seeing it for the first time.

"There's blankets enough for us both, if you want it that way." His voice was gentle.

"No," said she steadily.

He took her in his arms. Strangely, this was their first kiss. Events had, with them, moved too rapidly: the usual demonstrations were but just catching up. She raised her face simply and confidently. Their lips touched. She closed her eyes. And abruptly they were swept away, clinging to one another.

After a time they drew apart. John Murdock was bewildered and, at that moment, ashamed of himself. In John's world girls were either "nice" or "easy." This was not the way a man felt toward a "nice" girl. He had had his women here and there in the natural course of adventure; and he had learned to spot the "easy" ones; and the minute you found out they were "easy" the game was wide open, and you treated them in any way they would let you treat them. Some went farther than others, but the idea was the same, and they all played back. His desire had caught him unaware: he had yielded blindly to its impulsion. And this girl he had brought with him from Siler's Bend to the park under the Cascades had played back. A little belatedly, perhaps, but ardently. Her lips had widened to the passion in his kiss, her body had met eagerly the pressure of his. What had he done! He stared at her appalled.

But she did not perceive his panic; nor would she have understood it.

"I did not know it was so beautiful to love," she breathed.

Her eyes were starry: and John again was ashamed—ashamed of that in him which had caused his first shame. And he felt suddenly very humble, and a little reverent, which was quite a new feeling for John Murdock.

They camped together for two magic, ecstatic weeks. Their life was simple enough. Sarah Murdock's trousseau consisted of just what she had, which had not overburdened Sukey when they left Siler's Bend. The groom's presents to the bride were two: a pair of soft-leather, high-heeled short boots, stitched in a bright pattern; and a light stock saddle, a Visalia tree with silver conchas, the most expensive in town.

They rarely stirred outside the tiny park. The enclosure of its great trees contained an all-sufficing world. There is much to be said for after-marriage courtship. John could not get used to the idea. His eyes followed her as she moved about.

"Dog *gone!*" he marveled, "it's always seemed kind of wonderful to me to own a live thing like a horse, but to own a *woman*—all by myself . . ."

They caught their trout from behind the boulders, but the pool deepest and farthest downstream they kept for bathing. John had learned to swim in the Columbia, but Sally—she could not long remain Sarah—could only splash.

"Where would I learn to swim at Borland!" she cried indignantly. "You must teach me."

She was from the first serenely unself-conscious. John secretly marveled and puzzled over the mystery of women, whose modesty seems to be an affair of the moment's fashion, and whose giving carries whole-heartedly with it all the minor implications. In face of her matter-of-fact acceptance John actually felt an uneasy guilt that he could not so carelessly let fall tradition.

The afternoons passed quickly, for the ranges towered high to the west, and the sun must early touch their rims. From beneath the trees the shadows lengthened slowly, inch by inch. The shadows had chill fingers. They must dress, set about the necessary affairs of subsistence, postponed in deference to the day. It was the still time. The breeze had fallen. The pines held themselves straight and without movement in a compactness of silence. The birds drowsed. Even the heedless patter of the river seemed to have fallen in tone to a smooth, low muttering. And soon it was night.

One morning Sally was awakened by a touch on her shoulder. She opened her eyes sleepily and sat up in surprise and a little alarm. John was dressed and afoot. The hour was gray, the air chill, the tips of the pines as yet untouched by dawn.

"Time's up," said John briefly.

Sally had difficulty understanding. Yesterday had been like all the other yesterdays of this golden time. Now, it seemed, they had ended, suddenly, like that!

"We've got just about six days' grub left," John was telling her. "Way I figure it, that ought to get us quite a ways. Then I can rustle a job. Gosh," he answered Sally, "got to go sometime. Can't stay here forever!"

He grinned at her boyishly when she pleaded for another week, another day—it wouldn't take long to ride down to Siler's for more groceries—— "Broke," he interrupted. "No dinero." His eyes wrinkled humorously as he caught her dismay. "Don't worry, old lady," said he, "we'll eat."

"I'm not worrying!" she retorted indignantly.

John had, it seemed, thought it all out. They were going north, into Washington State. Why there? Dunno: hunch: never been there. Anyway John was sick of twisting cows and wrangling tenderfeet and pounding alkali. And anyway that's no life for a woman, and——

"Well, what is there different up in Washington State?" she wanted to know.

"It's green," said John. "I reckon this place has got me soft."

Small indignations were belatedly stirring in Sally. John had no right—he hadn't—he'd thought this all out and never said a word! And he was laughing at her! Her sense of bafflement focused on an irrelevancy.

"And you paid ninety-five dollars for *that!*" she cried.

He surveyed the beautiful silver-mounted saddle with complacency. "Sure! That's why we're broke," said he easily.

Then Sally noticed that the fire blazed, the breakfast was cooked: that the horses were up and tied to small trees: that, save for the saddling and packing, all was ready for departure.

"Come on!" cried John. "Rise and shine! We're hitting the trail!"

He was vibrating, exultant. He had no backward glances for what was ended. He lifted to the future, the unknown.

Sally threw aside the blankets. She was bewildered, hurt, a little sullen. He might have consulted her. He might at least have talked it over! To spring it like this! And he seemed so wholly oblivious. She had been treated as a child! It was not fair! Sally really knew nothing of men.

The grub supply saw them well up along the mountains toward Seattle. They might have gone farther had John any money with which to buy horse feed. As it was, he must graze them. He rejected Sally's suggestion that a trade-in of some of their superfluously fancy equipment—like the Visalia saddle—would put them in funds. He refused likewise to break the journey for any small-change jobs.

"Just delay us getting there," said he.

"Getting where?" asked Sally.

"Where we're going."

"Where's that?"

"I don't know." John laughed. He sobered a little at her expression. "No, I'm not fooling, honey. It's a hunch. A real hunch has never failed me yet. I always play 'em."

"That's just superstition."

"Oh, sure! Sure!"

A futile exasperation leaped within Sally at the facility of this concession. John invariably yielded to her opinions and rarely acted in accordance. As though opinion was not worth bothering about. He turned in his saddle to grin at her, and something leaped between them, something alive and warm and tender, as palpably real a substance as—as a hunch, flashed Sally humorously to herself and felt better.

On the sixth day they struck a wagon road that led up the mountain and followed it and so came at sundown to a sawmill and a dozen or so buildings of various sizes fashioned crudely from rough, unpainted lumber. The tall forest trees crowded close. Through them was a slant of sun. A pungency of dry pine needles and fresh lumber and old sawdust and hot tarweed hung in the air. No one was in sight. They might have thought the place deserted were it not for a clatter of dishes from one of the larger buildings.

John pulled up, hooked his leg over the pommel. Sally moved alongside him. She looked curiously about her, then up into John's face. His eyes were veiled. He was not seeing. He seemed to Sally curiously withdrawn. Only his nostrils dilated, quivering delicately as a wild beast tests the breeze for subtleties of danger or peace. Illogically Sally's paltry complacencies of education felt small. Here was a mysterious John to which humbly she must aspire. She did not know John. There were so many of him!

"Well, this is it!" John was saying. In his voice was an undertone of fulfillment.

CHAPTER II

THE SHANTY

HERE, it would seem, John Murdock had found the second element of completion. He had now the woman and the sufficing outlet for his abilities and energies. He had arrived at the place where, like his forebears, he could give over following the restlessness in his blood, could settle down and in real fact better his condition.

For accomplishing the latter was here real opportunity. John's nature inclined toward the stretch of his muscles in the vigorous out of doors, toward a varied practical application of his excellent brains, and toward the intricacies of mechanics. Here was wide outlet for all three. To be sure, the outfit was small, but it did things in the then modern manner. Bull Kirby drove hard and took no nonsense, nor fraternized with anybody; but he was skilled at placing men where they belonged. He started John as wood monkey for the donkey engine and apparently paid him no more attention. But within a week he transferred him to the mill.

"How much do you know about machinery, anyway?" he asked.

"Not much. Just what I picked up here and there," said John. "I like it," he added.

Bull Kirby grunted. "Well, you let it alone until you do."

13

John flushed. So Bull had caught him running the donkey! A wood monkey has no business fooling with the donkey. But Bull had not called him down: he had put him in the mill.

The outfit was a modest one. It had just one circular saw and a trimmer. Old Paddock, with the assistance of a gangling moron of sixteen, ran the engine room. John and the others constituted the floor crew. Charley Matson was sawyer, in the upper dimness, silent, detached, remote, in the calm weary patience of a god, high on his carriage, his hands resting on the levers, until John and the others had rolled the log in place. It was dim and wide and cool in the mill. The great saw, revolving so rapidly that it seemed to be standing still, hummed in expectancy. Strange black-hooked hands shot up from the floor, hovered hesitantly above the prostrate log, gripped it in savage decision, half turned it one way, quarter turned it the other, altered its position yet a few inches more. They loosed their grasp, hovered for a moment as though to be sure of their satisfaction, then swiftly, silently vanished down into the limbo whence they had been evoked. Of these strange and formidable creatures Charley was the overlord through the little levers beneath his hand.

And then abruptly it seemed that half of the floor leaped without warning into full swift motion, carrying the log and, with it, Charley on his elevated platform. And the humming peace of the dimness was shattered by the saw's wild shriek of exultance, and above the patient brown back of the log curved high a sawdust plume of triumph. As abruptly these things ceased. With a faint plop the detached slab fell on the moving rollers and was carried away. Like a ghost in silence the carriage shot back to position.

Next to Bull Kirby, Charley Matson was the most important man on the hill. His judgment, and his command of the strange familiars that his touch summoned, determined how much and how little could be made of each individual cut; whether he should "set" for a two-inch clear or a two-by-four or a six-by-six or just the one-inch mill run. Each run of the carriage on which he stood meant a new calculation, a new decision. A single uncertainty of touch or judgment could spoil the work of many men. He only was responsible.

Ordinarily Charley would have had no other duties. But here, largely of his own choice, and after the day's mill run was over, he saw to the comfort and well-being of his faithful djinns and daemons. He inspected and lubricated and tested the complicated mechanics that activated them; he filed and set the saws. Thus John was able to come into contact with him. And that is why, a month or so later, Charley Matson did a most unusual thing in expostulating to Bull Kirby when the latter ordered John out of the mill and into the woods.

"He'll make a good mill man, give him time. He might even," Charley went to the length of conceding, "make a sawyer. He's a born mechanic."

Bull Kirby grunted. He would not have explained himself to anybody else, but Charley was unique.

"I've a notion he may be a born lumberman," he growled. "Only way to know is to find out."

So John moved outdoors. It was not much of a mill; but it had seemed so to him. Likewise it was not much of a woods layout. They felled the trees by saw and by kerfs chopped from spring boards. They swamped and crosscut by hand. They yanked the logs out to arterial slideways either with horses or donkey engines, according to circumstances. The slideways converged on the mill, and the logs were slid along them by a wire cable hauled over a drum and returned, through blocks suspended to poles planted alongside the slideway, to the big he-donkey that furnished the power. At the mill the logs were sawed about as fast as they could be delivered. The fresh lumber was at once freighted down the mountain in wagons drawn by six, eight, ten mules, and the driver sitting asaddle of one of them, dim in the dust. There were no skidways, no drying yards, no flumes, no booming ponds, few of the customary facilities even of that time. But its lacks measured the strength of its challenge.

The men of the various crews slept in a two-story dormitory and ate at three oilcloth-covered tables running the full length of the cookhouse. Bull Kirby had a dog kennel of his own containing a bunk, a table and two chairs. He washed outside in a tin basin.

Charley Matson, the sawyer, Hugh Barkley, the bookkeeper, who also kept the company store, and old man Paddock, the engineer, shared a four-room shanty with a veranda, one of the houses built originally as married quarters. Of these there were half a dozen standing empty; and others, such as the scaler and the stable boss, would have rated separate quarters had they not preferred the vivacity of the bunk house. Indeed only one, other than the Murdocks', was occupied. Bull Kirby did not favor women about camp. Bull's experience with women was that they were pleasant but troublous. He had hired Mel Carter without knowing about Clara and had then kept him because he never went back on his word. Bull had no excuse of ignorance in the case of Murdock: a woman obviously accompanied him, and a damn good-looking one, too. Caught him after supper when he felt good natured.

John and Sally were given free pick of the empty shanties. These were all exactly alike: narrow veranda, three rooms in an L so a rectangular roof would cover the whole, rough lumber throughout except for the floors, which were dressed smooth; large room backing the veranda, two smaller rooms filling the L, one with a stovepipe hole as kitchen, one with a wide slatted bunk, built in, as sleeping quarters; off the kitchen an open lean-to with a rack at one end for the wood pile and a low wide shelf at the other for water pail, wash basin, laundry. Of furnishing there was little, and that home made.

To John there was not much choice, but Sally showed no hesitation. Her selection stood the last in the row, and an outcropping rock ledge had forced it just around the curve of the meadow so that it was to some degree separate. John was a little doubtful.

"Won't be so funny when the rain sets in," he pointed out. "Long way to the cookhouse, and the mud 'll be up to your neck."

"You don't think for a minute we're going to eat at the cookhouse!" cried Sally.

"Why—everybody else does."

"If," stated Sally with decision, "we're going to have a house of our own it's going to be home, and we're going to *live* in it."

"This lumber jackin' is hard work," he objected. "I got to have good cooking to keep up my strength."

"Well—of all the——" She caught on John's face the wooden expression she had begun to suspect. She made a rush at him which he dodged.

"Be good girl," he warned. "Papa spank!"

They came to this new home of theirs from opposite directions but with equal zest. To John it looked good and almost adequate just as it was. In the course of his wandering life John had learned to make himself comfortable, even luxurious, as he saw it, in many an old sod hut or line shack a heap smaller and dirtier and more scantily equipped than this. Needed a drastic cleaning, of course, it hadn't been occupied for a long time. The rusty old iron stove in the kitchen looked all right. He'd swipe a stove pipe from one of the other empty houses, and maybe a few more chairs and things; if not, he could knock them together out of hours. The camping outfit had most necessities for cooking and such. Might be a few doodads to get. A coal-oil lamp would be nice. Nice to get a mattress for the bunk, if they had any at the store. If not, John could get a donkey's breakfast from the stable boss and fix things up. At this point John's imagination ran off the deep end. They were all comfortably settled.

"Anything you need you can get at the company store," he told Sally, "or they'll order it for you. They'll charge it against wages." His mind ran beyond these immediate considerations to concern itself with Sally. Suddenly he was troubled about Sally.

"Going to be kind of tough here for you, I'm afraid," said he. "I don't know what you'll find to do. I could keep Pronto up. You might ride. How do you like Mis' Carter? Looks like a sort of nice little thing. Hope you and her—I have my job, of course, but you——"

He stopped. Sally stood squarely before him, her clenched hands on her hips.

"What's the matter?" he interrupted himself.

"Of all the stupid, conceited speeches I ever listened to!" she

cried. "You and your job! Just because you've camped out like a
Siwash all your life! Look at this!" She reached up to seize his shoulders and slowly revolved him in a complete circle. "Well? Do you
think I am going to live in *this?* Do you think I am going to let us
live in this? Don't you think we're going to have a *home,* a real
home? And don't you think it's a job, a real full-time job, to make
this into a home? No, you don't. You don't even know what a home
is. It's *us;* us and something else. And that something else is my
job. Dull! Why, I don't believe I'm going to have enough time!"
She gave his shoulders a little shake and dropped her hands. "You
poor goop!" she laughed in his face. She stood on tiptoe to bestow
a butterfly kiss. "You *do* need gentling! And that's another full-time
job!" she added.

Sally bought sparingly and improvised lavishly, measuring carefully her purchases against John's wages. Hugh Barkley, the bookkeeper and storekeeper, proved a real help. He had suggestions
to make out of his knowledge of stocks and prices, and he sent
to the city for things he did not keep, to be brought up by the
lumber wagons returning empty, and he charged against Sally at
the wholesale-cost price. Barkley examined her sternly over the
tops of his glasses when she expressed doubt of this arrangement.

"We don't keep it in stock, so there's no reason we should charge
a profit on it," said he.

The logic of this was obscure, but Sally accepted it with a thankful murmur. Her conscience was easily quieted on sixty dollars a
month.

But slowly the bare shack was taking on character. The stained
deal table had a top of blue-squared oilcloth. Sally's half-dozen
books she had packed from Siler's Bend made as brave a show as
they could on a shelf above the table. The shelf was Sally's most
heroic effort, for which she had appropriated the piece of dressed
lumber and borrowed the tools. John laughed at it and made it
over again. Spurred by derision, Sally next day put up another shelf,
a long shelf high up, taking enormous pains and pounding cruelly

her thumb. She held the thumb behind her while John that evening, his head appraisingly on one side, made his opinion.

"That's a good job, Sally," he had paid the compliment of a real inspection. "Plumb and true. Only thing you might do yet is to countersink the nails."

"How do you do that?" asked Sally. She glowed within. She could not have stood it if John had tried to be funny.

"Where's your hammer, and a big nail—a good big one."

He showed her, holding the square end of the old-fashioned cut spike against the head of the nail and tapping the spike until the nail was well countersunk below the surface of the wood. "Now with a little putty and a piece of sandpaper and maybe some wood stain . . ." John was getting interested. "Here, you try it." So he noticed the bruised thumb. "You got enough things to do without bunging yourself all up!" he cried indignantly. "If you got any more things to make, you leave 'em for me."

"But you've been working so hard all day," objected Sally.

"Shucks," John was scornful, "this ain't work, it's fun. What else you want done?"

Sally might do with another shelf or so in the kitchen. She showed John the place.

"What you want there is a cupboard," decided John. "If I had a T-square and chisel and plane—say, where'd you dig up these tools, anyway?"

"Mr Barkley loaned them to me."

"Well, you see if you can get him to let you have some more. I'll pick up some good scrap iron at the mill."

They returned to the main room, where John again admired the shelf. He reached up to run his hand over it, testing the surface dressing.

"Say," he seemed surprised, "what you tack on this edging for? Expecting an earthquake?"

Sally hesitated.

"Well, I was going to have them all up, for a surprise. What do you mean, coming home so early? But come here."

She led the way to the bedroom and threw back the old camp tarpaulin from a corner. It had concealed a set of blue and white china, a wonderful set. There were plates of three sizes and cups and saucers and four platters, and all were quaintly patterned alike with a willow tree and an arched bridge across a pond and a Chinaman about to cross the bridge and two great birds, one in the sky and one on the ground. She watched John with the pride of shining eyes.

John whistled. He was gratifyingly impressed. "Where in blazes did them come from?"

"The store. See!" Sally breathlessly scooped up a half dozen of the largest plates and flitted back to the large room. John, following, stopped in the doorway. Sally was standing tiptoe to reach the shelf, placing the plates one by one on edge, side by side, behind its shallow rails of edging. She could just make it, precariously. Sally looked mighty pretty that way, reaching up, thought John, and her dress straining against her that-away and her sleeves falling back. She had nice round arms. And when she looked over her shoulder at him, her cheeks all pink from reaching up . . .

"You come here!" ordered John peremptorily.

She dropped to her heels and turned, a little startled by his tone.

"Come here!" he repeated. "Now turn round. Just as I thought," said he; "funny I never noticed it before!"

She struggled to face him, but he held her tight.

"What are you talking about, you idiot!"

"Why," said he, "standin' straight and easy my chin is just an easy fit for the top of your head." He leisurely disengaged one arm and tilted her chin. "I bet that's so as to make it handy to kiss up-side down. Say," said he after the success of this experiment, "did anybody ever tell you that you're mighty cute?"

Laughing, she twisted to free herself. "Did anybody ever tell you that you're crazy? Let me go!"

"Nice crazy?" He squeezed her tighter. "Nice crazy?" he insisted. After a moment she nodded. "All right." He opened his arms.

"You're terrible," she said without conviction. "There, don't you think that looks nice? Help me put up the rest of them."

"They look fine," John agreed. They stepped back together when the row was completed.

"As soon as I can get some hooks we'll hang the cups underneath. See, they just match the oilcloth."

"Fine," repeated John. "Do we eat off them, or are they just pictures?"

"Of course we eat off them!"

"Well," said John placidly, "reckon then I'll have to build you a stepladder."

Sally's eyes flashed, but she made no retort. Evidently what was bothering her had not yet occurred to John. She must justify her conscience.

"I got the whole set for five ninety-eight," she said in a small voice.

"What!" cried John, aroused.

"I know it's extravagant, and we need so many things, and there's all the provisions to get yet, and——" The words poured from her with a rush.

But, it appeared, that was not John's emotion.

"You mean to say all that for six dollars?" He shook his head. "Somebody's crazy. Sure you understood right?"

"I know it sounds absurd," she hurried on breathlessly, "but Mr Barkley said we might just as well have it. It's no use to them. It was meant to sell to married hands, and then Mr Kirby decided not to have any more married hands, and they can't use it in the cookhouse, and they've had it for years, and Mr Barkley says he couldn't get much of anything for it if he sent it back——"

"Mr Barkley, Mr Barkley, Mr Barkley," John cut in. "Look here, young woman, I'm a nice easygoing cuss, and I like to live soft and easy and magnificent, but there's one thing I draw the line at." He eyed her severely. "I won't be no kept man."

She stared at him. And suddenly John threw himself into a chair and laughed and laughed and laughed. He tried to recover himself, dashed the tears from his eyes, was again overcome.

"If you could only see your face!" he gasped.

But Sally stood coldly waiting.

"I shall take the china back tomorrow," she told him when he had sobered.

Instantly John was on his feet. He tried to take her in his arms. She was rigid.

"Why, honey!" he cried all contrition, "you didn't think for one minute I meant—— Why, honey, that funny little bald-headed coot—— Of course I was fooling."

She shook her head obstinately. The plates were going back, the borrowed tools were going back, John could do his own buying at the store hereafter. She failed to see any joke in it. She was wholly unreasonable. She would not listen to John. And finally John began to warm a little into anger. Maybe it was a fool thing to say, he fumed to himself, but doggone it, he hadn't meant anything, and she ought to have sense enough to see it. He wanted to shake her into some sense. Damn the blue china! For one perilous moment John was tempted to smash the blue china. Luckily that impulse passed. He was bewildered, disillusioned, resentful.

Then his eyes widened, and his mouth dropped. Sally was laughing. She laughed and laughed and laughed.

"You goop!" she choked at last. " 'That funny little bald-headed coot!' " she quoted. "But he's nice," she added in justice. She chortled again at John's open mouth. He closed it, but he still looked crest-fallen.

"Keno!" he gave in. Then he rallied. "But you are kind of cute," said he.

Beside the blue plates Sally indulged also in another luxury. She bought some cheap gay-striped material and made curtains for the windows. Except for these two things, her purchases she kept within the bare necessities—and the sixty dollars a month. This was a matter of close figuring. Sixty dollars is not a great sum. The first month she must run over a little, but Barkley said that would be all right. It turned out there was a small rebate allowance if one did not eat at the cookhouse. That was a welcome help.

By now John had begun to be genuinely interested in the house.

"Well, what's new?" was his first greeting when he returned from work. He must be shown the day's accomplishment before he would begin to clean up. He marveled gratifyingly over the simplest things. "Well now, what do you know! I'd never have thought of that!" Particularly did he admire the bright curtains, once they were in place. Sally had mentioned curtains. What for curtains, John wanted to know. Keep people from looking in, for one thing. Nobody, pointed out John, was going to climb way out in the middle of that wet meadow just to look in. He did not urge this as an objection, however, merely as the reasonable point of view. If Sally wanted curtains that was all right. When he saw them, in place, he was vastly pleased and surprised. John had thought of curtains as things that wound up on a spring roller. These were pretty!

But Sally would not permit him to linger too long. The table was set. "I've got a good dinner, and I don't intend to let you spoil it," said she.

At the cookhouse the triangle had already rung, and the men were filing in. They looked scrubbed and clean. As a matter of fact, each had merely plunged over-ears into the basin so his head was slick and shining. If John had been eating at the cookhouse he would have been already at table.

"I've been working hard, honey, I'm hungry," he expostulated, "and honest, I'm perfectly clean—didn't even sweat my shirt! See!"

"If you didn't work hard enough to sweat your shirt you can't be as hungry as all that," said Sally with inexorable logic. "Shoo! Your clean shirt is all laid out. And don't dawdle; we've got a pot roast."

"Doggone schoolma'am!" accused John.

Sally chuckled. "Well, don't act like a small boy."

John retired in the direction of the lean-to back of the kitchen. Here was another of Sally's simple contrivances. Somewhere she had found an old garden watering pot with which one could sprinkle oneself in a kind of shower. John would never have thought of that. His idea of a bath was to set the wash tub in the middle of the floor and go to it. As that involved heating of water on the stove, considerable contortion, a liberal slopping over and a subsequent mopping up, it was a rite likely to be somewhat spaced in time. Like most out-of-door males John had a healthy instinct for cleanliness but was not bigoted on the subject. To be taken as needed. Sally's incomprehensible philosophy was more rigid. Whether needed or not, seemed to be her idea.

The flower-pot idea was ingenious, John admitted, but could be improved. Too much, said John, like pulling your own tooth. Again like most out-of-door men, he had a distaste for cold water. Don't mind jumping in all over, said John, but doggone this slow trickling! Now, if you hung up the flower pot and hitched a string to the end of the spout, then you'd get a steady shower just by pulling the string. He fell into a brown study.

"No, I got a better scheme," said he at last. "I'll rig you up, first chance I get."

The next Sunday he set about it. He refused to divulge his plan.

"You keep me from my work," she complained. "I've got to stay out here and see what you are up to."

The preliminaries, however, were sufficiently obvious. John was a deft handy man. Adjoining the lean-to, overlooking the meadow, he knocked together the framework of a small platform. This he floored with narrow slats set apart so the water would drain through. Atop it he erected a three-sided shelter, open toward the house. Sally thought this was all and agreed it was an improvement. She fetched her watering pot. John loftily waved it aside.

With a brad he punched dozens of holes in the bottom of a five-gallon coal-oil tin from which he had cut the top. He fastened the tin securely between two supports above his shelter.

"Now there," said he, climbing down from his lofty perch, "is a shower as *is* a shower: not one of your measly little trickles!"

"And how," asked Sally sweetly, "are you supposed to get any water into it? Or is this an air bath?"

"How about that stepladder you spoke of?" suggested John.

"If you think," said Sally with decision, "that I'm going to stagger up any stepladder lugging pails of water—and"—she pointed out, carried away by the triumph of her own common sense—"the minute you pour in the water it's going to begin to shower, isn't it, and how are you——" She broke off short. She had caught John's wooden expression. She had learned to know that expression.

John was tickled. He'd got a rise out of Sally. He was always solemnly badgering Sally, trying to get a rise out of her. It didn't work very often. Sally was pretty quick. And it didn't do to get brash. She generally got back at him. And she never got mad, like some folks would.

"Doggone," he complained once, after a particularly outrageous bit of fooling, "try my best, I can't seem to scare up a real good fight out of you nohow!"

"You wouldn't like it if you did," said Sally quietly. Somehow it sounded as though she meant that. But next moment she was laughing.

She was laughing now. John was satisfied: he'd got his rise; he was ready now to explain.

Over in the machine shop he'd found an old wing pump. This he would screw up, hand high, to the inside of the shelter. Its outlet he would lead up to the coal-oil can. Its inlet was a rubber hose that went out through an augur hole. You carried out a pail of water and set her down on an outside shelf John would build handy—or two pails of water, hot and cold, some style about this, he interpolated—and stick the hose in it, and then you got inside, under the coal-oil can, and worked the handle of the wing pump and pumped the water up into the can, and——

"The water comes out through all the cute little holes," mocked Sally, "and trickles excruciatingly, and you howl. Full set of directions with every package. But, oh, John, I think it's going to be *grand!*"

Completed, it turned out to be a weird-looking mechanical contraption. But it worked: and it was grand. John finished it early of a Sunday afternoon, and nothing would do but they must try it at once. The demonstration was entirely successful and delightful but was curtailed and complicated by a knock on the front door.

"Good lord!" whispered John in a panic, "it's Clara Carter. What are we going to do? All our clothes are in the front room."

But Sally remained calm.

"Put a towel around you and go get them," said she.

"She'll bust in, sure as shooting. The door ain't locked."

"You get 'em."

Sally gave him a shove. "If you don't hurry she *will* bust in."

John managed it. He was scared.

"Come in, Clara," Sally's voice was tranquil, "and sit down. Be with you in a minute."

John's demoralization lasted over.

"Just suppose she'd come in and caught me!" he said to Sally after Clara had gone.

"Well, suppose she had." Sally was matter of fact.

John was belatedly indignant.

"I think you might have done it," he grumbled. But, it seemed, that would not have done at all. John, with only a towel around him, was respectable enough. Sally, with only a towel around her, would not have been respectable at all: not at three o'clock in the afternoon. This seemed entirely axiomatic to Sally. John gave it up. Anybody who could understand a woman could breed a mule, thought John, reverting to an elegant simile of his cowboy days.

But Sally had news. Clara was going to have a baby. That's what she had really come for, to tell Sally about it. Clara couldn't stand it any longer: she had to talk about it to somebody, and Sally was the only other woman.

"Ain't she told Mel?" asked John, "or is it going to be a happy surprise?"

"Oh, Mel!" Sally's scorn dismissed Mel. Sally was all excited. She chattered on. John only half listened, wondering idly how a woman could get up all that steam over just a kid.

"Huh?" He was startled to full attention by a question. "Sure! Sure! It would be fine!" he agreed, trying for the heartiness he sensed as appropriate.

"I don't believe you think so at all!" she accused.

"Sure, sure I do!" repeated John. He was guiltily conscious that he really did not give a damn, so he covered the situation by the device that he had discovered sure fire in a crisis. He took her in his arms and patted her back. She snuggled against him.

"I wonder why we don't," she said wistfully, after a little.

But John was not wholly enlisted in the sentiment of this occasion.

"Well," he suggested with a laugh, "if at first we don't succeed, try, try again."

She flung away.

"*John!* You're outrageous!" she cried.

But he refused to be abashed.

"Only method I know of," he insisted.

The construction of the shower bath fired John's creative interest in nest building. Heretofore he had contented himself with admiring Sally's efforts. Now he wanted to take part. He spent all of every Sunday, and the hour or so of almost every evening, tinkering on the house. Had it not been known that they were new married, their almost complete self-absorption might have bred active unpopularity. He made a rocking chair with a back by cutting away a barrel and upholstering it with excelsior and sacking and nailing staves on the bottom for rockers.

"Try it," he urged Sally, misunderstanding her look of doubt. "Isn't that comfortable?"

"Most comfortable chair I ever sat in," agreed Sally surprisedly. It did not look comfortable.

"Then what's the matter?" John had by now learned to sense at least some of Sally's moods.

"Well," Sally hesitated, "it's a grand chair. But—do you think it quite goes with the curtains?"

John looked from the chair to the curtains to the blue china on the shelf.

"It'll go fine out on the porch." Sally hastened to soften the supposed disappointment. "And when we need it we can bring it in . . ."

But John was not hurt. He was, on the contrary, astounded and delighted by the sudden revelation of a point of view he had never before considered.

"Sure! I see!" he cried. "It looks sort of *clumsy!*"

Sally thought that crisis safely past. But some days later, lacking other occupation for the moment, she took down the rawhide kyacks from where, with the packsaddles, they hung overhead in the lean-to, with an idea of cleaning and wrapping the camp equipment they contained. Thus she laid hands on a paper obviously hidden there by John as the last place on earth she would be likely to rummage. Sally took the paper to the blue oilcloth-covered table, where she studied it with knitted brows.

On the face of it was nothing mysterious. The thing was merely a Montgomery Ward & Co. order form. In the space at the top John had printed his name and address. Below, in appropriate columns, he had written a list of numbers, and opposite each a price.

The matter was plain. John was ordering a number of things by mail from Montgomery Ward & Co. He did not want Sally to know about it. The proper thing for her to do, Sally realized, was to put back the paper, say nothing and be properly surprised. She would have done this except for that column of prices. For some moments she stared at them unbelieving. But they were written plainly enough. They totaled nearly two hundred dollars. Had John gone crazy—on sixty dollars a month?

Sally pondered for some time, then took the list and walked down to the company store. Barkley was back in the office.

"Have you a Montgomery Ward catalogue I could borrow?" asked Sally from the doorway.

She carried the catalogue to a counter in the empty store and looked in it for the item corresponding to the first number on the list. She stared unbelieving at the picture of it, for the catalogue was lavishly illustrated. It was of a clock, a large clock, that had started out to be round but had decided to break the line purity of its circumference by a succession of swooping convex baroque orna-mentations. The text informed her that it was covered with blue velvet.

"To match the china!" flashed Sally's appalled intuition.

Feverishly she turned to the next item. At the end of fifteen minutes she closed the thick volume and sat for some time collecting
her ideas and emotions, which were numerous and jumbled. Poor
John! Such awful things! Such terrible, *terrible* monstrosities of
"fanciness" and "elegance" and varnish and imitation carving and
fringe and dingle-dangle! Sally was overwhelmed by an impulse to
wild laughter as she recalled some of them. She had to stop thinking of them. She couldn't have hysterics on poor old Hugh Barkley.
What if she hadn't had that fool impulse to drop everything and
clean those kyacks, and that stuff had actually come! The thought
effectively sobered her. She stared at it and shuddered. Could she
have played up and been pleased and surprised, as John had planned?
She certainly would have been surprised, all right! Then suddenly a
tenderness flooded her heart, and the measure of it was precisely the
gap between John's eager secret anticipation and the atrocities of
the Montgomery Ward catalogue. She thought only of John, and his
poor, pitiful, blundering little plan; and of how puzzled and hurt
and disappointed he was going to be. For just the flash of an instant
it occurred to her that she really ought to let the transaction go
through. But that was only a flash.

She walked back through the deep dust disturbed and thoughtful.
How could she do it? John looked so like a hurt baby when he did
not understand. Her heart yearned over John. All the rest of that
day she moved apart, asking prayerfully and humbly that she be
given wisdom.

The whole crisis flattened out ridiculously. John's only show of
disappointment was when he caught sight of the order form laid out
prominently for his eyes.

"Oh, shucks!" said he disgustedly, "I meant that for a surprise!
You *would* go rummaging around those old kyacks!"

He broke through Sally's tactful circumlocutions when at last he
grasped their purport.

"Don't like 'em, eh?" said he. "Well, you go ahead and pick out
what suits you."

"Then—then you don't *care?*" faltered Sally.

He looked surprised.

"Why, I was just aiming to please you."

"Oh, John! John!" cried Sally, casting herself upon him.

John looked still more surprised. Then he grinned.

"Bad as all that, were they?" he surmised shrewdly. "Well, well. No call to cry about it."

He could not make out why she should weep so passionately. Will I ever understand Sally? thought John. Gosh, women are funny critters. What's all the shooting about? He patted her back. After a time she looked up at him wet faced. She had to know.

"John," she asked seriously, "tell me. Did you actually *like* those things? Did you really *want* them?"

The intensity of her question brought him up standing.

"Why—they looked to me kind of—kind of *fancy!* Nothing too good for us, old girl." He tried for the lighter touch.

She continued to stare at him. She thought of John as she had seen him once gazing rapt into a desert sunrise. Oh dear, thought Sally, will I ever understand John! Men are so funny!

That was at once emphasized for her.

"You order what suits you," repeated John. "But get the best. I want you to have the best."

This was Sally's chance to point a lesson.

"But we can't afford such things," she objected.

Then it appeared that John had money in the bank in Portland. He was, after all, still a Murdock. When it happened that his wanderings left him a few dollars over from wages, he had sent them in. Never very much, but it mounted up.

"You told me you were broke!" accused Sally, a trifle exasperated.

"I told you that?" John was genuinely astonished.

She reminded him of their journey, which they had curtailed for lack of funds with which to buy food.

"Oh, then!" said John. "I just meant I hadn't any money with me." And since then? "I never thought of it," said John. "Seemed like we had everything we wanted."

Sally's mind flashed back across her scrimping sixty-dollar-a-month economies. She looked at John, thought better of speech, threw her hands out in futility. She choked.

"What's funny?" John wanted to know. "What are you laughing at?"

"At myself," said Sally. "You wouldn't understand."

CHAPTER III

THE WOODS

NATURE always gets her way. Men, and the destinies of men, must move along her course. No price too high to pay. She creates and destroys a million individuals that one may carry her purpose. She safeguards him and sacrifices to him freely and is his fairy godmother of unblemished fortune, as long as he follows freely her urge. She spares him no spur of suffering or tragedy if he lags or strays. But when his impetus is spent she turns from him in divine disregard.

One of each generation, since old John Murdock had so unaccountably turned his face westward, had inherited and must forsake and go. He felt and was stirred by the first quiver of the waters; he was borne irresistibly forward with the wave; he rested only when the wave was spent. To this John had become the attunement. For ten years he had eddied with the indecisive whirls until the urge had defined its direction. He had lifted at last to it, and it had borne him here: and here, it seemed, he was content to rest. His nature was fulfilled. He had the woman, and the work that best suited him. It appeared to John that here, in the lumber woods, he had found all that he needed in life. For the moment he was too happily concerned with the immediate to think far ahead; but vaguely he saw

himself, in time, and with more experience, making his way, first as
a foreman, then maybe as owner and boss of an outfit like this, or
better. Bull Kirby made good money. Decidedly he had here every
opportunity any man could ask to better his condition; and that, be
it remembered, had ever been, for the Murdocks, the shining star in
the western sky.

He was satisfied; but the forces of his destiny were not.

Of a morning in early September John and Sally sat at breakfast.
It was just turned daylight, for the days were shortening, and work
began at seven o'clock. The door stood open. Sally liked to look out
and hear the few birds still singing and drink the cool air after the
stove. But it was John who caught sight of an approaching figure.

"Here comes Mel Carter," he told Sally. "Wonder what he wants."

Sally started to her feet, upsetting her chair.

"Clara!" she cried. "You don't suppose . . . ?" She ran out to
meet Mel. John followed more slowly. Sally was all excited, but John
was sure there was nothing seriously wrong. If there had been, Mel
would have come on the jump. He was just kind of dragging along.
Look at him, John grinned in secret amusement, the only other
critter in the universe that could look that worried and mournful is
an old-fashioned hound dog. You'd think this was the first baby
ever borned. Good thing if it *would* get borned, thought John, then
maybe Mel would stop being such a total loss.

John's reasoning was accurate. Everything was going all right. But
Mel was ashamed and embarrassed at his errand. Clara wanted them
to come on over. She *must* see them right away. Wouldn't give no
reason. Just notional. But she's all stirred up, and——

"Of course I'll go," agreed Sally soothingly. "Don't you fret for
a minute."

The young man's sallow face reddened slowly, and he shifted
boyishly from one foot to the other.

"Lord!" he blurted at length, "I feel like a fool!"

"You look just a little like one right now," agreed John with a
grin.

"She wants to see you, too," said Mel.

"Me!" John was plainly appalled. "What she want me for?"

"I don't know—well, it's a notion she has. It's just crazy. I told her it was crazy, but she took on so I got scared she'd have hysterics or something and that the baby might——" He appealed to Sally wistfully, "Is it always like this, Mis' Murdock?"

"Sometimes—not always—I don't know. Clara's high strung."

"Well, it ain't no fun," said Mel pathetically. He hesitated. "Would you mind coming over, just for a minute?" he asked.

"Of course he'll go," Sally answered for him. John looked uncomfortable and a trifle furtive. He would have liked to get out of this. He would not know what to do. This was woman's business.

"Sure! Sure!" he agreed with what heartiness he could summon. Sally disappeared. "I'll bring my work," she flung over her shoulder. "Just a minute."

"What seems to be the notion?" John wanted to know a little of what was ahead of him.

"She wants me to lay off work today."

"Why?" asked John.

"It's just crazy, I tell you."

"Don't she give no reason?"

"Nothing sensible."

"Well, what *did* she say?"

"Last night she asked me what I was doing today"—it came out at last—"and when I told her I was going to rig the blocks on the new chute way she near threw a fit."

"Why?" John was puzzled. "What's there about that?"

"I tell you it's crazy," protested Mel, "but you remember along last spring how Billy Miller was killed by getting smashed in the head by a block? Well, that was enough for her."

"But"—John was patently amazed—"that hadn't anything to do with rigging! That was just a snapback when the cable busted hauling logs!"

"I know it. I told her all that. But it was a block done it. That's enough." Mel's voice was bitter.

"It's just a notion." John repeated the word. "She'll get over it."

"She don't get over it," said Mel. "She was at it all last night. We didn't get hardly any sleep. I never saw her like that. It got me scared, I tell you, for fear she'd—— I had to halfway promise her—— Anyway, I wish you'd talk to her and see if you can't——"

"Can't what?" John was now looking at him with curious attention.

But Mel couldn't, or wouldn't, say. Sally rejoined them, carrying a bag of sewing. They ploughed through the light dust to the Carter's shanty.

Clara sat rigidly in the center of the little living room, a figure of tragedy. The table had not been cleared of an almost untouched breakfast. Sally crossed swiftly to her. The two men hung back near the door.

"I've come to keep you company a while, Clara," she greeted her cheerfully. "I've brought my work."

But Clara looked past her.

"Where's John? I want to talk to John." She paid no attention to the other woman's greeting.

"He's here." Sally impatiently motioned the reluctant men forward.

"Hullo, Clara!" John responded with a forced heartiness. He fumbled his cap and shifted his feet; but one eyebrow was quirked higher than the other, and his head was tilted the least bit to one side. Sally knew these symptoms of secret relish and appraisal. She cast upon John a glance full of warning that he must take this seriously. The eyebrow slowly subsided. "What's on your mind, Clara?" he asked. There was sympathy in his voice now. Sally flashed at him her appreciation of this. My sympathy is for Mel, you poor prune, he grimaced back. John and Sally did a great deal of this talking together without words. But he listened gravely enough to Clara.

"You're getting excited about nothing, Clara," said he. "There's no danger in this rigging job at all. None whatever. Why, all you do is to trim down small trees into poles and then splice the blocks to them for the cable return. They aren't even tall trees."

"There was Billy Miller," she choked on the words.

"But that wasn't the least bit like this. Then they were hauling on the chutes, and the strain was too much, so that a lashing parted, and the block snapped down." Patiently he continued to explain, showing logically and clearly that this job of Mel's and the accident to Miller had not one element in common except the presence in each of a block. "Like saying a jack rabbit's just as dangerous as a grizzly bear just because they've both got four legs!" he concluded with a laugh.

Clara uttered a low wail. "He'll be killed; I know he will be killed." Her voice was stifled.

Good lord! What did the woman want? He'd made it clear enough! And what was the matter with Sally? Why did she look at him that way? He knew that look of comical despair when she thought him exceptionally dense. And then he had his inspiration. Anyway, at the moment it seemed to him his inspiration. It might have been Sally's silent conveyance to him of what she expected. At least, almost with the first words he spoke, he felt distinctly in her mind an annoyance at his density change to a satisfaction.

"Look here, Clara"—he stooped to take the woman's two hands so that she must look up at him—"there's absolutely no danger in that job, as I told you. But if you feel that way about it, I tell you what let's do. I was going over today to the new chute we're putting in on Forty. You know the place. The chute logs are all hauled, and I was going to notch them. Well, Mel can do that just as well as I can, mebbe a little better. He can do that today; and I'll just rig those blocks. How's that? That suit you?"

"Oh, for Chris' sake!" Mel burst out, reddening angrily, but subsided under the sudden fierce pressure of Sally's hand.

"How about it, Clara? That suit you? Mel won't come to much grief on that job—unless he tries to cut his foot off with his own ax." Even Clara had to smile faintly at the absurdity, for these men were real woodsmen. "All right, that's all fixed!" cried John breezily. "Now you and Sally eat you some breakfast." Though apparently he had had eyes only for the forlorn figure in the chair, he must have noted every detail in the little room.

"Oh, haven't you had your breakfast?" For the first time the woman's tension relaxed in a pathetic concern of hospitality.

"She was just sitting down," put in John hastily. "Oh sure, I've et. I always eat first. Come on, you better get stepping. Whistle ought to go any minute now. So long, Clara. Don't let 'em get you down!" He made a great flourish of departure. The room was filled with bustle and heartiness. "What say?" he asked.

"I feel such a fool!" said Clara in a small voice. "I know you must think me such a fool! But it's just today. Just to get by today. Today is such a bad day." She began to cry a little, but softly and easily.

"That's all right. Don't you think about it. Easy as falling off a greased log. Safe now as a covered bridge." Under cover of these irrelevancies he made good his retreat. Outside the door he drew his sleeve across his forehead. "Whew!" he commented to himself. He felt the touch of Sally's hand on his arm. She had slipped out quietly after him. She squeezed the arm. Her eyes were shining.

"I'm proud of you!" she whispered.

He looked down at her, one eyebrow raised. "Shucks!" said he. He grinned maliciously. "Go back and eat your breakfast," he mocked. "You must be hungry—you've only had eight hot cakes this morning—that I saw."

"I love it in you," said she.

She flitted back into the house. John stared after her. Now what did she mean by *that*? Then he hurried to overtake Mel. They trudged along together in silence.

"Jees, I feel like a fool!" broke out Mel at last. "Of all the goddam—— As if I was a kid with a sharp knife . . ."

John listened to him for a few moments.

"Cuss ahead," he said at last, "if it does you any good. Get it out of your system." Mel muttered off into silence. "Well," said John after a while, "there's your trail. Be good."

The other hesitated. "Don't think I'm not grateful—to you and Sally," he blurted out at last. "You're white folks, both of you."

"Oh, go to hell," said John.

Sally stayed for an hour or so, then, as Clara seemed quite recovered and calm, she returned to her own work at home. She finished and was examining her few books with an idea that perhaps she might find something suited to Clara's amusement. Thus her back was to the door. John's voice startled her.

"Why, John!" she cried. "What on earth?"

"Mel Carter's dead," said John curtly. "Killed."

She stared at him.

"Dead—killed. Come. You got to tell Clara—before—they bring him in."

Sally snapped into control of herself now. She moved swiftly toward the door.

"What was it? What happened?"

They were hurrying together down the dusty road, Sally trotting to keep up with the man's long strides.

"What happened?" she panted.

"It was the darnedest thing I ever heard tell of. I wasn't there. The boys told me. Bat Hitchcock and Dick Barnes were felling an old stub. A hundred yards off the trail. Getting it out of the way for the new skidway. When it fell, near as we can make out, it flicked against a tree, and one of its rotten limbs snapped off, and the hard knot tore loose and came sailing through the air like someone had throwed it—like a bullet—and took Mel right behind the ear. He dropped like he was shot."

"Where is he?" she gasped, out of breath with the pace.

"The boys are bringing him in. They sent for me to——"

"Yes, yes, hurry! You must stop them—she mustn't see him until I——"

"They understand that." He indicated a little group waiting at the forest's edge.

After a little they moved slowly forward bearing their burden. Other men emerged from the office and store and from the mess house. The mill itself fell silent, and its crew appeared, one by one or in small groups, making their way up the road. Ordinarily an accident, even a fatal accident, could not have justified this wholesale desertion of the job. The work must go on. But already the extraordinary circumstances had become known. The men, gathered now in a group about the blanketed form, discussed it, low voiced. Hitchcock and Barnes, the eyewitnesses, had to tell over and over again what they had seen. It was hard to believe. They shook their heads, muttering, still half incredulous. "And him absolutely the only man on the trail—and twenty rod or more off!" "I never *heerd* of sich a thing!" One man bethought himself, looked right and left, half shamefacedly slid off his cap. One by one the others bared their heads. They waited, shifting uneasily, watching the closed door.

They stiffened slightly, half in apprehension, half in defiance, as a burly figure thrust from the forest and strode down toward them. This was Bull Kirby, the foreman, the driver of men and the work. How would he take this desertion of their jobs? But Bull Kirby's face had no anger in it, only concern. Somehow this unexpected and unprecedented forbearance deepened in the men's minds the unreal and fatal character of the tragedy. He spoke, low voiced, to the fallers and to John. "Mis' Murdock's in there," someone volunteered. Bull Kirby nodded. He, too, removed his narrow-brimmed felt hat and ran his fingers through his stiff short curls.

The door opened. Sally's face was very grave. She beckoned to John.

"Have them bring him in," she told him, low voiced, "and then all of you clear out. If I need any help I'll call for it. I'm taking Clara over to my house."

Thankfully they left the matter to her. The men went back to work. Only John and Bull Kirby and Hugh Barkley waited, seated on the edge of the narrow veranda. They did not talk. They had little to say to one another until Sally should return to them.

At the end of nearly two hours the door opened behind them. They looked up expectantly. Sally shook her head in warning. They walked away together out of hearing.

"She's quieted down," said Sally. "But she's in a daze."

"What she want done with Mel?" This from Bull Kirby.

"I don't know."

"Well, we got to do something. You'll have to ask her soon as you can."

"It won't do any good. She wouldn't understand. I tell you she's dazed."

"You mean off her head?" translated Bull Kirby bluntly. Sally nodded. Kirby pondered. "Know anything about Carter?" he asked the bookkeeper. "Where he come from or anything?" Barkley shook his head. "Well, inquire round, among the men."

"Clara has a sister in Seattle," volunteered Sally.

"Know her name?"

"What I came out here to say," Sally cut across him, "is that I think the sooner Mrs Carter gets down the mountain to where she can be taken care of, the better."

Bull Kirby's small eyes examined hers. "I see," said he. He pondered further, running his hand back and forth through his thick curls. They waited without suggestions.

"All right," said he presently. His voice was crisp with command. He knew what must be done. He was telling them. "Take her down in my light buckboard. You go along and take care of her, Mrs Murdock. John, you drive 'em down. Leave the team at Guffy's livery. Then you telegraph this sister at Seattle and start on the next train. Get the hospital telephone number from Hugh, here, case you don't make connection with the sister. Marshall House is decent and reasonable and will treat you right. It's on Second Street. Come back and pick up the buckboard when you get done, but not before. Hugh 'll give you some money. That's all."

"And—and poor Mel?" Sally gestured toward the other house.

"We'll tend to that," said Bull Kirby shortly. "Pack your duds. Get going."

Sally slipped away. Barkley started toward the office.

"Well?" Kirby challenged John's delay.

"It struck me—— Sally's pretty smart. She could get on all right after I got her to the railroad—— We're kind of short handed. I could——"

"You'll do nothing of the goddam sort," snapped Bull, without waiting to hear. "You ain't so goddam much I can't get along with-out you—or a dozen more like you. If I find you around here an hour from now, by God, I'll skin you!"

They drove down the mountain in Bull Kirby's buckboard. Sally, her arm about Clara, sat in the back seat. John drove alone. It was a long hard ride to the rails, which was one reason Bull Kirby did not make more money. The heavy lumber wagons had pulverized the road. The dust was terrible, for it was still alive with the day's heat. They breathed through handkerchiefs, and their skins turned gray; and they saw the forest in dim flat planes of slate blue, as through a fog. But evening arose from the valley, and its chill quieted the dust like a cool hand. They were more comfortable then; but the way was tense and long.

They drove in silence. Only once did Clara's apathy break for a moment. She turned on Sally, seizing her arm in a grip that hurt. "He *isn't* dead!" she denied insistently. "He'll be coming in a minute!" She stared intently into Sally's eyes, as though trying to see through clouded glass. Then her own eyes dulled.

Darkness had fallen before they arrived. The air was clear, and the trappings of the night were of velvet and silver.

Fortunately the sister had received the telegram. She and a compe-tent-looking husband met the train and took charge. But it was nearly four o'clock before John and Sally at last tumbled into bed at the Marshall House, numbed by the fatigues and emotions of the day.

Nevertheless, John slipped out of bed soon after seven. By habit of years he knew he would not sleep again. Moving softly, he dressed without disturbing Sally, scribbled two words for her reassurance—"back soon"—and so, shortly, found himself on Second Street. The sky was deep blue. From it came a taut vibrant wind, pungent as crab apples with a flavor strange to John's nostrils. He did not know the redolence of the sea. John was not wholly ignorant of cities, for occasion had once or twice brought him to Portland, and he had seen Salt Lake. But the substance of his life had been the open. He set off down Second Street, and everything he saw or heard or smelled delighted him.

At this hour the streets were not yet in full activity. Shops were opening, but not as yet settled into the day's business. John looked into their windows and was amazed and delighted at many of the things he saw, but remembered in time that Sally was funny about buying things. He came to a saloon on the corner and went in and had a glass of beer, which tasted very good even at this hour of the morning, and ate a handful of pretzels and had a few words with the barkeeper. The barkeeper told him to come back later and get a decent handout when the free lunch was going, and that in his opinion Sharkey was going to punch hell outta Fitzsimmons, and how was things in the woods; and John replied that he wouldn't bet on it, and that things were fine. There were more people in the street when he came out, all going in one direction; and a few wagons loaded with produce; and some wide, low drays drawn by massive horses. The drays one by one turned down a steep side street, and the air was rent by a shrieking of brakes. All these people and things were hurrying purposefully. They were going to work. John sauntered in a luxury of leisure. He was expansive with leisure. His narrow-brimmed lumberjack's felt hat had just a little cock to it. His movements were loose and slow and flowing with the indolence of trained muscles on vacation. His eyes roved speculatively and humorously. They met full those of the men hurrying. Some of the latter grinned a half response; others bristled like dogs, resenting differences and strangeness.

John came to a cross street. Looking down it, he caught a glint of blue. He turned toward it.

Two girls, on their way home from a dance hall, bent forward against the grade as they climbed the hill. They were wearied, drained of life. But the sight of John's tall figure plunging merrily down the steep slope brought a spark of interest to their eyes. They stopped short and looked at him, and when he had passed, with no more than an incurious glance, they turned and gazed after him. And then suddenly, seized by impulse, one took the other's hand, and they raced down the hill after him and separated either side of him, seizing him by the arms, so that all three were projected forward by the momentum, and John had considerable to do to keep his feet and bring them all to a halt. He swung them in front of him and looked down into their laughing faces.

"What you trying to do?" he asked. "Scare a man to death?"

"We like your looks," said the one with the frizzed yellow hair.

"Thanks," said John. He raised one eyebrow. "And what's your system when you catch 'em on level ground? Use a club?"

"Aw, go on!" giggled the one with the smooth yellow hair.

"You girls don't really need no such strong-arm stuff." John looked them over appraisingly from head to foot. "Just give 'em an eyeful and let nature take its course. I'm tellin' you in hopes of saving human lives. You mighty nigh jerked my head off!"

The two girls dissolved toward each other delightedly. There was nothing professional in their light-heartedness. Somehow their weariness was lifted. They were having a good time.

"I bet you're strong," said frizzed-hair, "the way you fetched us up." She laid her fingers on his upper arm. "Gawd, you've got muscle!" she cried. "Feel of that, Eloise. Like iron. What's your job—fishing?"

"No," said John, "my job's to get out mornings and hunt up little girls that get lost out and tell 'em to go straight on home and go to bed."

"Well, come on then," said Eloise. "Sounds all right to me." She took his arm with an air of proprietorship, warning off the other with her eyes. But John only laughed and disengaged her hand.

"You've got me all wrong, sister," said he. "I forgot to tell you: I'm a reformed character."

He gave them each a broad grin, and without other farewell, plunged on down the steep sidewalk, his body swinging back loosely in check of descent. The girls looked after him. They turned and resumed their climb.

John followed the street to its end and so came to the water front. Here were great warehouses. The wide-planked space between the warehouses and the city itself was crisscrossed by a network of railroad tracks. A stubby switch engine snorted back and forth on them, shunting freight cars. Before the warehouses stood the trucks, backed against their closed doors, waiting. The great horses dozed without attention to the puffing engine: the teamsters sat on the tails of the trucks, smoking. Over the roofs John could see the masts of ships. This excited him: he had never seen a ship. But the warehouses presented a blank front of wall and closed doors. John spoke to the teamsters. They answered him civilly enough, but briefly. They had no interest in John. Work began at eight o'clock. He could get out on the wharves when they opened up.

But John had a sudden new impulse. He turned to the left and set out more briskly. After a while he passed the last of the warehouses. An incline sloped steeply down to a long narrow float between tall piles. The float was empty, except for a sea gull atop each pile. From here John could see directly out into the Sound.

He paused for some moments to stare across its waters, lively in the breeze. Then he let himself cautiously down the ramp. The tide was low. He had to cling to the rail and catch his heels in the cross cleats. The tops of the piles were tall above him. He looked up at the gulls, amazed at their indifference to him, then walked out to the end of the float, where he knelt to wet his finger in taste of salt water. He got to his feet again and stood, hat in hand, the wind in his hair. Somehow he was deeply stirred; but he could not have told why.

The high prolonged note of a steam whistle brought him to himself. His interest leaped into lively attention. He climbed the incline and hurried down the water front.

Not until two hours later did he return to the hotel. Sally was still asleep. John hated to awaken her. Sally was sure pretty that way, with her hair soft on the pillow, and her cheeks that kind of faint pink she never had when she was awake, and one hand curled up under her chin. But the necessity of sharing drove John too hard for more than a moment's compunction. He snapped up the roller shade, and the sun flooded the room.

"What time is it?" asked Sally sleepily.

John sat on the side of the bed.

"Sally, wake up!" he cried. "Listen here. I want you to hear about this!"

She opened her eyes and saw that he was fully dressed. She sat up. "What time is it?" she repeated. "Good heavens, it's late!"

"What of it?" John was impatient.

"Clara!" She leaned forward to snatch at the old-fashioned chain that anchored John's watch. "I ought to have been there hours ago!" She tried to throw off one side of the coverlet. John firmly replaced it and sat on it to hold it down.

"Clara's in good hands," he told Sally. "And it don't matter one red cent whether you go round there now or this afternoon. You going to behave?"

Sally was going to behave. Now that the sleep was out of her brain she was sorry. John had come in full of enthusiasm about something. Now he was definitely off the boil. Cutting across John's enthusiasms with some other interest had that effect. Sally would never have done it if she had been fully awake. Now she must restart him.

But curiously enough, it was nothing she said that succeeded in this. She had sat up in bed and shaken loose her hair. Her nightdress had fallen a little way from her shoulders in a straight line just above her breasts. John hardly listened to what she was saying: he was filling his eyes.

"Doggone, Sally," he broke across what she was saying. "You look just like a little girl!" He stared at her, his appraisal somehow sharpening. "I'm glad your hair is brown," said he.

It was Sally's turn to stare. John told her about the two girls, and how they had tried to "kidnap me," as John expressed it; at which Sally felt a tiny leap of shock that she indignantly repressed as silly; and of what they said, and what John had said back.

"You ought to have seen their faces!" John was relishing his tale and laughing. "They had yellow hair," he added.

Now he was back easily and warmly on what he had wanted to tell Sally. He mentioned the float, and his sight of the Sound, and of how he had climbed down to the water level. He laughed at himself. "I knew it was salt, but I had to taste it!" But these things he passed over quickly.

"Then that whistle blowed," said he, "and I looked up. You wouldn't believe it, but I'd been so wropped up with that water, and all the rest, that I actually hadn't even seen that mill, laying right there next door, as you might say!"

John spoke of the mill with the same awe he might have felt at first sight of some great cathedral. Probably with more. John knew something of lumber mills.

"I hustled right over there," he told Sally. "You never saw anything like it!" For an hour he had wandered about, just looking. He tried to tell Sally what he had seen. There was no order or coherence in what he said. He jumped about, seizing upon what, unrelated, thrust to the foreground in his mind. Sally sank back again to her pillow and listened. She gave over trying to understand. Questions checked him. She was content to lie back and watch his face and dream upon the lovableness of John. Merely the surface of her attended his words, and that too only because they were John's words, and that he brought her his thrill to share. But in spite of that a picture did grow in her mind, drawn a little by John's words, but more by the leap of Sally's imagination.

Acres of low roof on posts, but with no walls. And a row of water barrels, against fire, spaced on the flattened roof tree. That was the mill. And under the roof a maze of machinery. Band saws working continuously in gangs to which, in unending procession, head on, came the brown logs and passed through them, without haste but without pause, and fell away on the other side in boards and beams.

"A whole log at a time," said John. "And the sawyer just stands there with a little row of levers in front of him and sizes up the log as it comes along and sets the saws wide or narrow, every which way. I tell you it's great!" He laughed, and Sally was fleetingly puzzled at an undernote of scorn. She could not know that John was remembering the dark coolness of the little mill on the mountain, and the carriage, with Charley Matson atop, moving back and forth, back and forth, the entire length of the mill, and a whole round trip for each board sawed.

John reached over to touch Sally impressively on the knee.

"One of these band saws turns out more in a day than Bull Kirby could cut in a month," said he. "And there are six of them!"

"Think of that!" said Sally. But she was not thinking of that: she was thinking that John was the best-looking thing she had ever seen when he was excited this way.

But she did see, in the corner of her mind's eye, the thick log, and its passing through the narrow, endless, swift bands of steel, and how it held together in the shape of a log until the last instant of its relinquishment and then suddenly fell apart into shining planks. What became of the planks then? Sally asked one of her few questions. Did men carry them away? Must take a lot of men.

There were no men, no men at all. Iron rollers, always revolving, carried them away unattended. You had to follow them down the whole length of the building, farther than you could see, out into the sunshine of the sorting yard. Here were men, in armor of leather, and flat leather palms strapped to their hands against the splinters. As the endless procession of boards came to them they must shunt each one to its own track of revolving rollers, according to its kind and quality. The tracks fanned out like fingers.

"*That's* some job!" marveled John. "You got to know all the grades there are and be able to tell 'em first off. There ain't much time. The lumber keeps coming. It waits for nobody. And you can't make a mistake, not and hold your job. Those fellers get high pay."

You followed the sorted lumber on out along the rollers until you came into the clear open, beyond all the buildings, to where they were piled in the drying yards. Acres of drying yards, as far as you could see, with the square piles of lumber, and streets between like a city, and the sweet shrill wind all through them carrying the spice of fresh pine, and in all the streets iron-rail tracks for flatcars drawn by horses, slow and large, like careful elephants. And over the tops of the lumber piles the masts of ships.

Sally would have liked to have heard about the ships, but John was away off at the other end of the mill. There the wide low opening framed the blue of sky and water. When you went up there and looked out there was an astonishing spread below you of spaced clumps of piles with the long boom poles chained end to end between them, and the pattern of logs floating in the pens thus formed. They lay crowded close in a brown crisscross pattern, content in sleep: but men, small in the distance, ran across them, so that they bobbed and turned, and urged them forward with pike poles, so that a continuous reluctant flow of them drifted toward the mill. Here were two men on the firmer footing of platforms on either side a narrow ramp. Their task it was to nose successive logs against the ramp. The logs obeyed sluggishly, grudgingly. And then all at once some great subaqueous power seized upon them, shook them from lethargy. They came alive. Sally's imagination was again fired. She saw them, brown and draining, rearing like great beasts out of the deep to follow one another in patient dignity up the incline to their destiny.

At the end of the hour John had, it seemed, fallen in with a man who was some kind of straw boss. At least he was not on any definite job. Name is Snell, Max Snell, said John. Something about John had attracted Max Snell's interest. He had taken time off to show John around. He had asked John a lot of questions. Finally he had taken John into the office to see the boss.

At this point John stopped short. Sally, raising her eyes to see why, perceived an embarrassment. He was looking at her almost with deprecation, it seemed, as though he had something to say that she was not going to like.

"They offered me a job there," he said at last in a small voice. "Wait a minute," he made haste to anticipate her comment. "I didn't say I was going to take it. I told 'em I was pretty well fixed."

Sally was startled, but for no more than a moment. Recovered, she examined John in secret amusement.

"Would you like to? Take a job there, I mean?" she asked. He asserted stoutly that he was perfectly satisfied where he was. "John!" She fixed him warningly.

"Well," he admitted, "some ways it wouldn't be such a bad idea. A man 'd learn a lot there, no doubt of that. And if he expected to come, by and by, into owning his own operation—even if it was a small one—why, that would come in handy. Wages are higher here. And of course in an outfit like that there's always a chance to work up . . ."

Under her accusing eye he ran down.

"You *do* want to," she brought him back to the point. He rallied.

"I don't want to do nothing you don't want to do!" he stated emphatically and with spirit. "And that settles it—no matter what it is!"

"What makes you think I wouldn't want to do this?" asked Sally.

John was taken aback. It had never occurred to him that Sally would approve a move so soon!

"So soon, what?" Sally was really curious.

The house. After all the fixing up she'd done. Tearing her away from her home. That was the gist of it. But it took a good many more words for John to tell it, and some time for Sally to grasp his conception of an insuperable obstacle. The idea hit her as a shock.

"That—that *shanty!*" she cried and broke into laughter, a compound of incredulity, relief, amusement and tenderness. A great deal of tenderness. John sat helpless, looking at her, his face slowly reddening.

"I thought it was kinda nice," he ventured after a while.

She sobered at once.

"It *was* nice," she insisted. John was hurt, or at least puzzled; she must reassure John. Nothing else was of importance until she had brought back John. "It was our home, and we could live there and be very happy. But don't you see," went on Sally, "that home is where *we* are, and that where that is isn't very important as long as we love each other; and after all we haven't lived there but a few months. And," continued Sally, shrewdly reading John's regrets, "we can bring down the things we have bought and have fun fitting them into a new house down here. Everything except the shower bath." Sally ventured to angle for a smile.

But she did not get it. John still looked doubtful. He was unable to believe that any woman could willingly abandon off-hand an abode on which she had lavished such pains, labor and taste to such an incredibly marvelous result. That is how the shanty on the mountain seemed to John. It looked good to him. The contrast to camp, line shack and the stark bare pioneer cabin, Sally, naturally, could not have realized; but she sensed it. She must burn her bridges.

"John," she said, "look at me. The house was lovely because it was ours, and you and I lived in it, and we had made it as nice as we could with what we had. And we could be happy in it because we are us. But don't you see we can be even happier here—with people and comforts and stores and shows to go to once in a while and places to go to and things to see and—and libraries——" Her voice died on the last word. She had begun solely in reassurance of John, but somehow the words had released stifled deeps in her own being.

"By God!" cried John, "I believe you'd *rather!*"

"Why, of course I'd rather!" Sally was almost sobbing with her own emotion. "Of *course* I'd rather! Oh, John!"

John uttered a great shout.

"Defend yourself, woman!" he cried. "I'm going to tousle you!"

Eagerly, breathlessly, they talked over ways and means. Sally would stay here, in the hotel. John would take the next train back and return the buckboard and fix things up with Bull Kirby.

"But if Mr Kirby needs you?" Sally was stricken. That thought had not before occurred to her. "It wouldn't be fair . . ."

John had not considered that either. It was a sobering idea. Naturally you couldn't double-cross Bull Kirby. But he did not long remain depressed. He was confident he could handle Bull Kirby. Bull Kirby was a good sort; he wouldn't stand in a man's way. John would fix that and pack up all their transportable goods and send them down with one of the lumber teams.

"Somebody's going to fall heir to a mighty good shower bath!" he grinned in delayed appreciation of Sally's effort at the shower-bath joke. "I'll get back soon as the Lord 'll let me," he promised. Shouldn't take long. Three or four days, maybe.

"Will they hold the mill job for you?" Sally suddenly had another practical thought.

But that was all right. They didn't want him for two weeks anyway. John was now all afire to get going.

"I'll look up a train while you're getting dressed," said he and was off. In ten minutes he was back, breathless with haste. "There's one leaves in twenty minutes," he shouted before he was fairly in the room. "Think I can just make it."

"Yes, yes!" Sally, too, was afire. "Go!"

He dumped a handful of money on the table. "I got my ticket. I won't need more!" He kissed her. "You'll be looking up Clara."

"But, John," Sally stopped him. "Suppose that Mr Kirby won't——"

"He will!" Then John's exuberance fell momentarily. "Well, then I'll telegraph you word, and you can come on up." They eyed each other soberly, afraid to say more. She ran to him and buried her face against his body. "John," she said in a muffled voice, "I'm going to pray."

PART II
THE TOWN

CHAPTER IV

THE CITY

JOHN WAS BACK within the promised four days. There had been no trouble arranging matters. Bull Kirby was reasonable. He sent his best wishes for Mrs Murdock. So did Hugh Barkley. Hugh was going to pack the stuff and see it was sent down. And John had found an unexpected purchaser for the horses. "Hated to see them go," said John; "but what use would we have for them? Got a hundred and fifty dollars for the four—cash. Pretty good for the mountains! How's Clara getting along?" he inquired belatedly after he had unloaded all his own news.

Clara was going to be all right—in time. She was over the first shock, had come to herself. "Of course, it's still terrible to her. But," said Sally, "deep down, she was sort of ready for it, somehow. You remember, that day, how she seemed to have a premonition? I like her sister and her brother-in-law," observed Sally; "they are kind, simple people, and they have no children, so they are really glad to have Clara."

The baby?

That, too, was all right. There had been no miscarriage, which was what they had feared. "I was out there twice," said Sally, "but it's a long way. He's some sort of watchman, and they really don't

55

live in Seattle. You have to take a train. It's out of town, up toward Everett."

"Well, we'll go see them," said John vaguely, in dismissal of the subject. He examined Sally more closely. "What you got up your sleeve, Pink Cheeks? Out with it! I don't know much, but I know them symptoms. You've got a gleam in your eye!"

But Sally would not tell.

"You come with me, and you'll find out!" said she.

They took a car line that went up Third Street and took them beyond the Washington Hotel, perched on its clifflike hill, and the steps leading up to it. They descended and walked for a short distance along a street-by-courtesy. In time it would become a real street, but now it was indicated merely by elevated sidewalks two planks wide, and the marks of wheels between them. Almost as far as one could see were evidences of an old forest. Fire-scarred stumps stood high, for the trees had been cut in the wasteful age. Around them the breeze stirred a sea of bracken and bright fireweed. It was typical logged-off land, except that the rectangular arrangement of the sidewalks and four widely scattered new houses insisted that some optimist considered it a real-estate addition.

Sally led the way to the first of the new houses. She had a key. She led John all through the house, which should not have taken long, for it had only four rooms. But it was fresh and clean with paint and varnish and the smell of newness. It had a bathroom with an enamel tub, opening both ways into two bedrooms. It had a front door with frosted glass in the upper half of it, and eight shiny glass windows that slid up and down almost at a touch. To Sally's impatience, John stopped short at the windows until he understood their system of counterweights. It had a front porch and a back porch, both under roof. The roofs were covered with sawed shingles, and there were gutters at their eaves that would carry rain to a barrel. The kitchen had a brand-new Agate stove, with shiny nickel curlicue ornamentations, and a commodious hot-water back that fed by thermal action into a cylindrical tank in the corner. John stuck there, also, while he figured out how it worked, making little admiring noises with his tongue against his teeth, while Sally plucked at his sleeve. She did not care how it worked, as long as it did work. There was also in the kitchen a deep white-enamel sink, flanked by drainboards of dazzling sandpapered white pine, and over them two nickel faucets. John turned one of the faucets, and it elicited a gasping gurgle, but no water.

"It isn't turned on yet," said Sally. "Neither is the gas."

There was gas! No more lamps! In every room, and a fearful and wonderful overhead affair, that pulled up and down with counterweights, in the ceiling of the living room. In spite of Sally's disclaimer, John tried one of the jets with a match. He grunted at his failure. John wasn't saying anything. Sally was doing all the talking. She flitted from room to room as she remembered things to show John. He followed her about more slowly and contemplated gravely what was pointed out to him, but made no comment.

"There!" Sally came at length to an end. "What do you think?"

"Think, what?" John had assumed his wooden expression.

She looked him over disgustedly.

"Don't be heavy sand!" said she.

"Why," John became satisfactorily human, "I think it's fine, of course. It's pretty grand." It's maybe a little too grand, Sally caught the unspoken comment in his voice.

"We can get it for twenty-five dollars a month."

"What?" John was startled and incredulous. "You sure?"

Sally nodded gravely. "Just that. Of course, it's worth more. But they're just starting here. They built these houses to get started. And they want somebody to live in them, you see, and so——"

"How did they come to pick out us?" John was still skeptical.

"They didn't. I picked out them," said Sally happily.

John looked down at her flushed cheeks and her eager dancing eyes.

"Reckon it's lucky it was you and not me they seen first," said he dryly.

"Then . . . ?"

"Grab it," said John.

"Then you *do* like it? We'll have to buy some things. It's unfurnished. And what we've got won't anywhere near——"

"Grab it," repeated John. "Before they find someone else. Let's go right on down and do it now. Where do they hang out?"

But, it seemed, such a course was beyond human nature, beyond Sally's human nature. She had to look over the house first. John supposed they had looked over the house. What more, for the love of Mike, was there to see?

"But now," said Sally quaintly, "don't you see, it's a *different* house. It's *our* house now!"

She moved about. She stood stock still in the middle of floors looking calculatingly about her, a finger on her lip. She perked her head sidewise, her eyes remote. John followed her patiently for a time, trying to make head or tail of the few snatches of phrase she threw out at him from an almost complete inner absorption. "Chintz," she said, "bright-colored chintz, I think. Not looped back. To draw, on curtain rods." She nodded her head twice. Then for some time she stared at the bare pine floor. "Rugs," she remarked and at once disappeared through the kitchen door. Only once did she appeal to John directly, and then he did not catch the drift of her question.

"Can you wax pine?" she wanted to know.

John got tired of it after a while and went outdoors. Sally finished with her vision at last and went in search of him. She found him grubbing about beneath the all-pervasive bracken with a stick. He looked up.

"Say," said he, "I bet you could grow good spuds in this soil!"

They closed with the real-estate firm. John paid a month's rent in advance to clinch the deal. He opened a banking account with the small balance of his wages from Bull Kirby and the hundred and fifty dollars from the sale of the horses. At the same time he arranged for the transfer of his savings from the Portland bank. The total made quite a respectable amount. At least they were well enough off so that Sally need not worry about spending money in fixing up the house.

She was eager to get at it and to move from the Marshall House, but she must first make an excursion with John. John had never laid eyes on the sea, and now he wanted to do so before he took up the new job at the mill.

Sally was willing enough, though the excursion was by no means either simple or cheap. It involved a roundabout train journey by way of Tacoma to circumvent the Sound and the towering Olympics. They must stay overnight at a hotel. Sally mentioned these things; but her intuition of John told her that, for some mysterious reason, this was to him more than a pleasure jaunt. She could not fathom the reason as yet, but the compulsion was clear. She sensed that he could not be content without it.

They arrived at the coast in the middle of the afternoon and came to the beach across broad dunes of yellow sand and gray verbena. The tide was low and the beach flat and wide. Sally stopped, partly to look, partly to catch her breath after the heavy going. John did not stop. He continued on across the wet sands and halted only at the very edge of the water, when the slow reaching wash hissed its warning to his feet. There he stood, planted, and gazed out to sea.

Sally caught up with him; but she did not join him. For once he had forgotten Sally, had left Sally behind. She stood apart, watching his rapt face. She perceived that he was far away, in a remoteness opened to him by the vastness of the sea. And it came to Sally that she was like a bird on shore watching a strange far flight; but that at the same time her spirit was merging with John's with a blending higher than themselves, not to be understood—at the border of mysticism. Sally's thoughts dissolved into pure feeling.

When John had touched its edge the sea had been at the poise of its ebb. Its forces caught their moment of repose, so that the waves were small and fell somnolently, and from beneath them the wash crept, reluctant, and drained back with the relief of a tired sigh. But presently a deeper note swelled in the voice of the surf. The slack was over. New power stirred. The sea quickened; and up over the flat of the sands ran a foam-edged crescent of its ever-renewed challenge to the land.

John was oblivious; but Sally was nearer earth. She seized his arm, and together they scuttled away, and the water snatched after their flying feet, but gave up at last and retired chuckling as though daring them to try again.

They turned, a little breathless from their scamper, and laughed at John's escape. If it hadn't been for Sally he would have been caught knee-deep. And him with his only pair of store shoes on, not to mention his new suit of store clothes! But the moment still lingered with John. He turned his eyes again to the far horizon.

"Well," said he and drew in a deep breath, "I reckon this is about as far as the Murdocks can go!"

They went back to the dry hot sand of the dunes and sat there and watched the hypnotic and ceaseless fall of the waves. They found themselves talking together soberly. John tried to express something of what he had sensed, but his perception had not been one of words, and they were difficult for him to find. However, since he spoke from the depths of him Sally did see and share and perhaps understood—if not better, at least more coherently than did John himself—the urge and fling that had lifted and let fall the chosen of each generation in this clan of Murdocks, but always westward, until now here stood this last of them at the sea!

Sally knew, for in her blood, too, that spirit stirred. She found herself telling John. Her own grandfather had crossed the Rockies in '51.

"What did he do, ranching?" asked John. "Funny if he'd run across my folks, wouldn't it?"

"I don't think he did." She shook her head. "He was a trader. He came in a wagon train with my grandmother and their little boy—my father—with him. He really started for California and the gold fields, but got switched off on the Oregon Trail, somehow, and they went down the Columbia and settled in Borland. I don't know why. Anyway, that's where we lived."

John was listening, but idly. He lay on his side watching Sally, who was sitting up straight.

"Say," said he, "I do like the way your mouth quirks up at the corners just the last thing! It's kind of cute."

"Oh, *you!*" Sally was impatient. This was not her mood.

"Well, it is!" insisted John. "Makes you look sort of happylike. Whether or no. At first it fooled me."

He continued to look her over. It was a good chance; Sally was gazing out absently across the sea. Her skin looked awful white, noted John, as though he had never seen her before. Too much indoors, he thought. No, some people are white like that no matter how much they are in the sun. Sort of showed off her mouth, with its startlingly red lips and that funny quirk at the corners. Kinda cute, he repeated to himself. Her face was fine cut, delicate looking —no, not delicate—like a flower, somehow. And she was slim. You'd think she might be weak, but she was strong as a horse; just tackle her, if you want to find out, John chuckled at reminiscence. He liked that up-tilt way she carried her head.

"How come," he asked suddenly, "you to be schoolma'am at Siler's, anyway?"

Why the question popped into his head he did not know. Now that he had asked it he wondered that he had never asked it before. But his attunement with Sally had sharpened more than he could have understood. He had cut accurately into her abstraction.

"Why, honey!" cried John, sitting up. Sally was dabbing at her eyes.

"I had to make a living," she said at last. "I was alone."

"I know that," said John gently. "I know lonesome. Want to tell me?" he asked after a little. "Here, blow your nose."

Sally dutifully blew her nose on the proffered handkerchief. John was very tender toward Sally. She was just like a little girl: a poor little girl. John had lived with this woman all these months and had learned something about this woman, but of the little girl he had known nothing, nothing at all; and now he wanted very much to know about her. He paused for a moment to remark on how extraordinary this was.

"Do you realize," said he to Sally, "that this is the very first time we've ever talked about us—our folks and all that, I mean? Don't you think that's funny? Wouldn't you think we would have?" Then he answered his own questions. "I reckon," said he, "we've been too busy on each other. I'd like to know," he said a little wistfully, "if it ain't too much for you."

"My father's name was Jefferson Slocum. He was a doctor, the only doctor in Borland, all his life. He brought me up. My mother died. He was the best man in the world. Everybody loved him. Why shouldn't they? He wore himself out for them. Day and night. All his life. He was so understanding, so gentle, so patient! *Everybody* loved him, I tell you. He hadn't an enemy in the world." She choked. John waited without comment. "He made a mistake," Sally continued, staring straight before her. "The child—it was a little girl—died because of it. Nobody held it against him. It was beautiful how everybody acted. But he held it against himself. It killed him. He was that sort. He'd lost all his money awhile back in some kind of a law suit. I had to do something."

"I see," said John. He laid his hand over hers, but offered no other caress. They sat side by side for a long time, looking over the sea. The sea breeze died. The sun turned huge and red and touched the horizon where, astonishingly, it flattened at the top into terraces of shifting fire. A line of black sea birds flew low across it. John's perceptions of Sally were acute. He sensed her restored peace.

"Helps a lot to bring 'em out where the sun can get at them," said he.

"What?" Sally aroused herself.

"Troubles. Grouches. Bothers. Blankets. Old clothes. Rutabagas," said John.

The winter that ensued on their establishment in the new house and the new job was not unusual; but this far to the northwest the days were short, the nights long, and there was a good deal of rain. The rain bothered John at first, for his wandering life in the semi-aridity of the Great Basin had not accustomed his mind to the wet. Sally, a daughter of the west slope of the Cascades, took it casually enough. She bought herself a scarlet waterproof with a hood that she could pull up over her head, and a short light pair of rubber boots. These protected her completely, so that she rarely bothered with an umbrella. She carried shoes or slippers in an inside pocket. John admired this outfit enormously. He had never before seen what he called a red slicker. It set off Sally's white skin and was just about a match for her lips. John actually liked to go out in the rain with Sally just to see the dew of mist on her cheeks, and how it brought into them a faint blush of color, and how her eyes seemed to darken somehow. With her hair all tucked away and the hood closely framing her face and the straight-lined fall of the red waterproof over her figure and the ridiculously tiny rubber boots, she looked just like a little girl. And John did especially like it when Sally looked like a little girl!

But it needed visibility for this particular esthetic gratification, and as John was away to work before daylight and back from work only after dark, they must make their walks of Sundays. No fun walking in the rain when it was dark! Therefore Sundays they tramped around looking over this city of their adoption. They even got as far out as Lake Washington under their own power; but they took the streetcar back. It was good training for John's catlike fastidiousness against the wet. Shortly he learned to ignore it, like any other webfoot. To do it justice, the rain was rarely heavy, little more than a mist; and of course there were some fine days.

Thus they climbed all the hills. There was plenty of interest for such as they. Merely the ordinary streets of commerce and the closed shops were fun. The city library was open of a Sunday, and John went there with Sally and was duly impressed by all those books, but there was really not much to do there, unless you wanted to sit down and read, and John certainly did not want to do that, not in the precious daylight hours. Sally had a library card and brought books home. The museum held him longer: he found quite a lot of interesting things in the museum. But he liked it better out of doors.

"Need exercise," he told Sally.

"I suppose you don't get any at the mill," said she ironically.

But that was different. That wasn't exercise, that was work. John was not entirely convincing on this point, nor was he able to explain to Sally, for the reason that he did not himself understand his in-

stinct for elbow room, for open air blowing from space unconfined.
The park was better, with its winding soggy paths and its trees and
bushes that shook off jewels when came a sudden breeze; or the
water front, shut and shrouded, and tall ships resting, and the water
cold and steel gray with winter. There was no life along the warehouses, but at the floats was life. There were the fishing boats, in
for the season. They were moored stem to stern the whole length
of the floats themselves; they were tied alongside of one another, row
after row, until all the water between was filled in one solid pack.
Their masts were like a bared forest. The owners lived aboard, in-
habiting dog-kennel cabins in the fore parts, above which arose slim
stovepipes. John and Sally stood ashore, high above, and looked
down. Wood smoke arose from the pipes. Occasionally a hatch slid
back, and a man crossed from boat to boat to reach a float or perhaps
to disappear in the cabin of a friend. Often, when the rain let up or
thinned, groups squatted together atop the houses, smoking pipes,
mending sails or gear. It was a community apart, sufficient unto
itself. From where they were, John and Sally could hear nothing,
and there was little to see. Nevertheless the place held some sort
of fascination for John.

He liked the zoo also, and, curiously enough, the wide maple-
shaded streets of what was known as the "residential district," in
aristocratic withdrawal on the hills over toward the lighthouse. He
liked to walk along them and look at the great houses with their
stretches of lawn about them. There was no snobbishness nor envy
nor even wonder in John's interest. Merely that here was something
different, and a spread of spaciousness. He did not care for church,
though he dutifully accompanied Sally for a time. Then he begged off.

"You go for both of us, honey," he pleaded. "I don't believe it
does me no good. Honest, I don't."

Sally was a little troubled. John, too, was troubled. He did not
want to worry Sally. And he did not want Sally to get the wrong
idea.

"It ain't that I don't think church is a fine thing," he protested,
"but somehow it don't hit me. I'm no heathen. I believe just like

you do." He groped for expression. "Doggone it!" he burst out at last. "Trouble is I just can't pump up ary idea that that little drawly-voice squirt knows nigh as much about God as he makes out. And I sure do hate a fourflusher! I'm sorry, honey," he pleaded with Sally, "but don't you see, when I have to set and listen to that fellow for two hours straight it just makes me mad. And *that* ain't a good thing to go to church for, now is it?"

In spite of herself, Sally had to laugh.

This was their first small separation in understanding, for to Sally church, as church, meant something, while to John church was the man who expressed it. Possibly that difference is fundamental in the sexes.

Thus John came into possession of Sunday-morning hours to be filled. He tried the experiment of staying home and doing something useful, but he did not like it without Sally. It occurred to him with a shock of compunction that Sally was alone there, without him, nearly the whole of every day. He wondered if Sally felt about it the same way as he did. She rejected the idea with spirit. If John imagined for one moment she sat around all day moping just because he wasn't there he had another guess coming. For the first time John learned that Sally had other activities besides keeping house and making things for the house and sitting in the house waiting for John. Indeed, it appeared that Sally was taking the house rather lightly, that she, that *any* woman with any gumption at all, could take care of such a house, with her right hand tied behind her, in two shakes of a lamb's tail. John had never thought of it at all, but his hazy acceptance of the scheme of things included woman's place as in the home. Not as a duty; merely that there was her natural habitat.

But Sally, it seemed, got through and locked up and went away immediately after her noon meal; sometimes before.

"I go downtown," she answered John. "I go to the park. Sometimes I take a walk in the country. Mostly downtown."

John learned of Sally's activities. Once she had well started talking about them, she kindled. She was reading, regularly, at the library.

"But I thought you could bring books home," said John.

Not some of these books. They were for reference only. Sally must consult them because they were part of a regular course of reading she was doing.

"What about?" asked John.

"I don't believe it would interest you," said Sally. The only reason she was interested was that it had been the doctor's one hobby. Chinese art, she replied to him. John looked blank. What little Chinese art he had seen—just lately, in their visits to the museum—had seemed to him just funny. It isn't just funny, insisted Sally; it all has significance. John cut short the beginning of a breathless little defense of formal symbolism with a laugh.

"Help! Help!" he cried, holding up both hands in surrender. "I can't even see your dust! Custer's Last Stand down in Casey's saloon is about my size."

Sally laughed, too. That was the best thing about it. They could both laugh with real relish. But John was still curious.

"How do you know what books to read?" he wanted to know.

That was easy. There were lists, all made out. And a professor from the university came to the library and gave lectures once a week. There were all kinds of lectures, on other things, too.

"What else do you do?" asked John.

He listened to her account of her doings in growing amazement. After living with her all these months he had imagined he knew Sally. Here was revealed to him a whole new Sally he had never suspected. She was seeing things, making friends of her own, feeding avidly on interests strange to him. Sally did not at first perceive what she was doing. John's comment enlightened her.

"I reckon you think I'm just an ignorant, uneducated mutt," said he.

She stood appalled.

"John!" she cried. "Don't you ever let me hear you say anything like that again! You! The finest, cleanest, straightest, strongest man I've ever seen! Uneducated! What do those silly little frills amount

to compared to what life has taught you! Any—any *sissy* can know
them! Why—why," she fairly stuttered in her emotion, "you have
more *real* education in your little finger than they have in their
whole brains! The things you know—*know!*" she repeated and threw
out her hands in despair of speech.

"What things?" asked John.

"The things that make me love you!" she cried passionately.

"I reckon that's enough for me," said John. But he was still
sobered. "But I'm sure glad," said he presently, "that things fixed
up so we come to Seattle. I can see now it must have been pretty
dry pickings for you up there on the mountain."

It took him several days to recover from a new awe of Sally. But
he did recover, as was indicated by the fact that he began to poke
gentle fun at her over her "high-brow" activities.

Nevertheless the episode did have one somewhat amusing result,
and one that took down a peg Sally's feminine conceit that by now
she knew all about John.

They were sitting together of an evening, on opposite sides of the
table, with an overhead light pulled down between them. Sally was
reading a book she had taken from the library; John was smoking
his pipe.

"Sally," he broke his silence abruptly, "I want you should take me
in hand."

She looked up vaguely, coming back from her book.

"Take you in hand?" she repeated.

"Just that. Fix me up. So people will take us to be the same breed
of cats, you and I."

"I don't quite understand," said Sally.

"Yes, you do—you ought to. I'm not up to the mark you were
raised by; and you know it just as well as I do."

He was entirely serious. Sally answered him soberly.

"I thought we had that all out. Do you want me to repeat what
I said? I really meant it."

"No. I don't mean that. Thinking it over I'm inclined to agree with you. You've got one kind of education; I've got another. Perhaps we can swap some of it. I'd like to. If you could start me off easy."

"Oh, I'd love that. We could begin on——" Sally's eyes began to sparkle. But John broke across.

"That wasn't what I was trying to talk about. Take that up later. That's for inside. What I mean is outsides—like clothes."

"Clothes? You want me to help you pick out some clothes?" John relaxed to a brief smile.

"Reckon I am kind of hazy. I meant outsides—*like* clothes. Things that people see and maybe size you up by. Get the idea?"

"I might, if you'd tell me exactly what it is you are driving at!"

"I want you to ride herd on my talk a little. Now listen," he forestalled any comment, "you can't deny that more 'n half the time I'm talkin' like a man who didn't know such a thing as grammar was ever invented. I say things like throwed for threw, and come for came, and them for those—all that sort of thing. You know better than that. Why don't you call me down when you hear me say those things? You don't like it."

He surveyed Sally's blank expression with a faint beginning of amusement.

"Don't want to get to shame me or get to be poking at me all the time. Don't want to do the schoolma'am on me," he answered himself shrewdly. "That it?"

Sally nodded slowly. She was watching him, fascinated by this unsuspected aspect of John. He continued to astonish her.

"That," he was saying, "would be all right if I didn't know any better. But I do. I know all about that grammar stuff. Or at least," he corrected himself, "as much as the Dalles had in stock. My old man was great on schooling, as far as he could give it to us kids. Wasn't far. But he did his best. He had a great idea of the Murdocks."

He looked at her as though he expected her to make some comment. But Sally was not yet that far oriented.

"I know better," he repeated, "but a man talks the language of the folks he deals with. And I've dealt with a tough bunch. And you get the habit so you don't really hear it no more." He chuckled. "There I go! Now what I want: when you catch me sailing off the reservation that away, I want you should stop me right there and mend my speech. Keno?"

"I see." Sally was doubtful. "Perhaps. I don't know—I don't know whether you'd like it quite that way. I don't know whether I'd like it. Can't you——"

"No, I can't," said John bluntly. "I've talked that talk so long it's second nature. And if I stop all the time to think that close how I'm saying it, then I ain't got a thing to say. Ain't—have not," he interrupted himself to contemplate the phrase. "Think I'll hang onto ain't," said he. "That one's a nice easy fit." He looked at her with one eyebrow raised in inquiry for her decision.

She had to laugh a little, but it was evident to John that she still hesitated.

"Look here," said he, "you'd hop me fast enough if I didn't shave my face for company. Well, *ain't,*" he emphasized the word defiantly, "I just as disgusting an object if I don't shave my language?"

They laughed together over this. John chose to take the laughter for assent.

"Don't worry, I won't get mad. Every time I make one of these here grammatical solecisms——" He paused to cock an eye so expectantly that Sally heroically swallowed her astonishment. "Learned *that* one in school," went on John parenthetically. "It's a peach. Well, you just stop me and make me back track. *Only,*" he sat up straight in his chair, "when I do like this," he held up two fingers from his clenched fist, "that means I aim to *express* myself. And you lay off!"

This somewhat fantastic arrangement worked out in practice much better than might have been expected. The imminence of Sally's veto sharpened John's own supervision of his speech. And the two-finger signal came into frequent use, for John often returned from work so full of things to tell Sally of his fascinating occupations at the mill that he must, as he said, get it out free, wide and handsome or bust.

For John, it seemed, was rapidly proving himself to be that most rare and valuable type of employee around a big operation, a quick and competent handy man. He caught on. When one of the specialists was so rushed as to need an assistant, John was called in. Thus he ran the whole gamut of the multitudinous jobs that intervene between the saw log and the finished product. He watched closely and intelligently and took hold deftly, so that, after a few experiences, he even got so far as to be trusted, on rare occasions of emergency, to do some things all by himself.

"They turned me in on the trimmer today," he bragged to Sally. The trimming saw, he explained, was a circular saw whose edge stuck up through a slot in a table, and you shoved the rough slabs against it and trimmed off the bark edges, or made of a plank, too full of knots to rate as clear or number two, slats or four-inch or six-inch or whatever, according to the situation on it of the knots. "You got to have a good eye and quick judgment to do that, or you waste a lot of valuable stuff," he boasted. "They don't give that job to everybody!"

He had a similar gratifying triumph in the planing mill and was often called upon to lend a hand with machinery: his flair for understanding mechanics stood him well there. Indeed he came perilously near being assigned a permanent job in the engine room. John was glad to get out of that. He much preferred the roving commission. To each new thing he came with the zest of exploration.

Some things were as yet beyond him, he acknowledged to Sally. But he had hopes; and, though he could not meddle in them, he sometimes snatched spare time to stand by and absorb wisdom at second hand. Harry Martin liked him and was good natured. Harry was one of those in the sorting yard who determined the grades of the lumber as it came from the saw, shunting it to one or another rollway. His judgment must be instantaneous; and it was final. If a plank of clear got onto the mill-run rollway, thenceforward it was mill run and would be sold as such, a loss to the firm. Harry permitted John to stand at his elbow and make his guess, just for practice.

"My batting average ain't so good—yet," confessed John.

Nor could he hope to get his hands on the levers that set the band saws. A miss there meant a spoiled log. But John could, and did, stand by and make his own guess to himself as to what he would do and then check himself against what the sawyer actually did. Another limit to his ambition was the booming ponds.

"I can fork a bad bronc," he acknowledged to Sally, "but I'd sure hate to tackle one of them logs." The two fingers were down. "They'd roll me into the water so fast I'd think I was born a fish!"

But one evening he burst into the house, the two fingers held high.

"By golly, Sally!" he cried, "what do you think! Today old Higgins let me gum a saw—all myself! And he said I done a damn good job, too!"

Sally rejoiced. But later, when the exuberance of the occasion had spent, she had to confess herself not very clear as to its reason. The term was quaint, but obscure.

"Why," said John, "after a while the teeth on a saw get wore down so far that sharpening and setting them don't do no more good. They ain't long enough to get shut of the sawdust. Then you've got to cut the notch between them deeper, which naturally makes the teeth long again. You cut down below the teeth into the saw's gums. That's gumming the saw." And, it seemed, it is a delicate job to get them all even again, so you could set them, and John had a right to be proud, for saws are expensive, and—— "Well, what you been doing with yourself today, honey?" asked John.

The long dark hours of winter were very pleasant. To John, returning from the mill, feeling his way along the plank sidewalk, the house, as he approached it, was like a brimming container of light. He went around by the kitchen door, for his mackinaw must be by now heavy with moisture. He hung it where it would dry out by morning. From that moment on he was in his own comfortable private world. For a little while he liked just to sit and smoke, resting up a bit. And if, as was often the case, a southeaster was hounding frightened scud across the skies, that was still better. Snug sanctuary from the weather was a thing to appeal to John. He liked the storms merely for the satisfaction of hearing rain on a roof that did not leak. He would stretch his powerful body and lean back in the sheer luxury of it and call out to Sally, finishing supper in the kitchen:

"How would you like to be making camp after a hard ride, and your blankets wet through, and a soggy tarp!"

The mill shut down at five; John was home soon after. While Sally cooked supper in the kitchen they talked back and forth through the open door. It was during that period, and while they were at table, that they cleared up the news of the day. Sally ran through her own day with zest, gaily. The town life stimulated her. She saw fun even in the marketing. She would imitate the slow, measured, groping accents of old Peterson, from whom she bought fish, that you'd swear the old cuss was out there in the kitchen with her. And that Wop who sold vegetables, talking fifteen to the dozen, glorifying his potatoes. Good as any vaudeville show you'd see on the stage. Then pretty soon Sally would come out all pink cheeked from the stove to say things were ready and disappear in the bedroom, and John would go out to get them and put them on the table; and by that time Sally was back looking fresh and starched and dainty as if she had never seen a stove. They played that fiction with entire gravity.

"Oh!" cried Sally in surprise. "There's fish for supper! *Isn't* that nice."

Bedtime must be early, for they must be early afoot so that John could get down to the mill when the whistle blew. It always caught them unaware. They had so much to talk about. This struck John forcibly.

"Before we got married," he told Sally, "if anybody'd told me I could think up enough things to say to any woman—any *nice* woman," he amended, then looked confused as Sally laughed, "for more than ten minutes at a stretch, I'd have told him he was crazy in the head. And here there ain't *time* enough!"

They had begun to explore each other's minds. John had always admired what he conceived to be Sally's enormous and mysterious erudition—Sally had had "advantages"—but from a distance. Now it began to look to him as though some of this mysterious region might be penetrable, with Sally to help him out. Not Chink art or such frills, John hastened to disclaim, but there was a lot of interesting stuff that Sally knew about and he didn't, and that proved to be not so doggone out of reach of a mutt like him as he had thought it. Furthermore, every once in a while, John was treated to a flash of secret smug complacency in discovering that Sally did not know as much as he thought she did. This was base! John was ashamed of himself. But he liked it, and it gave him somehow a warm feeling toward her.

Curiously enough, the contrary experience had the same effect on Sally. She was delighted over this new tendency of John's and entertained happily the prospect of "swapping educations," as he had expressed it. But promptly she discovered that John's humility had fooled her. John had a few unexplored areas of his own. She brought from the library books aimed at John's cultural innocence and was astonished to find that he had already read some of them! Quaintly enough he seemed to feel that he ought to apologize for this.

"You pick up stuff here and there, knocking about the way I did," said he.

His list was strangly haphazard, of course; but the thing that caught Sally was his point of view, which was entirely his own. As her quickened interest probed for his opinions, she realized how much weight has the convention of classic tradition on our own. To John, Shakespeare's characters were just folks, and he had known people—especially the men—just like them. Yes, he'd read Shakespeare, the whole business. There was a book of him somebody'd left in a bunk house up in the Galiuros, down in Arizona. The covers had been "tore off."

Sally glanced at the two fingers. They were folded. "Torn," said Sally softly.

"Torn off," agreed John equably, "but the reading was all there." John was chiefly astonished at the remarkable thinness of the paper. "Why, the whole thing wasn't thicker 'n that," he indicated.

"India paper," supplied Sally.

John's interest was caught.

"What's the difference from common paper? Do they make it in India?" he asked.

But Sally did not know: she'd look it up in the encyclopedia next time she went to the library.

Going back to Shakespeare: yes, John thought he was interesting. "*Othello;* that was a good yarn. That Iago was sure a son of a——" John choked, "sea cook," he caught himself. "But," added John, now fully under way, "if Othello had been sure of himself, Iago wouldn't have cut no ice. Oh, hell!" John thrust two fingers at Sally. "Let me be: I'm talking."

"Sure of Desdemona, you mean," said Sally.

"I do not. If he'd been sure of himself he'd have been sure of her. She was all right. But him being a nigger—well, a Moor then," all the same thing, far as John was concerned. "Anyway, if he'd been a white man, it would never have occurred to him that any white woman could go back on him. As I remember that coon he had pretty much of a swelled head. Shakespeare made him out as thinking he was pretty much the old he-wolf around them parts. If it hadn't been the color of his skin kind of made him touchy, far as women are concerned, he'd have kicked this Iago's backbone out of the top of his head and then gone home and told Desdemona all about it.

"Hamlet was just a nut. If the old man had had sense enough to put him in the bughouse early, they'd have avoided a lot of trouble."

Sally was a little taken aback at John's attitude toward Claudius and Gertrude and their murder of the king.

"Those were tough times," said he carelessly. "And what do you ever expect of politicians anyway? Look at Macbeth. And that Borgia outfit. Of course they were Wops," he acknowledged. He returned to Hamlet. "Polonius was the boy who ought to have had the job—he had the sabe, except he was a kind of weak sister when it came to handling men."

John's interest in the plays proved to be highly selective. He had not much use for the more fanciful—*Midsummer Night's Dream, The Tempest, As You Like It*. The historical plays had appealed to him most. He wanted to know if they were true, and if there were any more like that. They began to read history together. Shortly it became necessary to set the alarm clock nights as well as mornings, so they would know enough to go to bed.

CHAPTER V

THE FLOATS

JOHN BECAME a Sunday-morning habitué of the floats. For some time he remained merely a tolerated outsider to that quaint and self-contained community. For it was a community, apart from the city's population. Its members were a broad-shouldered, round-barreled lot, with hands that they carried at half grasp, and they all gave the impression of great strength, though possibly in many cases this appearance may have owed something to the thick, double-breasted pea jackets, which might well have been a uniform, so alike were they. Aboard their boats they moved with lightness and confidence, sensing and meeting the shifts of their footing; but ashore they stepped heavily, with slow accuracy, planting each foot. It was as though they distrusted the stability of the land.

This was off season for most of them. Accustomed, by necessity of tide and the habit of fish, to begin their day at north-latitude dawn, and at times to end it only when the dark waters sparkled with phosphorescence, they now luxuriated, lying in. Often John arrived, and there was not a sign of life except the blue plumes of wood smoke from the stovepipes, and here and there a dog, atop the house or in the bow, his nose flat to his paws, blinking sleepily but prepared to be vigilant should occasion require. Then hatches began to scrape back, heads to appear, men here and there to step on decks. There they stood for several moments and expanded their chests and shoulders and looked at the sky and all about them, sizing up the day. Their air of grand and spacious proprietorship tickled John. It was as though they owned the weather.

They moved about, stepping from boat to boat. The decks were an acknowledged common thoroughfare, so that even the guardian dogs did not lift their heads at one passing, though a stranger would have been clamorously challenged. A few seemed to have various small business to attend. To these slowly drifted idlers who roosted on house or combing. And there were always rows squatting on the stringers of the floats. They smoked and spat overside and stared straight ahead at nothing for a long time until someone was impelled to address a remark to empty space. Then ensued an exchange of gossip that might occasionally enliven into discussion or dispute for a while. It ran its course and sank below the companionable luxury of silence.

John, at first rather diffidently, ventured to join one of these groups on the stringers. They appeared not to object to John. One or two nodded briefly in his direction. Otherwise he might not have existed. It was not so much that they ignored him. He was negligible, like the sea gulls sitting there above, atop the tall piles. He was welcome to listen, if that pleased him, or just sit or smoke his pipe or go away. It was all one to them. This was a public float. His occasional experimental remark they paused gravely to attend. Perhaps after a while someone replied. But immediately they withdrew, as it were, to their own gossip or their own silence. It was better just to listen. John caught himself wondering humorously if he was real. Towards noon they got up, one by one, deliberately, and returned each to his own craft, where presently the smoke from the stovepipes thickened and blued for the noon meal. John was left alone, privileged to sit there or go away, just as he pleased.

Nevertheless he liked it. He was content to listen. There was a salty flavor to the talk. John developed an interest in the price of halibut, the injustices of cannery men. He discovered that there were certain subjects that were always good for an argument. The Fraser-river rig *versus* the sloop rig, for example. Each had its violent partisans. Like the single-cinch or the double-cinch saddle in the cow country, reflected John, and immediately felt a warm link of kinship. He came to know all the arguments on both sides, for they were standardized and repeated almost verbatim on each occasion, but as heatedly as though they were new. Nothing was ever settled. He tried hard to understand them. He wished he knew more about boats. Still he was learning something by listening and straight absorption and using his eyes. At first they had been just boats, just as all fishermen were fishermen. Slowly he began to sense the differences, and why certain groups were always the same. He commenced to understand the profound caste distinction between the deep-sea troller off Cape Flattery and the drift-net fisher of sheltered waters, and so to develop an eye for line and rig. He easily appreciated the vast difference between the compact, businesslike schooners that battled the seas off Flattery and the makeshifts that puttered inside on odd jobs of crabs, herrings, shrimps and the like. But some others must be more slowly puzzled out, such as the sturdy seiners with their low broad sterns for nets; and the Frasers with their low sweet lines.

Though John was not even a small part of this life it drew and held him. He returned to his customary existence refreshed as by wine. He liked it all. He liked the strangeness of it, the flavor of it. It opened a door. Even the breeze here was different. It snapped with a liveliness brought in from the sea, and of a fine day the wavelets danced, sparkling, and spoke with little voices against the timbers next to his feet. Nor did the rain, unless it was very heavy, interfere with the day. These men seemed wholly indifferent to wet. They owned the weather. And always a rich and pungent smell of tar and fish and strong tobacco, and John liked even that.

And then, one morning, without reason, quite smoothly and naturally, John was one of them. He had said nothing; he had done nothing. He was accepted. He did not know why, but the reason was simple enough. They had become accustomed to him. He was part of the landscape, like the gulls. The man next to him offered his pouch of tobacco.

Thereafter it was taken for granted that John belonged. The dogs knew this. He crossed decks under their noses on his way to someone's cabin in acceptance of an invitation to "mug up" on coffee in thick cups. Sometimes they acknowledged him by the slightest quiver of the tail, but they were neutral to his advances. It was not their business to make friends; only to recognize them.

John was interested in the tidy housekeeping. It was marvelously tidy, for he had been fortunate enough to fall in with the aristocracy of the trade, men who took pride in their craft. Everything had its place and was in it. Some of the contraptions and the economies of space delighted him with their ingenuity. Everything was compact, within hand's reach. John began to understand why these men stood still and threw back their shoulders and filled out their chests when they first came on deck. They were expanding to a new scale, a new dimension. The simplest things caught John's attention—such as a lamp in gimbals. He had never before been where a lamp needed anything but its solid base to stay upright. If this ignorance had been merely partial, it might have caused impatience or even contempt. But—as to nautical matters—it was so complete that it enlisted interest. It did not seem credible that a grown man should never have seen a deep-sea gurry rig: why, every longshore kid gets his pap to fix him a toy one on the dory and works it on blue perch! It was sort of amusing to think up something else to spring on John, the simpler the better. His naïve admiration gave a man a little swagger feeling inside. Obscurely they sensed John's quality, though they could not have defined it, so their self-esteem was the more warmed.

The season was waning. It was not yet time to begin fitting out in earnest, but here and there men began to tinker at odd jobs: replacing standing rigging, sandpapering in anticipation of painting weather, fitting new leathers in bilge pumps, cutting sheet brass into long rough blanks and tap-tap-tapping them to fit into a form carved in a block of hardwood. This was the artisan's model trolling spoon. After he had shaped it and smoothed it and fitted it with swivels at either end and attached the hook, he rigged it to a short line on a pole and dragged it back and forth overside. He watched critically its action in the water and retrieved it and tapped daintily a little here, a little there, modifying by a hair the overcurve of its tail, the up-tilt of its nose, perhaps the convexity of its medial line, and tried it again. Sometimes he hit what he wanted almost at once. Sometimes he must test over and over. But never did it dangle with its fellows, hung by the hooks on the wire in the cabin, until it performed to satisfaction. A row of self-appointed critics perched on cabin and rail and spat overside and proffered comment and suggestion, to which the artisan paid not the least attention. He had his own ideas and was willing to defend them, but not while he was busy. This matter of trolling spoons was one of the ever arguable subjects, never to be settled; whether they should be of the Stewart or the MacMahon type. But on one thing they did agree, an abysmal scorn for anyone who used anything store bought! John could not see any difference and said so, and they laughed at him tolerantly.

From time to time the close-packed integrity of the winter's lay-up between the floats began now to be disturbed. Somebody wanted to get out and later to get back in, after a low-tide session in the grid copper-painting the bottom. That involved much shifting of everybody else. John could lend a hand at this. He enjoyed it. They let him help in other small matters, much as one indulges a child. But here occasionally John surprised them. He could splice as well as they could, for instance; he was quick and deft with sail needle and palm; he could sew a neat grommet; he could throw a bowline; he seized rope ends competently; he got the laugh on old Svensen, elaborately preparing to teach him a Turk's Head, by taking the line from him and completing the knot before Svensen had barely begun. They did not know that all this was cowboy stuff as well as sailor stuff. It injected a wholesome doubt in their complacencies. They gave John more credit than he deserved. And indeed he was, in other things, an apt pupil. He caught on. It was never necessary to tell him or show him a thing twice. Sometimes he did not need to be told at all. He figured it out in advance. As the season neared, John was actually in demand on Sunday mornings.

"That feller, he's better 'n most hired hands," said old Svensen.

Sally was glad John had found something congenial to occupy the Sunday mornings. She was now playing the organ at the church and being paid for it. John was astonished to hear of this unsuspected accomplishment.

"It's a bluff," she confided to him. "I don't really play the organ. But it's enough like the piano so I can get by with simple things like hymns."

To John it was just as surprising and just as remarkable to learn that she could play the piano. Sally did not seem to think much of it; "not the little I can play," said she. He was fired with the desire to hear her perform, but he could not overcome his robust revulsion against the Reverend Morgan's exaggerated ecclesiastical elocution and his sanctimonious piety of manner. This was the fashion of the day, so that churchgoers accepted it as a part of church, without particularly noticing it; but John's inhabitude saw it fresh, as he had seen Hamlet and Othello. Sally did not try to combat his attitude. But she managed to get the keys to the church and to get hold of the boy who worked the pump and played for John on Sunday afternoon. He was enormously impressed. It was wonderful that Sally, his Sally, could sit up there so high and so little before that redoubtable gilded monster and cause it to roar mightily or sing small as she willed, as though it were a great obedient beast. John's heart swelled, for nothing more delighted him than to find something new to be proud of in Sally. She sure had that thing tamed!

He came away inspired with a wonderful idea. But inquiry, first chance he had, at Talman's Music Shop, on Fourth Street, ruined it, at least for the time being. He had no idea pianos cost anything like *that!*

He was proud of Sally, but at first he jibbed a little at the idea of her taking money. However, as that attitude was not really his own, but only a vague reflection of convention, he soon yielded. But on one point he was firm. They wanted Sally for the evening services also. He would not stand for that: nor, indeed, did the idea appeal to Sally herself.

"Then they probably won't want me mornings either," said she doubtfully.

However, the matter was arranged.

"I'm glad," said Sally. "You see I thought I'd use the money to rent a piano."

"Good lord!" cried John. "Can you rent the things? Nobody told me." He was disgusted with that fool clerk at Talman's; but he was glad Sally was going to have a piano anyway.

John's way home from the mill, after work, was by a streetcar on Second Street, just one block up from the water front. But quite often he would walk the extra short distance past the floats before turning up the hill. He did not stop; he wanted to get home for his hour before supper with Sally. But he liked to see the twinkle of lights and their reflected gleam and smell the cooking and catch the whiff of sea mingled with it and the dim loom of masts and the meditative lapping of waters. The floats were dark, save for the marking lights at their ends, and deserted. The life of the community had withdrawn within itself, like the sea anemones on its piles.

But on this particular night it had not withdrawn. On the contrary. John perceived the northerly float, the float ordinarily reserved for the aristocracy of the fleet, to be crowded with men, as were the decks of the boats in the immediate vicinity. Must be a full gathering, and an angry gathering, to judge by the voices. This was too much for John. He descended the ramp and stood for a minute or so trying to make out what it was all about. He could snatch only fragments. Too many men trying to talk each other down. Something about fish, of course. He touched the man next him.

"What's the row?" he asked.

The man turned so that John was able to see him clearly in the light from a street lamp above. John knew all the fishermen, but this was a stranger. He did not look like a fisherman; but neither did he look like a city man. In spite of a suit of somewhat baggy "store clothes," he carried an impress of the out of doors. In age he might have been anywhere between thirty and fifty. His figure was long and loose jointed and spare, but it looked strong and wiry. His face, too, was long and thin, the flesh at cheek and temple hollowed right down to the bony structure, but here, too, was no effect of emaciation, rather of hard carved leanness. His eyes, in deep sockets, surveyed John with lively and good-humored relish. John's interest quickened. He did not know this breed of cats.

"Same old thing," said the stranger. "Fish." He spat into the water. "The poor goddam fools," he added, an enormous contempt in his voice.

He spoke slowly, deliberately, without raising his voice, but John could hear him above—or below—the hubbub. He raised a hand to brush aside his long graying mustache. The hand was large and veined and knobby. And somehow at once the look of that hand added to the man a quality of deliberate competence that would never be hurried and would never fail. All the time John felt the stranger's eyes sizing him up in turn, and the stranger—slowly and competently—making up his mind.

"Every season same thing," the latter resumed presently. "Canners come out with the prices they are going to pay for fish, and the fishermen don't like them, and they get out like this and yowl like a lobo wolf that's going to tear up the moon by the roots, and then they go out and catch fish and sell 'em to the canners—at those prices," he added dryly.

"Well . . ." began John uncertainly.

"Little wuss than usual this year," admitted the stranger. "Six cents for reds, two for pinks, one cent for whites. Makes even me a little riled, and I don't give a damn, really, whether anybody ever catches another fish from now to doomsday. I've had to eat so many of the dang things I get to wish they'd forgot to invent 'em. God! At such prices I'd almost be inclined to turn fisherman myself just so I could catch them and throw them back. But that's goin' a leetle far." He acknowledged John's laugh with a slow smile. "Mebbe that 'll prod 'em so they'll do something," he resumed. "It sure would if they had the guts of a sea worm which hasn't hardly any at all, if that much. No, I take that back," said the stranger with an air of trying to be fair about it. "They got guts, or they wouldn't be goin' deep-sea in them rigs," he waved a hand in contemptuous dismissal of the whole fleet. "If they could agree together and stick to it for ten minutes . . ." he amended.

John's always eager interest in new things was greatly stirred. Here were plenty of new things. The man himself was new: John's experience of men was unable to place him. His various and apparently sincere scorns were new—for the fishermen on whom John had come near to bestowing a boyish hero worship, for their boats—what could possibly be criticized in them? Yet John liked this man; his opinions could not be dismissed. John must know them. As had happened to him before, a whole new world of some kind had suddenly opened before him. He must find out about it.

"What could they do?" he asked.

"I'll tell you if you want to know——" The stranger obviously had positive views. He stopped. "Jees," said he, "you can't hear yourself think here. Let's get out."

They mounted the ramp to the streets. At the top the man stopped and faced John.

"My name is Saunders," he announced formally.

"Mine's Murdock," said John.

"Pleased to meet you," said Saunders, with the air of encountering John for the first time, and solemnly thrust out his hand.

They shook, and at once Saunders' whole figure appeared to relax in sociable companionship.

"This is no good," he observed. "Let's go over to Casey's where we can set down and have a beer."

At this time of day Casey's was nearly empty, though Casey himself had already taken a place behind the bar. Daytimes he rarely bothered with personal supervision, but could always be produced at need from some mysterious back room. He was a burly man, the expression of whose face never changed, yet somehow one knew without mistake whether Casey liked him or not. Casey approved of a few, had no use whatever for a few, with most was indifferent and impersonal. He bounced efficiently but wholly without rancor. He knew all about everybody in his part of town. He knew John and nodded to him now, though, as we are aware, John had had little to do with the saloon. He knew Saunders and called him by name. "Here yet, hey, Len?" said he.

John and his new acquaintance sat at one of the round tables just off the bar. Casey himself brought their beer.

"Kelly not in yet," he half questioned.

"You'd be the first to know it if he was."

"I guess," agreed Casey. He jerked his head toward the float. "Strike?"

"I suppose. They're still jawing."

Casey moved the cloth in his hand round and round one spot, near the center of the table.

"What's the offer?" he asked Casey presently.

"Six, two and one."

The saloon keeper shook his head.

"Small pickings," said he. He moved slowly away. "There's yellow dogs in every pack," he said over his shoulder.

"And there's ways of handling yellow dogs," said Len Saunders, calling after him. Casey nodded his head without looking around. Len took a draft of his beer. "Where I came from they'd handle 'em all right," he muttered. He set down his glass and rested both elbows on the table and turned his attention to John. "I can't quite make you out, old timer," said he, "but you ain't any cheechako back where you belong from. Where's that?"

John chuckled.

"Back where I belong from we never ask strangers that question."

Saunders was still looking him over.

"Thought you had a look of hoss about you," said he, "though I ain't took notice of your legs."

John laughed outright.

"Keno!" he surrendered. "Well, I ain't stole away; I'm still a couple of jumps ahead of the sheriff. I'd as soon tell you. Call it from Montana to Mexico. I don't rightly belong anywhere—except here," he added.

"You don't belong here," stated Saunders positively. "I ain't prying," he added in half apology, "but I like to place a man in my mind."

"So do I," said John pointedly.

"Oh, me. I'm from Alaska."

"Alaska!" cried John, leaning forward.

But Len was not ready to talk about Alaska.

"You was asking about them poor dumb brutes." He jerked an elbow in the general direction of the water front. "It's simple, like I told you. All they got to do is quit. The canners got to have fish; they can't begin to get enough for a pack from the traps. They'd come around fast enough with decent prices. Ten or twelve cents for reds, say. Only they know damn well that all they got to do is to sit tight and pretty soon one or another of these yellow dogs Casey speaks of gets pinched kind of low and begins to sneak in a load or two, and some more of the yellow dogs hears about it and don't want to get left out, and before you know it the whole strike is busted wide open, and everybody's out hustling fish." Len spat disgustedly at a sawdust-filled box ten feet away—and hit it.

"I suppose those first poor devils got to eat," said John doubtfully.

"Why shouldn't they eat—if they stick together?" Saunders fired up belligerently. "That's what I'm telling you! But they got no notion of it. They talk big about it, but there ain't a half-dozen men in that whole fleet got brains enough to fork over a pound of grub or a dollar of his own to keep the show going. The canners stick together all right. Hey, Casey, fill 'em up."

"And bring some cigars," added John. "So it's different in Alaska, is it?"

"You're God a'mighty damn right it is!" said Len. "And so I've told these poor timid sand peeps plain enough. Trouble is, the ones among 'em with any get-up-and-git in 'em has already *gone* to Alaska. Them that's left hasn't got lime enough in their backbones to whitewash the backside of a muskeeter. There's better prices there, and steadier, there's more fish and bigger fish and easier got at. Say, you can't have no idee. In the run you can't wade across a stream without bracing your legs so they don't get knocked out from under you by salmon buttin' again you. If they'd hold still you could walk right across on their backs. I'm not fooling. You just ought to see a salmon run!"

"I have," said John. "I was raised on a ranch not far from the Dalles."

"Oh—yes." Len was momentarily deflated. It was slowly being borne in on John that Len was already somewhat tight. "Well, anyway," Len recovered himself, though he now spoke more reasonably, "there ain't no comparison at all, to a rational man, and if they had any sense they'd move on up out of this mess, and I've told 'em so till I've got tired of being sorry for such dumb critters." Len was losing interest in fish. He stared at his empty glass for a moment. "Let's make it whisky," he suggested abruptly. "It's a good chaser."

"All right," agreed John. But he did not want Saunders to run down. "Or don't the canners try it on up there?" he asked. The question worked.

"Bet your life they do," assented Len fervently. "But they don't get nowhere with it."

"Fishermen stick together?" suggested John.

Saunders laughed out loud, and John somehow was startled, as though at a rare phenomenon.

"Don't have to," he replied in the manner of one confiding a secret. "It's the canners that don't stick."

The situation, Len explained further, was the exact reverse. It was the canners who got together and set the scale and agreed solemnly with each other not to buy any fish from anybody at a higher price. And then the season began, and it was short—much shorter than here down south—and they had to have fish or put up a short pack. And it wasn't three days, said Len gleefully, after the run really started, before you could get your money, on the quiet, most anywhere you took your fish, if you just kept mum about it.

"Hell, they begin to plan double-crossing each other before they get out of their meeting!" said Len.

There were too many of them. Down here was only a few big companies, Len explained. Up there was the big companies and a whole raft of little fellows, one-line independents, all trying to cut each other's throats or gobble each other up. "I," observed Len parenthetically and without emotion, "was one of the little fellows; I got gobbled up. Fisherman's paradise, if they only knowed it. I don't give a damn one way or another," added Len. "I'm no fisherman. Nothing to it. All they need is a little brains, a few guts and maybe a strip of iron bark."

"Iron bark? What's that for?" John caught at this.

"Sheathin'. Along the waterline. Ice."

John's face kindled at the word.

"Spray freezin' to the rigging"—Len's voice was sarcastic—"grindin' of the floes. Franklin. Greeley. Bergs loomin' up through the fog. My hero! Rats!" He surveyed John a contemptuous moment. "All the ice you get is mebbe a little glacier ice workin' up some of the inlets."

"I bet it's pretty cold at that," volunteered John in retreat.

"Oh, my God." Len exhibited exaggerated weariness. "It must be awful cold," he said in a high, mimicking voice. "That's what they all spring on you, every damn one of 'em, just the minute you say 'Alaska' to them. Say!" He turned on John in startling belligerence. "Alaska's got a goddam sight better climate than this stinkin' wet hole, let me tell you! Rocks and ice—that's all you think. You and your country!" he dismissed the state of Washington. "What you got? We got it better and bigger and more room for it. Stick those damn measly little things you call mountains up there, and you'd never see 'em, less 'n you're looking for foothills. Let me tell you——" He gave it up suddenly. "Oh hell! Casey!"

"This is on me," said John.

This was the first time in many months John had sat at a table and had a lot of drinks. And it was also the first time he had swapped men-talk and cussed aplenty and smoked a see-gar and

swaggered spiritually in that expansive glow of comradeship possible only with another male. He had not missed these things. He
had not realized their absence. If confronted with the thought he
would have laughed at it. He saw plenty of men: the mill men, the
fishermen. But his instinct knew better. With the mill men he
worked. The fishermen were better, but them he visited in alien
country—their boats and their occupation and their very thoughts.
There had lacked a catalyst, some place like Casey's, with its saw-
dusted floor, its dingy bar and its big mirror covered with designs
traced in soap and the bottles and the pyramids in front of it and
the chromo of Custer's Last Stand on one wall and the fully matured
naked lady on the other and the flyblown garlands of colored paper
and the unventilated swirls of tobacco smoke, fully to release for him
the loud, rough, satisfactorily vulgar essence of masculinity in which
he could blend with a fellow being and wherein was the sustenance
necessary to their souls. Here it was, for John, because he and this
fellow, Len Saunders, spoke the language of the same tribe. He could
have stayed on until midnight swapping yarns with Len. He pulled
out his watch and looked at it. He got to his feet, uttering an exclamation of surprise. No idea it was so late, he told Len; must get
on home. He'd see Len some more, have him out to the house . . .

John stepped forth from Casey's into the street. Certain starved
psychic tissues were all plumped up. All departments of his being
were in balance, fed and satisfied. Therefore he felt top of the world.
He looked at his watch again. Gosh, it *was* late! He decided to walk
home. Another twenty minutes would not make any difference. He
felt like walking.

He climbed a block and set off along First Street, singing under
his breath snatches of cowboy ballads. He used the range versions
in preference to those offered the general public. They lacked re-
finement, but John felt ribald. He had his hat cocked over one eye.
People looked after him. Some of them laughed, but in amused
sympathy. John did not bother about them. He had much grander
things to occupy him, though he did not know what they were. Up
near Madison Street he encountered the two girls, Eloise and her

yellow-haired friend, who had stopped him on his way to the water front that first morning long ago. This was not remarkable, for here was their beat and hour. They recognized him at once in spite of the lapse of time and the change in his clothing.

"Hullo, lumberjack!" Eloise stepped before him. He came down from somewhere to recall them.

"Oh, hello," said he. "Ain't you girls gone home to bed *yet?*" He waved them majestically aside.

Somewhere beyond the Washington Hotel certain practical affairs of life began to loom in the fog. It was borne in on John that he must commence to lay a course or collide with them. There was Sally. He had not really forgotten Sally, of course; but up to this moment she had been hull down and becalmed, as it were. John paused to admire his nautical imagery. Regular sailor talk. This idea slipped him sideways into another realm of relativity, so that he glowed with extraordinary affection for his fishermen friends, whom he now perceived to be fine fellows, in spite of what Len had said about them. And when he got his boat—— He halted short to contemplate this thought. It had just popped into his mind, natural as you please. After a moment he walked on. Sure, he was going to get a boat. Always intended to get a boat.

Oh yes, Sally! Sally was going to be sore—at first. He couldn't blame Sally. She'd got supper all ready, and probably it had got cold waiting, or all burned up; and it was quite a chore cooking supper, and Sally always took a lot of pains over it. He'd be mad himself. Serve him right if she hadn't saved him any. That was all right: he wasn't hungry, or he could rustle in the new icebox.

"Gosh, I'm going to catch hell!" John was tickled. He'd never seen Sally really mad. He'd get what was coming to him, all right. John felt largely tolerant and magnanimous toward Sally because he was so willing to acknowledge that she had a right to get mad. But she didn't know about Len. When she knew about Len she'd be sorry she got mad.

The thought that Sally might have been worried about him never even cast a shadow on his mind.

The shades were up. He could see her sitting by the table under the lamp. She appeared to be doing nothing at all, just sitting there. "Laying for me with a stuffed club!" John chuckled to himself. He was in great feather. The situation was one of high comedy. It had worked around so that, somehow, the joke was on Sally. John cast about in his mind how to make the most of it and still smooth down Sally. He decided to be funny.

So he tilted his hat still farther and sneaked cautiously up the front steps and across the porch to the front door. Here he paused to get a good ready, then suddenly snatched open the door, leaped into the room and struck a pose.

"Hoopla!" shrilled John in conventional circus-clown entrance. "Here we are again!"

It seemed to him a good idea at the time; but somehow the scene fell flat. The comedy aside, his sudden appearance might have done the trick, were it not that his muffled footsteps across the front porch had not been quite as muffled as he had fondly believed them. Sally had heard. By the time the doorknob had ceased its careful turning, profound and thankful relief had passed its brief moment. She looked at John in such a way that the enormous imbecility of his posture was revealed to him as by a blinding light. He sank back on his heels and removed his hat from the side of his head and tossed it in the general direction of the davenport, after which stage business he turned to Sally a rather sickly smile of propitiation.

"I'm sorry to be so late, honey, honest I am," said John. He made a move toward Sally, but thought better of it. The climate did not seem right in that direction. "Gosh," said John, "you don't know how surprised I was when I looked at my watch and saw what time it was! I came right away then; but then I thought, 'Well, Sally wouldn't wait supper this long anyway, so I'll just walk home instead of taking the streetcar,' and that took me a little longer of course—— You did have supper, didn't you, honey?" No reply to this. "Oh!" John bethought himself. "You see I struck a fellow down at the floats, and we got to talking—the fishermen were having a big pow-wow over the prices of fish—that is, what the canneries were going to pay this next season—and of course they were pretty mad and talking pretty loud, so Len and I—Len's this fellow I was telling you about—Len Saunders is his name, and he's a fine fellow, different from anybody you ever saw before in your life, he's had so much experience. You'd like Len. He told me that in Alaska—you see he comes from Alaska—he went up there only about ten years after we took over from the Russians——" He stopped. Where was he? Doggone it, why didn't Sally say something and not just sit there like that looking at him that way? John was still standing in the middle of the floor, and he had a curious sensation that he was getting bigger and clumsier and more spraddled out and footless every second, while Sally became smaller and more compact and self-contained and competent. What he ought to do was walk over to the big armchair and set down and cross his legs and fill his pipe, easylike. But he couldn't. He had to stand there and let her look at him like—like a little small stick of giant powder with a short fuse. Somehow it had worked around so the joke was no longer on Sally. It was on him. If there was a joke. John cleared his throat. "So we went over to Casey's," he began again, "and got to talking, and you don't know how surprised I was when I looked at my watch——" Doggone, he was back right where he started from! A first faint warmth of indignation began to animate his abjectness. He had it coming to him all right, but why didn't she *say* something?

She was saying something in a tight, level voice.

"Did it occur to you that it was just possible I could not have one idea of what had happened to you?" she asked; then, before he could reply, "Did it enter your head that I might think something *had* happened to you?"

Obviously this had not occurred to John, as his bewildered face testified.

"Or," continued Sally, still evenly, but in one tone higher of intensity, "that I might be sitting here by myself, hour after hour, getting more and more frantic with worry? Imagining all sorts of things?" She stopped, bit her lip, caught back a control that was slipping.

She arose to her feet so quickly that John instinctively stepped back. Without a glance in his direction she went into the bedroom, but almost immediately returned. Her movements were staccato, as though each was a container of an energy that must be held in. She had jammed her small felt hat on her head and was struggling into her coat.

"Where—where are you going?" stammered John. Things were moving much too fast for him. "Honey! You aren't going *away!*" At last he was able to move. He made as though to stop her. She faced him squarely, her small chin thrust out.

"If you want to know," said she, "I'm going to the hotel. I must telephone."

"Telephone!" John was again all at sea.

"Yes, telephone. To the police. That you've got back."

She made as though to pass him.

"Hold on," said John. "Let's get this straight. What's this about the police?" Abruptly he was sober. His eyes had steadied on hers in a cool, level directness that some of his former associates back in the Great Basin had learned to think of as dangerous. Sally stood still waiting for him to give her passage. John's face slowly reddened, but he gave no other indication as yet that now he, too, was thoroughly angry. Indeed, his next remark was made with the silky gentleness that, to the Great Basin, had also been a danger signal.

"I asked you a question," said he.

"I telephoned the police that you had disappeared and to look for you," said Sally, as though to a child.

"I see," said John. His eyes did not leave her face. Nevertheless, for a moment, his gaze seemed to shift like a searchlight beacon to something hidden and then to swivel back. "And why," his voice was still gentle, "did you do that?"

In face of what she sensed to be a new and strange domination, Sally's long-held control gave way.

"What did you expect me to do?" she cried angrily. "Sit here like a ninny and wait your good pleasure, not knowing whether you'd been hurt or killed?"

"Hurt or killed?" John repeated the words in soft interrogation.

"You weren't at the mill, I telephoned there. You'd left the mill hours before. You might have been slugged and robbed, you might have—how was I to know where you were? You've never been late before. And you didn't come, and you didn't come—I couldn't stand it any longer. I went over to the Lonergans' and asked him to go down to the floats to see if you were there, but I couldn't believe you were there because I couldn't imagine your staying so late without sending me word, and Mr Lonergan thought so too, and he went with me over to the Washington, and we telephoned the hospitals, but they didn't know anything——" Sally had talked herself close to tears, which the right word from John would have released.

"Did Lonergan tell you to telephone the police?" He pursued his interrogation relentlessly.

"No. I had to do something, or I'd go crazy!" For the moment Sally was on the defensive. But only for a moment. "And while I was suffering torments, you sat there in a saloon, *drinking!*" She threw out the word scornfully, her anger rekindling. "Without one thought that I might be——"

"When I need a nurse to look after me I'll let you know," John cut her short. "I can take care of myself. I've managed to so far without any help." His own anger was getting away from him. The merits of the case were submerged by it. All John could see, right now, was the spectacle of himself—he, John Murdock—led home by a grinning cop like a strayed small boy. Suppose they'd happened to find him at the float or in Casey's or even had picked him up as he walked up Second Street. Nice thing that would be! He was getting madder every minute. Better look out! some remnant of sense warned him. "You go to bed," he told Sally curtly. "I'll do the telephoning."

"You needn't bother," said Sally with spirit.

He did not reply, but turned on his heel and went out. His anger was helpless, for there was nothing he could do about it. She stared at the door, her hands tight clenched, in a despair of complete bafflement.

When John returned Sally was in bed, and the light turned low in the living room. He undressed there, extinguished the lamp, entered the bedroom with an elaborate absence of any effort at quiet. In the dimness John could just make out her small figure huddled as far as it could get toward the edge of the bed. It lay very still, too still for sleep. Nevertheless, it did not stir when John thrust himself beneath the covers. He flopped on his side, also as near his edge of the bed as he could get. They lay there, back to back, rigid and motionless lest each should know the other was awake, and the space between them was as the space of astronomical distance.

When the alarm clock sounded the following morning John got up, made his own breakfast, packed his tin lunch box and departed for work. Sally did not stir.

The coolness of time passing at work that did not engage all his attention had its effect. John got over his heat and began a little to regret. But he did not see what was to be done, unless the night had brought Sally around so that she was now able to see things reasonably. John made generous allowances for Sally, for now that he had got over being mad he could see she had a lot of excuse for getting fussed up. But not to go all to pieces that way! John flushed for shame of Sally whenever that police business recurred to his mind. He held Sally so dear that he hated to have to feel ashamed of her about anything. She'd gone all to pieces over nothing! Well, practically nothing. Good lord! After ten years of the kind of life he'd led with the wild bunch he certainly might be held competent to handle the Seattle water front! Whenever his thoughts took that track he began to get mad all over again. He'd just have to accept the fact. But he could not see how things could ever be quite the same again. And as the day wore on a more immediate and therefore more dismaying thought bore ever the more swiftly down on him. He had to go home. How would they meet? What would she say? What was he to say? John's imagination constructed, released and discarded a dozen sketch dramas. As the closing hour neared he felt quick shoots of panic. He was scared. He had half a mind to go get drunk, good and drunk.

That was the best thing that could have happened to John. Not the getting drunk, but the thought of getting drunk as a way out. For it brought him an astounding illumination; so astounding that he stopped short in his tracks and nearly got bumped in the back of the head by a traveling block and did get cursed most profanely by Alex Hart, who was manipulating the block.

His idea of getting drunk was just his way of calling in the police! Yes, and Alex's explosion of profanity—same thing. Alex held no such considered opinion of his person and ancestors as he had expressed. Alex was a good friend of his. But Alex had been scared. And when he had yielded in thought to that impulse to get drunk, he had been scared. And none of them had meant any of it, really; it was just their different ways of getting scared.

He went on about his business of the moment—which was that of tally clerk—so absent-mindedly as to draw a call-down from the yard boss. There remained in him no trace of resentment, but the immediate realities had not bettered. He still had to go home; and the mess must be straightened out; and what Sally was going to say, and what he could say—to make Sally understand . . .

CHAPTER VI

LEN

BY THE closing whistle John was sunk. Instead of going at once to the car line he dragged miserably along the water front, lost in gloom. This extra excursion was made with no thought of pleasure, but merely to postpone by even a little the dreaded moment. He was oblivious of his surroundings. At the top of the ramp stood Len Saunders, looking down on the floats. Len greeted him. He replied glumly and passed on. He was completely off Len Saunders; which was unjust, but this is a world of injustices. Saunders looked after him in faint surprise.

John continued on a dozen paces. He came hurriedly back. He seized Len by the arm. He was no longer completely off Len. On the contrary. Never in his life had he been so glad to run across a man. Len must come home with him to supper. John would not take no. Len must meet his wife; Len must tell her, tell them both, more about Alaska. John was almost feverishly cordial, overriding Len's demurs.

"Your clothes are all right," he said impatiently. "Of course she'll be glad to see you. She doesn't have to know ahead; she always has plenty for supper. Oh, *anybody* can get along with Sally, she wouldn't scare a rabbit. She . . ."

Len surveyed him from under his thick brows, the corners of his eyes crinkled with amusement.

"Well," he drawled finally, "you mind me of a preacher who met him up with an old she-bear and cubs, and it looked like he'd better get to praying. 'Oh Lord,' sez he, 'vouchsafe thy servant a weepon to his hands, preferable a model 40–90 Winchester.' Then, as the bear was getting pretty close, and there wasn't any miracle yet, 'But anything 'll do,' yells the preacher, 'even a newspaper would come in handy.' Gave you hell for last night, did she?" Len chuckled.

John flushed. He was embarrassed. He wanted to defend himself. He wanted to explain. He wanted to defend Sally. Len waved all this aside.

"I'm tough," said he. "Any critter takes a bite at me just blunts his teeth. Let's get going."

But John felt that Len did not understand things as he should.

"Look here," interrupted Len, "this wife of yourn. She's a kid, like you, ain't she? She's a female woman, ain't she? That's all I want to know."

He refused further conversation until they had left the streetcar.

By that time John's spirits had again dropped to zero. What could this roughneck know about it? A woman like Sally was wholly outside his experience. His original idea of taking Len home as a buffer had seemed a good one; but if Len was going to butt in . . . John was getting disturbed.

"Rest easy, bub," Len broke the silence with another of his startling flashes of intuition. "I ain't going to make any breaks. But don't you make none either. Just ease along till we get a chance to try the water."

"You see," hesitated John, "Sally's sort of different, and she——"

"I know, I know," Len laid his hand on John's shoulder. "All you need is to hide behind me. That's what you brung me for, ain't it?" He chuckled indulgently; and John somehow felt like a lost small child, and Sally another lost small child, and them both taken by the hand, which was no way for a grown man to feel; but he liked it.

Sally received them brightly and agreeably. Too brightly: too agreeably. That was the trouble. Her conduct was impeccable. She was glad to meet Len; she was glad John had brought him home to supper; she talked; she seemed to display a polite interest in making Len talk. In all things her demeanor was correct. Nevertheless, John could have shaken her. She was too dang bright and chipper! She deliberately talked about things Len could not possibly know anything about. She was getting back at John through the unfortunate Len, by methods to which John could take no possible exception.

As for Len, in the interval before supper and at the meal itself he sat on the edges of chairs and said "yes ma'am" and "no ma'am." John was sorry for him. His brag had certainly been called. The only satisfaction to John was that Len was indeed finding out how little he knew about women like Sally.

But at the end of the meal Len unexpectedly asserted himself. He got to his feet and began to help Sally carry the dishes into the kitchen.

"You sit and smoke with John," said she. "This won't take two minutes."

He paid her no attention.

"I won't wash them now," Sally tried again, when finally they were all stacked on the drainboard. "I'll do them later, or in the morning when there is more time."

Len turned on a faucet and tested the water with his finger. He looked about him, spied two dishpans hanging under the sink, haled them forth.

"Poor business," said he. "No sense addin' dirty dishes to what's on your mind. Get them out of the way before you settle down. Then you can set comfortable."

He turned on the hot-water faucet into one of the dishpans; looked about for the soap, discovered it at last in a little wire cage with a handle, examined this arrangement with approval and a faint surprise.

"That's handy," he observed. He swished it about in the hot water, making suds, moved that dishpan aside and filled the other, made as though to test the water.

"Look out!" warned Sally.

He looked at her in slow inquiry.

"You'll scald your hands."

He turned them over, examining them on all sides as though he had never seen them before.

"What, *them?*" said Len. He smiled abstractedly and finished his test. "Oak tanned," he confided to Sally.

Sally caught at the cool ascendancy that somehow seemed to be escaping her.

"I should much prefer," said she, "to postpone this until later."

"You can wipe," said Len. "Where's your dishrags?"

John appeared in the doorway.

"What's going on here?" he wanted to know. "Oh—can I help?"

He was obviously nonplused. In John's world, as a matter of course, women did the women's work—when there were any women —just as men did the men's work. He would have been perfectly willing to help, but the thought had never even entered his head.

"You go sit down," said Len. "We'll tend to this."

John hovered a moment and disappeared. Len methodically washed a plate in the soapy water, swished it about in the rinsing water, handed it to Sally. After a moment's hesitation she took it and began slowly to dry it on one of the soft towels she made for this purpose from emptied flour bags. She was staring at Len with puzzled attention. His hands must indeed, as he said, be oak tanned. He plunged them in and out of the hot water indifferently. He did not look at Sally. Indeed he seemed quite unaware of her, except as a recipient for the cleaned utensils. His awkwardness had somehow evaporated. He was at ease in a native self-sufficing dignity of his own. Somehow, without a word said, the roles had been reversed. In spite of herself Sally felt diminished. Len had become a personality. She was puzzled.

The silence continued a long time. Len's serene detachment began slightly to annoy Sally. Somehow he had escaped her.

"John tells me you come from Alaska, Mr Saunders," she said abruptly.

Len turned a limpid blue eye in her direction.

"Yes ma'am." And then after a pause: "I know somethin' about *Alaska.*"

The timing and the slight emphasis on the last word seemed to give the phrase significance. Or did it? Sally glanced sharply at Len's face. Its expression was serene, bland and innocent. But she could not be sure. She flushed slightly.

"I suppose it's awfully cold up there?" She asked the usual banality from the surface uncertainty of her mind. But it did not arouse Len's indignation as when John had made the same remark.

"It ain't nigh so cold as it looks to people's minds," said Len. "Things is hardly ever as chilly as they look to be, outside." Another pause. "That was an extra-fine supper you gave us, especially and you not expecting company. I know: I'm a sort of a cook myself. Got to be." He reached out suddenly to take from her hand the plate she was about to dry, examined the bottom and plunged it again into the soapy water. "Condemned," he said briefly. Now how, wondered Sally, did he see that? He must have eyes in the side of his head. "Funny thing," Len was continuing placidly, "how a man gets to be a good cook just cooking for himself, but a woman she's got to have a man to cook for, or she's no good at it at all. Yes, that was sure a fine supper." He examined the bottom of the plate, tested a speck of black on it with his fingernail and plunged it into the rinsing water. "Growed there," he remarked briefly of the spot. Again the pause. "Appearances is generally deceitful, as the poet says," observed Len.

Sally stopped wiping dishes to attend to Len. She looked at him afresh, with new eyes. Here was now none of the embarrassment of awkwardness before which she had so strutted her superiorities. Len was quite at ease. Sally doubted if he had ever really felt otherwise. It came to her with a slight shock that the shoe was on the other foot, that all along he had been secretly enjoying himself. Playing a part, as it were. Sally had a quick mind. She caught the connection. He wasn't fooling her any more.

As though he sensed accurately the moment when she reached this point, Len's mild blue eyes swiveled in her direction. They were blank and bland and noncommittal. Then, as they held her own, an inquiry crept into them, succeeded after a moment by a faint twinkle deep down.

"Ain't that right?" asked Len.

"What?"

"That a woman ain't as mad as she looks when she cooks a man as good a supper as that?"

She gave back his gaze defiantly for a moment, then suddenly she laughed.

"He's real sorry," said Len.

The words reminded Sally of her grievances.

"Then I think he'd better tell me so!" she cried.

But Len did not at once meet this.

"How long you two been married?" he asked.

"Seven months."

Len sighed.

"That's not very long, is it, lookin' at it one way? And yet it's a long while sometimes, lookin' at it another. Now you take it wintertimes, back country, in Alaska—not on the coast; that's mild. You've no idee how long it can be when you're snowed up and can't get around none." Len laid aside his wash rag and perched one hip up on the drainboard, a feat his length made possible, and settled down as though for a long comfortable chat. "Gets you by and by," said he, "so you act like nothin' human, and when spring breaks and it's all behind you, you look back and wonder if you're the same fellow." Len paused to chuckle reminiscently. "There was two old cusses I knew been pardners twenty years. They lived together and summered together and wintered together and got drunk together and stuck to each other like death to a dead nigger. Cuss out ary one of them, and you had the other one crawlin' your hump. And they never had no differences between themselves.

"They'd wintered it together a lot of times, like I said, but they got out and around a lot, for they were running trap lines. And then one year they got snowed in, good and plenty. One of them bad blizzard years. Couldn't stick their noses out for three solid months. They were all right: plenty of grub. But you know what? They got so they weren't speakin'. Fact! And then one morning one of 'em took a swallow from his cup and spit it out. 'That's rotten coffee,' says he, which was the fust words spoken in that cabin for a week. And the other fellow, who had made the coffee, didn't say nothing back, but he just pulled out his six shooter and——"

"Oh!" cried Sally.

"No ma'am. He put a hole plumb through that coffeepot. Now wa'n't that just plumb ridiculous?"

Len laughed and slipped down from the edge of the drainboard.

Sally did not pretend to misunderstand.

"But we haven't been cooped up together all the time," she objected. "John's had his work and I——"

"Have had your play," interjected Len with uncharacteristic swiftness.

"You mean . . ." Sally was thoughtful.

Len laid his hand on her arm.

"Now mind you, I don't know nothin' about it—John ain't said a word. But I'm guessin' he's stuck pretty close—off hours I mean." His eyes held hers compellingly. After a moment Sally bowed her head. "It's only nat'ral, Sally," said Len gently. "I think he's done damn well. Excuse me," he caught back the oath with quaint and incongruous primness.

"Oh, I'm not blaming him," burst out Sally. "I can see that. But why *couldn't* he have let me know! I nearly died!"

"He knows that," said Len. "He's sorry. But," he fixed her with an eye that for the first time proved itself capable of sternness, "don't you go for to make him say so. Understand?"

"Why shouldn't he say so? I'm sorry for being such an idiot—about the police, I mean."

"Police?"

"I—I reported to the police. I got so worried finally that I——"

"You sicked the police on him!" cried Len incredulously. "Oh, jeeker-snipes!" He began to laugh. He clung to the edge of the drainboard. He dissolved in laughter, doubling over helplessly. "That's *funny!*" said he, wiping his eyes with the back of his hand. He looked at her small figure with new compassion. "You pore kids. Seven months," said he.

"I suppose it *was* funny," said Sally in a doubtful voice.

"Not for you." Len sobered suddenly. "You were scairt."

He handed her the last of the dishes, emptied the dishpans, methodically wrung out the cloth and hung it up.

"Now," said he cheerfully, "we're goin' in and have a good time. And after I go, *you act nat'ral!*"

He started toward the door. Sally followed more slowly.

"Len," she said in a small voice.

He turned. She stood before him, very small below his great height. The eyes she raised to his were swimming.

"Huh?" asked Len.

"Nothing—only—Len, do you know, you're something of a dear!"

"Just act nat'ral," repeated Len.

Len now became the life of the party and was as garrulous as before he had been silent. John stared at him in puzzled amazement. And Sally! It was as though the two had known each other for years. She wanted to hear about Alaska. She insisted that Len tell about Alaska.

"It's never been anything to me but a space up north." She made a comical face. "I asked him whether it wasn't awfully cold up there," she confided parenthetically to John. He brightened visibly at this attention. "By the look of his face, I gathered he had trouble getting through the tropical vegetation!" She laughed, and Len chuckled. He pondered a moment collecting his thoughts.

"It's kinda hard to commence with a standing start that way," he confessed. "Alaska's too big. It's too many kinds of things. I've lived there twenty-odd years, and I ain't even begun to know about it."

"What is there about it that especially appeals to you?" prompted Sally. "Why do you like to live there?"

"It's big," said Len. "It's big—and it's brand-spang new. Nobody's spoiled it yet. Don't believe they can. It's like this country must have been, way back, when white folks fust come to it. Better," he amended. He groped painfully for expression. "I reckon I like it because a man's got room up there, and plenty of air, and he's his own boss, and he stands on his own feet. It's up to him. Everything's there for him, but he's got to have the sabe and the guts to go after it. If he gets in trouble, he's got to be quick on his feet getting out: there ain't no police for him to holler for——" He checked short as he realized the slip, but at once caught himself. "Safe place for John, here," he said boldly. He cast toward Sally a look of challenge.

"He'd better take me there." She laughed gaily and then flushed a little with pleasure at the profound approbation she caught in Len's eyes. "I think you have the makings of an Alaskan, all right," she hastened on, "quick on your feet getting out of trouble," she explained. "But you haven't told me yet what it's *like*," she urged.

She questioned him and continued to question, and Len answered until at last he kindled and was off under his own power. They listened in growing fascination as a picture took form. Mountains two miles high, not as isolated peaks as in the Cascades, but in range after range, up and up and back and back, unbroken ramparts shouldered together containing and guarding the unknown. About their feet illimitable forests of spruce and fir, garments let fall.

"Timber line's low in that country," said Len, "mebbe three or four thousand feet.

"Turquoise-blue glaciers, like big rivers awinding. Some places they run right down to the sea, and there the bergs break off and float away.

"Something to see, that," said Len, "and hear. Sounds like the world's busting up.

"Man wants to go where no man ever set foot before, there's his chance," said Len. "He could poke around for years and always somethin' new." Lakes swarming with trout. The meanderings of wooded canyons alive with rivers, and wide hidden valleys opening out. Great waterfalls—some of them taller 'n Niagara, Len assured them, dozens of them. Everywhere. The sound of them falling was never out of your ears. "Sort of big and solemn," said Len, "like mountains look."

"It must be lovely," sighed Sally, "but a little big—and frightening. Unfriendly."

"That's just the back country," Len hastened to assure her. "Along the coast it's friendly enough." He tried for an image. "You know that paper they use to put on shelves with the edges all scalloped and punched and cut out in fancy patterns? Well, the coast is like that, fifty mile deep in islands and bays and inlets, and passages between, so's a man could sail around in there till he grew gray whiskers and never cross his own wake." Hundreds of harbors, thousands of them, where a man can put in, and in every one of them rivers and long flats and meadows. "Man would never suspect he was anywhere near a high country at all," said Len, "less'n he caught an opening in the trees." Nothing big and frightening about that, he told Sally. Cozy as you please. Everything grows fine there account of the long hours of sunshine. In June the daylight's never out of the sky all night. Grass in the meadow higher'n your head. "And," Len addressed Sally directly, "you ought to see the flowers, hundreds of acres of them, solid; sure a pretty sight. Why," said Len, "I wouldn't live nowhere else if you give me the whole show and throwed in, a drink for good measure!"

"Good game country?" John asked his first question.

Best in the world. Len was positive about that, though at first he seemed to despair of his ability to express in words how good a game country it was. Swarms of small stuff. Ducks and geese by the million—that's where the whole population breeds. You don't hunt deer: you just go out and get one. Any man, said Len impressively, who kills him a deer more'n forty rods from his small boat is just a damn fool looking for hard work. No need to. Deer are so thick that the soft ground looks like a flock of sheep had trompled it. Get you a sheep or goat any time you want to climb for it. Bear everywhere. See a dozen a day if you look for 'em. John could not inhibit a look of doubt when Len said that some of them stood ten or twelve feet high on their hind legs.

"I ain't lying," said Len without heat. "Don't have to. I do lie a little sometimes, to some folks," he acknowledged, "but that's only to keep practiced so's I won't strain myself when I tell the truth. I ain't lying to you folks now. Honest I ain't. It's just like I say."

They had to believe him.

"Can a man make a good living up there?" asked John.

Len came off the boil. He examined this soberly.

"Depends on what you mean by a good living," he replied, picking his words with care. "If you mean getting a lot of money, I dunno. Some makes good money—canners and such. But they don't live there—only summers, in the season. Some mighty good stakes are made trapping; there's worlds of good fur. A fisherman gets off better there than he does here—like I told you. A good live man's got plenty of chances, I reckon. There's other things. You could grow most anything, but what you going to do with it? Same with lumber. There's too much of it down here, nearer home." Len pondered and shook his head. Then suddenly he looked up. His eyes flashed. "No," said he, "by and large a man 'll probably make more money here. *But,*" he extended his great gnarled hand, "what will he do with it? What does anybody do with money? I'll tell you. He buys *life* with it. That's all. Life, living. And there's a country where he gets it without money. He don't have to 'make a good living': it's all ready made. Tell me this," Len leaned forward, "if you had all the money in the world, where could you go to buy yourself a better chance to be a man? or do it safer."

"Safer?" echoed Sally dubiously.

"You'll never starve." Len relaxed and struck a match on his thumbnail to refire his pipe. "There's meat—anywhere—plenty of it for the shooting; and salmon and trout and halibut and cod for the catching; and clams and crabs more 'n you'd believe; and if you're right up agin it there's wild strawberries as big as the tame ones down here, and wild potatoes and Hudson Bay tea and wild rice and parsnips and goose tongue and celery and such, and not just something to eat, either—every bit as good as you can raise," he assured Sally earnestly, "and you can raise garden truck if you want to, as far as that goes. And there's good timber for a shack; and cordwood just outdoors——"

"Food, shelter, warmth," murmured Sally. "Thoreau said those were man's basic needs."

"Never met him," said Len, "but he was dead right. Barring maybe a few ca'tridges and a little coffee and sugar, a man can live like a king and never go near a store." He came off the boil again. "Leastwise suits me," said he. "I don't bother none about money—till I get down where I got to use it. I've made some, and I can't say it done me much good except to worry was I going to keep it." He grinned wryly. "Which I didn't," he added.

Sally sighed.

"It does sound wonderful and wide and free." Her eyes were dreamy.

Len made a motion as though to look at his watch, but withdrew his hand.

"Lord, I been doing a lot of talkin'! It must be scand'lous late," said he. "Seems like every time I git going about Alaska *some*body don't know enough to go home."

Both Sally and John laughed wholeheartedly at this thrust. Len's faded blue eyes lit with satisfaction. He arose.

"Thanks for a good supper, Sally," said he. "I've sure enjoyed myself."

"You must come again," said Sally.

"Just ask me."

"I will." There was more in her voice than the simple words conveyed.

They looked at one another. Len patted her shoulder.

"Comin' along far as the corner?" he asked John.

Outside the two men tramped in silence until safely beyond earshot. They must go single file because of the narrowness of the plank walk. Len stopped, halting John. He cut short what John started to say.

"You listen to me." He took an edge of John's coat between thumb and forefinger and shook it in emphasis of his words. "Things is all right now. All you got to do is to keep them that way. Forget the whole thing. Don't never refer to it again—leastwise not until you can laugh about it—together. And don't act gentle and forgiving and elaboratelike neither; that's worse. Go right ahead like it never happened."

John was serious and troubled. He understood exactly what Len meant. But he dreaded the first moments after he opened the door. How begin? What was a good thing to say? It would be all right after they got over the hump; but that was going to be no cinch.

"You don't need to say anything at all," said Len. "Just love her up. Good lord, that's one of the things they invented loving 'em for —to git over humps. And don't worry about its bein' awkward when you open the door," he decided to add. "She's thought of that, too. I'm betting she won't be there when you open that front door. She's gone to bed. You see if I ain't right." He hesitated a moment.

"You seem to know a lot about women." But John's voice was doubtful.

"I'm a wise old coot," returned Len complacently. "I didn't really invent the critters, but I might have been around when they done so." He turned serious again. "This ain't 'women,'" said he. "This is just you and Sally."

"Sally wants you to come again," John reminded, holding his hand in farewell. "Where you staying? Marshall House?"

"No, I left there. I'll see you around the floats." He disengaged his hand and turned away. "Now mind!" repeating, as seemed to be his habit. "No palaver. Just love her up; love her up *good*. Ought to be nothin' hard about that," he added, but so low that John failed to catch the words. "Well, good night," he said abruptly and swung away down the line toward the streetcars.

"Good night," John called after him. "Len, you've saved my life."

"Shucks," growled Len without looking back. "I'll be seein' you before long."

That happened sooner than either, at the moment, expected. The very next evening, after the supper dishes had been put away—John helped—and the two had returned to the main room, Sally drew her chair out to face John's. Her expression was determined. She had come to some sort of conclusion, that was evident, and John was at once alarmed. What now?

"John," she began seriously, "just what do you know about Len Saunders?"

"Why," John sat up straight in surprise, "he seems all right to me."

"Of course he's all right." Sally was impatient. "He's a dear. But what do you *know* about him?"

"Why, just what you heard him say, honey. But what you driving at? Seems to me——"

Sally cut him short.

"John, did you see how he ate last night? That man was hungry."

John relaxed. He was not the target after all.

"Sure he was. So was I. And that was extra-special grub, if I do brag up my wife's cooking."

"And did you see how, when he thought it was late, he reached for his watch, and then drew his hand back as if he remembered that it wasn't there? And his cuffs?"

"What about his cuffs?"

"They were held together by safety pins."

John whistled.

"By golly, Sally, I believe you're right," he said slowly, "now you mention it. I never noticed." Sally glanced at him scornfully, but said nothing. It was her theory that men never noticed anything. "Now I come to think of it," he sat up straight again, "he told me the other evening he was at the Marshall House, and last night he told me he'd left there, and when I asked him where I could get hold of him, he sort of put me off, said I'd find him at the float sometime. Say"— he was fully roused—"that won't do!"

"Of course it won't do."

"I'll look him up tomorrow, if I can find him."

"You find him," instructed Sally with decision.

"I can't figure how a man like him come to get in such a fix."

"You told me yourself, the other day, that it's almost impossible now to get any kind of a job anywhere," pointed out Sally.

"Yes, it's hard times; we're lucky," admitted John. "But that wasn't what I was thinkin' of. What I mean was, how'd he come to be here at all, broke flat? Seems like, if all he says about Alaska is true, that he wouldn't have——"

"Does all that matter?" asked Sally.

"Don't strike me like a drinkin' man who'd blew all his——"

"He's not," stated Sally positively. "You find him; and you bring him back to supper. Tell him—oh, tell him I've got a pot roast that we can't eat up ourselves. Anything. But get him."

"You bet!" cried John. He was getting indignant. "Why he couldn't have just give me a hint! He ought to know that I——"

"He wouldn't." Sally seemed determined that John should not finish a sentence.

"Well, he will now," promised John truculently.

"Now listen, John." Sally was very serious. "Don't you do anything but get him up here. Don't ask him questions, and above all don't offer him money. It wouldn't do. It just wouldn't *do*. You must trust me on that. And after we have supper, I want you to get out. Leave us. I'll tell you to go down and get some beer; and you go; and I don't want you to act surprised or say you never knew me to drink beer or anything like that. Just go. And don't come back before you're wanted."'

"All right." John was relieved. Sally's small erect figure looked like it meant business. John had great faith in Sally when she looked like that. "What you aimin' to do, Sally?" he asked curiously.

"Find out," her tone was brief. "Then we'll know what to do."

John sank back in his chair. Sally was in charge; he could leave it to Sally.

"If he needs money to get back home, or anything——" He began vaguely, then stopped. It was unnecessary to tell Sally that. "How'll I know when I'm wanted back?"

"I'll pull down the curtain shade."

John looked at her admiringly. She had it all figured out.

There was no difficulty. Len was at the floats. He was only too glad to accept the invitation. Furthermore, on the way to the house, he made unnecessary some of the questions Sally undoubtedly had in mind.

"I'm waiting for a fellow I know," he explained his making the float his headquarters. "Trader. He's headed down this way from Alaska. Thought I'd ketch me a ride with him back. He knows me pretty well and knows I'm handy with a boat. He's considerable overdue. Damn nuisance. Keeps a man waitin' around doin' nothing."

Supper went merrily, with a great deal of interchange between Len and Sally, and John sitting by. He enjoyed that. It was as good as watching a play, with Sally teasing Len like a humming bird darting in and out, and Len sitting there like a carved-out wooden image, but every once in a while saying something kind of quiet and drawly that got back at her plenty and made them all laugh. John had never seen Sally so keyed up and gay.

John did not say much, he was having too good a time, but when supper was over he got back at Sally, in a mild sort of fashion, but enough to make her flash a glance of amused appreciation in his direction.

"I got an idea," he beat her to it. "I'm going to trot down and get a few bottles of beer. That ought to go pretty good."

He grinned at her. Not much of a joke, merely grabbing off the cue she had given herself in this small arrangement of things; but these two did not need much of a joke to get that warm feeling inside.

However, John did not pursue undeviatingly his errand. Once outside, he stopped to watch for a moment or so. Through the window he saw Len ensconced by Sally in the big chair; he saw him fill his pipe, and Sally, still afoot, trying to light a match for it by snapping its head against her thumbnail the way Len had done the other evening, and Len reaching out to take the match away from her, evidently expostulating in alarm lest she trap a burning fragment beneath the nail, and himself snapping it alight, and Sally laughing at him. Then he saw Sally pick up the small chair and plant it squarely in front of Len and sit down; and John, recognizing the funny little tilt of her head, himself laughed.

"Poor old Len!" he said to himself, "ain't got a show in the world!" and tramped away contentedly to get the beer.

When he returned, the shade was still up, so he waited. Len wa sitting up straight now, leaning toward Sally. Their heads were close together, and they were talking seriously. The conversation continued a long time, so long that it seemed to John his protracted absence must be getting a little ridiculous. How long did they think it took to go down to Madison Street and back, anyway? But at last Sally arose and crossed the room to pull down the shade. John collected himself for a plausible stage entrance.

"Well, here we are," he made great business with paper bags at the table. "I got a few pretzels, too. Where's the glasses? What you two lazy lummoxes think you been doing all the time I've been running my legs off for you?" He made toward the kitchen to remedy the omission, all the time trying to catch Sally's eye.

"Len and I have been talking," said Sally; "we've got a scheme."

John stopped at the kitchen door.

"Yes?" he questioned.

"Len's waiting for a man, and he don't know when he'll get here, and I told him it was silly, while we had an extra room that we had no use for, for him to be living in some hotel all by himself, and that we'd love to have him here with us."

"We sure would!" cried John heartily. "I don't know of anybody I'd rather have. I was going," John looked Sally in the eye, "to suggest it myself. That's great!"

Sally gulped at this brazen statement, but recovered.

"That's what I told him. Isn't it lucky for us! Now we can get that truck garden spaded up and planted out that you've never had time to get at—Len says he'll do it for us."

"By golly, that's great!" cried John with enthusiasm. "Getting so late in the season I was just going to hunt me up somebody to do it. Saves us the hire." He grinned at her. "Get anywhere near this woman, she'll put you to work all right."

Len was smoking, staring straight ahead, his face expressionless. He appeared not to hear. Now he knocked out his pipe and turned his head toward them.

"You're a great pair of kids," said he. "You put on a good show."

Deliberately he unfolded his long gaunt frame from the chair and stood looking at them. They looked back. Somehow they felt like two small children caught out. They did not know what to say. Len picked up his old felt hat.

"I'll make you a good truck garden," said he. He moved toward the door. "We'll have the beer tomorrow night," said he. He stopped and turned to face them, looking from one to the other. "John Murdock," he said, and in his voice was a vibrant undertone of feeling, "if ever I hear you ain't treating this woman the way you ought to, I'm going to look you up and knock your damn head off!"

The door closed behind him. Sally rushed to John and burst into sudden tears.

"I don't know why I'm crying," she sniffed presently. "There's nothing to cry about. But somehow . . ."

"I know," said John. Queer! He felt a little choky himself. "What's it all about?" John asked after a while.

"I don't know why I should cry," Sally repeated, her wonder at herself growing. "I'm not a crying woman!"

The situation was not as pathetic as all that. It was something else; something about Len himself, and the way she felt toward him. "He's just a *dear,* that's all," said Sally. And something of a dear yourself, thought John, stroking her bright head. She calmed presently. They sat down and talked.

Len was broke, all right. He'd made no bones of that, once she accused him directly. He'd put all his money into a little independent cannery up north, and the big cannery companies had waited until he was well established and then had squeezed him out.

"Something to do with banks and mortgages, I didn't quite understand it all," said Sally.

"He said something about being 'gobbled up,' as he called it, first time we met," recalled John thoughtfully, "I didn't pay much attention at the time."

Len had come down to Seattle to see if he couldn't save something out of the wreck. He hadn't. Now he was hanging on until a man he knew, with a boat, got to Seattle. He'd get a ride back to Alaska with that man. That's all there was to it.

"He was entirely cheerful about it," said Sally. "He laughed at himself. Said he was a fool for bucking the canners and just got what was coming to him. He'd be all right once he got back. Only thing that bothered him was this man's being so late. I had to pin him down hard before he'd admit he was in any trouble at all. And if I hadn't thought of that truck-garden idea he wouldn't have given in."

"You're a wonder, Sally," said John. "But you didn't fool him. He was onto you all the time."

"I know it," confessed Sally. "I think that's what made me cry."

CHAPTER VII

THE BOAT

THE FOLLOWING SUNDAY morning Len went to church with Sally. He said he wanted to hear Sally play the organ. Furthermore, he instructed John in no uncertain terms to lay off messing around in his new truck garden. John felt no desire to do so, but had a sneaking feeling he ought to, so he slid away to the water front with only a slight and salutary guilty feeling.

There was something queer about the floats. No one was in sight. Furthermore, Svensen's boat, which, by right of seniority, had been all winter moored to the big float itself, was now moored aft, and a strange craft had taken its place.

John climbed down the ramp to look at her. She was of a type unknown to him. He examined her with curiosity. His eye had been trained to the fishing fleet, so that just at first he did not know whether he admired her or not. He walked back and forth the length of the float, sizing her up; and by the time he had done that a half-dozen times, he knew that he did admire her. She sort of grew on you. She looked so competent, as though she meant business.

The craft was somewhere about forty feet long, built lower to the water and with less beam than the fishing boats. She differed from them also in the lack of hamper. Indeed her decks were almost clean,

broken only by a low flat house amidships with solid-looking port
lights in its side and a shallow cockpit, not over a foot deep. Both
the top of the house and the deck itself were constructed with a
slight turtleback curve toward the sides.

Though her freeboard was less than the average fishing boat, her
draft was much deeper. John, peering down through the clear water
at her stern, was amazed. Must be a lot of head room below, thought
John; fellow 'd be living mostly underwater, he reflected whimsically
and then slapped his thigh in delight. Of course! She was made that
way, so she *could* be entirely underwater—for a brief period—and
none the worse! Hence the clean-curved decks and the absence of
anything on them to offer resistance. This was a deep-sea craft, built
to stay out in anything, without necessity of taking shelter as must
even the sturdiest of the fishing fleet at times.

This key idea gave John's inspection a fresh impetus. It supplied
him reasons for a lot of things. Everything was solid. He examined
the heavy double shrouds that stayed the masts, spliced neatly around
oval pieces of wood with little holes in them through which lighter
lines, threaded back and forth, connected them with other oval pieces
of wood attached to narrow iron plates down the ship's sides. John
had never seen deadeyes; but he appreciated at once their superiority
over the fisherman's stays and turnbuckles hitched to ring bolts. The
advantage of the belaying pins over the usual cleats was not at first
so clearly apparent to him, but he puzzled it out—he thought. Hang
the coils of running rigging over them, maybe, when the seas ran
high. John wished somebody would show up so he could talk about
some of these things. Funny nobody was about. Perhaps they'd all
gone to a meeting somewhere about this strike business.

He continued to look her over and to speculate. Little bit of a stub
bowsprit pointed almost straight forward. Looked kind of funny to
John after the longer bowsprits of the Cape Flattery trollers, tilted
upward to keep them out of the waves. Waves too big to keep out
of where this one goes; John figured that out with a little thrill of
delight; that's why it's so short and strong, so it can't be broken
off! And so he was now able to see why the mast was stepped so

much farther back, so's to give space for the jib! But he did not quite understand the other little mast farther back. It looked too small, out of proportion. There were plenty of schooner rigs among the fishermen, but the ketch was not used.

So intent was he that he jumped with surprise when, raising his eyes, he perceived that a hatch had slid back and that in it stood a man. In contrast to the craft's general air of neatness, its owner looked like a tough customer. He had a round head, thick brown hair, tousled and uncombed, and a bushy beard growing high up his cheek bones so stiff and wiry that it thrust forward at a truculent angle from his chin. His eyes were small, slightly bloodshot. They stared steadily and belligerently at John.

"Good morning." John recovered himself. "I was just admiring your boat."

The man made no reply, but continued to eye John.

"What firm you with?" he demanded after a moment. His voice was deep and hoarse.

"What firm?" John was puzzled.

"Firm!" the man growled back. "That's what I said. Ain't you a broker?"

"I am not!" John was getting tired of the man's manner.

"Then what the hell you doing here with my boat?" demanded the other harshly. "You're no fisherman." The last words were spat out contemptuously.

"I'm not on your boat," returned John with spirit. "I'm on a public float."

The stranger grunted. He heaved himself out from the hatch and sat on its combing. John saw that he was short and broad, with chest like a barrel. He wore a thin shirt and overalls—both dirty—and apparently nothing else. His feet were bare and so browned that evidently that was their usual state. He stared at them vaguely. He seemed to have forgotten John. But presently he looked up as though with a new thought.

"Maybe you're thinkin' of buyin' her?" he suggested, modifying his manner a little.

John laughed.

"Huh!" The man resumed contemplation of his feet. "Well!" He turned his massive head in John's direction. "What you hanging around for?"

"Because I like it here," returned John promptly.

"You looking for trouble?" the stranger snarled back.

"Aw, for God's sake!" John was disgusted.

The other heaved himself up on short bandy legs, slid shut the hatch, snapped a padlock, crossed the narrow deck, stepped over the rail to the float. John watched him warily. But he did not look at John. He turned his back and stumped off down the float, his heavy body rolling slightly from side to side. He seemed to have forgotten John's existence, but as he set foot on the ramp he spoke back over his shoulder.

"Come have a drink," he growled.

John stared after him in utter amazement; then, his sense of humor overcoming him, he chuckled. He was startled by an answering chuckle near at hand. He turned. Old Svensen had thrust his head on deck from his own boat, moored next astern the stranger. John looked about him. The fleet had not been deserted after all. Here and there were men popping up from below, like a lot of prairie dogs, thought John with growing amusement. They were all looking after the short powerful figure just topping the ramp.

"Who in hell is that?" John asked.

"Dot feller?" replied Svensen. "Don't you know dot feller? Dot feller he's Pirate Kelly. The old son of a bitch," added Svensen tranquilly, without rancor. "He's a tough."

Pirate Kelly, eh! Who was he? Why was he called "Pirate"? Old Svensen was vague. All he was sure of was that he was a son of a bitch. Some of the other fishermen, by now slowly zigzagging toward the float, were more informative. Pirate Kelly was just a tough character, a hard citizen. He'd done about everything that was both maritime and shady; including, it was said, piracy. Hence his name. Last time he was in he had mostly white fox, which he claimed to have bought in trade.

"If he bought them it was because he was outnumbered and out of ca'tridges," said Marvin. "Or maybe he dished out a few peanuts and such," he met John's look of skepticism, "but nothin' of any worth. And if they didn't feel like tradin' "—he shrugged his shoulder. "He purty well takes what he wants," ended Marvin.

"That's how he got Svensen's place at the float?" asked John. "What's the matter with you fellows? You all act scared to death of him."

They looked down and shifted their feet.

"He's a bad actor," mumbled someone.

John was slightly disgusted and more than a little incredulous, for he knew these fishermen to be good men. There was something queer about it. Tom Holt, one of the older men, enlightened him.

"Don't get the wrong idea, Jack," he said to John. "We ain't cowards. But it ain't worth while, that's all. This Kelly is only in for a short time, and it's easier to keep away from him."

"Strikes me a good licking would do him good," growled John.

"He's been licked a many times," returned Holt briefly. "He don't mind being licked.'"

"Don't know *when* he's licked," spoke up someone.

It was difficult for John to understand this attitude, and he could not come to full sympathy with it. John had never made it a point to avoid trouble.

But this was different, they all tried to tell him. The man was a savage fighter. He knew no rules. He used any weapon. He took on one man or a dozen, odds did not matter. He lit into a man on the slightest pretext. He seemed to take no count of time, place or consequences. He had not done so yet, but the impression appeared to be unanimous that he would kill; and that the only reason he had not done so, in the numerous rows in earlier days at the floats, was because either a deadly weapon had not been handy, or he had been prevented by numbers. All right to fight back if it does any good, but what's the use when you have to keep on doing it? Less 'n you make up to murder the man, it's better just to stay shut of him. What else you going to do?

The logic was irrefutable, but John shook his head, unconvinced. He'd never been walked on, and he didn't propose to begin. But he let it go. It was only when he was halfway home that it occurred to him that this must be the man Len had been waiting for, with whom he was to return to Alaska!

Obviously this must be the man! John thought to remember that Len had mentioned the name Kelly. Nevertheless he could not believe it. Pirate Kelly and Len! It just didn't go! That was the reason it had taken him so long to think of it. He hastened his steps.

Len listened to his description.

"Yes, that's the fellow," he said. He made no comment. "Didn't say when he expected to pull out, I suppose?"

"What he said was that he was going to sell the boat," said John. "He took me for a broker."

"What's that?" Len was startled. "He didn't say nothin' about that to me. I don't believe it," he added after a moment. "It's just a notion. Was he drunk?"

"I don't think so. Looked to me like he'd just rolled out."

Len pondered. He looked troubled.

"Might be," said he after a while, as though thinking aloud. "He's come south three months earlier 'n usual."

"I thought you said he was overdue," ventured John.

"Gettin' here," explained Len. "Him and me left Juneau same day, but I was on the steamer. I asked him why he was comin' south so early, but he ain't got what you might call a confidin' nature." He grinned faintly. "Have any talk with him?"

"Some."

"What you think of him?"

But John refused to be drawn concerning a friend of Len's.

"Oh, he's no friend of mine," disclaimed Len placidly. "I've just knowed him a long time. You don't need to hold back."

"Well," John yielded, "he acts to me like a tough hombre. He's got that bunch at the floats buffaloed. I don't know as I'd want to take a voyage with that cuss. Looks like it would be taking long chances."

"Yes, he's tough," admitted Len, "but him and me get on all right. I know how to handle him."

John examined Len with new interest. Certainly he did not look capable of "handling" Pirate Kelly. But Len had spoken with calm and matter-of-fact confidence. John wished he knew more of Len's history.

Sally came in from the kitchen to announce that dinner was ready if they wanted to get it. Len made no reference to Pirate Kelly's arrival, so John also said nothing. That was an etiquette strictly observed in the cow country. Len, to all appearance, had dismissed the matter from his mind. He talked to Sally about sour dough, evidently continuing an argument begun in John's absence. He wanted to convert Sally to sour dough.

"You make dang good bread, Sally," said he, "I'm not criticizing that. But it's yeast bread. It ain't got the fine grain and the sweet to it, and it ain't got the *chaw* to it. This is a heap better 'n most," he conceded, taking up a sample, "but when it comes to stickin' to your ribs, you might as well open your mouth and let the moon shine in it!"

"I notice you seem to get away with it all right." Sally laughed in his face.

"Yes ma'am," agreed Len gravely. "I'm mostly arguin' on your account."

"On *my* account!"

"Yes ma'am. Once you start a batch of sour dough a lot of your trouble is done and over. Once you get her started, all you got to do is to feed her a little flour every day. The older she gets the better she is. I know a fellow's kept his going ten years. And you take rising. You got to wrop up your yeast dough in blankets, or else near the fire, all night, to keep her warm, or she won't rise. But sour dough you just stick out anywhere, hot or cold, pay her no more attention, and in the morning there you be, all riz up ready and waiting! And as for hot cakes! I tell you, you just let me start you a batch."

"Go ahead," urged Sally. "I'll do even better. I'll let you do the rest of the cooking."

"All right," Len agreed, "and that way you can get to exercise the spade and mattock on them cedar roots. You'll find the best ones over near the north fence."

But after dinner he drew John aside. "I'll see you later," he told him. "I've got to go find out what that damn fool's got in his mind."

He did not return until almost suppertime. He looked troubled.

"You're right," he told John seriously. "He means it. I couldn't get it out of him what he's up to. But he has some idee he's workin' on. Anyway, he's not goin' north again. Kind of takes the wind out of me. I was countin' on him." Len hesitated, obviously embarrassed. "I don't want to impose on you folks," he blurted out, "but if——"

"You're welcome just as long as you want, and you know it!" John assured heartily.

Len nodded.

"I'll try to make it worth my keep. And as soon as I catch a job——"

"That's all right.'"

They wrangled a little. Len was firm. As soon as he got a job, he'd pay for his board and lodging—or go where he could do so. John had to give in.

"You'll have to fix that with Sally," he finally ducked from under.

Wouldn't be for very long, anyway, proffered Len. Just till he'd made a stake to get back. . . . Another small wrangle. Again John had to give in. No, Len would not take his money, as a loan or otherwise. That was flat and final, and he didn't want to hear any more of that kind of talk. All right, then, that was settled. They went in the house. Sally took one look at them.

"Out with it," she commanded them. She laughed when they pretended not to understand. "When *both* of you get on that expression!" said she derisively.

She found no embarrassment in the situation. Bad luck about Pirate Kelly, since Len was so impatient to get back. Of course he must continue to stay with the Murdocks. Indeed, that was one good thing about it; they wouldn't lose him so soon. Perhaps John could find him a job at the mill. Naturally Len would want to pay board when he got the job. Sally would figure out how much it ought to be.

"Hope he doesn't," laughed Sally. "Not too soon, anyway. I wouldn't dare charge him what a man would cost us. And I like his company. We're getting the best of it."

Len looked at Sally appreciatively from under his deep brows, but said nothing. She made the whole situation comfortable, matter of course.

"That's a funny name," she said of Pirate Kelly. "Why do you call him that?'"

"Mostly because it fits," said Len.

"But he wasn't actually a *pirate!*" expostulated Sally.

"Might have been. He's done about everything else mean and ornery in the catalogue, from seal poaching to smuggling Chinks, and he's been plenty tough about it."

"How do you mean, tough?" Sally was fascinated, largely because of Len's obvious reluctance to go into details.

"He ain't one to let little things stand in his way. He's comparatively respectable right now. He calls himself a trader, and I reckon that's straight enough—up to a certain point."

John broke in.

"Isn't that boat of his pretty small for trading?" he asked.

Len shook his head with derision.

"Don't let her size fool you. She can take anything the Gulf of Alaska's got, and that's good enough for any seas in the world."

"I don't mean that. I mean cargo space. How can he carry enough goods?"

"Oh," said Len, enlightened. "There's more room than you think; she's pretty deep. And anyway he don't need much space. What he gets is mostly fur, and that packs close. White fox mostly. And for trade," Len continued dryly, "what he needs don't take up much room. Not if what they say is true."

Sally took the off side on that. People were always saying things. It was never fair.

"That's the trouble with her," John confided to Len aside, "Sally's a fine gal, but she's mushy," and prepared to dodge.

But Sally ignored him, except to remind him with dignity that after all Kelly was a friend of Len's. Len disclaimed this. "We get along," said Len, "but I got no more use for him than most folks have."

"Why not?" asked Sally.

"I ain't finicky," Len told her, "and I got lots of good friends that —well—mebbe interest the Coast Guard a mite, but I do draw a line."

"How?" asked Sally.

Len surveyed her in comical despair.

"You're worse than a no-seeum," he complained. Then, as she opened her mouth for another question, he stopped her with a gesture of surrender. "What you trying to do, size up my moral standards or Kelly's?"

"Both," said Sally.

"Well, I ain't going into our past history," said Len. " 'Tain't fitten for a lady. But I got to clear my judgment. I'll make you a bargain. I'll tell you one thing about this fellow that I know ain't rumor. And then if you're satisfied will you subside?"

Sally nodded. Len settled back in his chair for a yarn.

"All right. Well, a few years ago Kelly took up smuggling, over the line from British Columbia. He worked a lone hand, like he always does. Kind of easy pickin', in a way, because there's so many islands and passages and inlets that it ain't no great trick to dodge across without getting caught. He took on his loads near Vancouver or in the Sound or sometimes on the Victoria side of the Gulf. Then he run them over and landed them most anywhere where the coast was clear. He made good money, they say, and he kept at it for about two years. Then he quit and went to tradin' up north." Len stopped in obvious expectation. Sally obliged.

"And why, Brudder Bones, did he quit and go to trading up north?" she mocked.

"Things got too hot for him," surmised John.

"Not the way you think." Len was enjoying his own yarn. "Kelly wa'n't skeered of the Coast Guard. He used to laugh at them to their faces when he saw 'em in town. Told 'em to go ahead and catch him if they could. It wouldn't do them no good. And it didn't."

"Then they did catch him?" asked John.

"They overhauled him two-three times. But he had nothing aboard. They couldn't prove a thing."

"You're the most exasperating man I ever saw!" cried Sally.

"Kelly was smuggling Chinks. He took 'em in three at a time, at a hundred dollars a head," said Len. "And when the guard boarded him he was the only human aboard. But the hold smelt like a Chinese laundry, and Cap'n Ellis told me himself that one time the smoke was still hanging in the air."

"I don't understand." Sally stared at him, unbelieving.

"Kelly carried a lot of pig iron in his cabin, under the bunks. For ballast, he said."

"You mean he drowned them?" Sally gasped.

"Suit yourself. Plenty of Chink smells, but no Chinks. Only three at a time, so they would handle easy. And," added Len dryly, "it's a good bet, a shortage of pig iron." He looked at Sally with a curious blend of drollery and sympathy. "Satisfied?" asked Len.

"That's—that's horrible!" Sally's eyes were wide.

"Yes ma'am," Len agreed placidly, "that's right. Pirate Kelly's a leetle mite severe."

However, when John next saw Pirate Kelly that worthy was anything but severe. This was four days later, and at noon. John often spent the hour between the twelve and one o'clock whistles at the floats. The mill was no more than two minutes away. Partly he went for companionship of the fishermen, whom he liked; but the attraction that drew him was deeper than that. He did not understand it himself. Something within him swung to rest with the satisfaction of the magnet regaining its pole. Indeed often, when the mood took him, he did not descend to the floats at all, but went out on the pile dock that towered above them on the city side, and there ate his lunch and smoked his pipe in solitude and looked down on the pattern of hulls and the forest of masts and out across Elliott Bay and communed beneath his mind with something of the sea. He never missed this high perch when, as today, the sun shone; for in the planking of the dock was a small square hole, and if John lay flat on his stomach and looked through the hole he could see strange and wonderful things. The piles ran down like pillars into dimness, and below the surface the utilitarian clean hardness of above water was clothed in a dull velvet of sea growth, on which blazed bright anemones, like jewels, and starfish clinging, and, if John watched closely, once in a while he caught glimpses of tiny lively crawling creatures that popped out and scurried and popped in again. From them, too, streamed pennants of seaweed that moved slowly, as though half asleep. On a dull day these things were secret, for the surface of the water was blank, like gun metal. But the sun poured from without the screen of the wharf an infusion of soft light, so that the water dissolved into green lucence—like that in the sky sometimes after sunset—a kind of atmosphere in a strange world of suspension without the power of gravity. On every side, and straight down, it deepened until John could see no farther than dimness. Occasionally a school of fish swam by, or paused, resting, and then it seemed they must surely fall, so clear was the medium by which they were sustained. John never tired of staring down through the hole in the plank. There was something hypnotic about the slow, still weaving of this submarine life. The sun passed behind a cloud: it was gone. The sun came out again: there it was once more.

On this day he lay there as usual, concealed by the heavy stringers at the wharf's edge, when he was aroused by the sound of voices on the float below. At first he paid no attention. Then he recognized one of them as that of Pirate Kelly. He rolled over and looked down.

Kelly was accompanied by two other men. One was a tall lean individual, dressed in neat gray clothes and wearing a gray soft hat. John could see little of his face, but it was evident that this was of the city type. The other was burly, rough looking, in Mackinaw and half boots, just the ordinary bull-necked roustabout who might be anything from a lumberjack to a water-front loafer. He stood throughout a little apart, his hands thrust into his side pockets, staring off into space, apparently content to leave the talking to his companion. But what caught John's attention, and held it to what followed, was the attitude of Pirate Kelly himself. It was not in character. His domineering truculence had vanished.

John was interested. He dropped back prone behind the stringer and shamelessly listened. At first he thought Kelly was entertaining a possible purchaser and was amused that the prospect of a sale should so completely alter his manners.

"There she is," he was saying, "and just like I said, she's fit and able, and I can take her anywhere."

"Won't do," returned the other crisply.

"I'd like to know why not," complained Kelly.

"I've told you. I don't care how good she is. This is no job for sail. When we want to move we'll have to move; without any *ifs* or *ands*. And move fast. That means steam."

"But I tell you I know the coast like the back of my hand. I can take you where you won't *have* to move, and——"

"Won't do, and that's final," the other cut him short.

"I don't know nothin' about steam," objected Kelly sullenly.

"Who said you did? You know the coast. That's all I want out of you. Sell her."

"I've been tryin'," muttered Kelly.

"Borrow on her."

"I've tried that: can't get a cent. Nobody's lendin' these times. Money's too tight."

"Give her away, sink her. Get rid of her. But kick through. You've monkeyed around long enough."

A pause.

"I ain't got the money," said Kelly at last.

Another pause. Then the man in the gray suit exploded.

"Haven't got the money!" he repeated, and his tone was belligerent. "God almighty! Have you been trying to four-flush me, you misbegotten bastard? Look here, Kelly, that don't pay. Didn't you tell me——"

"I counted on sellin' and gettin' at least——"

"You told me, in so many words, that you had the money ready and waiting. Don't you tell me different. There wasn't a word said about selling this boat, or anything about this boat, and you know it. Do you think for one minute I'd have—— Look here, Kelly," his voice was level, "you'd better begin thinking. This thing is all lined up, and our money is down. You raise that money or——"

"I got some," Kelly interposed hastily. "Take that and make me a smaller cut."

Another silence.

"You damn fool," the other then resumed disgustedly. "Don't you realize it isn't a matter of a smaller cut? We've got to lay down the cash. And we've two days to do it in. And if we don't the whole thing is off." He stopped again, then burst out exasperatedly. "Cash! Cash down! Or we don't get that boat! And I don't know where to find another that fills the bill. And before I could find another it would be too late."

"Can't you——" ventured Kelly.

"No, I can't. And that's flat. I couldn't raise another nickel on my immortal soul. I've hocked my watch. God damn it, Kelly, I've a mind——"

"Hold on," and John chuckled at the deprecation in Pirate Kelly's voice, "give a man a chance. We got two days. That broker says——"

"Broker, hell!" the other snorted.

John heard the sound of retreating footsteps. He peered over the stringer. The two strangers were halfway up the ramp. Pirate Kelly followed slowly.

John could hardly wait for closing time. He went straight home. "That Pirate Kelly of yours ain't so tough," he told Len gleefully. Len listened with interest.

"Now I'd admire to know what that's all about," said he. "Can't be just seal poachin'," he speculated thoughtfully, "nor fish piratin', nor ordinary smugglin'. Steam would be fine for any of them, of course. But there ain't no such almighty rush about them. Less 'n it might be some special cargo that won't keep."

That seemed the most likely, though far from convincing. Sail had always done well enough before. What was there so special about this? They gave it up. But it was sure amusing to hear about Pirate Kelly's taking it lying down that way. *That* had never happened before.

"I'd like to meet that cuss with the gray clothes," said Len, "he must be quite a feller."

"Oh, I forgot," said John, "they can take you on at the mill, but not until next week. In the yards. Not much of a job. Handling and piling. And they don't pay much, I'm afraid."

Len nodded his thanks.

"What are you going to do, Len, when you get back up north?" asked Sally. "Where will you go?"

"I dunno." Len shook his head vaguely. "Depends. If I get enough stake I may take a try over in the interior for fun. I may look for a job for a while till I can get started."

"What jobs are to be had in that country?" John was interested.

"Most any sort, right now. They're building a new town on Klakan Island they figure is going to be the center of somethin'-or-other. Till they get that put up—and busted," interpolated Len dryly, "a man can get good wages for most anything he can put his hand to. I might take on for carpenter or painter or somethin'! I'm moderate handy. Then there's the cannery, of course; but that's a short season. Might be long enough for me, though. Just so I get a grub stake. What I want right now," said Len confidentially, "is to find me a place where I can set and watch the mountains to be sure none of them gets stole."

"I think I'd like that, too." Sally sighed and looked wistful.

"Yes," John mocked her. "You lead a hard life, especially now you've got Len to wash your dishes."

Sentimentality never got very far with these two.

After work time the following afternoon John was curious enough to veer aside to the floats on his way home. He wanted to see whether the ketch was still there, whether anything had developed. It was, and so was Kelly, seated hunched atop the deckhouse. The sight amused John. He descended the ramp. Kelly looked up, stared at him a moment, recognized him and stepped to the float. All truculence was gone from his bearing.

"Look here," said he, "you said you liked this boat. Why don't you buy her? I'll let her go cheap."

An imp of perversity danced in John. He was enormously amused. Knowing what he did, and Pirate Kelly unaware of his knowledge, made a situation that tickled John's sense of humor.

"I don't know," he assumed indecision, "I ain't even looked her over yet."

He suppressed a grin at the eagerness with which Kelly rose even to this bit of encouragement. John mentally agreed with Len that the man in the gray suit must be quite a fellow, in which he was probably right. He added to himself, somewhat contemptuously, that Kelly was merely another bully; overrated and collapsible by anybody who would call his bluff. In this John was wrong, as he was to find out, but only many months later.

"Help yourself," said Kelly.

John stepped aboard and looked fore and aft with a knowing air. He saw little more than he had seen from the float, but somehow he had a different feeling now that he was on the deck. This was no mere humdrum boat. She was a real little ship, and the small boy in John spread his feet a little apart and cocked his eyes knowingly aloft and for a brief moment filled him with a play-acting sensation as though he were a captain pacing his quarter deck. He himself had to grin at this, for two paces on the quarter deck would have landed him overside. But it was fun!

He slid back the hatch and went below. Kelly seemed inclined to leave him to his own devices. John was glad of that. He poked around at random. Kelly, whatever his own dishevelment, was a true sailor. Everything was shipshape and Bristol fashion, tidied down and in its place. There proved to be an astonishing amount of room. John was tall, but he could stand almost at his full height. There were two bunks, with high sideboards to hold you in and a table that doubled in the middle and folded up against the bulkhead out of the way. Two lamps hung in gimbals. John tipped them with his fingers and admired how they would always remain upright no matter what the boat's motion. The dishes stood on edge in racks. The doors of the lockers and drawers had latches, but also buttons to hold them securely shut. John prowled, admiring all the hundred and one gadgets, time-tried by the sea, unknown to the land. Some were strange to him; with many he had made acquaintance on the fishing craft. But the equipment of the fishing boats was hybrid. They borrowed and used many of the familiarities of the land. Here everything was of the sea.

Forward of the bulkhead was the galley, and here John admired the supreme of compactness and ingenuity. Here was everything a man could think of. Nothing essential lacked. Sally herself could ask for nothing better. All in a space not one tenth the size of her kitchen. And a lot handier, thought John; you could reach out and get anything you needed without taking a step!

For some time he admired the galley in detail. Then he slid aside a door in the next bulkhead. It was not exactly a door, but merely a square opening about large enough for a man to crawl through. John lighted a match to see, for there were no port lights here. Evidently the cargo hold, he decided. There seemed to be a hatch overhead. The hold contained nothing except some sails and coils of rope and an anchor. He returned to the main cabin.

Here he sat down on one of the bunks. For a few moments he looked about him, noting with fresh enjoyment more novelties. Gradually he drifted into a brown study, a blank subjective state, without thought, but alive with sensation. He was no longer seeing the details of the little cabin. He was just enjoying the feel of it.

He was in a curious state of being. Everything was strange. The immobility of the little ship beneath him was unlike the immobility of the land. It was alive. The voice of its quiet was not the shrilling of the land's quiet times, as at night, but an incessant breathless lap-lap-lapping of wavelets against the hull. He just sat quiet and absorbed. It seeped in and filled him.

He came to with a start and looked about him again. Somehow

things had changed. He felt queer, all excited deep down, a funny eager sensation. Recollection came to him. When he was a little shaver he had felt just like that every time he stood in front of the harness shop kept by Al Baxter, at the Dalles, and flattened his nose against the window and worshiped the silver-inlaid Mexican spurs with the carved-leather straps. He'd felt *just* like this! Something had gripped him, compelled him, a desire against which he was powerless, which he must satisfy. It was the way he felt about Sally sometimes. Suddenly he felt that way about Sally now, but the feeling was all mixed up with the silver spurs and the something that had come into him here. John was a little breathless.

He went on deck and paused for a moment to capture a proper appearance of indifference. John had that much sense left. As he stepped to the float, he touched, almost with tenderness, the miniature ratlines.

"Looks all right," said he. "How much you want for her?"

"Four hundred. Cash." Pirate Kelly thrust his beard forward aggressively.

John's heart bounded into his throat. He had asked the question almost perfunctorily, without expectation. He drew a deep breath.

"I'll take her," he found himself saying in a voice he did not recognize.

"She's yours—soon as you gimme the money."

"I'll have it in the morning—no, at noon. I'll go to the bank at the noon hour. Or I can give you a check."

"Here, you!" Kelly's belligerence was back. "I said cash, and I mean cash, and I mean now! Why, you little squirt, why do you think I'm taking a measly four hundred? You know goddam well she's worth fifteen. If you want her, produce! Otherwise I'm takin' her out of here on the next tide, and that's in about three hours."

"That's not reasonable," expostulated John. "You don't expect me to be carrying around any such amount in my pants, do you? The bank's closed." He reflected. He understood more of the situation than Kelly suspected, so he knew Kelly was not bluffing. Obviously if he could not meet the mysterious deadline set by the man in the gray suit, he intended to duck out, probably back to the north. John thought of Casey. Casey might cash a check. Then he remembered that Carghill was working over hours at the mill.

"Come with me," he told Kelly.

They mounted the ramp and proceeded along the water front to the mill. Sure enough, Carghill was there, working on the books. He heard John through without comment, then walked across the office to the wall telephone.

"Nobody at the bank but the watchman," he reported briefly after making his call. He waited a moment for John to say something. "I can't just fork out four hundred dollars without authority, you know."

John nodded. "I tell you," said he, "can't you call up the boss? He might— Hold on!" He had a better thought. "Try Casper. He has a phone at his house. He ought to remember anyway that I got a savings account. That's all you want to know, ain't it? Whether I'm good for it or not? It's a case of push," he urged, as Carghill hesitated. "Kelly aims to pull out on the next tide if I don't get it for him now."

Carghill grunted. He had paid Kelly no attention whatever. He paid him none now. After a moment he returned to the telephone and flipped through its directory in search of the saving teller's number. He spoke so guardedly into the receiver that John could not overhear, listened for a moment, hung up the hook and crossed to his desk. His face was expressionless. John was afraid to ask.

Carghill rummaged a moment, produced a slip of paper, laid it on the desk.

"Sit down and make out your check," he told John.

He recrossed the office to a big steel safe and began expertly to twirl the combination.

John sank into the chair before the desk. For ten seconds he sat there without moving. This was the high point of John's necessity for that boat. He took up the pen and wrote out the check. Carghill returned. He scrutinized the check, took it to the opened safe and deposited it in a shallow drawer with others. He counted out green-backs in John's hand.

"There you are," said he. He went back to the desk and drew the ledger forward under the hanging shaded light. "That's all right," he stopped John's thanks. He did not look up again from the ledger, but after John had in turn tallied the amount to Kelly, he spoke over his shoulder.

"Better take a bill of sale." Still without looking up he reached with his left hand for a sheet of paper, scribbled for a minute, passed it to John. "Tell him to sign that," said he. He waved his hand toward the tally desk against the wall.

"Thanks," said John. He would not have thought of that. Carghill grunted; he was already absorbed in his columns of figures.

Kelly awkwardly scratched his name on the document. He fished a key from the pockets of his disreputable jeans and thrust it at John. He was in a hurry.

"Better get your stuff out now," John called after him.

"Nothin' I want," growled Kelly and disappeared.

John looked uncertainly at Carghill's back. He followed.

It was by now nearing twilight. He drew a deep breath. He was tingling all over with satisfaction. In that moment he gave no odds to life.

But during the slow and jolting ride in the Second Street car his inner glory began a little to fade in afterthought. His mind was still on the little ship, and he wouldn't have her one bit different, and he was glad he had bought her. But he began to be just a trifle ashamed of himself that he had gone off half cocked that way. The fishermen would laugh at him if they knew. Not one of them would buy a boat that way. He ought, for instance, to have lifted the floor boards and dug into the frames and sheathing with the point of his knife, testing for dry rot. She looked fine: but you couldn't tell just by looks. John knew that. He had a moment of indecision whether he'd better go on back and see. But almost instantly he rejected that. His elation returned. Deep down he knew it would not have made any difference. He'd have bought her anyway.

However, another thought sobered him completely. There was Sally. How was she going to like it? Sally would like it, John replied to himself confidently. Everybody, most, had a boat, living right here on the Sound this way. That's all very well, insisted his newly stirred uneasiness, but this isn't just a sailboat, like folks keep here on the Sound. It's a ship. No getting around that. But look at how cheap I got her, argued John, weakening. Four hundred dollars, stated his conscience; and added bluntly and brutally, *just the price of that piano you couldn't afford!*

John got off the streetcar at his intersection a changed man. His footsteps became slower and slower. When Sally and Len looked up at his laggard entrance, they saw a wretched and beaten man.

"Well! We began to think you'd run away and left us——" Sally had begun and stopped. "Why, John!" she cried. "What in the world is the matter?"

"I've bought a boat," said John miserably.

Sally stared.

"She cost four hundred dollars," he confessed.

For ten seconds longer Sally continued to stare. Then she began to laugh. She laughed and laughed and stopped and had to laugh again. John was abashed by the laughter; but his heart stirred. He had never loved Sally more than at that moment. His conscience, however, was unappeased.

"I thought you'd robbed a bank, at least," Sally gasped finally.

"That's an awful lot of money," said John, "and the piano——"

"What in the world would we do with a piano—compared to a boat!" cried Sally. "Oh, what *fun!*"

"She's an awful good boat." John was plucking up a little courage. "You could live on her."

"What boat is it?" asked Len.

"Kelly's," replied John.

Len sat up. "Kelly's!" he repeated with an air of astonishment. "You got her for four hundred! Well! He *must* have been up against it!" He whistled. "You sure won't lose nothing on that!"

Good old Len! He had saved the day, thought John.

"Sure I can't," he returned confidently. "That's what I thought."

Sally laughed, briefly and skeptically, but brushed the whole matter aside.

"How big is she? Where is she? I've got to see her. 1 can't wait." She was all afire. She ran to the kitchen.

"Come on, you," she called back. "Feed yourselves. I want to see that boat."

"You'll like her," said Len. "She's a little beauty."

They gobbled hastily and piled up the dishes unwashed and locked the house and hurried away. It was by now dark, but the city light at the head of the ramp gave them enough illumination. John unlocked the padlock, and they went below. They lit the lamps hanging in the gimbals. Sally was the most excited of the three. She squealed with delight over everything. Her cheeks were pink, her eyes sparkled, she glowed. John was his own man again. He followed and explained the boat.

She must open every locker, examine every cranny. She even insisted on crawling through the little square door into the cargo hold and squatted there like a little small tree frog, thought John, and looked about her while he held up a match.

After a long time they put out the lamps and locked the hatch and came out on the float, and stood side by side at the end of it, their arms around each other. Len had discreetly vanished.

The lights of the city pricked out its hills like jewels on velvet. They shone fixed and constant, children of the land. But across the waters were other, single, lights, near and far, on wharf ends, on craft at anchor; and each of these seemed to be supported on slim living reflections that wavered and wriggled and danced forward and danced back, children of the restless sea. Beneath them the float moved gently. Sally's arm tightened in an ecstatic squeeze.

"Oh, John," she breathed, "I'm so *happy!*"

John squeezed in response. He felt calm and exalted and benevolent. He had bought Sally a boat.

CHAPTER VIII

EXCURSION

THIS WAS of a Wednesday. That left three days to wait. On Sunday Len would take them sailing if the weather was halfway decent, said he. Whereupon Sally and John both looked obstinate. They said nothing to Len, but they were secretly determined that indecency should have nothing to do with it. They were going sailing on Sunday! Sally would get a substitute for the organ.

"While you are about it, you might as well tell 'em to make it permanent," John told her. "Sundays ain't so many we can waste part of 'em to oblige that little pip-squeak. We'll want to be off all day."

He spoke with emphasis and was prepared to do battle; but to his surprise Sally agreed without demur.

"But," she warned him, "don't you begin to get skipperish just because you've bought a boat! At least not until you can sail her."

"Keno!" John laughed—at himself. He felt sometimes, with Sally, as if he were made of glass. She had a way of seeing things in him before he saw them himself. Unwise to try to boss Sally just because she hadn't hopped on him when he had thought she was going to.

At breakfast Sally demanded the key.

"I want to see her again. I want to play with her. It's a shame you have to work," said she regretfully. "We could have such fun. Len and I . . ."

But Len shook his head. He was going to be busy. He went downtown with John and did not reappear until evening, after both the others had been home for some time, and until well past the supper hour. As a matter of fact that was unimportant, for supper was going to be late anyway. Sally had waited at the floats for John, and only her housewife's conscience had torn them away at last.

Len's face was grave; so grave that Sally cut short abruptly what she was about to say. He sat down and surveyed in turn their growing concern.

"I hope," he addressed John, but without any symptoms of hope, "you looked into this business before you bought that boat? She's all clear?"

"Clear?" repeated John. "Why—I've got the bill of sale."

"I saw that. But did you know what you were buying?"

"Why—I looked her over. We all looked her over." The thought he had so summarily dismissed returned to John's mind with new force. He really ought to have tested her condition. "Ain't she sound?" he faltered.

"She's sound enough," said Len, "but don't it strike you funny to get a two-thousand-dollar boat for four hundred dollars?"

"Kelly was in a jam. He had to have it. I told you about that." Uncertainty was growing in John like a small panic. What was Len driving at? He looked mighty serious.

"How do you know he hadn't raised all he could on her already?" asked Len bluntly. "How do you know you ain't bought a good stiff mortgage along with the boat—that you'll have to pay? How do you know she ain't got libels agin her?"

He looked at John's appalled face in severe disapproval. Sally was standing in the kitchen door, her eyes wide with dismay.

"I—I never thought of that," stammered John.

"Well, I did," said Len severely. "Let this be a lesson to you." He paused, then added in a matter-of-fact voice, "Well, she ain't." The hard carved lines of his face relaxed. He chuckled. "Had to skeer you a little," said Len. "Pay you back. I was skeered last night—good and plenty. Couldn't hardly sleep for figgerin' you'd got yourself in a sweet mess."

The color was coming back into Sally's cheeks. John's recapture of himself was slower.

"That's where I been all day," continued Len, "Custom House. Hall of Records. Projectin' around ships chandlers' and such, where money might be owed. Findin' out. It's all right. She's clear." Len shook his head. "I can't figger it; he ought to have been able to raise four hundred on her."

John filled his lungs and expelled the air with a whoosh of relief.

"That's one of the things I heard him say," said John, "that he couldn't borrow on her. 'Money's too tight,' that's what he said."

"You might have thought of that afore," accused Len.

"That's right." John was shamefaced.

But Sally flamed.

"You ought to be scalped, Len Saunders!" she cried in indignation.

Len fumbled at his side pockets.

"Now hold on! Hold on!" he begged in mock alarm. He disengaged a bulky package from the pocket. "You wait!" He untwisted the newspaper wrapped about a bottle which he held up for them to see.

"Champagne!" Sally was awed.

"Right off'n the ice," said Len.

"How in the devil——" began John and stopped.

"Sure, I'm broke," Len placidly finished the thought for him. "Compliments of Casey. I was in at Casey's asking around; and he'd heerd about your gittin' the boat; and he says to me, 'Here, Len, you take this along to the missus, and you tell her compliments of Casey, with love and a Merry Christmas—or somethin' like that—to christen the boat.'"

"But I don't understand why he—I never saw Mr Casey . . ." Sally was at complete loss. "I don't understand . . ."

"I didn't understand myself, much," admitted Len. "Anyway, there you be—to christen the boat, says he."

"I—I don't know exactly what to say. It is wonderful of Mr Casey, but——"

"Shucks." Len was impatient of such hesitancies. "It's nothin' to Casey. He's all right. Casey and I are old-timers. I've knowed Casey since he started out in Juneau. He just likes young folks. And he likes John. He told me that once. Casey means all right. Matter of fact, what I think, he knows Kelly, and he just wanted to take the curse off the boat."

"I do appreciate it. I'm just surprised," said Sally. She picked up the bottle and turned it slowly about. "I've never tasted champagne." She turned to Len, still holding the bottle. "But you break it over the bow to christen a boat, don't you?"

"Hold on!" Len sat up.

"I've read about it," persisted Sally, her eyes beginning to dance. "It's bad luck without. And anyway, if Mr Casey gave it to me to take the curse off the boat, we've got to do it, haven't we?"

But Len was resourceful.

"I tell you," said he, "it ain't quantity that counts. You look around and find us a little small bottle—mebbe a pill bottle——" He broke off. "Dang these women!" he grumbled to John. "You go git your supper ready," he told Sally, "and I'll show you how to pop this stuff."

The "little small bottle" must have been effective in removing the curse of Pirate Kelly from the Tillicum, as they finally decided to name her. Or rather Sally decided. Both John and Len could see nothing the matter with calling her the Sarah M, or anyway the Sally M. But Sally herself hooted at such an idea. This must be an Indian name. Len supplied *tillicum,* which means friend. That the Tillicum had now become a lucky ship, Sunday demonstrated to their satisfaction. The sky was clear. Every sign promised the first of those clear, sparkling days that mark the break of the season, when the air softens, and the soil smells warm and damp, and the brown earth seems to swell in expectancy.

They saw its dawn from the water, for Len had routed them out at an unearthly hour, long before daybreak. It had something to do with the tides. Len had it all figured out.

Len tacked a rough sign on one of the float piles—COMING BACK—in order to hold their place. He cast off, and he and John maneuvered into the open by shoving with boat hooks. A tiny land breeze was filling in the time before sunrise. They drifted slowly out while Len, assisted by John, began to set the sails.

Sally sat in the shallow cockpit, her back against the combing, doing nothing, saying nothing, out of the way of the men. Every little while she shivered slightly, and then she hugged her arms close around her body. For the life of her Sally could not have said whether the shiver was of cold or ecstasy. Probably both. There was still a night chill in the air, and it was quite a different night chill from that of the land, more penetrating, but at the same time clean as a draft of cold water. Still, she had on her warmest clothes. Everything was so exciting. The first faint gray of dawn silhouetted the sky line of the city's hills, and the night lights on their slopes were paling. The surface of the water, too, was beginning to catch a hint of the coming day, so that it was no longer black and polished, but like pewter or dull frosted silver. Everything was so different from anything Sally had ever experienced before. She might fancy herself in a fairy tale. Indeed, there seemed to be some kind of enchantment, in which certain sounds—such as the creak of the blocks and the crackle of arousing canvas—were natural and permitted; but all others forbidden and profane. She wanted to hold herself hushed and still while night drained out of the world.

John and Len must unconsciously have felt this. They moved softly and spoke to each other in low voices, and only brief words that had to do with the things permitted, though there was no reason other than the enchantment why they should not have shouted aloud, had they so wished. Presently they both came back to the cockpit. John sat down by her. Len went farther aft, to the tiller and the sheets. Neither spoke. Sally's spirit warmed to her menfolk for their silence.

Len did mysterious manipulation of ropes and tiller. And magically the sensitive structure became alive and began to move.

The land breeze was light, almost imperceptible, little more than an air. It had barely enough weight to shape the sails. Nevertheless the lights ashore were changing pattern; the black wall of Magnolia Bluffs off the bow was growing in mass; the water alongside was passing astern in tiny gurglings and whisperings.

Sally shivered again. Never in all her life had she so tingled in every fiber of her body. She all but held her breath. In this shadowy silent motion was something almost furtive, as though of escape. And yet Sally felt no urgency of escape. She did not want it to end.

To starboard the hills now hung above them like a black cloud. Their lee had almost killed the breeze; yet the Tillicum continued to slip ahead. Now they were beyond Fourmile Rock and could see the light of West Point. It was still flashing its red and white intervals, but its brilliance was dimmed, and out beyond it lay a broad band of bright silver. And then, abruptly, everything changed. It was as though they had passed through a door into another room. The ship heeled far over, hesitated and seemed fairly to leap ahead. A burst of spray hovered a moment over the bow and pelted aft like a sheet of rain straight into Sally's face. She gasped and clung half terrified to John. John himself looked toward Len. Len grinned at them reassuringly. They settled back. John put his arm around Sally and hung on. It was all right; they trusted Len; but their instincts were still doubtful. Their world had always been one of level stability.

West Point had already dropped back to the quarter. They could see straight up Possession Sound, miles and miles of it. It ran like an enormous highway between Whidbey Island and the mainland, spread out with the gold and silver of the rising sun and the blue and white of a lively breeze for the triumphant march of the new day. The spell of night was broken. John filled his lungs and uttered a shrill cowboy yell. Len, one hand on the tiller, fumbled in his side pocket for his pipe.

"Good steady breeze," said Len. "We're going to have a fine sail."

Sally, too, drew a deep breath, but she said nothing. With her a remnant of the spell lingered. It was still somehow queer to hear a voice aloud.

"Come on here and take hold," Len was saying to John. "You got to learn to sail."

John took hold. At first he was pretty gingerly about it. The thing felt mighty skittish to him. Felt as though it might tip over any minute. He did an inordinate amount of exaggerated luffing, bringing her up all shaking whenever a puff gave the wind a little extra weight. That was the only thing Len told him how to do at first: if you feel you have to straighten up, just shove the tiller away from you, said Len. Once he got her in irons, and Len had to take charge and back off the jib and give her way again. Len was patient.

"You'll get the feel of her," said he. "She does her best with her lee rail awash."

Nevertheless, it was difficult to hold back when it felt to you like the whole dang thing was going right on over.

"She *can't,* I tell you," insisted Len. "She's too deep. She's got at least two thousand pounds on her keel. She'll lay way over and spill the wind first. That's the way she's built. Only thing is, she don't sail so well when she's flat. Hope nobody's watchin' us," added Len. "That wake would break a snake's back."

John quickly gained some confidence, but he did not satisfy Len. "Come here, Sally, you try," said he.

Sally tried. She took the tiller. It was wonderful. Immediately the Tillicum ceased to be to her merely a man-made structure of wood and canvas. It became a sentient being, alive beneath her hand, quivering in response to her most delicate touch, a very part of herself, so that she need merely to will it to obey. A friendly thing, eager only to do her pleasure. She was not afraid of its tipping over. She was not afraid of it at all. Len was enthusiastic.

"By glory, Sally," he cried, "you're a sailor!"

He sat by her and told her things he had not bothered to tell John yet. He showed her what was the luff of the sail.

"You hold her so it's just quiverin', kind of; just the least little bit," he instructed. "Then you're gittin' the best she's got. You can tell pretty well by the telltale," he indicated the little pointed pennant at the mast head. "Keep it flyin' just outside the peak of the gaff."

"How do you turn around?" asked Sally. She was very intent and serious, gripping the tiller with both hands, her feet braced against the combing, her eyes glued unwaveringly to the luff of the sail. Mighty purty, thought Len of her, with her hair blowing, for she had tossed her hat impatiently down the hatch. But he had to grin.

"Take it easy," he advised. "You'll git all tired out. She ain't goin' to bite you."

As for turning around, that came later. One thing at a time. Lots of things to learn yet.

John watched Sally with pride and also a little mortification. Finally he could not stand it any longer.

"Here," said John, "gimme that thing. I'll show you!"

They beat slowly up the channel, each trying it in turn, and soon progressed so far as to rate instruction on sail trimming and coming about. Len's canniness in getting them out so early was proved justified: the land breeze and the last of the ebb left them at the junction of Admiralty Inlet, and the sea breeze and the new flood boosted them up Possession Sound toward Everett. This gave them a fair wind, which was a new game entirely, for a little following sea kicked up, and Len thought it wise to sit behind his pupils lest they yaw or jibe. John's initial awkwardness promptly wore off, after which his years of doing things came into their own, and he gave Sally a close race in proficiency. She was glad of this. It gave her no great pleasure to triumph over John in his world; only in hers.

Now that the sun was up and the wind astern, it was warm. Between tricks Sally basked in the forward part of the cockpit. The leech of the sail struck her as making an admirable back for a seat on the boom, but Len sternly squashed that idea. He gave her quite a lecture—ruin the set of the sail. And possibly dangerous.

"That," said Len of the boom, "is one thing to keep in mind. It's loose: it can swing—you may have noticed. And it's heavy. If you don't see it coming or forget to duck, it'll sweep you overboard or knock your head off. Remember that." Len was seriously impressive.

"Yes, teacher," said Sally meekly. Never had she had so good a time. The waves danced, and the wind sang, and the sun shone and sparkled. Across the way the shores of Whidbey Island passed, dark with forest. Astern, miles distant now, she could just make out an elusive glimmer of buildings that Len said were on West Point. So Seattle must be just around the corner. She could hardly believe they had come so far. Beyond that, the islands blended into a black ribbon that appeared to close the passage; and still beyond them, but now so far that they seemed not to belong to the same world, rose the granite and snow and ice of the mighty Olympics. Only it did not look like granite and snow and ice, but rather some more ethereal substance that could float in the sky. By bending forward she could see under the boom and across to the mainland with its low littoral, and the scar of the railroad just above waterline, and patches of cutover lands with their stubs and green dense second growth and occasional pine clumps and cleared farms and white smokes here and there. As the Tillicum rolled gently in courtesy to the following sea, the boom lifted and fell. The sail was like a curtain raised and lowered. Each time it went up, Sally caught her breath. She had only a glimpse, but so overpowering a glimpse that it seemed to her she could not have stood more. The great mountain appeared actually to be sucking the earth upward in its majestic lift to the sky.

Ahead glimmered in half mirage a long, low, yellowish-looking patch that must be Everett, held—again at enormous distance—by a slate-blue rampart.

Nevertheless, though in every direction she looked Sally's eyes were stopped by the presence of the land, she had no feeling of the land, but of the limitless spaces of the sea. So when the apparently unbroken shore circle ahead of them opened at the last moment a broad reach angling off to the left, she had no sense of surprise. Imprison it as you would, the sea would yet escape. And she looked up Saratoga Passage to where Gedney Island divided it right and left, and her imagination leaped to follow through the channel, beyond and beyond. What was beyond? More islands? More channels? Out into the blue, over the edge of the world, following the lure, never turning back?

But Len was hauling in on sheets, thrusting the tiller down, so that the Tillicum was rounding into the wind. At once the breeze seemed to increase in strength, the waves in speed. The laziness of the reach livened to spray and dash and eagerness.

"Oh!" cried Sally, dismayed, "must we go back? Can't we anyway go as far as that island?"

She was disappointed. Somehow she felt if she could just see what was beyond the island . . .

But Len was obdurate. Something to do with tides again, and the afternoon breeze. If we want to get in tonight at all, said Len, and get back on the job. Sally for a moment was a little forlorn. The word jerked her back too suddenly to a world she had forgotten from another world where there were no clocks and no jobs, but only space and deep winds and enticements onward. But since she must yield to the practical, her reaction was complete.

"How about food?" said Sally. "I'm starved!"

Len's calculations proved almost exact. They rounded West Point just before sunset. Sally and John congratulated him, but he refused to accept much credit. Too many variables for anything but a guess. It's the boat, said Len: obviously she's a lucky ship now that she's rid of Kelly. That's the way it was: there are lucky ships and unlucky ships, and you can't get around it. Len sailed her toward the float under jib only and at the proper moment spoke to John, who let fall smartly so that their way carried them into the berth. They made fast and snugged down and locked up. John was conscious of the many eyes watching from the other boats, so he stood as close alongside of Len as he could and imitated what the older man did. Len advised him out of the corner of his mouth. From a short distance, the show they put on at furling the sails was very creditable.

They stepped ashore. No one came near them except old Svensen.

The fishermen did not lack friendliness or interest; but there was Sally. Old Svensen was not shy of Sally's kind; but, then, he was a squarehead.

"You bane got a fine boat there, mom," said old Svensen. "And you bane got a fine man; and I tank mebbe he bane got a fine woman." So, having covered the whole situation most gallantly, old Svensen chuckled and went below.

Sally continued to thrill with the excitement of the day. But it was not exactly excitement. It was more like being tuned up so that she might vibrate to a pitch higher than normal. Or more as though she had bathed in effervescence and her skin still tingled from it. This had been no mere excursion, but a venture into a new life so wholly strange that the old life must take its chance in comparison. However, that was a matter for sober times. Sally was not sober. She washed and changed her clothes and cooked a simple supper; she set the table; but she had not yet touched earth in these commonplaces. She floated in a breathless excitement, without form and which she did not try to understand. And it was a mounting and not a waning excitement, somehow. Sally was almost frightened of it, it was swelling so inside her. Yet she was not really frightened. She rose on it gladly, borne in exhilaration. Like the champagne; only this was even finer and more of the upper air. She was fey.

John and Len could not keep up with her. They were like grinning, slow earth-creatures, a little dazzled, more than a little bewildered, wholly fascinated, unable to parry the swift teasing raids of her fancy. She was vivid as a play of light, mischievous as an imp, shining eyed, mocking, restless of spirit and body. She seemed unable to sit still, but was up and down and flitting about from one thing to another. She was at once strange and adorable.

"Oh!" she cried at last, "I don't know what's got into me; I'm so restless! I've got to do something or bust out all over, and I don't know what it is!"

"Well," said John practically, "I'd go get drunk—at least I would have a year ago. But I reckon what you need is exercise. How about taking a walk to work off steam?"

Sally leaped at the suggestion.

"It's lovely out!" she cried. "See, there's a moon."

Len shook his head.

"Not me!" he negatived with decision. "I'm only a poor old sour-dough that's been raised soft, and I've only been up since four o'clock. What I need is rest."

They left him and stepped off the little veranda and turned up the street away from the car line into the wilderness of the cut-over lands. Sally clasped John's upper arm in both her hands.

"Oh, John!" she breathed.

The night was clear and tranquil. No cloud marred the brilliance of the sky. No alien sound disturbed the stillness. No movement troubled the repose of the earth. Yet the vitality of life brimmed full as in a steadied cup; and the stars twinkled with it, and the silence shrilled with it, and in the moonlight the dead bracken and the charred tall stumps and the scattered firs upheld themselves in a silvered fragility as though through them an essence flowed upward to its source. Low in the east hung the moon.

Suddenly Sally turned John to face her.

"Hold me, John!" she whispered fiercely. "Hold me close—*close*—closer! Oh! It's so big and beautiful! I can't stand it! I can't *stand* it, I tell you!"

She clasped her hands back of his head and pulled it forcibly down to her. Her eyes closed. "Kiss me, John!" she breathed. All the day and the reaches of its spaciousness, all the night and the splendor of its beauty, swept through her and lifted her up and up to the breathless ecstasy that all evening had swelled beneath her heart.

At length they stood apart. Her excitement had not diminished, but it had deepened and widened. And its restlessness had gone. She felt somehow stilled and wide open to something that flowed in.

And then there seemed to sketch across the night, like a fine thin line, a distant tiny something, high up there in the sky. At first it barely reached her consciousness. But as her senses woke it defined itself within her, small and faint; and then, as she recognized it for what it was, it grew and grew until its crying filled for her the whole cup of the heavens, the chirping and calling of migrating birds. She strained her eyes upward, but could see nothing. Yet somehow she thought to see. At least she sensed them, a mighty host of tiny creatures braving the vastnesses. And then, just for the fraction of an instant, she did see. Across the bland, placid disc of the moon winged the swift shapes of wild fowl and were gone. But strangely her spirit followed, caught up into their mysterious air lanes.

They found Len sitting as they had left him. He peered at them shrewdly from beneath his deep brows.

"Times is," said Len, "when glory burns." He arose to his great height, and his carved brown old face took on the lines of a beneficent god. "You kids better go to bed," said Len.

Midway through the night Sally came to herself from a deep sleep. The moon was looking in through the window. Sally sat up in bed, listening. Yes, there it was again, far away and faint; rising to a crescendo overhead, slowly dying in the distance again; a confused, eager, throaty, conversational cackling. She touched John on the shoulder. As is the habit of outdoor men, he came awake, completely and all over at once.

"Listen!" said Sally.

She held him from question, one hand on his shoulder. John clasped his hands behind his head and lay flat, looking at Sally outlined against the window. Her head was tilted back a little, and the moon edged out her hair, sort of, so she reminded him of a little small saint in a church window with a halo on her. John luxuriously stretched all his muscles lengthwise and grinned secretly at the conceit. Sally 'd make a hot saint! thought John, but then, he didn't think much of saints, anyway. He was not obeying commands by listening: he was not even wondering why he had been awakened. He was enjoying his own thoughts, which were pleasant.

"There it is again!" Sally whispered.

Once more the faint wild clamor swelled to populate the air above them, and once more it died to silence, passing somewhere over the edge of the world.

"Wild geese," said John, in a voice that was low only so as not to disturb Len in the next room.

"Yes," agreed Sally in a hushed voice. "Wild geese! Wild geese! Going north! We've got to go!"

For a moment longer she listened, then shivered slightly and slid down beneath the bedclothes. She was still trembling, but not with the cold.

"Let's; let's do it," she resumed. "Let's go! Why not? We have the boat; we have Len. Let's go see!"

But John's spirit was not winged to so instant a decision. They lay side by side and talked in undertones, he expostulatively, she in eager argument.

"You see," John spoke aloud after a while, "you don't know these rough new countries. I do. It's taking a big chance."

"Oh," Sally beat her hands together softly in despair, "I can't say it! I don't know how! But I feel it, all through me. I *know* I'm right. Don't you feel it, too? Just a little?" she pleaded.

"Of course I feel it," said John. "That sort of thing's been my life, and the life of my people, always, from way back. But you—I can't help thinking how you'd miss——"

"It's in my blood, too!" she reminded him passionately. "And what are the things I might miss compared with—— Hush!" she broke off. "Listen, John! Wild geese calling!"

PART III
MIGRATION

CHAPTER IX

DEPARTURE

THE NEWS, imparted to Len at early breakfast the next morning, had a different effect than they had anticipated. Len was appalled.

"Oh now, look here!" cried Len. "You don't want to decide a thing like that off-hand! You ought to think it over."

"We have," returned Sally.

"But you're so mighty well fixed here. You ought to think it over good before you throw all this over for something you don't know nothing about."

"Oh, but we do!" cried Sally. "Think of all the things you've been telling us!"

Len looked dismayed. Sally pounced on him.

"You haven't been deceiving us, have you, Len?" she reproached him incredulously. "All you've been telling us about Alaska—all the mountains and the glaciers and the game and the fish and the big chances! Don't tell me they aren't true! You *said* you weren't lying!"

"I wasn't lyin', honest Injun, I wasn't!" protested Len in distress. "But there's a lot of other things. It's a tough life, and you can't get around it. Might be all right for old sourdoughs like me, and young tough ones like John, but for a woman——"

155

"Aren't there any women at all in Alaska?" Sally interrupted. "I never heard of such a thing."

"There's some," admitted Len reluctantly.

"Well?" challenged Sally.

Len cast an eye toward John in mute appeal for help.

"She's pushin' me in a corner," he complained. But John continued to apply himself to his breakfast. He was by now wholly tuned to Sally. Sally was not arguing: she was having fun with Len. Far be it from John to interfere. Len braced up. "I tell you, Sally, there's a lot you ain't thought of. Unless you want to siwash it, it's hard work. There ain't no comforts, and no company like you're used to, or books or—or——"

"Go on," prodded Sally.

"It rains an awful lot sometimes," Len continued more lamely, "and winters there ain't more than about six hours daylight; and honest, Sally, it's just plumb foolish for John to quit a good job like he's got—he says they've raised him twice already—and go traipsing off where there's nothin' certain——"

"Man needn't look for a job up there," Sally reminded him, "and they pay three-four times the wages you get down here. That's what you *said*," she added.

"Sure, that's right," admitted Len, "but them jobs don't git you nowhere. You do them, and they're done. And when they get Klakan built and finished up——"

"But," Sally interrupted again sweetly, "barring maybe a few cartridges and a little coffee and sugar, you can live like a king up there and never go near a store. You said that, too. I'd *love* to live like a king," said she dreamily.

This was going almost too far. Len darted toward her a glance of suspicion. But Sally could look convincingly innocent, and Len was seriously alarmed.

He had a bright idea. "How you going to git there?"

"We told you. On the Tillicum. You'll take us."

"I don't know one dang thing about navigation." Len cheered up a little. "No," he caught their skepticism. "I can putter around in pilot waters all right. But piloting and navigating is different things. You see," Len was now easy enough in his mind to relax into dissertation, "piloting means goin' around by what you see; but navigatin' is sextant work and calculatin' and things I ain't never learned."

He sat back with an air of satisfaction. But Sally was unimpressed. "What of it?" she wanted to know.

"Why," said Len, "it's all offshore work, going to Alaska—the Pacific Ocean, the Gulf. Takes a sailor for that sort of thing. Never make it in the world."

"What's the matter with going up inside?" contributed John lazily. He was enjoying himself and, as usual, leaving it to Sally.

Len became earnest indeed, ludicrously earnest. He explained carefully, almost in words of one syllable, as it were. The mere idea was untenable. Heavy tides, strong currents, baffling winds reflected off the mountains from all directions. Never get anywhere. Might take a week beating somewhere and then lose it all in a day. Steam, yes; but sail . . . Len's picture was more conclusively prohibitive than the prospects held out to the wily Ulysses of getting through Scylla and Charybdis.

Apparently he had at last made his point. Sally looked depressed. "I suppose," she murmured, "that that is why there are no fishing boats in Alaska—or is it that fishermen know about sextants and those things?"

John burst out laughing. He could stand it no longer.

"I've got to get down to the mill," said he, arising. "I'll be back soon's I can. Perhaps I can get off right away, but if they need me I'll have to hang on till they fill my place." He put his hand on Len's shoulder. "No use," he advised Len. "She's got you winging. We're going. And," he stopped at the door to remind Len of something obvious, "we *could* go by steamer, you know."

The moment the door had closed behind him Sally's demeanor changed. She came round the table and placed the small chair squarely in front of Len.

"John is right, Len. We are going. We can't do anything else. That is the way we are made, both of us. And all the things you have said, yes, and all the other things you might say—I know there must be many more—do not matter *that!*" She snapped her fingers.

She paused a moment to draw a deep breath.

"Listen to me, Len. I'm going to try to make you understand, because I love you very much, and I want you to understand. I lay a long time awake last night, after John and I had decided, and thought about it. I know now why it must be, and I'm going to try very hard to tell you, and when he comes back I'm going to try very hard to tell John. Perhaps neither of you will know what I mean, but I think John will, for he feels it, even if he hasn't thought it out. Promise you'll listen and try not to think I'm foolish."

"I'd never think you foolish, Sally," said Len soberly.

"It started by something you said—you remember?—about buying life: that that's all money can do for you, buy life, living. That is very beautiful, Len, and it's true. And, no matter how much money you have or can make, it is no good to you unless you are where you can buy your kind of life with it. Remember?"

Len nodded slowly.

"Well, that's it, all of it. Our kind of life—John's and mine—cannot be bought here. It's taken me all winter to find that out. At first it seemed to me that here, in the city, is everything I'd been missing all my life. Some of it is. But there's something little and drab and respectable and—and *worthy* about the people. At least our kind of people, John's and mine. When I found that out it made me think still harder, for I could see what we would be coming to. Don't mistake me. John would get on; you are right about his chances here They think a lot of him at the mill. In time he'd own his own mill and forests and ships, and we'd live on Magnolia Heights. We'd be 'successful.' And perhaps you may be right in the thing you feared, but did not tell us—that if we go to Alaska we'd be beaten, we'd 'fail,' as they'd call it. But even if we *knew* that, we'd have to go. Can you see why?"

Len shook his head. "Mebbe just a little—I don't know." Sally hesitated, colored a little.

"It's because," she said slowly, "we'd mean nothing here—no matter how we succeed, because here are only ready-made, old, small things to shine through us. What would we *be?* What would we *mean?* By ourselves, we are really no different from all the other drab, commonplace little couples. Oh no we're not!"—as Len stirred —"not by ourselves, with only drab, commonplace little things to express. But there!" Her eyes were shining. "I can't say it. You must know!" she appealed.

Len rose to his feet. He put the flat of his hands under Sally's elbows and swung her from her chair and held her for a moment off the floor at the height of his eyes. He kissed her on the forehead.

"God bless you, Sally," said he, "you're a fine woman."

He set her down gently and passed the back of his hand across his eyes.

"How long you figger it 'll take you to close out here?" he asked. "We ought to get off in about two weeks."

John returned before noon.

"No trouble at all!" he cried to them from afar. "I offered to stay on if they needed me, but Snell was fine about it. Guess I ain't so important as you might think," he laughed. "Well, we ought to be off in a couple of days!"

Both Len and Sally hooted.

"You're stark, staring mad," Sally told him bluntly. "With all there is to do first!"

"What things?" asked John. "How long is it going to take us to stock up that little boat? I could be ready tomorrow."

"Well, I couldn't. For one thing, we have to do something about this house. There's three months yet on the lease."

"Pay it and let it go," said John largely.

Sally ignored this fatuous suggestion.

"What about all the furniture and things we've bought?" she pursued. "Do you expect to lug them along or just go off and leave them for anybody who wants them? And there are a *few* things, just a few, to be bought besides groceries, if we're going for keeps."

"Yes," struck in Len unexpectedly, "and I got a little interest in this myself; and I ain't going to be hurried by no kid stuff neither. I ain't nothing much in the way of a sailor, but I'm a reg'lar Cap'n Cook alongside of you two, and if I'm going to tackle this proposition I'm going to have at least a *chance* of gitting there. We got a lot to do on that boat yet afore we shove off."

"Why, Len!" cried Sally in amazement at his gloom, "I thought you——" She stopped as she caught his slow and solemn wink—on the side away from John.

"I don't see what there is, much, to do on the boat," objected John.

"No?" Len wheeled on him pugnaciously. "What's the state of her riggin'? You know that? Is her bottom clean? Any bare spots in the copper paint? What shape is her sails in? Any leaks? Bilge pump workin' all right? How about a skiff? You aimin' to start off without a skiff? How about charts? Compass p'inting correct? Such things as wax and palm and sail twine and caulking and marline all present and accounted for?" He eyed John sardonically. "Noticed mebbe what accommodations she has?" he pursued his relentless interrogation. "Where you expectin' me to sleep? Or are you aimin' to tow me along behind?" He held John under his ironic eye for a moment. "You're out of the cow country," he concluded crushingly. "So, Sally and me, we're going to be plenty busy for some time to come. I judge you're goin' t' be plenty lucky if you pull out of here in less 'n a month." He winked again reassuringly at Sally, who also was beginning to look a little dashed.

However, things moved not only faster than Len predicted, but more smoothly than his own private expectations. Sally, for instance, had surprisingly little difficulty with the house. The agent knew of a tenant all ready to take the remainder of the lease; and Sally was able, by payment of a small commission, to turn over the whole affair. The matter of the furniture was equally simple. Remembering the capacity of the Tillicum's cargo hold, Sally listed much of it to take along for whatever new home they might establish. The small remainder she disposed of to the new tenant at not too great a loss. Sally felt very busy and efficient and was—both John and Len agreed —a wonder, which made her still happier.

One thing she did of which she said nothing to John, and only after somewhat of a struggle with herself. She strapped up compactly the beautiful carved-leather saddle and lugged it all the way downtown—quite a feat, that—and sold it. This was John's first gift to her, away back in those prehistoric times, nearly a year ago, when she had emerged from nothingness into life. Her heart cried out as at a sacrifice; but her common sense ruefully contemplated the saddle's size and awkwardness and general unsuitability in a horseless country, even as a souvenir. And the money she got for it was to be special money, for which she had a secret use.

"Only I do wish John had given me something small," she reflected a little tearfully.

Now she was free to join the men in the preparations at the float. They, too, had been very busy: and they had made wonderful accomplishment. Much of this was due to the fact that they had plenty of assistance. The fishermen took enormous interest. They roosted about and gave advice and lent a hand. John and Len had hardly to lift a finger in the more nautical matters of rerigging, splicing, seizing and the like. Sally's first appearance rather threatened this fellowship. The seamen fell silent and wary or moved away. But this did not last. Sally had a way with her. They fell for Sally; and, while most of them never quite lost a slight awkwardness when on occasion they addressed her directly, most of the time the relationship was easy and warm. They called her "Missus," and made her small presents: braided lanyards for her knife or to hold on her hat, especial wobblers for catching salmon, anything their limited imaginations could suggest as femininely appropriate. Old Svensen was saving his present, but he had it "going"—a glass jar of sour dough.

"He bane six year old!" said Svensen proudly.

They had one bit of luck. One afternoon a man from upshore rowed around the end of the pile dock.

"Look here," he called, "anybody know who this dinghy belongs to? Somebody left it at my float a few days ago."

For a split second everybody looked blank. Then up spoke Marvin.

"Sure!" said he challengingly. "She b'longs to this ketch here."

It took ten seconds for the idea to sink in. Then everybody piped up at once.

"That's right!" "We was lookin' for her!" "Wondering what had become of her."

The man looked a trifle bewildered at the eagerness of this. He sculled slowly alongside the float.

"Well, here she is," said he, "but I don't see why——"

He was overwhelmed by a chorus of explanation: that the ketch had just been sold; that must 've been the old owner left it, Pirate Kelly, you've heard of Pirate Kelly; this is the new owner, here, he'd been searching for her everywhere.

The stranger looked still more bewildered. "Well, glad to be of service," said he vaguely at last. He stepped to the float.

"No, that's all right," he waved aside John, who had recovered sufficiently to make some feeble gesture of payment or reward. "Glad to have found her for you." He departed on foot up the ramp.

"Look here, you fellows—I don't believe——" began John. He got no further.

In his turn he was overwhelmed by asseveration. Every man there, it seemed, had seen that dinghy a thousand times in the possession of Pirate Kelly and was ready to swear it on a stack of Bibles a mile high. They waxed indignant that John should think . . .

Look at the empty chocks there on deck! That's where she fits. Still he did think, and so did Sally. Len argued against them.

"It might have been Kelly's at that," said he. "Who else is there would go off and leave a good boat like that tied up?"

"Funny he didn't paint her the same color as the ship," grumbled John.

"Just the same, even a drunk would have been looking for her by now if he'd left her and forgot," pointed out Len.

There was nothing to be done about it. She was a good dinghy, bluff and broad, with lots of carrying capacity, but slipping easily through the water. And when they hoisted her aboard, by a sling on the main boom, she did fit the chocks. Len seemed to think that settled it. Nobody appeared to claim the little craft, so they kept her: but Sally and John named her the Foundling.

John and Len were nearly ready when Sally was free to join them; and of this fact they were justly proud. They showed her what they had done. She was gratifyingly appreciative, but she laughed a little over what she described as the ridiculously drab masculinity of everything and was truly concerned over Len's sleeping quarters, which consisted solely of a bunk of rough lumber, fitted snugly into the triangular compartment forward of the cargo hold, and a narrow shelf above it.

"There's no light, there isn't room to turn around, there's no ventilation at all. How are you going to breathe?" she cried, aghast.

They pointed out to her that Len would be using it only when they were at anchor. Then he could leave open the hatch. As for room, all he needed was space to stretch out in, and they'd made the bunk oversize. He had a lamp and the shelf. Wasn't as if he had to *live* there, only to sleep there. Sally yielded, with reservations. But on the question of the feminine touch she held firm. She demanded paint. She bought curtain rods and cut down one of the house curtains for the portholes. She bought outright bright-colored spreads for the bunks.

"I'd make them if I had time," said she, "but they don't cost much, and after we've lived here a little while—you'll see!"

The cabin certainly did look brighter and cozier, more homelike. Nevertheless, the men were relieved when she had finished. Both had suffered from horrible uncertainty as to how far she would go. It would not have surprised them if she had added window boxes of flowers outside the portholes.

Shortly a day was upon them when the house was so stripped that it was no longer livable. They must move down to the Tillicum, even though some days were yet to elapse before they could set sail. This must be made a little of a ceremony. John bought a bottle of wine—not champagne. Sally put on the red-checked overall she had purchased in substitute for the kitchen apron. She shooed out the men.

"Go talk to your friends. Go take a walk. Do anything, but get out. There's little enough room as it is, without you big lummoxes getting in my way. When I cook I want the place to myself. I'll call you when I'm ready."

"What are you going to do about it when we get going and there ain't any floats and such for us to go to?" grumbled John. He had rather fancied the picture of himself loafing on the bunk, watching Sally flitting about.

"Then you can go on deck," said Sally.

"Even when it rains?" inquired John on the note of pathos.

"Even when it rains!" Sally was firm. "Well," she relented, "you can go sit in the cargo hold with the furniture, if you want to."

"Come on, Len." John looked hurt. "Let's go over to Casey's and get drunk."

But Sally only laughed at this threat.

"Go ahead. Get drunk if you think that'll do you any good. But I'd advise you to be somewhere in hearing when——"

She broke off abruptly. The clock against the bulkhead was striking. Sally and John were not yet used to the clock. Whenever it sounded the hour, they stopped whatever they were doing and listened. It struck briskly, two at a time, and yet its bell had a slow solemn undertone that spoke to them somehow of great ships and the deep sea, and the last note vibrated on and on. They still had to count up mentally to know what time it was. Sally did so now.

"Six o'clock!" she cried, scandalized. "Shoo! Get out!"

She listened until their footsteps had quit the deck above. Then she shut the hatch and bolted it and drew the new curtains across the portholes and set eagerly about her preparations.

After a time she took a last satisfied look about, slid back the hatch and stood for a moment on the companionway, head and shoulders out, breathing deep of the fresh salt air, savoring the strangeness. The clock struck six bells.

She had no need to call. Two figures rose from the stringer at the edge of the float.

"About time!" John's voice was reproachful. "What in the world you been doing? We're starved!"

Sally backed down the companionway and stood to one side. The cabin looked very attractive like this, with the lamp in its gimbals lighted, and everything bright and fresh with paint and color and the sparkle from metal and glass. The table, unfolded from the bulkhead, she had covered with a blue-and-white-patterned oilcloth to match her own china, which was already in the racks. It was all set and ready, with the bottle of wine prominently in a place of honor. Sally waited pridefully for comment; nor was she disappointed.

"Will you look at that!" cried John. "Flowers! Now where did you dig them up?"

"This is an occasion," said Sally.

"And, say, I never saw that tablecloth before!"

"That's one of my surprises. Like it?"

John moved forward.

"What you giving us?" he asked hungrily. He looked over the crowded table, reporting back over his shoulder to Len, "Corn pudding! Whoops! Hot biscuits and honey! Fried sweet potatoes! Yipee! How the devil did you work in all that on that little bit o' stove?"

"Well, you needn't get your hopes up," warned Sally. "You won't get anything like this again. This is a special celebration."

"I'll say it is! What you got here?" John reached to uncover a platter in the center of the table, the contents of which were concealed by a large roasting cover. But Sally stopped him.

"That's my other surprise. No, wait. Come up here, Len." She poured some of the wine and handed to each a glass.

"Can't we sit down?" complained John. "I'm getting a crick in my neck!"

Sally held out her glass.

"Here's to *us!*" she proposed. "Us three!"

The words were simple, but to both John and Len they held somehow a prayer for the future. They drank and stood for a moment in silence.

"Now," Sally broke it gaily at last, "for my other surprise!" She placed a hand on the roasting cover. "This is Len's surprise. It's a going-away present from me to Len. I want everybody to understand that I got it with my very own money. And," she fixed Len with a threatening eye, "I want no back talk!"

She lifted the cover. John uttered an exclamation of surprise. In the center of the platter lay a short-barreled Colt's .45 revolver flanked by a thick old-fashioned gold watch and chain and a pair of onyx square cuff buttons set in gold.

Sally stood, the cover suspended in her right hand, looking steadily at Len. For several moments no one moved.

"Please, Len," pleaded Sally.

Len turned away blindly and in three long strides had reached the companionway and was on deck.

John leaped upon Sally—taking a sharp crack on the head from the carlings above—and swept her into an enthusiastic hug. The roasting cover fell with a mighty clang.

"Look out!" warned Sally, struggling.

"You damn little—little chuckawalla! Why didn't I come to think of *that* myself!"

"Look *out!*" cried Sally in a muffled voice. "You'll bump your head —you'll upset the table!"

"To hell with my head! To hell with the table! That's the most gorgeous, splendiferous, all-around——" He strained her to him in the sudden passion that always, for them, accompanied any big moment of life. "I could—I could——" For a moment she yielded. Their lips met. Then she thrust him away.

"John, behave!" she warned, but a little breathlessly. "It was nothing really. I knew you wouldn't mind."

"Mind! You know that I've been trying all along to——"

"I know. But this had to be from me."

John was getting calmer and curious.

"How did you manage to get them without the tickets?" he wanted to know.

"I didn't. I got the tickets."

John looked at her with dawning comprehension and burst into delighted laughter.

"You dam' little pickpocket!" he cried. Another thought: "What was it, piano money?"

Sally shook her head. "I'd used that." She crept close to him again. "I sold the saddle," she confessed. "It was only sensible," she hastened on. "I'd never use it again. And I didn't want to spend the money just on—just on *anything*. So I thought . . ."

But Sally was to learn that, unlike women, men, especially men like John, who have traveled light through roving lives, ordinarily feel sentiment only as to equipment in actual use.

"Great!" approved John heartily; and Sally, in an upsurge of relief, in her turn was drawn . . . She snatched herself back.

"The dinner will be spoiled!" she cried. "Len! Len! Come and get it!" she called.

They were ready in two days more. After the furniture had all been stowed, room must be found for a number of good-sized boxes belonging to Sally.

"My piano money, as you call it," she explained briefly. "Books." She refused the suggestion to open the boxes. "We'll read books when there's nothing else to read—in winter. Right now there's plenty else."

The day before their planned departure the Tillicum again proved herself a good-luck boat, at least in Len's estimation. Svensen appeared, towing a younger edition of himself whom he introduced as his son.

"Oscar he bane skipper of tug boat," Svensen mentioned with pride.

It developed that Oscar had business, with his tug boat, at Port Townsend. He was offering to tow the Tillicum that far—gratis, for love—because old Svensen was his father, and old Svensen liked the Tillicum and her crew. Len thought that a great idea. Both John and Sally felt secretly a little disappointment. Towing behind a tug seemed to them an unromantic way of starting off on a great adventure. But before either could think of a tactful refusal, Len had accepted with enthusiasm and had made arrangements to anchor out in the stream that night so Oscar could pick them up easily in the morning. At this they felt still more flattened, for in the back of their minds had been a nebulous picture of setting out from the float and spreading their wings, and their fishermen friends waving their caps and cheering: and here they were sneaking off after dark as though they were ashamed of something. Not even a sail up! Len towed from the dinghy. To be sure, a few were afoot to give them a hand; but it was late, and they had already said good-by to those of the fishermen they knew well, and almost everybody had turned in. The occasion had no inspiration whatever. Even the Tillicum seemed to have lost the feel of buoyant vitality that had never before forsaken her, even when she was lying motionless at the float. She crept with sluggish indifference through leaden waters.

Satisfied at last with her position, Len rowed back and climbed aboard. He let down the anchor over the bow, slowly, until he felt the bottom. Then calculatingly he payed out more cable, until the scope seemed to him sufficient, and made it fast to the bitts. He led the dinghy by her painter around to the port side where, with John's help, he slung her aboard and into her chocks.

"We won't need to lash her," said Len. "We'll tow her when we get going on our own."

He moved forward once more, a dim shadow.

"I'll just coil down the towing cable handy," he called back to them. Len was cheerful enough. But, irrationally, it did not seem right, somehow, for him to be talking out loud like that. He was striking a match and lighting a lantern, and the spot of light picked him out of the gloom. He hoisted the lantern to the mast head.

"There," he observed with satisfaction, coming aft and squatting down beside them. "Now we're snug and all ready for a good start in the morning." He appeared to sense the atmosphere of depression. Indeed, he could hardly fail to do so. "What's the matter? Little sorry to leave after all?"

"Not one little bit!" denied Sally, aroused. "It's just—— I'm tired, I guess."

"Sure," agreed Len, "I don't wonder." But he spoke absently. "We're lucky about young Svensen," said he after a moment. "Gets us to where we want to start. Like getting to the edge of the city on a streetcar. That's what it's like getting out of Puget Sound, just workin' loose to where you can make a start. Gosh!" said Len fervently, "I sure did dread buckin' those tides in Admiralty Inlet!" he pronounced it "Admiráliy." "Between here and Townsend is nothin'—just a chore. It's when you leave Townsend that you're really setting sail!" He arose to his feet. "Let's turn in and get a good sleep," said he.

Sally paused in the hatchway to look after his long figure. Her heart was warm toward Len. How surely he had guessed! But she still regretted that imagined grand departure. John felt the same way. She knew that from his silence. It was silly, but they were as disappointed as children.

The tow to Port Townsend did much to alleviate the disappointment, but little to lift her absurd depression. Without the tug they could not have set out at all that day, for they awoke to a thick fog and a flat calm. Nevertheless, Oscar and the tug managed to find them somehow. They hoisted and stowed the anchor and passed the cable to the tug and were off. They could not see a thing. Sally's anticipated farewell sight of Seattle and Magnolia Heights and West Point joined the grand departure dream; and as the day wore on so did the Olympics and Mt Rainier and the glittering reaches of Possession Sound and the delight of unknown waters after they had turned into Admiralty Inlet. How Oscar found his way she could not imagine. Except for various melancholy wails and hootings, near and sharp or distant and muffled, they might have been alone in illimitable space. It was shivery and damp. Sally almost regretted her refusal of Oscar's invitation to the tug's pilot house. But she had had some vague and sentimental idea of sticking by the ship. It would have been warm and cozy in the pilot house. For that matter, it would have been much warmer and cozier below in the cabin of the Tillicum. But for some reason she did not want to go below. She must stay on deck and stare into the blankness. Sometimes she could see plainly the blunt, powerful stern of the tug, and again the impalpable veil of fog drifted across it so she could just imagine it. It might have been a ghost except for the lusty wake that boiled from under its counter and swept by them in a swift, live current.

Len, in oilskins, crouched over the tiller, and John sat beside him. They conversed together in low voices. Sally had no desire to talk. John appeared to have recovered his spirits, which somehow made Sally at once more forlorn. It was absurd; there was really nothing to be forlorn about. But she couldn't help it. She finally shook herself into going below to make some sandwiches and coffee and brought them on deck and perforce for a little while joined in with John and Len. But she could not arouse to real attention of what they were saying—something about hooters and sirens and echoes and compass courses and signal whistles. John had come alive with interest. She ought to have been interested, but she was not. At times a brief spurt of anger at herself upsurged within her, but it did not last.

She lost all sense of time. She was surprised when somebody on the tug cast overboard the end of the cable, and the tug rounded back toward them. Oscar was leaning out of the pilot house shouting something and pointing. Len was shouting something back. Oscar reached inside and pulled a whistle rope in farewell. Len went forward to drop anchor. Sally gathered they had reached Port Townsend. They might have been in the middle of the Pacific Ocean as far as she could see. Len went below and got a thing like a big dinner bell. He and John took turns ringing it, at intervals of a minute or two. Sally might have volunteered to do her share of this, but she didn't. She went below and lay down on the bunk. John came down after a while to see if anything was the matter. But Sally told him she was just tired. He returned to the deck looking troubled. After a time they stopped ringing the bell. Sally supposed the fog must have thinned, but she did not go on deck. She had no curiosity about Port Townsend. She was being thoroughly obstinate and childish and unreasonable, and she knew it; but she did not care. She took a perverse satisfaction in the men's anxiety and bewilderment.

She could have cried over them; but at the same time she wanted to hurt them. When John finally blew out the lamp and crawled dispiritedly into his bunk she did cry, and what she was crying about she could not have told, except that she was a little fool, a little *devil*—she told herself savagely—and she couldn't help it, and why she couldn't help it she did not know. She looked across at John's back, which she could just make out in the dimness, and she had a sudden impulse to cross over and cuddle against him for comfort, but something held her from it. She sniffed forlornly. This was to have been such a wonderful day! What in the *world* had got into her!

CHAPTER X

VOYAGE

SALLY STAYED AWAKE for some time, then sank into a sleep so profound that when morning came she must gather her wits to realize where she was. She lay on her back and stared at the deck planking just above her head. Discs of sunlight, reflected from the water through the portholes, moved back and forth and round and about in a curiously hesitant gay and eccentric dance. The air outside hummed contentedly, as though bees: but it was a wind in the rigging. The lapping of wavelets against the boat's side spaced faster than the usual tempo. It must be a fine day. She turned her head slightly. John's bunk was empty. A warming, utterly delicious feeling of guilt tingled all through her. She ought to be up preparing the breakfast; she ought to have been up long ago so they could be taking advantage of this fine breeze. She ought to get up right now and set about it. Instead, she snuggled down deeper in the blankets and wriggled her toes. Sally was enjoying being naughty. Last night she had been ugly-naughty; but this morning she was being happy-naughty, and then only for an impish moment or so more. She chuckled a little.

"I'm certainly terrible when roused!" she told herself amusedly. She pictured to herself John and Len, completely cowed by her

ferocity of the evening before, tiptoeing about afraid to awaken
her before her own royal good pleasure. This entertained her for
a moment. Then her fundamental common sense took charge. "Has
it occurred to you," this Sally asked of the other, "that it is barely
possible they may have thought you were tired and are simply letting
you rest?"

Smitten to the quick, Sally leaped out of the bunk and tore
through her toilet and into her clothes. Before starting the belated
breakfast she popped her head out of the hatch to see what the men
were doing, and to assure them she was awake and trying to make
up time. They were seated side by side on the combing smoking
their pipes.

"I'm so sorry," Sally flung at them. "I overslept."

Later in the day she would remember and relish the slow spread
of relief over the uncertain faces they turned to her appearance. But
now she was all breathless concern at the delay she had caused.

"Get a good rest?" asked John. "How you feeling?"

"Top of the world! I'll have things ready in a jiffy."

"Don't hurry," Len called after her. "We can't be leaving for an
hour yet, anyway."

This stopped her. She stuck her head out again to hear the rest
of it.

"Why not?" she asked.

"No sense going till the last of the ebb," said Len. "That'll get us
off Point Pa'tridge by slack, and then we'll get the fresh of the flood
all the way up the straits. Tide divides at Pa'tridge."

Sally stared a moment and then began to laugh. Her imagined
importance was all deflated.

"What's so funny?" asked John, grinning at the sheer contagion of
her sudden amusement.

"Nothing. You wouldn't understand." Sally filled her lungs and
for the first time looked about her at the little town piled against
its low bluffs, and the wide blue dancing sparkle of the bay, and
the arms of it tipped bravely with the lights on Marrowstone and
Wilson Points. What a day! It sang through her spirit with the lift

of the wind and carried her awing. "You poor lambs," she cried, "you must be starved!"

"Take your time," repeated Len; "we'll just get the skiff overboard, now you're awake."

The wind was a little south of west, so that, once Point Wilson was passed, it came to them down the Straits of San Juan de Fuca direct from Japan. Or so Len said. The Tillicum lay far over so that the water streamed aft inches deep along her lee rail. Nevertheless the *feel* of her was eagerly ahead, as though only good manners held her back at all.

"Old girl's glad to get back to it!" shouted Len, wiping the spray from his mustache.

"Isn't it a little dangerous?" gasped Sally, which saved John from asking the same question.

Len laughed at them. Just a good wholesale breeze. He called their attention to the fact that there were three rows of reef points on the mainsail, and that he hadn't even tied in the first.

"She's just beginning to show what she can do," said he. "Here, take hold and feel her."

But this proposal was emphatically and fervently turned down by both. That first sailing excursion inside had proved them so apt that Len had been deceived. He could not appreciate how strange to them was everything to do with the sea. They must become habituated to it one thing at a time. For today it was quite sufficient to get used to big waves. They were not really big waves, but they looked so to Sally and John: monstrous. As each bore massively down on the Tillicum, there was a moment when it hung so high and menacing above the poor little craft as to seem about to engulf her. Then Sally's breath caught in a queer mixture of sheer terror and exquisite ecstasy, and John did his best to look unconcerned. In reality it was not so much the waves they had to get used to as the action of buoyancy. For a time it was like a major miracle to them when, at the last split second, the stern of the ketch lifted; and the wave rolled smoothly beneath her; and then the bow tilted up and the stern dropped, and the wave passed on ahead. That was not the way the land acted when anything threatened. There you had to look out for yourself, but here the Tillicum did it for you. So, as is proper to all good ships, she began to take on to them her personality as one of their comradeship.

That, although Len could not quite realize it, was quite sufficient for one day. It occupied them almost wholly. To be sure, they managed to tear away a momentary attention to minor matters of which Len made mention, and so may have retained certain dim impressions of other things besides the oncoming, unhurrying, unending ranks of the sea. The great combers presented themselves one after the other in an indifferent sort of majesty, seemed to pause the space of a caught breath as though for inspection and rolled mightily on, resuming their aloofness. Each was individual and different. Both Sally and John were held to them by a mysterious compulsion, as though it were the lift of their hearts alone that buoyed the Tillicum over the ceaseless rhythm. If they were to miss just one!

It was exciting, breathless, exhilarating and deliciously just off the edge of terror. They were not really afraid. All they had to do for reassurance was to look at Len. Len smoked his pipe and steered and kept a critical eye on the telltale flying from the truck; but he vouchsafed the waves only an occasional glance over his shoulder. Apparently he considered them of minor importance. But only toward the close of the afternoon did Sally and John begin to feel in them a certain large, good-natured friendliness. Which was indeed achievement sufficient for a first experience.

This was for them the whole of that day. Space, time and the minor contents of those dimensions were all but lost to them. The only vivid outside memory they retained was of the bell buoy tolling solemnly its warnings on Partridge Banks. That presented itself clearly as someone brave and alone. The glittering magnificence of the Olympics, the rises of Vancouver Island, the low white littoral of the mainland that accompanied them to starboard, the San Juans lifting slowly above the horizon ahead, were all there for the looking, but of them they retained no memory. Of the gradual opening out and closing in again that marked their steady progress, they were unaware. They passed Smith Island with its sounding board to echo back in fog, and Len called their attention to it and to the wide-flung kelp beds that revealed its shoals; and they answered back that yes, it was interesting; but that was politeness off the surface of their minds. It did not even occur to them that they should be hungry; and as Len had the woodsman's indifference to food at noon, they all went without lunch.

As for time, that seemed either to be endless or to have stopped. There was no sense of its movement. Therefore they were surprised to wake up to the fact that, unexplainably, land had appeared all about them, and that the water had flattened out, and the wind moderated. Len was standing up, steering with his leg against the tiller.

"Well, we've about used up the flood tide," Len was remarking in a congratulatory tone of voice. "We done mighty well with it. Might as well call it a day."

They looked about them dazed, as though awakening. To port lay a beach, low and white, and beyond it a fringe of green forest, and beyond that, at considerable distance, a round-topped blue hill. Astern, through a rapidly narrowing opening, they could still see the waves hurrying by. They were sailing into a wide bay, somewhat like a round lake, the circumference broken on their starboard side by a projecting rocky point like a miniature promontory.

"Where are we?" asked Sally.

"That's Iceberg Point," said Len. "There's a good small bight beyond the cliff there. We'll drop the hook there for the night."

The little promontory cut off the last traces of breeze. The Tillicum coasted the last hundred yards. The sails hung so slack that Len proposed to leave them hoisted for a little while to dry out from the spray. He lighted his pipe, looked about him with an air of satisfaction.

"Well, we certainly come across there mighty lucky!" said he. "Couldn't have had a better day for it."

"Pretty rough," suggested Sally.

"Rough!" Len's astonishment seemed genuine. "If we don't strike anything worse than that . . ." He warmed to a kind of exasperation. "I got to keep telling you kids that this voyage ain't going to be no picnic, and you might as well make up your minds to it and get a good ready. We got to pick our wind and weather, and we're bound to get it dirty. Lucky thing is we got all the time there is. And one thing you got to get used to keeping in mind all the time, and that is, if you ever go overboard it's going to be tough for everybody. No matter what happens, *hang on to yourselves.* It's mighty easy to slip on a wet deck." Len spoke very seriously. Lines of anxiety seamed his face. John must answer him in proportion.

"It's a lot of responsibility for you, Len," said he, "and we know it, and we're going to do our level best to help. And it can't be rough all the time. A lot of it *is* inside."

Len admitted this: some of it was like a long meandering narrow lane between mountains. Never rough there. But strong tides and the winds blow up them or down them, and there was no use at all trying to buck it when either was from ahead. A lot of this so-called inside stuff could raise an awful ruckus. Johnstone Straits, for example.

"We ought to come to her in two-three days," said Len. "Look at her on the chart, and she looks like she's landlocked, and she's only a couple or three mile wide. But she runs a hundred mile or so east and west, and the high land on both sides makes a suction wind that mostly blows right in your face. And when the tide runs agin it, it raises a high chop that really does make it tough. I'd ruther—anybody 'd ruther—take open ocean any time. There the seas run regular even when it blows. With a good boat like this you can snug down and sort of rely on 'em. Kelly always made it outside. That's the good of this rig: one man can handle it."

"I've been wondering about that." Sally perked up from the delicious laziness that was stealing through her every fiber. "If you're alone how about when you want to sleep or anything?"

"Lay her to," said Len promptly.

Here was something new and of the greatest interest. Len must explain how the sails could be trimmed in such fashion that their

effects would balance one against the other, and then the tiller could
be lashed in such position as to keep her "sailin' without goin'
ahead," as Len expressed it.

"Don't she drift?" asked John.

"Some," admitted Len, "but you'd be surprised how little. You can
go below and turn in and get you a good night's sleep, and she won't
be far off where you left her, come morning. But," he added, "that's
why you got to give yourself sea room—git way offshore; and that
means navigation, which I ain't got."

Sally's eyes shone. Her imagination was fired. What a picture!—the
tiny ship maintaining itself in the vastness of the sea, with no aid
but its own gallant sufficiency: just those two antagonists alone together, and man's hand withdrawn from guidance. Sally's sense of
the Tillicum as a personality was properly deepened.

Len knocked out his pipe.

"Come on, John," said he. "May as well snug down."

The ship's clock struck its brisk yet solemn pairs of bells. Sally
stirred reluctantly. The sun was getting low, but its warmth still
had strength. It was delicious to lie there in it all relaxed. Now she
must go below and start a fire in the galley and cook something.
Suddenly she realized how long it had been since any of them had
eaten. But Len intervened.

"You lay still," he ordered her with authority. "I'm doing the
cooking tonight."

Sally roused herself to protest. Len had done all the work that
day. It was her turn.

"No," insisted Len. "You lay still. I aim to try old Svensen's sour
dough. Hot cakes." He held her sternly for a moment. "Besides,"
said Len, "you're all wore out pushin' back waves." Still chuckling,
he went forward to where John was already tying stops over
the jib.

Sally sank back with a grateful sigh. Surprisedly she realized she
was tired, very tired, as though she had done a hard day's work. And
she had not done a thing—except, as Len said, to "push back waves."
Len was pretty shrewd. The last shred of her active mind spared

a tender little thought for good old Len. Then she relapsed into a deeper absorption than that of the mind.

The water was still and polished, and in the westering sun, low to the horizon, the depth of its very substance was changing to a curious deep purple. A stray phrase from a translation of Homer popped up in Sally's mind: "The wine-dark sea." It was like that. The last breeze had died. There seemed to be no wind at all any more, anywhere. A brooding peace that was to become evening breathed from the earth into the upper airs. Sally seemed to herself to be basking in quietness, just as a few moments before she had basked in sun warmth. But, paradoxically, it was not at all quiet. All about were both life and motion. She rolled over on her stomach and propped her chin in her hands.

Here and there, as far as she could see, were birds, both on the water and in the air. Nearest the boat swam numbers of small, chubby brown ones, quaint, bright eyed, busy, confiding, enchanting, never in flocks, but faithfully two by two. Then farther off, elegant and trim, floated larger gray and white fowl with long necks curved genteelly, like question marks. Their coloring made them seem as insubstantial as mist, and they rested on the water like thistledown, and they had a way of slipping underwater so neatly that now Sally saw them, and now she didn't. One moment they were there, the next showed a surface clean and untroubled. And there they were again, as though materialized. Still farther away were ducks, rafts of them, different from any ducks Sally had ever seen. They were big and bumbling and fat and clumsy; and when occasionally one of them decided to go from here to there he had to bump and splatter and skitter for a hundred yards or so before he lifted into the air. And then he generally forgot for some time to tuck up his feet, which were red. There were other kinds, many others; but Sally did not know the names of any of them, and these then were the most amusing.

And, just as the quietude of the scene before her was undisturbed by these moving creatures, so the stillness of the air was undisturbed by the medley of sound. Against a background of continuous low cluckering, sudden wild cries flung and fell. They ought to have startled, but did not. Far across the bay a patch of white gulls on rocks exchanged broad jokes and shrieking ribald laughter. They struck Sally as a coarse and vulgar lot, but she liked them. Out in the middle a large black-and-white bird swam slowly back and forth and occasionally uttered a long peal of laughter that sounded insane. Sally felt that on another occasion she would get shivers down her spine. Just now these things were only small brilliances on the texture of the stillness that clothed the world.

The days following were not far off the key of this propitious start. As John pointed out—and Len agreed with him heartily—some trips are lucky, and things cannot go wrong; and some trips start unlucky and never change. This was one of the lucky ones. For several days the wind held fair; and then, instead of following the usual sequence to southeast and storm, it swung to westward and clear skies.

This spell of fine weather shook them the more quickly into ship's routine. So few people in so small a compass demanded, not a segregation, but a sharing of duties, turn and turn about. Len could not steer all the time. It was a proud day for Sally, and a little terrifying, when both men went below and left her in charge. She must have got away with it satisfactorily, for thenceforward she stood her regular trick of two hours. After the first, it was rather wonderful to be alone on deck with the sea and the winds and the sky as playmates. They were so big, so powerful and docile to the command of her little hands, but not to be presumed upon or treated carelessly without due deference.

This rotation of the watches extended over into most of life's other activities. The land divided its tasks into man's work and woman's work. The sea made few such distinctions. They all three cooked supper, turn about and with considerable rivalry. The cook of yesterday was the dishwasher of today; the dishwasher of today scrubbed down the deck tomorrow. Sally overrode the men's objection and took her day at this also.

"It's no different from scrubbing a kitchen floor," she insisted stoutly, "and I've done more of them than you have! And if I don't get some exercise I'll get fat."

Nevertheless it was different, done properly. Sally found that out at once. There is quite a knack to flipping the bucket overside so it will fill. Wrongly done, it usually floats in airy emptiness on the surface. Sally's success at about her tenth attempt so caught her by surprise that the unexpected weight dragged the rope through her hands. Helpless she watched the dratted thing waver slowly out of sight into the depths. Then she had to confess. John pretended to have lost all trust in her and held out the only other bucket for a day or two. She had to kneel down and dip the swab overside. Once that crisis was past, the enormously gratifying satisfaction of holding up her end got Sally through a lot worse things. There were days—when the wind blew cold, and the spray seemed to level at her with a vindictive and personal ferocity, and the tiller pulled at her until her back ached, and her hands were blue and cramped, and she could not spare one of them to brush the wet hair out of her eyes—when this thought was all that got her through the last interminable half-hour. And when her watch ended, it had occasionally to carry over for some time until the day decided to change her mood. Curious that: she could not change her mood; the day did it for her. Often she relinquished the tiller after a tough watch, cramped in the narrow confines of unreasoning and childish irritation. She resented being continually banged about, flaring back as though some rude person had jostled her. She was sick to death of living forever on a slant. And then suddenly, without cause, her spirit was released into great spaces and expanded forth to its serene equilibrium with them, and there were no little things, only the vast satisfying simplicities of the mountains and the sea.

The days were strange that way, alternate of vexation and sublimity, and Sally never knew which it was to be. She often looked curiously at the men, moving slowly about their tasks or hunched over, smoking their pipes, and wondered whether they felt these things, too, or whether it was to them all in the day's work. Or whether she herself was silly and fanciful—"soft." This was so fertile a time of the spirit for Sally, such a wonderful new texture of bold contrast of bright and dark, of great and small. She so longed to share it that she was afraid to try. And that was a silly thought which she herself could not understand. Not only physically was she wandering in strange lands. She had queer, unreal moments when she seemed to herself to be sailing out of reality into a mist of illusion. As though she were dreaming. She came to welcome the little sharp hard actualities that rapped her into focus. Then she came to and looked about her almost with surprise. That was where routine came in. The value of routine. Things to be done: solid markers in the day.

They got up in the morning. Sally cooked breakfast while the men rowed ashore to cut the stove wood for the next twenty-four hours. All the movables were stowed. They set forth into what wide flow of triumph or bafflement, ease or toil, comfort or anxiety, none could guess. They were back home again. For, whatever the adventuring, once the anchor was down they had returned. Then familiar life resumed where it had left off. It was leisured once more for small things. They could do what they pleased. The still, homely comfort of the little harbors! Curious, that traveler's sense of a constant, no matter where he is! On land it is the campfire.

Their gateway into this new state of being was really opened to them by an adventure that happened to them on their fourth day out, when they had reached Cape Mudge. Here they left the Straits of Georgia to one side and entered a straight wide channel that looked like a river. Everything seemed propitious. The wind that had been abeam now sucked around the cape to dead astern. A heavy tide seized them. They began to move fast and faster. The low shores at either hand took on speed. John and Sally thought this was great.

"If we could have it like this all the way we'd beat the steamer!" shouted John. He had to shout, because by now the water was making so much noise. It was running ahead at great speed; but it was also whirling and turning on itself so that suction holes and small whirlpools were continually half forming and smoothing away again; and every moment or so a boil heaved up from below and spilled away in all directions. But Len did not seem so pleased.

"She's going too dang fast to suit me." He shook his head uneasily.

"Long as she goes our way," said John.

Len wrinkled his face and looked about him.

"I'm going to put into that bight yonder till she slacks off," he decided.

He put down the helm and trimmed sheets. But as the Tillicum headed into her new course toward the bight they began to feel the real strength of the current. The Tillicum moved sidewise like a crab, much faster than she footed it ahead.

"She won't make it," said Len. "We're in for it."

"In for what?" John was scornful.

"I don't know."

"Shucks," repeated John, "she's going our way."

The point of a shallow S-bend opened, and at last they could see ahead. An island partly blocked the channel. To the left of it roared the water in a tossing cascade. Near the center of that choked passage reared two white broken surges, tossing and pulling as though struggling to be freed from the powerful detaining grasp of some submarine monster.

"Rocks, by God!" yelled Len. "Git down them sails!"

The three worked like mad. Even the two landlubbers were able to grasp the situation so far as to realize the imbecility of trying to steer a course. They cast loose the halyards and fell on the canvas anyhow and smothered it down.

"Look out! Lie down!" shrieked Len. "For God's sake hang on!"

In twenty seconds it was all over, but exactly what had happened none of them could have told. All they knew was that there was a great roaring and a giddy whirling about and clouds of spray and water slopping aboard, now on one side, now on the other. The Tillicum careened far over as the undercurrent pressed her keel one way while the overcurrent pressed it the other. It seemed she was going to upset, and then she recovered and careened as far on the other side. Now she struggled heavily as though resisting some inexorable down pull; and the next moment she quivered in giddy and unnatural lightness, as though deprived of vitally necessary stabilities. The rushing shores were a blur of confusion.

Then all at once things cleared up. The Tillicum floated sedately on an even keel, revolving slowly in an eddy.

They arose from the deck and looked about, trying to recapture their scattered wits. Len stared back upstream and cursed fluently, steadily, without apparently drawing breath. He did not direct his remarks at anything or anybody, not even himself. He just cursed. By and by he remembered Sally and stopped. Sally had recovered herself and was laughing at him.

"Don't mind me," she reassured Len. "I've been raised rough."

John, too, was laughing.

"You're wasting your time up north, Len," said he. "You ought to be a mule skinner."

Len looked properly ashamed.

"Well," he half apologized, "you ain't never going to be closer to Kingdom Come without gittin' there." He began to loosen the improvised stops on the mainsail. "Wonder if there's any more like that there," he grumbled. "I tell you one thing, next time things look like they're going our way too good, I'm goin' to duck!"

"I thought you knew all this coast," jeered John.

"I do," said Len stoutly. "That there's part of it!" He grinned. "I been up and down on steamers," said he. "Anyways, we are out of the banana belt. You've got into new country now."

They were also, at least as far as Sally was concerned, in a new form of life. It seemed to her thenceforward, until they reached the end of the voyage, that the gateway at Seymour Narrows had blocked back all sequence, either of time or geography. It was as though they had sailed into a mist. There was no time, in the sense that neither beginning nor end was in sight, and the days had no particular relation to one another. There was no geography, in the sense that they would never be able to string recollection in due order, to say that this followed that or was before it. They did not move forward to a goal: they lived.

This separateness of experience was exemplified to Sally soon after they left the "banana belt." So she knew it must have happened somewhere in or near Johnstone Straits. But where the harbor was, or what harbors preceded it or succeeded it, she could not for the life of her have told, nor even whether it was before or after the storm when they had met Mike, the hand logger. Each was clear and vivid in her memory, but they were separate things.

The anchorage for that day—Sally could picture that well enough —was in a tiny intimate cove, held close by low hills. Sally had sat on deck until dark, for it was warm and no air stirring and the water burnished in copper green. A seal kept her company, its head appearing now here, now there, in the unruffled surface of the water, examining her intently for long moments and then sinking backward with hardly a ripple.

After turning in she lay awake for a long time enjoying the absolute stillness. This night there were no sounds, not even the usual sleepy wash against the bilges. She could see stars through the open hatch, and she stared at them, and they stared back. Gradually her eyes drooped, and she was just drifting out of consciousness when she was snapped awake by something going on outside. She thought to hear a furtive small gurgling sound. There it was! And a deep and tired sigh, and then the gurgling again. She held her breath, listening into the profound silence. There it was again!

She slipped from between the blankets and up the companionway and looked about her. The night, save for the blazing banners, was black dark. She could see nothing, but presently she made out a faint glow on the forward deck.

"Len!" she whispered, when presently she had identified the glow as from his pipe.

He crept back to her cautiously. They talked in whispers so as not to awaken John.

"What is it?" asked Sally.

"Whales," said Len, "goin' by outside."

Sally strained her eyes toward the opening from the little harbor, and sometimes she thought she could make out against the black of the channel a gleam and swirl, but she could not be sure. Anew she felt the absolute stillness of the night so that there was no sound at all, save this spaced and mighty breathing as the great beasts rolled to the surface.

"I wish I could see them!" regretted Sally and instantly was glad she could not see them. This was more fitting, that these great harmless hunted creatures, returning to the open sea from the landlocked danger of the land, should pass thus secure in the enwrapment of the night. Her eyes filled with sudden tears, for somehow in those deep slow sighs seemed to breathe a weariness and a relief. This was silly, but that was to her the mood of the night.

As to Mike, the hand logger, that experience was more definite in future results. It came as indirect result of the one spell of really bad weather they encountered short of the Alaska border. Incidentally, this was the only occasion that drove them to shelter.

They found it in one of the numerous small bays so completely landlocked that for a few moments, after the howl of the southeaster and the fling of the combers outside, it seemed unreal. The cove proved already inhabited. A raft of huge cedar logs was tethered to the precipitous side of a cliff, and on the raft stood a house and a flower garden. The house was a well-built structure, and, as far as they could see, possessed everything a land dwelling possessed. It had a front yard and a back yard, a low picket fence about them both, a veranda with a rail, and the bright flower garden—in boxes. An admirable arrangement! When one is through with a location, or tired of it, he can be towed to another. They were delighted with the idea; but Len was not much impressed. He had seen whole towns built this way, with post office and stores and saloons and houses and little narrow streets: and sometimes you found that town in one place, and next year it might be fifty miles off, and you had to hunt for it.

"On a raft?" John was incredulous.

On a lot of rafts, Len explained, but then when they got where they were going they shackled them together with chains, so it was practically one raft. Generally have a high fence to keep the kids in—and the drunks from going overboard—added Len. This fellow here? Probably a hand logger.

John pricked up his ears. Anything to do with logs interested him. What did Len mean by a hand logger? Len grunted contemptuously. Just what he said. Feller did his logging by hand. Cut and trimmed his trees on steep slopes next the water and slid the logs down into the chuck. Strictly a Canuck proposition. Never see it anywhere else.

They rowed over to the float house. Nobody was at home. The door was unlocked, but they did not venture in. They returned to the Tillicum for the afternoon. Toward evening the owner appeared in a dory from around the bend of the cliff. He was standing up, facing forward, using the long oars after the manner of a fisherman. When he caught sight of the Tillicum he stopped rowing for a moment, then changed course to come alongside.

He proved to be a big-framed, rawboned man with huge hands. His nose had been smashed nearly flat with his face by fight or accident, but speculative humorous eyes relieved it of any sinister effect. He was wearing a faded Mackinaw coat, heavy with moisture, overalls so stiff with grease as to have turned black, laced half boots. A small felt hat was pushed back on his head to expose a mop of tousled thick brown hair.

He thrust the blades of his oars to stop his way and nodded a greeting without shifting his eyes.

"Come aboard," invited John.

The man shook his head and lifted one foot to expose the sole, armed with long caulks; and then John noticed on the bottom of the dory a protective sheath of boards eaten half through by the sharp spikes. He was, however, willing enough to chat. He stood there for a long time, occasionally thrusting at an oar as the dory drifted, apparently unaware of the heavy rain that was now beginning to pelt down in earnest. Yes, he was hand-logging. Without any help? Alone? No, he had a cat, said he gravely. He flickered at Sally when she laughed, but his face did not change. Doing all right, he answered John's technical question; had in about one swifter already. He looked at John with more interest.

"You a logger?" he wanted to know. He listened gravely to John's reply. "Little different from my kind," was his only comment. He cast an eye at the weather. "You won't get off for a while," said he. "I'll stop for you in the morning, if you'd like to see how it's done."

"You bet I would," John accepted promptly.

" 'Bout six o'clock. What time you got?"

Sally glanced down the hatch.

"Five-twenty," she reported. If the man wasn't coming aboard she wished he would go and not keep them all out there in the wet.

He fumbled about inside his Mackinaw and produced a fat silver watch.

"Huh," said he, "been cheatin' myself." He deliberately reset the hands of the watch. " 'Bout six," he repeated. He made a little swirl in the water with the blades of the oars, preparing to depart.

"It doesn't look to me as though you'll get in the woods tomorrow," said Sally. "This rain looks as if it's going to keep up."

The man examined each of their faces in turn. Only in Len's did he find a flicker of understanding.

"Quit for rain in this country a man 'd never get *nothing* done, ma'am," he told Sally. "Come over and get a cup of coffee and meet my cat," he invited as he swung the dory away.

They watched him a moment longer before going below out of the weather.

"He's a queer-looking man," commented Sally.

"All Canucks is queer," stated Len with conviction.

John spent all of the next day in the woods with Mike. They never learned his last name. He came back soaked, but he did not seem to mind. He was full of enthusiasm. This was a new game. It took a lot of *sabe*. It wasn't so simple as just knocking down a tree and having it slide of its own accord down the mountain into the water. There was a lot more to it than that.

"You go get off those wet things," said Sally, "before you get cold."

When he had changed, and they were all three at supper, he had to tell them more.

"This fellow's *good!*" said John. "He can pick a tree and figure out just how it's going to slide. All by eye, too. Just how the butt's going to bounce off a stump or another tree or a rock, maybe; and how that's going to point her for a new start.

"Sometimes," continued John, "he builds him something special for her to nudge off from. And he's an axman!" cried John. "He has to be. He's got to drop his tree to a gnat's hair, or all his other calculations are no good at all. These Washington and Oregon fellows are good, but Mike's got 'em skinned a mile!"

"I'm glad you had a good time," said Sally. "Len and I had a good time, too."

John's enthusiasm apparently slid right over Len.

"Well, the wind's dropping," said Len. "We can get off in the morning."

"No," said John, "I just got to stay another day or two."

Len roused up.

"Oh, look here," he expostulated, "we don't want to do that! After this southeaster quits she'll swing around to westward, dead ahead. We got to catch the last of it while she's with us."

But John brushed this aside. No, he wanted to see how Mike was going to handle a tree that had failed to slide. He paid no attention to Len's argument that they were missing their God-given chance to get down the length of the straits in favorable conditions. Len insisted, finally with some heat. They came near quarreling about it. Or, at least, Len came near quarreling. Sally watched them with secret anxiety until she discovered that John was merely obstinate, good-naturedly impervious to Len's irritation with him. Secretly she agreed with Len's irrefutable logic; but she had to side with John for the sake of peace.

"I'd like to go with you and see, tomorrow—if the rain stops," said she to John. "You better come along," she urged Len.

"It won't," predicted Len, "not till it begins to blow westerly— right in our faces," said he bitterly. "You go if you want to. Not me. When I go out in wet brush it'll be for something worth while. I'd just as soon jump overboard and get good and honest wet; but I sure do despise getting wet trickly."

This was his last word. He withdrew from the whole childish episode.

John returned from his second day in the woods full of talk.

"He did it!" he told them. "I wouldn't have thought it possible. Prettiest thing you ever saw!"

He explained to Sally in detail. Len sat sardonically apart. First Mike had trimmed off all the branches and then peeled off the bark, exposing the moist slippery sapwood. Then he'd greased the trunk all over with dogfish oil——

"Oh!" cried Sally, enlightened, "so *that's* that awful smell, and those awful overalls!"

"And when he'd got the tree all ready," continued John, "he made a trail all the way down the slope to the water—or, rather, a slideway —cutting out smaller trees, grubbing out hummocks and roots, laying skidways across hollows.

"He greased all them, too," said John. "You never saw a man take such pains to get a good ready." He paused for dramatic effect. "Then," concluded John simply, "he just blocked a jack under the butt end and gave her a little heave, and off she went, slick as you please! It was wonderful!"

He had to explain to Sally why this was so wonderful. It did not seem at all wonderful to her at first. "But," insisted John, "just think!" One little man and a tiny iron jack, and the enormous inert mass of the tree—tons and tons it must be. One little man against the huge inertias of nature! That was not how John expressed it; but that is what he managed to convey to Sally at last, so that to a certain extent she was able to see dirty old Mike with his battered face through John's eyes.

"Shucks!" Len was scornful. "Nobody but a Canuck would be damn fool to kill himself working that hard for what he gits."

"Don't fool yourself," said John. "I was talking to him. He makes good money. When prices are right, he says, he gets fifteen hundred or two thousand for a season sometimes. And he's got no expenses, much."

"Mebbe—mebbe." Len shrugged this aside. "If a man wants to

make money that way." His air implied that that sort of money must be tainted. "Hope you're satisfied."

"I'm going to try one myself tomorrow," said John.

"Oh, for God's sake!" cried Len.

"Why are you so scornful of Canadians?" Sally asked Len curiously.

Len had no use for them. He could give no reasons. Just didn't like them.

"Like one good dog bristling at another good dog just because he's a stranger," laughed Sally to John later when they were alone.

They pulled out only after two days. Len's good nature gradually returned; but he seemed to retain some sort of underlying resentment that puzzled Sally. It was not, she soon realized, in the smallest degree against themselves.

They sailed north, and deeper and deeper into the curious enchantment of space and time, with only the little harbors and occasional single adventures to break it. Then they bobbed up to the surface, so to speak. Sometimes, when Sally was alone at the tiller, there came to her a strange detachment, so that all the world simplified to a single quality of bigness that enveloped and permeated her as water a fish or atmosphere a breathing creature. Sometimes she expanded to it in a joyous lift of the spirit. At other times the dark mountains and the gloomy channels and the leaden skies swelled into a menace that almost terrified her. These things she could not control. They were like cloud shadows moving across the world.

But always the blessed harbors at end of day, sanctuaries of the familiar. There, at last, the spirit laid aside its arms.

Sally would have said, before starting out, that she would have been eager to go ashore when the chance offered. As a matter of fact, the shore did not tempt her in the least. After the vicissitudes of the day she found it much more pleasant to rest on deck, enjoying the harbor peace and its familiar inhabitants of birds and seals and accompanying in spirit the creeping incidence of evening. This hour or two of refreshment was too precious to be wasted on activities of any kind.

Sally and Len got their renewal from the little harbors by just plain loafing; but John discovered hand-lining overside. He had caught trout aplenty in running water, but this grab-bag business off the front porch, so to speak, tickled him immensely. In a trout stream, reflected John, as he tested for bottom with the heavy sinker, you know exactly what you are going to get—and that is trout. But here nobody can ever tell what he's going to get. Might be a rock cod or a ling or a stray red snapper, if the water was deep enough, or a skate or some other kind of flat fish, like a sole or flounder, or a dogfish; and then the other two woke up and barked at him in derision. But John's catch was a welcome addition to the commissary, at that.

This matter of food was one that required attention on so long a voyage. Once the men took the rifle and went ashore. They returned with venison, already skinned and butchered. Len was a little uneasy until the meat was safely hung in the coolness of the cargo hold.

"The old girl wouldn't like this!" he said. By "the old girl" he meant Queen Victoria. He seemed to consider this attitude on the part of Her Majesty as of a piece with the unwarranted unreasonableness of British Columbia—"grudgin' a man his meat!"

The weather continued favorable, on the whole. And Sally, noticing Len's reactions to its changes and adding in his remarks on the deer question, had an illumination. So pleased was she that she could hardly wait to get John by himself.

"I've found out what ails Len!" she cried when they were alone.

"I'd admire to know!" said John fervently. "I don't know what we've done. Time's come he's as grouchy as a bear with a sore ear."

"It isn't us. It's the way things are going. He doesn't like it because things are going so well. We're having too good luck."

John looked justifiably bewildered at this. Sally chuckled.

"Don't you see? He resents that because it's British Columbia, and it has no business to behave so nicely. Just stop and think. First there was Johnstone Straits, and that *did* hold us up a few days; but when it did clear up it was lovely and not rough at all. And then there was going to be Queen Charlotte Sound. Remember what he told us about Queen Charlotte Sound?" She held up a hand and ticked the items off on her fingers. "'Shoal water. Open to the sea—really a part of the ocean. Enormous seas made by the deep-sea rollers lifting into shallow water.' That was very interesting," she interposed a parenthesis, "the way he explained how that worked. 'Tides pouring out from the big inlets and jumbling up the winds and ground swells.'"

"'Bob and slat around like a cork,'" John took up the quotation with relish. "'Take all day and all night to get across, and no place to stop. It's always thick and gloomy, and you can't see nothin' until you are right on top of it.'"

"'Why, sometimes even the big ships turn tail and run back to Mamma,'" Sally took up the litany.

"Well," confessed John, "he did have me a little mite uneasy, I admit."

They dissolved into laughter together.

"Poor Len! He was actually glum!" Sally wiped her eyes.

They had rounded Scarlet Point Light, their hearts in their mouths, prepared for the worst. They met only a broad ground swell that lifted them high, high, higher, and set them gently down again. The atmosphere was clear. Once free of Storm Island and the Deserters, visibility was limited only by the curve of the earth. It was unnecessary to set a compass course. Cape Caution, on the mainland, and Egg Island were both in sight at the same time. The Sea Otter reefs were breaking seaward and were marked for them in white. They could even make out, dim and low, the headland of Cape Calvert, all the way across, and could steer for it direct. The crossing took only ten hours; and they were in Safety Cove under twelve! As a reliable character in a horror drama Queen Charlotte was a decided flop.

Len was disconcerted. But his pessimism was only transferred. They were back in comparatively sheltered waters—for a while. They had to come out in the open again at Millbank Sound. That was another place where sometimes the big ships turned around and scuttled back home to Mamma. Len managed to impress them with Millbank Sound. Beneath their pretense both Sally and John

realized that Len had not really been bluffing. They had had the
luck of the devil. Len was right: they wouldn't strike another day
like that one in a hundred. The thing that made Millbank terrific
was the course that must be steered. That, Len explained, brought
the seas abaft the beam. The implication was not clear to Sally, but
the words had a sinister sound. When she asked Len, he merely
muttered darkly something about landlubbers.

"Remember Millbank?" Sally reminded John. "And how we
laughed?"

They had to laugh again at the recollection. They had set sail from
a charming little harbor behind two islands early of a misty pearl-
gray day. It was not really foggy: they could see well enough for a
mile or two, but there was no horizon, and Len brought up the compass and set it in its chocks. After a time a dark blob of land
defined itself on the starboard side.

"Ivory Island," Len grudgingly answered their question.

It was a nice name, but it meant nothing to them. They passed,
and the island's solidity gradually refined in substance until it
matched the pearl gray and was gone. For a long time they continued. The breeze was light and steady. The seas were broad and
low and slumbrous; of what Sally called the upsy-daisy variety.
Nothing at all was to be seen. Sense of progress faded, as had Ivory
Island, into the luminous mist. A sense of detachment replaced it.
After a little, time itself dissolved away. They might have been out
an hour or ten; it did not matter. There they were! John and Sally sat
dreaming side by side. Len humped over the tiller, staring at the
compass card.

Then unexpectedly something appeared to be forming in the
nothingness ahead. At first it seemed merely a thickening in tone
that slowly condensed into a flat gray silhouette. The silhouette, still
flat, changed to slate. Abruptly it took on another dimension. There
were outlines of trees, and below them a rim of rocks bared by storms
and whitened by a line of surf, which now they could hear. A moment
ago they had heard nothing. On one of the rocks against the shore
stood the shaft of a small lighthouse.

"What's that?" asked John.

For a moment Len did not reply.

"Jergen's Point," he finally acknowledged.

Recollection of the name came to John.

"Then we must be across Millbank!" he cried, but incredulously.

That was when they had laughed. Len looked at them sourly.

"You darn kids make me sick!" he muttered bitterly. "We're just shot with luck. I don't like it. It's dang bad luck to have it so good *all* the way." They continued to laugh at this; and Len had to grin, though a little wryly, over his paradox.

"But I still don't see why he's so grouchy about it," said John.

"That's the point," said Sally. "He wouldn't know it, but it's jealousy."

"Jealousy!"

"Of Canada, of British Columbia. It's behaving too well, showing off. Len's all for Alaska. And acting this way it's sort of proving him a liar, in a way of speaking. See what I mean?"

John chuckled. "I see. That's funny. Things go all wrong whenever they go right. Even the rainy belt."

Sally looked inquiry.

"Weren't you there when he talked rainy belt? Three hundred miles wide. Rains practically all the time. See nothing until you get through on the other side of it." John looked up at the cloudless sky and cocked one eyebrow up at Sally. She laughed amusedly.

"Poor Len!" said she. "No, he didn't mention that one to me."

"Reckon he's give up," said John.

But when each morning the Tillicum spread her wings and half sailed, half drifted, from the protection of the night's home into the open and squared away on her course, then the enchantment enfolded her, as though it had been waiting outside for them. The shores of the harbor and its low surrounding forested hills and the higher mountains, sometimes to be seen at a distance, were all solid and permanent. They formed a definite place. But once outside, the whole world changed for Sally. It was a world suitably furnished out with topography that changed. But change was unimportant; the stage-set at the moment did not matter. There was plenty of variety. Sometimes high mountains overhung, and the channel ahead seemed closed. Again the waters opened spaciously, as though they had swept the mountains back to give room for their islands. And then came wide-flung stretches of open sea. The mountains were austere and rugged with splintered granite and snow; and, again, they were lower and rounded and furred with forests like gentle beasts. The islands were of all sizes and shapes. Some were no bigger than the Tillicum herself and looked like milliners' hats with their tufts of vegetation atop. Others might have been mainland, and days passed before the little ship rounded the heads of them into new channels. Sally, who had the pictorial imagination, fell into the strange fancy at times that they were fixed in space, and that around them the scenery was shifted in a slow, mighty and continuous illusion of change. The solid realities were drawn in, focused in the tiny compass of themselves.

At the time of her great discovery about Len they were sailing— had been sailing for some days—in narrow channels, like rivers, between steep wooded mountains, like walls of almost unbroken green, rising perpendicular from the water's edge. A mere strip of sky showed overhead. Occasional white waterfalls and cascades thundered down straight into the sea. At still rarer intervals the walls parted grudgingly, so that, as the Tillicum sailed by, its crew could see, as through a gateway, up short canyons into huge granite cirques and bare gray granite mountains with snow. The day's journeys in this place were unpredictable. The tides ran strongly, like currents; and the wind sucked as strongly up or down the channel. Our voyagers must have one or the other in their favor to get on at all. Preferably both. Coves and shelters were far apart. Sometimes shift of wind and tide caught them short of any place they could hang on. Then there was nothing for it but to turn tail and run back. The youngsters did not mind, but Len grumbled. His attitude was aggrieved; and, though he did not say so, his implication was plain that this could not happen anywhere but in Canada.

But at last the country opened out again. The channel widened to

accommodate islands once more and then expanded and spread until
the whole balance was reversed. The predominance was no longer
land, but sea, with only enough land for seemly furnishment. And as
the day wore on, the mainland fell farther and farther away to the
starboard, until it lay low as distant blue ranges, and the fringe of
islands withdrew farther and farther to port until they looked like
little ships on the horizon, and the Tillicum shook her spray about
her and rose delightedly to the ground swell of open water again.

They made wonderful footing that day. Islands, more nearly on
their course, grew one after the other out of the distance and came
alongside and passed astern. Rapidly they drew nearer the shores of
one so large they could not make out the end of it. It slanted out to
meet them, and they cruised along it for some distance and raised a
little one, like a satellite, bare and round off the coast. Len pointed
the bowsprit for the gap between the two.

Len had changed.

They looked at him curiously. His grumpy lethargy had given way
to something like suppressed eagerness. His attitude suggested impatience.

"Looks like a small boy going to the circus," whispered John to
Sally.

They questioned him and got monosyllabic replies. The big one?
Dundas Island. The little one? Green Island. Yes, that was a lighthouse. They wanted to see the chart. Len yielded it as though he
grudged doing so. They looked at him surprised, but he would not
meet their eyes. The head of Dundas Island just touched the top of
the chart. John went below and rummaged in the chart locker for
the next chart north. It was not there. He returned on deck and told
Len. Len grunted.

"Must be there," he growled. He appeared to dismiss the matter
from his mind.

"He's sitting on it," whispered Sally. "Why do you suppose he
doesn't want us to see it?"

John shook his head.

"Prickly as a porcupine. I wouldn't ask!"

Sally was examining Len speculatively.

"Let him alone," she advised.

They drew up on Green Island and passed it and came to the head of the big island. Before them stretched wide tumbling waters, an open sea, whose horizon was broken only by what appeared to be a sparse scattering of small islets over the rim of the world.

Len rose to his feet, steadying the tiller with his knee.

"Thar she lies, folks!" said he. "Thar's Alaska!"

For some moments he stared to the north, then sat down again. Suddenly he was all animation, as voluble now as he had been silent. He radiated. They had never seen Len like this, had not known that Len could *be* like this!

"Ain't that *great!*" cried Len. "Now we got room enough to take exercise!"

They looked across the sea and tried to be impressed. This was a trifle difficult: the stage-set was meager. There certainly was plenty of room. Indeed there was little else. But most of the space seemed to have mounted into the sky, which soared into unguessed eternities. Even the sea had been reduced to a narrow band at its skirts, ornamented with the tiny spots of isles, a fringe of clouds and here and there certain ghost-white flecks of radiance which might well have been imagination.

But Len needed nothing more.

"Islands?" he repeated scornfully. "Islands nothing! Them are the top peaks of mountains, so far off they don't show, and headlands of the big capes. All p'inting down this way. That there one, way out, that's Muzon. There ain't once in a dozen times you can see old Muzon. She's a hell of a ways out. The next one's Chacon. And then Duke Island. When we get closer you'll see; they're all connected up."

Len had a lot more names, each of which helped their imaginations to body forth the invisible land: capes and points and islands waiting below the horizon like actors in the wings—Annette Island, Mary Island, Dall Head, Bold Point. But the flame to their imaginations was Len's reply to Sally's question as to the flecks of radiance she fancied she was seeing just above the rim of the sea.

"No," Len assured her, "you ain't imagining it. It's real. It's reflection from the ice in the glaciers."

Sally clasped John's hand ecstatically. He squeezed it in an answering thrill of understanding. So, from the time of Moses and before, have lifted the hearts of adventurers at first sight of their promised land.

Len was trimming the sheets. Unnoticing, they had rounded the head of Dundas.

"We'll lie the night under the Gnarled Islands yonder," said Len. "Have to turn out early tomorrow. Two o'clock. That's Dixon's Entrance. We got a long beat and a tough one. Hope to God this weather holds." He spoke soberly and did not elaborate, as he had done on the terrors of Queen Charlotte and Millbank, but Sally and John were both much more impressed. So much so that they asked questions. He answered without histrionics.

Dixon's Entrance was a bad stretch for small boats. Its width made it really a part of the open sea, at a latitude where the open sea is notoriously turbulent. But here the conditions were further complicated by the confluence of three mighty tidal bodies whose ebb swept from Chatham Sound on the southeast, from the gash of the Portland Canal, that penetrated the mountains a matter of nearly a hundred miles to the east and drained all that part of Alaska from the north.

"That's an awful amount of water moves in and out two times a day," said Len. "Figger it for yourself. Up in this part of the country the average tide is twelve or fifteen feet, and the big ones more 'n twenty. Straight up and down. Got to move a lot of water to take care of that much difference; and you got to move it mighty fast to get it done in six hours!"

The rushing together of these three streams made trouble, always, without the further complication of the incoming swells and whatever the wind might be doing. The division of them on the flooding tide made trouble, too, added Len, though that was not quite so bad.

"That's why I want to get out early," he explained, "to catch the flood when we pass Cape Fox. And to get pretty well along before the wind stiffens. She generally takes a good holt middle of the morning. Trouble is, there's no shelter. Once we start we got to keep going."

He stood up in the cockpit and shaded his eyes.

"You can just make her out, if you look close. Down low and dim, there to the right. That's Cape Fox. Once you round her it smooths out some."

That evening at anchor he went over the Tillicum from stem to stern, inside and out, stowing and lashing everything movable.

They were off the following morning by starlight, before three o'clock. A breeze was blowing from the direction of the mainland. It was stronger than the usual night wind and bitterly cold. That, Len told them, was because of the Portland Canal. Through unguessed miles away across open water the draft from its snows and glaciers held its nozzle-like integrity, even so far out to sea. This and the strong ebb tide appreciably flattened the usually heavy ocean roll, but even at that a considerable and confused chop was running. The Tillicum rode well, but with a curious feeling of unstable giddiness beneath them that the pressure of the sails could not steady.

It was very dark and very cold and very lonely out there, surrounded by strange menacing forces which they could not see. Both John and Len wanted Sally to go below. But that was impossible. She must stay on deck, even though she could do nothing, and it was most uncomfortable, and there was nothing to see.

The confusion increased, and the giddiness. There was no reason or order to the waves. They came from all directions, it seemed, rushing together, rising straight up in sharp peaks and dropping straight down again, swirling ahead at enormous speed, stopping suddenly, to break with a roar and a cascade of white. In the darkness they looked gigantic. The Tillicum did not know what to do. It was impossible to ride them. She slapped and slatted and reeled and plunged drunkenly, and water came aboard apparently from every direction at once. John and Sally hung on desperately. Len clung to the tiller, tense and concentrated. From time to time he flung them a terse sentence.

"Rip tide," he grunted; and as the Tillicum jerked upright when the wind lulled momentarily: "Watch that boom!"

But he was calm and cool enough, and the feel of him was competent, like a boxer attending his adversary. He knew what he was about. They watched Len, taking heart from his confidence, for without him, frankly, they would not have known what to do.

"There's the light," muttered Len after a while.

They turned their eyes and perceived it just off the starboard bow, low on the rim of blackness, like a star touching the horizon.

"Cape Fox,"* added Len. "Once we round that——"

He did not finish the sentence, but from that moment Sally and John could not take their eyes off the tiny spark. Once around Cape Fox . . . They stared and stared at it, as though the very strength of their desire could draw it nearer. But it did not change. There it flickered, distant and low, and long hours passed, and the ship plunged and rose dizzily up and down, apparently in one place, without further progress. Indeed for a short period they had the illusion that the light was actually receding. It seemed dimmer and farther away. And then, all at once, they realized that this was because the day had been stealing on them unawares. The sky, too, was paling. They began to make out the coast. Soon they could see it clearly, low and wooded, and a great surf hurtling against rocks and reefs and boulders and breaking and spouting high and cascading back. It was fully two miles away, but the sight of it was shuddery even at that safe distance. And there was the lighthouse itself, miraculously drawn near.

They looked back. Dundas Island was fallen low and blue in distance. They *had* been going ahead! They had *not* been held fast in dark and turbulent enchantment! They imagined that the very wildness of the sea was falling under the sanity of the blessed daylight.

But no, Len assured them, this was not imagination.

"Gittin' toward the slack of the tide," he explained. "Pretty soon we'll catch the flood. Then we're on our way."

---

*Cape Fox is actually a little south, on the chart, but all Alaskans thus designate Tree Point.

The lighthouse was now square abeam, was discernibly falling astern.

"We're past." Len drew a deep breath and stretched his arms and legs. Tension lifted.

"Good-by, old socks!" cried John, waving his hand.

Sally uttered a shaky little laugh.

"Reckon there's many a man felt the same way," said Len.

To their surprise they learned that Len thought they had had a pretty easy time of it. "Just add on a good gale of wind," said he darkly, "or even a stiff breeze, like you'd expect." Ordinarily the night wind out of the canal dropped flat about dawn.

"Then's when you hop about with nothin' to steady you!" said Len. After which it turned westerly, right off the open. This morning it had swung, without falling, around to the southeast, which, Len pointed out, was a fair wind and had boosted them along.

"Best crossing I ever seen!" said Len with pride. For some obscure reason he seemed to put this down to Alaska's credit.

The sun came up. They ran with started sheets over a broad, low following sea that diminished with every mile. The landmark mountain tops of the day before had reared higher into the sky and had thrown across to one another connecting links of smaller ranges, except straight ahead. There the water horizon still held nearly unbroken. But, Len assured them, this was an illusion.

"We'll be raising Mary Island shortly," said he.

They loafed in the warming sunshine. It was a fine day. Len expanded. He pointed out landmarks with a modest air of proprietorship, taking satisfaction that Alaska was at least doing herself as proud as British Columbia.

They raised Mary Island, a flat low strip of blue that completed the landfall ahead.

"Pretty soon we'll be seeing the light," began Len and stopped with an exclamation of disgust. "Aw, hell!" cried Len fervently.

They looked up in surprised inquiry.

"Just look at that!" Len waved a hand toward the prospect ahead. "I might have knowed, with the wind southeast!"

They followed his gesture, but could see nothing, except that the clarity had a little dimmed as though by an invisible mist at the horizon. But as they watched, fairly between the ticks of the clock, the mist thickened and darkened until it had blotted out completely everything but the surface of the water. Then the sky turned black. The blackness spread toward the zenith, worked toward them against the wind.

"Here," said Len, "take her a minute while I get the compass and the slickers. *Hell!*" he repeated.

By the time he was back the first drops were already falling. He resumed the tiller over John's protest, mumbling something about keeping track of where he was. It began to rain in earnest.

"Better go below," grumbled Len. "No sense gittin' wet."

Sally nudged John vigorously.

"Well—if you need me . . ." said John.

"I'll call ye," Len growled.

They went below.

"He's been at that tiller since three o'clock," protested John. "I could just as well——"

"Leave him alone," said Sally. "Poor Len!" she added, half amusedly, half tenderly.

John caught the point. They chuckled together like children.

"Rainy belt sort of slipped on him!" said John.

Sally made some coffee and took it, with food, to Len on deck, but immediately returned. Then she and John ate and, as there was nothing else to do, lay down on their bunks. Shortly the early rising and the emotional strain overcame them. They slept. They were very tired and might have continued on indefinitely, but Len's hail aroused them. They returned to the deck. The wind had dropped to a whisper, and it was still raining. Through its veil they saw land close aboard. The Tillicum was rounding a point to enter a narrow bay penetrating, in two fingers, deep through the forest.

"Head of Mary Island," scowled Len. "We'll stop here."

They found bottom and dropped the hook and took in the sails. Len moved without snap or spirit and without a word said. When all was snug he went forward to his own quarters. John stood for a moment looking about him before himself going below.

But here was Sally in her short slicker and rubber boots. John looked at her distrustfully.

"What you think you're going to do?" he wanted to know.

"I'm going ashore," replied Sally.

"Ashore! For God's sake, what for? It's raining, and everything's as wet as sops!"

"A little rain won't hurt." Sally was firm. "And you needn't bother yourself. You're not going. I'm going with Len."

"But, Sally!" John was aroused. "You're crazy! The man's tired out! He needs a sleep!"

"He needs something besides sleep," said Sally. She went forward determinedly and rapped on the hatch. "Come on, Len, let's go ashore!" she called. "I've waited a long time to touch Alaska with my own two feet. Get on your boots and slicker and come on!"

After a few moments Len reappeared, rather uncertainly, as though just awakened. Sally was sitting in the Foundling alongside, holding on by the rail.

"Where's John?" he asked. "Ain't he going?"

"No, just you and me." Sally did not explain further.

Len squinted sleepily at the shore, but less to see than in effort to recall.

"There's a beach around the point. We might get us some clams," he ventured, though doubtfully. "But I dunno. The tide ain't much ebbed yet."

"Let's try," urged Sally. "It'll be fun anyway."

"I'll fetch the clam gun," said Len. He slipped down through the cabin and galley and into the cargo hatch, to return with an implement that elsewhere would be called a potato fork. This he deposited carefully in the dinghy. "John's asleep," he explained his caution. He stepped aboard and took up the oars. John, who had not been asleep at all, watched through a porthole until they had disappeared around the westernmost point of the little bay. Then he arose, put on his slicker and went on deck to drop the hand line overside. He was glad he did not have to go ashore. He could pump up no enthusiasm about setting foot on Alaskan soil. Looked like any other beach, what you could see of it through the rain. Much more fun here, wondering lazily what you might hook onto. But it was not the expectation of fish that kept him out in the wet. John could not seem to care much whether he hooked onto anything or not. The cabin would have been more comfortable physically, but here somehow was more comfortable spiritually. He liked sitting there, humped over sociably with himself. He got something out of it that was soothing and grateful to him—feeling that there was nobody around. They'd all been cooped up together a long time.

The shore party was gone more than an hour, nevertheless, John was surprised by the sound of the oars. He had to shake himself and bring himself back. He discovered that he was glad to see them, as though they—or he—had been gone a long time. Sally's cheeks glowed. She hailed joyously. Len said nothing, but he exuded satisfaction. Obviously everybody felt better.

"See what we've got!" cried Sally.

John looked down into the bottom of the dinghy.

"What kind of junk do you call that?" said he scornfully.

"Junk nothing!" Sally was indignant. "Bring a sail cover or something."

Len held the Foundling close alongside while Sally passed up treasure to the canvas John laid on the deck. John was derisive. "When we get to Klakan, I'll buy you kids some marbles to play with," said he.

"Goose tang," enumerated Sally, depositing aboard a double handful of green, "the stuff Len told us about, lily-bulb rice, wild celery, Hudson Bay tea. Len says we could have got wild rhubarb and wild potatoes if we'd looked long enough. The new ferns aren't up yet. We've been all over the woods. We saw some deer," she added.

"Well, I see you got some clams, anyway." John accented the last word.

Sally's eyes flashed at the implication, but she made no retort. She picked up a short stick lying in the bottom of the boat and stooped over to poke about beneath the stern thwart. After a moment she succeeded in urging forth an enormous crab that at once began to rattle about and to threaten in all directions with claws formidable as steel traps. Sally squealed and squirmed up on the seat. Len, with a grin, reached forward to seize the creature firmly from behind and deposited it with one swift motion at John's feet. They both laughed as John jumped.

"Did you ever see such a monster? We've got two more!"

Sally chattered on excitedly. Their capture had been a real triumph.

"We saw them when we were going in," said she, "lying on the bottom in shallow water, and Len was saying that if we only had a dip net or a spear or something we could get some, and we drifted around and watched them for a while, and all of a sudden we got a bright idea."

"It was Sally's idea," corrected Len.

"Well, anyway, we went ashore and I took all the ribbons out of my underclothes, and we tied them together, and we tied a stone on the end; and we went back, and we let the stone down very carefully, right in front of the crab, and when he grabbed at it we slacked out on the ribbon very fast and wound it around and around and then pulled him up quickly while he was all tangled up in it. It was so *exciting*. Of course we missed a lot—but we got three!"

"I never see crabs caught *that* way before!" said Len admiringly. "I bet nobody but Sally would have thought of it."

"I just thought what I would do if I was a crab and somebody dropped a rock on me," Sally disclaimed credit. "I do wish you'd gone along," she lamented, superbly disregarding the fact that she herself had ordered John to stay aboard. "You missed it."

"Oh, I don't know," said John coolly. He made a long arm to hook a finger through the gills of a fish, which he held up for inspection. "How do you like that?"

"What is it?" asked Sally.

Len was aroused.

"By gum!" he cried, "a chicken halibut! Thar's *eatin'!*"

"Well," said John loftily, "if you're through sitting in that wet boat and will come aboard and clean up your mess, we'll eat him."

Sally scrambled over the rail.

"We'll have an Alaska supper!" she cried, "nothing but Alaska. Not a thing else. We've got every last thing we need. Come on. Everybody get busy."

"I'll make some sour-dough hot cakes," offered Len. "They're Alaska, too."

He followed Sally aboard and made fast the dinghy's painter. Sally gestured to John, with her eyes, toward Len. Len's manner was cocky, informed, with a large air of satisfied proprietorship.

"He was *so* disappointed, poor dear!" said Sally to John in an undertone.

CHAPTER XI

KLAKAN

THE END OF THE VOYAGE found Sally very tired. She could see no sense to this. The last day's sail had been both short and easy, and the Tillicum had slid into a vacant float not long after noon. However, there it was. Indeed so weary did she unexpectedly find herself, both in body and spirit, that she let the men go without her for the first look-see. The decision bothered John, for it did not square with Sally's usual eagerness. But her recollection of how she had felt that first depressing day out of Seattle enabled her to reassure him—and herself.

"It's just reaction—letdown. Because we've got here; and, until an hour ago, it seemed we'd never get here. It's nothing. I've got to catch my breath."

"I should think you'd be curious——" began John doubtfully, and then remembered his own hour or two of solitude the other afternoon when Len and Sally had gone ashore at Mary Island. "Sure!" he amended, "I know how you feel. Len and I'll just take a little look around."

They put on their heavy Mackinaws and clambered up the steep cleated ramp to the street level. Thence they waved at Sally and disappeared. All she could see from here was piles and the undersides of things. South the view was cut off by a flat-faced wharf plastered against the shore. Evidently the water was deep close in. What might be atop the wharf she could only guess. The angle of her vision was too near vertical. Indeed, of most things she had, from here, a worm's-eye view. A sea worm, she added with a flicker of humor. This was undoubtedly because the tide was low. Sally could hardly credit that it could ever come in to lift her to a level so far above. But the float's tall frame piles showed barnacles much higher than the top of the Tillicum's mainmast; and the deep marks scored in the float's planking indicated that the butt of the ramp, at high tide, slid right out to the very end. Then it would probably be almost flat. Right now it was as vertical as a ladder. There were several other floats to the north, so that, in that direction, their clustering frame piles looked like a stark and denuded forest. Here and there a boat was moored; but nobody seemed to be aboard any of them. Otherwise the prospect was blued by a fine mist that was not quite a rain.

Sally went below and lay down, hoping for sleep. She had the good sense to realize that this hopeless feeling of weariness was, as she had told John, nothing but natural reaction. Nevertheless it was real, and there was no use trying to argue with herself.

The men gained the street level only after somewhat of a crab scramble, sidewise, to keep footing on the narrow cleats.

"Some tides!" said John, when finally they both had made it. "Glad Sally decided to wait."

He looked about him with curiosity.

"By golly!" he cried, and laughed. "Why didn't they pick it straight up and down?"

Apparently the steep slope of the mountain rose directly from the water. At its lower edge they had tried to glue a town. If any level ground existed at all, it was too narrow to accommodate even the single street that meandered along the front. A good half or three quarters of the roadway was supported on piles and planked, so that the thoroughfare resembled a long, narrow, winding dock. This impression was underscored by the fact that most of the buildings were lined up in a row on the land side, huddled back as far as they could go against the mountain, like a crowd at a fire. Some of the more timid had even burrowed holes for their tails.

"Well, I've seen some fool town sites in my time," said John, "but this takes the cake! Ain't there any level land in Alaska?"

He continued to stand stock still, trying to take it all in. The buildings were unpainted, but well built and very new. They touched elbows. A wooden awning, stoutly supported, ran unbroken along the whole front, and under its shelter people were moving.

"For the love of Pete!" John was still amazed. He had cast his eyes upward. Against the side of the mountain, almost overhead, extended a spider web of piling in support of a second platform, paralleling that on which they stood. It was obviously still in construction, for it ended abruptly in a pile driver overhanging space. When finally John comprehended that this platform was another street, he began again to laugh.

"I've heard of chucking a man into the middle of the next block," said he, "but a man could actually do it here!"

He sobered as the magnitude of the whole fantastic undertaking caught at the practical part of his mind.

"Jeez, what a piece of construction!" he marveled. For some moments he was lost in appraisal of the enterprise in terms of men and materials. "Where in hell do they get their piling and lumber?" he asked Len.

Len did not know. He'd never been here before, except just when the steamer stopped on his way down. Must be a mill somewhere. Or maybe they shipped it in on schooners or barges—from British Columbia, maybe.

"We'll have to see about that," said John. He was interested in this.

"Come on," said Len. "Let's see what they *have* got."

He started to move away. But John was still held in his amazement at the fantastic irrationality, as it seemed to him.

"What *for?*" he insisted. "What do all these folks *do?* What's the idea, anyway?"

Len shook his head. "Don't ask me why anybody does anything.

All I know is that Nelson Cole had him his cannery here—but there's lots of other places where there's canneries," added Len.

They crossed the plank street and walked along under the shelter of the wooden awnings. Most of the buildings in this part were either stores or offices of some kind, though occasionally an obvious but incongruous dwelling house had thrust itself in. There were no display fronts to the stores. One had to peer through the rather dingy panes of ordinary windows or through the open door, to know what kind of a store or office it was. Len and John sauntered slowly along, looking in.

The sidewalks were almost deserted of people. Indeed, except for a half-dozen stolid Indians squatted against the walls, only two white men returned their greetings, with an unmistakably Scandinavian accent.

"Wrong time of day," surmised Len. "Everybody at work."

They continued to saunter. Both men were experienced in the matter of new towns. They catalogued to each other what they saw and commented on its significance.

"Must be minin' around here," observed Len. "Here's an assay office."

"Or hopes of it," amended John. "I've seen a heap of that stuff. We might ask the fellow."

But the door was locked. The next double window held them longer. Through it they could just make out a dark interior crammed with an astounding jumble of all sorts of things. It might have been a peculiarly disorderly general store, except that a lot of the stuff was without doubt secondhand, and the stock seemed to lack certain things—such as foodstuffs—that one would expect.

"Pawn shop?" queried John after a while.

"Fur trader," said Len. "Take a sniff. He ain't sent out his fur yet for this year."

John would have liked to talk with the fur trader, but this place, too, was locked.

"Well, I see one I'll bet is open," said John. "How about a drink?"

The saloon was indeed open, but that was about all. That is to say, it was empty except for a man behind the bar who was sitting on a high stool, his elbows propped, reading a newspaper. When he saw John and Len in the doorway he slipped off the stool, deftly substituted a towel for the newspaper and began to revolve it on the surface of the bar. John looked about with interest, for by his experience he had learned that its saloon was the best indication of a new town's expectations. The higher the latter, the more startlingly flamboyant the former. But there was nothing spectacular here.

The bartender was a burly individual, in conventional shirt sleeves and apron, with bald head, florid round face and a long black mustache. Apparently this casual custom failed to excite him. He did not look up.

"What'll it be, gents?" he rumbled mechanically. He smothered a yawn.

"Well, for God's sake!" exclaimed Len. "What the hell are you doing down here?"

The burly man came alive. His head jerked up. He stared at Len incredulously.

"Len Saunders," he cried, "by all that's holy! Why, you damned old double-crossin', two-timin', leather-bellied son of a bitch! I ain't seen you since they propped up the North Pole!"

He stretched across the bar to seize Len's hand and pumped it up and down. He patted Len's shoulder with the other hand, and Len patted back, and they looked into each other's eyes delightedly and exchanged appalling epithets.

"This here's my pardner, John Murdock," said Len, recollecting himself after a while. "Meet a real old-timer, John. This old outlaw calls himself Mush Mahoney for some reason or other."

"Pleased to meet you," said Mush, extending a hand.

Mahoney reached far down under the bar to produce what was evidently a special bottle, enveloped three glasses in a capacious paw, moved with astonishing lightness, for one so bulky, around the end of the bar, rattled the bottle and glasses on one of the three round tables, shut and locked the curtained doors.

"Set down! Set down!" he urged. "Well, for God's sake! I thought they must have killed you off long ago! What's the matter with these fellows!"

John slid into his chair and took his drink. For some time he was content to sit in the side lines. They had forgotten all about him, absorbed in rapid exchange of their news.

"How come you quit Treadwell?" inquired Len presently. "Did they get onto you and run you out?"

"Well, I tell you. This looked pretty good down here."

"You was doin' pretty good there. Or wasn't you?"

"I was doin' all right," admitted Mush, "but there was gettin' to be too much competition."

"Probably got 'em a town marshal!" jeered Len.

Mush accorded this a fleeting grin.

"They're developin' a good mine there, all right. And I kept an interest. But the place to make your real money is where things is new."

"I don't see no tables," said Len, glancing around.

"Next door." Mush jerked his head toward closed double doors in the wall. "Always believed in separatin' your tables and your bar. Less trouble. Come around after supper. I'll show you. This is dead time now."

"What you got?"

"Oh, chuck-a-luck. Faro. Craps. Couple of roulette."

"How many gamblers you got?"

"Five—and three lookouts and a couple of barkeeps."

"Well, that looks prosperous," admitted Len. "Anybody I know?"

"Same old Treadwell crew."

"I'll have to come around and say hullo."

"So do. I'll tell you who's here. Annabelle."

"No!" Len slapped his leg. "That old bitch?" But he said the words with tolerant affection.

"Have another," said Mahoncy, pouring.

"Thanks. Don't mind. Well, you sure got me winging!" He looked bout the crude room. "Sure don't look it—after your Treadwell utfit!"

"Oh," said Mush, "don't need to look much as long as you're the whole works. That's why I come here. Bimeby mebbe I'll have to spruce up a little. Just now I'm gittin' on. Why"—Mush leaned forward impressively—"already my turnover's near twice what it was at the Treadwell. You'd be surprised."

"I am surprised," said Len. "Say," he turned to John, "here's the feller who can tell us! You can tell us," he returned to Mahoney, "what's this all about? This ain't just a cannery proposition. They's lots other canneries. Where's all the money comin' from? And why in hell do they think they got to have a town right here?"

"Have another." Mahoney reached for the bottle. "This is real stuff," he added.

"I seen where you got it from," said Len. He shoved forward his glass. John covered the top of his own. "Thanks. But leave me out." The others looked at him reproachfully.

"Real Canada liquor," urged Mahoney.

"Thanks," said John. "Why Canada?"

They stared at him.

"You wouldn't want to drink hoochnihoo!" said Len reproachfully.

"What's that? Moonshine?" asked John, struck by the quaint name.

Both Len and Mush Mahoney laughed.

"Corn liquor's all right, if it's made right," rumbled Mahoney, "but this stuff . . ." He half turned in his chair and scrutinized the shelves back of the bar. "I keep all kinds. Some is better 'n others. Various brands, just like real liquor, so you'll know what to call for. It's made out of molasses or beans or rice or flour or anything that 'll ferment. I call it squirrel whisky, because two drinks of it makes you want to climb a tree. I wouldn't touch a drop of it on a bet. But they get away with it, so I sell it." Mahoney spoke with contempt.

"If it's got more authority than moonshine, I'd sure like to see what it's like," suggested John. "I don't want a drink," he forestalled protest. "Just a taste."

Mahoney trundled to the bar, selected a bottle, brought it back. The bottle bore no label.

"That's Aurora Borealis," said he. "That's the best of it. I got, besides this, Nitric Acid and Chain Lightning and Snake Juice and Battle Ax."

"Wow!" John spat it out vigorously. "You mean to say anybody *drinks* that stuff?"

Len and the saloonkeeper were laughing at him. The latter did not seem in the least offended by the implied criticism of his wares.

"Man 'll drink anything, if he can't get anything else," said Mahoney placidly. "*I* can't get anything better, not at a price that 'll sell it."

"But there's nothing the matter with this," protested John, touching his glass.

"You bet there ain't," agreed Mush heartily.

John laughed, but a little in vexation.

"When you fellers get through kidding me, maybe you'll tell me the answer. What's the matter with Seattle, then? Plenty to be had there, cheap enough."

They eyed him curiously, decided he was in earnest.

"Didn't you know Alaska's prohibition?" asked Len presently. "You can't bring liquor in here, legal. It's agin the law."

"Everything you have is either smuggled or homemade," supplemented Mush.

"But—but you're running wide open; ain't it illegal to sell?"

"Oh, sure! You can't sell no liquor in Alaska. That's what the law says. But who's goin' to stop you? There's forty saloons running wide open in Juneau and Treadwell."

"We're mostly our own law yet, John." Len took pity on him. "They's one marshal—he at Sitka, Mush?"

"Wrangell," Mush corrected.

"That's right, Wrangell. I dunno how good he is in his home town, but he don't drag his wings anywheres that I've been. You been to Wrangell, Mush? They got any saloons there?"

"Sure," said Mush.

John laughed.

"Well, sounds like this is a good country. I never had enough law to get a taste for it."

They looked at him approvingly.

"You ain't give me an answer," Len reverted to his question. "How come anybody but a lunatic to start this town on a side hill? Ain't there no flats in this part of Alaska?"

"Why," said Mush, in answer to Len, "I reckon it's mostly Nels Cole. And he's got his cannery on the flat. You know Cole?" Len shook his head. "He owns the cannery."

"I know that. But how's it different from any other cannery?"

"It's owned by Nels Cole." Mush answered this with a chuckle. Someone rattled the door, trying to get in. "Go away!" roared Mush, "I'm busy! Well, Nels got the idea of halibut."

"You don't can halibut," objected Len.

"That's just it. There's millions of halibut out in the Gulf; banks that's never been fished. Reason is, it's too long a haul to market for fresh fish. So Nels gets the idee of buildin' a real old he-size icin' plant, big enough to furnish all the schooners ice, and then icin' down the fish again for the steamers when the fishermen bring 'em in and sendin' 'em south."

"Where's he get his ice?"

"That's it. He's got a little lake right in his back yard, four-five hundred feet up. He can cut the ice and slide it down chutes right into his icehouse. It's pretty slick. And man named Orford's got a little sawmill right next, so he gets his packing sawdust handy. It's pretty slick."

Len nodded. "That meant him a dock, and an all-year crew to git in the ice in winter and handle the icing in summer. I suppose Nels put up a company store?"

"Sure!" Mush shook with appreciative laughter. "And you bet you it's the only store!"

"Why?" asked John.

The eyes of both men swiveled in his direction.

"Why," said Len gently, as though explaining to a child, "because Nels had took up all the land and wouldn't sell to no one without he told him what he could do with it." He cocked an eye at his friend for corroboration.

"Yeah, I've seen that done," said John, "but he can't make that stick very long."

"Long enough," said Len carelessly. He returned to his friend. "Must be payin' good," said he. "I see he's puttin' in another street up the hill."

"Git 'em once started comin' and you're set. Trouble is to start 'em."

"What they got besides fish and ice?"

Mahoney laughed.

"Mining," said he.

"What mining?" Len was skeptical. "I never heard of no mine down here."

"Oh, they's a few little propositions on some of the other islands. But mostly it's what they're *goin'* to find. There's a lot come lookin', and they've all got to trade and have their fun. That's some money. And there's pulpboard—to make paper, you know. Why, what with woods crews and factory crews and handlin' crews, you have no idee what a pay roll it mounts up to! And for such a big show as that it pays better to use water power than steam; and that means more big crews for construction. And all them has to be housed and fed and have their fun."

"Paper mill located anywhere near the mines?" queried Len, poker faced.

"Right plumb squar' next door!" chuckled Mahoney. He held the bottle up to the light. "Better change your mind," he advised John.

"In other words," said John, nodding acceptance, "what it boils down to is Cole." Len looked at him with approval.

"Cannin' fish, icin' fish, keepin' store, sellin' building lots," he summarized.

"And the rest is moonshine? Bait?" asked John.

But the other two men would not go so far as this.

"You never can tell," said Mahoney. He took John more seriously now. "Nobody knows. I've seen aplenty of these things start. Some of them just fade out, and some of 'em keep on growing even when the bait gives out. But it's good pickin' while it lasts. That's why I'm here. That's why . . ." He waved his hand inclusively at the surroundings. "I got a real swell joint at Treadwell. Ask Len. There's something solid to bank on in a place like that. There's enough good proved ore blocked out there to last a hundred years. It's steady. But a place like this is where to clean up big and quick. And there's always a gamble she might make good. I'm a gambler. That's my business. Come back here in fifty years, and you may find a town, and you may find only salmonberries and bear. But you'd still find Treadwell; because she's got something proved and solid."*

"Well," said John, "that's all mighty interesting." He turned his empty glass in his fingers, reflecting on what he had heard. He remembered something. "You said something about a sawmill."

"Cole's?" surmised Len.

Mahoney chuckled. "Only bet he overlooked. Or mebbe he didn't. No, Orford owns it himself. Looks all right, but it'll only last as long as the town is building. There's no other market. Mebbe he figures to let Orford hold the bag."

"John, here, was a lumberman down where he come from," Len explained.

Mahoney turned square to examine John more attentively. John was surprised at the cold keenness of the scrutiny.

"Wouldn't have said so," said Mahoney.

"Keno!" John laughed. "I'm not really. Just worked at it since I got married—about a year ago."

"You been mostly where you had to take care of yourself better 'n that," said Mahoney. He did not pursue the subject further, for to have done so would have been frontier discourtesy; but John felt that he had been moved into an inner circle of esteem. The door was rattled again and again, with growing impatience. "All right! All right!" bellowed Mahoney. "Keep your shirts on!" He heaved out of his chair. "Reckon I'll have to open up. Some of the boys are comin' off shift. Set still."

*Klakan today is a thriving little city; Treadwell is a ghost town. In 1917 the mines sprung a leak, and it was found impossible to pump out the whole Pacific Ocean.

"We'll be going along," said John, also rising. "We got to look over the town." He took the bottle from the table and handed it to Mahoney. Len looked reproachful. "We'll be seeing you."

"Come in when we're really going," invited Mush. He hesitated, then added briefly, "Better not play the tables." John grinned at this. They continued their walk. More people were abroad. Except in occasional minor detail, they did not greatly differ from the men of any border town. For instance, John especially noticed their footgear. A great many wore high oiled moccasin shoe pacs instead of the caulk boots of the woods or the high heels of the horse country to which he had been accustomed. They all seemed to know Len. They threw him a greeting as they passed; heartily, as though they meant it.

"You seem pretty well acquainted," commented John at length. "Thought you said you'd never been here before."

"Me?" Len looked surprised. "Never saw 'em before in my life."

John gathered from Len that this cordiality to strangers was a characteristic of Alaskans. He thought it most pleasant. Where he had been raised strangers were treated only a trifle less warily than rattlesnakes. He was enjoying himself. Especially was he tickled, in secret, by the metamorphosis of Len. Slow-moving, kindly old sober-sides had become actually jaunty. Part of this was the drinks: he'd put away a good many more than had John. But it was more because he was back where he belonged and to hell with everybody! For the first time in their acquaintance the thought came to John that a man'd be foolish to pick on Len too far. "I'd hate to mix with that bird, if he once got waked up," thought John.

They came to a bigger painted building just at the end of the road, distinguished by four show windows across the whole front. As far as they had seen, these were the only show windows in town. Obviously the company store. They went in to look around.

It was an airy, clean, well-stocked store, with deep shelves around the sides behind counters and two long display tables occupying the space in the middle and a great variety of pails, pans and steel traps hung from the rafters. John saw rifles in racks, and revolvers and razors and knives in glass cases; canned goods, groceries, utensils; a small butcher shop; shelves of folded clothes; peajackets, Mackinaws and slickers on hangers; pasteboard boxes probably containing hats and boots and shoes; fishing tackle, both sporting and professional; barrels of various provisions; bolts of cloth and canvas; light and heavy hardware—about everything a man could want, and a few more, and all neatly arranged in order.

No one appeared to be in charge, but as they moved down the center aisle between the long tables they could see that the far end had been glassed off into a number of offices, in which sat a half-dozen men busy at clerical work. John surmised that here was the business end, not only of the store, but of the cannery and all the other company activities. One of the clerks caught sight of them and came out.

"Nothing," said John. "We're strangers. Just looking around."

The clerk nodded busily and turned back.

"You got a fine store," John called after him, by way of politeness. He laughed to Len as the man hurried on without reply, "Nobody *could* be as busy as he looks!"

They were as far as the door on the way out when a hail stopped them. They looked back. The clerk had again emerged from his glass case.

"Hey you!" he called. "Come back. Mr Ashley wants to see you!"

Len looked at John comically.

"S'pose he means us? Who in hell's Mr Ashley?" He raised his voice for the clerk.

The latter glanced behind him and came rapidly down the aisle.

"Mr Ashley," he repeated, when near enough to moderate his voice. "Mr Herbert Ashley, the general manager. Come back to his office."

Len looked at John once more.

"You been stealin' things again, you little rascal!" accused Len reproachfully. His manner changed. "Now," he proposed to the clerk, with the sprightly geniality of one amusing a child, "you tell me three reasons why we should come back to Mr Herbert Ashley, the general manager's office. Wait!" He stopped the man with upraised admonishing finger. "I'll help you; I'll give you two myself. He's Mr Ashley, and he's general manager. Now you're going to tell me the other reason, aren't you!" Len waited in exaggerated expectation.

John laughed.

"Oh, come on, Len. Let's go see what he wants."

"No. Hold on." Len stopped him with a hand on his arm. "We got to get to the bottom of this." He drew himself up to his full height. The clerk began to look a trifle apprehensive and to back away. Len followed him step for step. "There's more to it," said Len to John. "You see, when Algernon's told me that one reason why we got to come back to Mr Herbert Ashley, the general manager's office, just because he says so, I got to tell him just ninety-one and a half reasons why we ain't got to do no such goddam thing: and if Mr Herbert Ashley, the general manager, has anything to say to us, he can damn well got off his pratt and come out here where we are!" He glared down at the man for a terrific moment, then thrust him aside with a sweep of the arm. "Come on, John," said Len mildly, "let's just you and me go pay our respects to our general manager, Mr Herbert Ashley."

He strode grandly away. The poor clerk stared after them, undecided whether to call for help or not. John followed, laughing and interested.

They could see Ashley sitting at his desk in the innermost glass cubicle, a slim, olive dark of complexion, black-mustached, black-haired man. The mustache was clipped to a stubble, and the hair parted in the middle and plastered close to his head. These things, and the fact that his clothes fitted him, gave him somewhat of an urban air. Also, he looked too young for so responsible a job.

"Looks fool you, or else he's a pet of the old man," surmised Len happily. "I don't like him. I never did like dudes."

"Well, don't get too fresh," warned John as they entered the inner office. "They might throw us out."

"Say!" cried Len, much cheered. "That would be fun!"

But when they filed through the door to the inner office Len quieted to his normal manner. The clerk, who had followed them, looked relieved. Undoubtedly he ascribed the change to proper awe of The Presence; but John wondered what next.

Ashley looked at them for a moment. The keenness of the scrutiny impressed John. This fellow might be young and a dude, but he was competent.

"Still don't like him," muttered Len. Ashley evidently did not catch this. John nudged Len to silence, but he agreed. The man was too damn self-assured and bossy. Of course being bossy was his job . . .

"You men are strangers here," Ashley stated rather than asked.

"What of it?" John bristled. This was a free country, wasn't it?

"I know everybody in town. I never saw you before," explained the manager. "What I want to know is, is either of you men an engineer?"

"No," said John.

"Sorry. I hoped you might be. I'm in a jam. I need a mechanic—bad."

John stopped Len, who seemed about to swing into some kind of action, probably fantastic.

"You said 'engineer,' " said John to Ashley. "I know something about mechanics."

"Me, too," chimed in Len unexpectedly. "I have some every morning for breakfast."

Ashley ignored this. "How good are you?" he asked John.

"Depends on what you want done," said John.

"It's this way," Ashley swiftly explained. "We've always contracted for our cans. This year we're going to make them ourselves. The man sent up to install the machine took sick. We had to send him out. It'll take two weeks anyway to get another man in. I want to begin making cans before two weeks. I can't spare an hour. So I've been combing the country for someone who could finish setting up the machine. I'm asking everybody."

John nodded. He was beginning to like the man's direct incisiveness.

"You must have engineers of your own in a plant like this," he pointed out; and instantly perceived the common sense of the question had made a good impression.

"He runs his boiler room on Christian Science," murmured Len.

"Shut up, Len," said John. "Never mind him," he told Ashley, "he's a little drunk."

"Me, drunk!" Len roused up. "Why, boy, you don't know one first thing about me drunk! Say, that's a good idea!" he cried with enthusiasm. "Let's dem'nstrate! Perhaps," he became elaborately polite, "Mr Herbert Ashley, our general manager 'll join us."

"Oh, keep quiet," said John impatiently. "I'm interested."

Len fell into the background.

"Oh all right, all right," Len yielded. "But first thing you know you're going to be one of these here wage slaves. I can see it comin' on."

"Best thing is to take a look at it," suggested John to Ashley.

Ashley took down his hat from a nail on the wall and led the way. They went out through the store to the street. Here they turned to the left, rounded a bend, descended a steep dip, like a ramp, proceeded along a narrow railed sidewalk fronting a row of small red-painted shacks and came out on an extensive flat of several acres, composed partly of foreshore, but mostly of a heavy-planked platform on piles, where were the many buildings, large and small, that made up the cannery plant. John would have liked to look around, but Ashley gave him no chance. He threaded his way quickly to a narrow outside stairway, skipped nimbly up it into the dim spaciousness of a second-story loft, where men were working on nets, and to a room built in one of the angles at the far end. He unlocked the door of this.

In the center of the room stood the machine, partly assembled. Its heavy base was already bolted to the floor, and overhead the power leads had been installed ready for the belts. Tools and parts strewed the floor. Across one wall was a machinist's bench and equipment.

"There you are," said Ashley.

John stood still looking the thing over, trying to comprehend the principle of its working before tackling details. But Len made a great show of walking around and around it, stooping, cocking his head to one side with an air of owlish wisdom, reaching out to twiddle a nut or a bolt. Finally he straightened up with so convincing an air of decision that Ashley was betrayed.

"Well?" Ashley turned to Len.

"Very nice, very nice," Len gave his verdict. "I'm sure it's going to make you very, very happy." An expression of deep satisfaction overspread his face when Ashley disgustedly abandoned him for John. He threw his head back and began to stare blankly at the rafters.

"I tell you," John said to Ashley, "I never saw a machine like this, but I think I see how it ought to work. Anyway, I can figger it out. It ain't very complicated. You must have some sort of directions or blueprints or something."

He spread out the blueprints on the bench. Ashley waited. Len continued to stare at the rafters.

"I think I can do it," said John quietly after a while. "No harm to try. When you say your new man'll get here?"

"In about two weeks."

"I'll have her ready for him," said John.

For a moment Ashley looked faintly pleased. Then he stirred doubtfully, hesitating. Unexpectedly Len spoke up. He must have sensed the indecision, for he had not lowered his eyes from the ceiling.

"If John says he can handle it, he can; but damn if I can figger why he wants to!" He lowered his eyes. "Come on, John, I'm gittin' dry again."

John laughed.

"All right," Ashley made up his mind, "I'll chance it. Can't do any damage, and we might be that much ahead."

"Huh," observed Len and returned to Nirvana.

"If you need anything," Ashley was addressing John to the exclusion of Len, "let me know. I can give you a helper."

"We can handle it," said John. He caught Ashley's glance. "The two of us work together," he stated firmly, "or not at all." And after a moment: "Don't worry about him. He's all right when he's sober."

"Well . . ." conceded Ashley. "Look her over. Lock up when you leave. Stop at the office on your way back and sign in." He made as though to go.

"Wages?" spoke up Len, still contemplating the rafters.

"Eight dollars."

John's eyes opened. Len had told him in Seattle that wages were high up here. But eight dollars a day! Why, down there he had been getting only a hundred a month and had been raised twice at that.

"Ten," said Len, unperturbed.

"Ten!" repeated Ashley. He stared at Len, reddening. He turned to John. But Len came to life. He wheeled on the indignant manager.

"Look here, you," he told the latter. "Nobody I know of drug you up here. And we come only because you asked us to. Purty soon, when I get it thought up, I'm going to tell you where you can go to." For a long moment the two men's eyes clashed. "Come on, John," said Len, "I'm gittin' dry again. Let's go."

Ashley looked from one man to the other, then shrugged.

"Very well," he yielded. "It's a holdup, but I've no choice." He spoke without heat, from a dry impersonality into which he seemed to have withdrawn. "Ten it is. But," he warned, "you'd better be good."

"We are good," said Len placidly. "Why, sonny," he warmed to a large paternalism, "I didn't tell you before, but it was me *invented* that there machine."

"Hell!" said Ashley.

Len's eyes followed the retreating figure until the door slammed behind it.

"That fetched him," chuckled Len. "You know," he confided to John, "I don't think that feller likes me, somehow. That's all right, I don't much like him." He chuckled again. "I bet he's gone out to bite himself up a snack of ten-penny nails. Now look what you went and did," he reproached John. "You went and got us into a job. And I was just beginnin' to have a lot of fun!" Abruptly he became serious. "Think we can make it, John?" he asked.

John looked at him sharply. To all appearance he was completely sober. "I think so," said John. "It may take time. But I like machinery. It interests me. I'd pretty near have taken this job for nothing."

"Not me," said Len. "But I'm fairly handy myself. I've tinkered. I'm really a Yankee, if you was to scrape me down. How you goin' at it?"

"Well," said John, "first thing I'm going to do is to lock that door and keep it locked. We likely won't lay spanner to bolt for several days, and there's no sense in anybody's knowing *that*."

"What 'll we be doin'?" asked Len.

"Why, this." John walked across the shop to the blueprints. For a moment he examined them. "See that piece?" said he, pointing. He penciled on it the figure *1*. "That's number one. And this one's number two, and so on, till every piece on the plans has got its number. Then we'll compare them up with the actual pieces. They must be all here somewhere, either set up or loose. As fast as we find one we'll chalk its number on it. And we won't begin to work until we've found and numbered every last part that shows on the blueprint. Then all we have to do is to build her by the numbers. Can't go wrong that way, if we take our time."

"By cracky," cried Len, "that's smart!"

CHAPTER XII

CHILKAT HARRY

SALLY DOZED for a time. She awakened somewhat refreshed, but still feeling far from ambitious. She looked out the hatch. The float had risen halfway to the street level, and the ramp had correspondingly flattened. The mist had ceased falling, but dark clouds hung low. There did not seem to be much incentive to action. Nevertheless, Sally was curious enough to walk up the ramp for a look up and down the street. She did not go farther. The arrangements were curious, but they would keep. She would rather explore in company with the men when things were livelier. They were pretty dead right now. Indeed, at this moment, the only living creature nearer than the men working on the pile driver so nearly overhead seemed to be a dog lying in the middle of the planked roadway. He was a big dog, with long brindle-gray hair and a noble wide velvet-looking head and wise drowsy eyes. Sally liked his looks. Here was someone to talk to. She spoke to him and was about to pat the velvet head when she was brought up all standing by the suddenness and vehemence of a chorus of shouts. She drew back, her hand on her heart, startled not only by the warning, but by the realization that unguessed people must have been watching her from beneath the obscurity of the wooden awning.

227

A bearded man in a short faded Mackinaw and half boots sauntered across to her.

"Don't go to fooling with strange dogs, lady. It ain't safe."

"Why—why . . ." Sally was still a little startled.

"You can't trust malemutes," the bearded man insisted.

The dog rolled his eyes sleepily toward them.

"He looks to me good natured enough." Sally was incredulous.

"A malemute is part wolf. And maybe he is good natured, and maybe, if he takes the notion, he'll tear you to pieces," stated the man positively. "I'm tellin' you!"

"Then if that is so," cried Sally spiritedly, for she half suspected this man was having fun with her, "why do they allow such a dangerous animal to run loose?"

The bearded man eyed Sally appreciatively and chuckled. Indignation was becoming to Sally.

"You don't believe me, do you, lady?" said he tolerantly. "That's all right. But just as a favor to me, you let 'em be till you ask your menfolks. I don't want to have to shoot no man's sled dog. He won't bother you long as you let him be."

"Thank you," said Sally at length in a small voice.

She continued to stare at the malemute—from a safe distance—after the bearded man had left her. The dog stared indifferently back. There *was* something queer and aloof in his yellow eyes. Sally liked dogs: and dogs ordinarily liked her. The disappointment, small as it was, was sufficient in her present mood to determine her irresolution. She returned to the snug familiarity of the cabin.

A short time later she was summoned by a hail. She started toward the deck, but stopped short halfway up the companion, frozen by amazement. On the float stood a man holding at half ready, just above his hip, a long blue revolver, the muzzle covering the hatch. For several seconds Sally saw nothing but the sinister round orifice. Then it moved slightly to one side, but did not lower. She recovered her scattered wits sufficiently to raise her eyes.

This was a young man. Thin, keen face. Clean shaven except for a little mustache. Very blue eyes, narrowed together in a compact wari-

ness that even the obvious surprise of Sally's appearar
slacken.

"Where's Kelly?" he demanded curtly.

"Well!" Sally breathed out in relief. "He's not here," she
rather inanely, for she had not yet entirely recovered.

But the young man seemed not to accept this. He held the revo
still at the ready, though he shifted it still more from her direction.

"No?" said he. "Come on deck," he ordered. "Stand one side." Sally
obeyed. She was beginning to be both indignant and amused. He
leaped to the deck in one swift catlike movement and crouched to
one side of the hatch, peering down into the cabin, the muzzle of
the revolver thrust around the edge of the combing. For ten seconds
his eyes swept the interior, then he looked up at her puzzled.

"This is Kelly's boat," he stated, but with a trace of uncertainty in
his voice. "Isn't it?" he asked, the uncertainty growing.

"It was," corrected Sally. "He sold it to us."

He continued to crouch alongside the open hatch, his head turned
sideways, his blue eyes, detached and frosty, examining her face.

"Where is he?" he demanded.

"In Seattle, last I heard," said Sally.

He got to his feet in one quick and graceful motion and thrust the
revolver in a leather holster at his belt.

"Sorry," said he. He raised his hat briefly. He did not appear to be
in the least embarrassed, nor did he seem inclined either to explain or
apologize further. But Sally had no intention of letting it go at that.

"Possibly you wouldn't mind telling me what this is all about?" she
suggested with a touch of irony.

"I had business to discuss with Kelly," said he in a tone that implied it was none of hers.

"So I gathered," said Sally dryly. She waited. The young man
leaned gracefully against a shroud and contemplated her with a faint
air of amusement—the same amusement, thought Sally, one accords
the pretty ignorances of a child. She flushed and was indignant with
herself for doing so and so flushed deeper.

"I had no intention of murdering the man in cold blood, if that

u mean," he vouchsafed after a moment. "But I do choose
ways the integrity of my own skin, if possible. A sensible
no chances with Kelly." He continued to eye her with an
al raillery that left Sally a little at a loss. She had in her no
than normal of the deliberate coquette, but she was used to a
tain small impact on men. There was nothing personal in her
expectation of this. It was an especial masculine reaction to the feminine, as much a normal element to her as the atmosphere. She noticed
it only when, as now, it lacked. She returned his scrutiny with just
a trifle of recurring indignation.

Having so far explained—or justified—himself, the young man
began to roll himself a cigarette. He did not seem to expect any reply
or comment. But he showed no intention of going away. His head
was down over the cigarette. She looked him over, her intuition bor-
ing down through surface detail of appearance in search of a single
impression. She was pretty good at this with most people. But here all
she could sense was a trace of swagger, with a hard bright deflecting
surface of challenge about it. And that was evident enough on the
outside.

He finished rolling the cigarette and licked the edge of the paper
and began to fumble in his pocket for matches. He seemed entirely
absorbed in this, as though he had forgotten all about Sally. If he's
waiting for me to speak first, he's going to wait! resolved Sally. She
was enormously piqued and aroused and interested—a fact she would
have indignantly denied. She had to admit to herself that he was attractive looking; but she diluted the admission by pretending objec-
tivity. Handsome, in a dark, thin, nervous fashion. He had on a
Mackinaw shirt open at the throat and thick woolen trousers, tucked
into heavy socks that came nearly to the knees; nevertheless, even so
muffled, his figure kept its impression of quick, wiry slimness. On his
head was a small felt hat, about his waist a broad leather belt studded
with silver, and on his feet, instead of the usual leather boots or shoe
pacs, brilliantly ornamented moccasins of some thin tough-looking
material strange to Sally. She recalled the man's noiseless, catlike

spring to the deck. Undoubtedly picturesque. Stagy-picturesque, added Sally to recapture a proper scorn.

Then she perceived that he was perfectly aware of her scrutiny, and that he knew she intended to make him speak first, and that he was amused. So then she had to say something, and she could not quickly think of anything to say that would sound natural; and she felt he knew that also and was still further amused. It was intolerable.

Then her wandering eye fell upon something. Now, for the first time, she realized with something of a start that the young man had not come unaccompanied. On the float, patiently waiting, sat a dog. Sally might have thought this the same malemute from which she had been warned a short time before, were it not for a dark patch encircling this one's left eye.

"Oh," she cried, "what a beautiful dog! Is he yours?"

The young man deliberately lighted his cigarette and threw away the match.

"Yes," said he.

But Sally had her opening, and she was going through.

"What's his name?"

"Chilkat," replied the young man.

Sally laughed with a gaiety she tried desperately to keep from sounding forced.

"He doesn't look much like any kind of a cat. Is he like the rest? Dare I pat him?"

She moved tentatively in the dog's direction. He stared at her with enigmatical, unwavering yellow eyes. The corner of his mouth lifted slightly in warning.

"Wait a minute," the young man intervened. "Here, Chilkat!" The malemute leaped to the deck. His master stooped, took the animal's head between the flats of his hands, directed its muzzle at Sally, spoke to it in a jargon strange to her, held it a moment immobile and released it.

"Chinook," he explained. "I told him you're a friend. Go ahead."

Sally reached forth a doubtful hand. Chilkat gravely offered a paw;

and as she took it, he dropped his head and gave her hand one swift
lick of the tongue.

"Oh!" cried Sally, "you're adorable!"

She fell on her knees and gathered the great head to her breast.
Sally's heart went out to Chilkat in a rush of release. He talked small
things back to her under his breath in response. She gave him a final
hug of gratitude and arose to her feet. She was her own woman again.

But the strange young man remained unaffected. He waited coolly
until the little scene was finished.

"My apologies again for disturbing you," said he. He removed again
his little felt hat, bowed, turned his back, leaped over the rail to the
float with a soft pat-pat of his moccasined feet and, without looking
back, disappeared up the ramp, followed by the dog. Sally stared after
him, biting her lip. She had no right to be indignant. The young man
had been impeccably polite. But Sally was not accustomed to such
complete indifference. And she was, she knew, looking rather well,
for she had not yet taken off her little red slicker, and that was
always most becoming to her. Why, he had not even asked who she
was and where she had come from!

Shortly the men returned, John with a roll of blueprints under his
arm and full of talk about the job. But they kept quiet and listened to
her account of the visitor and her description of the dramatic little
scene. John chuckled with approval of the man's tactics.

"Sounds like he'd been raised down in my country," said he.

"I *told* him Kelly wasn't here, but he came aboard anyway!" cried
Sally. Only as she told of it did it occur to her that her word had
been doubted. John looked at her teasingly.

"How'd he know you wasn't Kelly's new woman?" he said.

"Oh!" Sally was completely taken aback. "I never thought of that!"
Her cheeks flamed. "How could he dare? Do I look like——"

"If you had on that red slicker, you do," interrupted John firmly.

"I'll never——" began Sally, then stopped and swallowed hard.
John looked disappointed: he had nearly caught her that time.

When she came to the dog named Chilkat, Len spoke up.

"Oh, that feller!" he cried, enlightened. "That's Chilkat Harry!"

"Friend of yours?" asked John.

"Oh, I know him. Everybody knows him."

"Well, don't be a clam! Tell us about him. Who is he? What does he do?" demanded Sally impatiently.

"I ain't really seen much of him. Anything that comes along, I reckon, like the rest of us. Last I knew he was dealin' faro up at Treadwell," replied Len vaguely. "I've heerd tell he's a pretty hard citizen."

"Oh, a gambler!" cried Sally.

"Nothin' agin that," said Len. "I been one, too. This feller ain't a professional, if that's what you mean. He does lots of things. What's he doin' here? Didn't he say?"

"He didn't say anything. He's worse than you are."

"So he was gunnin' for Pirate Kelly! Well, well, well!" Len seemed suddenly to find an exquisite entertainment in this thought and began to shake all over with soundless laughter. Sally could not see that the bare situation was as humorous as all that. John looked amused: he had thought Len was all sobered up.

"What's so funny?" asked Sally after a little, as Len continued his silent chuckling.

Len did not reply in words. From an inside pocket he extracted his old leather wallet, fished around in it and produced a newspaper clipping.

"I been saving this," said he. "Here, Sally, read it out loud."

Sally took the clipping wonderingly. It was from the Seattle *Times,* with a date line of nearly a month before.

"Go on, read it!" urged Len.

" 'Banker kidnaped,' " began Sally slowly. "But what has this got to do——"

"Here, gimme back." Len recaptured the slip. "They grabbed this man, Otis—he's the banker," he began to epitomize rapidly, "when he was comin' home, up his front walk, after dark—now read it from there." He returned the clipping to Sally, marking the place with his finger.

" 'Though no direct clue has been uncovered as yet,' " she obeyed,

" 'James Wilson, of 823 Packard Street, testifies to the presence at the time of three men in the immediate vicinity of the Otis place. Because of the dusk, Wilson was unable to see clearly enough for accurate description. He states that one was tall and slender and the other two shorter and thick set——' "

"So," Len interrupted, "I don't reckon Chilkat Harry's likely to see his friend for a while."

"By cracky!" John slapped his thigh. "So that's what they were up to!" He, too, began to laugh. "That explains it! Say, why the devil didn't you show us this before?"

"Account of her."

"Account of Sally?" John was puzzled. "What she got to do with it?"

Len avoided Sally's eye, in which was growing accusation.

"We was all ready to go," said he defensively, "and I knowed it was all right as far as you and me were concerned, but I was kind of skeered of her." He stole a glance at Sally and looked away hastily. "Once you git tangled with the police and the law you never know how long they'll keep you hangin' around. Might be all summer. Sure as shootin' she'd have made us go tell 'em what you heard. Women are mostly that way. I know. None of our business. You would, wouldn't you, Sally?" Len's manner was humble.

For a moment Sally did not reply. She eyed Len, who cringed exaggeratedly. But Sally did not smile at this.

"It isn't funny in the least. I suppose you never thought of what that information might mean to this poor man's family? What happened? Isn't there any news?"

"I asked around when we got in," said Len. "They ain't none."

"Well!" said Sally. "I—I don't know what to say. I'm ashamed of you, Len Saunders."

"Hold on," interposed John, "after all I don't see where we would have helped much. I didn't really know anything."

"You knew the name of one of them, and that they were going to use a steam boat," countered Sally swiftly. "At least that would have given something to look for."

"I writ them that much in a letter," submitted Len.

"What?" Sally stopped what she was going to say next. "I should think then we'd have heard from it. Everybody knew where *we* were going."

"I didn't sign the letter," said Len. His assurance revived suddenly. Len was through being humble. "Anyway, I don't like the law; and I ain't any too fond of bankers; we don't have 'em up here. I've kept shy of 'em all my life, and I don't aim to tangle up with them now. I'm a fair man, and I done what is right. They got all the dope to go on, if they ain't too dumb to use it. And that lets us out." He glared uncompromisingly at Sally.

"Why, Len!" Sally stared at him a moment and then began to laugh.

Len looked at her reproachfully and departed for his own quarters, mumbling something about fixing up for supper.

"Well!" said Sally. "What's struck Len? I didn't know he could be so sassy!"

John chuckled.

"Len's back on his home grounds. He's an old he-wolf up here, and he's out to howl. You mustn't mind him," added John, "he's had a few drinks."

"Oh, I *like* it," said Sally.

CHAPTER XIII

ANNABELLE

THE MEN WENT TO WORK the following morning. Len took his bundle of personal effects with him. He was not coming back to the Tillicum, not as a resident, that is. On this he was firm. He'd crowded them long enough, and now he was where he could take care of himself. They needn't think they'd got rid of him, though. The Murdocks did not object too strongly. That improvised forecastle could not be very comfortable for Len, they told one another. But secretly, and a little guiltily, they were very glad of this arrangement. It had been a long time since they had had a whole place to themselves, so they could celebrate in any way they wanted and make as much noise about it as they wanted, without having to think about being overheard.

Immediately she had finished the boatkeeping chores, Sally started out by herself to see the town. She was now rested and curious. Its picturesque strangeness delighted her, especially the new street being built on piles up there against the side of the mountain. So fascinated was she by this that she postponed other exploration in order to climb to its level by a long flight of stairs, the lower end of which she ferreted out at the end of a short dark alley between two buildings. Since the stairs were built against the side hill, they ran up beneath

236

the new road and its forest of pilings and cross timbers. The lumber of which they were made looked raw and new; but the wild growth was already crowding between the steps and pressing close to the rail on either side. Sally found it quite a climb. "I ought to have counted the steps," she regretted when halfway up. She had to stop for breath, but she did not mind that, for it gave her excuse to look about. However, she deferred fuller enjoyment of the view, for she had first to find out where they thought they were going to put the houses, and how you were supposed to get down from there— surely not by those interminable and break-neck stairs!—and maybe this wasn't to be a street with houses, but a road leading somewhere, to a mine perhaps; her mind raced on to a hundred questions of avid curiosity; so she must walk out to the end where they were working with the pile driver and find someone to question.

The pile driver was thumping away at a great rate, but she found one young man with his hands in his pockets. He returned her greet- ing affably and without surprise at her being what she was and where she was. He answered her questions as though they were a continua- tion of a former conversation and she an old friend. Unexpectedly Sally found it pleasant to be so instantly taken for granted, as it were, instead of having to break in an acquaintance like a new shoe. He did not look at her as he talked, but kept his eyes most of the time fixed on the work going forward, though when he did glance in her direction it was with approval. After a little it was borne in on Sally that he was really not idle at all, but had charge of this construction and was watching vigilantly every detail of its progress. Nevertheless he replied to her without apparent preoccupation.

This was a street, all right. "Kind of a funny street," he admitted. But they had to have one somewhere. Filled up below. Houses? Oh, more room than you'd think just to look at it. Blast back into the hill if you want a back yard. Didn't you see 'em down at the other end? There's three built there already. Oh, came up by the stairs! Quite a climb that way. Easier to stick to the grade. Slants up from just beyond Cole's store. He broke off to shout an order to the man at the throttle of the engine. "What say?"

Sally liked this young man. He had a nice clear, clean, competent air about him. She admired the astounding cleverness with which the crew upended the great piles and poised them, and the massive iron chunk of the hammer crawling to the top of the derrick and hesitating and falling free with a thump. There was a rhythm to it—swish-swish-swish-swish-*thump!* swish-swish-swish-swish-*thump!* over and over. It caught at her and could have held her for hours in its hypnosis. But she tore herself away.

"Good-by," she said to the young man.

"Good-by," said he. He turned on her a brief flashing smile, his first acknowledgment of her femininity; but instantly his eyes were back to the work.

Sally wandered slowly down the high platform of the street. The pinched long stringer of the town lay directly below her, all roofs and twists and turns. From up here she did not need to see it unless she wanted to. She could look out and across where were wide waters and islands and the bases of mountains whose tops were lost in clouds. It was nice up here, deep breathed, solitary. She decided that this enterprise was not so fantastic after all, and that if she were to have a house in Klakan she would like to have it up here.

After a few hundred feet the level of the planking began to dip, so that shortly she found herself again at shore level. As the young man had said, she came out behind a large square building, which, she concluded, must be the store. On a still lower level, spread out across apparently the only flat along this coast, were many red structures she knew must be the cannery, where Len and John were at work. But her watch surprised her with the statement that the morning was almost gone. She hurried back to the float after little more than a glance at the town itself. That must wait. But she looked forward eagerly to the afternoon.

The men were to take their noon meal at the cannery mess room, so Sally was soon free to continue her explorations. She stepped off the Tillicum almost at the level of the street. She was not yet accustomed to this enormous difference between high and low water, that sometimes forced her to scramble up like an acrobat and at others permitted her to step directly ashore like a lady. For a moment she hesitated which way it was to be—right or left, and then she remembered the cannery, so turned in that direction.

Sally took her time, peering curiously into such windows as looked commercial, stepping with care a respectful distance around a sleepy malemute, smiling timidly at the occasional Indian squatting against a wall, in vain hope of some response. Two men only did she encounter, and these she would have passed in the fitting demureness of those days, but they threw her a cheery greeting. Very doubtfully she returned it. However, they went right on by; and Sally belatedly recognized the same impersonal friendliness she had liked so much in the foreman at the pile driver. She wondered if all Alaskans were that way.

Shortly she came across an acquaintance. This was the dog Chilkat. He lay on the sidewalk near the wide door of a saloon. Sally recognized him by the shadowed marking around his eye; and Chilkat himself acknowledged his identity by waving a tail of welcome. Sally extended the back of her hand for him to smell at.

"Oh, he remembers you all right," came a voice from within the saloon.

Against all propriety, Sally peered inside. The dim low room was empty except for the man Len had called Chilkat Harry. He stood at the bar, but behind it. When he perceived that she saw him, he nodded to her and came out to the doorway.

He leaned his shoulder against the jamb and crossed one foot over the other and ran a hand through his hair and looked down at Sally below him. His performances of the evening before had left Sally still a little impatient with this young man. Nevertheless, unwillingly, she had to admit he stirred her. Quite impersonally, merely on the esthetic side, and not in the least by his good looks, which were striking enough. Sally had no use for that theatrical sort of good looks. Rather by the way he moved and flowed—that was the only word—flowed naturally into grace when he came to rest, like a panther she had seen in the zoo at Seattle.

The beast, too, had stopped its prowl back and forth and had stood still and looked at her. Chilkat Harry's surface manner was today easy and friendly, but his eyes were as remote.

"I see you know dogs," Chilkat Harry was saying. "Mighty few are mean if you give them a good smell first."

"How mean *are* they?" asked Sally. "I never know how much to believe."

"The malemutes?" Harry glanced reflectively down the street. "That depends. They won't hurt you, ordinarily. And yet—if you should happen to stumble and fall, for instance, and three or four of them happened to be near, and they happened to feel like it, they just might pile in on you—unless you could get to your feet before they reached you. Then you'd be all right."

"I don't think it's right to allow such creatures to run around loose!" flared Sally with one of her characteristic quick indignations.

"Probably not," agreed Chilkat Harry indifferently.

She looked at him with sudden suspicion.

"You're trying to scare me, like all the rest," she accused.

"I don't think there's anything to be scared of," agreed Harry. "But they are best left alone and treated with respect." The cold surface light of his eyes flickered with a momentary amusement. "You can't judge by looks. I found that out again yesterday. Had you all set down and bracketed as a yachting party, out for a summer's amusement. That was twice I had to change my mind."

Sally flushed, remembering John's teasing surmise that she might have been taken for "Kelly's woman"; and she perceived that the young man saw she understood and was entertained. But she refused to be routed.

"Are you sure you're right at last?" she challenged.

"Not one bit," disclaimed Chilkat Harry. "Now I *am* puzzled." He looked at her with a bold admiration that deepened her flush and for the first time aroused her defensive instincts. But she could not retreat on this.

"By the way," she said, "I don't think you need hope to see your friend, Kelly." She started to tell him about Kelly, but he interrupted.

"Yes, I know all about that," said he, "but I'm not so sure I won't see him."

"You know?" repeated Sally, thrown off her stride. "Then why yesterday did you——"

"I didn't know then. Your friend Two-Step—Saunders, I mean. Last evening. He was giving himself quite a time."

"Oh!" said Sally blankly. She wondered how much Len had talked. She turned away with as much dignity as she could summon, conscious without looking that the man was again surveying her with that hateful detached, amused, superior air of his. The dog, Chilkat, got to his feet and fell in beside her.

"Go back," she commanded without looking round.

Chilkat waved his tail respectfully, but continued with her.

"Better call your dog," she advised coldly.

"That's all right," returned the man. "I sent him. He'll take care of you. He's boss around here."

Sally hesitated. Whether it were worse to accept or reject she was too vexed to decide. "Thank you," she said finally in her primmest voice. But this annoying young man delivered a final shot.

"By the way," his voice floated after her, "I'm not a bartender. Just filling in an hour for a friend. Guess again," and then a soft laugh.

As if she cared who or what he was! But she did! And he knew it!

Sally was thoroughly exasperated. She turned blindly up the street, and it was some time before she had recovered sufficiently again to attend her surroundings. Chilkat had a good deal to do with this. Chilkat proved to be a person who took his instructions seriously. He walked soberly alongside, but a shade to the rear, so that she had but to drop her hand to touch his velvet head. But when, as twice happened, they must pass stranger malemutes, sprawled out comfortably on the thoroughfare, Chilkat quickened his pace to draw level with the other dog, where he would halt and stand until Sally had passed, when he would resume his place at her side. So far as Sally could see, no threats passed. Chilkat did not even look at the other; he stared blankly off into space; and as for the recumbent one, he merely rolled upward a lazy eye. The performance was absurdly stylized. It tickled Sally's humor and consequently did much to lift her irritation. She tried to joke about it with Chilkat. Chilkat acknowledged her remarks with one brief wave of the tail, but Sally perceived that he considered them in bad taste.

She had by now come near to the end of the planked street, or so it seemed; but it proved to extend on in a kind of sidewalk, with a rail on one side and a row of a half-dozen small detached houses on the other. The latter were set on a level with the sidewalk, but a little back, so that one must cross bridges to get to them; and in the spaces between the bridges, ten feet below, Sally saw tidewaters and the wash of miscellaneous debris they carried. This situation amused her. One could, she reflected, keep a rowboat right in one's front yard!

The houses were small, square and all alike. Each had a door and one window showing from the front. They were painted dull red, and their trimmings were of white. Back of the glassed upper parts of the doors each displayed an engraved portrait. These were all of the same size and placed in the same position. They differed only in subject. She and Chilkat sauntered along, and she peered at the doorways cataloguing, with growing interest, the worthies these people had picked to distinguish their places one from the other. For their exact uniformity in all other respects convinced her that such must be one of the reasons for the portraits. The latter were all of well-known Americans—Benjamin Franklin, George Washington, General Grant, President McKinley, Old Hickory. She came to the last house. At this point the sidewalk curved in to end in a stout railing, so the house stood fairly on the sidewalk itself. But as Sally neared, she perceived she was not going to be able to complete her roster of American heroes, for the door stood open.

Nevertheless, she continued to the end, and having done so, she must at least glance in to see what the interior of these houses might be like. In a rocking chair by a stove sat a woman knitting. Her head was bent over her work, and Sally could make out little except that she was rather large and dressed in gingham.

Sally hesitated. She found herself overcome by a desire to go in and talk to this woman and was astonished at herself that she had not realized how completely masculine her world had been and how much she had missed, without knowing it, just what this rocking chair and the knitting and the big warm-looking stove and the seated comfortable feminine figure represented in life. She waited a few moments for the woman to look up, but as she continued absorbed in the knitting, Sally ventured a cough.

"Mind if I come in?" she asked.

The woman raised her head with a jerk, thrust back the wide-bowed spectacles she was wearing and stared. Sally, whose native intuitions were quick, got the impression that she was not so much startled as incredulous. The woman's first speech seemed to confirm that idea.

"Glory be!" she cried heartily. "And where out of heaven *you* fell from, the saints only know, but the sight of you would cure sore eyes, only, thanks be, me eyes are fine."

She tossed the knitting toward some invisible landing place, bounced to her feet so vigorously that the chair continued rocking and threw wide the screen door.

"Come in! Come in, do!" she urged.

Sally liked her on sight. She was, indeed, a large woman, but square and compact and solid. In late youth or very early middle age. Her dress was crisp with starch. Black hair, florid. Good-humored looking, comfortable, obviously Irish. Tolerantly humorous eyes, just now snapping with a delight that was almost extravagant. She was holding the screen door open with the flat of one hand.

"Come in! Come in, do!" she repeated. "And I was just this minute sittin' there and saying to meself, sure if ever I get to paradise it'll be a spot where I'll never hear the words 'man' and 'fish' and 'boat' again; and here ye come along like an answer to prayer to save me from purgatory just when I was makin' up me mind to put poison in their soup!" She caught sight of Chilkat. Without transition or change of voice she turned on him. "Skat you! Keep your dirty feet out of here!" She flapped her apron in his face with a snap; and Sally laughed aloud when the haughty malemute looked abashed and meekly went back to the center of the sidewalk and lay down.

She slipped past the woman, still hospitably holding open the screen. "Abraham Lincoln," her mind registered as her eyes came in range of the picture on the door. The roster was complete.

The room proved to be larger than she had anticipated and was furnished in surprising comfort, she thought. Beside the rocking chair were two others and a sofa, all deep in overstuffed upholstery, and a table. The floor was carpeted, the walls papered. A door indicated a room, or rooms, in the rear. The front window and another at the side were curtained with imitation lace and could be darkened by pulling down roller shades. Next to the inner door stood the stove, a huge cast-iron affair, with nickeled curlicue ornamentations and a curved nickeled bar across the bottom on which one might rest his feet. Its dampers were closed, but from it diffused a soft warmth that made Sally realize for the first time the raw chill of the out of doors. On its flat top, at the back, simmered an enamelware coffeepot of at least three-gallon capacity.

"My, but it's warm and cozy in here!" she exclaimed.

The woman looked gratified at this.

"That's what they crave most, the poor cr'atures," said she. She let the screen close of its spring and shut the door.

"Set! Set!" she cried hospitably. "Set and warm yourself! I'll have some coffee in two shakes of a lamb's tail!"

She disappeared through the inner door, to return almost immediately with a smaller coffeepot, which she placed atop the stove. She took off a stove lid, peered within the fire box, thrust within it fresh fuel from a wood box at the back, opened dampers, substituted a ring for the lid, moved the coffeepot to the open flame, disappeared again to bring back cups and saucers, spoons, a sugar bowl, a tin can of milk, all of which she disposed on the table. During these activities, whenever she was in the room, she talked steadily.

"Two shakes of a lamb's tail," she repeated. "Sure, there's coffee in the big pot, and plenty good enough for them hairy apes to mug up on, but it's fresh made for me and my specials, or I want no

truck wid it at all; and when maybe one of 'em hollers he likes it fresh
made too, I tells him, take it or leave it, sez I; I ain't invitin' you
here just to fill your belly; and if ye come sneakin' around here for
a handout ye'll take what's handed; and, anyway, who are you to be
talkin' after swillin' down yer gullet that hoochnihoo Mush Mahoney
sells you——" She broke off to utter a jolly laugh. She looked over her
shoulder at Sally, and her manner turned confidential. "Not that I
grudge the lads, ye mind, but you can't encourage them too much, or
your place will be all tromped up wid loafers, and that I *cannot*
stand. I don't take in everybody that comes, mind ye, like some, but
I have me own. And," she recurred to the subject of the big coffeepot, "if it's really cold and wet they are, then they're better off wid
this stuff anyway. It's got power. Sure, it's strong enough to float a
wedge!" She laughed again her jolly laugh, chattering on as she
moved about, so ceaselessly that Sally had no word to say. Nor did
the woman seem to expect any. Finally she trundled over to the
table, turned the thick china cups right side up with a clatter, carried
the steaming pot from the stove, poured.

"All set!" she cried. "Drug up a chair!" Then, as Sally struggled
with the huge overstuffed contraption, she came around the table to
lend a hand. "My, but you're the little bit of a thing!" But she said
it with her big jolly laugh. She whirled her own chair into place with
a deft twist of the wrist. Her strength seemed enormous.

"There!" she cried with a small air of triumph. But at once she
bustled to her feet again to cross the room to the front window. She
pulled down the roller shade with a snap.

"There!" she repeated. "Now we can talk. Don't you know that
one?" she asked, catching Sally's puzzlement. "It's me sign and signal to them hairy apes—'keep away, git out, no coffee, no nothin',
busy.' We all work that. Don't you——" She stopped suddenly, and
look of horror overspread her face. "Saints alive!" she cried.

"What is it? What's the matter?" Sally was alarmed. The woman
looked stricken.

"Oh, the poor dumb fool I am!" the other wailed.

"What *are* you talking about?"

"O' course! You're from the Big House!" It was a statement rather than a question.

Sally stared. She was wholly at sea. Her quick mind darted here and there in search of some explanation. Was the woman crazy? The Big House? Then she felt her face reddening. Sally was young, but she was not so unsophisticated. She knew about such things. She knew that each city had its own name for them. In Seattle it was the Red Light. This woman evidently thought that Sally was . . .

But her dismay was short lived. Her sense of humor was too lively. She laughed. Instantly the other, who had been watching her face intently, laughed too. Her tenseness relaxed.

"Whoosh!" she exclaimed. "But I give myself a turn! But I might have knowed it was too early in the season yet. Am I the poor dumb one!" She fanned herself with a corner of her apron.

"Suppose I *had* been from the 'Big House,'" Sally teased. "Would your reputation have been ruined entirely? After all, I don't think anybody saw me come in."

Now it was the other woman who stared.

"Me reputation?" she repeated. Comprehension dawned in her eyes. She uttered a wild Irish whoop. "Oh, this'll be the death of me!" she cried. She rocked her body back and forth. "Oh, oh!" She wiped her eyes with the corner of her apron. "Give me a minute. I ain't laughed so much since Shaughnessy slid off the roof. Listen, dearie. You got it all twisted. There ain't no regular houses here. Not like you mean. The Big House is the boss's place—Nels Cole's—up on the hill back of the cannery. They call it the Big House." She began to laugh again. "Now ain't we both the dumb ones!"

They enjoyed the joke together.

"Here," the woman reached across to Sally's cup. "We gone and let our coffee get all cold."

"It's all right," protested Sally.

"It's slops," the other negatived decisively.

She arose, threw the contents out the front door, refilled the cups. Silently they put in the cream and sugar. Sally sipped.

"It's delicious!" she cried and sipped again. "I never tasted any so good. I can't make anything as good as that."

"You can that!" denied the woman positively. "Anybody can."

"Then I wish you'd tell me how," begged Sally.

Her hostess thrust aside her own cup to make space for her elbows on the table. She leaned across the better to impress Sally. Her eyes sparkled with interest and gratification. She was wholly engrossed in telling Sally how to make coffee.

"You put your cold water in the pot, and you use a heapin' spoon of coffee for each cup and one for the pot, and you dump it in on top of the water. And mind you don't stir it in. Let it float. And you bring it up to a boil; but the minute it boils, you set it off till it quits bubblin', and then you set it back. When she boils up three times like that, she's done. That's all there is to it, and don't you let anybody tell you anything different and fancy."

"I'll try it," said Sally.

They drank the coffee and talked. It was warm and cozy in here. The Irishwoman had that rare quality of making one feel clever. She listened to Sally's sprightly accounts of some of her adventures with admiring clacking of her tongue. Under this encouragement Sally expanded. She was really brilliant, she felt, and vastly stimulated and released. The deep-down sensible part of her stirred vaguely, trying to call to her attention that she was not actually as good as all that; but she refused to listen. She was having much too grand a feminine time. Finally she came to asking about things she wanted to know, one of which was why the founders of this town seemed to have gone out of their way to pick out the steepest and most difficult location for it.

"That's Nels Cole," replied the woman. "He already had the cannery and all down on the flat beyant; and it was he thought of the town, and so he would place it near."

"Yes, but I don't see how he got people started coming here."

"Sure, he built the streets and wharves and the store to sell what people wanted and so made it handy for them to come. There's a power of people"—she waved her hand vaguely—"living out, to come in for their grub—and their fun. Trappers and miners and prospectors and fishermen. And of course the Injuns," she added.

"I don't see," Sally was still doubtful, "how there can be enough to make it pay—I don't see how there can be enough business . . ." She was remembering the construction work still going on. All the towns and villages she had known had some solid economic reason for being, and the size of them corresponded roughly to the importance of that backing. But this crazy place seemed booming ahead regardless.

"Aren't you the one to ask questions now!" exclaimed the woman in admiration. "But why do you bother your pretty head with them things? I don't bother mine. All I know is that here's men; and where there's men, there's business. And as for the rest, I dunno; but I do know Nels Cole; and you can bet that where there's Nels Cole, there's something that pays. You're just in from outside, ain't you, dearie?" She broke abruptly from the subject. "Seattle? Why ain't I heard of you before?"

"We just got in yesterday." She saw the woman looked puzzled and remembered that probably no steamer had lately arrived. "We sailed up," she explained, "with Len Saunders," she added, in afterthought that perhaps her hostess might have heard of Len. But she was not prepared for the wild whoop of recognition that greeted Len's name.

"Old Two-Step!" the woman cried in delighted amazement. "You kem up wid old Two-Step! Why, the ould rapscallion: he always was shot in the tail wid luck." She caught Sally's baffled expression and hastened to reassure her. "Don't get me wrong. Two-Step's a grand old scout. You can rest easy about that. He hands it out when he's got it. But I'd heerd he'd got skun aplenty and was flat. And where, now, did he make *this* raise?"

"I'm afraid he is—'flat,' I mean," said Sally. "Why do you call Len 'Two-Step?' "

"Sure, that's what everybody calls him up here."

"Why is that?" asked Sally.

The woman chuckled reminiscently.

"Cost him ten thousand dollars awhile back to learn how to dance the two-step. Sure, that girl, she was a one!"

Well! gasped Sally, but to herself. Len! Who'd have thought—— Then she laughed. The woman laughed too.

"Don't you worry," she said comfortingly after a moment. "Old Two-Step always manages to light on his feet somehow. Ain't we the ones!" she cried, veering suddenly. "Here we sit clackin' away for an hour, and we can't yet call the other out of our names! Mine is Annabelle."

"I'm Sally—Sally Murdock."

"Niver mind the Murdock; Sally will do. Sure, Sally's a grand name." Annabelle volunteered no more of her own. She refilled their empty cups. Sally again praised the coffee. "Do you know," confided Annabelle, "coffee is all I keep. No liquor here. If they want that they can go somewhere else, and bad cess to them. Sure, they're welcome to their fling onct in a while wid the hooch and the ragtime and the per-oxides, but it's only onct in a while. This country is different; and what a man wants here is differ from what he wants outside. You got to learn that. What holds them steady, you'll find, is a warm stove and a comfortable chair and a real home-cooked meal that'll stick to their ribs—and I'm a good cook, if I do say it as shouldn't—and why not, when they come in froze and wet and tired all out from the sea and the mountains, and them livin' all cramped up in little cabins you wouldn't put your dog there into, or stinkin' little shacks wid mebbe a packin' box or an ould stump to sit on! This ain't much—compared to your Big House"—she paused to laugh at the double meaning their little joke had read into the words— "but it looks snug and homey to thim; and that's what they want more 'n all the rest put together. And, dearie," Annabelle leaned forward as though in confidence, "times is when that's all they want. And I give it to 'em." Her seriousness broke, and she gave vent to her jolly laugh. "Sometimes it comes to me like I'm a reg'lar philan —philan—what do you call it?"

"Philanthropist," murmured Sally.

"That's the way you best make your reg'lar friends—and keep 'em," said Annabelle.

Without reason a curious bafflement was growing in Sally, a sense of talking at cross-purposes, somehow. It was in the back of her mind, but it refused to emerge. To escape what was almost a discomfort she recurred to something that had slipped out of the conversation before she could ask about it.

"Why did you act so queerly when you thought I might be staying at Mr Cole's house?" she asked. "What difference could that make?"

"Wait till you run across that old beggar," said Annabelle darkly. "He'd bite your head off quick as look at you."

"I don't see . . ."

"Why, if you'd been one of his folks, and he found out I'd had you in here talkin' to you and havin' a mug of coffee sociablelike this way together, he'd run me out of town so fast I'd lose all me tail feathers in the breeze." Sally laughed a little at this, but Annabelle did not even smile. "Oh, he could do it!" she assured Sally. "He builded these houses here for us, and the rent is low, but don't you fool yourself: we stay only so long as we keep ourselves to ourselves, and make no mistake about that, dearie!"

"Why!" Sally was up in arms, for her upbringing had left her intolerant of any form of snobbery. "I think that is atrocious!"

"And him what he is!" agreed Annabelle virtuously.

Sally thought it over.

"I suppose it's his wife," she must conclude.

Annabelle uttered a derisive hoot.

"Oh, Nels ain't married," said she. She seemed to be relishing something. But she did not, yet, tell Sally what it was. "It's a pretty grand house," she deflected in her bewildering fashion. "He's carpets and a pianny and chiny bath tubs and the like, such as you've never seed. Mostly, till the summer warms," she informed Sally discursively, "he lives in a room in the boardinghouse he keeps special —when he's here off and on. But when he opens up the Big House, and the folks come up from outside, then there's the big doings, what wid fishin' and skyhootin' over the chuck in fancy launches and lyin' around on the rocks half nekkid. The folks," observed Annabelle with a short scornful laugh, were also pretty grand; "too grand for the likes of us." She allowed a dramatic pause. "They are," she observed dryly, "mostly nieces and mebbe some of their friends." Annabelle looked out the side window. "No," she repeated, "Nels Cole ain't married. But this I will say: his brothers sure has a mighty good-lookin' lot of gurrls."

She turned a humorous eye toward Sally. Sally's eyes widened, then she laughed. "And you thought I was one of them!" she gasped. Annabelle hooted again with delight.

"*Wasn't* I the dumb one!" she cried. "But, dearie, you're so awful pretty."

"Well," chuckled Sally, "be that as it may, I'll have you know I'm nobody's niece, but a nice respectable married woman; and my husband is working down at the machine shop somewhere right now. Why, what is it?"

Annabelle was staring at her with an expression Sally could not understand.

"Good lord!" said Annabelle.

Her whole manner changed. It was as though a curtain had fallen between them. She did not explain. The conversation fell flat and cold. Sally was puzzled. She tried to think back on what had been said, but could recall nothing for which she could blame herself that would account for this. The natural thing would have been to have asked what was the matter, but Sally found herself unable to do that. She could have asked the Annabelle of a few moments ago, but not this woman who answered everything she said so curtly and looked at her so strangely. But it was plain she was no longer welcome. Annabelle did not offer even conventional objections when she arose to go.

Sally took her leave forlornly. She had had such a good heartwarming time, and it had flattened out so suddenly without any reason at all. She was hurt and rebuffed and, in due sequence, resentful, as was only human. But part way to the door she took her courage in her two hands and turned back to confront Annabelle, still sitting in her chair.

"You've got to tell me what's the matter," said she. "It isn't fair."

Their eyes met and held. In the older woman's Sally fancied, for a brief moment, a flick of something soft and human; but it was only a flash.

"There's nothing the matter that I know of," said Annabelle.

"Well—good-by," faltered Sally after a pause.

"Good-by," returned Annabelle uncompromisingly. "And thank you kindly for your call."

But Sally had a gallant spirit. It rallied. She must make a final effort.

"We are living on our boat—at the float," said she. "And I hope you'll come and see me. I've had *such* a good time," she added almost pleadingly.

The woman came alive. She made an exasperated movement.

"Oh, for God's sake!" she snapped, "don't be a fool! What would your man say? You know damn well you've no business foolin' around wid an old whore like me." She caught Sally's stunned expression and sat bolt upright. "Mother of Mary!" she breathed. Then her eyes narrowed watchfully. From the cynical and almost hostile remoteness of her kind, she waited Sally's reaction. Obviously it had never entered Annabelle's mind that she had not known.

Sally turned red, then pale; hot, then cold. Her mind was confused. But it was not her mind that spoke.

"I don't care. I can't help it," she was saying stoutly. "I like you. I *want* you to come."

Her eyes blurred. She wanted to cry. She could not see Annabelle's face. But Annabelle's voice was very gentle.

"You blessed lamb." That was all Annabelle said; but unreasonably Sally felt like a small child that has been hurt and is comforted; and then she did cry; and Annabelle was patting her soothingly on the back.

"I'm sorry," gulped Sally, dabbing at her eyes.

The Irishwoman thrust her away, holding her firmly by her two shoulders, at arm's length, as though the better to rivet her attention.

"Listen to what I say, dearie," said Annabelle soberly. "I wouldn't have had this happen for all the glories of heaven, and it's a stupid fool I am to mistake you so. I should have seen that you wasn't, me wid eyes in me head; but somehow, wid everybody knowin' Annabelle the len'th of the coast, and you comin' down the row in broad daylight, bould as brass, and comin' up to me door, and you saying 'may I come in and talk to you,' so sweet and friendly like." Annabelle's eyes grew vague for a moment. "And me wid eyes in me head!" she repeated. "Take blame to yourself, you old fool, and tell the truth to yerself if ye're going to talk at all!" She looked at Sally fiercely; but Sally knew the fierceness was all self-directed. "Ye knew ye didn't *want* to see," she continued to address herself. "You was that hungry at sight of a woman that——" Her voice turned slightly bitter. "Oh yes, they's female crathures here—the cows! I take blame," she resumed her thread, "but what is done is spilt. But what I want to say to you is this: that you must not try to see me again."

"But——" began Sally.

"I know what you would say," the woman cut her short, "and the saints in heaven will smile on you for the unspoken wurruds. But it will not do. I know. This end of town is not for the likes of you. There's trubble enough in this world—— No!" she cut short Sally again, "I shall not come to see you, and you shall not try to come to see me. That is flat!" She softened. "As if I would have it so!" she mourned.

"But I certainly don't intend to have it so," put in Sally with spirit. "It will be all right. John is different. I *know* that when I explain to John he'll——"

Annabelle had seemed about to dissolve, but this brought her up. She uttered her derisive hoot.

"You poor innocent lamb of God!" she cried. "You poor baby!" She looked at Sally with tender pity. "You don't know the craytures. They're all alike, and that you'll find soon enough. 'John is different,'" she repeated Sally's words. Her eyes misted briefly. "It's good hearing that that's how it is between you." She shook herself briskly. "Now you run along. And if folks see you, what more nat'ral than that a stranger is takin' a stroll to see all the place—and you not knowin'— I hope! Oh now, look here," as Sally still looked obstinate, "you don't want to drive me out of here—where me friends are. And that's what I must do if you're foolish . . ." She faltered. "Git out!" she cried fiercely. "Do you hear! Is it fools you would make of us both?" She thrust Sally out of the door and banged it shut behind her. Sally looked for a moment into the infinite sad pity of Lincoln's face. She turned blindly away. Chilkat arose, stretched and yawned. He fell in beside her. They walked slowly down the street.

Sally did not know when she came to the ramp, nor that she turned down it to the float, nor did she say good-by to Chilkat, who left her at this point to return to his master. Chilkat did not blame her for this. He sensed her preoccupation perfectly.

Her quandary was simple enough, but difficult because it involved radical rearrangement of Sally's tidy world. Sally was no simple-minded innocent. Even before she was married she had known what were prostitutes. They were "bad" women, painted, brazen and what was known as "bedizened." Annabelle was none of these things: she was not "bad."

That was Sally's first passionate instinctive reaction, and she tried to stop on it; but certain facts were plain, and she had to look at them. Because of her unusual upbringing, her mind was, for those days, singularly tolerant. She could understand promiscuity, but only in connection with what she thought of as "a certain type," that was so different as to be almost another species. Her relations with John were so singly possessive, not only in body but in every tiniest thought, that she was not even remotely able to imagine promiscuity in anyone like herself.

And Annabelle *was* like herself—there was no getting around it— more so than any woman she had ever met, she told herself in a passionate exaggeration of the moment. How *could* Annabelle— Here Sally had to stop short. She shook herself and resolutely attacked preparation of the evening meal.

By keeping busy she managed to hold the stark fact itself below the threshold. But she could not dismiss Annabelle from her mind. She had to think of Annabelle. She *liked* Annabelle. She was so human and kindly and good natured and jolly and understanding. She woke you up: she had the gift of making you feel attractive and bright and clever—much more clever than you actually were. *Comfortable,* that was the word. But how *could* she be comfortable, how could anybody be comfortable in mind when—— And there Sally had rounded the circle again. She was ready to cry she was so bewildered and lost.

The hatch slid back. John, returning from work, backed down the companionway. As he turned around he was almost knocked from his feet.

"Well, well!" he cried, a little surprised at the warmth of his reception. She pressed against him, burrowing fiercely into his chest. He looked down humorously at her small head. "What is the——"

"Don't talk! Hold me tight, *tight!*" Her voice was muffled.

He put his arms around her. John was always ready for love-making, and Sally always quickened eagerly to response, but she did not often take the initiative. He was enormously pleased, but a little perplexed. He felt instinctively something unusual back of this. Puzzling, his arms slackened.

"Closer! Hold me close!" Sally's own arms instantly tightened.

John could not know what it was all about, but he obeyed and stood there in patience, occasionally patting Sally on the back.

She clung to him, her face buried in the heavy Mackinaw. After a little her tight muscles began to relax. The world was not all gone strange. Here was John, her John. Here was her stability and her refuge, and from it she could look out and be safe, no matter what the world. Nothing could alter that. And with the familiar warmth, there stirred in her just a trace of that high ecstasy into which emotion transmuted just for these two, so that to Sally it was a herald of the exaltation of life; but today its luster had been breathed upon, and now it was bright again. Such thoughts raced through Sally's heart, while her cheek pressed the hardness of John's Mackinaw in comfort. And then one thought came, pleading and timid. For just the flash of a moment Sally seemed to catch a meaning—comfort; comfort in cold; comfort from the harshness of a life unbelievably harsh; comfort of warmth and the luxury of ease and refuge, a fire, food, coffee, the stretch-out of ease; illusion of home; someone who made you talk and feel clever and funny; someone who understood and gave . . . It was a vague glimpse, deprecating, one sided. But it brought to Sally a sense of relief. She understood no better than before. But now she did not have to understand.

She looked up at John's puzzled face with a shaky little smile.

"I'm silly," said she. "I couldn't help it."

She tried to disengage herself, but his arms held her.

"What ails you? What's the matter?" John insisted.

She shook her head.

"Nothing. Nothing at all, really. Just a silly fit."

John was not at all convinced. Sally had never acted like this before. There *was* something back of it. He cast about him wildly. Only one thing suggested itself from John's abysmal ignorance of women.

"Are we going to have a baby?" asked John in an awed voice.

CHAPTER XIV

THE MACHINE

IN SPITE of the common-sense aspects of the situation, Sally had every intention of going again to see Annabelle, and soon. But circumstances combined to postpone the visit.

The next day John returned from work to announce that he had decided to move the Tillicum around the bend to the cannery float. This, he said, would be much pleasanter and more convenient than the present situation. For one thing, water was piped to the float itself. Here it had to be carried down in pails. He and Len towed the ketch from the dinghy while Sally steered. The cannery float, unlike most, ran parallel to the beach and close inshore. Its outer face was in constant use by company craft; but inside ran a narrow strip of water in which the Tillicum could lie snug and protected.

It was, as John had promised, much pleasanter. At the city float Sally had felt closed in. Here she could see abroad in all directions; here were things going on. She could sit on deck and be entertained. Tugs were always bringing in scows or barges or pile drivers and edging them, with much churning of the water, against the piling, where they lay for a while only to be taken out again. Cannery tenders returned from mysterious day's work out in the blue somewhere, to stay overnight and be off again early in the morning. Sally soon came to know the crews of these various craft. They exchanged with her gay and hearty banterings while they were making landings or preparing departures, but none of them ever stopped long enough really to talk to her. Sally wondered whether this was because they were too busy, or because of some frontier etiquette with which she was not familiar.

As she extended her explorations, Sally became more and more impressed with the enormous labor of preparation. Everywhere she went were men getting things ready, tinkering on machines, caulking dories, painting, mending and tarring nets, unloading and trucking away all manner of supplies—foodstuffs, box lumber, great rolls of chicken wire, bales of sheet tin, huge packing cases of unidentified contents. Some of this they stowed in warehouses, some they reloaded on the cannery tenders. They worked busily, as though time lacked. Thus they had been working, Sally learned, since May. When one has but the precious few weeks of the salmon run to make or break his season, it is well to be ready.

As Sally wandered about among the many buildings she began to understand this, and why the men she took to be the various foremen seemed so rapt and intent, so wholly preoccupied, and she herself awakened to a vicarious excitement of anticipation. She began to understand, too, why, in spite of all this activity, she sensed a curious feeling of vacancy. What these men were doing sounded to her lonesome and hollow against a huge emptiness. The larger buildings were full of it. Actually in them were quite a number of men doing various things, but the dimness and the long narrow tables and the strange-looking machines and the great boiler-looking affairs, with wrapped steam pipes running to them, and the escalators and elevators disappearing above and the little cars on tracks seemed aloof from them, asleep and waiting.

"Oh, sure," John told her when she spoke of this, "they won't bring in the crew till the first part of August—last of July, anyway. Wait till the run begins. Then you'll see things hum. Day and night, when the fish are in. Won't be so dull for you then."

Sally had not yet found it dull right now. After she had pretty well looked over the cannery proper she discovered the halibut wharf and the icehouse, where the sturdy schooners came in off the sea; and then the back country and the charming little lake whence came the ice, and soaring peaks beyond it that lifted her to the skies. She liked that place best of all and liked to sit there, just looking. It was a place of great simplicity and solitude, owned by a black-and-white loon, who swam about in small circles near the middle of the lake and eyed her cynically and every so often laughed derisively at the mere thought of her. On her way to the lake she passed below the Big House, shuttered atop a little hill. At sight of it she chuckled a little and reminded herself anew that she would go to see Annabelle at the first opportunity. But the hermit thrushes were just beginning to sing and the tips of the bracken to uncoil; and here was a chuckle of little waters and a flickering of small shy birds and a taste of clean coolness; and behind her, whence she had come, an organ undertone of the waterfall from the lake. The little town, for the moment, had no temptations for her. A week slipped by; and then things happened so that it was too late.

During this week John and Len worked away busily on the machine to make cans. John's idea of numbering the parts to correspond with similar numbers on the blueprints was sound enough as far as it went. By its means they at least came to understand exactly how the thing was supposed to work. But it told them nothing of how those parts were to be assembled. They had to be put together in an exact order or something was sure to be left over, and no way to get it in short of backtracking to a certain point. So a considerable portion of the time—and the overtime—for which the two men were being paid, they passed squatted on their heels in apparent idleness staring at the structure before them, brows furrowed in speculation, arguing as to how this or that was supposed to work or to fit on; and a further considerable portion they spent tearing down what they had been building up. After a fashion they were really reinventing. For this reason they kept the door locked against visitors.

Occasionally Ashley looked in on them. When his key in the lock caught them in one of their periods of puzzling things out, they seized wrench or spanner and set to in an appearance of activity. Ashley had not much to say. He looked the machine over, with the air of examining it in detail, and went away, springing the lock of the door behind him. He puzzled the two men.

"I can't make out whether he knows anything about this thing or not," said John. "He acts like it; but if he does, he must see we got to yank that second gear out before we can get in that little jack shaft. I saw him looking at it. But he didn't say anything."

"He ain't fired us yet," Len pointed out.

"Say," said John, "it's funny the boss hasn't come around yet. Come to think of it, I ain't laid eyes on him since I been here."

"The boss? Ashley's boss."

"He's straw boss," corrected John. "I mean Cole."

"Oh, him. He ain't here. He's outside yet. You'll see him soon enough."

"Know him? What sort of a cuss is he?" John was faintly surprised that this was his first curiosity as to Cole.

But Len shook his head. Too far south for Len. His tromping grounds had always been farther upcoast.

In spite of their necessary gropings they made good progress. The thing was beginning to look like its pictures. They were enormously interested. Even if there had been no question of overtime pay they would have gravitated back to the machine shop after supper. They could not keep away. Sally put in her protest for a nine-o'clock deadline. John had a moment's twinge of conscience about Sally; but she assured him she was all right and having a good time.

"Well, we'll be through with this thing in a few days now," said John.

He told the same thing to Ashley, who had begun to show signs of impatience.

"I want that thing running by the twenty-fifth," said the manager.

Len fired up.

"We're working as hard as we know how," he told Ashley bluntly. "If you got anybody can do it any quicker, send 'em around. A man's got to eat and sleep."

There was nobody else: all three knew that.

"That feller makes me sick," grumbled Len when the manager had gone. "Why the twenty-fifth? What's so goddam important about the twenty-fifth? There won't be a fish in for six weeks anyway. What's he expect to can between now and then? Fresh air?" He glowered at the inoffensive machine. "I dunno why we should be tearin' our shirts just to humor that slick-haired dude's fool notions!" He arose to his feet. "I'll be damned if I'm goin' to!"

John looked up at him curiously.

"You ain't going to quit on me, are you?" he asked. "Right in the middle of the job?"

This brought Len up short.

"No," he conceded reluctantly, "I suppose I'll see her through. But," he bristled up again, "I'll be te-totally chawed up and spit out if I'm goin' to *marry* the dang thing! You can suit yourself, but six o'clock is quittin' time for the day, and that's when I quit. Why," Len's indignation warmed, "here I been back now most a week, and just on account of that god-damn lily-livered, pasty-faced, slave-drivin' squirt I ain't seen a soul or turned a card or—or—why, I ain't even had a chance to swap a yarn or shake a foot or get respectable drunk yet, and all because——"

John was laughing at him.

"All because you're interested in getting this thing to go—and you know it," said he.

"Well," Len was deflated, but he stuck to his point, "she'll be there just as well in the morning."

Sally approved heartily of this revolt.

"You've been working much too hard, both of you. Len is right. There's no sense to it."

But she put down a firm foot on John's idea that at last they were to have a nice quiet evening together. She had things to do.

"You get Len and go uptown and have a good time," said she. "Bring me the news. See what's going on."

"Don't you want me?" asked John, taken aback.

"No," said Sally. "I'm busy. Mrs Durkin is coming down to see the boat."

"Who's she?"

"She's the woman at the cookhouse."

"Good lord!" groaned John. "I've seen her!"

"I thought you'd be away—you generally are. There'll be other evenings."

"Well . . ." John yielded, trying hard to be reluctant.

But he did not have to go out looking for Len. Len showed up after supper. He carried a small package which he thrust at Sally.

"What's this? Peace offering for neglect?" she teased.

"I reckon," agreed Len. "Open her up."

Sally undid the parcel. It contained a pair of moccasins. Only these were not ordinary moccasins. They were made of some paperthin semitransparent material, were lined and topped with fur, and the tongue across the instep was heavily ornamented with beads, bright steel and dyed porcupine quills.

"Mukluks," said Len. "Leastwise a kind of what you'd call a slipper mukluk. The real mukluks got legs on 'em. That's whale gut—or walrus gut—they're made of. You wouldn't think it, but they'll wear like iron."

"They're beautiful," said Sally. "What is the fur? It's so soft."

Len took the moccasins from her. "That lining is caribou," said he, "and this other is otter." He handed them back. "You can wear them around the boat. They're waterproof."

"I'll wear them right now," said Sally, seating herself on the bunk and beginning to take off her shoes.

"What I really came by for right now," Len turned to John, "was to tell you I got onto what that 'twenty-fifth' business is all about. Seems the Portland gets in that day, and Nels Cole is comin' on her. Well, that's why."

"And I suppose Nels Cole's got to have a can the minute he steps foot on shore," said John with sarcasm. "Next day wouldn't do!"

"I don't quite gather the plot," observed Sally from the bunk.

"Why," Len turned to her, "this Ashley's been proddin' John and me to get that machine running by the twenty-fifth, and we couldn't quite figger the rush; there's no fish for a long while yet."

"And he'd like to show it off to Mr Cole the minute he arrives." Sally nodded comprehension.

"Yes. But it's worse 'n that. Seems like this idee is a special pet of Ashley's, and Cole had no use for it at all. The old ways was good enough for him. Began with an argument and ended with a good old-fashion knockdown-and-drag-out. And Cole had to give in, by gum! You know," he addressed John, "I'm beginning almost to like that dude. Anybody who tells Nels Cole where to get off has guts, anyway. And he must be pretty good other ways, or he'd have been fired right then and there. The old man was plenty mad, and he's used to having his own way."

"Where'd you get all this?" asked John.

"Bookkeeper. Up at the bunkhouse."

"Are you going to get it going by the twenty-fifth?" Sally wanted to know.

"Mebbe. Mebbe not." Len was indifferent. "But we ain't going to break our necks. It's no skin off our hide if we don't." He arose to his feet. "Well, I'll be gitting on. I—I got to see a man . . ." He looked at John, surprised. "You comin' along?"

"Sally's got a visitor." He hesitated awkwardly. "You sure you wouldn't like me to . . ."

Sally laughed.

"Run along, you two, and have a good time." She eyed them derisively. "Be good, if you can; but anyway, have a good time."

"I won't be late," promised John.

"I'll expect you when I see you," said Sally.

But John was not late. He returned before Sally had put out the light, though she was already in her bunk. He sat on its edge to tell her about it. He was in high spirits. They had had a grand time. No, nothing special. Just ramming around. Len's friend, Mush Mahoney, ran quite a place, once you saw it lit up and going. The saloon was only the lesser part of it; no, not exactly a lesser part, but a smaller part.

"How they drink that stuff and get away with it is beyond me," John paused to wonder. "These Alaskans are sure a hardy race!"

The big show was in the room closed off during the daytime. Gambling. Plenty of it.

"Layout for every game *I* ever ran up against, and a Chinese one I never heard of," said John.

"Did you play?" asked Sally.

John shook his head.

"I was sort of tempted to," he confessed. "Sometimes I used to get a good streak. But I hadn't any pardner then." Sally's hand stole toward his arm. John did not notice. He chuckled in relishing reminiscence. "But you ought to have seen old Len!"

"Len!" echoed Sally. "I thought . . ."

"I staked him to ten dollars. He ran it up to somewhere near three hundred in no time at all. You ought to have seen him! Top of the world! Do you know," said John, "that old coot is a perpetual surprise to me. Men don't often fool me much, but I sure was fooled in Len. Kind we used to call 'Pop' down in the cow country, steady as a tote horse." He laughed. Then he caught Sally's eye. "Don't get me wrong," he said hastily. "Len came home with me, and he's cold sober. It isn't that. But he knew a lot of that gang up there, and somehow they weren't treating him like anybody you'd call 'Pop.' " He mused a moment. "You know," he said, "I'd sure admire to see Len in action."

Sally snuggled down closer under the blankets. Why she should feel so absurdly happy and satisfied she could not have told. If anybody had told her baldly that it was because John—and to a lesser degree Len—her two men—had returned early and sober, she would have retorted indignantly that she expected no otherwise. Nor did she. But still—well, it was a nice world, and this a nice day even if Mrs Durkin had proved inexpressibly dreary.

"What else?" she asked John.

"Nothing much. Oh yes, saw your mysterious friend Chilkat Harry. What do you suppose? He deals stud. One of Mush Mahoney's regulars. Gambler. He's a cool customer. I think," said John, "I'd kind of admire to see him in action, too—if I was on the sidelines!" He laughed. "Chilkat?" he repeated Sally's question. "Oh, the dog! Yes, he was there, lying by his master's chair. Perfectly quiet and well-behaved. Never moved.

"But," said John, "I noticed folks kind of stepped around him. Struck me, in case of trouble he'd be there with the bells on. Kind of bodyguard—or lookout."

Nevertheless, in spite of this pugnacious declaration of independence and celebration thereof, the next evening found Len and John as usual back at the machine shop. They gave various excuses to one another, and to Sally, who was greatly amused. Not a steady thing. Only a couple of days more anyway. The real reason was that they had run a blazer on Ashley in getting this job, and now their pride was enlisted. They wanted mightily to make that bluff good. John, with a flourish, gave a last twist of the wrench just before whistle time on the twenty-fourth. He and Len shook hands.

"Grandstand finish," said John.

Ashley let himself in. He had been in and out all that day.

"She's done," John told him.

Ashley's ordinarily expressionless face lit with gratification. For the moment he turned human.

"That's fine work, men!" he cried heartily. He walked around the machine, admiring it. "You haven't tried her yet?" He looked about him. "I'll get in some sheet tin, and we'll see how she works."

He started for the door, but John stopped him.

"Hold on," said John, "I said she was done, and she is; but there's an hour or so's work oiling and greasing before we can start her up. She's dry yet."

"You can do that this evening," said Ashley, but he made the mistake of taking the tone of a command rather than suggestion.

"The hell we can!" John bristled.

Ashley stared at him for a moment, shrugged and went out. John continued belligerent. He held forth to Len. They'd broken their necks to get this thing done in time, and look at what thanks they got for it! Len grinned. "Go home and ketch up on your sleep," advised Len; "you'll feel better in the morning."

John did feel better in the morning. Only sufficient of his reaction remained to cause him to take his time getting down to work. This gesture of a free and independent spirit restored his good humor. He arrived at the shop ten minutes late, but again eager in anticipation.

"Come on, old-timer!" he greeted Len boisterously. "Tie into her. I want to make me a can!"

Len did not respond in kind. He was standing by a window, examining something in the palm of his hand. When he turned to John his face was sober.

"Look at what I found," said he to John.

John looked at the piece of metal.

"What is it?" he asked.

"I ain't figgered yet. But," Len was positive, "it belongs somewhere in that there machine."

"How do you know?" John's voice was like a pistol shot.

"It's new. It was in the packin' some of the machine parts come in."

"I went through that a dozen times myself."

"I was bringing in some boxes of tin to try her out on and run across some boxes that was unpacked before we came. Manufacturer's name on them," he forestalled John's question.

He watched John thinking this over.

"Don't know how I come to paw around in that excelsior," he proffered more discursively. "Hunch, I reckon."

John made no reply to this. He took the piece of metal from Len and looked at it frowningly.

"Looks like some kind of cam," said Len.

John walked across the floor to the machine. Len followed disconsolately.

"I been all over the thing from top to bottom a dozen times," said he. "I come early and got the greasing all done so we could start her up," he added in parenthesis. "A dozen times," he continued, "and danged if I can see any reason why she won't run and do her stuff just as she is."

"They didn't make this for fun," said John curtly.

"Mebbe it's a spare," Len brightened with a new thought. "Let's slip the belt on her and see."

"Might see more'n we wanted to." John shook his head. "Let me be."

He continued for some time to stand motionless, staring steadily at the machine as though he could extract its secret by sheer concentration of will. Once he crossed to the bench, opened a drawer, consulted a blueprint for a moment and returned to his intent frowning preoccupation. Len waited. Finally John drew a deep breath.

"Got it?" asked Len.

John nodded. Silently he pointed. Len groaned.

"Means we mighty nigh tear her to pieces!"

"That's right," said John.

"It'll take a week."

"About two days," corrected John.

"Ashley'll throw a fit!"

"Let him," said John. "He'd throw a heap more of a fit if we'd tried to start up the way she is now." He brooded for a moment, then turned toward where his coat hung on the wall.

"You ain't quitting?" said Len incredulously.

"No," said John. He put on the coat. "I'm taking time off to spit on my hands. We'll make a fresh start after dinner."

"I'll trail," agreed Len.

"From now on," said John in a compressed voice, "we're going to take our own time." He whirled on Len, flashing out, "Why, goddam it all, don't you see why we're in this jam? Hustling too fast so that dude could show off. If we had took our time, we'd have *seen* we needed a cam on that jack shaft. Hurry! I'd like to hear any son of a bitch say hurry to me again!" He glared belligerently at Len.

Halfway between the cannery and the company store they passed Ashley and threw him a growl. Ashley did not stop or question them. Whatever their opinion of him, he did not hold his present job without qualifications, one of which was the ability to handle men. He knew a chip on the shoulder when he saw one; and he was much too shrewd to oblige by knocking it off. So he did not question their absence from work in midmorning. They had really been working hard and overtime. A loose rein was indicated for the moment. It did not occur to Ashley that they were abroad for any other reason than that the job was finished.

He continued on down to the cannery and let himself into the locked room. For some time he stood examining the machine, reviewing the different steps of its operation as they had been demonstrated to him by the salesman at the factory last winter. He thought he recalled them all.

The power belt was running on the idler. He shunted it, by a thrust of the hanging bar, to the driving wheel of the machine. He found a hammer and cold chisel and pried open one of the boxes Len had piled against the farther wall. From it he slid a piece of sheet tin. This he inserted in the feed slot of the shaper and pulled a lever.

The wheels turned, the sheet of tin disappeared down the slot— and an instant later with a grinding crash the machine slowed.

Ashley had the virtue of facing situations instantly and coolly. He did not pause on the certainty that he had precipitated a major disaster. There was no mistaking that something had gone smash. Unflurried, he shut off the power. He stooped, peering into the mechanism, trying to see what was broken. Some teeth had been stripped from one of the gears—he could see that much—there might be other things. The expression of his face did not change. He dusted his hands, crossed the room, locked the door behind him.

It did not remain long closed. Presently Len returned. He had parted from John shortly after they had passed Ashley. He said nothing to John about it; but he recalled, belatedly, that the manager was uninformed of the situation. He hurried back, but arrived only in time to see, from a distance, Ashley's quick compact figure descending the outside stairway. Len watched him away, then ascended the steps two at a time. He flung open the door of the shop, took one look and closed it again. He had guessed it. No use looking into danger without John. First thing was to find John.

Surprisingly, John's first reaction to the news was of amusement. "Well, that lets us out!" he shrugged. "Not our fault!"

But Len was a fair man. He did not think it so funny. After all, Ashley could hardly be blamed. Last he knew the machine was all ready except for greasing, and obviously it was now greased. "Not so sure it *ain't* our fault, in a manner of speaking," argued Len; "we ought to have warned him. And," Len clinched the matter, "if we hadn't walked out in the middle of the morning, we'd have been there, and it couldn't have happened."

"That's right," agreed John thoughtfully. He was a fair man, too.

They were strolling slowly in the general direction of the cannery while they talked. John quickened his steps.

"Come on," he urged. "Let's see how much damage is done."

At the shop, after opening the door, he withdrew the key from the lock and looked at it humorously.

"Anybody asks you what's the matter," he observed to Len, "just tell 'em it's a case of too many keys to a door."

He crossed the shop, returned with one of the heavy boxes of sheet tin and propped it against the open door. He picked up a nail from the floor.

"What you think you're doing?" asked Len curiously.

John did not answer directly.

"Gimme a hammer," he requested. He drove the nail part way into the wall outside and on it hung the key. "There!" said he. "Now if I can find me some paint and a brush I'll paint 'welcome' over the door, and everything 'll be just dandy!"

They drew on their overalls, spread wrenches and spanners about them on the floor and began to back off nuts and bolts. For some time they worked in silence, laying aside one by one the various parts as they succeeded in detaching them.

"Funny," muttered John after a while, "how quick you can tear a thing down compared to putting it together."

Finally they reached the center of damage. John punched out a key, carefully drew a gear from a shaft. Both men examined it as it lay on the floor; peered into the machine.

"Not so bad," said John. "Three teeth gone. All we need is one gear wheel. Everything else is all right."

"Yeah—that's all," agreed Len dryly.

John laughed. He sprang to his feet, fumbled in a drawer at the bench, produced the cam that had caused all the trouble.

"Well," said he, "one thing, now we can put this doo-hickey where it belongs."

"Yeah," said Len still dryly. "That helps a lot."

John disdained reply. He thrust his head and shoulders into the intricacies of the machine and began to fit on the missing part. Len squatted by, handing tools.

They were snatched out of their absorption by a voice.

"I thought this thing was supposed to be ready to run."

Len turned, startled. John carefully withdrew his head and shoulders. He looked up at a stranger.

For a moment the two eyed one another coolly and appraisingly. John saw a short, four-square bulldog of a man, with a red face and a level, frosty blue eye. "A scrapper," thought John. "Won't stand any monkey work. Reminds you of Bull Kirby. But a lot more *sabe* than Bull Kirby," he amended. Not a man to go off half cocked. Knows where he's at before he moves. John was getting slowly to his feet. Len remained squatted on the floor. John wiped his hands on a bit of waste. He knew who this must be; but he wondered where he had sprung from—the Portland must have got in during the night. And where was Ashley?

"Not ready yet," said John in reply.

"What's the matter?"

John touched the gear wheel with his foot.

"Defective part?"

"No defect," returned John placidly.

The man considered this.

"What happened?" he barked. "I'm Nelson Cole," he added.

John nodded.

"That gear was stripped because someone turned on the power before things were ready." He waited for accusation. But none came. Cole merely looked him in the eye.

"Who did it?" he asked after a moment.

"I wasn't here," said John. He looked toward the door. "Maybe Mr Ashley might know."

Cole's eyes followed his.

"Oh, there you are," he snarled ungraciously at the manager. "Well, I hope now you're satisfied. There's your worthless newfangled contraption! What you got to say now?"

"Just what I've always said," replied Ashley firmly. "This is unfortunate. Accidents will happen. The machine is all right."

Cole glared at him. Ashley withstood the impact with a coolness that elicited John's unwilling admiration.

Cole turned on John.

"Why in hell you let every Tom, Dick and Harry in here is beyond me!" he growled. "Haven't you any sense? There's a key to the door, isn't there?"

John waited, staring at Ashley. The manager's sallow face flushed faintly, but he said nothing.

"That was a mistake," said John steadily at last.

"Mistake! I should think it was! I ought to fire somebody!" Abruptly Cole seemed to dismiss all thoughts of blame or recrimination. Almost visibly his mind shifted to concentration on the practical. "That all that's the matter?" He indicated the stripped gear wheel.

"That's all," said John.

"If we had another we could go ahead?"

"That's right."

"Any spares?"

"Not that I know of." John looked at Ashley, who came to with a start and shook his head.

"I've already written to Seattle," he ventured.

"Seattle! Hell!" snorted Cole. "Take three weeks. We got to have cans." He pondered. "Couldn't you make one?" He ignored Ashley thenceforward and addressed himself exclusively to John. John's cold detachment softened. He liked Cole's hard directness. He wanted to help Cole. He shook his head reluctantly.

"Not with what we've got. It takes a real machine shop to cut gears."

Cole pounced on this.

"A machine shop could do it?" he persisted.

"Oh sure; it ain't much of a job if you've got the tools."

"Good," said Cole. "The Portland goes north at eleven-thirty. There's machine shops at the mines, both at Juneau and Treadwell. They'll fix you up. Just say you come from me. You can catch the Portland back on her down trip." He dove into his trousers pocket to produce a roll of bills, from which he peeled two. "That ought to cover everything. Keep an account and settle the balance when you get back. And hereafter you lock that door, and you keep it locked. Then we'll know who's responsible. You're to blame there. Now, Ashley, regarding that shipment of trap wire . . ." He turned away, apparently dismissing all this matter as settled and finished. John uttered an exclamation and took a step after him.

"Take it easy," said Len. "I'll go."

This stopped John, but he remained for a moment staring at the retreating figures.

"Who's responsible!" he repeated Cole's words. "We're to blame there!" His face congested with disgust and anger. "And that fellow stood there and said not one word!"

"Why didn't you speak up?" asked Len curiously. "I was expecting you to."

"Not my business to," returned John shortly. "Up to him. Well, he sure showed himself up for a yellow dog!"

Len was taking off his overalls.

"I'm kind of sorry for him at that," said Len.

"What?" blazed John. "You mean to say you defend——"

"Keep your hair on," said Len. "I don't defend nothin'. I just said I was sorry for him, and I am. I'm sorry for any man that gets put in a fix where he thinks he has to pull somethin' yellow like that. Our Mr Herbert Ashley, the general manager, ain't so bad. He was just backed in a corner. It was a case of keepin' quiet or losin' his job. Or so he thought. I ain't sure he was so far off. Strikes me Cole could be mighty sudden."

"Hell!" John was just a trifle impatient at this unexpected return of the easygoing philosophic Len. "You make me tired!"

Len had finished folding his overalls, and now he deposited them in one of the drawers. He held out a hand.

"Produce!" he said to John. "The dough." He prodded John's comprehension. "Think you're going to get away with that? Don't expect me to traipse all over Alaska doin' your errands at my own expense, do you?"

"Oh!" John dove into his pocket for the two bills Cole had handed him. "Look here," he said to Len before he withdrew his hand, "you sure you want to? I suppose I could—— How long would it take?"

"And turn you loose in Juneau without Sally? Not a chance!" mocked Len. He became serious. "No, if I can get this thing made prompt so's I can catch the return trip I can be back in four days. But if I run against a snag and have to wait over for the Queen it'll take a couple of weeks. You can't take a chance of leaving Sally that long. We got to finish this job, now we've took hold of it."

"I'd quit it in a holy minute——"

"Shucks!" Len stopped him decisively. "Come on, shell out! I know your fingers cramp when they get around a dollar, but cough up!"

John withdrew his hand from his pocket. The two men stared at the bills, which were of fifty-dollar denomination. Len whistled.

"The man's a damn fool!" cried John, astonished. "Wonder somebody hasn't lifted his eye teeth off 'n him, if that's the way he hands it out to every stranger."

But Len shook his head.

"I sort of suspicion he knows what he's doin'," said he thoughtfully. "He's no damn fool. He's what I call a 'sizer-up.' They're scarce. I saw him sizin' you up pretty sharp. He ain't never goin' to lose any money on strangers! Not that feller!" He chuckled. "Better keep it dark it's me that's going," he advised. "He'd call out the militia. I ain't got your shinin' honest face."

"Oh, shut up!" John flushed. He picked up the gear wheel. "Just have them copy that: exact. You're right. We got to make good. And we will. And then——"

"Yeah?" drawled Len, "and then . . . ?" He cocked a quizzical eye in John's direction. "I suppose then you aim to take up somethin' serious? Like Mr Herbert Ashley, our general manager? Fine—if you think skunks is worth while."

John's belligerence fell. He had to laugh.

"Len, you got me winging," he confessed. "I can't make out whether you're a man or a mouse."

"Mouse—mostly," said Len.

"Well," observed John, beginning to strip his own overalls, "if Cole is so good as a 'sizer-up,' like you say, I'd advise him to take a good look at his friend Mr Ashley."

"I'm not so sure he ain't," said Len. He looked at his old silver watch. "Jeeker snipes!" he cried. "I better get a move on! Tell Sally I'm sorry not to say good-by."

"I'll get her. We'll come down to see you off."

As they hurried out Len paused to take the key from the nail.

"Now the hoss is stole we might as well lock up," he commented.

John and Sally arrived at the wharf breathless and only just in time. Len was already aboard. He leaned over the rail on the upper deck. They exchanged brief shouted remarks with him, but the noise of escaping steam blurred their words. So they grimaced amicably and wished the Portland would pull out. There was some small delay. The gangway was still overside, but two deck hands stood ready to haul it aboard. A last passenger hurried across the wharf.

"Hello," said John, surprised, "Len's going to have company!"

Sally recognized the young man they called Chilkat Harry, and at the same instant his eyes met hers. The gangplank was already rising beneath his feet, but he stopped short to sweep his hat from his head. In the gesture was a trace, just a trace, of exaggeration. Sally flushed, for it was impossible for her to guess whether the extravagance was unconscious or intentional in subtle mockery. She turned away in vexation.

She was glad that he was going away, that this was the last of him. Or was she?

"He's talking to you." John nudged her.

She looked back. The young man was at the rail. He had his hands cupped over his mouth trying to make himself heard.

"What's he saying?" she asked.

"Something about his dog," said John.

Abruptly the safety valve closed, and the roar of escaping steam fell.

"Mrs Murdock!" his voice came clearly now.

"Yes?" said Sally.

"I'll be back on the return trip. Could you take care of Chilkat while I'm away? He's at Mahoney's."

It was John who had finally to reply.

"Sure!" he shouted. "We'll look after him."

He turned to Sally as the hawsers slipped into the water, puzzled by some reluctance he belatedly sensed in her.

"What's the matter? Isn't that all right? I thought you said you liked the dog."

"I do," said Sally slowly; "I love him."

"He'll be good company for you," said John.

CHAPTER XV

PIRATE KELLY

RETURNING from the wharf to the planks of the street, John stopped abruptly and uttered a short laugh. Sally looked up, curious.

"See that bunch of tough-looking customers?" He indicated a group of four men talking together up the street to the left a short distance. "Well, that big fellow in the middle is our friend Kelly—Pirate Kelly."

"For heaven's sake!" Sally turned to look.

"Better keep moving," warned John. "I don't know whether he'd be glad to see us or not." He chuckled again. "Your other friend, Chilkat Harry, left just too soon." He turned to the right and moved on.

Sally followed, but she continued to look over her shoulder.

"How do you suppose he dares come back here—openly, like this— they must be after him—after Len's letter to the police."

"He may not know that," said John, "and, anyway, here's just the place he would head for. I'd admire to know how that last *business* deal of his came out, and where his two friends scattered to—especially that fellow in the gray suit. I could be interested in that bird. Something ought to be in the papers. I'll inquire about." He was wondering at himself that the kidnaping had so completely slipped out of all of their minds. But Sally had a more immediate interest.

Now, she demanded of John, perhaps he would kindly explain what this was all about? Why was she snatched from her cooking and fairly run off her legs? Where was Len going and why, and how long would he be gone?

Recalled to the events of the morning, John's brow darkened. As he proceeded with the narrative his anger and disgust rekindled. Sally listened thoughtfully, without comment, except when he mentioned Nelson Cole.

"I saw him," said she. "He came down on the float and looked at the boat. I didn't know who he was. I liked him," she added, "in spite of everything."

"In spite of what?" John was exasperated at this feminine inconsequence. "What has he got to do with it? He's all right. It was Ashley, I tell you . . ."

Sally allowed John to run on concerning Ashley. She had for the moment forgotten that he knew nothing about the "nieces," and smiled a humorous secret smile over the reflection that it would probably not have made any difference if he had!

"He was in a pretty difficult situation," she said of Ashley when John had finished.

John stopped in his tracks.

"Oh, for God's sake!" he cried. "Are you going to stand up for that yellow skunk too?"

He stumped on.. First Len, and now Sally! You'd think, before you got through, that it was all his, John's, fault! He'd taken it from Len; but this was too much! Sally followed, now a pace or so behind him. She was puzzled and a little indignant at his sudden flare of wrath. She did not know about Len; but even if she had, he was probably still not far enough along in matrimony to realize that when a man is angry he wants only endorsement from a wife. Contrary opinion is best postponed.

"You're too cross for words!" she told John. "I'm going for a walk."

"All right with me," grumbled John.

She turned off toward the waterfall. John continued on to the float. Then he climbed aboard the Tillicum. His impatience with Sally soon evaporated. But he was crisscross, pugnacious and independent. He did not know what his status was supposed to be until Len returned; and he did not bother to find out. If he was continuously on the pay roll, he supposed he owed the company his time; and in that case he ought to report to the boss for assignment to a job. But the boss was Ashley. To hell with Ashley! The more he thought about Ashley the madder he got! He had half a mind to go right now and hunt up that son of a bitch and cuff him up to a peak. His fists clenched.

That was the mood he was in when, in answer to a hail, he came on deck and faced Pirate Kelly. John surveyed Kelly with open and obvious distaste. Kelly's greeting gave him no reason: it was entirely friendly.

"I didn't expect to see *you* here," grunted John ungraciously in reply.

Kelly ignored this.

"I heerd you'd come north," said he. "I just heerd you were here. I was lookin' for you."

"Sake of old times," said John.

Kelly's little eyes glowed red for an instant at the sarcasm.

"I got use for this boat again. I want her back," he came directly to his point.

"Just like that!" said John. "Trouble is, she's my boat now. You sold her to me. Remember?"

"For nothing!" growled Kelly.

"Your own offer," reminded John.

His manner was hard to take, but Kelly took it.

"Look here," he managed a reasonable tone, though with an obvious effort. "You really got no use for a boat like this, now you're up here. You can easy pick up a dozen that'd suit you better for 'inside,' if you want a boat at all. I'll give you double what you give me for her—I'll give you three times. That's fair enough. Treble your money. What more could you expect?"

"I might expect to get what she's worth," pointed out John.

"Well, I'll pay you what you think that is, within reason," conceded Kelly.

John eyed the man.

"What you want her for?" he asked bluntly.

"What business is that of yours?"

Kelly flared for an instant at John's brusqueness.

"None—except that she's my boat, and if I'm selling it's going to be for what she's worth—to you." John emphasized the last two words. There was no sense to this. He had not the slightest intention of selling the boat. Nor had he an earthly reason for acting this way—except that he felt cross and was taking it out on Kelly.

Kelly had, apparently, much the same idea.

"Say, what's biting you anyway?" he complained. "All I want to know is will you, or will you not, sell this here boat back, and you act like you're trying to pick a fight."

They were at this point interrupted. A great red-painted scow glided along the other side of the float and slowed. Atop its rail stood a man with a coil of rope. A fuss in the water and a smoke in the air attested the presence of the tender, Sea Imp; but she was on the other side of the scow. The man cast a loop at one of the huge mooring cleats and missed.

"Hi!" he called to Kelly. "Give us a hand, will you!"

Kelly retrieved the rope and flipped it over the cleat. John sprang to the float and went down to the other end, prepared to take the second rope when the man was ready to pass it to him.

The little interruption broke the sequence of John's irritated reactions. "Actin' like a kid," said John to himself. All might have been well, but unfortunately at this moment his indirect motive in the person of Ashley came bustling over the rail of the scow from the Sea Imp. He climbed down to the float and disappeared up the ramp. He said nothing, but the mere sight of him was enough to stir John's indignation again. John even took a step after him, in two minds whether to follow Ashley and have it out or not. But he checked himself. Wouldn't do! It wasn't all Ashley. There was Len, and Nels Cole. Had to think of them. And the machine to make cans. Couldn't get bounced until that job was done. Thus he put his thoughts in sober order. But, he flared up again inside, Ashley better keep out of his way! God! how John hated a double-crosser! He stood staring at the ramp up which Ashley had disappeared.

"Say you!" Pirate Kelly came alongside and claimed his attention. "I'm offering you twenty-five hundred, cash, for this boat. I want an answer. I'm getting sick of this."

"Not for sale," said John curtly.

Without warning or change of expression or shift of position, Kelly's heavy boot shot out. So instant and unexpected was the attack that it only just failed of landing on its intended mark. Indeed, John's slight twist that saved his groin was more a reflex than a considered movement. But the kick did land squarely, with a thud, against the front of his thigh. The impact nearly knocked him off his feet. He felt it through all his body, so that, between the surprise and the physical shock, he stood for what seemed to him a long time, staring dumfounded at the man before him. As a matter of fact it was not even a matter of seconds. Kelly's foot had not fully swung back from the kick when John sprang at him, delivering his first blow.

Kelly took it, and several more like it, with an evil grin. Blows in the face did not bother him. He was tough: he had taken aplenty in his time. He did not even trouble to guard against them. He hunched his head down and extended his gorilla arms and snatched at John's quick figure as he struck. That was not Pirate Kelly's way of fighting—standing off and bobbing in and out. He could swap punches with anybody, but there was no such foolish thing as fair play in Kelly's fighting, which was rough and tumble. He used his fists, but also his feet and his thumbs and even his teeth when he had a chance. Or any weapon lying around handy. He wanted to get his hands on John. He couldn't quite do that yet. John was too fast for him. But he'd get his chance. Kelly knew what he was about. He was as angry as was John, but he was cool, which John was not. His pig eyes narrowed, awaiting the end of this first flurry. John had

no conscious thought of this, though instinctively he kept away and
avoided the other's grasping hands. All he knew was the relief at
last of action after bafflement. Into each of his tiger-quick blows he
threw all the pent-up exasperations of the morning.

The crew of the Sea Imp, who at once swarmed to the rail of the
barge, estimated the situation well enough. They shouted to John,
trying to advise. "Keep away from him! If he gets his hands on you
he'll break you in two! Get off the float! Make a run for it!" they
besought John urgently. "Get him up on the wharf! Make him follow you up on the wharf where there's room!" Room: that's what
John's style of fighting needed against a man like Kelly. They saw
that. For Christ's sake, man, use some sense! They were for John,
to a man; and they saw that John hadn't a chance—they thought;
but it would not occur to them to interfere. That wouldn't do at
all. A man must do his own fighting. John heard nothing: he was
not even aware of their existence. They saw this and resigned themselves rather glumly to what seemed to them must be the inevitable
outcome.

The finish did not long delay. Kelly's hairy hand darted up to
clip John's left wrist. For the first time he uttered a sound, a grunt
of satisfaction. The audience groaned.

The sheer pressure of the man's steel grip startled John into realization of his predicament. He brought his right fist across with all
his force. He felt the hard impact to his shoulder. Kelly grinned.

"Try again," he sneered.

He held John's wrist immovable and thrust his face forward in-
vitingly, sure now, pausing for a moment's indulgence. This was his
mistake.

"You would, would you," muttered John. He did not repeat the
blow. Fair play—as John knew it—had had its chance. He kicked
Kelly's shinbone as hard as he could, wrenched his wrist free as the
latter winced. His flash of panic as he had realized the man's enormous strength gave place to a wild, blind rage. He rushed in recklessly, hitting with both hands.

Up to now Kelly had stood in his tracks. The sheer impetus of the

attack forced him to give ground. His heels came against the low
stringer of the float. He toppled backward into the water. John narrowly escaped following. He caught himself back with a wrench,
dropped to his knees, leaning out, eager as a terrier at a rat hole,
waiting for Kelly to come to the surface. When he did, sputtering
and thrashing wildly, grasping for the edge of the float, John
promptly thrust his head under. And again. And yet a third time.

Someone had hold of his arm, was shaking it. Someone was saying
something to him. He was dimly aware of arms extended on either
side of him toward Kelly, who was thrashing on the surface. John
came to consciousness of his surroundings as a man comes out of a
dense fog.

"Easy, man, easy!" the voice was repeating next to his ear. "You
don't want to kill him!"

John rose to his feet and shook himself like a dog, as though it had
been he, and not Pirate Kelly, who had been in the water. The float
seemed full of people, and more were coming toward the ramp
from various parts of the cannery. As yet they were to John a mere
confusion, just people; but now he saw Sally. She was among them,
looking anxious and pushing a way through the men, trying to see
what had caused all this excitement at the float. John waved a hand
at her. She saw him and slowed at once, her anxiety relieved. Some
accident to someone on the Sea Imp, she supposed.

John drew a deep breath and looked about him. The man who had
hold of his arm he now saw to be Nelson Cole. Some of the crew
had hauled Kelly's bulky form over the edge of the float. They
dumped him down unceremoniously and left him to his own re-
covery. He lay there gasping, unable as yet to do more than try to
get his breath back. For the moment nobody paid him any attention. Cole still retained his grasp on John's arm.

"What's this about?" Cole was demanding. "I'll have no brawling."

"He started it," said John. "A man has to defend himself."

"That's right, sir—Kelly hit him first," came an eager burst of
corroboration. Seemingly every man on the float had been a per-

sonal eyewitness of the whole affair. John looked up, startled, for as he recalled it there had not been a man in sight when Kelly delivered that kick at his groin. Indeed, so patently absurd was this unanimity that even Cole smiled grimly.

Kelly struggled to his feet. He had recovered his breath. He lurched toward them cursing.

"Shut up," said Cole. He did not look around. "See this man gets off the premises—and stays off," he ordered, to no one in particular. He released John's arm. "Now as for you——" he began. "This is no place for you, ma'am," he interrupted himself. It was Sally, who had managed a way for herself through the crowd. She paid him no attention.

"What is it, John?" She was all anxiety again. "What's happened?"

"Nothing serious. Just a little argument with our friend Kelly. All over now." This from John.

"Are you hurt? Did he hurt you?" She had eyes only for him.

"Not one little bit," said John cheerfully. "My wife," he explained to Cole. "We live on this boat," he explained further. "I'm Murdock—in the machine shop," he reminded.

Cole looked briefly at Sally, but he made no other acknowledgment nor did he sweeten his manner.

"I don't care who you are," he said bluntly. "I tolerate no fighting on cannery premises." He turned on the men grouped silently. "Did any of you eyewitnesses actually see this row start?" he demanded with some sarcasm.

But, contrary to his expectation, one man spoke up.

"I did, sir," said he.

This, it developed, was the one who had handled the mooring lines. Cole listened to his testimony.

"All right," he grunted when he had heard. He turned on the crowd. "Now get back to work, the lot of you." He addressed himself again to John. "I'm not asking what it's all about," said he. "Fights don't start on nothing. But let it go at that. But I want no more trouble around here."

"John's no troublemaker!" spoke up Sally with spirit.

Cole looked at her again, and the wrinkles at the corners of his eyes deepened.

"No ma'am," he agreed, "I hope not."

"But if that man comes back—you can't expect . . ." continued Sally, undaunted.

"He won't," said Cole.

"I don't see how you can say that. And if he does——"

"Do you see, over there, where the street comes down from the town, just by the store building?" Cole turned her about gently to face the shore. "Well, that marks the limit of what I call the cannery property; and that's the only way—except by water—that anybody can get into the cannery property. Nobody's coming down that, day or night, without I want they should do so. I have men hired just to see to that. I don't want Kelly back here, and I'll see that he don't come back. As long as you're here you're safe from being bothered any more by Kelly. Satisfied?" He relinquished his grasp of her shoulder with a final reassuring pat.

Sally nodded, but she was not wholly satisfied. Cole turned away.

"Now," began Sally to John, "what in the world——"

But John interrupted her.

"Just a minute. I've got to speak to Cole. Tell you when I get back."

He hurried after Cole's brisk figure. Sally looked after him helplessly, vexed and puzzled. She saw John catch up. Cole slowed his steps. They strolled together up the ramp.

"Well!" said Sally. She sat on the rail of the Tillicum to wait, but after a few moments, as the two men showed no signs of separating, she went slowly down the companion into the cabin and began to light the galley fire.

"Drat these men!" said Sally to herself, half humorously, half ruefully. "Why must all male critters be such idiots!" She was impatient over the delay, for she was alive with curiosity and speculation. What was it all about? What had made John so mad? She had never seen him like that. Annoyed, irritated, indignant, even outraged—she remembered that time she had sent for the police—lord, how green she was then in men's ways!—but never crazy, fighting mad, as he had been just now. What could Kelly have done to make him so mad? She remembered the kidnaping. Had he found out that John had known something about that? But how could he? And what about the kidnaping, anyway? Why had Kelly shown up here? Why couldn't John come back? She thrust her head out of the hatch for a look. The two men were seated on pile heads, up on the wharf. John was swinging his leg and chewing a sliver. She had a notion to call to him to hurry up, but thought better of it. This was no time to stir up the animals!

John hurried to catch up with Cole. He was still breathing a little quickly.

"I'd like a word," he told the cannery man, at the same time jerking his head backward in caution toward Sally. Cole nodded. They mounted the ramp in silence to the level of the wharf. There they stopped.

"Well?" said Cole.

"This ain't settled yet, not by a damn sight, you know!" said John.

"I've got nothing to do with that," disclaimed Cole. "I'm interested only in cannery property. I'll have no trouble there. That's the best I can do."

John's eyes blazed.

"The best you can do!" he burst out. "Say, do you think that I'm asking you to——"

"What are you asking?" asked Cole.

John checked himself with an effort.

"I'm not dodging Kelly," he stated emphatically. "What I'm trying to tell you is that this town's too small for the two of us. One's got to go, and I don't intend it's going to be me. Got that straight?"

Cole seemed faintly amused.

"I've got that," said he. "What *are* you asking?" he repeated his question.

"This bum is a dirty fighter," stated John bluntly. "I know that. Where I come from I'd know what to expect. But I'm new here. I had a notion you might give me a steer."

"What kind of a steer?" Cole asked curiously. Here was a type new to him.

"I know Kelly's kicked and slugged them around up here until he's got everybody buffaloed. But how far does he go? Is he a killer? That's what I want to know."

Cole's grim sense of humor was tickled.

"Don't worry," he replied dryly, "he'll kill you quick enough."

"Thanks." John actually looked as though the information had eased his mind. Certainly it calmed him from the last traces of excitement. He plucked a sliver from a pile head and thrust it in the corner of his mouth. "In my country that bum wouldn't last a week," he proffered almost casually.

Cole began to feel a stir of uneasiness. As long as this young man had spoken quickly out of anger and excitement Cole had viewed the affair with sardonic detachment. He had seen many men angry and excited from fighting. He understood them and could guess what they would do. But back of this quiet, deliberate, almost humorous drawl was something from a life outside his experience, that he did not understand, but whose deadliness he sensed. The hands-off idea was all very well—up to a certain point!

"Hold on!" he cried. "You can't set out deliberately to shoot a man! At first I thought this was not my business, but I can't have that! In a way I'm responsible around here. I'd have to stop that!"

"Yes?" John's voice was low, but his words had edge. "How do you figure on doing that?"

He looked down at Cole from his greater height, and Cole could not fight off an impression of dominance, which was a curious feeling in an employer, and especially in Nelson Cole.

"Look here, Mr Cole," John went on, after a moment, almost indulgently, "this is *not* your business. Stop and think. If I know Kelly, he's bragging right now that I don't dare stick my nose in town, and if I do, what he's going to do about it. I aim to live in this country, Mr Cole, and I don't aim to go around dodging Kelly all the rest of my life. And"—a snap came into his voice—"I don't aim to go around being pointed out as one more man Kelly has buffaloed, like these other jack rabbits up here," he drawled with faint contempt. "And get this through your head," he continued presently. "I ain't got the slightest idea of going gunning for Kelly! I don't have to. I'm not out after trouble, but I've got to call his bluff. So what I aim to do is to walk quietly and peaceably up to Mahoney's about suppertime and buy a drink and walk back again. And I'll take it kindly of you if you'll pass that news around."

"I tell you the man will murder you!" protested Cole.

"There'll be no killing," John assured him quietly.

"For God's sake, man, talk sense!" Cole was jolted into exasperation. "He'll pot you from behind a door or out of a window. What chance have you then?"

"He won't," said John.

"I'd like to know how you'd keep him from it!" cried Cole disgustedly.

"Every man's got his ways and tricks," said John with finality.

Cole looked at the grim straight line of his mouth.

"I don't like it," he said grudgingly, but more to his conscience than to John. An unholy curiosity was commencing to stir in his vitals. Here might be a show worth seeing. He'd be at Mahoney's!

John sensed the yielding. He laid his hand on Cole's arm.

"There'll be no killing," he repeated. "I'll guarantee it."

"Humph!" Cole uttered a short vexed bark. "Who'd I collect from?"

Sally heard John's returning steps on the float and came eagerly on deck to hear about it. No, he reassured her again, he was *not* hurt; and as for what Kelly was doing here and the reason for the fight and all the rest of her tumbling questions: "Why, he'd come down to try to buy the boat back, and when I wouldn't sell he got mad and took a kick at me, and then, of course, we went to it." As he told it, in bare statement, that did not make sense to Sally, and she said so.

"Sure it wasn't something to do with that kidnaping business?" she suggested doubtfully.

"How could it be?" John's look of surprise was genuine.

"Well . . ." Sally was vague. "Len wrote the police. . . ."

"No." John brushed this aside. "He wanted the boat pretty bad. Y'd like to know what he's got up his sleeve this time."

"You've been spoiling for a fight all the morning," surmised Sally shrewdly. John did not meet or deny the implication. "Well, I hope you've got it out of your system—both of you. Aren't you coming below? It wouldn't hurt you to straighten yourself up a little."

"I'll be right on down," said John. He seated himself atop the deckhouse and began to roll a brown-paper cigarette, cowboy fashion, with the fingers of one hand. Sally paused a moment to admire this. Its dexterity always fascinated her. Then she disappeared down the hatch. "Dinner 'll be ready in ten-fifteen minutes," she called back. "You clam!" she added half vexedly, half humorously, in reference to his masculine brevity of narration.

John smoked his cigarette and kept his eye on the viaduct from the cannery to the town. He was taking no chances. But, apparently, neither was Nelson Cole. Presently a man, whom John recognized as one of the winter caretakers, took his place on a stump at the foot of the broad rise. Satisfied, John flipped his cigarette overboard and went below. Sally was in the galley, but heard him.

"You can get down the table as soon as you've brushed up," she called.

"All right," said John.

But he made no move to do either. He knelt and pulled open the locker drawer beneath his bunk, in which he rummaged. Presently he laid hands on what he wanted. He closed the drawer and seated himself on the bunk. He drew from its holster a heavy Colt revolver. It was thick with protective grease, for John had laid it away a long time back. He laid it down carefully and went to the galley door.

"Let me have a piece of clean flour sack?" he asked of Sally.

He returned to the bunk and set himself to wipe off the grease. This was quite a task, and John was carefully methodical, searching out every corner and crevice in the mechanism. He had to remove the cylinder to get at the bore, for this was an old model, the original—and historical—single-action .45 that had been nicknamed the "Peacemaker." He reassembled it and tried the strength of the mainspring, cocking and uncocking the hammer, listening critically to the click of the gears. He held the hammer halfway back and twirled the cylinder. It ran freely. He was satisfied. Not much to look at: the original bluing was almost worn away, and the wooden side plates of its handle were scarred and chipped; but its bore was as bright and its mechanism as true as ever. A good gun. He wouldn't have traded it for a new one, double action and all. He knew it: he was used to it. He'd carried that gun since he was a kid. He folded his fingers almost lovingly about the butt, sensing delicately its familiar balance. He had himself carved the wood just to fit. His eyes unfocused: all his perceptions were in the feel of his fingers.

He thought of old Wong, the Chinese cook, at Carstair's ranch, whence he had quit his first job for no reason at all except restlessness. It was old Wong who had given him this gun, again for no reason at all, except that he must have liked something about that kid. John had not thought of Wong for years. But he had had a soft spot for Chinamen ever since. Why! he recalled, a Chink had been the occasion for his first serious use of the gun! That had happened so much later that the poetic justice of it had not occurred to him until this moment. Those "Cousin Jacks"* bedeviling that forlorn little laundryman! He smiled now rather tenderly at the angry but half-scared kid, lugging out that young cannon in face of the brutish Welsh miners, and the mixture of surprise and gratification and relief when the assiduously practiced "draw" worked so smoothly, and the "Cousin Jacks" had wilted. He'd never had any use for mines or miners. That was the reason; but he had not known that either until now. He drifted on through the past, he and this old gun in the hollow of his hand. He had not visited those years for a long time. The present had him so wholly that it was as though they were the years of another life, and he had died from it, and they no longer concerned him because he had become a different person entirely who belonged to the present. But as he sat there on the edge of the bunk, balancing the old Colt .45, gradually the past reclaimed him.

*Welshmen.

Here was no longer the John Murdock Sally knew, but the Trigger Jack the Great Basin had known, hard, wary, solitary, competent, sometimes dangerous. His very appearance changed. His eyes narrowed, his brow drew into an intent frown, the line of his mouth thinned and straightened.

Sally, at the galley door, gasped as though someone had thrown cold water in her face. In the place of her teasing, dancing-eyed John she saw a grim-faced stranger. A stranger with a gun! She had dismissed the whole episode as over and done with. For a moment her heart sank, but instantly she rallied.

"That won't do!" she heard herself saying with decision.

The stranger looked up swiftly, but with the very motion of his head the strangeness vanished, and it was her accustomed John who was eyeing her small determined figure with quizzical amusement.

"What won't do?"

She checked at the easy good-natured tolerance in his voice. Was she jumping too fast to conclusion? Going off half cocked, as John called it? Doing the tragedy queen over nothing? John's attitude seemed to imply so. He was making fun of her.

"What are you doing with that thing?" she demanded nevertheless. "You haven't looked at it for months."

"Oh, that?" John examined the revolver with a faint air of surprise, as if he had not seen it until this moment. "Cleaning it. Why?" He made innocent wide eyes at her, but modified his tone to her impatient movement. "No sense in not being heeled," said he. He looked at her more closely. "Good lord! You didn't think this thing was over and settled, did you? I believe you did!" His voice was incredulous.

"There's no sense to it!" cried Sally indignantly. "Two grown men mauling each other over nothing, like small boys squabbling in the street! That's bad enough. But this!"

John was now laughing at her openly.

"The fighting blood of the Slocums!" he cheered her on. "Sic 'em, Sally! Quite a scrapper yourself!"

Sally flushed. He was trying to tease her. But this was no matter for teasing. It was serious, or at any rate it might easily become so. It was time to put a stop to it.

"You put that thing away," she ordered with decision.

"And how about Kelly?" asked John. He shook his head. "No, thanks."

"John Murdock," Sally summoned all her forces, "if you think I'm going to stand by and allow you deliberately to make yourself a——" She stopped. She could not add the word.

John stared at her. He whistled. Then he chuckled.

"So that's what's biting you!" he cried. "Well, keep your shirt on. I haven't the slightest idea in the world of going gunning for Kelly. For the love of Mike, what would I want to do that for?"

"Then why . . . ?" Sally was unconvinced.

John glanced down at the weapon.

"Oh, that!" said he. "Well, that's just a persuader for him to keep his hands off me. He's strong as a gorilla. I don't aim to let that happen again. Don't you fret; he understands that argument. And it's the only one he does understand. There won't be any trouble."

Sally drew a deep breath. It might be. But . . .

"Why can't you just keep away from him entirely?" she begged, but without conviction. "You haven't any particular business to take you uptown."

John looked up in blank wonder.

"Why, Sally," he reproached her gently, "you wouldn't like for me to do that!"

Her cheeks reddened at the disappointment in his voice. No, she wouldn't like for him to do that. Dodging an issue was not her way, either. It could not be, with her background of inheritance.

"And, anyway," John was continuing, "I don't aim to go roaming around promiscuous looking for it. But I got to show once, anyway."

Sally hesitated. Perhaps she was making too much of it, she forced herself to believe. Perhaps John was right: there would be no trouble. Unless . . .

"Suppose he has a gun, too?" She had to get rid of that haunting thought from the bottom of her mind.

John snorted.

"He won't use it. I'll just beat him to it," he explained when he saw she did not comprehend.

"But suppose——" continued Sally doubtfully.

"Suppose nothing!" John's scorn was final. "That clumsy drunken bum!"

His confidence in himself was so complete and at the same time so matter of fact that, for the moment at least, it diminished the whole situation to a commonplace. Sally bit her lip.

"I expect you're hungry," she said after a moment.

"I could eat," agreed John. He arose from the bunk and began to unlatch the folding table from the bulkhead.

After the meal—of which Sally ate little—John returned to the weapon. Sally, clearing up in the galley, looked in on him from time to time. It was hard to hold herself steady and not think of possibilities, and the sight of John reassured her. He was at the moment removing the wooden side plates to the grip in order to get at the mainspring. His head was bent over the small screw driver. He was half humming, half whistling between his teeth, very intent in what he was doing, but apparently without a care in the world. By the time she had finished the dishes he had laid the gun aside and was pushing the cartridges one by one from their loops in the leather belt. He sensed her in the doorway.

"Finished?" he muttered without looking up.

"Pretty near. All but wiping up."

"I'll wipe up. I wish you'd do something for me."

Sally took off her apron.

"I wish you'd just run up to the store and get me a box of Colt .45s. These things are all verdigris."

"Colt .45s," Sally repeated to show she had it correctly.

"That's right. I'd go myself, but I don't like to show up in town just yet."

Returning to the boat from this errand, she paused to look down the hatch at John. He had strapped the cartridge belt loosely around his waist, she saw, and had slipped the revolver into its holster. At the moment she first caught sight of him he was standing beneath the hatch opening, which was the only place in the cabin that gave him head room. His body was relaxed; his arms hung loosely at his side; his head was bent thoughtfully; he seemed to be half asleep. So lost was he that apparently he had not heard Sally come aboard. She said nothing, stopping for the moment to admire him, to indulge the little upsurge of love for him and pride in him that always choked her throat when she caught him, as now, off guard. Silly that, to feel the tears rise, she did not know why—— Her tender musing was broken as by a clash of cymbals. There was no warning, no smallest shift of position, no preliminary tension, at least that she had discerned. But there he stood, his head up, his whole body taut and alert, in his half-extended hand the leveled Colt revolver. And his face was again the face of the grim, hard, tight-lipped stranger.

It was amazing, incredible. Her startled faculties recalled no hesitation. She thought she had not seen him move.

For an instant only he held the pose. Then the stranger faded. His form slackened. He dropped the Colt .45 into the holster and reassumed the posture of relaxed detachment in which she had discovered him.

She crouched, fascinated, while again and again, over and over, he repeated the maneuver. Now that she was watching with attention she could follow his hand. The transformation was no longer a magic, but not the less amazing. The movement was as smooth and swift and sure as the flash of a lightning stroke, as the strike of a rattlesnake. Sally had never seen a good stage juggler of any kind, so she had no conception of the ultimate dexterities possible to practice and training. She thought this the most wonderful thing she had ever seen. She was amazed and, at the same time, enormously comforted and reassured. John's words returned to her mind, and she repeated them, re-echoing his scorn—"clumsy drunken bum"—I should think so!

But John did not seem satisfied. He shook his head, muttering to himself, apparently casting about in his mind. At length his brow cleared.

"I think I've got it, Sally," he said. So he had known all the time that she was there! He gave no other indication of it, however, but came on deck and disappeared down the cargo hatch without a glance at her. After a while he reappeared carrying the high-heeled, soft-leather cowboy boots he had packed away when he and Sally had quit horses for the Washington forests, but to the possession of which he had obstinately clung. He descended to the cabin again, kicked off the low elastic-sided fisherman's slippers he had worn on the boat and drew on the boots. Then he once more went through the motions of the "draw."

"That's it!" he cried, pleased.

He tossed the revolver to the bunk and sat down beside it.

"Come on down!" he called. His intent preoccupation was over. "Did you get them? That's good!" He took the package and laid it beside the gun. He held his foot sidewise, admiring the boots. They were very fancy boots, with much silver and silk embroidery on the soft-leather uppers. John laughed at them amusedly.

"Damn-fool kid! Must have thought considerable of myself when I blew myself to them," he observed. "Never thought they'd come in handy again. It's the heels," he explained chattily to Sally. "I knew there was something wrong, but I couldn't figure it. Felt off balance somehow. Needed the high heels." He got up and stamped his feet contentedly. "Now I feel natural!" said he. He picked up the gun and almost carelessly flashed it again into position.

Sally's eyes glowed. In this moment she showed all John's superb confidence.

"John, I think you're wonderful!" she breathed.

"Keno." John laughed at her. "Take you all this time to find that out?"

He spent the afternoon going over the boat and her rigging. "Do you realize," he observed to Sally, "how long we've been here already, and I actually haven't had a minute until now? And after so long a voyage up the coast—got to have things shipshape for when we start out again." He sat crosslegged next the shroud and worked at the seizing of the deadeye lanyards and talked to Sally over his shoulder. "Stay here?" He looked around at her question. "Haven't any idea of doing that, have you? Oh yes, for a while maybe. But we certainly want to see more of Alaska than this before we light!" He finished the deadeye and moved to the fantail, where he squatted down to examine the jigger's rigging. "When Len gets back, and we finish up that job, then we'll see." He chatted on at random or whistled cheerfully as he worked. Apparently, after making his preparations, he had dismissed the whole Kelly business from his mind as too trivial to bother about further at the moment. Sally stayed near him. Once in a while she handed him something which, by making a long arm, he could quite well have reached himself, and so preserved the fiction that she was helping. As long as she was with him she was all right. Bad hour coming, she knew, when she was to be alone and waiting; but even that thought she thrust resolutely below hatches. Time enough then to summon the Slocum pioneer spirit, she told herself, with a flash of rueful humor, as she battened down her mind.

The whistle blew at the engine house. John looked at his watch. "Most time to call it a day," said he; but he continued his tinkering for a half-hour longer. Then he got to his feet and stood for a moment flexing the muscles of his long legs. "Gives a man the kinks, doubled up that way," he remarked. He looked down the deck. "Done pretty well. I can finish up in the morning."

Curiously the last words shot a pang through Sally's heart. In the morning . . .

She ousted the implication indignantly and refused to look at it again, but she felt it thrusting for admission and knew that the bad hour had begun, and she could no longer avoid it. So she set her resolution to face it and get it over.

"I suppose now you'll be going uptown," she said steadily.

"Keno," said John. He stopped in his gathering up of the materials he had been using. For a moment Sally feared he was going to joke or say something too serious. If he had done either, she might have broken down and boohooed. However, as respects Sally, John's instincts were true. He said nothing. But his eyes spoke plainly of pride in her; and in a flash she realized that his detachment had been only apparent, and that his thoughts had held her all along, worrying a little about her; and a great rush of thankfulness lifted her that she had measured up. This, too, John must have sensed. He chuckled delightedly.

"Pretty nice to be the same breed of cats," said he.

He went below. Sally waited on deck. Presently he climbed out of the cabin, wearing the belt and holster. He grinned at her. She smiled at him. Now don't be a silly fool, Sally kept telling herself sternly. Same breed of cats—she clung to that.

"But you *will* be careful, won't you?" She could not help that.

"Oh, sure!" said John. "Consider it done."

He walked briskly down the float and up the ramp and so to the slope of the viaduct leading into the town. There he waved his hand. Sally waved back. She kept her eyes on the top of the rise until he had disappeared, then she buried her face in her hands.

John stopped for a moment at the top of the viaduct to look down the street. It was empty, except for the usual malemutes sprawled lazily about. After the moment he moved on. He walked now more slowly. His glance searched quickly in all directions. Two lines of concentration deepened between his eyes, and the muscles of his face and the line of his mouth hardened.

Outside the door of Mush Mahoney's saloon he paused. The place was crowded. Mush Mahoney and one bartender stood behind the bar. Opposite them leaned a dozen or so, toying with whisky glasses, but by far the greater number of those present had clustered singly or in groups well across on the opposite side of the room. There they stood in idleness, evidently waiting. John smiled grimly at this. His eyes passed over them rapidly in appraisal, lingering only for a moment as he recognized Nelson Cole. Finally he located the man for whom he sought. Pirate Kelly was there, at the far end of the bar, and with him the two rough-looking customers John had seen that morning in his company. John's scrutiny did not linger on Pirate Kelly, but he examined his companions with care. Then he stepped swiftly into the doorway and stopped.

At sight of him fell a dead silence. For a second no one moved. Then one by one the drinkers melted unobtrusively away into the crowd across the room. Only Kelly and his two companions were left at the bar. Presently, under John's stare, the latter also fell back. Kelly remained alone.

John walked down the room until he stood facing Kelly, and about ten feet distant from him. He held his hands ostentatiously away from the revolver at his side.

"Well, Kelly!" said John.

His whole attitude made it evident that he was giving the man a chance to declare himself. But if this was indeed a challenge it was not accepted. Kelly merely glared murderously, but made no movement toward the revolver at his belt.

The room held its breath in a frozen immobility. Mush Mahoney moved to spread his shirt-sleeved elbows on the bar. He rested his chin on his clasped hands, watching both men with the detached interest of the connoisseur.

For perhaps twenty seconds the two men eyed each other. Then John uttered a short contemptuous laugh and turned his shoulder to Kelly.

"Give me a drink," he said to Mahoney.

An audible gasp went up from the crowd.

"You goddam fool!" growled Mahoney in abysmal disgust.

John slowly turned back to look down the barrel of a revolver into Kelly's eyes, blazing with ferocious triumph.

"Now," Kelly ripped out a string of descriptive oaths, "I've got you where I want you. And I'd like to see you wiggle out of it this time." His voice fell soft. "It's Kelly you're dealin' wid, if you hadn't heard; and in just about ten seconds I'm goin' to pull this trigger and send you to hell. How do you like that, me bucko?"

He leered at John, gloating. John made no reply, nor moved a muscle, but stood there, body relaxed, hands hanging loosely at his side, gazing reflectively, almost absently, into Kelly's face. The latter congested with blood.

"You think I won't do it!" he snarled. "Well, don't ye——"

The words were cut short by the roar of an explosion and the splintering of glass. In the confined space the concussion was shattering. To a man the bystanders leaped convulsively. They had tuned to it, for they knew Kelly's murderous nature; nevertheless it caught them unprepared. And they were most certainly unprepared for what they saw. There John still stood, erect and unharmed. Their immediately previous impression of him had been of relaxed, almost lazy indifference. Now he was back against the bar, pistol half extended, every muscle strung. It was amazing. No one had seen him move, largely because nothing about him had suggested movement. So startling was the mere fact of this transition that for the space of a short breath all eyes were on John. Then they swung to Kelly. Kelly, too, was still afoot. He stood there, swaying slightly, staring in blank incredulity. His right arm hung limp, and from the ends of his fingers blood began to drip, at first slowly, but in increasing volume. His revolver lay on the floor. At the far end of the room lay a heap of broken glass where the bullet had ended its flight.

John's eyes darted here and there about the room. They came to rest on Kelly's two companions.

"Anybody else?" His voice snapped like a whip.

"If there is . . ." spoke up Mush Mahoney unexpectedly at his elbow.

John flashed sidewise a brief and somewhat startled glance. Mahoney still leaned against the bar, but he had dropped his hands from his chin. They rested now, idly, flat on the polished top of the bar, and between them lay a convincing-looking bulldog revolver.

For perhaps ten seconds a dead heavy silence. John took a step forward to face Kelly squarely.

"You've run a blazer around here long enough," said he crisply. "It's called."

He held Kelly a contemptuous moment with his eye. The two

might have been alone together. So still was the room that now the steady drip from Kelly's wounded arm was distinctly audible.

"If this man has any friends they'd better take care of him." John broke the spell. Then, as no one moved, he indicated pointedly the two who had been drinking with Kelly, "I mean you," he specified. "Take him away. Step out!" he ordered curtly as they hesitated. He watched the three out the door and at last slipped the Colt .45 back into its holster. "Now, Mahoney, I'll have that drink," said he.

The room broke into uproar. John was surrounded. Men bawled at him, pounded him on the back, crowding to get near enough to grasp his hand. They shouted at one another, red faced, excited, trying to vent their amazement. "Never saw anything so quick in my life!" "*Didn't* see it, nobody could see it!" "God, I thought sure he was a goner, and then——" "Reckon Kelly's got his bellyful at last!" They were exultant at the downfall of Kelly, punching one another in congratulation, each as proud as though he had done this feat himself! John was a hero. Everybody wanted to buy him a drink. He was pushed and shoved about. He grinned and protested. No one could hear him. A dozen men clamored at Mush Mahoney and his bartender, insisting that they give John a drink. Mush Mahoney at last put a stop to the dispute.

"It's on the house!" he roared, pounding the bar with the butt of his pistol.

John managed to shake himself free.

"Thanks, boys, thanks!" He raised his glass. "Here's how! No, I can't. Not now. Another time." He would not yield. No, it was nothing. Anybody could have called that bum's bluff.

"Yeah—from now on," growled Mahoney. "Have another!" He motioned his bartender to refill the glasses, helping John's escape.

Out the door at last, John spread his arms and drew a deep breath. For all his confidence, this thing had been a good deal of a strain. He felt tired, let down. And there was Sally, waiting . . .

He snapped his fingers in sudden recollection and turned back. After a little he managed to catch Mush Mahoney's eye across the milling hubbub. Mahoney slipped around the end of the bar to him, and the two drew aside and out of sight.

"I just remembered," said John to him, "I promised that fellow, Chilkat Harry, I'd take care of his dog for him while he's gone."

"Yeah," agreed Mahoney. "He spoke to me about it."

Without further speech he led the way around the corner into the planked narrow alley between the buildings. There an outside staircase ascended to a door in the second story.

"Harry's room." Mahoney motioned with his head.

They climbed the staircase. On the platform at its top lay the dog, Chilkat. He raised his head and looked at them, and the corners of his lips lifted slightly.

"Come on, old boy," John invited.

Chilkat gave no sign that he had heard. He continued to gaze at them from a guarded neutrality. John tried again. He cajoled, commanded, even experimented with mild threat.

"He don't know you," said Mahoney. "He's funny that way."

They contemplated the beast in perplexity. Then Mush had an idea.

"He knows your wife," he suggested. "I seen him following her around." They returned to the street. Mahoney turned in at the saloon door. "I take back that damn fool," was his only comment on the previous episode as they parted.

John quickened his pace. By the strength of his own reaction he began to appreciate Sally's courage at its true value. He was proud of Sally.

He heard himself hailed and recognized Nelson Cole's voice behind him, but he did not answer nor turn his head. Cole had caught up and was trotting along at his elbow, trying to match his long strides. John was being cursed heartily and fluently by Cole for some reason he did not bother to understand and in words he did not bother to hear. He had no time for Cole. He must get to Sally.

Where the viaduct to the cannery grounds began, he could look down and across to the Tillicum. Sally was there, on deck. She saw him instantly. John realized she must have been watching just this spot ever since he had here disappeared from her view. He waved his hand in a wide semaphore circle of reassurance, then, remembering the dog, swept a horizontal circle of beckoning. He watched until he saw she understood.

"Were you saying something?" he then asked mildly of Cole.

"Saying something!" Cole echoed in disgust.

"Sorry, I didn't hear."

"Just as well," said Cole wryly. "I was blowing off steam. I ain't often scared, and I don't like it. God damn it, boy," his voice rose again, "don't you know better than to turn your back on a man like Kelly? You ought to have a nursemaid."

"But I had to," said John. "He wouldn't draw until I did. I gave him every chance to. You could see that for yourself."

Cole stared at him, dumfounded.

"For Christ's sake!" he almost whispered. "You mean to say you did it apurpose?"

"Sure!"

"But—but *why?*" Cole had not recovered.

"I told you. So's he'd make the first move," John repeated with an air of patience. "That's sense. I wasn't out to pick no fight," he added quaintly. But Cole was in no frame of mind to see the humor of this.

"You crazy fool!" he exploded in exasperation. "It gave him the cold, dead drop on you. Is that sense?"

John glanced toward the wharves in search of Sally's small hurrying figure. She had a long way around to go yet. He half perched on the viaduct rail and swung one leg.

"Let me give you a tip, Mr Cole," said he. "When a man's got the drop on you, you just watch his eyes. No man alive can keep strung up top-notch steady for very long. You watch his eyes. Sooner or later they're going to flicker. When they flicker, *you get him.*" He spoke reflectively, with the calm competence of authority. Cole looked at him with something like awe, which was a new sensation for Cole, as respects his fellow man. "I knew what I was about," added John presently.

"That's taking an awful chance—unnecessarily!" Cole's exasperation returned in the last word.

"No chance at all!" defended John, roused to a little indignation on his own behalf. "Especially with that bird. He's slow as molasses. No," he fell back to his slow drawl. "Unless a man starts shootin' right off, chances are you can take him—if you know your business."

Cole pounced on this.

"Exactly!" he cried. "And what was keeping him from shooting you in the back?"

"Why, he was," answered John tranquilly.

"I guess I'm crazy," said Cole.

"Listen here, Mr Cole." John came down from the railing and stood on his two feet in order to tackle the unaccustomed job of analysis. "Just figure your man. Here's this Kelly. He's buffaloed everybody up and down the coast so long he's got the notion that he's the old he-coon, and nobody's got a right to look cross-eyed at him, and he can lick the world, and all that stuff. He's all puffed up with it, and he's kind of sensitive on the subject. That right?"

"Proceed." Cole was listening attentively.

"Well, what happens? He takes me on, and he has a little bad luck. That's what it was," admitted John frankly. "He gets licked— or it looks like it—in front of a lot of men. So he's out to kill the man who did it." He glanced aside to see how near was Sally. She was threading her way through piles of nets on the cannery platform. He perched again on the railing. "That's to get even. But Kelly's a grandstand player," continued John, hurrying his words a little. "Sticks out all over him. Wouldn't satisfy him just to shoot me. *He'd want me to know when he's going to do it*. That's why I was sartin he wouldn't shoot me in the back. I wasn't such a dam' fool as you think," John defended himself almost plaintively. "I figgered it out."

"I'd hate to gamble on that sort of figuring!"

"It wasn't a gamble," John protested. "It was a sure thing. I've run against these birds before. They're all alike. They just *got* to strut. I forgot to tell you," he brightened as he recalled something overlooked in his argument, "I got a good line on him in our scrap this morning. He got his hands on me, and I don't mind telling you I thought I was a gone goose. He's got a grip like a bear trap. And I would have been if he'd gone right on from there. But no, he had to stop and enjoy it. That gave me a chance. So I had him pegged. Just size up your man and figger things out," concluded John.

"By God!" breathed Cole, and then again, "By God!" He could not take his eyes off John, as though he were incredulous of John's reality. John was looking toward the far end of the viaduct for Sally to appear. "You're a cool customer, Murdock." He knew better than to ask questions. This, too, was a frontier, and Cole knew its etiquette. But he was enormously curious. "You must have had a lot of experience," he allowed himself to suggest.

"Oh, I've roamed," said John indifferently. His face lighted, and he hopped down from the rail. "There's my wife!" said he and left Cole without ceremony and went with long strides down the planked viaduct to meet Sally.

She came to him with a little rush, breathless with hurrying.

"Are you all right? What happened?" Her eyes searched his face.

"Sure, I'm all right." He grinned at her with tender mockery. "Can't you see me?"

"What happened? Was there any trouble? Was he there?"

They were together now. She had seized his arm in both her hands. He squeezed them to his side and held them there.

"He showed up," said John. "But don't fret, he won't bother us any more."

"You didn't—— Oh, John!"

"Had to wing him a little," admitted John. "He got mean and pulled his gun. Couldn't help it. Here, here!" he cried in alarm. "There! That's better. I just busted an arm on him, that's all." He looked down at her head against his arm. "Nothing to it," said he. "I think you done darn well—feel a little that way myself."

Somehow the admission steadied her. Surreptitiously she wiped her eyes.

"I can't help thinking," she half apologized. "Suppose that he——"

"Not in a thousand years!" said John. He held her for a moment.

"Tell me about it," she begged presently.

"There ain't much to tell. Wait till we get home. Right now we got to get that damn dog. You know," as she did not instantly focus on dogs, "we told Harry we'd take care of him."

"Oh, Chilkat!"

"Yeah. He's up back at Mahoney's. He won't come with me. Maybe he will with you. That's why I called you over."

They turned back to the town. Cole had disappeared. The street was still deserted, but the saloon buzzed. Sally looked toward it a little fearfully.

"I didn't hear any shot," said she. It was her first reference to the subject since they had left the viaduct.

"Let's sneak on by," said John.

Chilkat still lay on the platform at the top of the stairs. At sight of Sally he raised his head, and the curve of his tail swept the boards. At her invitation he arose and followed, taking his place at Sally's side, his head pressed close against her thigh.

"Here," said John to Chilkat, "you better get used to me. I'm still one of the family!"

Sally stopped. She patted John's sleeve.

"*Tillicum,* Chilkat," she repeated the form of Harry's introduction.

With some caution John extended his hand. Chilkat sniffed at it deeply. He withdrew his muzzle, wrinkled his nose, ducked his head and sneezed twice. They resumed their journey. Chilkat now walked between them.

PART IV
THE VALLEY

CHAPTER XVI

THE HOLE

LEN AND CHILKAT HARRY returned on the down trip of the Portland. She docked early in the morning, but both men came at once to the float. Len had the new gear for the can machine, all right, but he brushed that aside. He had news. Such important news that he scarcely greeted John and Sally. Chilkat Harry stood one side, acknowledging Chilkat's gentlemanly raptures.

At Juneau, said Len, they had run into a sheriff or a marshal or a federal—or, anyway, some kind of peace officer up from the outside—from Seattle.

"How do you know?" asked John. "Does he advertise?"

Len looked disgusted at the frivolity of that question. John grinned, pleased that his small insult had struck. Anybody could tell a "bull," of course!

"Well, what of him?" asked John.

He'd come down with them as far as Wrangell, Len continued, where he had been met by McClintock. Wrangell, Len shot in parenthetically, was the present seat of what government there was in Alaska; and McClintock was the one and only marshal for the territory. And—unless both Chilkat Harry and Len missed their guess —the two would shortly blow in here at Klakan on the government steam launch. At most any minute.

"Important if true," said John ironically. "But why all the excitement about that?"

This man was looking for Pirate Kelly!

"He won't need to look any further," said John. "He'll find him here."

"So we've just heerd," observed Len dryly. "Point is, they'll find you here, too."

"Me!" John aroused. "Why should they want me? What kind of a country is this? Ain't a man supposed to defend himself?"

"They couldn't possibly know anything about that," cut in Sally swiftly. She caught Chilkat Harry's flash of admiration at her keenness. "What do you mean?" she pressed Len.

Harry intervened across Len's slowness to come to the point. It was the kidnap business. The police were after Kelly on that count. Undercover. Working on a secret tip—he flashed an amused glance toward Len. They'd want John too—as a witness.

"I don't see how I'm mixed up in it," said John.

"No?" Chilkat Harry raised one eyebrow.

Sally was looking reproachfully at Len. Len's leathery cheek flushed.

"I mout have done a little talking that mebbe I ought not to have," he confessed shamefacedly. "Sometimes," he added, "I think I reelly ought not to drink."

At any rate—both men were in emphatic agreement on that point —John had better not be here when the government boat arrived. Not unless he wanted to be taken back to Seattle as a material witness. And kept there God knows how long. Maybe all winter. How'd you like that?

John wouldn't like that at all. He sat revolving the matter in his mind. He'd just got here. There was the boat. And how about Sally?

"But I've never been drove out of a place before," he objected doubtfully.

"Nobody's driving you out now, you touchy little damn fool!"— this from Len. "We can come back, can't we? Just take a cruise around, till this outfit goes south next trip of the Queen, and see something of the country. Wouldn't you like that?" Len had a flash of inspiration and asked this of Sally.

"Like it?" cried she. "Good heavens! You don't know how *bored* I've been!"

Well—John yielded more to her instant kindling than to Len's arguments, which seemed to him a little farfetched. It *would* be fun to see something of the country. They ought to be able to finish up the can machine in three or four days, and then——

"Three or four days!" Len echoed the words in comical despair. "Can't you get it through your head? How long do you think it will take that pair of bulls to comb out Wrangell? And where would they naturally look next, except Klakan? Three or four days! Why, they might be in at any minute! You're going to pull your freight to-day, right now; and if you don't you might as well not go at all, and to hell with you. I quit; go your own gait; I never could get on with a squarehead!" Even Sally had to laugh at Len's vehemence: he was so unlike any Len she had ever seen before, though she agreed with him.

"What about the machine?" said John.

"Damn the machine! To hell with the machine!"

"I'm not going to let Nels Cole down."

"Aw, for Chris' sake!" pleaded Len. "We'll be coming back. We can do it when we get back."

"The Queen don't go south for three weeks," John pointed out.

They sat for a few moments in silence. Len looked completely baffled. Chilkat Harry lounged back against the after bulkhead in amused detachment, idly fondling one of Chilkat's ears between his thumb and forefinger. Sally watched John. She knew the obstinate slant of his jaw, and that this was his affair, and that whatever she could say must be later.

"All right," said Len at last, in a resigned voice. "Dang it, I wanted to go along! I can fix up your dang machine." He turned to John with a new belligerence, as though John had disputed the statement, although John had made no indication that he intended to do anything of the sort. "I know that thing backward and forward and up and down and sideways, just as well as you do, you pusillanimous little whelp, and don't you let me hear a peep out of you to the contrary. Now are you going to get out of here, or ain't you?"

John laughed.

"All right! All right! You win! But I warn you, it's on you if we run on a rock and sink. And"—he was beginning to enjoy himself—"if your friends really want to get hold of me, like you say, they'll come out looking for me with that government launch of theirs. I don't know this country: I don't know where to go. They ought not to have much trouble finding me."

But if he hoped to tease Len he was disappointed.

"Not where Harry's takin' you, they won't," said Len. "He's got a hole over acrost here that most nobody knows."

At this both Sally and John swung in startled inquiry.

"I hope you don't mind," spoke up Harry suavely, before either could speak. "It isn't far. I have a trap line I run there some winters, and a pretty substantial little shack, so I won't be any bother to you. You can be quite independent. And, as Len says, there's hardly a chance in a million of anybody's looking there, except by accident."

"Why, that's mighty kind of you, I'm sure," said John slowly, "but I don't like to feel that just on our account you're——"

"You needn't," Chilkat Harry cut him short. "This proposal is no burst of altruism on my part. It's the long arm of coincidence. It isn't even my own idea. Len, here, pointed out its advantages. It just so happened that I had already arranged to retire for a season to this winter residence of mine. In fact my recent trip to Juneau was to engage a substitute or successor for myself in the establishment of the estimable Mahoney. So you see we are of mutual advantage. You come into possession of a desirable sanctuary: I gain transportation and am spared the necessity of a long row in a heavy pirogue—a prospect to which I have not looked forward with any great pleasure. There is no obligation, I assure you."

He said all this while leaning against the bulkhead, one hand idling over the soft head of the malemute. His tone of lazy indulgence and the precise elaboration of his words brought a faint flush to John's cheek. He had no resentment except against himself. "Gon off half cocked again, you damn fool!" he cursed himself in half-humorous mortification. But Sally was irritated. She stared at Harry with furious eyes that he should dare treat John so. His own met them briefly with the amused, hard, surface mockery that, as always, held her outside and baffled. For an instant the whole situation hung. Then abruptly Chilkat Harry arose to his feet. He clapped John on the shoulder.

"And, anyway, we'll have a good time!" he cried heartily. "You'll like it. Game! Trout! Mountains! Prettiest place you ever saw in your life!" He stretched his arms and flashed down at them a boyish smile. "God, it'll be great to breathe clean air after this stinking hole! How's your shooting eye, John? Wait till you see our deer!"

The man's charm was enormous. John brightened to it instantly. Even Sally felt its power, though deep within her lingered a faint and baffled unease.

The matter was settled. Len showed his relief.

"Sooner you get going the better," he urged.

"I'm ready—after I've seen Cole. I've got to see Cole," said John.

"Make it short," said Harry. "We better catch this tide. I'll run up and get my plunder. Twenty minutes—half an hour."

"How you fixed for grub?" asked Len.

"We'll need some sugar and coffee," said Sally. "That's all. Come on, Len, help me carry them down." Her spirits were rising. New adventure, like fresh and untracked snow.

John was the last one back. He had found Nelson Cole on the cannery wharf. Cole heard him through without comment.

"You're doing just right," he approved. He accepted John's assurance that Len would be able to assemble the machine. He agreed to arrange with the office about John's pay. "I have a job for you when you get back," he told John. John was embarrassed. He did not want to tell Cole that he could not work under Ashley. He made some vague excuse about not wanting to be tied down. "You wouldn't need worry about working under anyone," said Cole, "except me, of course," he added. John looked at him sharply. "Have to overlook some things in favor of others, sometimes," observed Cole. John wondered whether this meant that after all Cole knew about the role Ashley had played in this matter of the machine to make cans. Sounded a little like it. But Cole was continuing, "You're just the man for the job I had in mind." He explained briefly: fish pirates—getting bold—time something was done. "I'm sick of it," said Cole, "and I've about made up my mind to go to war." John was in a hurry to get back, but he must hear about this. Idea was, Cole answered his questions, to send out a small fast launch on night patrol to make the rounds of the traps. "These fellows work at night," he reminded John. But John knew nothing whatever of the methods of fish pirates, nor even that there were such things, and he said so.

"Why," said Cole, "it's simple enough. They pick their time and raid one or another trap at night and brail out the fish and sail up the coast and sell them to some other cannery as their own catch. They carry an old seine net, generally full of holes, as a bluff," explained Cole further. He spat over the end of the wharf. "Hell!" he exploded disgustedly, "if the canners would stick together and refuse to buy they wouldn't last a week. They all agree not to and claim they don't, but there ain't a one in the lot that won't if he gets hard up for a pack."

"How could you tell the difference?" John wanted to know.

"Seined fish have net marks on them; trapped fish don't."

"Well, what do you think of that!" cried John admiringly. Here was something brand new to him. His imagination and interest were caught. He thought it over a moment.

"Haven't you got trap watchmen?" he wanted to know.

"Oh, sure! That's what they're there for. But short of putting an armed garrison on each trap——" Cole brushed this aside. "Can't really expect a man to put up a fight when he's jumped by armed men, in the night; not for sixty dollars a month. Sure, sure!" Cole anticipated John's speech, "pay more to more men—there's your garrison again, and with a lot of traps it would cost you more than the stolen fish are worth. May come to that. But the patrol-boat idea—— Look here, Murdock," said Cole directly, "I've seen you in action, and this is right down your alley."

It was down John's alley. His eyes brightened at the adventure of
it. Lord, what fun it would be! Like old times. For a brief instant
he breathed the night, and the sage was ghostly gray, and the stars
watched the moving dim forms of armed posses searching; and the
pistol holster against his thigh beneath his hand——But that was the
past; and here was the present—and Sally. He shook his head.

"No go, Mr Cole," said he regretfully.

Cole did not press him.

"Well, think it over," said he. "The job's there when you get back."

"By the way," he added carelessly, as John was about to turn
away, "that place Harry's taking you: I put up a little sort of hunting shack there a couple of years ago. Harry knows where it is. I
don't know what kind of shape it's in, but help yourself. Your wife
might like to get on shore for a change."

"Why, thanks," said John, "but we're coming right back. And don't
worry about the machine. Len 'll fix you up all right. It 'll work."

"Oh, that!" grunted Cole. "It 'd better!"

It came to John, with some humor, that—through Len—he was
working on Ashley's behalf after all. In case of failure it would not
be Len who would catch it. There was a gleam in Cole's eye.

He returned to the float in a high good humor of anticipation.
The others were waiting. They cast off, eased the boat by hand and
pike pole from behind the float into the open water, hoisted the
canvas. It caught the light breeze blowing from off the land. The
Tillicum yielded to it in a graceful curtsy of farewell, righted and
began to slip through the water. Harry's pirogue and the dinghy
strung out behind. The ebb tide caught her. She picked up speed.
Len waved at them from the float.

"We're off!" shouted John and unexpectedly uttered a sudden
wild shrill cowboy yell.

"Good heavens, John!" cried Sally, startled. The malemute raised
his head, his ears cocked in inquiry. Chilkat Harry looked amused.

The tide carried them smoothly toward the foot of the island,
slackening from moment to moment in anticipation of the turn.
The day was brilliant. The gods are with us, thought Sally happily.

She sat right up in the nose of the Tillicum, as far forward as she could get. Her eyes were not wide enough, her lungs not deep enough, her being had not the sheer cubic capacity to take in everything to which her spirit leaped. But it was to the imponderable that Sally at first responded rather than to beauty of seascape or the physical glories of the day. From dull murk into clarity. From close gray walls into space. From stifling suffocation into cool breeze. From torpid numbness into life. Something held suddenly let fly. She could not find words, she could not find thoughts, but somehow she had the strange fancy that these things came to her through the very fabric of the structure beneath her: that she shared the rejoicing of the little ship released from apathy to the movement of the sea.

She would have liked to share this enormous expansion of spirit with John, but John was steering, and Chilkat Harry was perched on the combing next to him, so she contented herself with squeezing the dog and patting the deck and feeling as though in another minute she was going to burst. Then suddenly she began to laugh, and once she had begun she could not stop. She wiped her eyes. Both men were looking at her in inquiry.

"What's so funny?" asked John. She shook her head. "Must be something," he insisted. "Let us in on it. Don't be a tightwad!"

She turned her head and examined John attentively. Good old honest, direct, busy, absorbed, masculine John! It would never occur to him—he'd never understand . . . Nevertheless, to her surprise, she heard herself speaking.

"It's been raining," said she. "I've sat there in the cabin. Then I've put on my boots and my slicker, and I've walked up past the mill as far as I could go, and I've walked back again until I've got cold and wet, and then I've come back and sat in the cabin and read until it was time to cook something. And all those piles and that little row of houses stayed just exactly where they'd been all the time. What a—a *wharf rat* of a life!" She stopped herself short and laughed again, but now with amusement. John looked so astonished. "Don't mind me," she hastened to add. "It's just that I'm having such a good time."

They had reached the foot of the island. As they rounded the point, the new tide was just beginning to stir and with it the first of a favoring breeze from the sea. John slackened the mainsheet. Now the malemute, who had been lying flat just under the foot of the jib, sat up. His ears cocked forward, his eyes fixed on the broad channel ahead, his nostrils worked delicately, as though searching.

"He knows where he's headed," said Chilkat Harry. "He thinks Klakan's no place for a dog."

"Well, I don't think it's much of a place for anybody," said Sally. She made a little face at John. Her good humor was now complete. She turned her back on Klakan. Its dullness had no place in this joyous venturing. She was comfortable enough now in spirit to chuckle at her own unreasonableness. Considering the brevity of her sojourn at Klakan, it could hardly be described as dull, what with Pirate Kelly and Ashley and Nelson Cole. And Annabelle. She suddenly remembered Annabelle. She was sorry she had not seen Annabelle again.

For the first time she began to look about her with the outer eye, and she caught her breath in the sheer glory of what she saw. The channel sparkled wide in the sun. Klakan Island was now on the left, dark and wooded. On the other side were bare cliffs, like walls until Sally raised her eyes and saw above them mountains, so high and remote that the cliffs became mere pediments for their serenity. They were gray and capped with snow, and in crevices here and there were white frozen rivers that at first she thought were more snow, until she caught the gleam of blue in them. Then with a quick thrill she knew them for ice, glaciers: Sally had never seen a glacier. And suddenly the Tillicum seemed to her small and negligible: a nothing in the presence of still immensity. She glanced a little wistfully toward John, wondering if he was feeling this too; but John and Chilkat Harry were examining the face of the opposite cliffs with eyes obviously of practicality, so she hugged the impassive Chilkat again.

But shortly her more practical curiosity was stirred. The breeze, by now considerably freshened, blew straight up the channel. Nevertheless John—under Chilkat Harry's direction—instead of running free, was reaching in a long slant toward the mainland shore. There seemed no reason for this. Sally examined the formidable wall of the cliffs but could discern no break in their continuity.

The channel proved much wider than she had supposed. As the ketch drew nearer, the cliffs rose until the mountains behind them were obscured. Then Sally could appreciate them at their true height. It was a matter of scale. The Tillicum and its passengers shrank still more in significance.

Details began to show, some of them surprising. What from across the way had looked like a strip of white beach along the shore soon disclosed itself as a long stringer of ice. This was enormously interesting. It became more so at nearer view. Then Sally could see that the ice was not continuous, as had at first appeared. Soon the Tillicum was threading her way through what proved but a narrow strip of chunks and bergs of all sizes. This was sufficiently exciting in itself, but what caught Sally's breath was the color. It was too incredible: she had to talk about it, so she deserted Chilkat and went aft to the two men.

"Did you ever dream of such a blue!" she cried. "Why—why—it's actually *indigo!*"

"Sure is pretty," agreed John, but a little absently, for he was intent on picking his course; and as all the ice was shifting in the tide this took doing.

"And, look, it doesn't look like just reflection. It seems as if it were all *through* it. It's the most marvelous illusion."

"It isn't an illusion," returned Harry.

"Like a jewel! like sapphires!" she breathed. "Only it's deeper than sapphires! Blue ice! I never would have believed it. I did not know there *was* any such thing!" She looked up at Harry, puzzled.

"Glacier ice," said he. "Made by pressure. So its substance is fractured, full of tiny prisms. That breaks up the light that shines through it, and you get the blue. You notice it's white where there's nothing but reflected light. Get the idea?"

"Of course. But it's wonderful!"

The strip that from across the way had looked like the beach itself now proved to be narrow and well offshore. Shortly they emerged from it into clear water.

"I'd hate to tackle that stuff in thick weather or on a dark night," observed John, looking back.

"It doesn't get this far down very often," said Harry. "Comes out about ten miles up the coast. Plenty of it there. Drifts back and forth with the tide until it melts. What the pilot book calls a 'menace to navigation.'"

"I never saw anything so lovely," said Sally. She took a last look back, then ahead. "Why are we going this way?" she asked.

Chilkat Harry moved to her side and sighted over her shoulder. "Look close, just through that second shroud," he advised. "See that narrow dark slanting line down the cliff? That's our hole. That's where we're going."

Sally obeyed. She could see no indication of a "hole," only the slanting line, and that looked to her no more than a tiny crevice, a notch, down which a watercourse might run. The boulder-strewn beach, which now showed plainly, ran unbroken. She made a movement which Harry correctly interpreted.

"No use," he told her. "Not charted around here. Wait and you'll see," he assured her.

Nevertheless she did not see until the ketch seemed about to pile itself up on the coast. Then miraculously a narrow gut disclosed itself, running at a sharp angle to the right, behind a knife-edge spur, as between the wings in a theater.

"I better take her for a while," said Harry. He and John changed places. A strong inflowing tide caught the keel. A great shadow fell across them. Enormous naked cliffs squeezed close upon them. The ketch was seized, flung forward. Sally caught her breath, for the great walls menaced, and in the twist of the narrow channel and the rush of the tide it seemed that any instant would crush the tiny craft against them. She glanced apprehensively at Chilkat Harry. He was intent, but unperturbed. And abruptly the gut widened; the flow slackened. She looked about her again to find they had been spewed forth into a round pond.

It was a small pond, not over two hundred yards in diameter, and seemed completely enclosed in precipices of dark rock so lofty that the sky was only a tiny patch directly overhead. The light was dusk as twilight, and the water a polished black, turning in the tide sluggishly, like oil. It was a chill and solemn place, an abyss filled with a roar of falling waters, and yet Sally had a queer impression of immense and timeless silence. She shivered. It was wonderful, but . . .

"We aren't going to stay here!" she cried in dismay. "How are we going to get out of here? There's no way out!"

But both men were laughing at her.

"Where do you suppose all this water's going to?" mocked John.

She joined their laughter, though uncertainly and a trifle vexed with herself. Of course: how stupid! Even landlubber John had thought of that. The little instinctive panic was over; but she could not yet free herself from the awful austerity. She looked at the men: they were lounging back and had produced tobacco. Nice, sometimes, to be a man, uninvadable by the dread forces that lie in wait behind the screen of the visible. These things that had so assailed her had glanced from the clean surface of their masculine practicality without impression.

"We'll be out of here where it's warmer shortly," Chilkat Harry assured her.

There was no stir of air. The Tillicum revolved slowly, turning now one way, now another, following the lazy eddies, but always drifting toward the lower end of the pond. Presently a gleam of light revealed an opening there; and shortly after, caught by a new current, the ketch straightened out and moved more purposefully again into another passage. This, however, was wider, straighter, less precipitously walled than the entrance, more like a river than a gut. Here, also, a breeze recaptured them; and in a half-minute or so they coasted between wooded knobs into open water again.

Or, at least at first dazzling glance, so it seemed to Sally, after the gloom and shadow of the gateway through the mountains. But an instant later she perceived that it was an impression of sunshine and space rather than of the sea. The ketch had emerged at about the middle point of what appeared to be a big lake: how big Sally found herself curiously unable to estimate. As long as she looked merely at the lake itself it seemed to her immense. At any rate it had room for two wooded islands of considerable size to the left, and the curve of the littoral to the right glimmered in the soft focus of distance. But when she raised her eyes to take in its surroundings, the lake shrank. It was a pond: one could swim across it—that is, Sally chuckled in one of her whimsical swift conceits—if one could only keep one's own size and not shrink too! This strange impression was due to the fact, she continued the conceit, that the mountains, which completely ringed the place, did not intend to alter their scale for anybody. They had been that size for a long time, and they were going to stay that size, and interlopers like herself must do the changing.

"All right," said Sally, "I'll be small. You got here first."

She did not realize she had spoken aloud. The men turned to her in inquiry. She laughed.

"I was just talking to the mountains," said she.

"You nut!" said John resignedly. Sally was always saying things like that. Chilkat Harry flicked toward her a glance of quickened interest.

"You'll be surprised how much room there is," said he. "Now over there, where that narrow green strip is, looks as if the foot of the mountain came almost right down to the water. But that green strip is a forest, and it would take you a good two hours to get through it." He looked about him with an air of gratification, almost of pride. "In Europe this would probably be a separate country, with a population and a king and an army and all the fixings," he was saying. "It's bigger than some of them, and it's more lavish. A kingdom. And here we are—just we three!"

Sally looked at him with curiosity. This was a man she did not know, had not suspected. She liked this man. He was simple and human. And he had so instantly caught the real meaning of her silly remark. For an instant she experienced a warmth of something shared. But it was only a flash. He was eyeing her again with his old mocking detachment.

"Good safe hide-out," said he. "Very few know about it at all, certainly nobody you need worry about." He turned to John. "You can take her now. Clear water. Just head her for that light green patch down at the end."

For no reason at all Sally felt irritated, as though a door had been slammed in her face. But that reaction, too, was momentary. She recovered as one recovers from a dash of cold water. John was talking.

"Certainly would be a hard place for a stranger to figure," he was saying. "Have to pick your tide to get through that gut."

"Sometimes a strong enough breeze sucks through so you can buck it," returned Harry. He was still looking at Sally as though secretly diverted. This would not do. She must say something.

"I never *dreamed* of such a place," she proffered. "It was overwhelming!"

"Kind of a Dante's inferno," assented Harry easily, "only somehow there isn't much inferno in it."

"It had eleven waterfalls," observed John.

Harry looked at Sally impishly. She refused his glance and after a moment rejoined Chilkat on the forward deck.

The water was smooth except for the silver ripple of a light breeze. The Tillicum glided steadily, without disturbance, heading to the right. As she drew out from the shore the whole circle of the mountains became visible. They ran in unbroken rampart all the way around; but at one end, the end toward which the ketch had headed, they had drawn back to give space to flat country. Except for a thin line of lighter green next the shore—and which Sally could not yet identify—this flat country was covered with forest that met the foot of the mountain wall and crowded into a canyon and thinned and straggled up its narrow steeps to a final timber line above which was only the bleakness of rock, snow and ice. Sally recalled what Chilkat Harry had said about that negligible strip of woods under the eastern mountains: take two hours to cross! If she believed that, then this must be a day's journey! Only she could not believe it. A narrow dark shadow and a gleam seemed to indicate the outlet of a stream. She half turned, about to ask Chilkat Harry, but changed her mind. Her zest was rising in anticipation.

They rounded a point, and a single great mountain came into view. It was apparently detached from the ranges that made the wall, much nearer the shore and, therefore, optically soared high above its neighbors in the background. The illusion was helped by the fact that its timber line was low. It rose steep and naked, as though it had dropped its forest garment to its feet. By the very boldness of its isolation it commanded recognition as an individual—as a *person* —that thought flowed into Sally's heart with a little rush. She made a gesture of greeting and obeisance. "Live forever, O Protector of the Wilderness!" she murmured and chuckled delightedly at herself, for the mountain certainly looked as though it had every intention of doing so. "I'll see you later," she promised it gravely and mentally backed out of the Presence to pay attention to the shore line, which they were rapidly nearing.

She saw now that the thin strip of light green was a willow fringe to the forest; and that it, in turn, was bordered by a wide meadow of sedge; and that the grass ran out into extensive flats exposed by the low tide; and that there was indeed a river. It came from a black cleft in the forest and wormed, broad and shallow, across the flats.

Here, on land and water, were myriads of birds—ducks, grebes, gulls, terns, long-legged shore birds—and as they were all running about or swimming or flap-skittering or flying, and everyone squawking and quacking and whistling and crying at the top of its voice, they had established a nice, noisy, cheerful, vulgar, self-centered coziness of commonplace life. It seemed to Sally that the Tillicum sailed into it as from chill into warm air. She glanced around at the Protector of the Wilderness. He looked as if he did not mind.

But John was coming forward, and she must get out of the way.

He let fall the jib. The Tillicum rounded into the wind, lost way. The pirogue and the dinghy caught up, nuzzled the stern, swung alongside. John let go the anchor and began to cast loose the halyards of the mainsail. Chilkat arose to his feet. He stretched, pressing his chest to the deck between his forepaws, his hindquarters high and rigid, yawning luxuriously. He looked briefly at Sally, his pink tongue hanging, and waved his feathered tail twice and settled on his haunches, his ears pricked and his eyes fixed on the shore. He seemed to think that they had arrived.

Sally felt a faint and momentary disappointment. Unreasonably, she had anticipated putting foot directly on shore. Ferrying back and forth in a small boat was too much like cruising. Unknown to herself, passionately she had longed for the good earth. And they were a long way from shore. And then there were the wide bare flats. This was silly, she realized at once, now she thought about it. Nevertheless, she was disappointed. The day, by ever so little, had let her down.

But it had not let her down. Chilkat Harry, helping John furl the mainsail, spoke to her over his shoulder.

"We'll have to wait a couple of hours for the tide," said he. "Then we'll be able to tow in. I'd suggest it's a good time to get something to eat, if it's not too much trouble."

"Tow in? Where? Don't we stay here?" Sally stopped.

"Lord, no! Can't be rowing back and forth all the time. At high tide we can go right up the river and tie up to a cut bank in the meadow."

Sally made a surreptitious gesture of apology toward the Protector of the Wilderness. "It's perfect!" she breathed.

They ate lunch on deck in the sun. It was wonderful how fast and yet how imperceptibly the tide came in. Between raising and lowering the eyes broad stretches of the flats were covered. The shore birds and the gulls and terns and ravens fell back before it, protesting indignantly. Finally the gulls rose in a white cloud and flew away to some great boulders on the steep-to shore across the way, where they perched and held a noisy indignation meeting over this diurnal outrage, as though it had never happened before. Soon the ravens followed them; but the ravens flew into the woods. Only the shore birds remained, and they said nothing, but ran about more busily, making the most of the narrowing strip of tidelands.

But suddenly Sally exclaimed. She had caught sight of the figure of a man, moving in the grass near the mouth of the river.

"Oh *dear!*" she cried in dismay. "Somebody's here!" She was indignant at this outrage, like the gulls.

Harry turned to look.

"Oh, that's just Johnny," said he carelessly, "Johnny Mackamoose. Indian. He hangs out here a good deal of the time." Another figure appeared by the first. "That 'll be Susy, his squaw. They won't bother you. They'll be coming off presently." He laughed. "This 'll be a shock to them," he observed. "They must think this is Kelly come in to trade."

Presently the high, graceful, carved and painted prow of an old-fashioned Alaskan canoe thrust out from the grass and came bouncing down the shallow current of the river. Amidships it was completely filled—overflowed—by the ample figure of the squaw. In contrast, Johnny looked to be small and wiry. He perched on the elevated stern, steering. As soon as the canoe floated free of the stream Susy produced another paddle, which she dipped reflectively from time to time. Sally had never had to do with Indians. She watched with eager curiosity their approach.

On closer inspection, Johnny proved to be lean and dressed in a faded shirt and overalls. Susy was fat and dressed shapelessly in flowered calico, also so faded that its pattern was almost lost. Both were bareheaded and barefooted. Certainly at first glance there was nothing romantic about them. Nevertheless Sally thought they looked exceptionally and incredibly wise and benevolent: an effect, she was sensible enough to realize, that was probably due merely to deep lines and innumerable fine wrinkles.

When a dozen yards off they stopped paddling and allowed the canoe to drift toward the ketch. Their bright small eyes remained riveted on Chilkat Harry; but their intentness was the only indication—if indication it was—of the predicted shock.

"Hi-yah, Johnny." Chilkat Harry sang out a greeting.

"How do you do, Johnny. How do you do, Susy." Sally was gracious.

As far as Johnny was concerned she might have been addressing a cigar-store Indian. His small bright eyes did not flicker from Chilkat Harry's face. Nor did the woman reply, but she did turn her head slowly in Sally's direction. Sally smiled at her. Susy's expression did not change, and her eyes were blank. Singularly enough Sally had no sense of rebuff, but she did have a momentary queer feeling that she did not exist, at least in any visible body. She looked at John to assure herself that he was still there.

"My *tillicum.*" Chilkat Harry indicated his companions.

This introduction, if such it might be called, sank into the static of the occasion without a trace. But after an interval Johnny Macka-moose said hi-yah, which might have meant acknowledgment or might—Sally told herself with an impulse toward hysterical laughter —have been intended merely as an indication that he was alive. A long silence fell. Chilkat Harry perched atop the deckhouse, lounged at ease. John leaned against the mast, also at ease. Only Sally fidgeted within, casting about for something to do or say.

"You got tobacco?" Johnny Mackamoose spoke up so suddenly that she jumped.

Chilkat Harry fished a half-filled sack of Durham from the pocket of his shirt and tossed it into the canoe.

"You got meat?" he asked in his turn.

Apparently Johnny did not hear this. He picked up his paddle.

"Ai-ee," he then replied. He dipped the paddle. "Mowitch,"* he then added.

Chilkat Harry stirred into authority.

"Listen," he commanded, "bimeby salt chuck come in. I take boat in river. Deep pool by cut bank. Understand?" Johnny Mackamoose showed he was listening now. "Stay there. You bring meat."

The Indian considered this.

"Ai-ee," he assented at last.

Mowitch—deer—venison.

This simple arrangement appeared to have smothered out any intention of departure. The occasion relapsed into the blankness and the silences. The men did not seem to mind, but Sally had a desperate feeling that unless something was done thus they would all squat there forever, and that shortly she was about to hop up and down or jump overboard or shake the bars with all four hands and scream. Then she had a sudden inspiration. She darted into the cabin, rummaged in her hanging locker and from it took something put away carefully in a pillow slip. She returned to the deck. In her hand she carried a hat: a wide hat of light pliable straw, and around its crown was a pink ostrich feather. This she held out over the Tillicum's low rail to Susy. Susy took the hat and placed it on her knees. She did not look at Sally. She expressed no thanks. The expression of her face did not change. Johnny Mackamoose now thrust his paddle strongly. The canoe glided away.

"Well!" John managed to recover from an astonishment that had stricken him dumb. "Of all the——"

"I'd never in the world have any more use for it," interposed Sally swiftly. "What could I do with it up here?"

"But that fat old squaw . . ." John's indignation was rising, not because Sally had given away the hat, but because John's strong point was common sense, and he was always both mortified and defensive whenever Sally showed any lack of it, especially before someone else. And if there was anything more senseless than giving a picture hat to a backwoods Indian—— But Sally declined to be abashed.

"She's a woman, and *any* woman likes a new hat," she insisted stoutly.

This was even sillier, and probably John was about to say so when Chilkat Harry intervened.

"She's right, Murdock," he chuckled. "Take a look." He waved a hand toward the canoe, which was halfway to the shore. Susy Mackamoose had lifted the frivolous hat with the pink ostrich plume from her knees and had placed it on her head. At this fabulous spectacle John collapsed. "My sainted aunt!" he gasped incredulously. "But there's no *sense* to it!" He rallied a trifle.

Chilkat Harry arose to his feet and squinted toward the shore, calculating the state of the tide.

"There's never any sense to it," said he, "except that it works. It's what they call feminine instinct. You'll learn in time that it's no good to buck it." He spoke with the lazy mockery Sally knew and resented. She glanced at John. He did not see it. It had gone right over his head; and suddenly it came to Sally that Chilkat Harry knew this perfectly and knew that she resented it and gauged the subtlety of his ironies with just this end in view. And the worst of it was she suspected that her resentment was part of his intention. Well! She would not give him that satisfaction! She smiled brilliantly at Harry.

"Timeo Danaos et dona ferentes," said she and hugged herself secretly at the young man's expression of startled surprise. "If you know what I mean," she added maliciously.

Presently Harry adjudged the tide right. The men towed from the pirogue. Sally steered, trying to carry out her instructions to follow accurately lest she run upon the mud. The current now had brimmed toward slack but was still moving slowly in their direction. It brought them to the sedge. The outer fringes were already half inundated. The grass swayed languidly where its lower parts had been taken over by the water. It rose now, as the bottom shallowed, until finally the hard land emerged, and Sally could no longer see over it. The men now went ashore. The ketch, drifting, sidled sidewise and bumped softly against the bank. Sally leaned across the rail to touch the earth, black and dripping beneath the thick sod of the sedges. Suddenly she realized that for the first time since Seattle her habitation had a connection with the soil. A content of homely satisfaction diffused itself all through her. Her spirit gave itself a little ecstatic stretch and shake, as a bird, alighting, folds its wings.

Harry passed the towline around the base of a huge bunch of sedge grass and drew it tight. John was demanding the end of the mainsheet to do the same thing astern. Thus the Tillicum was held moored after a fashion against the cut bank. Sally did not think it very secure, but who was she to butt in on masculine arrangements? So she said nothing. Chilkat Harry leaped down to the deck and dropped the lead line over, both fore and aft. In the meantime John went down the forward hatch to reappear with the double-bitted ax and the heavy sledge hammer he used to drive wedges when splitting timber for firewood. The malemute watched prick eared from the forward deck. He, as well as Sally, knew enough to keep quiet when men were busy.

"There!" John looked about him. He turned at last to Sally. "We're going over to the timber to cut some mooring stakes. Won't take long."

"She'll lie all right for a while," said Harry. "That grass is tough. If it shouldn't happen to hold, just dump over the anchor."

John threw the ax and sledge ashore. The men vaulted up to the bank's level. Chilkat made to follow.

"You stay take care of the lady," Harry motioned him back. Chilkat obeyed without demur, but his eyes remained fixed on the spot where the men had disappeared.

"Never mind, old boy," Sally comforted him. "This is pretty nice." She stretched herself luxuriously in the cockpit and clasped her hands behind her neck. After a moment Chilkat picked his way daintily to her side and lay down, his nose between his paws. She placed a hand on the velvet of his head.

For a long while she basked. This was a simple world: just warm sun and the bending green of the sedge grass. That was all she could see: that and the clean sky. And, alongside, the small surreptitious busy gurglings of water: but she could not see that. The clamor of the wild fowl had ceased. By and by she fancied that even the sound of the waters was growing fainter. It seemed to her that silence was creeping up the channel like a twilight. She sat up to look and was surprised to find that the Tillicum's deck was now above the level of the bank. The water of the channel was still and burnished. It had covered the flats. It gleamed in points of silver all through the grasses. Sally perceived that this place, where the Tillicum had been moored, was now the extreme outpost of the dry land. There was no breeze. There was no motion. There was no sound. Her world rested its brief moment in the hush of fulfillment vouchsafed the unwearying tides.

CHAPTER XVII

THE STAR

THE MEN RETURNED shortly with stakes which they sharpened and drove deep into the earth. To them they moored the Tillicum, more strongly than Sally would have thought necessary until she learned that at low tide the craft would be aground and must be held upright. Chilkat Harry then drew the pirogue next to the bank and made it fast. He unbound and threw back the tarpaulin and from his belongings made certain selections. These he rolled into a pack, leaned a rifle against it and came back to the Tillicum carrying a shotgun.

"Mind keeping this in the cabin for me?" he requested. "The rest of the stuff is all right, but I'm afraid this might rust out before I get back."

"But aren't you going to——" began John. Sally laid her hand on his forearm. He stopped. Chilkat Harry grinned.

"No, you're rid of me," said he. He gave no space for reply. "Johnny Mackamoose will be bringing over some venison. Don't pay him or give him anything for it, and don't let him beg. No, it's for you," he forestalled the protest he saw coming. "We'll kill a deer and return it to him when I get back. That's the way we do it." He whistled Chilkat to the bank. "Help yourselves to the country." He picked up the pack and rifle and pushed his way through the sedge toward the fringe of willows. They stared after him.

"Well!" Sally breathed out sharply and uttered a vexed little laugh. "That's sudden! Where do you suppose he's going? And when he's coming back? Why didn't you ask him?"

"I just didn't like to, somehow," confessed John. "He's a queer customer," he said presently, and with this seemed to dismiss the thought of Chilkat Harry. "It's early yet; let's take a look-see."

"I'm dying to explore," agreed Sally.

They started out at random through the sedge, with the general idea of following the shore line. But within fifty paces they came out abruptly on the brink of a narrow winding channel filled with tide-water: so abruptly, indeed, that they all but fell into it. Perforce they turned inland, skirting it, until it had narrowed sufficiently for them to jump across. This they did and almost immediately came to another.

"This won't do," said John. "The damn place is full of these things. Take us a week to walk around them all. We'll have to get up next the brush and stay there."

"It looks so nice!" Sally looked regretfully across the green expanse.

"At low tide they will all be dry," suggested John. "Then you can go anywhere."

"Why, that's so!" agreed Sally, much cheered.

They set their faces toward the brush line and began to plow their way through the coarse grasses, which became tougher and thicker farther inland until at last they opposed real difficulty to progress. John went first, picking a way, intent on the ground, which was hummocky and split. Sally, following him, could look around; but as the grass was now above her head, she could see little except the tips of the brush fringe to the forest and the forest itself above. But now she saw that the great height of the latter was due, not merely to the tallness of the trees, but to the fact that they grew on a shelf, or plateau, that arose here abruptly at the edge of the marsh. And at the same moment she made another discovery.

"Look, John!" she cried. "There's a house!"

John looked. It was indeed a house, up on the shelf, back among the trees, which seemed to have been trimmed high immediately about it.

"That must be the place Nels Cole was talking about," said he. "He told me he had a kind of hunting shack over here. He told me we could have it, if we had any use for it," he added. "What's the matter?"

"Why didn't you tell me about it before?" Sally was surveying him with humorous despair.

"Why—I don't know . . ." John groped for some reason why he had not mentioned the house to Sally. There was no particular reason. It just hadn't happened. Got back to the boat late, hustled to get off, and then Sally was up forward, and he was talking to Chilkat Harry —and then it just slipped his mind. Sally was always prodding him this way about his not telling her things, as if he were deliberately hoarding them from her. He'd just as soon tell her anything worth while, of course; but a man doesn't go around blabbing just to hear his head roar. They had argued about that before and never got much of anywhere. It was a point in understanding to which they had not yet grown. "I didn't think it was particularly important," said John.

Sally looked at the house nestled in the trees and then back at John. "Important!" she echoed in half-comic resignation.

"He just said he had a hunting shack here," said John defensively. "I don't know why that should be so dang interesting." An expression of surprise dawned in his face. "You wasn't actually thinking you might want to *use* the place?" he cried. "Why, we're only here for two weeks!"

"Two weeks!" she caught the words from him. "Two weeks— fourteen whole days!" Then she laughed: she had to at the sight of John's honest masculine simplicity. "Listen, you goop," said she, "it's a house, a genuine house, anchored to earth, with rooms in it and space to move about and spread your elbows and scatter things around in and step out from onto solid ground and back into. After that little boat where you can't lift your head without bumping it. Two weeks! Why, I'd do it for two days. Wouldn't you?"

"Why," stumbled John, taken aback, "I thought we were pretty well fixed. . . ."

"It's a *house!*" insisted Sally.

But by now John had recovered. He cocked a humorous eye at Sally.

"Mebbe," said he dryly. "Nobody's been there for a couple of years. Likely the roof's caved in."

"Oh!" Sally looked dashed.

"Well," said John, "let's go look at it."

They found a half-obliterated path slanting up the face of the elevation. John, leading the way, stopped when he reached the top and whistled.

"This man Cole is sure no piker!" said he. Sally drew level with him. " 'Hunting shack,' " John quoted derisively. This was no hunting shack as John knew them. A hunting shack was a sort of makeshift you crawled into to keep out of the weather. It might—it just might—have a window, but no more than one. It certainly would not have a wide covered veranda. The structure before them had both and likewise a stone chimney. Deprived of those features, it was nothing noteworthy: merely a log cabin, and of no great size. But with them it was, as Sally had said, a house.

"Come on!" cried Sally, snatching at John's hand.

They ran like children, ending in a rush up three steps to the veranda. The door, of eight-inch undressed pine, was furnished with no knob or handle.

"Shuts with a latch—and the string's inside." John pointed out the hole through which the string should hang.

Sally was trying to see through the smirched window. She cupped her hands around her eyes. "I can't see a thing," she reported. "How are we going to get in?"

"You've got a black smudge on your nose," said John. "Let's try out back."

They followed the veranda. It proved to run around three sides of the log structure. Its ends were blocked by wings, as though a second cabin had been built across the end of the first, like a T. There were three windows on the other side of the main house, but no door. John tested the windows. "Nailed shut—or bolted," said he.

"There must be another way in," insisted Sally.

"Sure," agreed John.

They stepped off the veranda to make their way around the projecting wing. The ground for some distance about had evidently been cleared, but the brush was already beginning to take over again. They must pick their way a little, swinging wide. Thus they discovered that what they had thought to be the general level of forest was in reality a neck of land, and that the cabin had been built on a flat wooded promontory. They looked down upon and across a broad green meadow, clean of forest except for occasional scattered single trees or small clumps of two or three. John showed excitement.

"That's no salt grass!" said he. "I bet that's good feed!"

Sally laughed. "What you going to feed?" she mocked.

Recalled to the present John grinned. "Once a hoss wrangler, always a hoss wrangler, I reckon," said he. But he lingered, squinting appraisingly. "It's a pretty piece of country, just the same. I bet there's five hundred acres. Just needs a few stumps to look like somebody's cleared it."

"Well, I'm glad there are no stumps!" said Sally decidedly. "I've seen enough stumps to last me the rest of my life. Come on, I want to see that house. I'm going to get in if I have to break a window."

They found another door at the back of the cross wing. At first glance this, too, seemed closed against them.

"How in the world do you suppose they get in themselves?" Sally cried, bewildered. "There must be some way!" She squinted into the hole for the latchstring, and so caught a reflection from its frayed end just inside the orifice.

"Sure!" cried John, enlightened. He began to laugh. "That's one on Nels Cole! I'll josh him on that one when I see him! He ought to have thought of that!"

"What?" Sally was all at sea.

"Birds—chipmunks—such-like critters. They'd be sure to chew off the string for their nests."

He produced his knife, opened a slim reamer blade, squatted down and began cautiously to poke its point into the hole. Sally leaned over his shoulder, her head close to his.

"Lose that thing inside, we're sunk," grunted John, and presently, "Hope to God there's some slack." He breathed heavily. "If we could only get a fingernail on her——"

"I think if you'd just——" began Sally.

"Oh, hush up!" John had almost managed to touch the string with the point of his knife. Sally smiled secretly. "Oh *damn!*" John exploded finally. "Let's go bust a window. I'd like to bust something!" He arose, flexing his knees.

"You all through?" asked Sally. She fell swiftly to her knees, produced a hairpin and in a moment had deftly teased forth the obstinate cord. She grinned up at him impishly. "Is that what you wanted?" she asked sweetly.

But John yielded nothing.

"Shucks, woman, what you expect? Want me to grow long hair like Buffalo Bill?" They pulled the latch and entered. "Well," observed John, "the mice sure had no trouble getting in!"

They looked about. The kitchen, their point of entrance, had shelves, cupboards, a sink, a pump, a stove. The latter was a huge affair, extending all along one side of the room, and was red with rust. John's interest was caught by the stove. He pulled out the dampers and found they worked in spite of the rust. "Big enough to roller-skate on," observed John admiringly. "Nels must have lifted that out of some camp. You could feed a crew of men off that thing!" He showed curiosity next about the pump, but Sally was impatient. The kitchen gave into a small living room with a stone fireplace at one end, and that in turn into two bedrooms flanking the kitchen. The first was empty except for an iron bed frame with springs, which John promptly tested with his fist.

"I'll be damned!" said he.

"What?" asked Sally.

"You'd think they'd squawk by now—rust," John explained. He showed symptoms of being deflected by the condition of the springs, but Sally haled him away again. She wanted to see everything. The second bedroom justified her. Two big bundles wrapped in canvas hung from its rafters by wires—"to keep the mice from getting at them," said John: and on the floor had been piled a miscellany of furnishings of no possible interest to mice. These were such things as a number of simple chairs, a pendant lamp, hand lamps—Sally pounced with eager curiosity, but now it was John's turn to be impatient.

"Aw, you don't want to paw all that stuff over *now*," he protested. "Leave it lay until we can clean up enough place to put it."

This was common sense, but she drew off with reluctance. She poked one of the hanging bundles.

"What do you suppose is in there?" she speculated.

"Mattresses," decided John promptly.

They returned to the living room, and John stood stock still and looked about him. It was a small and simple little cabin, but there were a lot of things about it that caught John's attention. He commented on them fragmentarily, as though to himself. Sally would never have thought of them at all. They were things you took for granted in a house. But now she began to see them, through John, in new value, not at all to be taken for granted in a house. Her thoughts had to follow his: that was the curse of being so closely attuned to him. And she saw what he was seeing: that was the curse of her vivid imagination. Beds! he muttered: the beds were whisked into limbo to give place to deep, narrow, hard bunks, nailed against the wall. Dressed floors, for God's sake!—presto! she felt rough splintering planks beneath her feet, or was it packed earth? Fireplace!—it vanished, and in its stead glowered a squat, sheet-iron airtight, or was it a coal-oil can perched on stones? She saw him look toward the three windows set horizontal, instead of vertical, and end to end, in spacious outlook across nearly all one side of the room. In another split second she would have no windows.

"Stop it! Stop it!" she cried.

John turned to her in surprise. After a moment he grinned.

"Well," said he, "you must admit that Nels is no piker when it comes to hunting."

A flood of love for John welled up in Sally. Her cry of protest had been involuntary. Yet he had instantly and surely caught the point. As though he had been herself. He had those strange intuitive flashes, and such things were what set him apart for her from all other men. And, curiously to her, her mind swung to the thought of Chilkat Harry. You see! She confronted that mocking image with pride.

But John was through with the cabin for that day.

"It's going to be a man's job to clean up this dump," he was saying with decision, "and we aren't going to start on it now." He unlatched the front door and propped it back. "Smells like a menagerie in here," said he. "Tomorrow's a new day. And do you realize what time it is?"

"Then you do want to move up here!" cried Sally.

"Oh sure, if that's what you want."

They stepped to the edge of the veranda. Through the trimmed trees they could look out across the flats and the waters of the inland sea. The tide was dropping again; the sea birds and the ravens were back at their noisy affairs. The breeze had fallen flat, and the water shone silver and faint rose-pink. The mountain wall to the west was black in shadow; that to the east was wrapped in deepening purple.

"Good lord!" said John, "I told you it was late!" He fished out his thick silver watch, looked at it, whistled. "Nine o'clock!" he yelled. "What do you mean keeping me out to this time of night! What you trying to do? Starve me, woman?"

"It can't be!" expostulated Sally.

"Look for yourself." They hurried down the trail.

They climbed to the deck of the Tillicum with some difficulty. The tide had gone out, and the ketch, strapped tight against the cut bank, perched up on her keel, nearly dry. Sally peered wonderingly overside down to the brawling, tumbling ripples of a brook, so shallow that she could almost have waded across it.

"Like as if we'd taken up a homestead right here!" chuckled John. "Look out you don't fall overboard: you'd break a leg!"

It did not seem possible that the Tillicum would ever float again; and that impression was underscored by the extent of the exposed tide flats, so that now they looked as across the width of plains to the distant blue line of salt water.

Atop the deckhouse lay a shoulder of venison. Johnny Mackamoose had made good his promise—or Chilkat Harry's command. John was struck by a thought.

"You know," he told Sally, "when you stop to think of it, these must be a pretty honest lot of Injuns around here. Paiutes would have had that cabin looted ten minutes after it was empty."

They agreed they must look up Johnny Mackamoose and Susy and find out where and how they lived. But in the meantime they made a belated meal of some of the venison and tumbled into their bunks. This had been a long day. John fell instantly to sleep, but Sally lay for a long time on her back, thinking about it. This morning she had thought of herself as settled down for the summer, at least, and was preparing philosophically to make the best of it. That was fourteen or fifteen hours ago. And here she was: and there could hardly be anything more different, not if she had traveled to the other side of the world, instead of only ten, or possibly fifteen, miles. So, reflected Sally, getting sleepy, time and space in themselves don't count at all—it is change—and the unexpected—that make the realities in space and time.

She slept lightly, held on the border by a sense of strangeness that she could not analyze, and was awakened hours later by a feeling of change. She leaned on her elbow, trying to focus her wits. Pretty soon she had it. The sense of strangeness had been due to the immovable solidity beneath her of the Tillicum, supported by the bottom beneath her keel: the change that had aroused her was the first faint stir of returning buoyancy. She listened and could hear the small delighted chucklings of the tide.

Sally reached for her blanket wrapper, thrust her feet in the mukluk slippers and stole to the deck. John did not stir. Sally never ceased to marvel at the selectivity, so to speak, of John's arousings. He was broad awake and in full possession of his faculties at a whisper: he slept peacefully through the most outrageous disturbances with which he could have no concern. It was the outdoor man's lifetime training in vigilance. John had once told her that certain silences could awaken him as effectively, as when the bell on his grazing horse stopped ringing.

The last daylight had left the earth, but not completely the sky. Over the westward rim, close down, was a gun-metal burnish of a quality different from anything owned by the night. By and by that, too, would absorb into the deep cobalt of night sky; but by that time, Sally knew, the east would begin to lighten. This persistence of the day, though the rest of the heavens blazed with stars, never failed to stir her somehow. She had at Klakan several times arisen, as now, to crouch, huddled cozily in her blanket wrapper, to see this miracle of the change of guard. As though the day did not dare relinquish all its claim, lest night take over completely and forever.

But at Klakan the eastward hills had been so near; and here was all the wide spaciousness of the sky; and the mountains were a black rim and seemed so much lower, as though they crouched or had lain down, like the rest of the world, to their repose. All but the steep high peak at the back of the valley. Detached from the range, set apart by the illumination of starlight, it had refused the cloak of darkness. Sally could make out dimly a sheen of its granite, a whiteness of its snow and the trace of trees in the crevices; and there came to her fancifully a sense of companionship, as of a living presence.

Next morning they attacked the cabin vigorously. The pump proved not to work, but John followed its pipe through the brush to a still cold spring. This discovery filled him with admiration—fairly atop the hill that away, must be some kind of vein or crevice that forced it up. "Needs cleaning out," he told Sally, setting down the brimming pail, "and reboxing. Had to dip awful careful to keep the silt out of this. Take it easy till I can get her fixed up." For this reason Sally contented herself with a good sweep of the floors: she had cherished some notion of soapsuds. By noon everything was spick and span and the windows washed. By late afternoon they were settled in. The cabin's equipment included all necessities, but some, the utensils especially, had deteriorated beyond use. These they replaced from the Tillicum. Sally also carried up the bright-checkered tablecloth and insisted that John suspend from its hook in the crossbeam the big hanging lamp, though John pointed out that at this time of year there could be no use for lamps, and they had not oil enough for this one anyway.

"It looks nice," said Sally. She cast about her a speculative eye. John laughed.

"What you laughing at?" she complained.

"Curtains. You've got to the curtain stage. I can see it in your eye."

"Dark gold—I think," murmured Sally.

She drew a deep sigh of satisfaction. *"Aren't* we going to have a good time! Let's go sit on the porch."

But it was not in John's temperament to interrupt jobs before they were finished.

"You intending to cook up here or down at the boat?" he wanted to know.

"Why here, of course! We're going to *live* here."

"That's what I thought. Then I better go get some grub. What'll you want—besides the rest of the venison?"

"I'll go down with you."

"No," said John, "you sit here on your porch and take a rest. You ought to be tired."

He was gone for some little time, for once he had begun to make up his back pack he thought of many small items, not immediately necessary, but which he might as well take along while he was about it. It was only a short heat up the hill. His return was heavily burdened, and consequently he did not raise his head until he had topped the rise. Then he dropped the pack with a crash and sprinted to the cabin, for from its door and from every window poured dense clouds of smoke. As he leaped to the veranda Sally, carrying the empty water pail, staggered from the doorway, choking, the tears running down her cheeks. John seized the pail.

"What's happened?" he cried, on poise for a dash to the spring.

"It's the fireplace—the chimney—it won't draw," gasped Sally.

"Huh?" said John. He stared at her incredulously. Then he set down the pail and began to laugh. "You'll be the death of me yet, Sally."

Sally was clearing her eyes of the smoke tears.

"I thought it would be so nice and cheerful to have a fire."

"You come with me," commanded John. He led her by the wrist down from the veranda, across the little clearing to a point of vantage. He took her face between the palms of his hands and directed it upward.

"Oh!" said Sally in a feeble voice.

"Where were you raised?" he demanded severely. "Don't they cover the chimneys down in your country when they go away?" He withdrew his hands from her cheeks. "Must be a ladder somewhere," said he. He chuckled again, immensely pleased over getting one on Sally. "Anyway, you've got us all fumigated. Now I reckon we *will* sit on your porch for a while till she gets cleared out."

"I'm ashamed of myself," said Sally, but she did not look especially ashamed.

John found the ladder and made another trip to the boat for hammer and nails, for it was pretty rickety, and climbed up to remove the planks with the heavy stones atop that had covered the flue. The fire flamed up. The smoke sucked out. Together they stoked up the huge stove in the kitchen.

"You're sure a grand piece of ordnance!" John admired it. "To-morrow I'll blow you to some stove polish—reckon we've got enough to make a little showing, anyway." He surveyed humorously the modest set-out of foodstuffs to be cooked. "Don't suppose he's going to feel insulted, do you?" he inquired of Sally. "Think it's safe to leave you?"

"He looks nice and gentle to me," she returned, "big, but gentle, like elephants."

"You treat the lady right," promised John, "and someday I'll let you cook a whale."

While Sally tested the efficacy of this promise John prowled around, satisfying various small curiosities. The pump had quit because the pipe to the spring had burst: hadn't buried it deep enough, ought to be down at least four feet in this climate. Hard popple wood below there in the basin: heap better and cleaner burning than this jack-pine stuff John had found out behind the house; he'd split some of that out, first chance he got. He circled toward the inland hill edge and once there could not resist dropping down to the level of the big meadow. It was dry, not marshy as he had suspected it might be. It *was* good feed, no doubt of it, and thick and tall. He found a stout stick and prodded up the sod and crumbled the soil beneath it between his thumb and finger. John was no farmer, but he had had plenty to do with ranches. He knew this for good soil. Couldn't be otherwise: the luxuriance of the grass proved that. "Bet you could grow anything," muttered John to himself. He came upon deer tracks and examined them. Doe and fawns, he identified them. He pushed farther out into the meadow and found more deer tracks, plenty of them. The place was full of deer. But all does. John could not find a grown-buck track in the lot. Bucks all up in the high country hardening their horns, he decided. He came across a beaten-down trough meandering through the high grass, as though somebody had dragged a good-sized log. This puzzled him. He turned and followed it in the direction the grass had been inclined. After a time he came to a bit of bare earth. For several moments he stared incredulously at what he saw. Then he whistled.

"Gee-jumping holy Christmas!" he said in awe.

He stooped and laid his forearm lengthwise in the imprint. It just filled the impression, from the point of his elbow to the bone of his wrist. He arose to his feet and stood looking down at it.

"I don't believe it," he muttered.

He was aroused by the sound of Sally's voice. She was standing on the edge of the hill waving at him. He was surprised to discover how far away his wanderings about had taken him.

"Well," reproached Sally as he mounted the slope, "I thought I was never going to make you hear me!"

"There's been the biggest bear in the world across that meadow!" cried John. He was breathing hard, partly from haste and the climb, but more from excitement. "His track's as long as my arm. He must be as big as a moose! No, I mean it. Literally. I measured." He showed Sally the exact length of the track. She was suitably impressed, but a trifle skeptical.

"Must have slipped," she ventured.

"No, no," John insisted, "clean and clear. Come and see for yourself." Suddenly he was all eagerness for Sally to come and see. "I'll get the rifle," said John, "and we might—— He hasn't been gone long. The grass is still flat——"

"Supper has been on the table ten minutes," Sally quashed this scheme firmly. "It's getting stone cold. Besides," she added sensibly when John looked reluctant, "what would be the sense of shooting the bear—what would you do with him? The skin's no good at this time of year; I know enough to know that," added Sally.

"I suppose not," agreed John. His deep-seated hunter instinct died slowly. "But he's such a sock-dolager!"

It took him some time to get over the idea of that bear. Critter that size down in the States would be famous, make history. Any more like that around, Nels Cole sure picked a good country for a hunting camp. That reminded him of the deer. He told Sally of their abundance. "I bet this basin is a paradise for game," said he. Only gradually did his mind detach itself from such speculation and settle down to rejoin Sally.

It was very pleasant there at the table covered with the red-checked cloth, and the fireplace blazing at one end of the room, and sweet breezes stealing in the open door and wandering idly and stealing out the open window on the other side. John commented ironically on this arrangement. "You can't warm up all outdoors," he pointed out.

"We'll shut them when it begins to get chilly," said Sally absently. She barely heard the words. Indeed all her senses were in abeyance as far as conscious attention to them was concerned. Or perhaps it was her mind; for the senses continued faithfully their reports, and she accepted them, but not as identifiable facts. Outside in a near-by spruce a hermit thrush was singing; and here was the brisk cheerful crackle of the fire; and a fragile shell of faint sound far away was where the sea birds were crying. She did not hear them; but she received them into herself. Just as she was aware of the feel of John near her and the touch of air on her cheeks and the long slant of sun through the windows and the trees. Something empty in her was slowly filling, and she must sit rapt and quiet until it brimmed to its full and was still, like the marshes and the tide.

After a long time she took a deep breath and stirred. How long she had sat caught in this strange replenishment she did not know. John had finished his meal and was smoking. She was thankful to John that he had not moved or spoken. John's blunt practicalities concealed some beautiful intuitions. But they were instincts rather than understandings, as his next words proved.

"You've been working too hard," said he, when he saw she had come back. "You're all tired out. You haven't eaten a thing!"

But Sally was not in the least tired. She said so. "I was enjoying the feel of it," she offered a groping explanation. "It's so—so peaceful. I feel as if I'd lived here forever."

"Well, you eat your supper," commanded John severely.

He insisted on washing the dishes at once when she had finished. At first Sally begged to postpone them. Just for once. But this was scandalously contrary to all John's habits. Get 'em done with, and then you won't have them hanging over you. Then she wanted to expedite matters by helping. But John would have none of this either.

"You take your rocking chair and sit out on the porch. You're tired," said he firmly. He was still convinced she was tired.

Sally objected no further. But she did not take the rocking chair to the veranda. Instead she moved over to the long narrow window and stood there leaning against the frame. She could see out through the trees to the meadow, and over across it to the great mountain she called to herself the Protector of the Wilderness. Against the clear green sky of approaching evening he looked high and remote, as though at this close of day he had taken to himself the privilege of his estate for the refreshment of his simplicity. Sally sat there rapt, utterly still. This was a rare moment, for he shared with her his privilege; and the tumblings of the waters and the winds in the trees and the enormous stirrings and restlessness of life had dropped away from her and lay far below her at her feet, and her spirit was one with the serene spirit of the mountain.

She turned her head at John's entrance from the kitchen. He stopped short, his eyes widened at the clear outlined grace of her standing there.

"Gosh, Sally, but you look pretty tonight!" he exclaimed. "I've never seen you look so pretty!" he cried. Abruptly he took fire. In four strides he was across the room and had snatched her. She clung to him in a sudden frenzy of passion. After a time she drew back her head from his breast. "John, John," she begged breathlessly, "don't let's ever, *ever* get old!"

"Consider it done." John's laughter was shaky. He, too, was a little breathless.

She shook him fiercely.

"No, no, I mean it! We must never *let* ourselves get old!"

That night she came broad awake. It was in the dark hours, but there was light enough so that she could make out dimly the rafters overhead. She stared up at them, thinking softly of the many satisfactions, missed without her knowing it, now in with this new uplifting tide. Simple matters that it was silly to miss: common space, the privilege of stepping out in any direction, the reassurance of firm footing, the indulgence of carelessness in leaving things lying around instead of eternally stowed or strapped down, the open fire, the luxury even of that absurd big stove with room atop for everything at once.

"I'm afraid I wasn't really cut out to be a sailor," Sally acknowledged to herself. She veered to a moment's loyalty toward the Tillicum, recalling her first delight with the ship's compactness and handiness and coziness. They'd had good times on the Tillicum. She turned on her side and threw her arm across John's body. He stirred slightly.

She drew herself closer to him. This was such a large part of living, this peaceful sleepy "snuggling," as Sally called it. Not much snuggling to be done on that boat! She purred contentedly and added snuggling to her little list of the comfortable satisfactions of shore.

Across John's shoulder she could see the square of the window. Near its top were stars. All the rest was black. But at once, as though her attention had been awaited, a change began to take place. The dark mass began slowly to gray. As though, was Sally's drowsy conceit, into the cup of darkness a steady hand were pouring, drop by drop, some subtle solution of light. Perhaps, she followed the fancy idly, from dissolving of stars: some of them had disappeared. More of them were disappearing, and the gray was strengthening, until now there was only one great star left.

"Oh!" breathed Sally.

She was tempted to awaken John to share with her this wonder of the rising moon; but something restrained her. Something was here for herself alone. She must keep very still. She lay with her eyes wide, her spirit huddled within her quiet as a mouse, while the moonlight crept downward, until at last the movement of a mighty change seemed to her to stop, as though with a faintly audible jar, and rested.

The single blazing star was all that remained of black night. The world was silver. The great mountain rose still and remote and fragile as frost crystals; and for a space Sally was small and chilled by the perfection of its austere purity. She felt abashed and shivered a little and drew closer to John's body. But shortly a warmth began to enwrap her that was not a warmth of the body but a warmth of peace. She was no longer abashed. The mountain was not really remote, only wise.

"You *do* like your people to love, don't you?" murmured Sally. She was cradled in reassurances; and with the comfort of it she fell slowly into drowsiness. Her thoughts became confused. The star seemed to blaze brighter. Once there had been another Star . . . She was content to slip away, leaving the world to its guardians. She was content to have loved so much. . . .

CHAPTER XVIII

THE RIVER

THEY AROSE luxuriously late—for them. Sally was still tempted to fuss about fixing things, for the novelty of having again a shore habitation had not yet worn off; but John had had enough of houses, he wanted to explore. So did Sally, for that matter.

"Which way shall we go?" John made a large sweeping gesture of invitation.

The whole country seemed open to choice. But surprisingly that proved not to be the case. The tide flats would best be postponed because the tide was coming in, so that, John pointed out, shortly all the entangling little water courses through the sedge would be filled. But the tide was not yet in far enough to float out the boat for a water excursion. Up the coast? Well—Chilkat Harry lived that way, and seemed like, if he'd wanted them . . . Through the forest back of the house? That was tough going: "A tangle of salmon brush and devil's club, thicker 'n hair," said John. "Man 'd have to cut trail to get anywhere in that stuff!" Sally laughed vexedly as each of her suggestions fell flat.

"This country certainly does order you about!" she cried. "Anyway, let's go down to the Tillicum first. I want my boots."

Sally was proud of her boots. They represented one of her few Seattle extravagances. They laced high, nearly to her knee, and at the top was a flap that buckled across to protect the knot of the laces from the snatchings of brush. As their uppers were of soft leather that fitted snugly, Sally thought them very smart and snappy and outdoor looking. Only unfortunately, until today, she had had no occasion to wear them. Their Hungarian hobnails were business-like, but ill adapted to decks. Now at last she put them on and stood on the cut bank above the Tillicum and stamped her feet and craned her neck, trying for different angles to see how well they followed the lines of her legs, until John began to laugh at her.

Since they had descended to the level of the stream it seemed a good idea to follow it up a little. Sally remembered that the two Indians must live up that way somewhere. And, anyway, in that direction ran the line of least resistance.

The going proved comparatively easy. At least it was simple. All they had to do was to push a way through the grass. That was all! But the farther they went, the higher and heavier it grew, so that at last they could barely see over it, and John had almost to lean against it to break passage. He stopped and wiped his forehead.

"This sailoring business makes a man soft," said he.

"Are we getting anywhere?" asked Sally. She was having an easier time than John, for she did not have to break trail; but she was a little thing and could see nothing but grass.

"Well," said John, "I should say we're about halfway to the woods. This seems to be part of that big meadow back of the house; but I reckon by the looks of the willows the river bears off to the right. How are the boots making it?"

"Fine!" said Sally. "Let's go on."

"The going's easier up in the meadow," decided John, "but I reckon we better follow the river. That goes somewhere. It 'll probably open up when it gets into the woods. By golly!" He had a sudden thought. "We ought to cut that bear track I was telling you about!" He pushed on so eagerly that Sally had to hurry to keep up. "I told you!" cried John.

They stood side by side, a little awed, comparing the wide clean-pressed tunnel made by the animal with the comparatively slight trace of their own progress, already growing fainter as the grass sprang back.

"You're not going to——" cried Sally in sudden alarm that died at once when she remembered that the beast must have passed at least twenty-four hours ago.

"I want to find you a track," explained John.

This brought them back to the river, which they had been paralleling. The tidewater had already drained out.

"Here 'd be the way to go, if you didn't mind getting wet," said John.

Sally said she did not mind getting wet, but John shook his head. "That stuff's too cold to drink," said he. "I know: I've tried it. What a man needs is rubber boots."

But he found his track, in the loose small gravel of a bar. It was not so well defined as in soft earth, but, as John pointed out, it was therefore the more impressive. "Think how much weight it takes," he reminded Sally, "to make any track at all in that stuff! Maybe I ought to have brought the rifle." He looked about him with a sudden slight uneasiness. But Sally refused to be bothered.

"He's too big. Big things are always sleepy and good natured."

"It's the little ones you want to look out for. Yeah, I found that out," John grinned down at her. "You look hot. Want to go on?"

"Of course I'm hot," retorted Sally. "Of course I want to go on! This is fun!"

After a little John stopped so suddenly that Sally bumped into him from behind. "There we are!" said he. He held Sally up, an arm under either elbow, so that she could see.

They had by now neared the forest. A stringer of willows reached out from it to indicate the course of the stream. Concealed by them until now, elevated on a hummock, stood a small and remarkably ramshackle shanty. It looked as though it had a cupola atop! Sally had no more than a glimpse before John set her down.

"Our friends, Johnny and Susy," said John.

"Do you suppose they're home?" she asked doubtfully. She had seen no sign of life.

"You bet they're home—or Susy is, anyway," he amended. "Low tide," he explained. "Can't use the canoe except at high tide. And I can't see that old fatty doing much walking."

"Everything seems to be tide around here," complained Sally.

"Pretty much," agreed John.

Shortly they came out into full view of the shack, but even then there seemed to be no sign of occupation: no life, no smoke, no nothing. But the canoe, tied to a stake, lay on its side in a shallow.

The cabin was small, built of logs and shakes. It had no windows and no chimney, and likewise no parallel and no perpendicular lines, and so suggested ramshackle and ruin. Across its front, also rakishly off the vertical, ran a shade or shelter supported by slender poles. Sufficient courtesy might have called it a veranda. The ground immediately before it was flat and clear, but elsewhere a thick high growth of nettles crowded close in from all sides. Except for the evidence of this clear ground, and the canoe, the place looked as though it might have been abandoned for years.

Nevertheless, after a moment's scrutiny John uttered a surprised exclamation and laughed. His eyes were keener than Sally's. Presently she, too, made out, in the dimness under the veranda roof, seated upright on either side of the door, two figures, solid, planted, motionless, as though carved from wood. Johnny and Susy Mackamoose were at home.

Nor did they stir or show the faintest indication of either surprise or emotion until the visitors had crossed the river and the cleared patch and stood—rather doubtfully—side by side below them.

"Thanks for the meat," said John.

"How do you do," said Sally.

These conversational gambits elicited no return for at least twenty seconds.

"You ketch mowitch," then said Johnny Mackamoose, but nobody could have told whether as a suggestion, a demand or a question. John chose to take it as the last.

"Pretty soon," he replied. "Maybe tomorrow."

"Ai-ee," approved Johnny Mackamoose, "plenty mowitch."

"Big bear go across down there." John tried again. He struggled to convey some idea of the size and importance of that bear. Johnny Mackamoose was willing to acknowledge the bear, but evidently did not think it of much importance.

"*Cultus,*" said he briefly. Then, as John looked puzzled, "*Cultus,*" he repeated, "now, no good. Bimeby: good—maybe."

This was his longest speech. Susy said nothing at all. Sally's efforts directed at her Susy silently referred to Johnny. Socially the occasion was not lively. After a time the visitors gave up and resumed their excursion. And yet, as Sally said, there was nothing sullen or unfriendly about the taciturnity. Rather the contrary. One sensed an underlying kindliness. It was underlying merely because there was in this occasion nothing special to bring it out.

"Do you suppose they sit there like that all day?" she wondered to John.

"Shouldn't be surprised. What I think is, they're waiting for the salmon to come in. Let's go on up the river. It ought to be easy going once we're in the woods."

But it was not easy going. To be sure, once they had passed the willow fringe they were able to look up a long stretch of wide gravel bars with narrow beaches between them; but before they could enter it they must get by a tangle of log jams and windfalls; and then after that was a long still pool walled right to the bank by salmon brush. The log jam was not so bad, though they had to do considerable climbing, scrambling and crawling to pass it by; but the other proved almost impassable. The salmon brush did not look particularly unfriendly, but when they tried to buck it they had to lean their whole weight to move at all; and each foot forward built up a closer weave of thickness and thorn. They tried circling it inland, through the woods, and ran into a mess of down trees and thickets of spiky devil's club and willow stringers bound with vines. But John's blood was up, and Sally followed John, so that finally they burst through the last clinging screen back again to that open stretch

of river. They were hot, red faced and thankful. There they sat
on a log for a few moments to get their breath. John rolled a cigarette.

"God, that's a tough country to get through!" said John. "If the
back country's all like that . . ."

They rested a little and went on. Now, it seemed, they were to
have the reward for their hard work. The course of the river between
the walls of trees was as wide as a city street and as clear of obstruction. The stream had good size and ran swiftly over riffles and rapids
from one long narrow pool to another, turning and twisting around
the gravel spits and bars kept bare by its spring freshets. The water
was extraordinarily clear. Except for its surface gleams and the re-
fractions of its motion it might not have been there at all. Only in
the deeper pools did it seem to take on a substance of its own, a peculiar milky gray, as though silt had been disturbed. But as they
came opposite the first of these pools John, who was walking a little
ahead, uttered an exclamation.

"For the love of Mike, Sally, do you see what I see?" he cried.

She joined him and peered into the pool and so saw that the gray
was not silt, but the backs of fish lying motionless, side to side,
nose to tail, a solid pack, hundreds of them, thousands of them. John's
face was thrust forward in eager examination.

"My God, Sally, they look like trout!" His voice was awed. "They
are trout! Saw you ever the like!"

He was fascinated by the spectacle. He left that pool reluctantly.
Sally was sufficiently impressed, but pretty soon she wanted to move
on. She had not John's background of life and could not quite appreciate what a sportsman's marvel such abundance could be.

"They look as though they intended to stay here," she hinted after
a while.

"I'm sure coming back after some of these babies!" said John,
yielding. "*What* a country!" he cried.

They continued. The river wore well on further acquaintance.
Each bend had its disclosures. Sally found herself hurrying just a
little to see what was going to be around the corner. She was delighted with the river. It was alive with people. A mother duck pre-

tended to be wing broken, but when that did not lure them to pursuit, she skittered madly past them, returning downstream just above the water's surface, and a downy brood came out of concealment and spattered after her. A kingfisher rattled up the river ahead of them.

"Settles it," said John disgustedly. "Now everything knows we're coming."

But if so they did not care, for around the very next bend two does stood on the gravel, their ears pointed inquiringly. For ten seconds they stared, then bounced into the woods, leaping high, as though suspended on rubber bands, tucking their feet under them with a neat air of deliberation. And while the intruders watched, charmed by the deer, they were so startled they presently had to laugh at themselves by a burst of commotion overhead, and they looked up at an eagle that had been perched only just above them. Neither had ever seen an eagle so near. It seemed enormous, as though the spread of its wings and the penumbra of its flapping to gain altitude above the forest filled all the river course from trees to trees. After the bird had gained its sky and, with a sudden access of majesty, had soared away, they went on, aquiver for new excitements. There were no new excitements; nevertheless, the lure continued strong in smaller things: cool airs and warm airs, amicably side by side; a winter wren bursting forth, slightly mad, but ecstatically so, and abruptly falling silent; a hermit thrush, unseen voice of the shadows; far down in the forest ravens talking across distances. Sally laid her hand on John's arm.

"Listen a minute, John," she begged. And after a little, "Did you ever hear such a variety of talk? I know it must be a language." She increased the pressure on his arm, holding him motionless. One of the great black birds came sailing down the opening of the stream, caught sight of them in spite of their immobility and fetched up awkwardly on a limb near by.

"*Kla-wock!*" cried the raven, with a strong accent on the last syllable.

"*Kla-wock!*" promptly returned Sally in almost exact imitation, whereupon the raven became very angry and, after jabbering at her excitedly, flew away. "Now I *know* it's a language!" cried Sally delightedly. "I wonder what *kla-wock* means?"

"Something uncomplimentary," surmised John.

"Well, he said it to us first," said Sally. "I wonder what we'll find next?"

What they found next was another stretch of water without either bar or beach for their footing. If they wished to continue they must either wade or take to the brush again. And they could not see how far it extended. John eyed it with disgust.

"If we only had rubber boots!" he grumbled. "This is sure a rubber-boot proposition. I reckon we'd better call it a day."

"I'd like to go on," said Sally wistfully. "It can't be much farther. How far do you think we've come?"

John grinned at her.

"About half a mile."

"It *must* be more than that!"

"Just about—and it's the same half-mile back."

"All right," Sally agreed reluctantly; but in her secret heart she determined that she was going up that river if she had to swim.

"Thing to do is to brush out a trail," John met this thought. He had a bright idea. "Suppose," he suggested, "I hike back and get the ax and cut out a way in this far, anyway."

Sally laughed. "Don't forget to bring some fishing tackle," she jibed. "And," she added, "there's some cold venison and some biscuits— we could have a picnic . . ."

"I'll beat that," promised John.

He was back within the hour, threw down the ax and a small pack. "Let lay," he told Sally as she moved to open the pack. "Fish for lunch." He made a beeline for the pool, strung his rod, cast, got an instant rush of response and, after a surprisingly spirited struggle, floated the tired-out fish into the shallows. John stood looking down at it speculatively. Then he stooped, wet his hands, carefully disengaged the hook and deposited the trout right side up in deep water.

THE RIVER 353

"Why did you do that?" Sally wanted to know. "I thought it was a beautiful fish."

"He was," agreed John, "but did you see the size of him? Two pounds, if he's an ounce. We couldn't handle that size fish—not for a picnic. We *could,* of course, but not unless we had to." He examined the depths of the pool as well as he could without too closely approaching it. "Near as I can make out that fellow was about mill run; I don't see any smaller. There's plenty that looks bigger. Say!" he cried as a new idea struck him, "remember I promised that stove that someday I'd let him cook a whale? Well, there's some of those trout down there that would mighty near qualify." He seemed in two minds, but evidently made up one of them. He reeled his line short and turned away.

"You aren't going to *stop!*" cried Sally, unbelieving. "Why don't you try up there where the riffles come down?"

John shook his head. "That's precisely where I'd be *sure* to tie into that whale."

He went downstream and began to cast in the shallows at the lower end just where the water broke over into rapids. It did not look to Sally like a good place to fish; nor did John's casts stir any response. She watched him for a moment or so, then seated herself on a smooth rock and gave herself over to vague and delicious enjoyment of tepid air and the sound of running water. She was presently jerked back by a wild whoop. Startled, she came into focus. John was crowhopping about, waving his rod in one hand and an eight-inch trout in the other.

"Eatin' fish!" he cried in triumph. He broke the troutlet's neck, threw it up on the bank and resumed casting. He was very skillful, dropping the fly delicately behind the tiny swirls that indicated a sunken stone. Sally watched him now. She was amused by his intentness. Every once in a while, apparently, he coaxed a rise; she could see his wrist flex, striking back daintily, as he must if he hoped to hook small fish with a number-six fly. Twice he snatched the fly hastily from the water with so audible and hearty a curse that Sally laughed aloud. He looked up and grinned. "One of these here armored cruisers wanted in," he explained. He returned to his casting. It took enormous patience, and Sally felt her own wearying in sympathy. Nevertheless, every once in a while he did connect and then he uttered his wild shrill cowboy yell of exultation, ridiculously out of all proportion to the size of the catch. Once he failed to snatch the fly away quickly enough and was forced to fight for ten minutes before he could get his hands on the culprit to turn it loose. From time to time he grinned at Sally. He was having a wonderful time: like a small boy, Sally reflected amusedly, but with tenderness.

"There!" he cried at last, reeling in. "That ought to hold us." He laid aside the rod and began to gather together the half-dozen small trout he had tossed up the bank. Sally arose from her rock and joined him. "Ain't this the most ridiculous country?" said he happily. "Anywhere else you'd be tickled to death to tie into a two-pound trout—I bet there's some down there that weigh five. Anywhere else you'd keep the big ones and throw back the little ones." He produced his pocketknife and began expertly to dress the fish.

He built a fire and cut and peeled willow switches and on each threaded a trout, nose up, and on the ends impaled chunks of raw pork from the pack, so that, when the switches were planted before the coals, the pork fat ran down over the roasting fish. "Now," predicted John, "you're going to have eatin' fish as *are* eatin' fish, and no fooling!"

He produced from the pack the biscuits, a kettle, two cups and a small packet of tea.

"What else did you bring?" asked Sally.

"Nothing," said John. "And for the first trout that's all you'd want even if you'd cooked up half of Nels Cole's store."

Which, on trial, Sally found to be true.

After the meal for some time they sat together drowsily side by side. But when John had finished his second cigarette, he arose with an air of purpose.

"Now," said he, "I'm thinking of going fishing."

He pressed flat the barb of his hook between two stones and returned to the big pool. It was really very exciting, Sally had to

acknowledge to herself, though in the back of her mind was a doubtful reservation. But John dispelled that.

"As long as you wet your hands before you touch them, it doesn't
hurt 'em one little bit," he told her emphatically. "By tomorrow those
same fish would bite again."

"I wouldn't like a hook in my mouth," objected Sally.

"Their mouths are all cartilage; they don't feel a thing. Doggone,"
said John, "it's good for them: just gives them some much-needed
exercise. Here, you try it."

Sally tried it. Her only fishing experience had been with John during that honeymoon week in the Cascades. She tried to remember
his few lessons in casting the fly. John laughed at her first attempt.
"Might as well do it up in a bundle and send it to them by mail," he
jeered. "Well, I'll be doggoned!" he broke off. The flies, the leader
and a liberal two yards of line had slapped the surface of the water
in one demoralized mess. Nevertheless a half-dozen swift forms converged on it, rising from the gray ranks lying along the bottom.
"Strike! Strike!" agonized John as Sally stood staring helplessly at
the commotion. But Sally did not even have to do that: the fish
attended to his own striking. The very speed of his rush drove the
hook home; and Sally found herself clasping desperately a rod that
suddenly seemed charged with electricity, attached to a darting,
diving, turning, jumping streak of sheer velocity that seemed everywhere at once; and married to an imbecile that leaped around back
of her and implored her to reel in and let him run and snub him and
keep the tip up and—in a shriek of agony—for God's sake not to give
him any slack. All of this was much too bewildering. So she merely
hung on tight and pulled and was confusedly conscious that the fish
in front of her and John behind her had both gone raving mad.
Nevertheless her blood was up now, and she would not give way
to either of them, though at moments the rush of the fish was too
much for her. The strength of her wrists could not hold the rod
upright: that was the single thing to which her consciousness fastened
—she must keep the rod upright. Tug as she would, the astonishing
sheer power at the other end was forcing it down inch by inch. She

gritted her teeth and presently found herself nearly waist deep in water. But the rod was still upright, and abruptly the pressure ceased. "He's coming at you! He's coming at you!" John was howling. So she backed out of the water, not because she heard John—she was beyond all that now—but because the drag on her wrists had eased. And John was now at her elbow and trying to take the rod out of her hands; and she flared out at John in a sort of side blast that swept him aside; and she continued to tug at the fish.

Sally came gradually to the surface of haze as one comes up from the depths of water. She was standing at the edge of the stream, and on its side in the shallows at her feet lay a huge creature, its gills moving slowly. To her faint surprise she realized that she was wet to the waist. She looked around. John was seated on the gravel bar, holding his head between his hands and shaking it slowly from side to side. She stared at him, puzzled, her wits still confused. What was the matter with John?

Presently he got to his feet. He looked at Sally: he looked down at the fish. John was not a profane man, as outdoor men go. He spoke, spacing his words slowly.

"You did every goddamn thing wrong," said he. Awe was in his voice. He stooped and picked up a stone and rapped the trout over the nose. "Sorry," said he, "but you're going with us—if we have to eat fish for a week." He raised his head quickly and so caught Sally in the beginnings of smugness. She might have done every goddamn thing wrong—but there was the fish! "Don't you be getting proud," he warned severely. "You ought to be ashamed. You've got yourself sopping wet, and you've scared out the whole pool, and why you didn't bust my rod, I don't know! Why didn't you use the reel?"

"I didn't have to," said Sally with suspicious meekness.

They dropped fooling and laughed together. John cut a willow fork on which to carry the trout. He hefted it thoughtfully. "Wish we had scales; he must go at least five pounds—maybe six. That was an astonishing performance. I don't know what we are going to *do* with so much fish."

"We could give half to the Indians," proposed Sally.

They started downstream at once, for John insisted Sally must get home and get dry. They found Johnny and Susy Mackamoose just as they had left them several hours before. The Indians accepted half the big trout. They expressed no thanks; nor, on the other hand, did they mention the light net under the shanty, laid away because they were sick of trout. Johnny stirred himself to haul in the canoe and ferry them across to their own side of the river, now tide full. They had not thought of the tide. They returned to the cabin directly across the meadow and found that much easier going than the bottom land along the river. Already their short residence had begun to materialize a mist of welcome-home.

CHAPTER XIX

GUN PLAY

"I ONLY WISH now we had that shower you fixed up at the shanty," said she.

"Well, if we were going to be here longer, I'd fix up something," said John. "You'll have to take it from a pail, if you're set on having it. And," he grinned, "believe you me, that spring turns out ice water. Why don't you just take a good rubdown and let it go at that?"

But Sally could not let it go at that. She wanted a bath—now. John had not yet arrived at complete sympathy with this insistence on immediate baths the minute you got through doing anything. Sure, it had been hot at times, bucking the brush up the river. But you'd cooled off, hadn't you? On her part Sally could never quite understand such a point of view. You feel so much more *comfortable!* "I'm comfortable enough now," countered John. Actually John's instincts were for cleanliness, and he would have his bath, but what sense going to all that bother now? And, too, this was one of the few points, he had early discovered, on which he could tease Sally, and she never seemed to get onto it.

"You ought to have been a cowboy, Sally," said he, "and learned that one good sweat washes off another."

358

"I think you are absolutely *disgusting!*" she cried.

Chuckling over his success, John filled the pail at the spring. But Sally's warmth of indignation could not overcome a gasp and a yelp as the icy water dashed over her. She turned with fury on the grinning John, holding the empty pail. "If you think you're going to get out of it! You go fill that pail," she ordered, trying desperately to keep her teeth from chattering. Her eye was dangerous. John hastily capitulated. "All right—all right! Keep your shirt on!" He caught at the words with a laugh, "or go get it on," he amended.

From the bedroom Sally heard him return and set the pail down. There followed other sounds.

"What are you doing?" she called.

"I'm stoking up old Jumbo here," John's voice came back to her. "I aim to warm up this water. I'm no polar bear."

Sally stopped stock still, outraged at the duplicity of John.

"You *pig!*" she managed at last.

Then she resumed dressing at top speed. John was going to get that pail of water just as soon as she could get there, whatever its temperature, and if he wouldn't take it with his clothes off, then he'd get it with his clothes on! So far with a splendid indignation. Then she uttered a vexed and helpless exclamation at her own foolishness. It was a gorgeous idea, only unfortunately she'd be the one to get it with her clothes on if she tried anything like that! John wouldn't hesitate for a minute! She finished her dressing more slowly, reflecting on various ways of putting one over on John. He was two up on her lately. But her inspiration was out. Nothing occurred to her. She was now in no hurry. She paused to primp a little, then stepped into the living room on her way to the kitchen. At any rate he was going to take that bath, and now, not later. That was a minor victory. She glanced out the narrow window as she passed. She stopped, stared, then threw out both hands in humorous surrender. No use: this was John's day.

"John," she called to him, "here comes your friend, Chilkat Harry, across the meadow."

Chilkat Harry was evidently headed for the Tillicum, but must have caught sight of the smoke from John's newly lighted fire in the stove. He swerved and mounted the slope at the back of the house. Sally could see that he carried a rifle and a small pack; and presently, when the malemute had emerged from the tall grass, she saw that Chilkat also had his little pack. Sally had never heard of packing a dog like a horse or a mule, and she was vastly entertained. The young man skirted the house and appeared at the front door just as John came out from the kitchen. His return of greeting was absent minded, almost perfunctory. He looked about him.

"Looks as if you people had moved in here," said he; and there was something of disapproval in his manner that caught Sally back, so that she kept silent and left the talking to John. The malemute must have shared her instinct: at any rate he sat down quietly in the background.

"Yes; we thought it would be more comfortable," returned John equably.

"Humph!" grunted Chilkat Harry. He kept silent for a moment; and then, "You know, it may be different where you came from, but we don't do that sort of thing in this country."

"What sort of thing?" John's voice was gentle.

"Breaking into another's property and taking possession, and he not there. Only if a man is freezing or starving would he even consider it."

"Thanks for telling me," said John. "It's the same way down in my country. But Cole told me to use this place."

"You mean to say Nelson Cole offered you the use of this place?" returned Chilkat Harry sharply. Sally ruffled at his air of incredulity, but the flat of John's hand toward her held her silent. Nor did John make any further assurance. He waited tranquilly. "Humph," grumbled the young man, "I never knew him to loosen up with his playthings to anybody before."

"No?" said John. "Then I suppose we should feel flattered." Nothing in his manner acknowledged the remotest possibility that Chilkat Harry, even secretly, might be doubting his word. Only Sally, watching a little anxiously now, caught the set of his jaw and the fine white line where the muscle tightened. But having said this, he said nothing more.

Surprisingly Chilkat Harry dropped the subject there. He eased the pack from his shoulders and laid it down, but he did not leave the doorway.

"What I came to see you about," said he, "was returning that meat to the Indian. Those people are particular about things like that, and it pays to keep on the right side of them. We'd better go shoot a mowitch tomorrow, if that suits you." There was still an edge of ill-humor in his voice, as though he spoke grudgingly.

"Suits me," said John.

"Well"—Chilkat Harry stooped to lift his pack—"we better start early," he flung out, as though in afterthought. "Be at my place about four o'clock. Bring your dinghy. Row along shore," he indicated the direction. "You'll see me." He slung the pack on his shoulders again.

"Aren't you going to come in a while?" invited John. "We'll be having supper pretty soon." Sally compressed her lips. She'd have died before she invited Chilkat Harry, she told herself indignantly. He was impossible. He was acting like a petulant small boy. For no reason. She resented Chilkat Harry.

"I've got to get back," the latter refused shortly. But he did not go at once, hesitating—again like a small boy—Sally's indignation was turning to scorn—who is vaguely becoming ashamed of his petulance. "A cache—of any kind—is pretty near sacred in this country. It has to be," he muttered, half in explanation, half in apology. Then, as though regretting even this much, he turned away. "Four o'clock then," he reminded John. "Come on, you!" to the malemute harshly. He swung down the trail. Chilkat arose and followed, bearing his little pack. He had made no sign of recognition to his friend, Sally: strictly the business-dog.

At once Sally's indignation found voice. She was not accustomed to such treatment on the part of a grown man. She resented it. She resented his attitude toward John. "He acted as if he did not believe you," she cried. She even resented a little—as a side issue—that John had taken it the way he did!

John was enormously amused at Sally's indignation. "Regular little spitfire! Gosh, you sure do touch off easy, worse 'n gunpowder! You look," said John, cocking his head sidewise in appraisal, "just like an outraged dicky bird. I'm scared. As for Chilkat Harry"—he brushed that aside—"Oh, he's just tired: probably been on a long hike." Which did not seem to Sally much of an excuse, and she said so.

"I think he was insulting," Sally finished. John agreed to the first part of this.

"I'm beginning to think that in some ways he ain't quite a grown man," said John.

Sally fell thoughtful.

"So there's no sense getting all het up," continued John. "And it ain't very safe. That's the funny part of it. Sally, let me tell you this: the man you got to step careful with ain't the man most folks would label as dangerous—he's a simple proposition; it's the fellow with a streak of play-acting in him. You can't guess how to handle him until you figure out what kind of a part he admires himself in, because that's how he's going to perform when the time comes."

"You think Chilkat Harry is a play actor?" asked Sally anxiously.

"I don't know yet what he is," confessed John. "That's why I'm interested. I'll know about him before I get through. But until you've got a man sized up it don't pay to get far off base. So," he admonished in conclusion, "keep your hair on about being 'insulted,' until you find out. Me, right now, I don't figure he meant anything like that. He was just cross; and, as I say, in that way he maybe ain't quite grown up enough to keep it to himself, and he ain't never been called down for it. As I figger him, he don't stand being called down very well."

"Spoiled," snapped Sally.

"Something like that," John nodded. "And," he added, "man enough to make it stick. Don't make any mistake there. This fellow's a good man. Get the point?"

"Of course I do!" cried Sally. She looked at John with new respect. "Why—you're wonderful!" ("Check" interposed John with his usual grin.) "You're a psychologist!" She was filled with admiration. Here was another John, one whose existence she had heretofore only vaguely sensed. Her own keen mind quickened exultantly at its discovery. The problem of Chilkat Harry sank to insignificance in her eager desire to partake of this new association with John. But, like most men of his type, John shied from frontal attack.

"You know what 'll happen to you if you get to calling me names!" he warned.

He returned from the deer hunt rather late the following afternoon. Sally saw him rowing by toward the mouth of the stream and at once set about cooking as more practical than going down to meet him. Of this he heartily approved: it had been a long day.

"Sure," he answered one of Sally's first questions. "He's as sweet as cream." He chuckled. "I just let him show me how to hunt deer."

Sure they got a deer, two of them in fact. "They aren't very big up here, and we picked us 'spikes'—leave the tough old record heads to the sportsmen," said John, with the faint contempt of the professional for the amateur. "No trick at all: killed 'em not over four hundred yards up from where we left the boat." He lounged against the side of the kitchen doorway while Sally did things at the stove.

"What kept you so long then?" she asked. "You better sit down. You must be tired."

John made a long arm back of him and dragged a chair into the doorway, which he straddled, resting his forearms on its back.

"Exploring around. Taking a look-see," he answered the question. "We clumb mighty near to the top of the ridge. I have a kind of suspicion he aimed to walk me down. And," confessed John frankly, "he mighty near did! I was raised more on a hoss than on my feet. And that fellow's a regular chipmunk." He stretched out one of his long legs and laughed. "I managed to stay with it, but he saw plain enough I was having tough sledding. Oh, he's all thawed out now. Was calling me 'Jack' toward the last."

But it had been worth getting a little tired for. Soon as you got up a little way, just beyond timber line, then you began really to see game. Bucks: it was ridiculous! The whole lower ridges swarmed with them. Counted fourteen in plain sight at one time, all along toward midday at that. John was much impressed, for even in the wild countries of his youth he had had to work for a sight of game. Up higher, among the cliffs, they saw goats. When you got that high you got a great view of the country——

"Shoo!" interrupted Sally, "you're blocking traffic!" John moved over to the table. "What sort of a place does he live in?" she asked.

"I don't know," confessed John. "He met me at the shore, and I didn't get to see." He fell to hungrily on the food. "I got him to come over to supper tomorrow," he mumbled. "Didn't seem to want to at first. Queer bird. Seems friendly enough, too."

He finished eating and at once insisted, over Sally's protest, on returning to the stream.

"You deserve a rest," said Sally.

"Got to take care of the meat first," said John.

He made three trips back and forth. Chilkat Harry had kept the saddle and haunches of the smaller: John purposed dividing the rest with the Indians. "I'll take it over at high tide in the morning," he said to Sally over his shoulder. He was standing beneath one of the taller trees, his attention absorbed in trying to cast a coil of light line from the Tillicum over the lowest branch left by the trimming. This was a delicate matter, for the limbs grew close together. "May have to climb it," he muttered. "There!" he cried in triumph. He caught the other end of the rope as it fell and shortly had hauled all the meat high off the ground. Sally wondered against what sort of animals he was taking the precaution; but John was at the moment too busy to be questioned. Only when he had finished did she inquire.

"Blowflies," said John.

He rolled a cigarette. Apparently he was somewhat astonished that he had to explain. Everybody, in John's opinion, must know about blowflies. Sally said impatiently that of course she knew about blowflies. But how did this performance help with blowflies? Her manner indicated more than a suspicion that John was trying to be funny. He examined her carefully while he lighted the cigarette, with more than a suspicion, on his own part, that it was she who was trying to be funny.

"Blowflies," he said with sardonic brevity, "never fly higher than eight or ten feet off the ground."

"Oh!" cried Sally, "I never knew that!" Her sincerity was evident. "What are we going to do with it all?" she gave voice to a speculation that had been bothering her from the first.

"Why, eat it." John looked surprised.

"But a whole deer—three quarters of a deer, anyway—— We haven't any ice. I do hate to waste things——"

Ice! John re-examined her attentively. No, she meant it! Here was another of Sally's astounding ignorances of the ordinary expedients of life—as John knew it. He was always running against them and explaining to her. Still, it was fun explaining to her: she caught on so quickly and was so flatteringly enthusiastic over learning how to do the simplest things.

"You leave the meat hang nighttimes, and that gets it chilled all through; and then daytimes you take it down and wrap it up in a couple of blankets or something, and that keeps the chill in—and so on. Why, even when you're traveling, if you put it somewhere in the middle of a pack it 'll stay good for a couple of weeks. And of course up here—— And anyway," John interrupted himself to point out, "you can always make jerky."

"Can I?" said Sally, with a comical grimace.

John stared at her a moment.

"No, come to think of it, I don't suppose you can," he said slowly. "But it does seem kind of funny, first off. Lord, you sure need educating!"

His use of the word stopped short the spirited reply she was about to make. She had always taken for granted that as between John and herself she was better educated. That assumption carried no littlest taint of superiority, for John was and had so many finer things. Sometimes she felt humble minded when she contemplated John. But was she? What was education anyway? This was quite a new thought. She must ponder on it.

"It's no trick," John was saying. "I'll show you."

"I wish you would," said Sally.

John's view out from the ridge had inspired him with the idea of exploring the inland waters with the small boat. "There's a lot of islands and coves and bays and things at the far end and another stream," said John. But when morning came he postponed the expedition a day. "I told you that boat life made a man soft," he reminded Sally. He was half ashamed that the deer hunt had left him a little stiff and tired. Nevertheless, a day of rest would be pleasant, they agreed. So again they got up late—for them—and after breakfast John loafed for at least half an hour. Then he must deliver Johnny Mackamoose his share of the meat before the tide dropped. Returning from that errand he remembered the popple wood in the bottom land and took his ax down there and spent most of the rest of the morning cutting and splitting out what he called proper stovewood. This gave him great satisfaction, for the pitchy quick-burning fuel they had been using had offended his sense of artistic fitness.

By now the tide was low. This gave John another idea. He went back into the bush and chopped and trimmed a number of long slender poles and carried them, two or three at a time, down to the mouth of the stream below the Tillicum. When he had accumulated there a dozen and a half or so of the poles, he next began to plant them upright at intervals along the bank of the stream, out toward the flat, thus marking the channel for high tide.

"When I get this done," he told Sally, "we'll be able to get in and out when we want to, without fussing with a lead or sticking our nose in the mud."

He was thoroughly interested, so Sally gave no expression to her thoughts. But she could not help being a little amused at John's idea of a day of rest, nor reflecting that there could be no reason for getting in and out—not until they went out for keeps on their way back to Klakan. While John happily dug holes and lugged his trimmed saplings and then rocks to tamp them strongly upright, she wandered about and so found herself on the bare part of the flats. It was bare, but far from dry; water trickled and oozed from the spongelike soil under her every step. Still, the footing was firm and hard. Except for here and there a sprawling orange patch of stranded kelp, the prevailing tone was brown. Far out toward the line of blue that marked the edge of the salt water were compact drifts of white and an occasional flurry upward like a tiny localized snow squall; and Sally remembered the gulls and terns and sandpipers she had seen on the way in. They looked to be a long distance away, and only when she stopped squnching her feet could she hear their busy and sociable clamor. She hesitated whether to go out there, but decided it too far and curved back toward John—who was planting his last pole well out on the flat—spying interestedly on small things by the way. There was not much to see, but she was not unrewarded. She came upon a small pool of water that had not drained, and around it and in it stalked a half-dozen long-legged dowitchers; only, so still was the water, that there were a dozen dowitchers, half of them upside down. Sally tried to decide which image was clearer, but gave it up. They were so wholly absorbed in their business that they reminded her of John, so she took great pains to circle them wide to avoid disturbing them.

"Got that last one in just about in time," said John to her with satisfaction as she rejoined him. "Tide must be on the turn."

"We ought to find some clams," said Sally. "There's an awful lot of empty shells."

After this exchange of local gossip they stood side by side looking out seaward. As John said, the tide must be on the turn, though as yet there were few indications. The distant blue line of the salt water looked as far away as ever, but it seemed more distinct. The gurgling rush of fresh water down the stream bed might have slackened by ever so little its speed. And then, at the turn of a little drained bayou to their right, there crept hesitatingly an exploratory finger of the new flood. It stopped, stole forward, stopped, as though unsure. After a moment it began to flow, advancing by little rushes, gaining confidence.

"About time we pulled our freight," said John, gathering up his tools.

To their surprise it had become midafternoon. John was mortified that the noon hour had passed without his knowing it. "Forgot the tide was later every day," he muttered. Sally was less orderly in her time sense: she did not mind.

"As long as Harry is coming for supper, we'd better just have a light snack now. What time did you say he'd be over?"

They tramped back together toward the cabin, still a little bewildered that the day was about done. And each of these days had become curiously valuable to Sally. The way the days of vacations used to be. That was it: their supply was limited.

Chilkat Harry and the malemute arrived about six o'clock. He greeted Sally without trace of embarrassment or apology. Indeed, he looked her so blandly in the eye, with such a limpid innocence of any recollection at all of anything disagreeable, that she was forced to play up. Or make herself out less magnanimous, less willing to forget than—— Drat the man! He had a diabolical cleverness in making her feel defensive, whether there was any justice in it or not. Or was it self-conceit?

She avoided the occasion by exchanging greetings with Chilkat, who was now off the job and could again follow his social inclinations. He wrinkled his nose and ducked his head and sneezed to Sally, as though to say that he hoped she had understood. After that he began to go over the interior of the cabin systematically, storing away in his memory sniffs for possible future use.

"Yes," Chilkat Harry agreed with Sally's comment, "he takes his job seriously. He'd be no good if he didn't."

"He's pretty nice just as a person," suggested Sally.

"Oh yes," Harry agreed, so indifferently that Sally was tempted to probe deeper. Didn't that count, she asked—being a nice person, she explained. "Not much." Harry was frank. His eyes followed the malemute thoughtfully. "Chilkat's a good dog. He knows what's expected of him, and he does it. He carries a pack—as you saw. He'd make a good sled dog in a team, if I needed that. He does what I tell him. He's friends with nobody but my friends. He'd fight for me. But it's a simple job, after all. I wouldn't keep him for a holy minute if he wasn't up to that much."

"But you're fond of him," Sally must persist, "as a person."

"As long as he does his job." For a brief instant Harry's eyes narrowed and hardened. Then he laughed, almost visibly turning on his gay charm as one would turn on a light. Sally perceived this; yet, in spite of herself, she must respond to the charm. "You see this is a pretty practical kind of a country, Mrs Murdock, without any luxuries." His confidential manner gathered her in. "You can't afford to keep pets, either men or dogs. Your husband knows how it is," he referred himself to John. "He's been where he has to travel light and keep his elbows close to his side. When you are fixed where you have to strip life down, a lot of things have to go overboard."

"Even friendship?" asked Sally quietly.

Chilkat Harry preferred to avoid generalizing so widely. He recurred to the malemute.

"Aren't you getting pretty serious about nothing?" he suggested good-naturedly. "After all Chilkat *does* do his job. Look at him"—as the dog raised his eyes at the sound of his name. "I think he feels hurt that you've even implied he might do otherwise. Why theorize on something impossible? That's not fair."

Sally experienced a momentary dizziness. How had the conversation worked around to this? so that once more she had been put, somehow, on the defensive? Was it again the man's diabolical cleverness, or was that suspicion also fantastic? If it was indeed cleverness, Chilkat Harry continued to exhibit it.

"As a matter of fact," he turned the whole subject to the impersonal, "you'd be amused to know how completely off the wrong foot intelligent and well-meaning people can get on subjects they do not know. Last time I was in Boston some very nice, but somewhat idle, ladies were occupying themselves with just what we were talking about. The sled dog, I mean. They were starting some sort of an organization or agitating some sort of a law—I never did know exactly what—to put a stop to the terrible cruelty. And they had their facts right, too. . . ."

"What facts?" asked Sally, for obviously he intended her to ask.

"They drag heavy loads over terrible country, sometimes for long hours, fairly to the point of exhaustion; they are fed one or two frozen fish and then must curl up and sleep out without shelter in below-zero weather, sometimes in blizzards, so that by morning they are completely buried in snow."

He paused. His eyes were twinkling with expectancy of Sally's reaction to this list of inhumanities. Perceiving this, she refused to oblige.

"All that is true," went on Chilkat Harry, a trifle disappointed. "But they'd left out one thing. The dogs like it." He ignored her derisively raised eyebrow. "A dog—any dog"—he veered without transition to a new attack—"in his relationship with mankind, has to have a regular job, even if it's only bringing in the morning paper. If he isn't given one he invents one; and sometimes what he invents is pretty absurd and even annoying."

"That's right," John spoke up unexpectedly. "I remember a dog who made up his mind his mission in life was to keep tumbleweed off the place. Never paid any attention to it anywhere else. Comical sight to see him."

Chilkat Harry nodded.

"The happiest dogs, you'll find, are the professionals," he continued his argument: "Specialists, like pointers and setters and hounds and such things—when they're used. Of course hunting is fun. But that includes dogs doing things that don't look like fun. Turnspits. The Flemish dogs that pull carts. And malemutes—sled dogs. They love their life. And if you don't believe it wait till sometime you see them fairly fight to be harnessed. That's the one item the Boston ladies overlooked; but it's the one that makes all the difference."

"They overlook quite a few things," John chuckled at a recollection. "There was another lot from Boston—or maybe it was the same lot— that wanted to do away with branding cattle. They wanted cows marked with a nice little brass tag hitched to their ears. Can't you see it! 'So, bossie! Hold still now, while I read your tag!' "

They all laughed at this picture. Sally arose to attend to the supper. The occasion somehow had warmed to easy good fellowship. Sally and Chilkat Harry chatted animatedly back and forth. John threw in an occasional comment, but contented himself most of the time—

especially after supper was finished, and they sat before the fire—with listening. This sort of brilliant gay fooling was too fast for him, and some of the allusions were over his head. But he liked it, and he was quietly tickled that Sally could return as good as was sent, and that Chilkat Harry hadn't been able to spring anything yet that she did not know something about—or at least recognize. His eyes twinkled secretly under his heavy brows, for he could see that Chilkat Harry was showing off and was probably trying to do just that. And, too, John was enjoying Sally's enjoyment. She was having such a good time, her eyes sparkling, all stimulated and stirred up like a—like a terrier waiting for the ball to bring back, was the best John could do. She was good at this sort of a game—she must have missed it—— Gosh, she sure did know a lot! He was glad she had found somebody who could play it. He was wholly sincere in this thought. In it was no trace of envy or jealousy; for John's solid sense of reality knew it for what it was—a game, fluff, fireworks—nothing to do with the fundamentals of relationship.

And while he was enjoying wholeheartedly the toss back and forth between the two, he was at the same time sitting coolly apart, studying Chilkat Harry, sizing him up, filing away what significant fragments he could catch. They were curiously few. The man was certainly an engaging cuss, frank, gay, lighthearted, friendly, admitted John—when, as now, he wanted to be, was the added corollary. He had had apparently wide experiences in all parts of the world, and he touched upon them entertainingly—but without consecutiveness or real body: you couldn't reconstruct from them a thing about the man's past life. The same might be said of his casual references to himself. Apparently frank, they actually told nothing, though each of them opened wide vistas for speculation. Which, was John's shrewd comment, was probably just what he intended. The man loves to show off; and you can show off a lot better by giving people just enough to guess on. The way this fellow left it, he might be anything—preferably romantic. Mysterious-past stuff, reflected John placidly. Fugitive from justice—some nice tidy noble crime, of course; or maybe you hadn't done it and were falsely accused. Rich, haughty family, and the wild young son breaking free from it all. Busted heart. Any of these things, or a dozen more. John knew them all: they were the backbone of plot in the tattered paperbacks the average cow-camp stuffs into flour sacks and calls its "library."

But—and this to John was a significant distinction—though the man had a streak of vanity, liked to preen, to show off, he did not brag. And because he noted this, John would never make the mistake of underrating Chilkat Harry. The man might pose, but he was no bluffer.

The evening was half over before John was brought front and center in the conversation. Something was said of Klakan, and that reminded Chilkat Harry. He turned directly to John.

"I owe you something there," said he, with all his engaging openness of manner, "but I can't for the life of me make out whether it's gratitude or grudge."

"Yeah?" John raised his heavy eyebrows. "What's that?"

"Kelly. If you hadn't attended to him the way you did I would undoubtedly have killed him. And," his face turned grim for a fleeting moment, "let me tell you it would have been plain murder. I'd never have given a chance I didn't have to. He didn't deserve it. Like potting a rattlesnake or a mad dog." He caught Sally's expression. "Well," he continued, more lightly, to John, "you kept me out of that much. But, as I say, I don't know whether I want to thank you or not."

"If I had known, I'd have saved him for you," said John gravely, but with a twinkle. "I'd never think of poaching on another man's property," he added.

Chilkat Harry did not notice this, or passed it by.

"Tell me," he begged, "did I get the straight story? Was it a fact that Kelly had the straight drop on you?"

"Oh yes," acknowledged John.

"I didn't know that!" cried Sally, startled.

"That's what Mush Mahoney told me. You must be pretty quick with a gun."

"Don't have to be so extra quick with that kind of a bum."

"Well," said Chilkat Harry, "that may be, but I'd hate to have to try it—with a holster gun."

John pricked up his attention at the addition of the last four words.

"There's no better way to have a gun handy than in a holster," he stated.

Chilkat Harry laughed amusedly.

"I'd have been planted years ago if I'd believed that. In my business you don't want a gun near as often as they make out; but when you do, you want it next your hand and not hanging down on your leg somewhere."

"That's interesting," observed John mildly.

Chilkat Harry explained. He took no attitude of offensive superiority, but it was evident that he liked to explain. In his business, said he, the only serious trouble a gambler is likely to get into is when some loser—generally more or less drunk—becomes convinced he has been cheated and tries to shoot it out. Then, he repeated, he needed his gun right next his hand, where he could get at it while still sitting down and get a dead drop before the troublemaker can go into action.

"Then," said Chilkat Harry, "he can shoot or not shoot, depending on circumstances. It's mighty rare he has to. I never have; and I've had my share of bellyachers, of course. Goes with the job. I may have to sometime or other. But by the time a man's made up his mind I've seen symptoms; and by the time he's got to his feet I've the muzzle of my gun in his belly, and the show's over."

John nodded agreement. "That's right. Matter of quickness. And, as you say, with the average bum out for a time, you don't have to move very fast. With most of them you'd have plenty of time to wheel in a six-inch cannon. But you can't count on that forever. I don't know how it is up here, but down where I came from there's a scattering of serious-minded hombres that don't rattle. If I sat in on your game and made up my mind something was crooked—oh, right or wrong, right or wrong"—John interpolated easily—"I wouldn't give you any symptoms. I'd lay doggo until I was ready, and then I'd act *pronto,* and you'd never have a chance, unless you were a better man than I, no matter where you kept your gun. Chances are you'd never get to touch it."

"So?" said Chilkat Harry, "and just how would you accomplish that?" John had spoken with the lazy tolerance of amusement; but Chilkat Harry's voice had a challenging purr.

"Oh, I'd probably begin by dumping the whole table over in your lap," said John.

"I should not misinterpret your effort. My tables are screwed to the floor, my friend. I wasn't born yesterday."

"In that case I wouldn't try it. Don't you suppose that the first thing I'd do when I sat down would be to find out if they were screwed down or not? I wasn't born yesterday either." So far John replied with some spirit, but immediately reverted to his lazy drawl. "I reckon you know your business," he acknowledged. "Comes back to what we were talking about—who can get at his gun the fastest—you or me."

"Other things being equal, probably you," Chilkat Harry made his own acknowledgment, "from what I heard. But I wear my gun under my left armpit, and in a clip, so that would give me my advantage, you see."

John shook his head.

"I'd hate to see you depending on that, Harry," said he, as though regretfully.

Chilkat Harry flushed.

"I must say you don't hate yourself," he returned with some sarcasm.

"Now don't take me wrong," John protested good-humoredly, "I wasn't trying to brag. I wasn't thinking of us. But take any two good fast men, one just as quick and practiced as the other, and one of them carrying his gun in a proper holster, and the other in a clip under his arm, like you describe, and start 'em at the word, and the holster man will get the other fellow every time. It stands to reason."

"I don't believe I like this kind of talk," spoke up Sally, who had been watching Chilkat Harry's face.

"Shucks, Sally," said John placidly, "let us alone. We're just having fun." He turned to Harry and now spoke seriously. "It's like this, Harry: you see, when you pull a gun from a leg holster you can bring it to position with one clean curve; and when you reach for your clip your hand has to make two angles, and you can't make angles without checking and starting over again, and that's where you lose time. And, besides, there's your coat. You don't want to advertise by not wearing a coat—or do you?"

"I think you're talking nonsense." Chilkat Harry was impatient. "You've got to make at least two of your famous 'angles' lifting your gun out of its holster, and you've much farther to reach."

"Sure—if you lift it." John turned earnest; he was beginning to want to prove his point. "That's where the tenderfoot makes his mistake. I've even seen 'em tie the holster to their leg—— Wait," John broke off, "I'll show you."

He disappeared for a moment into the bedroom, returned carrying the belt and holster and the Colt .45. He emptied the latter of its cartridges, buckled on the belt. "Now watch," said he. He dropped his hand to the butt of the weapon. "Notice," he instructed, "that at the same time I hunch my shoulder well forward; and when my hand hits the gun it swings the bottom end of the holster back, and then you've got a straight draw forward, and you swing the muzzle down and up in one curve—and there you are!" John was demonstrating slowly as he talked. "It's all in starting with throwing your shoulder forward," said he, thrusting the weapon back in place. "Now I'll do it all at once, so you can see."

He repeated the motions of his draw as he had described them, but now consecutively and without pause. Sally watched, fascinated as always by the easy grace of the man when he engaged himself in the performance of any physical feat to which he had been accustomed—riding a horse, swinging an ax, throwing a pack hitch, casting a fly, as the other day, against the background of the forest. He was moving now with the precision of an oiled machine. There was no visible check in rhythm, but Sally perceived at once that, promptly as the muzzle came into position, this was nothing like that lightning flash of action she remembered. John had slowed down, by ever so little, for the purpose of his demonstration.

Chilkat Harry, of course, could not know this. He watched interestedly enough, and even with a growing admiration as his good humor was restored very simply by a return of self-confidence. Pretty: but he could beat that a mile.

"I still know I would come out first best," he recurred to their argument.

"Well," said John, "there's one way to find out. Got your gun on you?"

Chilkat Harry stared, then laughed. John grinned a little sheepishly. "No, of course not. Too bad." His grin became quizzical. "I'd hate to have you show me up before Sally."

Something in his tone caused the other to fire up.

"You don't get off that easy!" said he, rising. "It's not much of a chore to *get* my gun." There was an edge in his voice.

"Shucks, sit down," urged John. " 'Tain't worth while, all that walk way up to your place and back. Another time's just as good."

"No, we'll try it now." Chilkat Harry's manner was almost violent. He started for the door, moving on the balls of his moccasined feet, after his light pantherlike manner. "I won't be long," he added over his shoulder. "I don't have to go to my place. It's in the pirogue."

Sally looked after him uneasily and back to John sprawling in exaggerated laziness.

"I don't understand. I don't like it. What is it you are going to do?"

"Kid games," said John. "Just going to snap our guns at each other like a couple of kid waddys in a bunkhouse. See who can get there first. Never thought to play *that* game again. But it ain't a bad game," he added judicially. "Good enough practice."

"I don't like it," repeated Sally. "Why do you persist in keeping him all stirred up so?"

"Stirred up?" John repeated. "I hadn't noticed."

"Don't try that on me, John Murdock!" warned Sally. "Let him alone. He wants to be friendly——"

"Does he?" John interrupted quietly at this point.

"Why—why—doesn't he?" Sally was stopped.

"How friendly?" John persisted. "With who?" Sally sat up straight. "Now hold on," he checked her, "don't you get to going off half cocked too. One's enough. If you do, I might join in and make it unanimous." He had one eyebrow higher than the other as he looked at her. It fell slowly to the level as she sank against the back of her chair.

"If you suspect that he——" she began in a more reasonable tone of discussion.

"I expect nothing about him," John interrupted firmly. "But I don't know anything about him, either, and a man's a fool in Injun country if he don't scout from the hills."

"But I don't see why you have to . . ." Sally did not pretend to misunderstand.

"He's never said one word or done one thing—or even *looked* at me as though—— Just the opposite," she said thoughtfully.

"I've sometimes had pretty good luck taking that line myself," said John with a chuckle. "But that was the other fellow," he added quickly, "the one that sort of drug along through life before I met up with you. You don't give a damn about that low-down ornery critter, do you, Sally?"

She had to laugh. "No, of course not." She recurred to her first uneasiness. "But I can't see how deliberately goading the man is going to——"

"Here he comes," John interrupted.

He tilted his chair back again. Chilkat Harry re-entered the room, crossed to the table, flung on it a pack of cards, twirled a chair to face it. He moved in the staccato restraint of exasperation.

"All right," said he to John, "come on."

John unfolded his long figure and moved leisurely to the opposite side of the table, dragging his chair after him. He did not sit.

"Let's see," he requested. He extended his left hand, and at the same time with his right hand he drew the Colt .45 from its holster and laid it on the table.

"Of course they're unloaded," he told this to Sally, "but it's etiquette to let the other fellow see."

Harry, a trifle grudgingly, reached under his jacket to give John a short-barreled nickel-plated weapon, which the latter examined with interest. He broke it, twirled the cylinder about, handed it back to its owner.

"Double action sure saves you a lot of practicing," he observed pleasantly. "I was raised single action, and I never got over it. When I try double action I find myself thumbing the hammer just the same. So I stick to old spitfire, here." He slid the .45 back into its holster and dropped easily into his chair. He turned his head to Sally. "You be umpire," said he.

"I'll be nothing of the kind. I think this is all just silly."

"Silly yourself," rejoined John, still pleasantly. "Can't we have a little fun? You got to be umpire. There's nobody else. That right, Harry?"

"If you please, Mrs Murdock," the latter assented. There might have been the least shade of iron in the tone: Sally could not be sure, but she flushed at its implication—if it were there—that her decisions might be partial. Or was there such an implication? She flushed still more, but now with vexation. This man had a diabolical knack of involving her in subtleties. But the vexation burned away her hesitancy.

"All right, what do I do?" she asked.

"Why, Harry and I are playing cards here, and you just have to decide whose gun snaps first. You'll have to notice sharp because the clicks 'll be mighty close together."

"Who gives the signal—to begin, I mean?" asked Sally.

"There's no signal," said John. "Harry can go into action any time he thinks I'm making a suspicious move. That was the idea, wasn't it, Harry?" The young man nodded. "Well, then, deal 'em out," said John. "We're supposed to be playing cards, you know."

Except for the fact that he manipulated the pasteboards entirely with his left hand, nothing in John's posture or actions indicated that he was in the least on the alert. He sprawled back loosely in his chair, which was balanced on two legs. But so abruptly, so without a slightest preliminary flicker, so without transition, did he move, that sheer surprise checked Chilkat Harry's reach toward the shoulder holster beneath his coat. The check could have been gauged in a small fraction of a second: but it was enough. He stared into the muzzle of the .45 just as his hand touched the butt of his own gun. John laughed.

"I'll spare your life this time," said he.

But Chilkat Harry protested. John had caught him unaware. He hadn't understood. It was he, not John, who was to start the game. Wasn't that what John had said?

"What I said was that you were to go into action any time you thought I was making a suspicious move. Well," John glanced at the .45, which he still held in his hand, "strikes me the move I made might be considered by some as a leetle mite suspicious?"

Harry flushed angrily at the dry irony. But Sally interposed.

"Harry's right," she said, "it was a mistake."

"There generally ain't chance for but about one such mistake. After that a man ain't interested," said John. "However . . ." He slipped the revolver back in its holster and reached for the cards. Sally tried to catch his eye. This was unlike John, to labor a mere technicality. It was obvious to Sally that he was deliberately baiting the other man. She could not understand why Harry did not see this. She was vexed with John. The latter was speaking.

"Now let's get this straight," said he. "We're playing cards. You're running the game. I'm the sucker. But I got a suspicious nature. Somewhere along the line I'm going to think I catch you in some funny business. I want my money back, and I'm going after it. Maybe I'm wrong, but that don't alter my actions. That clear? All right. Now for you. You're dealing with a tough bunch, and you got to protect yourself. If you see anything that even *looks* like trouble, you are the one that's going into action. Maybe *you* are wrong. Maybe I'm just aiming to blow my nose. But you can't take chances. Simpler to get the drop on me and apologize if it's a false alarm. Nobody holds that against a gambler. Nowhere *I've* ever been. That right, too? Fair enough. Now for me again. If I see you beginning to make a mistake like that, I'm not going to wait to see if you mean to shoot or not. A good many folks got a principle never to pull a gun unless they mean to use it. Pretty good principle, too," observed John parenthetically, "bluffing with a six gun is poor business. So if, as I say, I think I see you starting to make a mistake about me, this time it's me tries to beat you to it." He turned to Sally. "Just about half of shooting trouble is mistakes," he said conversationally. "Ain't that right, Harry?" he asked the latter in genial disregard of the other's obvious impatience. "All set, umpire? Of course," he added, "you've got a little the best of it. In real life you'd have a tableful to keep track of. Here you've got only me. Snap out of it, Sally! Let's go."

Sally came to attention with a start. She had been staring at John, puzzled, trying to make out what he was driving at. So long a speech was not like him. Deliberately arousing enmity was not like him, especially as she was perfectly aware that, by and large, he did like Chilkat Harry. It was not merely for amusement: John was not that kind either. He had some purpose, but she could not guess it.

The men pretended to play cards, Chilkat Harry wary and tense, John apparently half asleep. Abruptly both men flashed into action. But this time there was no question of getting a drop on the other. Chilkat Harry's short weapon appeared from under his coat at the same instant the muzzle of John's .45 came over the edge of the table. But the sharp clicks of the hammers were well spaced. John looked toward Sally. However, she was not needed for decision.

"Yours," acknowledged Harry briefly.

"Get it?" asked John. "You got your gun out about as quick as mine, but you had to turn it to point it. Mine came out pointed."

"Try again," said Harry.

They tried again and again and yet again, but with always the same result. Sally's uneasiness and disapproval melted into the interest of sheer admiration. Anything done superlatively—anything at all, no matter how uncouth in nature when done less than superlatively —must be done with both grace and ease; and these are pretty things to watch. The result of each essay was the same. After a little she thought she noticed that John was "telegraphing," as boxers say: making slight, almost imperceptible movements of warning a split second before going after his gun. She was not sure of that, though the fall of the hammers seemed to her closer together. She sharpened her alertness in case she might be called upon as umpire. Some, toward the last, she thought might have been open to debate. Even these, however, Harry acknowledged.

"Yours," said he without hesitation. But with each repetition Sally fancied the word lost some of its curtness, and glancing at John, she thought to catch a shadow of approval in his eyes. Finally Chilkat Harry burst out laughing and tossed his revolver to the middle of the table.

"'You're a better man than I am, Gungha Din'!" said he. "Gosh, you've got a whole graveyard of me laid out. If ever I get around to shooting you, it'll be from ambush!"

John slid his own weapon into its holster and unbuckled the belt.

"I got to brag to tell you that you're plenty fast with that thing. Even the way you carry it, you're faster than anybody I ever saw, bar two or three. Of which I'm one." He made a droll face. "That's the brag. I reckon nobody in this country will crawl your hump."

Harry left shortly after, whistling down the trail. John stood a moment in the doorway looking after him. Then he turned back to Sally.

"He's quite a feller after all," observed John with an air of gratification.

"I thought I understood men," she confessed. "I don't believe I do."

"That's the stuff!" said John. "Keep 'em guessing."

"I think I see, just a little," said Sally, two lines between her eyes, "but would you mind telling—why were you trying to quarrel with him? Don't tell me you weren't," she headed off denial, "I know *you,* anyway."

"Why," said John, "looked to me like we're due to see a good deal of this feller, and I had to know what to expect. That's only sensible."

"How?"

"Well," John groped, as always when it came to explaining himself, "I had to find out whether it was all just outside, or whether maybe it was inside, too."

"What?"

"Why, being a kid," said John. "Don't you see? Outside he's mostly kid—likes to show off, touchy a little, stuck on—well—play-acting a little. I had to find out whether he was really that way. You got to know what a man *is* before you can tell how he's going to act when things get tough—or something."

"And he isn't?"

"No. He's all right. A kid would have stayed mad."

Sally laughed.

"I'm glad you're satisfied," said she.

"Oh, I ain't," returned John unexpectedly. "I haven't seen him drunk yet."

CHAPTER XX

PICNIC

ALTHOUGH neither could be aware of that fact, the following day proved to be one that definitely ended one phase of their life together. In a way it was like the end of a honeymoon, but only in the sense of swinging to the direction they must henceforth take, as the needle of the compass steadies. They would always remain lovers.

For that reason it was well that the day should be fortunate, both in weather and adventure. When Alaska really gives her mind to it she can contrive a brilliance not elsewhere to be equaled. Her sparkles of water and snow and sky are more eager, her colors are cleaner, her air so crystalline it should ring like a bell, but the secret of her magic is that she can, and does, evoke in her children also a heightening of the senses to receive. The austerity of her native vastness she throws aside like a heavy cloak, so that the very hills dance together, and the sea laughs, and the somber brooding forests arouse to joy.

At least that is how Sally described the day, as the two of them shoved off in the dinghy early the following morning. John felt the same way about it, but he could not have said it. He had a curious diffidence about words that conveyed feeling. Almost as though there were something shameful about them, like exposing nakedness. Sally just said things like that, right out. He could never quite get used to her unself-consciousness. As John shipped oars and began to pull away from the mouth of the stream he was thinking of that. It had been that way right from the start, way back there in the little grass park above Siler's Bend, where they had spent their first weeks together. That second day, when they'd found the big pool downstream and gone swimming. He was remembering. He'd made the proposal in a sort of panicky daring. He grinned secretly as he recalled how promptly and joyously Sally had greeted the suggestion, and how unconcernedly she had dropped her garments while he was still overcoming embarrassments.

"What are you grinning at, all by yourself?" demanded Sally now.

"I was remembering that first time we went swimming together—in the Cascades—and how rattled I was, and how you weren't rattled the least bit."

"Why should I have been? We belonged to each other, didn't we?" Sally was really surprised. She examined John more narrowly. "Why!" she cried, "it never occurred to me—I never thought——"

"Don't, Sally, don't!" pleaded John. "I thought it was beautiful—your being so—well, so kind of——"

Sally burst out laughing.

"You began to think I was a shameless hussy!" she accused.

"I did not so!" protested John. "That wasn't it at all. But you see it sort of upset all the ideas I'd been brought up on . . ."

"Go on!" prodded Sally inexorably. Her eyes were dancing with mischief over this rare opportunity of getting John in a corner.

"Well," blurted the latter desperately, "I'd always had it rubbed in about women being so naturally modest as compared with men; and all the ones I'd known had—you couldn't say 'garter' at 'em without getting throwed out." John's grammar was weakening, always a sure sign to Sally of stress. "That is, the nice ones," he had to add in the interests of accuracy.

Sally pounced on this.

"And it was such a shock to find I wasn't a 'nice' one," she accused hopefully and hugged herself when this suggestion did the trick. John exploded.

"No!" he roared. "You know better." He stopped himself as he caught Sally's expression. "Keno," he made his usual acknowledgment of defeat. "But that learned me one thing . . ."

"Yes? What was that?"

"That this modesty-of-women stuff is the bunk," John counterattacked boldly, "that men are naturally more modest than women."

"And how do you know that?" asked Sally quietly. Too quietly. John looked at her in uncertainty.

"Why—I just been telling you."

"I consider that a most immodest idea," stated Sally. "It would never have occurred to a woman—a 'nice' woman," added Sally with a touch of malice, "not if she loved a man. I should think," she concluded in virtuous reproof, "that you'd be thoroughly ashamed of yourself."

"Well I'll be doggoned!" John stared at her. It had again worked around to be all his fault, and he could not see how. Not offhand. How did Sally do it?

"How did you happen to think of that?" asked Sally presently, offering a commonplace as a peace offering. "Want to go swimming? It *would* be fun."

"Not me!" John's reply was emphatic. "Have you felt this water? Dip your hand."

The purpose of the excursion was exploratory. The first idea was to hug close the shore of this inland sea all the way around, but that was soon abandoned. "Take about a week," said John, though that was an exaggeration. Looked small enough until you got out there, and then you found it was you who were small! However, the dinghy was light, and they had their lunch, so they kept on to the other end. From the water the fringe of the valley looked to be only a narrow strip before the rise of the mountains. There was a stream, but it was not much of a stream. They thought they would follow it up to its source, but they walked until nearly noon and had not yet come to its steep confinement in canyon walls.

"Looks like they've got different scales here for your eyes and your legs," said John.

They arrived back at the beach hot from bucking brush. It would have been pleasant to sit down and cool off, but the tide was dropping. If they lounged much longer they would have to trundle the dinghy overland on rollers—heaven knows how far. So they embarked, and John rowed slowly, skirting the coast, now on the west side. This was behind the two islands they had passed north of the entrance coming in. The shore itself was of rounded boulders. Evidently the water ran deep here. Between two of the boulders Sally caught a glimpse. She exclaimed and pointed. John nodded and whirled the bow of the dinghy. There was not much to spare between the boulders. John made three strong strokes with the oars, then held them aloft while the little craft scraped through.

They were in a tiny lake, or pond. It was only about a hundred yards or so in diameter and comparatively shallow—possibly twenty or twenty-five feet deep at this state of the tide, though it was difficult to estimate that. A sort of pothole, generously scattered with boulders. Some of them rounded above the water, like the backs of beasts; others were dim green down below; several were but just below the surface. John gingerly ran the bow of the dinghy on the slope of one of these latter. They looked about them.

There was no breath of air: the place was completely enclosed. The sun had both strength and laziness.

"If there was even a few feet of beach we could picnic," said John.

"We don't need a beach," said Sally. "What could be nicer than one of these big rocks?" She trailed her fingers overside and uttered a delighted squeal.

"Hey, look out!" warned John. "What do you think you're doing? What's the matter? Yellow jacket?"

Sally was precariously afoot, snatching off her clothes.

"Feel! Feel!" she cried. "No, you goop!" as John, puzzled, made a cautious move in her direction. "The water! The water!"

In twenty seconds she was overside, almost kicking the dinghy out from under John and splashing him heavily. She came to the surface and tossed her wet hair back with a quick fling of the head.

"It's heavenly, perfectly heavenly. As warm as warm!"

They swam about over the green depths, leaving the dinghy to drift. Shortly they came upon a great rock, not rounded like the others, but flat and level on top. Over it the water was at that moment exactly so deep that when Sally sat down her chin just touched its surface. John's height gave him margin, of course; and he laughed at Sally's intent and earnest concentration on keeping her nose out, and he tried to make wavelets to force her to arise. But she gulped and gasped and stuck it out, as though somehow it were very important that she thwart John; and shortly it became evident that the greater powers were on her side. They had forgotten the tide; and now she experienced a wholly irrational personal triumph as the fall of the water freed her. After the long hesitation, as though of uncertainty, at the slack, it was like magic, now that it had made up its mind. She need no longer hold her chin up. It was down to her shoulders, her breast. They sat there side by side, unable to leave the big flat rock, held by the fascination of this mysterious and silent refluence. But it did not seem like a refluence. The water remained the same, but the great rock was rising, slowly, very gently, beneath them. It yellowed as the water shoaled; and soon over it scurried only distracted shallow ripples seeking escape; and then it drained, and Sally and John stretched out on it luxuriously in the sun.

By and by John swam over and brought back the dinghy, which had drifted to the shore; and they ate the lunch they had brought; and then, reluctantly, but compelled by consideration of time and sunburn, they dressed and resumed the excursion. By now they had to scramble down into the small boat as from a wharf. At the entrance the guardian boulders, too, stood high above them, and the inflowing water between was swift and shallow. Sally turned for a last look. She was very happy. This was the one thing needed, the one thing that lacked, to make the whole place perfect.

Once in the open, John rowed rapidly. They passed the two islands and were again in familiar water. The best of the day was over; remained now only to get home. John headed directly across the open.

But the projecting point below the entrance brought them again close inshore. The steep forests overhung them. John hesitated on his oars, then turned the boat toward the shore. It was a momentous decision, though of course neither knew it at the time.

"I want to take a look," he answered Sally's inquiry.

"At what?" was her natural question.

"The woods. I got an idea."

She pressed him for the idea. He said merely that he wanted to climb the ridge. Sally did not feel that energetic. They'd already had a long day. The ridge would probably stay there. . . . But John wanted to do it now.

"Then," said Sally, "I'll wait here in the boat."

"I won't be long," said John. He nosed the dinghy against the bank, which was steep-to. There was no beach; the side of the mountain continued almost straight down in the water. He made fast the dinghy painter to a bush. Then he began to scramble.

Sally looked after him with faint curiosity. Something beside exercise was behind this whim. She'd find it out soon enough. She lay down in the bottom of the dinghy and rested her head on the stern thwarts. There was not much to see from this position, except the sky—in which two soaring eagles traced slow intricate patterns—and the forest wall before her and just the top of the Protector of the Wilderness to her left. But there was plenty to hear. She closed her eyes to listen: whisper of water against the stony shore; quick lapping of water against the boat; ravens in the woods; a winter wren, hermit thrushes; voices of the shadow—the quick lapping of water . . . She fell asleep.

John broke through the screen of brush next the shore and found himself, as he had anticipated, in a clear forest. He looked about him for a moment and then started to climb. It was a a steep scramble to which he had to address himself with a single mind. After ten minutes of it he came on a narrow shelf, or miniature plateau, of level ground. Here he stopped to look.

Through a break in the trees he could see the inlet. It looked like gun metal, and from this height its wavelets did not seem to move.

The skiff was almost directly below. He could see that, too, and Sally lying down in it. So nearly under him was it that he had the quaint fancy that he could take a running jump and leap right over it into deep water. That would surprise Sally! He slapped his thigh with delight, for that was exactly what he had suspected and what he had come to verify. As usual he was fired with the desire to share his splendid inspiration with Sally. He plunged down the mountain side so heedlessly that twice he barely saved himself from pitching forward. If he fell, then he *would* surprise her, for there was little to stop him short of the salt chuck.

"You'll break your fool neck!" he admonished himself and slowed to proper caution.

The moment he reached the shore he began to talk. Sally, abruptly awakened, was a little dazed.

"Minute I saw that slope, the idea struck me!" was the first she understood, "and as soon as I got up where I could see I found it would work. I'm going to try it!"

"Try what?" She had not the least notion of what John was talking about.

"The time we were stormed in, in British Columbia. That fellow who was trying to bust the cat—you remember—Mike what's-his-name—the hand logger. You and Len wouldn't wait." If she and Len had been willing to wait Mike was going to let John try to run a log. He'd wanted to see if he could do it. Sally's wits were focusing. She recalled now John's almost boyish admiration of the hand logger's skill. She could see it now: of course he had wanted to try it!

"I'll bet I could 'run' one of those trees; and, by gosh, I'm going to do it!" cried John happily.

He loosed the dinghy and got aboard and picked up the oars and began to row. He dipped the blades and kept his direction mechanically. His mind was occupied with inner speculations, fragments of which he threw out to Sally from time to time. He'd picked the tree for his experiment, and sort of halfway picked the course of its run. Have to go back and figure on it more carefully, of course—calculate where he'd have to figure on deflections—and make a "bed"—his

mind trailed off into silences and technicalities which Sally did not
understand. But it was very busy: she could see that. She gave over
trying to understand and contented herself with looking at John. He
was all lit up. She liked him like that, and she was glad he had
found something to interest himself this way, and she understood
a little why he was interested—something new, but still in line with
his practical upbringing—a challenge to the very qualities his life
had bred in him. A new game to play. But even her intuition did not
fathom why this thing seemed so flamingly to have possessed him.
Nor could John have told her. He was not self-analytical and could
not himself have realized that the deep-hidden spring of his enthusiasm lay in the simple fact that this was the first reality offered his
hand, since he had left the Big Basin, of which he was the Boss and
not the Hired Man. The first Job, that is; even if it did not mean
anything!

"Don't you have to have tools?" asked Sally, to show interest.

John thought he could get by with his ax—for the tree he had
selected.

But this started him on a new line of speculation. The job *might*
be made to mean something!

"By golly, Sally," he burst out presently, "I'm not so sure we
haven't got something here!"

If he could "run" one tree, he could "run" more. Logs! Lumber!
"They're using a heap of lumber in that fool town, and they'll use
a lot more. Orford—the fellow with the mill—he's always hollering
for more logs. I'll bet he'd take 'em—and send a tug after them. I'll
bet he'd pay a good price: stands to reason. Soon as we get out of
quarantine"—John grinned—"we'll run over to Klakan and find out.
And get tools. We'll need tools, if the thing works out." John retired
again to consider tools. Grindstone. Some of those big jacks—"'Gil-
christs' they call them," he told Sally. Boom chains. Iron dogs.
("Whatever they are!" interjected Sally to herself.) Crowbars. Barking bars.

"Dogfish oil," interposed Sally, wrinkling her nose, "and you can
go sleep in the brush."

John laughed, but briefly. He could not be deflected.

"There ought to be a good stake in it," he speculated. "We can use some money."

He was happy and looked it. He had found something real, something to get his teeth in. It had all been wonderful, but somehow intangible. A man's world must be solid. Anything will do, as long as it is solid.

"Then we're going to stay here," surmised Sally. Suited her: she liked it here.

But John was not ready for that.

"Oh, we'll be moving on. Want to see the country. But here's a chance to make a stake . . ."

He did not have to see farther ahead than the immediate thing: the task next to his hand. That was all that was needed. But it had to be real and worth while. This was worth while. John was at heart a pioneer. The pioneer is driven by an urge, not persuaded by a plan. If he thought things away out to conclusion he would never be a pioneer.

The picnic was over.

CHAPTER XXI

THE JOB

WITHOUT opportunity for adjustment Sally was now to learn how completely a job peculiarly his own can absorb a man, especially if it is new and baffling. She was amazed and a little hurt. John was away all of every long day, up on that side hill. There he did physical work much harder than any slave could have been whipped to, accomplished brilliant prodigies of planning, most of which did not work first off and must be modified, returned to the cabin late and dog tired. That part of it might not have been so bad, but he brought home a complete preoccupation. He appeared to listen to what Sally was saying, but she came to doubt if he heard. He tumbled into bed like a log and might as well have been a log, as far as Sally was concerned. Next morning he hurried to be off early, eager to try out some new expedient.

For, Sally gathered, things were not going so well in the woods as he had hoped. Trees did queer and unexpected things. The causes of failure were various. John studied them and eliminated them one by one, but always a new one developed on the next attempt. John was not in the least dashed by these setbacks. On the contrary. Each seemed to add zest to his interest in winning a new and fascinating game.

"I'll get there! I'll get one in—if the trees hold out!" he said to Sally with a laugh.

"How much do you expect to get for one tree?" she asked, with the first genuine edge of irony she had ever turned on John. Instantly she regretted it, but as instantly saw that it had not penetrated his single-mindedness. "I hate to see them come down uselessly," she added as a compromise to herself.

"They're not wasted," returned John. "I'll get them in when I have the tools."

"Oh," said Sally faintly. She had forgotten. Then this was to go on. She caught herself up. She was being childish. What did she expect? A man must have his work. Nevertheless, she felt forlornly like a child, left outside where it was chilly. And it had been so warm and cozy inside, and . . .

But she took reassurance from John's next words.

"Of course as soon as I can get proper tools it won't be near such hard work."

"Then why not wait until you have the tools?" she suggested.

"Oh, I'm having fun," returned John.

It was on Sally's lips to say that she was not having fun, but she snatched that back in a flare of real contempt for herself. Little fool, little self-centered fool! Spoiled little fool! She went outside and looked at the Protector of the Wilderness and regained her common sense.

So—for the time being, she told herself—she set herself resolutely to fashioning her own days—and nights—apart from John. He was in his own world, his man's world. It was not hers, but she should be able to share it, partially at least, because it was John's. So she went one day with John into the woods; but there was nothing to do but sit on a log or wander about. She was not really with John; or, rather, he was not really with her. He was wholly possessed by the practical things he was groping toward doing. When she tried to ask questions he answered vaguely. Her intuitions sensed an inner annoyance at questions, but they did not go quite deep enough to make her understand that the real reason for the annoyance was that

John himself did not know the answers: he was fumbling for them, and questions broke the thread. Sally was above all things candid. She did not shrink from confessing to herself that she was just plain bored.

To be sure, it was exciting when a tree fell. That was worth the waiting—once—almost. But it was so soon over; and the preparations were so dull and so long; and the succeeding operations were so dull and so long. And, to Sally, the thrill was shot with pain of regret that so noble and ancient a dignity should be laid low. It was exquisite, like a great and noble tragedy. She would not have missed the experience; but she did not want to repeat it.

There was the tiny human creature and the movements of his futility against serene and age-old stabilities. But as she watched the serenity somehow was flawed. She seemed to catch far aloft a fine quivering, as though of a strange breeze; and then—then—yes, there was no doubt of it—the tipmost top of the tree was shifting, sketching the beginning of an arc across the sky.

"Tim-ber!" John was uttering the long woodsman's call, though there was nobody there but Sally, perched safely aside; and she did not hear. All her being was caught in the mighty drama.

The tree moved toward the crescendo of its fall with the slow quiet dignity of a prelude of music. It yielded; but it yielded in its own good time, hesitant to abandon itself to gravity's upreaching arms until it had composed itself to fate. Then came the breathless moment of its acceptance. Faster and faster! A crackling through the branches of the trees! Crashing, plunging in a wild and swirling turmoil, strangely blended, of both sight and sound! And then a mighty thump and the abashed retreat of echoes and a light fine dust-mist hanging in the sun and the hushed reverence of memorial silence.

But the silence was for only an instant. It was broken by a deep murmur, then by a groaning and a grinding.

"She's going to run!" cried John.

Indeed, the great mass was sliding, but the motion was deliberate, and it gained but slowly. To Sally there was in the prostrate tree still something disdainful. Though fallen, it was not yet conquered. In it was an enormous power still. Down the slope it moved, without haste, inexorably grinding down, thrusting aside the brush and small timber in its path. Then it stopped.

"Hell!" said John fervently.

That was all.

Sally did not go to the woods again. She was rather at loose ends. The time until, as John expressed it, the "quarantine would be lifted" at Klakan was short. It was like one of those railway journeys that is too brief to tempt one to settle down and too long not to be boresome. She put in the first few days just wandering about: but the possibilities even of this were limited by her lack of rubber boots and the fact that John had the dinghy. Twice she went at low tide —when she could cross the river—to see the Mackamoose family. Her interchange with them could not be described as voluble, but she had a good visit nevertheless. It came to her afterward, as an astonishing discovery, that for satisfactory companionship language may be wholly unimportant! Her best bet, she found, was out on the tide flats or the grass meadow behind the house. Amazingly brilliant blankets of wild flowers were in the weaving. There were curious, small, elusive but friendly birds who slipped in and out between the grass stems. There were blue herons, ancient, serious, preoccupied in meditation. Sally was amused by their air of humorless importance and named them "Grandpa Grumps."

In the back of her mind was an expectation that Chilkat Harry might be coming over; and she found herself wondering a little how he would conduct himself, and whether he might be a nuisance. But he did not appear. This, Sally thought, was a relief. It simplified matters—perhaps. Still, Chilkat Harry was fun: he was quick and intelligent and obviously of education. He quickened and stimulated her, made her feel especially clever. It did not occur to her to be afraid of him: he had about him somehow the air of being what is known as a "gentleman"—possessed innately of certain fastidiousness of conduct. Even if he "had intentions"—and Sally was by no means certain in her own mind as to that—he was the kind who would find more satisfaction in siege than assault. He admired himself enough for that! Sally had no doubts she could handle Chilkat Harry. It would be rather fun, she yielded momentarily to the idea and at once threw it out in disgust at herself. She turned her thoughts from Chilkat Harry; but the mere fact of his continued absence brought them back. Perhaps John had misread, and Harry was more deeply angered than he had thought. Whatever the man's present seeming, he had origins. Race and breeding showed in his every movement. Such people were, she supposed, more touchy. She drifted into speculation. Where did he come from? Who and what were his people? What was his past? He'd given small glimpses of that—he seemed to have been a little of everywhere—but they were unrelated, did not make a picture. What had brought him here and into this wild life? What kept him? Love of adventure? Escapade? Desire—or necessity. "No, I don't believe that," said Sally to herself, "he's not one tamely to accept necessity, *any* necessity. Why did he make himself so scarce? she thought in the frontier vernacular, and they the only three white people in the valley. It wasn't natural. Just independent, indifferent? Or was it his game to pique her interest—Sally checked herself at this point with a vexed laugh. She was indeed thinking an awful lot about Chilkat Harry! She stamped her foot in humorous derision at herself. "Drat the man!" she cried aloud so emphatically that a near-by Grandpa Grumps, who had trustingly accepted her as a fellow in meditation, uttered a disillusioned squawk and flew away. Then and there she resolutely dismissed Chilkat Harry from her mind. He shouldn't have that satisfaction!

That night the miraculous spell of weather broke. The wind shifted. The cabin roof resounded to a rush of rain. Next morning disclosed a changed world. The bright spacious valley had become a prison of gloom with dark green walls and a ceiling of driving gray. Alaska had withdrawn her glad adventure, her excitement, her promise, as though suddenly unfriendly. Surely, thought Sally, John would stay in, weather like this. But he put on his heavy Mackinaw and set forth. The cabin was dreary. Sally's mood was absurdly disconsolate. She recognized the absurdity—they would be going back to Klakan in five more days—perhaps to stay—she could not make out whether John was still planning to buy tools and come back, or not. But she did not care. She found pleasure in indulging the mood.

The storm cleared the day before the Queen was due to sail south, taking with her, presumably, the peace officer. That afternoon Chilkat Harry and the dog made their first appearance since the six-gun contest. He timed his arrival with John's, probably had been watching for the dinghy. They came up the trail together. It suddenly occurred to Sally that John had not once bothered to ask her about Chilkat Harry—whether or not she had been seeing anything of him. If that's all he cares about it! Sally's head reared back. Such was the unreason of her mood. In a happier moment her proud thought would have dwelt on his complete confidence in her. Sally was not yet completely adjusted to the idea of a man's world.

She retired to the kitchen. It was to be supposed that the visitor would stay for supper. She called back gaily to John's greeting. The malemute came to the sound of her voice. She hugged his head briefly. The dog's master had made no indication of his presence. Sally was vexed over having to make the first advance; but the evidence of Chilkat forced her hand. She paused to compose herself, then stepped to the doorway. John had gone into the bedroom.

"Well, Harry," she greeted him, "I thought we'd lost you. What have you been doing with yourself?" Unnatural to ignore the fact, better to acknowledge boldly: that was exactly what he was angling for—color burned bright in her cheeks that again his lazy clever maneuvering had put her on the defensive. But the necessity of setting another place at the table enabled her to avoid seeing that usual and exasperating look of amusement.

"I've been busy," said he. He stopped at that, leaving suspended the obvious explanation of what could possibly be busying him.

"So has John: it's been pretty dull," said Sally and looked toward Chilkat Harry with comradely frankness—she hoped. She was resentful of the baffling nuances, the vague and artificial complicities he managed to evoke between them out of nothing. She passed her hand impatiently across her face, as though brushing away cobwebs.

John reappeared, ready for supper. Sally presently brought in the supper. They ate. The men furnished the talk. John told Harry of his plans. He came out from his shell of preoccupation. He was talking now of man's work to a man. Harry had to poke a little fun at John. Sounded to Harry like an awful lot of hard work. "When I want to do any hard work," remarked Chilkat Harry, "I'll start rolling rocks down a mountain to hear them crash: at least I'd get some fun out of that. Hard work wasn't put in the world to be *done,* but to test a man's cleverness in avoiding it." He elaborated this fantastic idea for a moment or so, but sobered down to give the matter serious attention. "It ought to be a good thing," he agreed, "if a man wants to work that hard," he reverted to his argument: but why do it? They went into technicalities—what to buy, how much it cost Orford to get in his logs and how much reasonably he would pay . . .

"How do you get to buy the timber—the stumpage, I mean?" asked John.

Harry stared.

"Buy it?" he repeated. "Why should you buy it? Just take it. Who's going to stop you?"

"Somebody must own it."

"Oh," Harry dismissed this, "it's government land."

So they *were* coming back here. Abruptly Sally spoke up.

"I think I'll wait here until you get back." The decision came to her suddenly out of her vague dissatisfactions.

John looked at her astonished.

"But, Sally," he protested, "what for?"

"I just want to."

"But—but——" John groped. "How about—— Look here, you've got to do some buying too, you know that. And how about Len? Don't you want to see Len? I thought——"

"I want to stay here," repeated Sally.

"But all alone——"

"She'll be all right," Chilkat Harry spoke up unexpectedly. "Why not? I agree with you," he turned to Sally. "Klakan's no treat." He turned back to John. "She'd be all right. Nothing here to bother her.

And there's Johnny Mackamoose. And I'll leave Chilkat for company."

"But——" Both had the same thought.

"Oh, I'm coming back, too," said Chilkat Harry.

The men were gone only four days; but that was more than sufficient to dissipate Sally's vapors. There was the wide and luxurious expansion of being all by herself: paradoxically there was also the aloneness of her first separation from John, for up to now they had not spent a night apart. There was the perfect weather. There was the Buddhistic calm of Johnny and Susy Mackamoose, seated side by side, apparently waiting for eternity. There was, Sally thought, a sort of benign amusement wreathing the serenity of her Protector of the Wilderness, like a cloud. She raised her eyes to the peak, and even to herself her perturbations became small and funny. By the time the Tillicum's sails showed around the point her welcome-home had in it no alloy.

And the interlude seemed to have cracked the shell that was forming around John. Again he was outside and outgoing, the old John. Sally linked her arm in his and hugged it to her breast, and they walked up the narrow trail close together. Harry would follow, he said: he wanted to make up a pack of his purchases. Oh yes, he'd stay and eat. Chilkat looked back and forth, uncertain. Finally he seemed to decide that his job was over, though he had had no formal release. So he squatted, waiting for his master.

The two, with one accord, looked back just before rounding the brush to their first real kiss.

"What's he here for? Why did he come back? What does he *do*? Did you find out?"

"No, I didn't," confessed John. "Everything else, about, but not that. Says he trapped here last winter. There's no trapping now. I've made me a guess or two . . . ." He raised one eyebrow at her.

"I made the same guess—at first," returned Sally candidly, "but in two weeks he's been near us just twice—three times, if you count the day he came by with a pack. And only when you were here. What does he do all the rest of the time? And he must have known you were off all day in the woods. It doesn't make sense."

"Maybe he's onto some prospect he's keeping dark," surmised John vaguely. "Aw, to hell with him—you come here!"

Having settled that more immediately important question, they strolled on to the cabin, freed for a quieter exchange of news. The expedition had been a complete success. John welled up in triumph over his justification.

"Sure I was right," he told Sally, "Orford will take all the saw logs he can get—from anywhere. Gosh, they're using a lot of lumber, more 'n I had any idea of. They're going to put in another of those plank streets, for one thing; and then there 'll be the buildings along them, of course. And piles. Orford can't begin to handle it." John named impressively the price Orford would pay for saw logs—in the boom—John's boom: Orford would send for them.

Sally's knowledge was sufficient to cause her to look incredulous.

"Are you sure?" she asked. "Did you get it in writing?"

Of course John was sure.

"Well!" exclaimed Sally. "Did you see Len?" she wanted to know.

John laughed. "Len! The old coot! What do you suppose Len is up to? You'd never guess!" He paused, but more to impress Sally than to let her guess.

"They've made him town marshal! He's running around with a star and a gun. And I bet he makes them toe the mark. Len's got a streak in him—fools you, first sight—but these folks up here aren't fooled. For why else did they pick Len? They're serious about this business. I reckon Kelly and his like have about played out their hand. Reminds me," said John, "I got a present for you." He thrust his hand into the side pocket of his Mackinaw.

They had reached the cabin. Sally, on her way into the kitchen, stopped. John produced a small blued revolver which he laid in the palm of his hand and surveyed with pride. So evidently sincere was his admiration that Sally choked down a wild impulse to laugh at John's choice of a present.

"Police model," said John, "double-action .32 I just happened to see it. Here. Isn't that cute?"

Sally took the weapon and turned it over and over.

"What would I shoot with it?" she ventured doubtfully. The amusement bubbled up. "Suppose it would attract a bear's attention?"

"That's all right." John brushed frivolity aside. "You ought to have a gun. And you just might need it sometime." He looked at her steadily. She raised her eyes, startled at the note in his voice. But he was speaking lightly again. "You wear it when you go out. I have a belt holster for it. It's good if you want to signal, ain't it? And," he grinned at her, "there's nothing better if you get yourself all snarled up with one of those big he-trout again and want him to be good. Beats one of those dude landing nets all hollow. His name," concluded John gravely, "is Black Mike. Oh! I found you a pair of rubber boots!" he called to her in the kitchen.

CHAPTER XXII

SOMETHING UNLEARNED

THAT AFTERNOON and night Sally was happily back in her familiar and comfortable world. But the return was temporary.

Up to now these two had not experienced spiritual separation. To be sure, John had been away on his job—Bull Kirby's, the mill, the cannery—for many hours of the day; but that was merely physical absence, a sort of interruption; she knew he was thinking of her a good deal of that time, as she was thinking of him; and when he got home they took up right from where they had left off, and the job forgotten. But this was different. John had thrown his whole being into his problem of using the forces of Nature against herself. Sally had no part. She knew he was not thinking of her during his long hours in the woods: his every faculty was absorbed in kerfs and slides and deflections and angles and various bafflements for which his naked ingenuity must evolve solution—all the things he talked about when at last he returned to the cabin—the only things he talked about—when he did talk! Sally's efforts to get off the subject met little response.

"I suppose," agreed John apathetically to whatever she said. "But, gosh, I'm tired!"

Only when she returned to the one subject did John's animation revive. She could still touch elbows by keeping to that. But she was sick of it. She resented it. She did not go into the woods with John. Silly, but the work had to her an element of tragedy. She could shut her eyes now and feel again that quiver of noble resignation before the great tree fell. Oh, she knew it must be done—she was living right now in a house made of trees—but she did not like to see it. It hurt her. Just as she could not stand seeing a deer killed, though she recognized the necessity and ate the venison. John used to tease her about that.

"You're just mushy!" he accused, which always made her indignant. No one likes to be called mushy.

It was not the mere fact of John's physical absence, she told herself. She was not that spoiled; and she had sense enough to realize that a man had to work; and here was a good chance, as John said, to make a needed stake; and anyway it wouldn't last forever. No, it wasn't that. It was the discovery that John could give himself completely to something in which she had no part. She could not have done that! Women have not a man's ability to divide life's interests into watertight compartments. That this was a general masculine trait, Sally had not yet gained the wisdom to know. She thought only in terms of John. She was hurt; at loose ends. Life had drained out, like the tide. Sally was aghast to discover how everything had grown into dependence on John. Extraordinary how empty the ebb!

But shortly, being a woman of spirit, her vitality stirred. "Here, you," she berated herself, "don't be a little fool! You are a person, all by yourself. You ought to be ashamed of yourself to be such a spineless jellyfish, such a—such a *barnacle* on anyone!" She shook herself vigorously and put on her new rubber boots and forced herself to an excursion into the bright and welcoming world outside. The exercise did her good, but try as she would she could not recapture the rapture of intimacy with her surroundings. She was outside: and she could not get in. Just as with John! The thought overwhelmed her in a small momentary panic. A terrible feeling came to her of being very small and all alone in an unfriendly universe. Lowest point for Sally, and of course quite absurd.

Her small accomplishment of induced tranquillity fell flat. She bent her steps in return, mounted forlornly the short trail to the cabin. Chilkat Harry was perched on the edge of the veranda, swinging his legs and whistling. The malemute sat beside him. He hailed her cheerfully, then his eyes narrowed.

"You look all tired out," said he.

Somehow he managed to hit the right note, of solicitude, but just short of sympathy. She flung herself alongside the malemute.

"I'm not tired," she burst out, "but I'm bored—bored to tears!"

"Hm . . ." Chilkat Harry made no comment. She laughed with an undernote of derisive bitterness.

"Sounds silly, I suppose, but it's a fact." She met his eye challengingly. "Cook two meals and do a little washing. And then what? Go for a nice long chatty visit with Susy Mackamoose, I suppose." She moved her whole body as a petulant child moves. The man still kept silence. There stirred in the back of Sally's mind the necessity of justification. That's the way she must sound—like a petulant child. This man must be remembering the rhapsodies of only a week ago. Sally remembered them!

"It's no fun doing things alone," she proffered defensively.

"I don't know," demurred Chilkat Harry slowly. He pulled the packet of Durham from the breast pocket of his shirt and began to roll a cigarette. He watched her from under cover of this small operation, trying to make things out. Something back of this more than mere separation for a few hours out of the twenty-four; the man must have had jobs before. And they had been married more than a year . . . "Had a quarrel?" asked Chilkat Harry abruptly.

Sally's body jerked upright.

"Good heavens, no!" she cried. She turned startled eyes toward Harry. But in his was no gleam of the ironic amusement she had feared. They were sober and friendly. Sally relaxed; but now she must explain herself. "But you don't know John. When he gets interested in something new to him like this, he's in it head over heels.

He can't see anything else or talk of anything else or think of anything else until he gets it. I honestly believe that nothing else in the world really exists for him——" She checked herself on the verge of what might sound like disloyalty.

But Chilkat Harry made no sign that now the situation was clear to him. Nor, apparently, did he intend—or perhaps desire—to press it. He arose to his feet.

"Well, it's a valuable trait," said he. "It gets things done. Wish I had more of it." He did not comment further, but stood looking down at her for a moment. "Well, got to be moving," said he presently. "Cheerio." He spoke to the dog, and the two moved off down the trail.

Sally looked after him. She was vexed with herself for having burst out so. "No fun doing things alone!" she mimicked herself scornfully; some men might have construed that as a broad enough hint. Most men would have done so. But Chilkat Harry had not tried to take advantage. On the contrary he had exhibited a delicacy and tact and understanding of which she had not suspected him; yes, and a certain unexpressed sympathy which was very warming just at this moment.

Filled with this new kindliness toward Chilkat Harry, she got to her feet and entered the cabin. It was time to be thinking of supper. But as she opened the door of Jumbo's firebox a new thought stopped her short—or a sensation, rather than a thought. It was a familiar sensation; and the suspicion that it generated was ungrateful and unworthy. But there it was.

"Well, we'll see!" said Sally grimly, yanking open the firebox.

But day followed day, and Chilkat Harry did not follow up any advantage his fancied tactics might have gained. Sally scorned herself as an egotistical little fool. How the man would laugh at her if he knew what she had thought he was up to! Sally's cheeks burned when she thought of it. "Pretty stuck on yourself, aren't you?" she told herself in scorn. And, inconsistently, down deep she was honest enough to realize that she was just a little chagrined that he had not been playing a game—had not considered her worth it, perhaps.

And then, in sequence, she had to laugh at herself: here she was back again among the same old baffling subtleties he always seemed to evoke. She began to suspect that it might be she, and not Chilkat Harry, who evoked them. "Better get simple!" she admonished herself. When she had absorbed that idea she found herself liking Chilkat Harry. She wished he *would* come around and do things with her!

But scolding herself had little effect on the restlessness that possessed her. It had no sense to it. She could argue that. In fact she was rather amazed when she faced herself squarely. "Is that the sort of person I am?" she demanded. "With all I have, inside and outside of myself, can't I do anything but wander about like a lost chicken? Is that the sort of a cowardly custard I'm turning out to be, can't even do my share? What did I expect anyway—one long picnic?" John's words came back to her with a pang. "Picnic's over," John had said when they came back from that glorious day up the inlet. "Oh dear!" said Sally and headed wearily back to the cabin to get things ready for John's return. She felt almost as tired as John looked.

John was very tired. He'd tackled something big, and he was right in the middle of his fight with it. Things had not yet worked out. She gathered small details of various discomfitures, things he had figured that did not pan out. Had the "run" all fixed down to the salt chuck, had a good angle; but when the tree came down, a heavy limb deflected her, and she "hung," and that meant three days' chopping and work with the Gilchrist; and then she did run, but at that point there was an underwater shoal, and of course the log had to hit that, and it had split and buried its nose and stood up on end against the cliff.

"Ought to have taken soundings," said John. "It's no good there. But I've figured out a new route."

"How many logs have you got in?" Sally aroused herself to ask, but listlessly. She was dulled by the succession of frustrations.

"None—yet," confessed John.

"None!" she echoed after a moment. And he'd been at it now for nearly two weeks. At this rate . . .

"Oh, I'll get there!" John was saying, "I'm not going to be licked by a tree!"

But he was close to licked, thought Sally. He had not much left in him by night. Nothing for her. He ate and mumbled abstractedly for a little while, always about the work, and went to bed early. Sally lay beside him, staring out the square of the window. He might not have been there at all, as far as she was concerned. She tried for companionship with the great mountain, the Protector of the Wilderness. He had never failed her before. Now he stood aloof in his own serenity, benign as always, but waiting for her to come to understanding. If only John would just lay his arm across her. But he was like a log, dead to the world.

CHAPTER XXIII

SMOKED FISH

SALLY FINISHED the few house chores and, for lack of a better idea, wandered down to the stream bank. The tide was half on the ebb, so the pools and riffles were defining. She had intended, vaguely, to cross and explore on the other side; but at the bank she stopped short, amazed.

The pool was gray with fish, lying side by side, like wavering shadows. As she reached the bank a half-dozen or so, as though on signal, detached themselves to rush the riffles. There the water was not deep enough to cover them, so that as they rose to the shallows their backs looked like emerged submarines. With so little purchase against the fast current, the rush must be determined. From their vibrating tails the water flew in white spray. They arrived and abruptly fell quiet and became the wavering gray shadows of the upper pool.

Sally sat down on the cut bank, her interest fixed. For a long time she waited and had almost made up her mind to go on, when the maneuver was repeated, but this time by at least fifty of the great fish. Like a gallant and concerted charge against the unintermitting dynamics of the river. A forlorn hope. Sally wanted to cheer. She leaned forward, lips parted, following the fortunes of the attack.

Each must keep his line: she saw that. Cleave the current straight; or be carried back. At times, when the flow momentarily strength- ened, hold the onrush poised and motionless. And then with a heart-bursting spurt of effort they tore themselves free. All but three. The direct line of their attack had brought them hurtling hard on against a wide spit of gravel.

"Oh!" cried Sally in dismay, for she was heart and soul with the gallant adventure.

It seemed only too clear to her what would happen when they must turn: the pounce of the exacting waters; the frantic and despairing struggle; the final ignominious tumbling over and over down the rapids back to the lower pool. But the dauntless three re- fused to make that fatal turn. Before Sally's unbelieving eyes they continued on, straight at the gravel bar and then overland, holding miraculously their vertical position of swimming by sheer speed and vigor, as a bicycle stays upright, and—it seemed to Sally—solely by the tenacity of their purpose. They must do so; for once on their sides, they must flop helpless, as any fish on land. She held her breath, urging them on with all the strength of her will. They made it; and then she did cheer.

She drew the air into her lungs and relaxed. A truce had been declared. The rapids ran white and empty; and in the pools the salmon rested, awaiting another upbuilding of the urge within them. She was awake again, alive again. How could she fail to catch the contagion? Here she had drawn near to the very flow of life itself, powerful, teeming and fecund, upswelling to its ordained fulfillment. She stared at the water, but was unaware of its bright surface. She was groping within herself for some meaning.

At first a great compassion flooded her. She knew that of all this great multitude not one would ever return to its sea. So gallant a struggle to die! But at once the compassion left her and was curiously succeeded by something almost like envy. It came to her like a revelation that the nature of the outcome was nothing; that the won- derful thing was to be so sure of one's destiny that none other could be either possible or desired. This was a consecration so utter that the very substance of its sacrifice must be tranquillity. There was something here for her: almost she had it . . .

She came back so far that for a moment she could not gather her wits. Then she realized at her elbow the presence of the old squaw, Susy Mackamoose. The wrinkles of Susy's usually impassive face were arranged in a broad grin.

"Plenty fish," observed Susy. "Much good!"

She squatted down comfortably and for some moments contemplated the salmon.

"Plenty good," she repeated with satisfaction. And then, after another long and typical pause: "My old Johnny bringum net. Catch 'em now, quick. Bimeby no good. Go soft. No good for smoke. You tell your man. You get your net."

Sally had never before heard Susy utter more than three words at a time. Even now Susy's outside appearance was as stolid as ever. But she was all lit up inside. It came to Sally that exactly this was what had been the business of Susy and Johnny Mackamoose for the past month, sitting smokily side by side on the narrow veranda of their hut, like a pair of Buddhas. They had been waiting for the salmon run.

"We haven't any net," she told Susy.

This, Sally imagined, was a simple statement of fact. But it took her some time to make Susy understand. Such a situation, it developed, was incomprehensible to Susy.

"*Cultus!* No good, no good!" Susy was emphatic when she was made to believe. "Bimeby winter. No fish."

She turned on Sally and asked questions. She probed the utter improvidence of Sally. She was incredulous. It was disclosed that Sally had dried and smoked no clams. Nor dried any berries. Sally gathered, rather vaguely, that she should be doing something with dried berries and deer fat. Susy shook her head.

"Man no work; no good," she pronounced dogmatically. "You make um work!"

Sally laughed delightedly. She pointed out to Susy in painfully simple phrases that John was working and working hard.

"He cut trees," she enunciated. "Lots trees. Over there. You go look."

But Susy was unimpressed.

"Tree no good," said she. "No eat tree."

She muttered to herself for some time under her breath, then heaved herself to her feet.

"I tell my Johnny catch you fish," she told Sally. "Plenty fish."

"But we don't want plenty fish!" protested Sally.

To this Susy paid no attention. Presently Johnny Mackamoose came, afoot; and Susy joined him, and the two set off toward the mouth of the stream.

"You come," ordered Susy; so Sally came, greatly amused; but she would have come anyway, without the command, to see what it was all about.

Johnny had brought the canoe down, while the water was high, and tied it to grass. In it, folded back and forth, was the seine net. He tied the ropes of one end of this to a stake and paddled in a big circle, allowing the net to slip overboard, and returned to his starting point. In the meantime Susy had waded in nearly waist deep and was pounding the water with the flat of the other paddle to frighten back the fish until Johnny could complete the circle and close the gap. This was fun; so Sally, who had on her rubber boots, joined in and did a lot of splashing. The net had corks on one edge and lead weights on the other, so that when Johnny again touched prow on the bank he had in effect put up a big underwater corral, enclosing —it was hoped—at least part of one of the schools of salmon finning about before starting upstream.

The next thing, Sally found, was simply to pull in both ends of the net at the same time; and slowly, so as not to upset the corral. That was all there was to it; but it was good hard work. Sally tugged away mightily; but she thought to detect a flicker of amusement, once, when she turned suddenly and caught Susy's stolidity off guard. It was tremendously exciting when the first gleam of silver flashed in the water against the red brown of the net!

A few last strong heaves drew the bight far up the beach. The

Indians laid back the fold of the net and examined the catch. Sally thought it wonderful—what could anybody do with so many fish?—but Susy and Johnny did not seem unduly impressed. There were a lot of salmon; but there were also other kinds of fish—flounders, skates, dogfish, quite a few trout. Sally was surprised at the trout; she had not known they ever took to salt water. Johnny threw aside the dogfish and skates and loaded the rest in the canoe. Susy and Sally trudged along the bank; Johnny paddled the canoe until he had reached the present head of navigation, just beyond the Tillicum. Here he drew up to the bank, and he and Susy went into a huddle over the fish. Sally waited to see what next.

She soon found out; and protests did no good at all. She found herself in possession of thirty or so big salmon tossed out on the grass at her feet.

"For you," said Susy.

"But I don't *want* them!" Sally almost wailed. "We can't *use* so many! What'll I *do* with them!"

Susy and Johnny fixed their beady eyes on her. It is probable they did not believe their ears, or were trying to determine if Sally was serious. They must have decided that she was.

"You smoke um," instructed Susy after a while.

"Smoke them!" Sally echoed in a dismay so genuine as this time to carry instant conviction.

"Tomorrow I come. I show," said Susy.

"Tomorrow—they'll spoil. No, you take them. I'll take a trout for supper: that's all we can use."

"You got knife. You cut um for smoke," Susy spoke firmly. "You got knife?" she inquired in a tone suspiciously near to irony.

Johnny stepped ashore, produced a sheath knife, flipped over a salmon, demonstrated. A few deft strokes, and there were two slabs of clean meat held together by a strip of skin at the tail. He tossed aside the gills and entrails, miraculously detached by one swift operation, and the backbone, as neatly sliced out by another, wiped the knife on the grass, dipped his hand in the water, re-embarked, resumed his paddle.

"You fix like that," repeated Susy. "I come tomorrow."

Unexpectedly the Indian woman reached forward and patted Sally on the shoulder. Then, without further speech, she turned away, moving with an ease and lightness surprising in one apparently so unwieldy. She paid no attention to what Sally called after her. At the foot of the riffles she waited for Johnny, and then the two, in the water, one on either side, set about easing the canoe over the shallows.

Sally looked after them in despair and indecision. Had it not been for the pat on her shoulder—— That had somehow touched her—a warmth of friendliness, and just now she was ripe for that—and in spite of herself she somehow wanted to redeem herself with Susy Mackamoose. She must have seemed a complete imbecile to Susy Mackamoose. . . . Abruptly she squared her shoulders and shook herself. She'd show Susy Mackamoose!

She went aboard the Tillicum and searched out the spare butcher knife. Then she rolled up her sleeves and set to work.

Watching Johnny Mackamoose, the job had looked simple. She remembered just how he had done it.

In five minutes Sally was gurry up to the elbows, and the one unfinished victim of her trials and errors was so hacked and disfigured that she threw it away and started in on another. The difficulty was not so much with the mere cleaning as with the fins and backbone. Their resistance against the knife was stronger than Sally's grip. She simply could not hang onto that slippery fish! And of course her nose had to itch; and she had nothing but her elbows to scratch it with! She must cry or laugh; so she laughed—but ruefully.

The laugh was repeated from the cut bank above. Startled, she looked up at Chilkat Harry and his dog. Of course *he* had to show up right now! That made it complete! She stared up at him belligerently.

"Enjoying yourself?" he asked after a moment.

"Decidedly not!" returned Sally with spirit.

"What do you think you are doing?"

"An astute observer might deduce that I am cleaning fish." Sally did not intend to be put upon. "What did you suppose I was doing?"

"Thanks," said Harry, "but I'm not very astute." He surveyed the mangled results of her efforts. "I didn't know. It might be practicing totem carving."

She made no reply to this, but looked dangerous.

"Would you mind telling me what you're going to do with all the fish—once you've got them cleaned, I mean?" His question was almost exaggeratedly respectful. "And how did you get hold of them, anyway?"

"Caught them," returned Sally briefly, "with Johnny and Susy," she added.

"Oh, I see!" Harry was enlightened. "And you're going to smoke them, without doubt."

"Exactly." Sally's reply was uncompromising.

"The complete Siwash," murmured Harry. "And I suppose later on you will be going in for hoolican."

"Yes?" Sally's manner was as elaborately polite as his own. "And what is hoolican?"

"Well," said Harry, taking his time, "you take coal-oil cans and fill them with a very fat, greasy little fish that comes in later in the season, and you stand them out in the sun, and when they've reached the proper state of decomposition—— Hullo!" he broke off. Sally had squarely turned her back. She had plucked a salmon from the pile and was squatting before it with her knife.

Harry dropped his bantering.

"Honestly, Sally," he told her earnestly, "it's no good. You're just wasting your time. You won't get decent smoked fish the way these Siwash do them. You have to have a smokehouse and quarter-ground salt and—— Good lord! All Susy does is to hang them on poles in the open air in a kind of smudge, and all you'll have is a sort of sun cure with a smoky flavor . . ."

"Yes, I know," murmured Sally sweetly; "she's coming over tomorrow to show me how."

The set of her shoulders looked obstinate. She was obstinate. It needed only Chilkat Harry. She'd finish this now in spite of hell and high water. The man looked down at her perplexed and just a little nettled by the utter absurdity of Sally.

"There are millions of them," he ventured at a guess, "and anyway, they won't be wasted. The crows and ravens will use them."

But this was no go. She said nothing, but went on hacking away, even more inefficiently, hampered now by resentment.

"You'll never get anywhere at this rate——" he began again.

She turned so suddenly that the malemute threw up his head. "I am going to finish these things if it takes me all day," she said furiously. "I wish you'd go away!"

"Well, for God's sake!"

She met his astonishment with cool contempt.

"I suppose," said she at length, "that it does not occur to you that old Susy is doing her best to be kind."

She did not look around again. She heard Chilkat Harry utter a short bark of a laugh and an exclamation; then he was beside her, leaning over her; his hand was disengaging her fingers from the knife, gently enough, but with decision.

"Here, gimme," said Chilkat Harry curtly.

She relinquished the knife and arose to her feet. Chilkat Harry's manner was indignant: he did not again even glance up at her. He attacked the pile of fish with the quick jerky motions of exasperation. It was obvious to Sally, in every line of his figure, that he was doing this solely to indulge a fool woman. She should have felt rebuked, but she did not: on the contrary she began to see the humor of the situation. She should say something, not only to make her manners, but to keep herself from laughing out loud.

"You do that well," said she.

And, indeed, Chilkat Harry was truly expert, more so than even Johnny Mackamoose; or perhaps it was that he worked faster. How did that happen—with Chilkat Harry? It seemed out of character. But he did not answer. He continued to clean fish. The set of his shoulders, the quick jerky rip of the knife, the fling of his hand as he tossed the offal one way, the slabs of flesh the other, told plainly what he thought of this job, and, incidentally, of himself for being involved in it. Sally tried again.

"You must have had a lot of practice," she suggested.

He ignored this also until the last salmon filet was laid on the pile, and he had cleaned the knife and washed his hands in the stream.

"I worked a while fishing. When I first came to the country. Before I got over being so much of a damn fool," he then vouchsafed.

He got to his feet and stretched his body. Apparently he had worked off his ill-humor. He surveyed Sally's small figure quizzically.

"I don't believe you have," said he.

"Have what?"

"Got over being a damn fool. As if that old Siwash——" He broke off. "All right," he said briskly, "you've begun it, and you've got me into it; and now, by glory, you're going to see it through. You don't know what you've got ahead of you, young lady!" He chuckled delightedly. "You wait here," he told Sally.

He disappeared in the direction of the brush. She looked after him, perplexed and a little indignant. She intended to "see it through," as he called it. What made him think she didn't?

Chilkat Harry returned shortly, carrying a willow pole. This he propped against the cut bank.

"Now," said he, "the next thing is to hang these sides of salmon across that pole." He hung one, to show her: a filet on each side, with the tail to hold them together. "Go ahead," he directed. He stood aside and began to roll a cigarette. Obviously he had no intention of helping further. Sally hesitated. Sounded a good deal like a command. She did not like to be ordered about. But she had no choice, not if she would save face. Resentfully, and with faint distaste, she set about handling the raw and slippery fish.

"Pick up one end of the pole," commanded Chilkat Harry when she had finished. He himself shouldered the other. They started up the meadow trail toward the cabin. Almost immediately Sally began to realize what she had let herself in for. There is weight to thirty-odd big salmon, even when they have been cleaned and trimmed. They flopped and dangled and slid on the slender pole. Sally stumbled. Her muscles ached. Soon it seemed to her that she could not go another step without a respite. But Harry neither slackened gait nor showed any intention of stopping for rest. Sally gritted her teeth. She'd make it or die! She did not die, and she did make it; but toward the last she had to summon all her resolution just to keep going. She came out of a kind of haze of concentration, when Harry at last stopped, and was surprised to find herself out back of the cabin and nearly dropped her end of the pole in reaction at the cessation of effort. But she hung on until Harry had carefully lowered his end to the top of a stump and had come back and taken her end to slew it around to the top of another stump, so that the fish hung suspended between. And even then she had to keep braced up to prevent his knowing how near collapse she was.

"All right," she managed, without gasping. "What now?"

He was looking at her with reluctant admiration.

"Nothing right now. Tomorrow Susy'll take charge." He grinned at her. He snapped his fingers at the malemute, preparing to go. "Wish you joy," said he and grinned again as though at some secret anticipation. Sally wished she knew what it was. She wished she could ask him what more was to be done to complete this horrible thing she had let herself in for. But of course she could not. She would have to wait for tomorrow.

Fortunately John was rather more tired than usual. He did not wander about; and as the two stumps that supported the pole with the fish were outside the blind end of the cabin, he need know nothing, as yet, about the new enterprise. This was a small favor, but to be accepted thankfully. Sally was in no mood for any more masculine superiority.

Susy Mackamoose appeared, as she had promised, early the following morning. Almost too early, indeed: John had but just departed. She eyed the cleaned fish with what Sally thought to detect as faint surprise, but she made no comment. In the thicket she cut willows and, in a clear space, put up two tripods just so far apart as to support the ends of the pole on which the fish were strung. She said nothing, nor paid any attention whatever to Sally, who followed her around helplessly. Susy cut and brought in a small supply of alder-wood fuel and some pitch pine for kindling and a quantity of moss.

"Ketchum." She briefly indicated one end of the pole. She lifted the other. They placed it across the tripods. Susy slivered some pitch pine for kindling, laid dry wood atop, and the green alder atop that. When the fire was going well she damped it down with handfuls of the moss. She surveyed the resultant smudge with satisfaction.

"Make smoke, plenty smoke. All time smoke. No hot. No fire. Alder wood. No dry wood. Smoke. All day, all night, smoke. Bimeby good."

She fixed Sally with her small beady eyes. Sally felt herself slipping. Only a few moments ago she had rallied her common sense. There was no earthly reason why she should keep on with this. Somehow a compulsion was on her. She simply could not hold out against Susy Mackamoose's expectation of her. The darn Injun took her so completely for granted!

"All right," she assented meekly. "How long?"

"Three day, four day," said Susy Mackamoose. Sally brightened; that was not so bad. But Susy had not finished. "Mebbe rain," she added, "then l-o-n-g time." She dragged out the adjective dramatically.

She departed without further attention to Sally. Well! Sally drew a deep sigh, she certainly *had* bit off something! All day, all night, eh? "Suppose I'll have to get up nights to keep that dratted fire going? Well, I'll do it!" she told her lazy reluctance with spirit. How about disturbing John? "Oh, John! He'd never know whether I was there or not," she answered this with perhaps just a trace of bitterness. "Pretty cold at night; I wonder how often I'll have to crawl out? Shucks, what's the matter with me! I can find out by watching how often today I have to tend to it to keep it going." She began to consider ways and means, which meant fuel. Plenty of fuel lying about—bonfire fuel—dry limbs and windfalls. "Bet I could make a good enough smudge by using enough moss," she speculated. "No," she squared her shoulders, "that would be fudging. You've tackled this, Sally Murdock," she told herself severely, "and you do it right!" John had cut a good pile of alder wood, and she cast a longing glance—but only a glance—in its direction. That wouldn't be playing the game either: and, besides, John worked hard enough now. What Susy had cut would probably last out the day, but Sally got the cabin ax and went at it—best not wait until she got some horse sense, she told herself sardonically.

Chilkat Harry traced her into the thicket by the sound of the ax. She was prepared to put Chilkat Harry in his place: she intended to stand no nonsense from Chilkat Harry. But, astonishingly, he was already in his place. He did not try to be funny. He now appeared to accept her occupation as a matter of course.

"You know, you're pretty good with an ax," he commended after watching for a few moments.

Sally could not repress an involuntary upsurge of gratification, though instantly she scoffed at herself for it. Falling for that stuff! But she *was* doing a pretty good job! Alder is a soft wood and splits easily; and Sally's youth had been near enough the backwoods to have acquainted her with the feel of an ax. There is a kind of elation that comes with measuring up to a job. Sally felt it; and it brought with it eagerness. Now she not only wanted to finish the job, but to do it properly.

Chilkat Harry did not offer to help; but he did lend a hand carrying the split wood. Sally was watchful. She had a chip on her shoulder. But presently she had to let it fall off of its own weight. Chilkat Harry was entirely respectful toward the situation. He even had a practical suggestion or two to offer. "Several smaller fires, in a row under the pole," said he, "lay the sticks of wood pointing toward common centers and then keep shoving them in as the ends burn off: saves fuel and labor." He even voluntarily supplied the one thing Sally lacked: a moderately sane reason for the performance; and in the most tactful way, for he proffered it through the malemute, and not directly to Sally herself.

"Looks as though you're going to live high this winter," he addressed Chilkat, "if the lady is kind. Makes the best dog food in the world," he assured Sally, as she caught eagerly at this.

Sally warmed to Chilkat Harry. She experienced a glow of comradeship, of shared understanding, new in their relationship. She was, for the first time, sorry when he departed, after his usual abrupt fashion.

The job was not so bad. Sally found that by going to bed a little late and turning out betimes, she did not have to get up nights. Nor, as a matter of fact, was there a lot to do daytimes, but Sally was by now really interested. She took unnecessary trouble. A dozen times a day she must pop out to take a look. She altered the fire. With a stick she poked the salmon into what she thought more favorable locations, shifting the thick ones to the ends and giving the end ones a chance near the middle. Within a few hours the slabs had begun to turn brown; and by morning the outsides were hardened. And then Sally became puzzled. How did one know when the things were done? They looked done now; but Susy Mackamoose had said three or four days. Susy had not come back. Sally wished she would, and then she would ask her—— "No!" decided Sally, "I hope she doesn't come back!" Sally wanted to do it all on her own. She wanted to show Susy Mackamoose! Cautiously she made little slits in the driest and separated the flesh and peered within. She even sliced off bits and nibbled them. It was hard to tell.

Of course, John noticed the smoke behind the cabin. He laughed a little when she told him what she was doing. He went around to take a look. But Sally disclaimed credit for the two things that particularly impressed him.

"Harry cut the fish that way; and Susy Mackamoose built the rack," said she. Sally was in a disclaiming mood in which was a slight admixture of defiance. "Harry says they're only good for dog food without salt and a smokehouse," she cut all support from under herself. Dryly, without humor, in short flat sentences, she catalogued to John the sequence of her tribulations, ignorances and dismays in dealing with fish. She spared herself nothing. She waited, braced for

John's comments. He was half perched on a stump, rolling a cigarette, and when she had finished looked up at her, frowning. "It's the first time you've looked at me, really looked at me, for days," was Sally's swift and resentful thought. But he was looking at her now; and it came to Sally that he was not going to laugh at her, but merely was puzzled and searching a reason.

"It must be kinda hard work for you," he groped slowly. "Good deal of chopping. Green wood's tough. Let me see your hands!" he commanded suddenly. He turned them over and gazed soberly at the palms, but said nothing of their condition. "You got to be careful," he said. "It's awful easy to cut your foot."

Sally softened to this forbearance.

"Harry says he can use them for Chilkat this winter," she volunteered.

"Hardly seems worth while," proffered John, but diffidently and without criticism.

Sally's hand flew to her breast, and her lips parted to the quick intake of her breath in the splendor of a great illumination. Her fish—hardly seems worth while, to John. Why! That was exactly what she had been saying to herself—about his trees! But her attitude had been of resentment and bitterness; and now in John's was none of these. Fish—trees—what difference which, or what? The significance was not in the material results. It was the challenge, and the meeting of it. What was it John had said?

"I wasn't going to be licked by a mere fish," she paraphrased it. John cried aloud delightedly.

"Atta girl!" he cheered.

He hopped down from the stump and gave her a mighty hug. They strolled together happily toward the cabin. Sally was feeling very humble toward John and very contemptuous of herself. John was so sure and simple. He was never bothered with the fog of complications and subtleties that had so beset her soul. And when the time came, he always reacted, as though by instinct, so certainly and so accurately. *He* would never get all darkened up with nothing; Sally had no mercy on herself.

Whether because the day's work had gone well, or whether John reacted to this change in Sally, he did not seem to be so tired. Or perhaps it was because Sally was now really listening. At any rate, soon she had pulled a chair up to the table and was sitting beside him, and he was drawing rough diagrams to illustrate. She would this evening have taken an emotional interest, just from the warmth of her new mood; but soon her enthusiasm was caught. She was amazed at herself for being so stupid.

Question of one big spruce, it seemed. Right in line of the natural runway down the mountain. Get that one in, and all the rest would be a cinch. *But*—John was emphatic—that was a tough one. And if she got jammed there she'd block the whole operation.

"That's what's been holding me up," said John, "I just didn't dare make a move with her and make a miscue. But I got her solved! Look here . . ." He began on his diagram.

It seemed that it would be impossible to fell the spruce straight downhill directly in the path of its run. That's how you'd do it with most of the others. Center of gravity wrong, John threw in briefly. But if you chopped the kerf real careful, so as to leave, just off center in the middle, a single strand of fiber, why, then when she fell that fiber would resist just enough to twist the trunk a little sideways.

"Sure, she'll tear loose, but she'll hang on *just long enough*—that is, if I've figgered right," said John.

That, pursued John, ought to throw her on a slant across the line of the "run." To straighten her out John had carefully trimmed a hemlock about twenty feet away, which the falling tree must scrape against—"again, if I've figgered right," added John.

"And that," he concluded, "ought to jump the butt sideways while it is still in the air, so she'll hit the ground straightened out on the run."

Sally stared at the diagram, her imagination kindling to the niceties of the problem. No wonder John had been absorbed! The whole thing depended on so many exact accuracies—of guess! Would the strand of fiber twist the tree just far enough to hit the hemlock on the right side and with the proper force? Was the hemlock strong enough and resilient enough to flip the heavy butt? John thought so.

"Oh, sure, it's taking a chance," he acknowledged.

Sally must come up tomorrow and see it tested. She assented eagerly, then wavered. She shook her head.

"I've got to keep up my fire," said she. Vexation misted her eyes. She wanted to go; she knew how it would please John to have her there at the moment of his triumph—or defeat. Those silly salmon! Silly, and not much use to anybody. But something deeper than common sense compelled her. It was something that was in John also; for he did not combat her.

"You and your fish!" he jeered.

"You and your trees!" jeered Sally back, but blinking tears.

Sally kept hoping Susy Mackamoose would make a visit of inspection. Sally was now getting really worried about her precious fish. They ought to be about ready. But the only thing she was sure of was that, whatever their condition, she herself was thoroughly smoked. She decided to sacrifice one in the interests of science and took it off the pole and boldly cut it in two and examined the cross section. The corpse itself was twisted and shrunken and pretty dark in color: something—Sally's sense of humor was reviving—any good Egyptologist would appreciate. But she was not so certain about the middle. Finally she abandoned her dream of flabbergasting Susy Mackamoose with the perfected article and took the half fish over for expert advice.

The Mackamoose shanty was closed. A heavy bit of log propped shut the door. The canoe was gone from its mooring post in the slough. Two long drying racks like Sally's stood empty. This was no temporary absence. But, conclusive testimony, no trace of smoke oozed from the boxlike ventilator on the roof. Johnny and Susy Mackamoose had pulled out!

Sally was childishly disappointed. She had wanted Susy's opinion— why, drat it, now she stopped to think of it, this whole silly enterprise had been aimed at Susy's opinion! She had wanted to see Susy's fish—whether they were like her product. And they'd gone without even saying good-by! That hurt a little.

She returned to the cabin and perched on the doorstep. Suddenly she felt drained. The bottom had dropped out. This fool performance of the fish had become to her just that: a fool performance, not an enterprise of merit because of its character content. It was just a fool performance.

Something nudged her softly on the elbow. She turned, startled, to find Chilkat, the malemute, looking down upon her gravely. Her immediate impulse was of flight, and she half rose. She was in no mood for Chilkat Harry right now. But he was nowhere in sight. She waited for him to appear. Presently she must conclude Chilkat's visit personal. She was touched by what she knew was an unusual evidence of doggy favor. She sank down again beside him and threw her arm around him. The feel of his coat, the warmth and strength of his powerful body, were grateful to her. Some instinct must have called him, she thought a little sentimentally. He had come just at the right moment, when she was feeling so disillusioned over the defection in friendliness of the Indians.

A more practical idea suddenly struck her. A brilliant idea! Chilkat had selected also another psychological moment. The fish were for Chilkat.

She sprang to her feet and raced around the cabin to the drying racks. Chilkat bounded alongside. He sensed something doing; and he was filled with a dog's instantaneous eagerness to take part. But when Sally detached one of the dried salmon from the pole and offered it his expectations fell. Nevertheless he took it from her. For ten seconds he held it daintily in his mouth, then as daintily laid it down.

"Go ahead! Eat it! Don't you want to eat it?" Sally made various motions of invitation toward the fish, reassuring Chilkat that this magnificent gift was really intended for him. Chilkat looked up at Sally. He wrinkled his nose and ducked his head deprecatingly and sneezed. The apology was most polite; but it was firm. Chilkat did not endorse the fish.

For some days reaction had been stealing up on Sally. Now it pounced. She snatched the mummified thing from under Chilkat's nose and hurled it as far as she could into the brush. From the rack she tore another and another and yet another and sent them hurtling after. She reacher for a fifth, but stopped, her hand outstretched. She had not kept track of Chilkat; she had seen nothing; she was blind in released exasperation; she was all concentrated on throwing away dried fish.

But here out of the brush came Chilkat. His tail was waving, his eyes sparkling. In his jaws he carried a dried salmon. He laid it at Sally's feet. Before she could recover he had plunged again into the brush after another. When he had retrieved all four he took up his position in front of her, tail going vigorously, muscles tense, eyes eagerly sparkling.

"Do it again!" urged Chilkat enthusiastically.

Sally sank down right where she was, in fish and ashes, and laughed and wiped her eyes and hugged Chilkat and laughed some more. All the sting was out of everything. It was a good world. She could hardly wait for John to come home so she could tell him about it. She did so, with gusto and humor; and John joined her laughter wholeheartedly and poked their sort of fun at her, just like old times.

"I knew the Injuns had gone," said he. "They stopped off to talk to me on their way out."

"They might have said good-by to me," complained Sally. "I really thought they were getting friendly."

"Oh, they are friendly, all right," reassured John. "They took a lot of trouble to come ashore, and Johnny climbed way up to where I was working, just to tell me——" He broke off, eyeing her teasingly, as he always did when there was more to follow, and he wanted her to ask.

"All right, Brudder Bones," she obliged. "What is it?"

"You ought to like this," said John. "I don't suppose an Injun pays a compliment very often. You must have made a hit."

"A compliment? For *me?*" Sally was surprised at how absurdly pleased she felt. "What was it? What did he say?"

John screwed up his face and harshened his voice in passable imitation of Johnny Mackamoose. " 'When I first ketchum Susy she didn't know nothin' either.' That's all. Every word. Then he went away." He whooped with laughter. "Now who do you suppose he was trying to encourage, you or me?"

They recovered slowly from their delight together of the whole preposterous episode. Sally suddenly bethought her.

"What luck? With the tree," she must add, for John was at a loss. He laughed.

"I'd forgotten all about the tree," he confessed.

"And I've forgotten all about the fish!" said Sally happily.

They looked at one another. What was it? What had happened? The tree had "run." John recovered himself to tell. It was floating, fastened by an iron dog and a chain so it could not get away. Everything had worked out just as John had calculated. The rest was going to be easy.

"You'll see a real boom before you know it!" John boasted. "Well, in a month or six weeks, anyway," his practical mind amended.

It was wonderful. It was a real victory. For the first time it occurred to Sally that he was back much earlier than usual. He must have rowed home bursting with it—success, after all that toil and disappointment. And he'd forgotten! A great wave of satisfaction flooded her. Just because he'd forgotten! That was absurd of her. Well, she liked feeling absurd! Everything was all right again.

CHAPTER XXIV

THE GRIZZLY BEAR

THE FREEING of Sally's spirit freed also her body, lifted the indifference that had tied her to the cabin. She—and her new rubber boots—set forth at the first opportunity to explore up the river.

The grass was at its highest and toughest now, so she started across by the old path to the Indian shanty, when she cut the river for the first time. Since her last visit the salmon run had reached its peak. The water was crowded with the great fish, resting or following indomitably their instinct toward the upstream shallows. Just opposite the Mackamoose shack were small riffles aside from the main stream, and here a dozen or so had stopped for their spawning. Sally stood on the cut bank to watch them.

She was enormously interested, for soon a number of her preconceptions had gone by the board. Her general idea had been that, with salmon, propagation was a detached and general sort of proposition: that the females laid the eggs and departed; and that the males then came along to fertilize them and also departed; and that the roe thereafter took a chance with the sun and whatever creatures fancied salmon eggs as a diet. Admirable, but without the charm of family life. But here were the fish in pairs, side by side, holding themselves miraculously motionless against the current. Looked like companionable married couples to Sally. A single fish came along and swam in front of one of these pairs and flirted his tail before the nose of one of them. At once the other dashed vigorously into action. He not only drove away the intruder, but he chased him upstream and out of sight. Sally was sure it was "he"; and that the one that remained was "she"; and that she, Sally, had witnessed a bachelor's brazen attempt to break up a happy marriage. This pleased Sally immensely because, she told herself, it made salmon so much more human. She sat down and hugged her knees and rested her chin on them, making herself comfortable to see what would happen next.

Nothing happened for a long while. Sally began to fear the rivals had annihilated each other, and the lady was bereft. But presently the male returned—it just *has* to be the male, insisted Sally—dropping down with the current, tail first, permitting it to carry him, and rounded up gracefully alongside the female—it *must* be the female— like a yacht coming into the wind; and the two again lay side by side, as though sharing some mysterious communion in which was no haste and no time. That seemed to be all there was to it, and Sally was about to resume her excursion when suddenly one of them—she was mixed up now and could not tell which—as though struck by a sudden idea, moved straight ahead the distance of one flirt of the tail, turned partly on its side, thrust its nose violently against the stony bottom and burst into a spasm of writhing energy.

Sally's eyes widened incredulously. What a thing to do! What a *painful* thing to do! And now she saw that what she had dismissed as mottlings and markings on the noses and sides of these fish were really places where the skin had been scraped from the flesh by the violence of abrasion against the harsh stream bed. And she realized something else: that the deep corrugations and potholes in the gravel were not natural inequalities of the stream bed, but had been excavated, and by precisely such maneuvers as the one she had just witnessed! It did not seem possible. Some of the potholes looked to her at least a foot deep and four or five feet wide; some of the up-stream mounds of gravel—protecting the nests against the current, she surmised—were piled nearly to the surface of the water. It certainly did not seem possible! But it was so! Now she thought of it, she remembered that this riffle had been a smooth sheet of gravel: she had crossed it with John! And scooped out by the soft bodies of the fish! No wonder they looked scraped and skinned and frazzled. Her mind was filled with awe and pity at the intent devotion, at the urge that compelled them.

"Oh, the poor things!" she breathed.

But instantly she knew that here was no call on compassion. It came to her again, that mystic sense of standing very close to the unhasting, upswelling, powerful flow of the very stream of life.

She came to herself. But the impression lingered. The tide of life! Exuberant life! It was rising to its peak; it poised at its flood; it hovered at the moment of culmination, toward which all the year had been quietly building. Released at last, as waters are released by the melting of snows in the mountains. She was caught up by it—she longed to have John with her. . . .

She shook herself. The ecstasy of it, for just an instant, had been almost too strong. It seemed to her she had been in danger of being swept away. She made an effort and looked about her, noticing things, so that she could catch back her equilibrium.

But everywhere she looked now she saw the same thing. The rush of the salmon had sucked in other life, as leaves are whirled behind a wind. As far as she could see, up and down the stream, the bars were white with flocks of gulls and terns, and the water bobbed with them floating high and light, like little ships. Crows and ravens stalked among them or flopped overhead, their wings swishing. The mergansers had marshaled their broods, now nearly full grown, out into the open pools. They all screamed and shouted. The whole air was restless, electric with excitement. High excitement. Too high: Sally, in almost frantic haste, plunged into the forest, following her necessity for a moment's respite.

Here it was quieter. She could draw her breath. The trees were calm; and they had not lost their power of bestowal. Nevertheless, even under their shadow the pitch of life was rising. The vanguard of the salmon must be by now far upstream: for here they were as crowded as in the lower stretches. The great flocks of birds predatory on them, and their eggs, were outside on the flats and meadows; but the ravens were accustomed to forests and had followed in, and the crows; and the eagles seemed to fancy this seclusion, for several of them rose up ahead with a mighty beating of pinions which startled Sally; and she was amused to discover, away off their beat, some of her marshland friends, the blue herons she had nicknamed Grandpa Grumps. All these, obviously, were following the salmon on business, and so were part of that ever-vibrant tide of life from which Sally sought moderation. But there were the other creatures who had nothing to do with salmon—the slate-gray water ouzels, the miniature bob-up-and-down sandpipers, the tiny forms of the migrant host flickering in the dimness of the forest—and they, too, seemed keyed to the bright vibrant spirit of culmination. Or so it appeared to Sally. They seemed to her to move more briskly, and in their voices she thought to detect a sharpened eagerness. She pushed on upstream, toward the headwaters where, she was sure, she would shake herself free.

The rubber boots proved to be a great comfort. Where she and John had been forced to a half-hour's detour through the thick brush—why, now she could wade it in about a minute. To be sure, the water was lower than it had been then; and its surface did lap pretty close to the Plimsoll mark; but she pulled the tops of the boots up hard and walked gingerly and assured herself she had got away with it in spite of a suspiciously cold streak down one leg. She got quite interested in getting up the stream without taking to the brush at all and performed some remarkable feats of squirming and tiptoeing and balancing on rocks. Thus she passed successfully four of the deep pools. In the fifth she slipped. She pulled her leg back sharply; but it was too late. After that she did not mind dipping over the top. It wasn't like wading. You sort of warm up to it, reflected Sally. She plowed along happily. She paid little attention to her surroundings, though the stream certainly offered lavishly. She was caught in the flow of her inner musings.

Therefore, when Chilkat Harry spoke from just behind her she was startled enough to cry out. She had not heard him; and this was the last place she would have thought to find him. He carried a rifle over the crook of his arm. Obviously he had been hurrying. He was splashed with water and streaked with sweat and his breath was short. He seemed angry.

"For God's sake, what do you mean coming up here!" he demanded without greeting.

"Why shouldn't I? Do you think you own the whole country?" She neither liked Chilkat Harry's manner, nor did she intend being ordered about. Who did he think he was? Chilkat Harry did not appear to notice her resentment. He dropped the butt of his rifle to the gravel and took off his hat and was passing his forearm across his forehead. He no longer looked angry. "Why, he looks relieved," thought Sally. "At catching up with me—stopping me—maybe I was spoiling something—spoiling the hunting—or—or something," her thoughts veered swiftly. Sally was naturally fair minded. "I'm sorry if I've been scaring things," said she. "I didn't know."

Chilkat Harry put on his hat and drew a deep breath.

"Lord!" he ejaculated, "I thought I'd never catch you!" He stamped his feet on the gravel, and his half boots gave out a squelching sound, and little jets of water came out through the eyelets. "You've no business here," said he. "Don't you know this is a grizzly basin?"

"A what?" asked Sally.

"Grizzlies. Grizzly bears."

"What of it?" Her question was sincere. "I'm not afraid of bears; I've seen lots of them," she proffered.

Suddenly Chilkat Harry became again himself as Sally had known him. He examined her from the vantage point of his customary sardonic amusement.

"Listen, tenderfoot," he admonished, mockingly didactic, "there is an enormous difference between the bear you've seen 'lots of,' which is the common black bear or *ursus Americanus,* and the grizzly

bear or *ursus horribilis,* with which you can have had no acquaintance whatever. The black bear is a peaceful, not to say timid, citizen,
and no more dangerous than a good dog. You can drive him away
simply by ordering him off; and you can scare him out of a year's
growth just by throwing your hat at him. On the other hand the
grizzly bear——"

"*Horribilis!*" she supplied sweetly.

"—may be very dangerous, especially if he is suddenly come upon
or disturbed," he refused her frivolity. "Furthermore, the grizzly will
not tolerate the black bear, so that when I say this is a grizzly basin,
I mean that any bear at all that you meet is sure to be a grizzly and
not a black bear."

"The *Americanus,*" she added with the air of a dutiful pupil. "Ain't
education wonderful!"

"You make me tired. I tell you the streams are dangerous now.
Every bear in the mountains is down here after the fish. The river
is lousy with them."

"I haven't even seen a sign of a bear." Sally had been impressed,
but now she was getting back to normal.

Chilkat Harry made a gesture of disgust.

"Well, you'd have seen more than you wanted if I hadn't caught
up to you. Look here, I'm serious. If you'd come up here last week,
while the salmon were lower down, you wouldn't have got this far.
Sign! The whole place is full of sign."

"I didn't see any." Sally was obstinate, but without conviction. As
a matter of fact she knew that if there had been sign she would not
have seen it. She had not been noticing things on the outside. She
had been wholly occupied within. Still, she was not going to be put
upon. "You can't scare me," she told Chilkat Harry, expressing this.

He snatched up the rifle into the crook of his arm.

"You come with me. And keep quiet," he commanded curtly.

He turned away and started up river. He did not look back to
see whether or not she intended to follow. She did follow. He
moved lithely and sure-footedly and so swiftly that in the open
stretches Sally could not keep up with him. But at each bend he

slowed and crept forward, close under the cover of the bank, and peered cautiously; and at such times Sally caught up. Thus they proceeded for nearly half a mile. Nothing happened. Sally's expectations were beginning to fade; but paradoxically her excitement was mounting.

Then suddenly Chilkat Harry was crouching low and peering around the bushes, and his hand was motioning her forward. She crept to his side.

"Good heavens!" she whispered when she could catch her breath. "He's so big! Oh!" she cried aloud. The great beast had made a sudden dash and pounce into the shallow water. She clapped her hand over her mouth. Chilkat Harry eased himself back against the low cut bank.

"Well, there he is! How do you like him? Want to go shake hands with him?"

"He's magnificent!" murmured Sally.

"You don't need to whisper," said Harry. "The water's making a lot of noise. Just keep your voice low. Well, there are at least a dozen —probably more—just like him on the river right at this moment."

But Sally was too excited to catch the reproof. She was all intent on the bear.

"What would he do if he saw us?" she asked presently.

"Go away, probably, after he'd taken a good look at us. Maybe try to bluff us out, if he's the sassy kind and still hungry."

"Might he attack us?"

"Oh, it's possible—just possible," Harry shrugged. "He's too far away. They don't want to fight unless you crowd 'em."

"He looks awfully close to me," said Sally doubtfully. "Suppose he should make up his mind to walk downstream?"

Harry had one eye on the bear, but he was looking at Sally. Her cheeks were red and her eyes sparkling. Her lips were parted in the excitement of her breathing.

"Had enough?" asked Harry. "Scared? Want to go?"

"Not for worlds! Oh, I've never had such a good time!" She seized Harry's wrist. "Oh, he *is* coming downstream!"

Harry shook aside her hand and cocked the rifle.

"Don't shoot him!" she implored.

"Not unless I have to," he muttered.

The animal had finished eating the fish he had caught. Now he had arisen to his feet and was slouching idly down the middle of the river. His eyes were sleepily vacant. Obviously his movements were without purpose, but they happened to be directed accurately toward the spot where the two were crouched. Nearer and nearer he came. Sally could see the drops of water glistening on the long hairs of his coat. Her heart began to pound, her breath came short. She tore her eyes away to look at Harry. Harry was watching the animal intently, and his rifle was forward at the ready, but his expression was one of amusement. He caught her glance upon him and uttered a low chuckle.

"Nothing on his mind but his hat!" said he.

Afterward, Sally chuckled too, in recollection of the creature's huge and colossal indolence, his fatuously somnolent self-satisfaction. But this was no time for levity.

The bear continued to wade down the center of the stream. In his progress he disturbed several pairs of salmon that had been lying side by side, nose to current. They darted past him. He swung his head toward them. Once he half turned as though to follow one of them, but gave up the idea after the halfhearted movement. He had no faintest suspicion of the presence of these human beings; nevertheless, the line of his sauntering was so accurately in their direction that, if he continued, it seemed as though he must actually run over them.

Sally was making desperate efforts to control herself. Something ought to be done! Left to herself, she would have fled or cried out. But this was Harry's business. Harry looked to be on the job. The muzzle of his rifle was forward, and his muscles tense. He must know: but—— Sally was surprised to hear her own voice. "He's getting awfully close! He's getting awfully close!" she was muttering under her breath, over and over. And, indeed, he was getting close. Sally could see every hair in his ruff, the lazy twinkle in his little eyes. Evidently Harry thought so too, for the butt of the rifle began slowly to rise toward his shoulder.

But, almost at the last minute, the bear stopped. He swung his head, looking back vaguely, as though he were trying to remind himself of something he had forgotten. For ten seconds he stood thus, then whirled into action so suddenly shattering that Sally only just managed not to scream. However, the charge—for such it was—was in the other direction; and its objective not the two humans, of whose presence the animal was still unaware, but one of the smaller pools just above the head of the rapids. Into this he hurled his enormous body. The water flew as though from the impact of a six-inch shell; at any rate that image would express Sally's impression. Then he raised his head calmly and looked back downstream; and in his jaws, firmly clamped, he held a salmon.

"They sure can make a savage rush!" remarked Chilkat Harry in his natural voice. "Don't worry," he reassured Sally. "He's right next the rapids: he can't hear us now. And he's right busy with his fish. Now's our time to pull out. Don't make any sudden moves." He let down the hammer of his rifle, eased himself slowly to his feet, as slowly drew back, inch by inch, until he had, so to speak, faded around the brush at the bend of the stream. Sally copied his movements. Once out of sight, Harry walked rapidly until he had gained the shelter of the next bend. There he stopped, dropped the butt of his rifle to the ground.

"Well," said he, "how do you like it?"

"I apologize," said Sally. "But wasn't he magnificent? And he did look so good natured, so sort of roly poly and lazy, not a bit fierce and dangerous. As if you could pat him!"

"I wouldn't advise it," said Harry dryly.

"I know. But wasn't it exciting!"

She was stimulated in every fiber of her being. Her eyes and cheeks were bright. She tingled. For the moment at least her human encasements had sprung a leak. She shared with the other creatures of nature their perviousness to the swift brimming flood of life. If, for the space of just a heartbeat, she could stop to think, she would understand. But she was carried with it far beyond that; and when such a thing happens, one may toe-dance, but one may not think. Harry surveyed approvingly the outward and visible signs of this inner state. However, he had a point to make, a serious point; and now was the time to make it. He fixed Sally's attention, facing her squarely.

"Now I hope you see what I mean. There are, I should say, at least a dozen, probably more, of these animals, somewhere along the course of this one stream, either fishing or lying up in the woods close by. And the same with every other salmon stream in the valley. It's heaven's own luck you didn't bump into one before I caught you. And they're dangerous: make no mistake about that. It isn't safe to go wandering around by yourself at this time of year. It simply won't do! You mustn't do it again. It isn't fair—to anybody. You've simply *got* to stay out of the woods for a while. I want you to promise."

He meant it. In his manner was no trace of the ironic detachment Sally had come to identify with the man. He seemed older, more mature—and somehow more solid, as a person.

Sally was sobered, as much by the change in the man as by his words.

"I promise," she agreed readily.

"Good girl!" he approved.

"But it *was* such fun! So deliciously scary," she added.

"You be good, and I'll take you to see him—or one of his pals—again," promised Chilkat Harry.

"Oh, can you—will you?" Sally was all aflame again. "Isn't it—that is, are you positive it would be all right?"

He did not quite catch her meaning at once.

"Oh, certainly," he then reassured her. "They're not really dangerous if you know their habits and how to handle them. I've been among them for years, and I've never had to kill one yet. I've had to come close to it at times," he added.

They were moving together, slowly, down toward the mouth of the stream. She pondered his last remark.

"Then you don't want to kill them?" she asked presently.

"Kill them?" Harry's surprise sounded genuine. "What would I want to do that for?"

Sally digested this for a further period of silence. Here was something new to think about. Such forbearance did not seem in character. If John were to come close onto huge bears like these he would want to kill one.

"Haven't you ever?" she asked after a while.

"Haven't I ever what?"

"Shot a bear."

"Heavens, yes—when I needed 'em."

Her thoughts groped a little further.

"You must have seen a lot of them," she ventured next.

"Hundreds," replied Chilkat Harry carelessly.

That was better. When John had seen "hundreds" he would not particularly want to kill any either. Comfortable, now that she had solved her anomalies, Sally trudged on after Chilkat Harry, enjoying herself.

"I should think you'd wear rubber boots," she spoke up suddenly out of a long silence, as they emerged to the gravel after wading along the edge of a pool. "Isn't the water awfully cold?"

"It is. And I do," Harry assured her dryly. "But it seemed inadvisable to take time to go get them."

"Oh!" Sally's voice was contrite. "I *am* grateful," she added.

"Think no more of it." Chilkat Harry waved his hand grandly. "Damsels in distress are right up my alley."

They came to the long riffles which they must wade down the middle. It was full of salmon, and they were well splashed by the panic-stricken fish. Some of them thumped so violently against Sally's legs that she had difficulty keeping her feet. Successfully by this hazard, another thought occurred to her.

"Where's Chilkat?" she inquired.

"Tied up. At your house. I left him. Chilkat's no asset when it comes to bears—unless you want a bear fight."

The mention of the dog reminded Sally of the smoked fish. She

told Chilkat Harry about it, and with relish and humor, for the day
had keyed her spirits high. She laughed delightedly at herself. But,
strangely, Chilkat Harry did not seem to see the humor. On the contrary, he frowned. Sally could not understand that. She stopped short
in her narrative.

"Damn that dog!" said Chilkat Harry.

Sally misunderstood.

"Why, I didn't mind. I thought it was very funny," she assured
him. But that was not it.

"He's never quit me before," the man was saying.

Sally could not take that seriously.

"Now don't get jealous!" she admonished.

"Jealous!" he repeated contemptuously. Then after a silence, "That
dog's business is to stay on the job—unless I order him different—
and he knows it!"

"Surely everybody gets their day off." She kept her teasing tone
with an effort: the man seemed deadly serious. "And he did refuse
my offering *so* politely; and he tried *so* hard to make a game of it."

Gradually the remote hardness of his eyes softened to her. But
beneath she felt uneasily still the cold disapproval.

"You wouldn't understand," he admitted. "In a country like this
you depend on your dog. You may have to depend on your dog—
for your life. He's got to be a one-man dog, or he's no good. He
isn't worth killing!" He spoke the last words, Sally thought, almost
with bitterness. But immediately he seemed to recover. "I admit he
was tempted," he said in a lighter tone. "Who wouldn't be?"

Nevertheless Sally finished the journey thoughtful and troubled.
She was sorry her friend Chilkat had got himself in wrong on her
account. She wouldn't have put Chilkat in wrong for anything in
the world.

And at the cabin Chilkat himself seemed to sense disapproval.
He ducked his head and sneezed; but his greeting lacked other
exuberances.

Sally put her hand on the man's arm.

"Please!" she begged.

He chuckled.

"All forgotten!" he assured her. "But you get the idea." Apparently he regretted the impression he might have made. "How'd you like to tackle 'em again?" he suggested. "Tomorrow? Put up a lunch and tie up the noble hound and make a day of it? The bears, I mean."

"I'd *love* it!" Sally was fairly breathless. "But you won't kill any, will you?" she pleaded. "I'd hate that."

"We'll just stand quiet and let them eat us," he laughed.

"I'm so excited!" cried Sally. "I think I'd rather go 'bearing' than anything in the world!"

CHAPTER XXV

THE MALEMUTE

THE HALCYON DAYS were here. There was neither cloud nor wind. In all probability fogs brooded outside, but they did not overtop the mountain barrier. Nothing troubled the serenity of the valley.

Its inhabitants shared the well-being of this happy time. Against the streams eager hordes of salmon struggled to their destiny's culmination and rested at last in fulfillment. The birds of the flats and the forest, the beasts, great and small, of the mountains, exulted in their season of abundance. The bushes were heavy with berries. The wild grasses bent under the browning weight of seed. John's operations were at last working smoothly: even from the cabin one could make out the white of peeled logs floating in his boom. Chilkat Harry came often, almost every day, to take Sally up the streams. She never tired of the interest and thrill at the privilege of attendance on the great animals about their daily business.

The calm was profound; and during its allotted period no disturbance could more than ruffle temporarily its surface. But in an imperfect world there must be disturbances. The salmon paid their toll to fang and claw; and even in lavishness the wilderness creatures must occasionally dispute ownership. Across the bright surface of

Sally's new days passed small brief troubling shadows. There was John. He was enormously interested in her account of the bears; so interested that for the first time his single tenacity of mind wavered. He'd like to see one of those bears! By glory, that must be something to see!

"Why don't you?" urged Sally.

"By golly, I will!" cried John.

But his first enthusiasm flickered away. The stronger, vital interest of his work held him. By and by. The big spruce was *just* about ready! And if it chanced to turn windy all of a sudden—— He explained to Sally what would happen if it turned windy. "Wait till I get the big spruce in . . ."

"Then there 'll be something else; there's always something else," said Sally resentfully. She was disappointed. She had allowed herself to believe John would carry out his impulse. It would be twice as much fun with John. "You don't know what fun it is," she added.

"The skins are no good right now, anyway," John pointed out.

Sally checked. She backtracked from the urging of John, softly, as she and Chilkat Harry sometimes withdrew from the presence of one of the bears. She had not thought of this: of course John would want to kill a bear. Sally's intuitions realized that. All men were that way; but John especially, by instinct and lifelong training. He was an outdoorsman, a hunter. He would have to kill a bear, just to get it out of his system. But not now, not on my stream, not my friends! Her recoil at the thought of such treachery settled to thankfulness to Chilkat Harry. He'd killed his bears; he had no temptations in the matter of killing bears. He'd long ago got it out of his system. In his company she could enjoy her bears with a free heart.

She had come finally to confidence in Chilkat Harry. For a long time she had had none at all. She had held herself very guardedly when in his company. But now she was ashamed of her first suspicions. Obviously he liked her, enjoyed being with her. Well, she liked him. He had light and gay wit; he was good company; he was inspiriting. He knew how to fool solemnly. He was quick to catch allusion. They had fun together. But not once, by a single word, by the smallest hint, had he ever indicated that he thought of her—well, the way you'd suppose he ought to think of her! Sally had to laugh at herself for this. The nearest he came to it was to tease her a little, sometimes, about being a neglected wife. And as for that, she was now able to take that so lightly that she teased back. "Don't lose your sense of humor, old girl," she warned herself.

Just at first she harbored a slight uneasiness as to how John would look at all this traipsing around together. Not that there was any reason; but men are so funny. But John was more concerned with the possible dangers; he catechized her as to the conduct of the bears and looked doubtful when he heard what close quarters these adventures seemed to require.

"I'd like to talk to Harry about that," he told Sally. "I wish you'd ask him to stay until I get back."

Sally invited Harry to supper; and he came; and John talked to him. What he learned must have satisfied John as to Harry's knowledge and competence, for he made no objections to the excursions. Sally had been ready to meet objections, not to the bears, but to Harry. Apparently that aspect had not occurred to John. This should have gratified Sally; and it did, really, but unreasonably it also vexed her just a little. Either John had exaggerated confidence in her ability to take care of herself; or he had read Harry more shrewdly than she thought he had; or else he was just too ingenuous for an imperfect world. That brief shadow passed. Sally knew how closely she and John were attuned; she did not doubt that he had caught intuitively her own feeling as to Chilkat Harry.

Curiously enough, another of the small brief troubling shadows across the bright surface of the days seemed at the time to Sally neither small nor destined to be brief. On the contrary, the episode carried apparently a shattering finality of disillusion. She could not conceive how she could ever again feel the same toward Chilkat Harry. Nevertheless, in final outcome the incident enhanced her confidence, not in the man, but in her relationship to the man.

This was one of the off days when they were not to go "bearing." Sally finished her small housework; and, as the tide was low, she put on the rubber boots and walked out on the flats. She had neglected the flats of late. The sun was out, the water sparkled, the air was crisp in her nostrils. The kelp bulbs popped under her feet. Before her a flock of turnstones fanned into the air, crying, and wheeled and settled like a sudden drift and rose again when she overtook them. She noticed them only because they were close at hand. Her old friends of the tidelands, she merely sensed, but outside of her focused consciousness. Later she might look about her and see things. At the moment she was simply enjoying herself, savoring the fun of striding along free limbed, head back, breathing deep, without thought.

Now here was a dead sea gull at her feet; newly dead it must be, for the tide had not wet it; and she must spare it a vague regret. But shortly there was another and then yet a third. She looked about her and saw other patches of white lying here and there. Startled and curious, she turned over the nearest with her foot. An obvious bullet hole told her the story. Revolt, indignant revolt, filled her, not against Chilkat Harry, but against men as a whole; and not so much against men as against the killer instinct common to all men. Why did they have to do it? Kill, kill! And so carelessly, without thought of the beautiful life they destroyed! There was a hard outside objectiveness to it. They never stopped to think. That was the trouble; they never stopped to think!

There was nothing to be done about it. "Oh well!" sighed Sally. The flats were no fun any more; not for today. She returned, rather forlornly, to the cabin.

From afar she discovered Chilkat, the malemute, at the top of the trail. For a moment she hesitated whether to go forward. Here was another of those occasions when she was in no mood for the dog's master. But she repressed that impulse, reminding herself that they were all that way, even the best of them. No sense in taking it out on Harry that he was a man. She continued on and climbed the trail. Chilkat greeted her enthusiastically. But Harry was not about. When she had assured herself of this she turned upon Chilkat sternly.

She remembered only too clearly the man's unmistakably deadly anger on that former occasion when Chilkat had made her an unauthorized visit. But perhaps this visit was authorized: he might have sent Chilkat to keep her company—— A sudden thought checked her for a moment: for Chilkat's sake she could not take a chance on that.

"Go home!" she ordered the malemute. "Go right home!" She extended her arm, pointing, and tried to look severe.

Chilkat ducked his head and sneezed apologetically; but he did not stir.

Sally's heart weakened within her, but outwardly she did not relent. She made it plain to Chilkat that she meant what she said. He looked at her in reproach, arose, turned his back and walked slowly away.

But at a dozen yards he stopped, turned again, sat down on his haunches.

"Go home!" ordered Sally again.

Chilkat eyed her. Then his tail stirred feebly. This would not do. Sally picked up a stick—a small stick—and advanced upon Chilkat. Chilkat rolled over delicately on his back and held up all four feet, inviting her to kick him in the stomach, if she would be so cruel. As she did not do so, he rolled back and placed his head between his paws and sighed.

"Go home!" ordered Sally for the third time. She tried her best to put some dynamics into it, but failed miserably. Chilkat caught the uncertainty, rolled his eyes at her in comical appreciation and wagged his tail, as if now electing to take the command as facetiously intended: a joke, though somewhat of a threadbare joke, to be sure.

Sally looked down at him, baffled and perplexed. "Oh well!" she half gave it up. She made no outward sign of yielding, but instantly Chilkat leaped to his feet and ran madly around and around her barking. In full career he snatched a stick from the ground. He dashed to her and deposited it at her feet and backed away inch

by inch, his hindquarters gathered tense and expectant beneath him.
"Oh well!" repeated Sally, giving way completely. She threw the
stick. She knew she should not do it.

Chilkat Harry burst up the trail. His face was congested with
anger. He paid no attention to Sally. Chilkat cowered humbly, but
made no effort to escape. The man kicked the dog twice in the side.
The blows were delivered heartily, with a wide free swing of the
leg: if they had been armed with boots instead of shoe pacs they
must have broken ribs. As it was, Chilkat whimpered under his
breath at each impact. Chilkat Harry jerked the malemute to his
feet, headed him down the trail, delivered another kick to start him
along. All the while he was cursing savagely, in the primitive terms
of the wilderness, without heed to Sally. When she seized his arm,
he shook her off with such violence that she staggered and nearly
fell. But it is doubtful if even then he was fully conscious of her.
He was wholly contained in his blind anger. He followed close after
Chilkat retreating abjectly. Chilkat made no effort to hasten ahead
—as he could easily have done—from the repeated urging of the
man's foot.

Sally sank to the ground. She was badly shaken. No man had
ever so laid hands on her before. It was as if he had struck her. He
would have struck her, without hesitation, if the sweep of his arm
had not sufficed to brush her away! The man was blind mad! He
would have shot the dog at her feet, had he been armed! She knew
he would! She was convinced of it! Sally's hand flew to her heart.
A sudden realization stopped her breath. She would have shot
Chilkat Harry—had she been armed! She had a distinct picture of
herself, fumbling at her waist, where—obeying John, in spite of the
other man's derision—she usually wore "Black Mike," the little thirty-
two caliber police model Colt revolver. She would have done it,
unhesitatingly. She had been blind mad, too! She was appalled, as
at escape, not from a small single episode, but from a cosmic blast
of destruction that had snatched and roared by. She felt his presence
and looked up. He had returned.

He was holding his hat in his hands before him. His bold eyes were contrite. His whole attitude was of apology, of humility, expecting her resentment.

But she had no resentment now; only hurt and bewilderment. "Why did you do it! Why! Why!" she lamented.

He was trying to apologize, to explain. He was begging forgiveness. Something about his rotten temper; something about missing the dog and looking for him and the sort of trouble a dog could get into; something again about the necessity of being able to depend on your dog. Just blew up. Inexcusable—oh, a lot more! Sally's mind could not focus on it. Unimportant, somehow. It wasn't the thing that had happened that was making her shiver in almost a physical sickness. It was the revelation that behind the fair surface of life were primitive forces that could seize so utterly. Sally was not angry; she was humble—and scared. She did not want to "forgive" Chilkat Harry. She had nothing to "forgive." She was in the same boat. She wanted him to stop talking, to go away. She wanted to be alone. Life had revealed another of its terrible simplicities. She wanted to look at life.

She must get rid of him. She told him she understood. She told him she was not angry. Anything to get him to go away. But she must rouse herself to put in a word for Chilkat. That came to her. Chilkat must not be further abused. "It was really my fault," said Sally. "I'm to blame." So far reasonably; then her nerves jangled. "Oh, go away! Go away!" she cried again passionately.

He hesitated, but went without a word, slowly and doubtfully.

She sat there for some time, her hands covering her face, sore spirited, very weary. She tried to remind herself of many things. She tried to understand. But always it came back to the one thing that she could not understand. These other things were life: they could not be escaped. Something ruthless, something lethal, so integral a part of life that men were blind to them. The dead sea gulls on the flat—so wanton, so cruel, such a senseless waste of beautiful life! It was not an affair of Chilkat Harry: she had got beyond Chilkat Harry. If she were to tell John about it, she knew what he would say. He would laugh at her indulgently. Plenty of sea gulls, he would dismiss the episode; probably targeting-in his rifle. That's the way he would react: reasonably, just like other men. It was not really cruelty: merely a curious incapacity. Thoughtlessness. Like small boys who stone cats and tie tin cans to dogs' tails, without seeing beyond the immediate fact. They were all small boys, just grown bigger; that's all. Sally felt very maternal toward all men. She felt maternal toward Chilkat Harry.

This would have considerably astounded that young man, had he known. He was back the next day, soberly bent on recovering lost ground. He brought Chilkat with him. He was very quiet, very contrite, very uncertain of how to approach Sally. He tried little jokes —quite small jokes—and watched her covertly to see if she was going to smile. As a matter of fact she had difficulty to keep from laughing at him. So like a small bad boy . . .

Then it was her turn to be astounded. It *sounded* as though he were trying to give her Chilkat. As a peace offering?

"I wouldn't think of such a thing!" she cried, aroused.

"But you like him, don't you?" insisted Chilkat Harry.

It wasn't a question of that—of course she liked him—but——

He cut short her protest.

"You needn't feel that way. It's no favor to you. If you won't take him, someone else will. I can dispose of him."

"Dispose of him!" echoed Sally, incredulous.

"He doesn't suit me. I was serious in what I told you. A dog is of no use to me unless I can depend on him completely. I don't keep pets. And I will not tolerate a divided loyalty."

He meant that last with a deadly seriousness too formidable to be doubted.

"Oh, I'm not blaming the old fool," he continued, but now in his customary tone of ironic mockery. "How could I? He's just fallen in love with you. Nobody could be blamed for that."

The swift impudent boldness of his smile put her—as usual—on the defensive.

"I'll—I'll ask John," she temporized weakly.

He seemed to take the affair as settled and at once departed, after his sudden fashion.

"Better keep him away from the river," he advised indifferently over his shoulder. "The salmon are beginning to die. They might poison him."

Whether from a dog's intuitive understanding of situations, or in obedience to some gesture of command, the malemute did not offer to follow.

CHAPTER XXVI

NEWS

LIFE SETS HER STAGE at her leisure: a touch here, a touch there, arranging and rearranging until everything is exactly so. Over long uneventful periods her unconscious protagonists carry on routine. Nothing happens. Then they are called. Everything happens. Fate seems to pounce. Actually this thing has been happening all along.

Now here, in this secluded Alaskan valley, just such a moment had come. Remained only to touch the signal of release.

Somebody must take a run to Klakan. It was time. There were a number of things to attend. John's boom would soon be ready; Orford must arrange to send a tug for it. The hunting season was at hand: was Nelson Cole going to need the cabin? John wanted to get in touch with Len to find out what he was going to do all winter. Too late in the season to explore on farther north. Do that in the spring. Perhaps Len could find a shanty in Klakan for the three of them. They both missed Len. These things ought to be done right away, but John hated to take time off right now. This good weather could not last forever. Lucky if it would last another week; but in a week John calculated he could have this "swifter" finished; and the business of Klakan would take just about that period of time.

Chilkat Harry offered. He had nothing to do until time to get organized for the trapping season. He took the Tillicum and the dinghy, leaving John the pirogue. It occurred to nobody that, as the ketch carried most of the Murdocks' worldly goods, this was a somewhat trustful arrangement on their part.

He left early, intending, he said, to get back in three or four days' time. Therefore Sally was surprised when the very following morning he pushed open the door of the cabin.

"Well!" she exclaimed, "what in the world are you doing back?" A glance out the window proved wrong her first misgiving: the Tillicum lay safely at anchor. "You *couldn't* have finished all you had to do——" she began incredulously, then stopped, and her eyes sharpened. He's been to Klakan, all right! decided Sally. He's drunk! Didn't show it much, but couldn't fool Sally. She'd seen all kinds. He was just being too careful; but that was enough. Sally was both amused and exasperated. The precision of his movements as he crossed the room and drew out a chair and lowered himself to it and deposited his hat, exactly so, alongside, and placed his hands palm down, one on each knee, and finally looked up at her and swung his mind ponderously toward her—that was funny. But his coming back without doing his errands—that was exasperating. Of course he hadn't done them. He hadn't had time; not to do them *and* get drunk.

She stood in front of him, her hands on her hips, perplexed and trying to master her vexation. These men! You never could tell about them! Or what idiotic impulse they'd follow when they got drunk. Now why on earth, of all things, should it occur to Harry to come back here? You'd think if he got started he'd want to keep going. Must have been pretty far gone not to have sobered up more by now. Or perhaps he'd had a bottle with him. She was disgusted and just a little disappointed. Somehow she hadn't thought it of Chilkat Harry.

Her first impulse was to go away and leave him to get over it. Then a thought occurred to her. Perhaps he *had* some reason for coming back. Can't imagine what it could be, but there just might be something important. Not likely, but she'd better find out. She moved a chair and sat down facing him.

"Look at me," she commanded sharply. Then as he slowly focused: "What have you got to say for yourself? I thought we could depend on you."

Chilkat Harry suddenly looked as though he were going to cry. He puckered his face at her aggrievedly.

"Now don't you be acting that way!" he objected in an injured tone. "Nice way to treat a man that takes all this trouble! I take all this trouble for you, and you go and act like this!"

"What trouble?" Sally tried to be patient.

"How about your dear old friend, Len Saunders?" inquired Harry bewilderingly. He pretended to look about. "Don't see Len Saunders. You'd think he'd be here."

"Now why should Len be here?" demanded Sally.

"Thought he was friend of yours, that's all. Thought *sure* he'd be first one to come tell you the news."

"News? What news?" So there *was* a reason. Her interest quickened. She must find out. "Harry! What news?"

But as yet he could not be deflected.

"Len Saunders!" he sneered with heavy sarcasm. "Bet he's halfway there by now! With the rest of them! That's the kind of a friend Len Saunders is! But I'm your friend. Did I go? No! And then you go and act that way!"

"Is it about John?" Something to do with the kidnaping matter or the affair of Pirate Kelly? Her mind flew to that.

"John *hell!*" He came more into focus than at any time since his arrival. "What in hell has John got to do with it? Where does John come in? You tell me that," he urged. "What we talking about John for?"

He rather had Sally there. It was just that her first anxiety was instinctively for John. Absurd!

"Well, what is this wonderful news?" she asked.

Chilkat Harry sat forward; he glanced from right to left as though assuring seclusion from the seething multitude. Almost, but not quite, he laid a finger on his lips. Sally controlled her amusement.

"Well, what is it?" she repeated.

"That Klondike thing is *so!*" Harry's voice was low and cautious. He sat back and surveyed her.

But his expected effect did not come off. Sally had never heard that queer word before and said so. Harry's face showed blank amazement. Where'd been her ears? Why, *everybody*'d been talking Klondike, ever since last fall; only they'd just thought it was another of those things . . .

"Suppose you begin simply, from the beginning," suggested Sally, "and tell me first of all what a Klondike is."

Harry did not take this lightly, as presented. He seemed to resent it.

"Sarcastic, aren't you!" he sneered. He cocked his head sideways and appeared to reflect. "Don't know as I blame you: it *does* sound wild."

Sally had the feeling of walking through heavy sand. But she controlled her impulse of exasperation. Wouldn't do! Emotions of that sort are too contagious.

"Please, Harry," she begged, "be good, and tell me, *what* is it that sounds wild?"

"That George Cormack yarn," vouchsafed Harry, as though that explained everything.

"Heaven bestow patience!" breathed Sally, but to herself.

She set herself to do more digging than even George Cormack had done the summer before on the Klondike (so the Klondike was a river!) in company with his brother-in-law, Skookum Charley, and the rest of the family. Indeed, the squaw man was reported to have done almost no digging at all—hadn't anything but frying pans to pan with——

"Oh, it's gold!" Sally at last began to understand. Her face showed her fall of interest.

"They took out seven hundred thousand!" Harry insisted. He seemed to think he now had to defend the story he had just denounced as "wild."

"You believe that?" asked Sally indifferently. (She'd been hearing that sort of story all her life. Oregon had not yet discovered that proximity to California did not make a gold state. Twice before she was fifteen years old she had seen Borland empty overnight of practically every one of its able-bodied male inhabitants. Following rumors even more fantastic than this one. Looked as if Borland were to be a ghost town. But the doctor, her father, was undisturbed. He locked his office door. "We'll just go fishing," said he, "until they get back." "Will they come back?" she had asked. "How do you know they will?" She was rather exact minded as a child and wanted to know things. He had wrinkled his eyes at her, as he did when he wanted to tease; but that was the only indication that he was not entirely serious. "Because I'm a doctor," he had said, "and this is a disease." "What kind of a disease?" for she was a doctor's only child, and no mother. "Let me see"—he frowned at her with his bushy brows—"it's—it's a febrile sciamachy epidemic in character, exceedingly contagious; characterized by hypertrophy of the mythogenic faculties. Yields readily to treatment by cold hard facts. Prognosis favorable—but busted!" Then she knew he was laughing at her.) All this flashed through the back of her mind while the front of it was being surprised that Chilkat Harry had fallen for that sort of thing. He did not seem that sort, somehow. (More like John, went on the swift undercurrent of her reflections. John shared her father's opinions on mining and prospecting. "Sucker's game," said John. "If you want to gamble, why work so hard to get it, as long as there's faro?")

But instantly she realized she was making a mistake. The effect of her idle comment was out of all proportion. He struck one hand into the palm of the other.

"God damn it!" he cried violently, "what do *you* know about it?"

Startled, she stared at him a moment, catching her breath. Except for the one outburst against the malemute, she had never heard him profane before; and in a country of easy profanity, this had, in a way, set him apart. Now he was swearing at her! And he was really angry. There was a little red flicker in the back of his eyes. Her natural affront died as promptly as it had flared. The man wasn't responsible. Watch out! Watch out! an inner instinct warned her. But she had no fear of him, as yet. Touchy. Just needed handling.

"Not a thing, not a thing," she hastened to answer. "But," she added, "you must admit it's a pretty tall story."

He took this under advisement. The red flicker died.

"That's right," he admitted, with a great air of fairness. "Come to think of it, I didn't pay much attention to it myself—at first. 'N I was hearing it all last winter, too. That's right." He reached forward to pat her on the knee in reassurance. She did not draw away; but she stiffened warily. " 'Just another of those things,' that's what I said myself last winter. That's what everybody said. You're all right: don't blame you."

That was better. Keep him talking. Maybe he'd talk himself sober, if she could keep him talking long enough. Wish John would come . . . No, I don't! Watch your step!

"Why do you believe it now?" asked Sally. "You must have some reason."

This worked. He veered again to argument.

"Purser on the Portland," he said impressively. "Friend of mine. He's all right. I got him out of a hole once. He wouldn't steer me wrong. It's straight goods. On her trip south she took out eight hundred thousand in dust and nuggets! Had 'em in her safe. Hard, cold fact. He showed me the entries to prove it. In his books. I tell you I saw them myself!"

He leaned back, spreading his arms in his chair, justifiably triumphant. Sally was impressed, in spite of herself, and showed it. Harry was gratified.

"Of course," he acknowledged magnanimously, "it wasn't all Cormack's. Probably the winter diggings of the whole district. Maybe some Treadwell stuff thrown in. But that's not the point. Point is, the stuff's there. And it's going to boost that Cormack yarn. Make people prick up their ears and take notice. But that isn't all. Do you know what?"

"No, what?" Sally was expected to reply and did so.

"Eight hundred thousand in one shipment—that sounds pretty good," Harry spoke with relish, "in a kind of way. But some bright lad on a newspaper figured out that made about a ton. 'A ton of gold,' that's the way he wrote his headline. 'The Portland docked yesterday carrying a ton of gold!' Whee! That hits your imagination! That'll bring 'em! They're piling in already. You can't get a berth even now. Pretty soon you can't get deck room. And by next year they'll be coming in dugouts—or swimming!"

"It sounds exciting," agreed Sally.

"Exciting! That the best you can do? I've been waiting for this. This is big!" In his sudden catlike fashion he leaped from his chair and began to pace up and down the room. Sally noticed for the first time that Chilkat lay in a corner, very quietly, his chin on his paws, his eyes following the man's every movement. She had not thought of it before, but now it struck her that the dog had been in that corner all the time; that he had shown no greeting when the man came in. The latter stopped, suddenly, before her. He must have caught her doubtful expression and misinterpreted it.

"You don't believe it yet," he accused. "Well—maybe I don't either—not all of it. But that isn't the point. The point is that it'll be believed. What difference does it make to us whether there's as much as they say? *We*'re not going to break our backs digging gold. Let the mugs do that. And some of them *will* get some gold, and all of them have got to eat and sleep and get lugged around the country and have their fun. Don't forget that! That's where we come in."

"We?"

"Sure. That's where we have it on 'em. We've got the ketch. Lay in what we need at Klakan or Treadwell or Juneau—prices haven't begun to boost there yet. Sell the boat at Skagway—no trouble doing that, they'll be just *hollering* for anything that'll float—and I know a man who'll take her. Pack over Chilkoot. We can get Indians now; but in another month a man'll do his own packing! Same way at the Lakes. Boats to be had there yet; but pretty *pronto* the next fellows'll have to build them, on the spot. Dawson's probably the place to head for. Find out when we get there."

He was talking rapidly and straightforwardly now that he was on something definite that he had planned out. It *did* sound alluring, as he told it. She'd never thought of a gold rush that way.

"We'll make a million!" bragged Chilkat Harry. "You've no idea. Why, that little one-horse rush to the Sapphire—back in Montana— why, in two months there I—— And my whole outfit was two packs of cards and a gun!" He laughed recklessly. "Anybody who can do *anything* can clean up big and not lay a hand to a pick."

"I'm pretty good at a washtub." It seemed to Sally he had at last "talked himself sober": that she could venture this much.

"You might smoke some fish," he retorted; and this return to the old easy and bantering relationship seemed to confirm her. "That's all right, my gal; any mitts you stick in a washtub 'll have diamonds on 'em. Little tough going getting there. The Chilkoot's no summer stroll. But you can make it. You'll eat it alive!"

"Of course I can make it!" cried indignantly Sarah Slocum, great-granddaughter of Joshua.

"Great!" he cried. "Let's go! We can make this tide!"

This brought Sally down to earth. She chuckled a little amusedly.

"Just like that!" she mocked. "Drop everything and go! And it's just possible John might have something to say."

All this time Chilkat Harry had continued his swift pacing back and forth. Now he stopped short and whirled on his moccasined feet to confront her.

"To hell with John!" he snapped.

Sally was still chuckling.

"That's all very well," said she, "but John might need a little persuading."

"I can persuade him—when it isn't play-acting." There was an under growl of sullenness to this.

"Well, let's go do it," suggested Sally, determinedly cheerful. "It won't take long to row over there."

"All right, all right! If that's the way you want it! But why in hell should we bother with him? I don't see any *point* to it. What can *he* do?"

Here was a new and strange crosscurrent.

"I don't believe I understand," said Sally slowly.

The man made an exasperated gesture.

"You understand, all right."

"I wonder if I do." She eyed him steadily, searching his face. The implication of his words seemed clear; but it was too fantastic. Even as an alcoholic vagary. But Harry himself cleared her doubts on that. He lurched forward as though to seize her wrist.

"Come along! Come along!" he insisted. "Hell, we can be fifty miles away before he even finds out!"

She caught her breath and snatched her hand behind her. For a moment she was unable to speak. He dared, he *dared*—— What had she ever done, what had she ever said that he should *dare*—— The conceit, the colossal, colossal *conceit*——

"You're absolutely mad!" she told him in an anger and contempt so utter that for a moment it brought him up standing. He focused on her in what her indignation knew for genuine amazement.

"Wh-what?" he stammered.

"Get out of here!" ordered Sally.

The incredulity drained from his eyes. The little dancing dangerous red flicker returned.

"Like hell!" he snarled. "No woman can do that to me! Not and get away with it. Who do you think you are? Deliberately teasing me all summer, and then——"

"I never!" cried Sally, her sense of outrage overleaping her growing panic. She could not move. The man's face was within a foot of her own, held her.

"Oh no?" he sneered elaborately. He swayed a little. "You!—and your 'neglected wife'—and playing around with whores—and your pants—and wiggling your little behind at me—and . . ." He trailed off, mumbling, gathered himself sharply. "You had your fun—you'll pay for it!"

He pounced so suddenly that he caught her wrist. She tried to twist it away. She struck at him with her free hand. She twisted and turned, kicked at him, threw herself about. She fought savagely in silence:

useless to cry out. For a brief space desperation gave her strength. He barely managed to hold her.

"No, you don't," he panted. He began to drag her. Toward the door into the bedroom. "You little hellcat!" He half raised his fist as though in mind to strike her. He was very strong.

Fear drowned her. Suddenly her powers deserted her. She went limp. The conviction of utter helplessness overcame her. She closed her eyes. She heard herself screaming. She knew it was useless to scream.

Something hurtled by. Her wrists were snatched free so violently as almost to throw her from her feet. She staggered and looked about her, dazed. What had happened?

The man lay flat on the floor. Over him stood the malemute. The dog's hair bristled on his spine; his teeth were bared; his muzzle thrust into Chilkat Harry's face. From deep in his chest issued a continuous rumbling, that changed in timbre, back and forth, as the animal breathed in and out. Chilkat Harry was very near to death; and he was aware of it; and the realization struck him cold sober. He had his wits about him now and knew enough to hold himself rigidly motionless. He had his eyes on Sally and spoke to her, quietly and steadily, as soon as he saw she would hear him.

"Call off the dog," he told her.

Sally wavered, doubtful, then darted into the bedroom, snatched John's .45 from its holster at the head of the bed, remembered it was unloaded, picked up the Winchester that stood in the corner. She threw its lever down and back, caught the gleam of brass as the cartridge slipped up into the chamber, ran back to the door. Nothing had happened. Chilkat still stood over the prostrate man, who continued to lie rigid. Sally drew a deep breath of relief. But she had had to chance it. She steadied herself. She had no great confidence in her power over Chilkat in a crisis such as this. Nevertheless she must try.

"Leave it, Chilkat!" she commanded.

The animal hesitated for a moment, then backed slowly away, inch by inch, until he stood clear. But he kept his eyes fixed on

Chilkat Harry, and the rumbling of his deep two-toned growling did not intermit.

"Good dog," commended Sally cautiously. "Come here! Now lie down!" Chilkat sunk at her feet. She leaned over to bestow a swift pat on his velvet head. But the rifle was ready in her other hand, and her eyes never flickered from the man on the floor.

"All right, I think you can get up now," she told Chilkat Harry. Then, as he got slowly to his feet: "Keep your hands out. I warn you!" She watched him vigilantly, her finger on the trigger. It surprised her that she felt no emotion. Even anger had died. She had no personal feeling whatever: merely a deadly coolness for the job in hand. If this man made the least move toward his weapon she would shoot. She knew that.

Chilkat Harry shook his shoulders. He stood quite still for what seemed like several minutes, his head down, as though in deep thought, studying the floor at his feet; then threw out both hands in a queer helpless gesture and turned toward the door. Then he paused as though about to say something, decided not and walked out through the door, across the veranda and the little flat, and disappeared down the trail. Not once did he look toward the woman or the dog.

Sally watched him go. She was filled to the throat with an enormous thankfulness; and for the moment it was enough. Then thought returned, and with it new anxieties. It was not finished. What next? The crisis was over; but a situation remained, murderous in its possibilities. She was afraid, with a fear even more deadly than the panic that had gripped her in her helplessness. She sped to the door. Chilkat bounded past her. She had to stop his pursuit. Wouldn't do to get Chilkat shot. From here she could see Chilkat Harry. The sudden idea that had come to her was only too true. He had not turned toward the right, to his cabin, but to the left, and was now out in the grass flats, headed toward the river. And he was running. In a moment he leaped into the dinghy and rowed rapidly toward the anchored ketch.

For a brief instant Sally's strength left her, and she leaned against the doorjamb, helpless. "You fool! You fool!" she berated herself. "Oh, you poor fool! You might have known that this would be what he would do!" She remembered a lot of things that meant nothing much at the time. There was that evening when the two men had competed at quickness with the six-shooters, and what Chilkat Harry had said. He had carried off his discomfiture very well at the last, but Sally recalled now a flash of vindictiveness, so instantly covered. And his words—delivered as a joke—"If I ever have to shoot you, it will be from ambush." He hated John!

She began to run. There was no boat; only the rough and indented shore. "Why didn't I have sense enough to hold him here until John came back?" she sobbed under her breath. "Why did I let him go? Why? Why?"

She plunged recklessly through the ebbing stream. The little bayous in the tide flat were still awash. The season had toughened and tangled the tall grasses. She tore through by main strength, in a blind instinct, though there was a sane part of her that told her it would be too late, that what was to happen would already have happened long before she could arrive, that her strength must soon exhaust itself in this insensate squandering of it. But she must do *something*.

Pretty soon she was forced to stop. Her lungs would take her no farther. She gasped and clutched her throat and fought the blindness that was blurring her eyes and fighting to possess her. She brushed it away with her hand, as she would have brushed away her hair, and parted the high grasses and looked.

The ketch was reaching toward the gateway opening, not toward the scene of John's operation, though for that also the wind was fair!

The relief was too much for her. She sank down in the grass. Every force in her was drained away. The past hour had shaken her to the depths, and a great variety of emotions were swirling inchoate within her, and each seized her and shook her in turn. Indignation, disillusionment, outrage, hurt, bewilderment, sheer relief and thankfulness—he had sailed by, he had not killed John: reviving anger— he had sailed away and taken with him almost everything they owned. She came back always to the same thing. "You little fool! Why, why, *why* did you let him go? You *had* him! You could have held him easily—you and Chilkat." Until John had returned! Oh— yes—John! What would have happened when John had returned and learned what had happened? She did not know: she feared to guess. Here was about John something she did not know. A few hours ago she would have said she knew all about John. Now she was humbled. She had been equally confident that she knew Chilkat Harry. Perhaps it was as well as it was——

A cold nose touched her cheek. She threw her arms passionately about the dog. He seemed to her at that moment the one stable object in a jumbled world.

For some time she sat there aware only of this and the grateful feel of the dog's rough coat. Then Chilkat barked.

She sprang to her feet. John was passing, close alongshore, in the pirogue. He was standing, facing forward, leaning against the oars in the graceful stroke he had learned from the fishermen.

He saw her at once and turned the prow inshore. She stumbled through the grass to meet him.

"What's up?" he called, then, as she neared: "I saw Harry come in; and then he went out again. I yelled at him, but he didn't pay any attention. Anything wrong?"

He stepped ashore, lifted the bow of the pirogue and slid it up on the grass.

"What's the matter?" he demanded sharply when he caught sight of her face.

"Plenty," said Sally. She collected herself. She sketched for John what had happened, briefly, dryly, stating merely the bare facts. He listened at first without comment; but his eyes narrowed, and the lines of his face hardened. Only once did he interrupt.

"Are you hurt? He didn't . . . ?"

"No, no," Sally assured him, "I'm all right."

He glanced toward her torn and wet garments; the rifle, still in her hands.

"Sure about that?" he insisted. "All right: go ahead."

He listened then to the end. Only as she concluded did Sally's control break by ever so little. "I thought at first he would come back and shoot Chilkat," said Sally, "and then I was afraid he was going to go and shoot you. And oh, John, John, I was terror stricken! He might do anything! How was I to know? How was I to guess? John, I swear to you I never did one thing, I never uttered one word, that could even remotely be *twisted*—— I can't see how he could *think* such a thing! Why, why—I never dreamed of it—he seemed to me just like a brother—I *trusted* him—I was just natural with him—— You've got to believe me, John!"

"Of course I believe you," John dismissed this curtly. He frowned for a moment. "The goddamn son of a bitch," said he, spacing the words. He took the rifle from her, thrust the lever half down, spilled the cartridge from the chamber, inserted it in the magazine, closed the gun and laid it in the bow of the pirogue. "Hop in," he told Sally.

"What are we going to do?" she ventured, though she had learned it was better not to question John when he looked that way.

He did not reply at once.

"You, too," he told Chilkat, who was waiting, his eyes eager. John delivered a caressing blow at the furry body as it leaped past him. "Diamond dog collar for you, old boy, if ever I see one." He gave the pirogue a mighty shove and leaped lightly to one knee on her bow as she glided from shore. He picked up the oars, thrust them in the water, turned the prow of the boat toward the stream's mouth. "We're going to get back our boat," he answered Sally grimly.

CHAPTER XXVII

THE TILLICUM RETURNS

A T THE CABIN John began methodically to throw together various items of equipment—blankets, clothing, a frying pan, a coffeepot.

"Rustle what grub you can," he told Sally, "and what you think you're going to need. And get our money."

She obeyed in silence, asking no questions until John made ready to shoulder one of the three packs he had got together and laid out on the veranda.

"How about the cabin?" she then ventured.

"Just shut it up. We'll be back."

She made fast the doors while he carried two of the packs down to the water. She could not guess what plan he could have. It seemed hopeless to her: oars and the heavy pirogue against sail—and already an hour's start! But she expressed no doubts.

"Hop in," said John again. This time Chilkat awaited no invitation, but jumped aboard and lay down amidships, his chin between his paws. The pirogue crawled out from the river mouth and headed toward the gap. Sally could no longer contain herself.

"We'll never in the world catch up with him!" She must express the futility.

"I'll take care of that," said John. But after a few minutes he fell into the rhythm of rowing, and his concentration of purpose could relax. "It'll take him two hours to Klakan," he relented, "if the wind 's right. I can make it in four."

"I don't believe he'll go to Klakan," said Sally.

"Mebbe not. But any reason for thinking so?"

She told John now about the Klondike. He listened, almost suspending his rowing in the fixity of his attention. "So he's more likely to sail straight north, isn't he?" she finished.

For some time he said nothing, but stood there, his eyes fixed on her face. They were frostily blue and remote, staring out from some inner speculation. Sally knew John was not seeing her at all. Presently he resumed rowing.

"He'll go to Klakan," he decided, so positively that Sally knew there must be some reasoning back of his certainty, though what it might be she could not guess. "Anyway," added John, "we'll know when we get to the entrance. He won't be out of sight."

He pushed on the oars, deliberately, steadily, without haste, conserving his strength for the long pull. His face was set in stern lines, but showed no emotion. Sally, on the forward thwart to balance the baggage astern, looked up at him and so slipped into a daydream of contemplation of his good looks, his clean-cut graceful strength. And presently this brought her again to indignation. The nerve of the man! Presuming to set himself up against John! Her face flushed again as she remembered the terrible things he had said. That a man—*any* man—should be capable of them—to a decent woman—— She caught herself back. This was going around in the same old circle. Wouldn't do. Strangely enough she was not in the least worried over the immediate future. She gave it no thought. Her man would take care of that.

The weather on the inland sea of the valley was never much of an indication of the weather outside. Often a vigorous wind proved to be local; or, as today, a few skittering cat's-paws across calm water were the only indication of trouble in the channel. The pirogue rounded the last sharp elbow of the entrance. They looked out upon angry whitecaps.

"Damn!" ejaculated John fervently; but he continued on. "There's the Tillicum," he indicated after a few moments more. "I told you he'd head for Klakan."

The tide still poured from the gap. Its strength was sufficient to kill the seas for a certain distance off the mouth. The limit of its influence was curiously exact. The purposeful gray waves ran by it as though it were a solid flat pavement. Across this flat the pirogue rushed headlong and fetched up with a bang, almost as if against a concrete wall. Sally was pitched off the thwart to the bottom boards on top of Chilkat. John staggered, but saved himself with the oars. A sheet of spray leaped straight up and was blown across them like a pelt of sleet.

Sally gasped as the cold water bit through her garments. She looked up anxiously at John. His face was streaming, but he merely shook his head and continued to push doggedly on the oars.

There was no sense to this: John acknowledged this—afterward. But he was obstinately angry: too angry to think. A really expert small-boatman might have made very doubtful headway against that headwind, for a little while; but John was no expert. He did well to hold his own. And then something happened that he had not thought of at all. The tide turned. And very soon thereafter he was brought to his senses by the realization that he was losing ground.

He cursed himself briefly and savagely and turned back toward the opening. He'd have to go back. But immediately it became too evident that it was not going to be easy to get back. The instant the pirogue ceased to face directly into the weather she began to act badly. She bucked against the oars. At the crest of the waves she swooped sideways. John had to throw all his strength against one oar to prevent her broaching to. It was a question now, not of making progress, but of staying afloat. But they had to make progress or be carried up the channel into the tumble of breaking seas. As it was, they were in instant danger of swamping. He escaped only by a series of minor miracles. They were drenched. The boat was quarter filled and already waterlogged and sluggish.

The situation was grave, but neither John nor Sally was as yet seriously frightened. Len had once remarked on another occasion that they were too ignorant to be frightened. John shook his head and shoulders like a savage bull. The veins stood out on his forehead, the muscles of his arms and chest corded beneath his thin shirt.

The tide gained in strength. Slowly, but inexorably, it pressed them back. The mouth of their inlet had been on their quarter; now it had fallen abeam.

Sally was the first fully to wake up to the fact that they were in serious danger. She began to attend the shore line, lining up the trees, to gauge loss or gain by their shift of bearings. It was by inches, one way or another.

"We're making it!" she screamed to John, or was silent and held her breath when the slow or jerky march of the trees past one another stopped or reversed.

This went on for a long time. But John couldn't keep this up forever. He began to tire. The wind and the sea did not tire. He looked rather wildly at Sally. Apparently nothing could save them.

This again was their ignorance. About when they had given up hope, a powerful back eddy seized the pirogue and shot it back toward the smoother water of the inpouring tide. It seemed like a miracle. They knew nothing of back eddies. Nor could they guess that John's dogged exertions had earned that miracle. Accurately the invisible hands beneath her keel bore the little craft into the mouth of the inlet.

John rested, panting, half leaning against the weight of the oars. He straightened his back gingerly.

"Well, I'll be doggoned!" he breathed fervently. He looked out at the sea. "Looks like the Old Man had his hands under us that time," he said presently. He dropped the oars and let them trail and flexed his arms. "You know, I feel better," he confided to Sally. So did she. Somehow they'd worked some of it off. Chilkat looked up at them reproachfully. He felt the returned cheerfulness, but he was unable to share it. "I don't mind lying in cold water as long as there's a good reason for it," Chilkat told them, "but . . . !" They both caught this at the same moment and laughed. John picked up the oars.

"Reckon we'd better go ashore and dry off," said he.

He rowed leisurely through the dark gorge and out into the bright sunlight. A hundred yards along the shore the steep drop of the mountains modified to a tiny grass plot. There was no beach, but John found a landing.

"This 'll do," said he. He unloaded the packs and built a fire. They sat close to it, drying off. "We'll camp here. Maybe overnight if it doesn't cool off outside. Damn that fellow, the devil's on his side." But he said it reflectively. "But he hasn't got away with anything yet. This wind won't last."

"He won't stop long at Klakan," said Sally.

"Then," said John, "we'll take a steamer, or catch us some kind of a boat, and keep after him." He spoke cheerfully, almost with relish, Sally thought, as was indeed the case. John had been on man hunts before. They were interesting. "We'll catch him!" he predicted with confidence.

"And then?" Sally hesitated, with a little catch of the breath.

"Why, that depends on him," replied John. "We're going to get our boat back."

Sally let it go at that. She did not want to examine possibilities too closely. She resolutely shut her mind to them.

"Better eat," said John. He set about preparing a meal. Sally knew this game. She could help. The movement and the exercise did her good, helped her shut her mind. The fatalistic philosophy of the wilderness is wisest after all: let each day take care of itself.

The simple meal was soon prepared and eaten. John sat in the grass and began painstakingly to clear his weapons of salt water. Chilkat hunted shade, for—now that he was dry—the sun was beginning to oppress him. Sally came to sit beside John. John paid her no particular attention. He was wholly concerned with his task. He hummed cheerfully under his breath. He did not appear to have a care in the world. Sally watched him, frowning slightly. It was always difficult for her to understand this frontiersman's habit of mind, that can so completely set aside whatever might happen, until again it became a basis for action. Sally could not do that. She could shut her mind to the future, but not the past. Things kept rising in it. Mostly she resented the injustice.

"How could you wear rubber boots with skirts?" she burst out resentfully.

"Eh?" John's hand stopped polishing. He looked up in mild surprise. It took him a moment to comprehend. Then he laughed.

"You couldn't," he agreed.

"But he said——"

"Shucks," John cut this short with easy contempt, "he was drunk."

"I can't see that that is any excuse——" began Sally indignantly.

"I wasn't excusing him," denied John.

"I feel so *mortified!*" cried Sally, her pent-up feelings welcoming an outlet at last. "I must have been so dumb not to have foreseen. But he's always been so—so *different!*"

John squinted down the barrel of the gun.

"Sure!" he agreed, "probably he *was* different. Whisky does that sometimes."

"But he must have had such—such ideas about me all the time!" lamented Sally, coming to the thought that had been nagging at her most. "I was so dumb!"

John glanced up at her briefly, then laid aside the weapon and deliberately spread out the rag to dry. He turned to face her.

"Now," said he slowly, "you mind what I say. You quit thinking about it. And quit worrying. You had nothing to do with it. Understand that? If you were dumb, then so was I. As for what ideas this fellow did or didn't have, you don't know, and no amount of guessing's going to make you know. There's a heap of brand-new ideas in a bottle of whisky. So let's just drop it for now. What say?"

"You act as if you actually didn't care!" said Sally bitterly. Suddenly she found herself close to tears: but this was because the relief of her outpouring had been checked.

"I care all right." For a brief moment John's face was grim. "We'll tend to that when the time comes," he stated briefly.

John seemed to think that settled it and should satisfy everybody.

He never could understand the safety-valve utility of talk. But to Sally right now it was a necessity. She hesitated.

"You seemed sure he'd go to Klakan and not straight north," she tried a new slant, less personal.

"Well, he did, didn't he?" countered John.

"Why were you so certain? Or was it a hunch?"

"No," John shook his head slowly, "when I stopped to figger I saw he wouldn't do different. If you're trailing a man—or a critter—you'll often save time by stopping to figger him a little. This Klondike thing," he reminded Sally, as though she might have forgotten, "that's where he'd head for, of course. That's plain. But you've got to think farther than that. What for? Not gold—not to dig gold, I mean. This Harry's no pick-and-shovel man. No more than I am. He's after the gold, all right; but he'd aim to let the other fellow do the hard work." He looked toward her for endorsement.

Sally nodded. John's processes of mind, when he set himself to "figgering," had always fascinated her. Nothing could have been more salutary to her than this reduction to cold logic.

"There's a lot surer—and easier—ways to make money on a gold rush than by digging it," said John.

"Yes, he said something like that himself," recalled Sally.

"Freighting. Storekeeping. Trading. Most anything. But my bet on Harry would be gambling. He'd start a gambling joint, or I've got him all wrong."

Sally agreed to that.

"Well, you can't start a gambling joint on a pack of cards. Not a plunger like Harry. So he's got to stop somewhere and pick up an outfit. Klakan. Sound reasonable?"

She nodded again. "I see. But suppose he doesn't?"

"Then we'll do some more figgering," said John, undisturbed. He arose to his feet and looked down at her humorously. "Don't you fret," he advised her, "I've worked out dimmer trails than this."

When the tide slacked John rowed out to the entrance to take a look. He came back, shaking his head.

"We'll have to stay the night," said he. "But it's dying. We'll make it on the morning tide. I bet I don't forget the tide again!" he promised grimly.

They were up early and packed and under way. Things looked propitious, but in this landlocked harbor you never could tell. The inlet and the tiny cliff-bound lake and the entrance were just at slack. As they neared the last point that screened from them view of the channel they craned their necks, peering eagerly for the first glimpse of what it was going to be like. John unconsciously leaned a little harder on the oars.

"It's calm!" he shouted; and at the same time Sally, in dismay: "Oh! Look!"

He swung to the left and saw. Not over a hundred yards away was the Tillicum, under every sail, headed almost directly toward them.

For a moment he stared.

"Well, I *will* be damned!" he breathed, incredulous.

He looked about him, swiftly planning. But here the coast was sheer. No place to beach the boat and land Sally. There'd be no time to do that in any case, was his instant second thought.

"Lie down and stay down!" he commanded her under his breath. He dropped the oars and let them trail and crouched down and picked up the rifle and threw its lever down and back. His eyes narrowed, his nostrils wide, his face set.

Unbelievable that Chilkat Harry should return: but John did not bother about that. Here he was: that was the important thing. Drunk yet, maybe; come back to fight it out—for Sally, maybe; he was the crazy-drunk sort: they'd told John that. John's eyes flamed. Suited him! Only he wished Sally wasn't there. His trigger hand tightened on the stock. Mustn't take chances, with Sally there!

Sally was touching his leg, trying to get his attention.

He shook his head impatiently, but without taking his eyes from the ketch. He moved his leg slightly to one side to get away from her insistence. She touched it again. She was whispering something. Finally he bent his ear to listen.

"He may be sober now." Finally he understood her.

Damn it, just like a woman to bring that up! Couldn't she understand? That he couldn't afford to take chances, not with her there? Drunk or sober, this fellow was quick with a gun. Didn't she remember? He wasn't going to wait while John inquired, made sure of his intentions. He'd go into action, soon as he saw them. Thing to do was to pot him quick, on sight, like a mad dog or a rattlesnake. Which he was.

Thus the flash of John's mind. But underneath John cursed in exasperated surrender, for she'd called the turn again. You can't shoot a man down cold, like that; not unless you're dead certain. And now John was not dead certain. He had been until Sally had whispered. But you can bet on one thing, John told himself savagely, he'd better not make one little move, not of *any* kind! He lifted the rifle stock to the level of his elbow and thrust forward the muzzle.

In the meantime the ketch continued to glide steadily toward them under the impulse of the light air. As she was nearly bow on, her structure as yet concealed the helmsman. That was an advantage. The nearer the better. Soon she would be broadside. But even then disclosure was postponed by a vagrant puff of wind that shot her ahead and at the same time heeled her far enough over so that her sides and combing continued to screen her occupant. This was luck. By the time she could come back to an even keel she should be not over ten yards away. John would have a dead drop. He got to his feet.

The puff of wind died. Slowly the craft rose to her bearings. John's rifle snapped into line with the man's chest.

"Goin' somewhere, folks, or do you want a lift?" drawled Len Saunders.

He inspected the blank faces of the two with amusement, thrust down the tiller, rounded to. Gradually the ketch lost way, lay, sails flapping, drifting on the new tide.

Of the two in the small boat, John recovered first.

"What in the name of hell and high water are *you* doing here?" he demanded.

"Same to you. Same to you," returned Len cheerfully. "Come aboard."

John picked up the oars and drew alongside. "What's all this about?"

"Well, I'd kind of like to know that myself," submitted Len. "Or do you always welcome folks this way?"

"How did you get hold of this boat?"

"Get hold of the boat?" Len repeated. He looked perplexed. "Say, what's goin' on here?" He turned toward Sally, as though to question her, but cut himself short with a howl of alarm. "Watch out! We're goin' ashore!" he yelled. "Grab hold!"

Sally seized the painter of the pirogue; John leaped to the jib sheet. They had to work fast. It was touch and go, for, unattended, the ketch had drifted perilously close to the beach. But they got her in hand.

"Here, where you heading?" demanded John, as Len, at the tiller, pointed the bow toward the entrance.

"Don't you folks live here?" Len looked surprised.

"We were going to Klakan."

"In that thing?" Len spared a glance toward the pirogue. But he reached for the mainsheet in preparation for coming about.

But abruptly Sally intervened.

"Keep going," she told Len. "We've changed our minds. Haven't we?" She turned to John. "Haven't we?" she repeated with more emphasis.

"I reckon so," he agreed after a moment.

Len was looking from one to the other in an exaggeration of despair. He thrust the tiller violently at John.

"Here, you take her!" he demanded. "Take her!" he howled suddenly. "I want to climb the mast and jibber a while. Take her, I tell you! She's your boat! Or ain't she? If I git any more mixed up you won't be able to tell me from a scrambled egg!"

John took the helm.

"Reckon a palaver is in order," he admitted; "we're a little mixed ourselves." He sighted over the stays, squinted at the entrance, glanced upward at the telltale, estimating the breeze. "Tide's just beginning to make against us," he observed, "but I think we'll fetch it in." He settled down in the cockpit, his elbow over the tiller. "Shoot!" said he

"Not any!" Len refused with vigor and indigation. *"You* shoot! Here I come doing a favor and making a friendly visit, and what do I get? Not a shake of the hand or a glad-to-see-you! Nothin' but the snout of a 30-40 in my belly, and a where-did-you-git-that-boat. You'd think I'd stole your dang boat! And then you ask *me* to explain! Why, gol-ding your pusillanimous soul——" He broke off to appeal to Sally. "I did take a mite of coffee and some bread and bacon early this morning, ma'am, but I'll pay for 'em. And I'll go! I can take a hint—when it's a 30-40 hint—I'll go!"

Sally burst into laughter at Len.

"That's more like old times," he approved, dropping his mock plaintiveness. "Now who's going to talk?"

They both were going to talk. Len listened without interruption, without expression. He did nod once or twice, but more as though corroborating some thought of his own than in direct comment.

"That's interesting," he said when the tale was at an end. "It fits. It's more interesting than you know. Say, this is purty!" he broke off as finally the slow tide released them into the valley.

"I thought you'd been here," observed John.

"I've heerd of it. I knowed where it was and how you get in. But I never *been* in."

But neither Sally nor John had patience for discussion of scenery. They reminded Len in no uncertain terms that now it was his turn.

"Well," he yielded, "I ain't got much to tell. All that happened to me was that Chilkat Harry hunted me up late yesterday and allowed as how you'd lent him the boat to get that far, on his way to the new diggin's, and he wanted to git somebody to bring it back to you, and would I do it, and I said sure, glad to, and I started early this morning 'count of the night breeze. And there I come sailing along, peaceful as a bear in a berry patch, and, without no rhyme or reason *I* can see, I look down the muzzle of a 30-40." Len's voice slowed to a drawl. "All the events of my past life flashed through my mind," he declaimed, " 'specially emphasizing all them times I'd secretly double-crossed you folks—leastwise I'd thought they was secret—and I says to my-self——"

"Oh, shut up!" John cut this off. "Said we'd *lent* him the boat!" he marveled. "Was he drunk?"

"Cold sober, far as I could judge," Len obediently returned to the matter-of-fact.

"I thought he acted sober when he left the cabin," supplied Sally, "but it didn't seem possible."

"Enough of a scare does it sometimes," Len told her. "And I reckon he took a scare all right! I wouldn't want no malemute breathing in my face! Well, that's what he done, anyway. And then he hopped the Portland goin' north, and that was the last I seen of him. Oh, yes," added Len, fumbling in the pocket of his Mackinaw, "he gave me this. For you," he told Sally.

Sally took the envelope doubtfully.

"Here, let me," said John, at her obvious reluctance. He read its enclosure, whistled. "I'll be damned!"

"What's it say? Read her out," urged Len. "That is, if you ought to," he added hastily.

"Oh, it's all right. But listen here: here's all it says: 'I'm more deeply sorry than I can express that you had to encounter that beast; but I am as deeply grateful that he did you no harm. I just want you to try to believe that his sentiments toward you are not, *and have never been,* those of the one who calls himself Chilkat Harry.' Now what do you know about that!" marveled John. "You'd think he was talking about someone else!" He looked from one to the other of them in honest perplexity.

Sally's face cleared with enlightenment. But it was Len who spoke up out of the typical magpie hodgepodge of unsuspected knowledge that stores the frontiersman's mind. He slapped his leg.

"By gum, it *was* some other feller!" he cried. "I read a story about it somewheres. Dang good story," he observed in parenthesis. "About a bird—he was a doctor—that learned how to mix up something, and when he drank it he turned into a regular hellion. He used drugs; but I'd bet on Mush Mahoney's barkeep doin' as good a job."

"*Doctor Jekyll and Mr Hyde,*" supplied Sally.

"That's it!" cried Len, delighted that Sally had read it, too. "And by and by this doctor got so he couldn't be anything *but* the hellion! Why!" he was carried away by the brilliance of his reasoning, "maybe Chilkat Harry read that story, too. Maybe that's why he's been generally so careful to lay off the drink. *I* ain't never seen him take a drink before. What you think, Sally?"

"Dual personality," Sally nodded thoughtfully. "Yes—I think that's right. . . ."

But John had already and completely lost interest in Chilkat Harry. John dealt with things that had to be dealt with. Chilkat Harry was no longer one of them. Of course, if they ever happened to cross trails again . . .

"What do you make of this Klondike thing, Len?" he cut impatiently across such idle speculations.

The ketch was at the moment drifting idly, not yet far enough out from the gorge to catch the inland breeze. The sun was warm. They had lots of time.

"Looks like they struck it," said Len. "It's a big rush, anyway. Boats crowded already."

"Figuring on going?"

"Sure! If she pans out. But I don't stampede easy. Besides, it's too late in the season."

"But if there is gold, don't you have to get in on the ground floor?" Sally, unconsciously, was quoting Chilkat Harry.

Len looked at her quizzically.

"Ground floor, as you call it, is likely already full up," said he. "They's pop'lation enough in the country to tend to that. *If* this thing is like they say, there's plenty more ground floor outlying. But it's got to be prospected for; and there ain't going to be no prospecting done in winter, not by the kind of wild-eyed cheechakos that's crowding in now. Next spring's good enough for me. And by then we'll know whether it's real or just another of them things. How about you, John? Figgered on it any?"

"Well, I'm no miner," said John slowly. He glanced toward Sally. Len caught the look.

"We could take care of Sally," he stated confidently.

"Likely to be pretty rough stuff for a woman."

"Nonsense!" Sally spoke up with spirit. "Stop talking drivel!"

"I'll bet on Sally," said Len. "And she'd eat it up."

"Well—I'll see . . ." It was obvious what John would see. His eyes were alight with adventure. The land breeze overtook them, and the ketch began to slip through the water. "I got to get my boom in anyway," he observed presently, out of a silence. He indicated the gleam of yellow white where the peeled logs floated.

Len glanced uninterestedly in that direction.

"Looks like a good boom," he admitted. "I wouldn't wish for none," he added.

His uninterest was marked. John gave it up.

"How's Klakan?" he changed the subject. "Anything new?"

"About the same," said Len, "except 'n some of the boys are beginning to get restless. This Klondike business," he explained. "But Mush Mahoney still hangs on, and as long as he sticks there's nothing very desperate about it. No, nothin' new. Oh yes, there is!" he amended. "We got a doctor now. Mighty nigh the first one in the territory, I reckon."

"Is he a genuine doctor?" asked John, out of cow-country experience.

"Looks genuine. Anyway, he's doctoring."

"What do you think of him, Len?" spoke up Sally, who had more interest in doctors than the men.

"I like him," said Len. "First off he's a kind of funny-lookin' rabbit, sort of gangly and slow and awkward looking. And he looks kind of young. But he's got a good steady eye and a sort of humorous slant to him. You got to cotton to the critter."

"But how much of a *doctor* is he?" persisted Sally.

"How should *I* know?" protested Len. "I ain't got sick yet. Folks that has had him say he's good."

The ketch rounded the last headland before the mouth of the river. Sally pointed it out; and the location of the cabin. Len had an interest in all this. He squinted his eyes, sizing up the country inch by inch. "Looks to me like it might be a good fur layout," he proffered finally.

"Chilkat Harry traps it," said Sally.

Len opened his eyes.

"Sho now! Did he! Wouldn't think of him trappin'." He continued his slow scrutiny. "Feller might do worse than to winter here. Pick up a purty good stake, maybe. Need a stake to tackle the Yukon. Nothin' but trial and tribulation without. Got to winter somewhere." He turned suddenly on John. "Why don't we?"

John was not quite ready to commit himself offhand, but Sally jumped at the idea. It solved delightfully a problem that had been worrying at the back of her mind, though she had not before realized it: that long dreary winter at Klakan! It would have been dreadful! But out here in the clean white open——

"Only how about the cabin?" she raised a sudden objection.

Len misunderstood the purport of her question. He hadn't seen the cabin yet; and of course it was built only for fall hunting and not for winter, but him and John could easy do any chinkin' necessary, and with lots of firewood—— Oh, Nels Cole! He looked rather blank when he comprehended Sally's doubts. Why should Nels Cole care?

"Well, it *does* belong to him," Sally pointed out.

It appeared to Len—and to John also, it developed—that mere ownership had little to do with it. The only question of the slightest importance was whether or not Nels intended to use it. Len was positive he did not: he was lighting out for Seattle soon as the pack was over. That settled it.

"How soon you got to get back?" asked Sally.

"Get back?" asked Len.

"To Klakan."

Len turned on her, pretending indignation.

"Doggone! You think you own this whole country? I got just as much right here as you have."

Sally laughed.

"How about your job?"

"Job?" Len looked as though he had never heard of such a thing. "Don't be a goop. Your job as marshal—at Klakan."

"Oh! That!" Len's air was of one reminded of some obscure forgotten episode in remote past history. "That's over."

"Had to fire you, did they?" This from John. "*Thought* they'd get onto you in time."

"No; didn't fire me. They thought I was doing all right." He was plainly waiting for questions. Sally obliged.

"Why did you resign?"

"I didn't resign. I just nat'rally evaporated. Seemed like a good thing to do before he got out. Chilkat Harry and the boat come along at just the psychological moment—ain't that what you call it, Sally?"

"I suppose you're going to tell us when you get good and ready," said Sally wearily.

"Hold the tiller a minute, Sally, while I throw him overboard," said John. "He's no earthly use to us."

"All right! All right!" Len held up a defensive elbow. "I never *see* such people! Won't let a man frisk and blow off steam, no matter how tickled he is. This feller come off the Portland pretty drunk—that was all right—but so godawful important I could see the boys takin' him apart in about ten minutes to find out what makes him tick. So I gathered him in—for his own good. And it turns out that I been doin' such a fine job that the gov'ment's been takin' notice of it and concluded it was a good thing, so they sent this feller along to do it official like, and here I'd gone and arrested the new U.S. marshal of the Klakan District, in person!"

He looked at them aggrievedly, but with a twinkle in the back of his eye. They responded to the twinkle with a burst of laughter. Len's face slowly relaxed.

"Didn't seem to me tactful," said he and at last joined their hilarity.

The ketch had been making progress. The mouth of the river was now discernible. The great mountain Sally called the Protector of the Wilderness came into view from behind its screening point. She told

Len what she called it and why; and Len nodded. You could tell Len things like that, and he would understand.

"*Aren't* we having fun!" cried Sally. She overflowed with satisfaction at having Len back; and making mock-solemn fun with Len; and the sun warm on the deck; and John there safe and sound; and she here safe and sound; and Chilkat sprawled out, basking and rolling a comical eye at her; and delightful strange adventures to look forward to; and nothing whatever to worry about.

"Sure is a purty country," said Len. "Now there's two of us dodgin' sheriffs we ought to name it Outlaws' Roost or something like that."

CHAPTER XXVIII

TRAP LINE

LEN DID his own settling down to suit himself. He had decided ideas and refused to listen to argument. For one thing, he declined even to consider living at the cabin. Didn't make any difference if there *was* a fine bedroom and all the fixings going to waste; didn't matter if he *wouldn't* be any extra trouble; didn't matter if they *did* want him; doggone it, it didn't matter even if *he,* himself, wanted to! Poor idea, living with other folks too much. Where would he live? Could always sleep in the ketch, till he could put up a shack of his own. "I'll eat with you," Len conceded that much, "but only till I get going. And I pay my share!" he warned belligerently.

"Isn't it funny!" Sally laughed to John. "But I like it," she added.

Len took a walk up the shore line and returned to face them in accusation.

"Hell's potatoes!" said he. "Why didn't you tell me this fellow has a shack here? That fixes me up like a mice."

He refused to take seriously any halfhearted objections based on property rights. Chilkat Harry had outlawed them by his own actions. "Anyway," said Len, "he'll never come back here. How's that bunch of traps he left strike you to start the winter on?"

"I've never been over there," confessed John.

480

"Nor I," added Sally.

"What?" Len was incredulous. "Why, it ain't over a quarter mile! How come?"

"Why—I don't know." John was a little at a loss, now he thought of it. "Just happened. Busy, and——"

"He never invited us," put in Sally.

"That's right! He never did!" Here was another thing that had not occurred to John until now.

"Well!" Len was scandalized. "You come on right over now and see my new house!"

They walked down the trail with Len; and Len showed them the house with an air of proprietorship, as if he had owned it always. They looked over the premises with growing interest and surprise. This was no mere shack. Though it had but one room, that was large, airy, with two windows and a smooth planked floor. The structure itself was solid and four square, of squared and mortised logs. The roof was stoutly timbered and shingled with split shakes. A wide, high veranda, almost as big as the body of the house itself, elevated and floored, ran across the entire front. On it one could take one's ease, looking out across the flats and the inland sea. Beneath the shelter of the veranda, suspended by their chains, hung a great number of steel traps; but somehow these gave an impression more of decoration than utility. Indeed the whole place had an air of leisure, of residence rather than the stark practicality of a trapper's usual winter quarters.

"Snug as a bug in a rug!" boasted Len triumphantly. "Everything here I need, and a lot I don't!"

"I suppose it's all right . . ." Sally could not dismiss all qualms. A lot of these things were very personal. There were even a few books —she must look them over.

"Sure not!" agreed Len unexpectedly. "But ain't John and me outlaws?"

It appeared that Len must all along have expected to stay. He had brought with him, aboard the Tillicum, everything he owned and in addition had laid in a stock of groceries.

"Didn't have much time to go shopping," he confessed. "But this 'll do until things cool off, so we can make a trip back."

He packed everything over, shot a deer and settled down. John went back to work in the woods. As far as he was concerned, Klakan could wait. Time enough when the boom was full. After all, he had Orford's agreement.

Len went over one day, with John, to the scene of operations. He professed himself interested, flabbergasted and in hearty approval. But to the suggestion that he go in partnership he gave a flat refusal.

"When I want to work that hard," said Len, "I'll get them to put me where I can bust rocks with a hammer. I could set down to that. No, this is all your show, son. I wouldn't deprive you. Anyway, I ain't got time: I got too much to do."

"Like hell!" jeered John. "You're just plain lazy."

"Well, I don't know anything better to be," submitted Len.

However, he managed to find plenty of occupation. First of all, he set to work cutting and splitting firewood, cords and cords of it. He seemed to Sally to have developed a mania for firewood, beyond all reason, until the stacked tiers of it extended across the entire length, at the back, of the cabin he had inherited from Chilkat Harry. Then he moved his operations over to the other house and started in with the obvious intention of repeating there. He paid little heed to Sally's protests.

"Going to winter here, ain't you?" said Len. "Well—you wait and see."

"But John will——"

"That lazy lummox!" snorted Len. However, he had a different reason to give to John when the latter returned from his work and discovered what was doing. "I know," John agreed to the necessity for plenty of winter fuel, "but I was going to put that in later in the season when I can't work any more in the woods." "Later in the season you and me is partners," returned Len, "and I ain't going to let you use our time on personal business. Let be, let be!"

He worked without haste. He seemed to have lots of time to stop and fill his pipe and lean against a tree and gossip with Sally. Even when he swung his ax or drove his wedges he did so with a deceitful air of indifferent leisure. Nevertheless, the wood along the back wall of the cabin piled up as though by magic.

"It's mostly not getting the job done in your head and then getting fretted because your hands are so far behind," Len told her when she remarked on this. "Keep your head and your hands about level, and you can take it easy."

It was pleasant to sit on a stump and watch Len. The long spell of clear weather still lasted—we'll get a come-uppance for that, was Len's comment; well, let's enjoy it while we've got it, was Sally's. Certainly she enjoyed it. The sun was just the right strength for basking: just warm enough to release pungent woodland smells. And Len was so comfortable! She had both her men with her again, and nobody else; and it was good not to have to think or speculate or be wary! Everything in her little world right now was *reliable;* and that was a wonderful feeling—to have things reliable.

Len finished the fuel supply to his satisfaction; but he scorned Sally's suggestion that now they go on a picnic together, up river. She had been waiting, just a little impatiently, for that: she wanted to show Len her bears.

"I've seen all I want of those critters—when I ain't got to," said Len. "Besides, you been up river lately?"

"Not for about ten days," admitted Sally.

"Well, go take a smell," advised Len. "I ain't got time to fuss around amusing you, anyway. I got all I can tend to."

"I'd like to know what you think you've got to do!" jeered Sally. But she had to take that back.

"Who's going to scout out the trap lines?" demanded Len.

He must explore. Follow the little streams. Read the sign and discover where the fur "used." Figure a route that would take in the best country, yet start from home and come back to home again. Blaze trees to mark that route: high up, against the time of deep snow.

"It's going to be mighty tough going, and I ain't going to linger helping no women over windfalls," he notified Sally when she wanted to go along. "I'm goin' to *travel!*"

Her indignation was instant.

"All right. Try it. Once," he had to concede. "But you show up at four o'clock prompt, or you get left. And if you tucker out you needn't look to me to baby you none. You'll get home best way you can, and if you get lost and starve or those bears of yours gobble you, don't you blame me!" He bent his brows at her; but she laughed at the twinkle beneath them. However, his scolding was real when, ten minutes before the hour, she reported the following morning.

"What kind of a rig-out do you call that!" he demanded severely. "You know better than that! You go straight back and take off that skirt—and put on your pants. Oh, I'll wait," he said, as she hesitated. "I suppose I got to!" he grumbled.

Sally sped back along the trail to the cabin. John was just getting up. Four o'clock was too early for him: he was just a common working man, he had said, and needed his sleep. He was surprised at Sally's return.

"Len wants me to put on pants," she explained breathlessly.

John surveyed her.

"Well, I should hope so!" said he.

Somehow this little episode lifted Sally's spirits enormously. The foul and reckless vulgarity had burned into her deeper than she had wanted to acknowledge. The words and the injustice would have been shocking enough from a barroom tough, but from a man such as she had conceived Chilkat Harry to be—she was all confusion. Were all men that way, underneath? Or *was* it her fault? It *must* have been in some degree her fault; innocently, unconsciously, of course, but hers nonetheless. And now here were her two men, her two *reliable* men, and apparently it had never occurred to them either that she should not wear pants! For, absurdly enough, that comparatively trivial reproach had the most persistently nagged Sally's mind.

That first day's scouting with Len proved—as he had warned—to be a tough one. Sally had a shrewd suspicion that he was deliberately making it so. He kept going, without resting pauses. Indeed, he

grudged no more than ten minutes for the sandwiches Sally had prepared. Nor did he pick the easiest country. By midafternoon Sally was
traveling on nerve. But that was sufficient. She not only managed to
stay with it, but she contrived a gay and energetic demeanor. Len
wasn't going to put *that* over on her! She'd die in her tracks first!

They got to the cabin sometime after John had returned from his
own work. Sally was never more glad of anything in her life than the
sight of its roof among the trees. She had never been more thankful
than to have finished lifting those two feet of hers—one after the
other, one after the other—up the slope to its level. It was over! At
last! She wanted to wilt right down where she was, perhaps even to
cry in the aching relief. And let Len know how tired she was? Not
she! Her head came up.

"We've had a grand day!" she cried to John.

John examined the pair of them quizzically.

"You look all in," said he. But he was not talking to her, he was
talking to Len! And Len was shaking his head with a lugubrious air
that was only half mockery.

"If ever I take that critter out in the woods with me again," he
told John, "I'm going to put hobbles on her! Why!" his voice warmed
with something like indignation, "I'm all tuckered out with her! She's
just like a dang little chipmunk!"

Sally's belief in her own ears skipped a beat; then her heart sang
within her. Suddenly she was not tired, not the least bit tired.

"Poor old Len!" she mocked. "You're going to stay for supper: I'll
go get it ready. Same time tomorrow?" she inquired.

Thereafter the excursions went much easier. Sally prided herself
that this was because Len had tried to walk her down and, having
failed, now had given up. There was a little truth in that; but as a
matter of fact he would have made that first expedition a long one,
even if he had been alone. He had first to get a notion of the country
in general. Having done so, his job was now to examine its possibilities
in detail. Sally learned a lot about fur-bearing animals and their
habits and the best places to catch them. This was interesting and
made for easy days, for often Len would spend an hour or so in a

single locality. Only after his explorations extended farther back must the day begin with an initial long walk. But pretty soon, Len pointed out, they'd be nearer the cabin again, for the whole idea of a proper trap line was to round a circle back home. "Pretty soon," said Len, "we'll begin working from the other end."

However, not long after, he modified that plan.

"This country back is bigger 'n it looks," he told Sally; and later, to John: "To get the best of her we really ought to run a bigger circle."

The men decided on that. Len was to build a line shack, good enough to stay in overnight, at the farthest point out. Coal-oil-can stove; and cache some blankets and grub, so a man could travel light. One day out: one day back. That would make it. The two could take turns. "Really easier when the snow comes," Len told Sally, "and we get our snowshoe trail broke and packed down. Just make a nice trip to get exercise."

Len's first haste and hurry seemed to have fizzled out. He spent considerable time just sitting on a windfall with Sally, smoking his pipe and talking. She herself liked nothing better than this, though she poked fun at him for the readiness with which he rounded to and came to anchor at her most trivial question.

"I can hear perfectly while I'm walking," she pointed out.

"I don't aim to let you run me off my legs a second time," said Len. He had adopted the fiction that Sally had deliberately set out to walk him down, that first day, and that such heartlessness saddened him: "And me a poor old man!"

Actually they both relished these long pauseful chats, with the sun warm and the air cool, and the mysterious voices and flittings of migrating birds in the trees. "And that poor deluded im-be*cile* back there workin' his guts out wrastling saw logs!" commiserated Len. "Oh well, he just ain't got common sense!"

But one day Sally turned to face him squarely and propounded what was, to Len, a complete heresy. Nor could he argue it out of her. Nor could John, when Len, in a real panic, appealed for aid. Sally remained obstinate. She had been thinking it over, and the more she had thought it over the more determined she grew. The whole trapping business had been to her, up to now, in the nature of an abstraction. It had had no body of actuality, had been, more or less, just a name. But now that she was right there, on the spot, her lively imagination went farther. She visualized. And she was horrified, not only at the thing itself, but at herself for not having thought of it before.

The men did not visualize. They dealt with the whole business only as any man deals with the materials of his job. Accepts them whole. But where Len—and John—thought only in terms of fur, and stopped at that, Sally saw too vividly a picture of a living creature, struggling, panting, broken legged, wild with terror, held fast hour after hour, even day after day—— She simply could not stand that! Sally put her foot down on trapping!

Len did not take her first outbreak too seriously. He merely looked indulgent. Women are that way, Len generalized: they have these queer fancies. But shortly he must realize that he was really up against a major crisis. This was no sentimental whim: it was a settled determination. If Sally meant that—— "Why, doggone it, don't you see, Sally, if you're going to act that way about it . . ."

He argued with Sally at great length. So did John. John finally got a little heated over her utter unreasonableness, as he looked at it. He could not understand. Just like women: they *wear* the furs fast enough! And how about all our plans? Oh, shucks, Sally, you'll get over——

But Sally could not understand either: this masculine obtuseness. She could comprehend their not having thought of it before; she had not thought of it herself. But now that they *had* thought of it—of the cruelty of it—how could they even consider going on? Their indifference to this aspect hurt her, in a way. Both John and Len were kind men; she knew that. And yet they seemed wholly unable to get her point of view.

They treated her like a child, proffering her absurdities, as one offers candy as distraction to the child.

"No, they don't," Len denied her picture of prolonged agonies. "Likely they freeze pretty quick after they're caught." But he had the air of one struck with a sudden bright idea. Sally merely looked at him.

"I'm sorry, but that's the way I feel about it. And I can't help it." She was almost in tears.

They were vexed with her, perhaps becoming a little more than vexed.

"Well, I'm sorry, too," returned John bluntly, "but we've got our living to make, and if you're going to act like a damn fool——"

"Hold on! Hold on! Take it easy!" Len interposed with sudden authority. "I got something to say here. Don't you forget that this trappin' idea was *mine*. It's my business, not yours, and it's going to be run the way I want, and I ain't going to have either one of you kids telling me how to run it. If you want to fight each other that's all right with me; but you find out something else to fight about. I'm settling this!" He held them sternly through an impressive pause. Then he turned to Sally. "I ain't going to quit trapping for nobody," he informed her. "It's agin all reason and common sense. Folks has wore furs since they came out of caves and always will." John looked gratified. Len whirled on John. "Wipe that smirk off your face. Whatever idees you may have you get no help from me makin' little small critters suffer. I never rightly considered it before; but Sally's right. It's kind of tough, when you start to think of it." He looked from one to the other. Sally was puzzled; but John caught Len's meaning at once. Len perceived this and began to argue with John.

"I know it's a lot harder work," he admitted, "and you mebbe don't make *quite* so big a ketch—after all, there's nothin' like a good 'Waterhouse'—for a lazy man; but if we take trouble and *sabe,* we'll do pretty well."

"Kid stuff," grumbled John.

"Yeah," agreed Len, "and Injun," he added. "Don't forget that! Injuns done pretty well at it, too: still do, here and there, when they've got no steel. Anyway, if Sally kicks on steel, that's what *I'm* goin' to do—or nothin'. I'm for Sally!" He looked at John and waited. John struggled a moment, but gave in.

"Oh, I suppose so!" shrugged John. "But it's going to be a hell of a nuisance!" He was still a little grumpy, but Sally knew she had won; John never harked back to anything once he had decided it or accepted it.

So the festoons of oiled steel traps hanging under the veranda of Chilkat Harry's cabin continued merely to supply ornamental atmosphere. Sally was happy. She could not have borne it. Sudden clean death she could accept, for she was no sentimentalist. But to wake up, winter nights, and think of small, frantic, broken-legged, gnawing creatures, dying by inches in the snow! And she was happy, too, that her men had indulged what they still secretly looked on as mere feminine squeamishness.

From then on she could take a real interest in this trapping business. And it *was* interesting. Len was enormously ingenious, and he had a vast store of woodcraft on which to draw. He himself warmed to the project. "Danged if this ain't more fun than steel trappin'," he confessed to Sally. "Feller's got to do more figgering. Now," he appealed to her, "if you was a marten and was sort of moseying along down your runway and come on a nice piece of fish bait lyin' right here, what would you think about it? Would you suspicion it?" He cocked his head sidewise. "To make good at this business, you really got to learn to *be* the critter," said Len.

Sally could offer no valuable opinion: she knew too little of the habits of mink and marten, of fisher and fox, of ermine and otter. But she liked being appealed to. And she was fascinated by the ingenuity of the boxes and deadfalls and spring nooses that Len constructed at his selected points along the trapping line. It had the fun of play: like the play building of children.

"There!" Len pronounced with pride, as he drove the last small stake in the wing "leads" that—it was hoped—would guide the victim to the bait in the cubby. "Ain't that sort of cute?"

Each trap he finished completely before moving on to the next location, even to the notched triggers that would release the weight or drop the gate or snatch the noose, as the case might be. He demonstrated to Sally how they would work; but he did not set them. Something new, he told her; they'll be shy of it at first. But by winter they'll be used to it. By and by we'll feed 'em up a little just to get 'em interested. Suddenly he looked sheepish.

"Tell you one thing, Sally," he confessed, "I'm glad we got this whole place to ourselves. If anybody was to come along and ketch me makin' these things, and a hundred or so perfectly good Waterhouse steel traps hanging right outside my door, he'd send for the boob-catcher to lock me up before I got dangerous!"

Then for a few days Sally was again left to her own devices. Len took a pack and camped out, at the apogee of the trapping circle, where he was to build the line shack. It was too far for Sally to walk and return. But soon Len was working back toward the cabin; and she could go out to meet him. She was glad of this. Her routine duties at the cabin did not amount to much; and it was not worth while to fuss much with other things. Not as if this were her own house. After all, they were just camping in it. They would be going north in the spring. And there was not much of any place to walk right now: the river was horrible with the annual and wholesale sacrifice of the rotting salmon.

CHAPTER XXIX

GRANDSTAND SEATS

BUT LEN'S community contributions did not end with the finishing of the trap line. He surprised—and amused—John and Sally by opening the Tillicum's cargo hold and producing therefrom a quantity of bright new tin cans.

"Made by our machine," he told John proudly. He'd put them aboard "just in case," he told them.

"In case what?" demanded John.

"Just in case you might be staying on for the winter."

"You expected to, right along," Sally accused him.

"Canned venison's mighty fine along toward spring when the deer get poor," said Len.

He killed several deer, one after the other, as fast as he and Sally could handle them. Some of the meat they canned; but most they made into jerky or smoked. The cans would really be more useful for other things, said Len. And as he had built a smokehouse for the venison, he suggested it would be well to lay in a few salmon—if we can get us any fresh run he qualified; kind of late in the year. He made an excursion to the shack of Johnny and Susy Mackamoose and returned with their net. One end he stretched above the first deep tidal pool to block the river. On either bank below the pool he drove stout stakes.

491

"Now," said Len, "if any fish come along, we'll lead the rest of the net around those posts and have us a nice little fish corral. If there *is* any fish, we'll gather 'em in."

The first thing, however, that they gathered in was John, returning in the dinghy. "Plumb forgot John," said Len to Sally, bending an ear toward the sound of language. "Reckon I'd better take to the brush? Or does he get over his mad easy?"

"I'll protect you," promised Sally.

But John merely looked them over sardonically, as he might have examined two guilty children, which, indeed, at that moment they much resembled.

"Saw a pretty good wolf trap hanging up over at your shack," he told Len, "might try that next time." He waved aside any apologies or explanations. "All right with me. But you'll have to fix it up with Johnny Mackamoose how his net got tore."

Next morning Len showed Sally how, and together they spread the net out on the grass and squatted down sociably together and mended it with some hand fish line from the Tillicum. Len seemed to know everything. Then they set it again and fastened it at one end to two stakes so John could untie it from one of them and slip through with the dinghy. All this was something to do and good fun; but Sally was lukewarm toward the salmon idea. Finally she told Len about the fish she had tried to smoke. She began a little shamefacedly, but warmed to the humor and made a good story of it. Len chuckled in appreciation, especially when she came to Chilkat's verdict on her efforts.

"I vowed I never wanted to *see* another smoked fish," ended Sally, "and I don't know that I do. But I'll help, if *you* want some," she added.

"You'll change your mind," Len predicted. "Proper smoked salmon beats fresh fish all hollow. But you need a white-man smokehouse."

"And quarter-ground salt," pointed out Sally, "so John says."

"Sure," agreed Len. He calmly produced salt, two bags of it, again from the hold of the Tillicum, where it had lain unsuspected all this time. "I thought of that."

"Well!" Sally was impressed by this further evidence of Len's forethoughtfulness. "What else have you got down there? Show me. I want to see. *Now.* I never knew such a secretive creature."

"Nothing much," protested Len. "Just a little coal oil and a few groceries and a parka or so, in case it gets to blowin' cold sometime, and such things. You see," he submitted with an air of deprecation, "that there U.S. marshal looked to me like a sort of pompous cuss, and I reckoned it might be a good idee to lay in what we was going to need for a while."

"I don't see how in the world you had time!" Sally was amazed, remembering the early hour of Len's arrival. "You must have stayed up all night!"

"I did," assented Len.

At the end of two days a belated small school of humpies bumped their noses against the obstruction and fell back into the pool to think it over. Len cautiously led the net around them.

"There's our smoked fish!" he told Sally triumphantly.

But it was not so simple as that. The pool was large and the salmon had ideas of their own. Len and Sally could work on them only at low tide. At first they tried to transfer the fish to dry land by means of one gaff and one small landing net, a process that involved much wild chasing and splashing and infrequent successes. This pleased Sally enormously, but filled Len with disgust.

"Had a stick of dynamite I'd fetch 'em!" he muttered viciously. "We'll be froze in here along with the fish if we keep this up!" He was disgruntled at John's attitude. John came home a little early one afternoon and caught them at it. Next day he made it a point to come home early and sat on the bank above them and laughed himself sick. He refused flatly to help.

"Spoil this show?" he disclaimed. "Not me! Haven't had so much fun since I saw my first circus!"

"I bet you eat your share of 'em all right—if we give you any!" growled Len.

"You look like a pair of trained seals!" mocked John, stretching back luxuriously. He took it all as a huge joke, and so did Sally. But shortly she realized that Len did not think it a joke. This was the first time she had ever seen Len really resentful. She did not like that; and she took the first occasion apart to talk seriously to John.

"Sho!" cried John, instantly contrite, "I thought he was joshing!"

He made amends by offering help, which Len ungraciously accepted, after a proper amount of grumbling. Now that he had another man to handle the other end of the net, the two of them could sweep it upstream to trap the salmon in a pocket. That, it appeared, was the usual procedure, but Len had said nothing of it, for Sally had not the strength.

"And you wouldn't call on me for anything in the world!" reproached John, in affectionate exasperation.

Len refused to meet his eye, mumbling something about lazy lummoxes, and any damn fool ought to be able to see what was required without being told, and then contradicted himself by something else about how hard John worked in the woods, and 'twan't right to ask a tired man to——

"Oh shut up!" John cut him short. "You'd think I was just out of a hospital."

Indeed, John was not now working nearly so hard. The days were growing shorter. He set out later and came home earlier. Daylight evenings were finished. Even before an early bedtime there were genuine night evenings to be spent. Len's coal oil now came in handy. They played a good deal of three-handed "rummy"—as did, and still do, most Alaskans—and read a little or just talked. Len brought over the books from Chilkat Harry's cabin. Sally was not ready to unpack the supply she had brought from Seattle, and which was still boxed, in the Tillicum's hold. She had a curious idea of hoarding them against the fantastically short daylight of real winter.

A hundred signs of that season were ready to be thrust on the notice of him who could read them. The river ran clear and empty of all life. Of the teeming, close-packed hordes, the trout had retired to the far upper reaches. The salmon had spawned and died and rotted to nothing. With their disappearance the gulls and ravens and mergansers had returned to the better pickings of the tide flats outside. Glutted and fattened for hibernation, the great bears had retired to the mountains. Their trails, worn deep and wide and hard, were left silent for the use of the deer. Sally, in the forest, a finger on her lips as though to still even her thoughts, stood very quiet, waiting.

And after a while she caught it, far away, like the merest breath of a whisper, so that she might have imagined it. But it took on the substance of sound and came ever nearer, as a wave sweeps in from a far horizon; and pretty soon she could make out its pattern of hurried small twitterings as the migrating flocks called back and forth lest they lose touch with one another and the wide thin front of their advance be broken. Then abruptly the chirping was all around her, and the forest was alive with small shapes. They flitted and darted back and forth, up and down, here and there, as though they searched, or perhaps as though they would have lingered; but this was not so, for the sum of their movement was on: and the moment of their presence with Sally was so brief that almost before she had grasped it, it was over; and the anxious furtive chattering was growing faint. It was gone. The forest was still.

Then Sally could draw breath. It seemed to her that all this time she had been holding it. She had strange delightful fancies. She held her spirit tiptoe. Almost she understood. Almost—almost! She groped. There came to her a feeling of the reluctance of children as recess ended, and her outspread arms shoving them in, and some of them pretending to hide or darting in mock escape, and their gurgling laughter, and her own . . . It was like that, somehow, a little . . . With another sharp intake of the breath, she crossed her forearms on her breast. She felt herself lifted. She was herself the spirit of the gentle outspread arms, and she moved through the forest sweeping it clear of these small reluctant creatures, and when there was no more forest to screen them away from the pure impulse, they must yield and be caught aloft and swept away down the southward air lanes.

She let the breath out again and looked about her, a little dazed. It was as brief as that, this one small moment of eternity. But it was wonderful. She would never again be quite the same. She wanted to share it with John. But it was not something she *knew*, it was something she felt.

Now that Len was again occupied on the farther limits of the trap line, Sally resumed her solitary walks. They were safe now that the bears had gone. To be sure, it rained a good deal; the halcyon days were done. But she did not mind that; she had been raised in a webfoot country. The woods were rather beautiful in the rain. Every twig and frond was jeweled. Her sou'wester and little red slicker and rubber boots were complete protection. Or nearly complete. Wet brush, as Len said, is wuss 'n falling in the river. Len, himself, as a seasoned Alaskan, paid no attention to the weather. Even John's desert-bred aversion to the wet was becoming accustomed. At times none of them could recall whether it had rained on a certain day, or not.

The latter part of the month, however, they decided that up to now they hadn't seen it rain. For two days a southeast wind blew. Early in the morning it fell to calm, and the black low sky opened. John and Sally stood in the doorway and looked out at the falling water. It came down so steadily and solidly that there was nothing to see beyond the group of fir on the edge of the bluff. And even they were grayed and dimmed. The world, however, was full of sound: the steady roar on the roof; the intermittent trickling from eave and branch; a background hiss given back from the earth. Already from the river came a roar and growl of menace. They bent an ear to it and were glad they had listened to Len's insistence, when the rains first started, and had anchored the Tillicum outside. They never would have thought of that.

"Pretty *sabe* old coot," said John affectionately.

Len slopped in, streaming, about an hour later. He professed to be shocked at finding John at home.

"Why ain't you out at work?" he demanded. "You gone sissy on us? You ought not to let a little rain stop you!"

But John had him there. The boom, he disclosed for the first time, was finished; done; the last peeled log "ran" successfully the afternoon before. Hadn't said anything because he'd sort of figured on taking them over and surprising them and celebrating—picnic, maybe, or something like that. Len and Sally exclaimed in congratulation. John beamed. He'd worked hard. He'd licked that game after all.

"How much you figger you've got in?" asked Len.

"Hard to say. Fifteen hundred dollars maybe."

"John, you're wonderful!" The phrase had long since become a joke, and Sally dutifully gave it the traditional mocking inflection; but her eyes shone.

"Keno!" John completed the formula; but he was really pleased.

"Well, we're not going to lose our celebration," said Sally decidedly. "Nor our picnic. We'll have it right here."

They offered to help, if she'd tell them what to do. She would have none of it.

"You sprawl: I'll cook," she vetoed. "Now it's my turn."

John agreed to this with alacrity. He had not sprawled for a long time. Len, however, kicked off his slipper moccasins and began to draw on his rubber boots.

"Goin' fishing," was all he would tell them. "I'll be back."

In a half-hour he returned, paused on the veranda only long enough to kick off his rubber boots and drop his slicker, marched straight across the room and planted in the middle of the table a bottle of wine, turned and surveyed them triumphantly.

"Where the devil did you get that?" asked John.

"Had it. On the Tillicum. Thought you might want to celebrate somethin'-or-other sometime."

"You certainly think of everything," said Sally in admiration.

"More 'n some folks do," Len unexpectedly rounded on them. "If I just hadn't happened to go after this, you wouldn't have had no small boats. Don't you know enough to haul 'em out when it rains?"

"I did!" protested John.

"You slid 'em out on the bank," corrected Len. "What's that amount to? Go take a look. Better had: it will learn you."

Later in the day Sally and John took his advice. They had waited, hoping for a letup. There was no letup. So they put on their weather armor and went anyhow. They suggested to Chilkat that it might do him good to go along; but Chilkat took one dainty sniff and retired to a corner. He was apologetic and deprecating, but he would not stir. "Looks to me like that dog's got the better sense," John had to shout at Sally once they were out in the thick of the deluge. Nevertheless, it was worth while. The river burst out from the forest with a roar, foam slavered, like a savage beast let loose. Its waters were chocolate brown. They reared up angrily, as though seeking prey, and rushed on and spread, so that the entire inlet was stained with them. Whole trees, roots and all, rolling and turning, were tossed from crest to crest like playthings. Beneath the exultant roar, without cessation, was an undernote of hoarse growling which, Sally learned, came from the grinding of boulders rolled down the river bed by a strength at last too powerful for their age-long resistances. It was an awesome sight, and they returned to the shelter of the cabin suitably impressed. John was full of congratulations to himself. Perfect timing! One day later and he'd have had a hell of a job finishing off the boom!

The rain lasted for two days and two nights. They made Len stay: no sense going out and getting all wet again, with an extra room and everything; and what would you do over there, all by yourself, anyway? They enjoyed it. John discovered enormous fun in having a real excuse to stay home for once. His reactions after the long period of overdrive were not restful. "You'd think the dang fool would want to rest," complained Len, forced into a corner with his pipe. But apparently John had to blow off steam. He roughhoused Sally scandalously. Chilkat's hair bristled on his spine, and he rose to his toes. "Watch out!" cried Sally; but at the same instant Chilkat perceived his mistake. His bristles fell. He joined enthusiastically, uttering little short barks and terrific growls. After a while John sobered down, but not before both Sally and Len professed themselves wholly exhausted. He began to putter around, examining the cabin in detail, speculating on small improvements. He'd not had time or a free mind for this before. Sally cooked elaborately, so they sat around like a trio of overstuffed anacondas, she said. There seemed to be a lot of nothing to talk about. And Len maintained it was absolutely necessary to take *some* time off to be lazy in! So pleasant was the intermission that almost they could regret the bright clear morning of the third day.

But that could not last. The world was new washed and jeweled. It quivered. It seemed somehow to be fresh-made and to possess new wonders crying out for them to come see. Chilkat found this out the first of them. Even while the three humans were at breakfast, he was out, questing about and about, sniffing long at every familiar tree and corner as though he had never smelled it before.

The men washed the dishes while Sally tidied up. Then they put on their rubber boots and sallied forth. They started toward Len's cabin, but were stopped by what Sally thought was a brand-new river pouring out from the woods. The men remembered it, however, as a tiny rivulet and tried to recall it to her, but she had not noticed. Anyway, there it was now: not much of a stream, to be sure, but too deep to wade easily.

"And there's four more just like it," said Len. "But they'll be gone down by night. No sense getting in over our boots now."

They backtracked and took a look at the main river. It was still over its banks, but not as high as it had been; and it seemed to have lost its truculence. The overflow sparkled in the grasses. Much too wet to slop around.

"Let's hop the dinghy and take a look at my boom," suggested John hopefully, which was what he had had in mind all along.

This was a good idea; but they decided on the pirogue. The dinghy would comfortably carry three, but would have mighty little freeboard with four. Chilkat counted, for he weighed nearly as much as Sally. No thought of leaving Chilkat. He had earned his permanent status as the fourth by force of arms—or teeth. It was a pleasant excursion. There was much to exclaim over. The blue of the bay had browned as far as they could see. All sorts of driftwood and debris, flung forth by the river, floated about. There was a deer—and Sally exclaimed in compassion—bulk of 'em took to high country, Len re-assured her—and even trout, belly up. Some current, to tear those fellows loose! marveled John.

By easy stages they came finally to the boom. Sally and Len com-plimented John on the boom; and indeed the great peeled logs, rank after rank of them, close huddled, floating patiently, awaiting the next pleasure of the tiny creature who had mastered them, were an im-pressive enough testimony. John said little; but his satisfaction was evident.

"Not a bad lot, not a bad lot," said he. He looked almost lovingly across the sleek yellow backs. "I'd better get over and talk to Orford while this good weather lasts. Tomorrow, I reckon. Want to go along?"

"Oh yes!" cried Sally.

"Not me!" said Len.

John landed and climbed a short distance up the hill with an idea of retrieving his tools, but soon returned.

"No go," he reported. "Got to wait until she dries up a little. The whole side of the mountain is running water. Ground is like mush. Soft as a muskeg, even on the steep slopes. A man would sink in up to his knees."

He came aboard and stepped past Len to Sally, in the stern. Len dipped the oars and began to row idly, straight away from shore. John turned his head, looking back, still admiring the results of his hard work.

"I'll bet there's fifteen hundred dollars in that boom," he calculated absently. "Well, we can sure use it!"

"Getting toward broke?" Unembarrassed, Len spoke without thought of giving embarrassment. Being broke—or not broke—is no criterion of competence on the frontier, as it often is made to be in established communities.

"Oh, I still got a little in the bank. And what Nels Cole owes me," John replied easily. "But my way of figuring these things is, that the better stake a man takes into a rush, the bigger stake he's likely to pull out. And it costs money to get there comfortable, too."

"That's right," agreed Len, "they's going to be a lot of those hopeful wild-eyes find that out. I been figgering a little, and the man who leaves the States without at least five thousand dollars is going to do that stunt they call 'sufferin' hardships,' before he gets through. And how many of them is going to have that?"

"That much?" John looked up surprised. "You're crazy! How could even the worst tenderfoot in the world get away with that?"

"Counting everything," insisted Len obstinately.

John was still skeptical, but he did not argue the point.

"Lets us out then: I never had that much money, at one time, in my life!"

"Oh hell," Len was weary and discouraged with such obtuseness, "you make me sick!" He appeared about to abandon the whole subject, but reconsidered. "You're here already, aren't you?" he explained carefully, as to a child, "and you're no cheechako. Or are you? I'm taking about cheechakos. But just the same, it's going to cost you that fifteen hundred dollars. You got Sally to think about."

"*Will* you stop everlastingly talking about me!" cried that lady, exasperated. "I can go anywhere you two can go. And you know it!" She looked remindingly at Len. "Besides," she challenged the latter, "I fail to see how *you*——" She broke off. "What was that?" she cried.

"Sounded like a tree falling, maybe." John was indifferent. But Len resumed his rowing toward the middle of the inlet. "Sounded to me more like a glacier cracking—only there ain't no glaciers around here. Probably a rock splittin' off. If it was winter, I'd say so for sure."

"Listen to the echoes," said Sally.

"I don't hear nothing rolling." Len rested on his oars. "But, anyway, I'm superstitious about hanging around underneath, when the Old Man begins rollin' rocks. Jeeker snipes!" His slow drawl was cut short by a sharp crack, succeeded by a long-drawn, rippling and tearing crash. This was instantly caught up by the nearer echoes and passed on to the farther and tossed back again, so that for a long time, in diminuendo, it continued to roll and grumble, back and forth, like thunder.

"For heaven's sake, Len!" John recovered presently. "If that's a rock splitting, it must be some rock! Sounds to me like the whole mountain split!"

It sounded to Sally like something volcanic. She had heard vaguely of Alaskan volcanic islands—or something—and she said so. She looked around the mountains a little apprehensively for signs of eruption.

Len did not reply directly. He cast an estimating eye on their distance from shore, which was now a good half mile, swung the pirogue broadside, dropped his oars and propped his elbows on his knees.

"Well," said he, "if she does fetch loose, we got grandstand seats." He squinted his eyes, searching swiftly along the mountain sides. "Just below that white rock face! She's going!" he cried with a trace of excitement. "Watch her!"

"What? An eruption? What is it!" She caught what Len had seen and interrupted her questioning in amazement. "Look! look!"

Below the face of the white rock a handful of the growing trees were vibrating rapidly. It was a peculiar motion. John expressed it. "Looks like somebody in a hurry was trying to shake him down a mess of pine cones," said he wonderingly. Sally, her mind still on her volcanoes, thought it like an earthquake. Only it must have been a remarkably local earthquake. The other trees, even those close about that little patch, were still. The agitation was increasing in intensity and even, she thought, extending a little in area, though of that she could not be sure. Then abruptly a single tree shot up half its length above its fellows, seemed to hover an instant and disappeared. To Sally there was something personal in that disappearance. Like a swimmer, exhausted and sucked down. She was utterly bewildered, without a clue as yet. She turned to Len, and Len said something to her, but she could not hear the words. There was too much noise. She actually had not been aware of the noise; not until she tried to hear Len! She had been so held by the sight of the monstrous and inexplicable thing going on up there on the mountain that the sound of it did not penetrate. That did not seem possible. The very substance of the air was shaking with a series of sharp cracking explosions, rendings, tearings, multiplied by the echoes against an undertone of continuous heavy rumblings. Sounded as though the whole world were going to blow up: Sally had a moment of involuntary terror. She looked anxiously toward the men and was reassured. John no longer seemed perplexed: Len had lighted his pipe, clasped his knees and was lounging back with the comfortable air of a connoisseur at a show. He leaned forward to repeat his remark.

"I said to keep an eye on it clost up under the cliff," he raised his voice. He pointed the stem of his pipe.

Sally followed the indication and saw now that a wide brown band had opened between the trees and the base of the cliff. It had not been there before. It looked a little like wet earth. It *was* wet earth! Why of course!—the bit of forest had slid downhill away from the rock. It was still sliding. By looking closely she could see, at the junction edge of the quaking forest with the still forest, the trees passing each other, though very slowly. And at once the puzzle fell into orderly explanation. "Perfectly obvious! How dumb of me!" thought Sally.

"Avalanche!" she screamed at Len.

He nodded. She twisted sidewise on the thwart, the better to see. This was too exciting!

Now came a change. The trees ceased the violent quivering of their resistance. The struggle was finished. They moved, rank by rank, proudly erect, as though to yield, if yield they must, at least in dignity. But even dignity they were not to maintain. Presently, here and there, a single tree was seen to stagger, to snatch at his footing, as it were. Momentum gained: those behind pressed more closely on those in front, crowded against the forest below. The downward flow was checked by this fresh resistance. Ensued a silent and invisible test of strength.

But it was short. With a shattering crash the forces of avalanche prevailed. The forest was no more. It collapsed, disintegrated, dissolved into a torrent of tree trunks and roots, of splintered timber and boulders, that plunged, headlong and roaring, down the steep slope and into the sea. Vaguely Sally heard Chilkat barking like mad, and afterward she was to recall how small and ridiculous it had sounded to her against the mighty salvos of the mountains. But that was afterward.

She was stunned, bewildered by the beat of sound, jostled and hurried by the crescendo of rhythm. In another minute she would burst with it—but it was slowing at last—it was dying. It was over! For a little the echoes continued on. Then silence. Beneath the white cliff, down to the water, an arrow-shaped gash of brown had been cut clean through the forest. It did not look to be a very large patch: there were hundreds of similar patches all over the hills, bleached white by time. Len had told them gravely that they were made by beavers sliding on their tails and had pretended to be hurt when she had laughed at him. On the blue waters of the bay below this one bubbled the debris, flung fanwise from the shore. Sally drew a deep breath of relief. Len was laughing quietly.

"Well, what do you think of that?" he asked Sally. He had an air of pride and satisfaction, as though he had himself engineered a show.

She laughed, partly at this, partly from excitement. She turned to share with John.

"Why, what's the matter?" she cried, suddenly alarmed.

He nodded his head soberly toward the rack and ruin that fringed the shore.

"Strikes me we pulled out of there just about in time," said he.

She had not thought of that. If the avalanche had occurred ten minutes sooner, or if they had pulled away from the shore ten minutes later, they must have been caught. It was a narrow escape and would seem sufficient reason for John's serious expression, but Sally knew better. John was not one to give a second thought to narrow escapes; certainly he would not brood over it, once it had passed. Suddenly it came to her.

"John!" she cried, aghast. "The boom!" She stared at him, but unseeing. The shock of the catastrophe stunned her. "All that work! All that—— Oh! oh!" She buried her face in John's shoulder and burst into a brief passion of tears. Sally was not a crying woman; she hated herself always for crying; but the suddenness, the completeness, crashed down on her like a wave. Immediately, however, she recovered. She shook her head angrily. John was looking down at her with concern. Len, too, was looking at her, very sober and compassionate. They were being sorry for her, for *her!* It was John they ought to be sorry for. She was ashamed of herself. You'd think it was she who had slaved week after week and come home all tired out, and—— Nor was Sally a dramatizing woman, so she caught herself back sharply. Don't be a fool! She threw back her head and turned to John a dauntless—but tear-stained—face.

"Don't you mind!" said Sally.

The concern faded from his face. He patted her shoulder.

"Atta girl!" he approved. "What the hell! Easy come, easy go."

CHAPTER XXX

CHANGE OF PLAN

IT SEEMED that the catastrophe was not to be as complete as
had at first appeared. The boom itself was, of course, smashed to
smithereens, and many of the logs buried or splintered. But when
Len rowed the pirogue over for a closer examination they found a
good many salvageable logs floating among the debris. John and
Len set about it as soon as they had made the round trip to the
cabin for tools and the dinghy. By the end of a week they had managed to herd into a tiny shore line notch perhaps a third of what the
boom had contained. This meant really hard work. They had no
proper equipment: most of it had been in the woods and had taken a
ride with the avalanche. But they improvised towing dogs from
splitting wedges and stole Sally's clothesline and chased the straying
logs one by one and bent their backs to it and towed them in. It was
slow work, too, for the heavy timbers could be moved through the
water only at their own gait, and the slightest head wind stopped
progress entirely.

"If I didn't have faith and prayer," said Len, wiping his brow, as he
and John happened to converge near the opening of their notch, each
with a captive, "I'd never suspicion I was moving an inch, just diggin' holes in the water." He was standing facing forward, rowing
fisherman fashion. Abruptly he sat down, hard. He glared back at the

round bland end of the log that had all but butted the pirogue out from under him. "Hang back like a mule when I want ye to go, and then don't know enough to quit when I stop!" he addressed it vindictively. "I promised my mother I'd never have nothing to do with saw logs; and now look at me!"

Nevertheless he stayed with it, from daylight to dark, apparently as tireless as John himself; nor did he fall in with John's own suggestion that they quit after they had gathered the logs drifting within reasonable distance of their new boom. As time went on drift and tide were scattering the last remnants far and wide.

"No sir," Len vetoed, "we're going to show who's boss."

With only makeshift boom chains and dogs, the new impoundment was by no means secure. They strengthened it as well as they could, but an extra high tide, or more flood waters, or even a heavy wind, could break the flimsy barrier. Better get Orford to send for his boom as soon as possible. John started for Klakan the next tide after the last log had been impounded. He sailed alone.

"Unless you really need me . . ." Len declined the trip. "I reckon I'm an old fool, but I'm superstitious about U.S. marshals when they're fat."

Surprisingly, Sally, too, thought she would stay home. She gave no reason, simply wanted to. John was disappointed. "Thought it would be kinda fun," he complained, "sort of a spree together; I should think you'd want a change—maybe buy things or something."

"I don't feel like it," said Sally.

John departed in somewhat of a resentful mood. Sally'd been moping around like a barn owl for mighty near a month. John had let it slide. No use fussing about women's mulligrubs. Leave 'em alone, and they got over it. And she'd had quite a jolt, after all. But damn it, you can carry a thing too far! He clambered aboard the Tillicum and made fast the dinghy and hoisted the sails and pulled up the anchor and trimmed the sheets without a glance in the direction of the two standing side by side on the shore to see him off.

Only after the sails had caught the wind, and the ketch had heeled and taken her course, did Len say anything.

"Now look here, Sally, what's the matter with you? You ain't acting like I'd expect. Why didn't you go along with John?"

"I'm all right," she protested dully.

He examined her, speculating, shook his head.

"No, you ain't *that* weak kneed," he decided against his first thought. "Must be you ain't feeling well. You ought to have gone with John and seen Doc Vincent."

"I tell you I'm all *right*," she repeated with a spark of impatience. "Let me alone," she begged. Len turned her to face him. He inspected her critically.

"Well, you look kind of peaked to me." She kept her face obstinately averted. Len held his grasp on her arm. He was puzzled what next to say. "Don't take things too serious," he ventured. He hesitated. This was a delicate matter. He'd better step cautious. "Bound to little things come up between folks sometimes. Don't want to be too proud. John ain't the kind to——" Len stopped. Now you've done it, you dang fool, he apostrophized himself. He looked at her in consternation. She was biting her lip to keep it from quivering. Suddenly she gave way. She flung herself against Len's rough Mackinaw. Len gave a sigh of relief. This was better. He could handle this.

"You go right ahead and have a good cry," he approved soothingly. He looked down at the small bright head and patted Sally's shoulder and waited. Have her cry out; then we can get somewhere.

By and by she raised her head a little and dabbed at her eyes.

"Oh, Len, I'm so miserable!"

He continued to pat her shoulder, but said nothing. Len was, as John had often pointed out, a pretty wise old coot. Presently Sally emerged from the Mackinaw and fumbled for her handkerchief.

"Want to tell me?" then Len offered gently. "Needn't to," he added.

"I think I'm going to have a baby," Sally informed him in a small voice.

"Well!" Len uttered an astonished whistle. "What's miserable about that?" he challenged, recovering himself.

"Oh, Len!" wailed Sally.

Len looked down at her bent head and shook his own regretfully.

He did not want Sally to disappoint him that way. But he must comfort her if he could. "No call to be scairt about it, after all," he reminded her, "there's a good many women had babies since the world began."

"I'm not scared," she protested with a flash of indignation that Len should so mistake her.

Len was stumped and looked it.

"John," murmured Sally, as though in complete explanation.

Len looked still more bewildered.

"John," he repeated. He thought he had an illumination.

"For God's sake! Ain't you told John yet?"

She shook her head.

So that was it! The poor little nut!

"For God's sake!" repeated Len, astounded. "Why should you be scared of John!"

"But right now—of all times! Oh dear! And his heart's so set on it. And it would have been such fun!"

"Right now—— Set on what?" He was again all at sea.

She threw out both hands in despair at the enormous stupidity of Len. She made as though to turn away up the trail, thought better of it.

"The Klondike." She yielded that much to Len's pathetic bewilderment. A sudden impatience seized her. Couldn't the man see his nose on his face?

Len saw all right. Sure, the Klondike was off. Self-evident. But why all the tragedy about it? Have to get that out of her head. He made her sit down beside him in the grass. "You listen to me," he began on Sally. "You got the tail wagging the dog. What's a gold rush more or less? Shucks, I've seen a dozen of 'em," argued Len. "They're fun, sure; and maybe you make a stake. And then again, likely not. I've done both; and here I am! What difference? Way you act, you'd think the whole world was going to cave in if you didn't git to go."

"But think of all the plans we made," lamented Sally, "and now we'll have to give them all up. And John is so excited about——"

"There's other things John can get just as excited about," Len repressed her severely. "Like having a baby. That's one thing," Len spaced his words drolly, "is a thrill them gold rushers 'll have to miss. They ain't qualified." He looked down at her sober face. "That's a joke, durn it; laugh!"

This elicited a brief smile.

"John's going to be so disappointed."

Len fired up.

"*Is* he?" he cried with indignant scorn. "Well then, if he turns out to be that much of an ungrateful, wrong-headed, ring-tailed budmash, he don't deserve no better than he's goin' to get, which is a swift kick in the pants, old as I am and young as he is! But he won't." Len suddenly cooled down. "He'll be as tickled as a cat with two tails. Why, *any* man would."

"Do you really think so?" Sally was a little comforted, but still doubtful.

"I *know* so," said Len dogmatically. "You'll see. And, anyway," he turned to accusation, "what you mean moping around all over the place and getting me all stirred up this-a-way before you even know what you're talking about? It ain't sense! Klondike! Good lord!"

Sally felt better. And there was not much sense in that either, when you stopped to think of it. But she did.

Len put on the finishing touch, casually, when his shrewd wisdom saw the exact moment.

"I reckon Chilkat Harry 'll feel relieved, anyway."

Sally's heart gave a leap. She had not thought of *that* compensation.

"You're always such a comfort, Len. You're just like a nice old Rock of Gibraltar," she told the latter.

She arose and shook off the grass seeds. "And you're funny," she added. "What was that you called him? That queer word"—as Len looked blank—"bud—bud—something."

"Budmash!" cried Len. "Ain't that a pip? I got it off a cannery worker, one of these here Orientals they bring in."

"What does it mean?"

"It means," Len informed her accusingly, "the kind of a skunk John would have been, if what you thought of him was so. You ought to be ashamed of yourself. And you up and tell him the minute he gets back. Understand?"

But that promise she did not find easy to fulfill. She knew something had gone wrong the moment she had caught sight of John coming up the trail. And she knew it was something serious because of the devil-may-care swing of his gait and the devil-may-care sardonic grin of his face. When Trigger Jack began to grin, look out!—that's what they used to say in the Big Basin; and John Murdock had become no different. So Sally said little in way of greeting and nothing at all of what Len had told her to say, waiting for John to volunteer his own news, whatever it was.

John entered the cabin, spoke to Chilkat, moved here and there, hanging up his Mackinaw, bestowing his hat, dumping a pack sack in the kitchen, all the time humming cheerfully. Sally was not deceived; she knew the undernote. At length he straddled a chair, ran his hand through his hair and turned the grin in Sally's direction.

"Well," said he to Sally genially, "it's nice and complete. Orford doesn't want the logs."

"Doesn't want the logs?" she echoed. "But—why, he *agreed* to take them——"

"Well, that's off." He seemed entirely good humored. It was Sally who blazed out. "Doesn't the man's *word* mean anything to him——"

"Orford's all right," John cut in. "He's as sorry as anybody."

"Sorry!" she repeated witheringly.

Having delivered bad news with sufficient impact, and successfully stirred up Sally, John felt better. He was ready to explain.

It wasn't Orford. It was just bad luck: more bad luck, like the avalanche. Orford's market for lumber was Klakan. Klakan was dead: dead as a last year's herring. "Lumber—Orford's got a yardful of it, and you couldn't sell a plank to a drowning man," said John. "Don't be dumb," he told her a little impatiently. "It's this Klondike business again. Everybody's pulled out for the mines. Why, the town is empty."

"I never thought of that," confessed Sally slowly.

"Me neither," said John, his spirits back to normal now that he and

Sally were together in the situation. That was plenty for John. But not for Sally: she had yet to recover.

At this moment Len entered the cabin. Sally frantically tried to catch his eye, but failed.

"Saw the Tillicum and came right over," said Len. "How you like the good news?"

"What the hell," shrugged John, "I reckon we'll still eat." He looked up in belated surprise. "How'd *you* know about it?"

Sally shook her head and pantomimed vigorously at Len to keep him quiet. Len merely looked blank.

"Ain't you told him yet?" he asked Sally.

"Told me what? What you two talking about?" John looked from one to the other.

"Never mind that now, that will keep." She fixed Len with so compelling an eye that he subsided—but unsubdued. He continued to survey Sally with reproach. "Orford's gone back on his word. He isn't going to buy the logs," she threw this news into Len's midst like a bombshell.

The diversion was successful. Len listened to John's tale. He asked just one question.

"Mush Mahoney gone?" he wanted to know. He nodded when he was told that Mahoney had gone. "Looks like there's something *to* it, then," said he. He pondered a moment. "Take his outfit away? Or just lock it up?"

"No," said John, to the first question.

"Then that's all right!" Len looked relieved. He turned to Sally. "Mush has a nose like a bird dog," explained Len. "Keep your hair on and lay low, my son," he turned back to John. "You'll sell your logs."

"I don't understand," said Sally.

"Mush don't leave no two-three-thousand-dollar outfit for nothing. He'd take it where he'd git use of it. I know that coot. He don't figger Klakan's dead: only winter-sleeping, like a b'ar. She's right in line on the way north. She's going to boom, come spring." He nodded again with satisfaction over his reasoning, which sounded fine spun to Sally.

"Anybody left at all?" he asked John. "They can't be *all* gone." John admitted it was not as complete as that. Nels Cole had hung on.

"How's your friend, Mr Herbert Ashley, our general manager?" interrupted Len.

"Didn't see him," said John curtly. Cole had managed to get in a small pack, but it wasn't much of a one. He had a hell of a time to get that. Cannery workers had lit out. Nels had scraped together some Indians, and he'd brought up a bunch of Orientals. Had to send the cannery tenders down after them: ships are jammed tighter'n a wood tick. And most of the fishermen had lit out, too. But Nels had stayed with it.

"He'll get treble for what he did put up," commented Len keenly.

"And of course there's Orford," John resumed his count, "and your new doc. But that's about the tally."

This seemed to catch Len's interest.

"The doc stuck, did he?" he wondered. "Now I'd have thought—— Nels and Orford, yes: you can't pack a sawmill and a cannery over Chilcoot Pass, like you can a black bag."

"That's what I told him," said John.

"What'd he say?" Len looked interested.

"He's a funny cuss." John did not reply directly. "I like him. He's kind of lazy talking, but he looks you in the eye. We had quite a palaver." He produced his sack of tobacco. At this symptom of deflection into safe gossip, Sally sighed relievedly. "I told him, like you said, and he said he'd come up here to make himself a practice; and I said he'd sure ought to get good pickings at a gold rush— especially a big one like this; and he said *that* wasn't building practice; and I asked him what was it, then; and he said it was all same going to war—lots to do while it lasts, but you're just alone in the wilderness when it's over. I asked him what he expected to find to do at Klakan, with nobody there. He just said it looked good to him, and he'd always wanted to be Senior Medical Adviser somewhere, and that he thought he'd wait and ketch 'em coming back." John fished out his packet of rice paper and began to make a cigarette.

"That doc's got more sense than I gave him credit for," said Len.

"Sounds like a solid citizen. Gold rushes is always a wild gamble."

"Yeah," agreed John indifferently, "but think what fun you get out of a good gamble!" He had talked himself out of his ill-humor. His eyes were alight with adventure. "How early in the spring can we make it?" The cigarette was rolled. John held it intact while he returned the packet of papers to the breast pocket of his shirt.

Len looked at Sally. "Here's your chance," he urged silently. Sally flushed. She felt just a stir of indignation at Len. What would John think? She shook her head, trying to get this to Len, but succeeded merely in making him look disappointed and reproachful. It could not occur to him that Sally might feel any delicacy. She'd talked to him about it, hadn't she? He cast on her a glance of reproach. It was up to him. He gave Sally a last chance.

"You can't git into that country with a baby," he told John bluntly.

John froze, the cigarette halfway to his lips. He looked steadily at Len: Len looked as steadily back. Neither spoke. Finally Len made the slightest movement of his head toward Sally. Blank and amazed incredulity dawned in John's eyes. He swung around to Sally. Her cheeks were ablaze.

"Well, I'll be damned!" ejaculated John slowly.

Sally did not raise her head. She felt his eyes on her. She must say something.

"I'm so sorry," was the best she could do.

"Sorry?" John repeated the word as though it puzzled him. His eye lighted with sudden excitement. "Is that right?" He turned on Sally. "Are we going to have a baby?"

"Yes," she answered directly. "I'm so sorry," she had to add. She raised her eyes at last, anxiously, almost in deprecation.

She could make nothing of him yet. She might foresee that; John never was one to "go off half cocked," as he expressed it.

"Why haven't you told me before?" he asked.

"I wasn't sure. I thought so; but I wasn't sure. I waited to be sure."

"You told Len," John pointed out, but with no censure. He merely wanted to get this all straight.

"I had to tell somebody. I was so miserable."

Another than John might have felt hurt and have deflected into bypaths of reproach at Len's unexplained priority, but John's eye was keen for main issues. He let that pass.

"Why?" he demanded. "Don't you *want* a baby?"

An edge of severity sharpened his voice. He was looking at her almost sternly. No, not sternly—that would not be John. As if in suspended judgment—no, not that either; but waiting—to see if he was going to have something to forgive—she could not stand that from John!

"You *know* I do!" she blurted frantically. "Only——" And stopped.

"Only, what?" John prompted. He still waited.

"After we'd lost the boom, to have to tell you that—— And we'd talked so much about it and made so many plans—— And of course now——" Sally stopped. She knew she was incoherent, but she was all stirred up. She gulped, ordering her emotions. "Don't you see——" She made a fresh start.

But John had turned to Len.

"Do you know what she's talking about?" he asked Len.

Len took his pipe out of his mouth.

"Frettin' about that Klondike trip," he informed John briefly. He put back the pipe.

"Well, for the love of Mike!" said John. Which was his whole comment, but somehow the way he said it brushed the Klondike off like a mosquito. There was almost no such thing as the Klondike.

"Then you don't mind?" gasped Sally, dumfounded.

"Mind!" John repeated. *"Mind!"* He suddenly leaped to his feet, sprang in the air, cracked his heels together.

"Yip—yip—yee—e—e!" He uttered his shrill cowboy call. Chilkat sprang from his corner, barking. John upset Chilkat and tousled him, rolling over and over. Chilkat bared his teeth and pretended to bite John and uttered ferocious mock growls deep in his throat and in a moment had escaped from John and tore around and around the room and made short dashes, daring John to catch him again, and John did catch him again and wrestled about with Chilkat. It made a glorious row. Sally clung to the table to keep it from being upset and crowed with joyous laughter now that she could be lighthearted again. Len balanced his chair on two legs and cradled the bowl of his pipe in his hand and looked on with what might be described as sardonic benevolence.

John gave Chilkat a final roll and got to his feet, panting. Len removed his pipe.

"I gather," he told Sally, "that John doesn't mind." He dropped the chair to all fours and unfolded his long frame. "Reckon I'll be pushing along," said he. He sat down again, violently, propelled by the flat of John's hand.

"Reckon you won't," vetoed John.

"But——" Len began to remonstrate.

"But, nothing! You don't leave this place until I've got you good and drunk. Who you think you are to run out on us that way?"

Len cast a look of appeal toward Sally, but got no help there.

"Oh well," said Len, "don't mind me: I'm gittin' just a mite deef, anyway."

He drew up to the table with an air of resignation. John stormed into the kitchen and out again, bringing a bottle and glasses. Len eyed them.

"Hell of a time of day to go to drinkin'," he grumbled to Sally.

"All right," agreed John unexpectedly, "you don't have to." He reached toward Len's glass.

"Hold on!" cried Len in alarm.

John laughed at him. He held his own glass high.

"Here's to Jefferson Murdock!" he cried.

Sally looked up, surprised. She flashed a pleased look at John.

They drank ceremoniously. Len set down his glass.

"That's all right." Len maintained his air of discontent. "Why Jefferson?"

"Sally's folks," said John.

Len grinned at him.

"Got it all fixed, eh?" said he.

John wheeled on him, arrested by the dry sarcasm of Len's voice.

"Occur to you that this here new Murdock might not be a boy?"

"Of course it's going to be a boy!" cried John violently. "It's got to be!"

"Bet you," said Len.

"Stop it! I won't have it! You're outrageous, both of you!" interposed Sally with indignation.

Len gazed into his glass, picked up the bottle.

"All right," he said sadly, "just as you say." He thrust forward his chin. "Just the same," he informed the world in general, "I'm going to drink to her. You can suit yourselves. Poor little friendless gal!"

He finished pouring and set the bottle down. John reached for it, but Sally was too quick for him. She filled her own glass to the top and shoved the bottle toward John. He did not take it.

"Hold on!" he cried, alarmed, "what you doing?"

"Same as you and Len."

"But you don't want to take a drink like that! And, besides, you just had one!"

"No," agreed Sally, to the first part of this remark. "So have you," she pointed out to the second. "But I'm in on this celebration, too."

John was too solicitous to meet that challenge. Sally had to take care of herself now: that was all he could think of. Sally was entirely pleasant about it, but firm. She had at least as much right to take drinks as had John, and a good deal more right than Len. "You see it is I who am having this baby," she reminded. And she was going to. Len suddenly burst out laughing.

"She's got us, John!" He made a long arm and retrieved the bottle. "Too good to waste," he muttered as he steadied his hand to pour back his drink. He managed this without losing a drop. "Thar!" he exclaimed. "Purty good! I ain't drunk yet!" He bent his bushy brows on Sally. "Purty cute!" he approved. "He *did* have a kind of reckless gleam in his eye!"

"I didn't see you show any symptoms of hanging back," said Sally dryly.

"Keno!" shouted John, delighted to score on Len. He swept aside the bottle and glasses heedlessly.

"Look out!" cried Len in alarm. "We ain't off liquor for life!"

John had gone away beyond the idea of liquor. That had been merely the nearest obvious thing. He could get just as drunk talking about it. Well, Sally was pretty excited, too.

"What do you think, Sally? You think it's going to be a boy?"

"How in the world do you suppose I'd know!" She was laughing at his eagerness, but delightedly, for now everything was all right. Her cheeks were bright.

"Ain't she pretty?" John shot an aside toward Len. "You got to think so," he told Sally earnestly. "If you keep on thinking so hard enough it's bound to be!" He caught her fleeting expression. "Not that a little girl wouldn't be nice, too."

"What's the matter with one each—twins?" suggested Len with some irony.

John missed the irony. He seemed to think this a sound notion, nevertheless looked doubtful. For some reason the idea of twins stirred anxieties. For Sally. He had not thought of that side of it. He went into such a panic about Sally's having a baby—maybe twins— that both she and Len burst out laughing at him.

"Just the same," John was obstinate, "the sooner I can get you out of here, the better!"

Len cocked one eyebrow humorously at Sally.

"Give him time: he'll light," said he, but he looked pleased. "I told you so," was Len's unspoken message.

"For heaven's sake, why?" demanded Sally, exasperated. "It won't be until spring!" Of *course* she could not have the baby here: never thought of such a thing! But there was no sense or reason to rush off now, lose all their plans for the winter and the trapping. "Talk about going off half cocked!" she used his own phrase witheringly. "Klakan's no distance," she pointed out.

But it seemed that John's idea was that he should take her back to Seattle! He was quite set on that.

At this evidence of complete and fatuous imbecility Sally lost all patience. His solicitude was gratifying, but it was getting ridiculous. Time she put a stop to it.

"I'm not going to be taken to Seattle," she informed him categorically. "What kind of a coward do you think I am? Did I try to make you run away just because Pirate Kelly came to Klakan?" John looked bewildered. "And you expect me to be run out of the country by a little *baby!* There's a perfectly good doctor in Klakan," she continued, more calmly. "And even if there weren't—my grandmother was born out on the prairies, in a covered wagon!"

"That was different," objected John.

"How different?" she snapped back. "Do you mean to say I'm not as good as my own grandmother?"

"Three cheers," spoke up Len. They had forgotten Len. "Would you like his hide tanned or just dry cured?" he asked Sally.

CHAPTER XXXI

THE WALL

THE SNOWS CAME EARLY that year, which was satisfactory to the men, for that meant early prime in the fur. They could begin their trapping. The country proved well stocked, and they began to catch immediately. By chance the first victim, in one of the deadfalls, was a marten; which so tickled Len, who had won the toss and so was making the first round of the trap lines, that he returned at once to the cabin to show it.

"Look at that pelt!" he cried with a near approach to excitement for Len—without a drink. He ruffled it back, showing its length and thickness; he smoothed it down to exhibit the richness of its coloring. "You git money for a thing like that. If furs are going to be as prime as this we're going to make the Klondike look like penny ante!"

"Beginner's luck," said John.

"I don't believe it. It's the season. Animals know a lot. They spotted this for an early winter; and I bet it's going to be a cold one."

"And bought a fur coat to match, I suppose!" jeered Sally.

"Surest thing you know!" Len was in earnest. "And if it was going to be an open winter, the fur wouldn't hardly be worth taking. And besides," he added, "if you start the season on a marten, it's good luck.

So the Injuns say. And Injuns knows an awful lot. About them things, I mean."

"Len, you're superstitious," Sally accused him.

"Sure I am!" agreed Len unexpectedly. "I've lived too much outdoors not to be." He gave the marten's sleek coat a last pat and went back to complete the round. He would not be home until the morrow, staying overnight at the little line shack. Then John would make the next trip. They would alternate thus all winter: one out to tend the traps; one in to do the chores and care for the pelts. Len had moved over from Chilkat Harry's cabin to occupy the other bedroom, for neither man thought that Sally should be left alone. Indeed, for a time John threatened to become absurd about Sally. If John had had his way he—or Len—would have cooked the meals and washed the dishes and made the beds and done all the other small things that were rightfully her province.

"And what am I supposed to do? Sit and twirl my thumbs?" demanded Sally. "I'm as well as I ever was in my life. And I *need* to do things."

Len was inclined to back her up—to a certain point. No reason at all why she should not carry out her customary occupations. She ought to keep busy. "Got to sit on John's head," he agreed with Sally privately, "or he'll have us all talkin' in whispers." They took John in hand and, between them, made him behave. However, Len was not a completely satisfactory ally. He sided with John on a good many things. Like carrying in stovewood and things like that.

"But I *need* exercise!" protested Sally. "And right now it won't hurt me one little bit. What do you know about such things?"

They knew nothing about such things! But they were taking no chances. It did no good to argue, once they had their heads set. Sally promptly found that out.

"Please, may I brush my own teeth?" she asked John.

She yielded to most of their idiocy without too much fuss. But she battled it out on a few things that she thought worth while. Thus when the men were fashioning themselves web snowshoes Sally wanted a pair also. What would Sally do with snowshoes?—she was going to have a baby, and—— That—by now—outworn remark touched off the fireworks. They decided that they would make Sally a pair of snowshoes!

"It's either snowshoes for Sally or wheel chairs for us," submitted Len ruefully to John. "Most likely she's right. Women know about them things."

But Sally ran against a stone wall when she proposed to accompany John on his first rounds of the traps. "Just once," pleaded Sally. She was really in earnest: she wanted so much to see that country she had tramped over with Len, now that it had wrapped itself in winter. So much in earnest that she reasoned with John apart, talked soberly to him, without emotional appeal, solely along the lines of what anatomical knowledge she had absorbed from her father, the doctor; proving to John that at this early stage of pregnancy it was not possible for her to come to harm. Her argument was irrefutable; but unfortunately John was impervious to argument. Sally tramped about defiantly near home and daily pointed out to John that she'd been just as far as if she'd gone with him to the line camp. No good. John remained a mule. So did Len. A pair of them. All she needed was a set of harness! They were equally impervious to sarcasm. Supposed they couldn't help Sally's doing fool things if she was set on it: couldn't very well put hobbles on her——

"Thank you!" said Sally with deceptive meekness.

But they withheld their approval. And obviously—very obviously —entertained dark forebodings. Sally 'd get her comeuppance: but they loved Sally, and they did not want her to get her comeuppance.

There was something touching about their concern: like a pair of big clumsy dogs. If she had not had Chilkat's moral support she might have given in to it. Chilkat approved and accompanied her at a decorous gait and lay down in the snow when she stopped and was generally an unobtrusive comfort.

On the whole, things went very well. Each second evening whichever was trap tender brought in a gratifying pack of pelts—the skins of yesterday's catch, skinned out the evening before—and the animals that had been picked up on the in-trip. But nothing like, they took pains to tell one another in Sally's presence, what could have been expected from a real good set of steel traps. Sally paid no attention to this grumbling. She took it for what it was worth—exactly nothing. Indeed, she shrewdly suspected that it was really a kind of left-hand bragging. A couple of small boys, tickled that they could actually catch things with their home-made contraptions! She played up to them, admiring their skill.

Time passed with surprising swiftness, as is always the case when a sound routine has been established. "Seem always to be gittin' up or goin' to bed," admired Len. The days grew shorter and shorter, until the daylight lasted through only seven or eight hours of the twenty-four. Now Sally saw why Len had made the trap lines so short; and why he had built the overnight line shack right in the middle of what had seemed to her only a good day's journey. "Poor old Len, getting lazy!" Now she saw he had merely been measuring winter daylight! She confessed to John. "It's going to be plenty far," he assured her, "especially when the winter storms begin." Sally had not thought of bad weather. The first sample was convincing; and it was a mild sample at that. The real thing was tough. The line-man of the day could not possibly get in before dark; and he arrived pretty much frozen and tuckered out. They kept hot coffee and a big fire for him and did not worry, no matter how late he might be. That is the way of the wilderness.

The men were occupied enough: but how, they inquired solic-itously, about Sally? Pretty dull doings for Sally.

She did not find it dull. Whenever the day was fine—and there were more fine days than she had anticipated—she and Chilkat were much out of doors. There were dark hours aplenty for the doing of other things. The men did not think highly of this. Get out for a little fresh air and exercise—sure! But to stay out for hours and hours, when you didn't have to, and you had a tight house and a good fire handy . . .

Go with her? Not they! Got enough of that on their day out. And besides, there was always plenty to do inside—skin the catch and scrape and stretch the pelts and make more stretching frames and repair or renew various tackle which they lugged up from the Tilli-cum and spread out all over the cabin floor and—and various tinker-ing. Sally accused them of lying awake nights trying to think of more things to do, so they would not have to accompany her. Then they were quite brazen in agreeing to that—you bet! And, anyway, what in blazes was there to do, to see, at this time of year?

Sally did not try very hard to persuade them. She enjoyed being alone. That there was nothing to do or to see—from the men's point of view—was part of it. As soon as she stepped from sight of the cabin she was privileged to utter simplicity. When she stopped mo-tionless and so· stilled the soft crunch of her snowshoes, there was not even sound. She never tired of doing that, of standing quiet. Chilkat knew: he stood quiet, too, with only the smoke of his breath rising. Thus she entered a fellowship of expectation. The dark trees, the benign Presence she called the Protector of the Wilderness; the aloof distant ranges, all waiting. For what? If only she could stand there long enough with them, in the calm faith of their pa-tience, she would know. But the deadly cold would not permit. Nevertheless, from even these brief permissions she drew a spiritual sustainment that shone. She returned to the cabin so glowing with it that even John admitted the excursions did her good and stopped worrying.

Sally had thought that the long evenings might drag, might be something that must be endured. The lamps had to be lighted now by four o'clock or so. It did not turn out that way at all. On the con-trary. She settled down with a purr of satisfaction to a nice long comfortable evening. One night there was John; the next night there were Len and John; the third night Len alone. At last the boxes of books had been broken out from the hold of the Tillicum. She was doing some very especial sewing. They played rummy when all three were together and wrangled delightfully, and John and Sally joshed Len, who growled, more than half in earnest over his bad luck. And astonishing how much absorbing small gossip the wilderness could yield! And the plans to make. In the spring, northward. A good deal of discussion before they came to that after all. "Next year," insisted

John. "*This* year," amended Sally stoutly. All right? Of course it would be all right! "Why, the baby'll be six weeks old by July. Plenty old enough: especially on a boat. Why, a boat is no different than a house. You ought to see what some women do with a young baby!" "That's right," contributed Len unexpectedly. "I seen a man travelin' on a hoss onct, with a baby hitched behind him to a harness ring in his belt. I dunno how old he was," Len answered John's challenge, "but anyways, it was a leetle small baby." Northward in the spring then; but spring was a long way off. Too far off to think about. "Let's take Len into camp for another two bits." They played their rummy for a cent a point. No, the long evenings did not drag. It was bedtime before you knew it. Astonishing, too, how much sleep you can use when you put your mind to it, especially when it gets good and cold.

One day Len came in with surprising information. "Buds startin' to swell. Nothin' much to look at, but I bet Old Man Winter's a mite worried." His eye turned remote in calculation. "By glory!" cried Len, "it's only three days off to March!"

Sally felt an impact almost as of a physical blow. March! Why, why —they were returning to Klakan in March! She could not take it in. It was as though a solid world had dissolved from about her. She looked from John to Len, to share astonishment. They did not look astonished. They were finding themselves suddenly at the end of things that seemed as though they were going to last forever. They were accustomed to turning their backs on things. That was the roving life. But Sally was not. She put on her rubber pacs and went out through the wet cloying snow as far as the edge of the hill. For some time now her growing heaviness had limited her customary excursions abroad, but from this near vantage point she could consult the Protector of the Wilderness. Sometimes she carried on quite long one-sided conversations with the Presence and extracted from them enormous comfort and sometimes illumination. He was serenely understanding in matters she could not discuss with John because they were too foolish. Like being so causelessly shaken now.

She looked across the valley to the great mountain.

"Why am I so dumb?" she propounded. "It isn't as if I were caught by surprise. I knew we were going away in March. And here it's March, and I act as if I'd never heard of it. I knew perfectly well we were only camping in the cabin, and I've gone and made curtains and bed slips and covers and things as if it were my own house forever." She paused. "I don't mind doing them so much; maybe somebody 'll like them." She chuckled. "I doubt it: a hunting camp!— but I do mind being such a ninny; and to settle down so cozily—in my mind—in that little space of time, as if it did not have any end at all! I don't like to be a ninny. I like to have a tidy mind, like John's." She was quite serious in all this, but an imp of humor tickled her funnybone at the paradox: if she had a tidy mind like John she wouldn't be out here in melting wet snow asking herself fool questions that got you nowhere, she reminded herself.

She appealed to the Protector of the Wilderness for appreciation of her little joke on herself. But the Presence did not seem to be amused. He waited in serene benevolence; so she knew she was supposed to continue. It was that way with the Protector: if you started something, you had to see it through.

"Funny," continued Sally thoughtfully, "now I think of it, it's always been that way with me. I must be nearsighted, inside, I mean. The end of things is always so dim, until I have my nose right up against it. So dim that I act as if it wasn't there. Give me ten minutes and I start a cathedral! Such a waste—and I might be doing something useful." She looked up, as though startled. "What was that? All people are that way? I don't believe it!"

She spoke now as though in direct answer to a living and present person, and she had a sense of happiness, for she knew her channel had opened. "Yes, I know," she would have been willing to admit— later—"I'm talking to myself." But to a deeper self. Locked from her, save when something—the Protector of the Wilderness?—opened the door. Or *was* it herself? Who knows?

"Well—maybe," she accepted dubiously. "Perhaps they are. But why? *Why* should we all act so like children? Because we are? Yes, I suppose so." She made a humorous grimace. "But even then, why?"

She pondered this for some time. "I suppose it *was* worth while—all those things I made—in a way," she mused, "and I suppose I *wouldn't* have made them, otherwise." She looked doubtful. "Is that it? So we will do the things that would not seem worth while—if we stopped to think?" She appealed to the Protector's serene crest. Yes, that was it! She caught back his response and felt the little warm elation that came when things clicked. Sally was pleased at this happy thought. But her satisfaction had little or nothing to do with her original quest—why she had been such a ninny. It was not that, but because here was a shining-new treasure for her that was going to be of use. She would not be fooled again by time! From now on she was going to do things without having to be fooled. That was something, like being considered grown up. The shining-new happy thought had been given her because she deserved it, like a medal.

She raised both arms in a gesture of gratitude to the Presence.

The movement must have aroused the child within her. It stirred; and Sally was invaded by the sudden small instinctive panic that seized her when she thought unexpectedly of her approaching ordeal. After all, this was her first baby: and she had no one with whom to talk reassurance. She called upon her common sense. Birth is a commonplace, she reminded herself stoutly. But back of that brave front lurked still the tiny stabbing fear. Women *do* die in childbirth. . . .

To help herself out of this threat of mood—which she had never permitted, and which she did not intend to permit—she lowered her eyes from the high austerities to the comfortable earth. Its surface still wore winter's appearance unbroken. But something beneath seemed to stir. Nothing the senses could identify, though undoubtedly composed of a thousand of their reports. The end of winter was at hand. Sally could see it now, as plainly as the nose on her face; and she gurgled with delight, her brief panic forgotten, at this perfect example of her happy thought. "I am certainly a profound thinker!" said Sally, in mock admiration of herself.

But here came to her another happy thought with which she was equally delighted. "I'm doing well," purred Sally. She loved these times—too rare—when some lucky chance opened her spirit and things flowed in. This new one came to her on the voice—just a tiny tinkle—of an unseen trickle of water. So small was it that she knew it instinctively for a new-born thing. "Why"—this was Sally's happy thought—"when you get there it isn't a wall: it can't be a wall, because things don't chop off clean like that. Nobody can look at the clock and say, this moment winter ends, spring begins. It isn't like that. They—they sort of blend"—groped Sally toward the idea of transition—"and you walk right on through. Not a wall—a kind of mist—and there you were, in another fair wide space of time!"

She began to chuckle at her simplicity, tenderly, as one is amused at a child. And it didn't teach you a thing, not a thing! she told herself. "That space is just like the other: and a wall of termination at the other end. You know the wall is there, but it's so far off and dim that you don't pay any attention to it: and it holds you in. Exactly as before! Like a horse that has eaten loco weed," thought Sally, "held by flat shadows on the earth because they look to him ten feet high! But it works. Because we're such children! The wall is only an idea— a sort of dread . . ."

Sally's eyes opened wider and wider: she could scarcely breathe: she thought her heart was going to stop beating.

"Why!" gasped Sally in her awe of realization, "that is what death is! Not a wall; hardly even a mist—when we get actually to it! Merely a dread. Put there to keep our interest from straying, so we will do the things that must be done, consider them worth while! If it were not for that we would skimp, or just wait!" ("Not John," was Sally's swift aside; and she felt humble, as often.) "When we grow up we won't need it." And Sally knew that never again was she to know fear of death.

She lifted shining eyes to the Protector of the Wilderness.

"Thank you," she breathed simply.

CHAPTER XXXII

THE DECISION

ON THE FIFTEENTH of the month Old Man Winter got so very worried, according to the doctrine of Len, that he gathered all his forces in a last desperate assault. For four days the skies had shone with a burnished and almost forgotten brilliance; the snow had been visibly melting; long black streaks had appeared on the southward slopes of the mountains; John, returning from his trick on the trap line, had brought with him a handful of pussy willows. But this morning the whole extent of the sky dimmed at once, as though it had been breathed on; by noon the mountain crests were hidden; by night the wind had risen cold and lashing; and by noon of the day following snow was driving horizontally before a typical December gale.

"She's a shrieker," John reported to Sally, shaking off his Mackinaw. "I've sure got it on old Len!" He chuckled relishingly as he contrasted his own lot with that of Len, struggling back from the line camp. He congratulated himself that it was Len's turn to be out. "How about tomorrow?" Sally suggested maliciously. "Your turn tomorrow—or are you going to stay in?" "She'll blow herself out by tomorrow," predicted John confidently. "These spring storms are always short."

"She came along just right to get it over before next week," said John. Next week they were to move to Klakan. Piece of luck, that, according to John. He had recovered to a state of expansive satisfaction over everything. The universe had withstood the tremendous shock of the new baby and seemed to be doing business as usual; the fur catch had exceeded expectations; Sally was fine. His first panic of ignorance had been succeeded by a sublime confidence—also of ignorance. And next week he was going to turn the whole business over to professional hands. His spirit swaggered. He had hard work to hold himself down.

About noon Sally went into the bedroom to lie down. This was not unusual. John paid no attention, except to prop open the connecting door so she could get some of the warmth. It was really cold. Cold as winter. Then he went cheerfully about his business; which was, largely, finding something to occupy him. Almost everything was done. There were a few things he could pack. He was pretty much preoccupied and was humming under his breath, and the storm outside had risen to a howl. Nevertheless he thought to catch a faint whimper. Some animal, sounded like—not Chilkat; Chilkat was snoozing near the fire, and now he had thrown up his head and had his ear cocked. So John had not imagined it. He listened a moment. The sound was not repeated. Some critter under the house for shelter, maybe. Wasn't important. Only an outdoorsman would have noticed it in the first place.

Chilkat arose from the fireside and stalked into the bedroom. He returned, inserted his nose beneath John's elbow and heaved.

"Get out!" said John: he was just finishing a knot. Chilkat nudged again; and John, dropping the rope ends to attend to Chilkat, heard again the queer little animal whimper. But it was not under the house: it was not some critter. It was in the bedroom. It was Sally!

John hurled from him the half-finished pack and in two bounds had reached the doorway. Sally was huddled in a tight little ball with the quilt around her. She did not move nor utter any more sounds. "Looks like she's asleep," thought John; "good for her, mustn't disturb her; must have been something else I heard." He was tiptoeing very cautiously to where he could see if she was asleep. She was not asleep—the face she turned up to him, as he came in sight over the billows of the quilt, looked small and white, and the eyes very large.

"Oh, John," she moaned, "I'm in such pain!"

And at once all the artificial surface of confidence and comfortableness crumbled away from beneath him, and he was back at his first primitive fears; and he saw they had not been banished but only been covered over; and he saw that he had been right all along—about Sally's having snowshoes and being so dang sure of herself and all— and that this situation of man and woman and the mechanisms of nature were not in truth commonplace things to be taken lightly merely because they were accustomed, but that each was a separate hazard with tragedy behind the mask, and—— Upon him descended the quiet wariness that meant crisis. No vain fussing about John then.

"Do you think it's——" He left the sentence unfinished.

"I don't know," gasped Sally. Her face twisted with a sudden agony. John's own face was setting in the grim competent lines with which he fronted emergency. He said nothing, but moved slowly toward the door, his forehead creased.

"Back in a jiffy," he reassured Sally.

He thrust firewood into Jumbo and opened the dampers and half emptied the kettle, so the water would heat the more quickly, and then pawed about until he found Sally's hot-water bag. Presently he filled it and returned to Sally. None of his movements were hurried. Time enough to hurry when he had figgered out what he ought to do.

"Try this. Might help," he told Sally briefly. He sat down beside her and rested his chin on his hand and looked at Sally; though he was not really seeing her. He was still figgering.

Well, there was one thing he could do—beside the hot-water bag. He went into Len's room and swept all the bed clothing off on the floor, moved the bedstead into the next room and set it across the fireplace. Then he swept Sally, quilt and all, into his strong arms and deposited her on the mattress.

"Warmer here," said he. "I'll fetch some more quilts. No sense bothering to make the bed, unless you get better."

"I'm feeling a little better now," said Sally faintly. She snuggled down with a tired sigh of relief and comfort now that she had no longer to fight alone against the growing terror of the pains. John was in charge. She looked gratefully at his somber, preoccupied face and waited. He sat beside the bed and stared into the fire. After a time he got to his feet.

"We've got to have that doctor." He had decided. "You can't possibly make it to Klakan in this storm. It 'd kill you." There was in his voice no note of interrogation, but he paused as though for her opinion.

"I don't believe I could," agreed Sally.

"Do you think you'll be all right alone for a few hours?"

"Oh!" Sally shrank from this.

"*Somebody's* got to get that doctor. It won't be long: Len will be in. I can send Chilkat to hurry him."

"Can't it wait until Len gets here?" pleaded Sally.

The grim lines of John's face twitched, turned to iron again.

"I thought of that. But it would miss a tide. And I think that doctor ought to get here as soon as possible. It's a guess. But I'll do as you say."

Sally felt very weak and cowardly. She knew deep down that John was right: and she felt—deep down—what it had cost him, and was costing him, to come to that decision. But she could not as yet emulate that complete and solitary self-control. She was afraid.

"Supposing"—she hesitated—"while I am all alone, it should——"

He would not permit her to finish.

"I thought of that," he cut her short briefly. "What say?"

She summoned all her courage. John's very curtness, his refusal even to consider a possibility once weighed in his decision, shamed her own cowardice. He suffered over that decision. She knew it by the look in his eyes. She mustn't let John down; she managed a smile.

"You'd better go," she told him. "I'll be all right. These first pains really don't mean anything very imminent, I believe. Just warnings. I'll be all right."

John's face cleared.

"That's the girl!" He began to move swiftly about, making his preparations. Sally lay quiet and watched him. She was feeling a lot more comfortable and confident. The pain was almost gone: and just making the decision had lightened her mind. She had been pretty frightened, but the fright had been a sudden instinctive panic. Now she was over it. She was not going to be afraid—of anything. Whatever happened. "I don't want to die," said Sally to herself; but that was not on her own account, but because of John.

John wrote a note and called Chilkat to him and tied it firmly in the ring of the malemute's collar. Then he let Chilkat smell of one of Len's garments and opened the door.

"Find!" he ordered. Chilkat quartered a moment, departed swift as an arrow, his nose down. Satisfied, John shut the door and returned to Sally. "That 'll fetch him," said John. "He'll be here by noon."

"What did you tell him?"

"Just to get a move on and come in. He'll be here. That dog's good. Wasn't sure he could catch the scent—under the new snow." He stopped a moment to listen as a savage gust howled past the eaves. "She's a humdinger," said he.

"Are you sure you can make it?" Sally had not thought of this part of it before. She was shot through with a new alarm, now on John's account.

"You bet your sweet life I'll make it!" For the first time John showed emotion.

The emotion died. He moved about, his eyes puckered, thinking of various small arrangements. He piled firewood—the small light sticks—on the floor next Sally's hand, so she could reach over and throw them on without having to get up. He filled the kettle and hung it on the crane and cut Sally a hooked stick with which to swing it out. He punched holes in the tops of several cans of milk— "Do you till Len gets here," said he. "I couldn't possibly eat," disclaimed Sally. John thought of everything. He even led a stout fishline, over nails, from the latch on the door to within hand's grasp. "So you can let in the dog," explained John: "he'll beat Len in, and Len might send a message." Then he cut a light pole long enough to reach from the bed to the door, so she could push it shut again and keep out the weather. "I can move about," protested Sally; "the pains have stopped now."

"That's good," said John briefly. "But you better not move any more than you have to." He straightened and looked about, but could think of nothing more. "Keep a-shining," he told Sally. Her eyes filled at the unconscious poetry of the thought. He was standing above her. Just for a moment he permitted—only a little—the tautness of his purpose to ease. "We'll make the grade!" he assured her confidently. "Ought to have gone before," he mused regretfully. "But it's a month early," protested Sally. He thrust vain regrets aside. "Things ain't so bad," said he, with determined cheerfulness. "Lucky we bent on the Tillicum's sails last week." Suddenly he grinned. "Notice that word? 'Bent?' Say I ain't a sailor!" He stooped to kiss her. "Keep a-shining," repeated John.

He was halfway to the door.

"John!" she called.

He returned. She held out her arms. He stooped.

"Oh, John, I do love you so!" breathed Sally.

CHAPTER XXXIII

THE STORM

UNTIL HE HAD POKED the Tillicum's nose beyond the entrance, John had no conception of the effect of a real winter gale on open water; nor had he appreciated how much the mountain ramparts sheltered the valley's inland sea. Fortunately he had hoisted only the jib and the jigger; but this had been more in the interest of easy one-man handling than in deference to the strength of the wind, and he had in the back of his mind an idea of setting the mainsail once he should be in the clear. He got over that idea promptly. The wind pounced upon the little craft, swirled her away down the channel like a fallen leaf.

The suddenness of it, and the fierceness of it, took John's breath. All he could do was to brace his feet and cling to the tiller with both hands and put all his strength into holding the Tillicum's stern toward the great seas that charged upon her and crested above her and seemed about to bury her and at the last split second lifted her and hurled her forward. She struggled frantically against John's control, shaking her head, lunging first one way, then the other, like a terror-stricken horse. He gritted his teeth and fought to hold her. Even his inexperience recognized what would happen if she should broach to. That was what the sea wanted; to that end she hurled after him, one after the other, these monstrous waves. He beat them in their purpose, one by one. They slipped away under him reluctantly, sullenly, and rolled away.

Just at first each escape seemed to him a separate miracle, not to be repeated. But after a little, finding himself still afloat, he began to gain a little confidence. A corner of his mind was freed for snatches of thought. "Why in hell didn't I know enough to leave the dinghy," muttered John. He thought the dinghy might make trouble; in which he wronged the dinghy, which bobbed gaily along after, perfectly dry and apparently having a good time. "God, I'm glad I didn't loosen the furl on the mainsail!" was his next thought. "That would have made a sweet mess!" And presently, with a certain grim satisfaction: "Anyway, we're sure travelin'!" Klakan Point was fairly leaping toward him. It looked bigger every time the waves lifted him to where he could see: nothing to see from the troughs but mountains of water. Nevertheless, the troughs were sort of friendly. Not so much wind. The ketch seemed to relax. John, too, could ease the muscles of his back and neck, shift his grip on the tiller. Kind of breathing space, like between rounds of a fight. Only this respite was so brief. It was as though they were hurled upward by a mighty hand into the fury of the wind. The Tillicum reeled under the shock. "That a girl!" muttered John in applause; but only a sailor could have appreciated fully the stoutness of hull and spar, of canvas and bolt rope, that withstood so gallantly these repeated and mighty blows. A craft less sturdy would have gone to pieces in the first half-mile.

However, he was getting there—he was going to get there. His exultation revealed to him that he had really been doubtful. No matter what he had said. "Damn fool!" John apostrophized himself, without quite knowing why. By now, naturally, he was wet through, for at each crest, horizontal sheets of water swept the little craft from stern to bow. Not rain. Sea water. Blown from the tops of the waves by the sheer strength of wind! John had never seen anything like that: he had not imagined anything like it. That, he discovered, was why he was cursing himself. Ought to have known enough to have put on his slicker. Just because the sky was clear, it never occurred to him. Well, too late now. It was down in the cabin, but it might as well have been at the North Pole. If only Len were along —or somebody—— Must be a mess down below, the way things were banging around—ought to have had sense enough to snug down before he started—— To hell with it—no time for that now—— "I'm *cold!*" discovered John. And it was not just ordinary shivering cold: something more deadly. The kind that stabs inside of you and works out to the surface and puts you out! He noted with dull astonishment that the rigging was gray with ice. "Salt water, freezing!" marveled John. "Wonder if I can stick it?" The misgiving pounced on him unaware. He threw it out. "By God, I've *got* to stick it!"

There was Klakan Point! And under its lee no more big waves, only a confusion of water. Cautiously John shifted course, feeling for the edge of disaster as the ketch turned her quarter toward the seas. He glided into the narrow strip of shelter. The ketch seemed to shake herself like an animal in out of the storm. John, too, shook himself and arose stiffly to his feet. Klakan was only a mile or so away now. He felt let down, as though he were already there.

He trimmed sheets for the new course and resumed his place at the tiller. In the brief truce before he entered the rough waters in the upchannel the front of his mind had thought of Sally. She had been in the back of it all along. Len ought to be with her by now . . . He refused to contemplate the return journey, except that the thought of her had given him strength for it—he'd get somebody to help him sail back——

A blast of wind and a rush of sea smote him in the face as he drew out from the shelter of the point. The Tillicum staggered, checked, heeled far over. A level sheet of almost solid water swept her decks. John's comfortable feeling of arrival dropped from under him. He had not thought of this: he had really been too numbed to think of anything. This woke him up with a vengeance. Klakan only a mile away—he could see the cannery buildings and the floats. But such a mile! Upwind, and the tide still running out.

Any sailor would have dropped back to the shelter of the point: but John was no sailor.

John was young, strong, had led a hardening life. In his earlier days he had been what he would have called up against it on several occasions. He discovered now that he had been mistaken. He'd never really been up against it. Being up against it means continuing automatically on blind nerve after your mind is completely blurred. He learned that now. He never was to remember how he got there. Only that somehow at last the tall piling of the floats loomed above him, and that eager boat hooks seized the rail, and somebody had jumped aboard and was slackening the sheets. He heard the loosened sails clap sharply in the wind, and the sound of many voices. The float was full of people. Someone behind him had a hand under either armpit and was trying to get him to his feet. Someone else was thrusting a whisky bottle at him. This aroused him a little. No whisky. He knew better than that—right now—and the job half finished.

"Coffee," he gasped.

"Sure! sure!" they promised. Someone hurried away. He felt himself being supported, half carried, up the ramp. The blood was returning into his cramped and stiffened limbs. He could help himself a little; he was beginning to function again. Two men had remained behind. They were lowering the two sails, furling them. John struggled free.

"Don't do that," he expostulated. "Don't let them do that. I got to start right back."

"Sure, sure," they agreed soothingly; then, as he hung back: "They'll slat themselves to pieces if you leave them."

At the top of the ramp he caught again the force of the wind. It cut like a knife. John realized with dull surprise that he was wet through; and when he moved his arm suddenly the fabric crackled with ice. They crossed the street; and John was seated in a small hot room with a stove. The room was full of people, and from time to time the door opened and more crowded in.

"Keep that door shut!" somebody was calling hoarsely.

A hand thrust on him a steaming mug of coffee.

"My God, man, you're froze," said a voice pityingly. It was a woman's voice. John gulped down the hot coffee. The woman took the cup. He saw this was Mrs Oldstrom, the wife of one of the older fishermen.

Oldstrom himself was there with an armful of heavy clothing. He dumped it at John's feet.

"You bane get those duds off'n you," he ordered. Mrs Oldstrom disappeared. John fumbled at the buttons of his Mackinaw. His whole hand ached and tingled. He could not control his fingers. Other hands reached to help him. They got him to his feet, stripped him. They rubbed his body vigorously with a towel rough as a nutmeg grater and tried to pull the coarse woolen undergarment over his head. He took it from them.

"Here, let me. I'm all right," he muttered.

He reclothed himself; and the simple accustomed movements helped. Here was Mrs Oldstrom back with more coffee. His head cleared. He remembered.

"Somebody get the doctor!" he cried. All his vigor suddenly came back. He was his own man again. "Where's he live?" Then, as they merely looked blankly one to the other, his voice sharpened. "Speak up! This is serious! I've got to get back!"

It was Oldstrom who replied.

"Get back?" he repeated John's words. "You don't be gone get back. You gone crazy? Better thank God you got here! We watch you two hours, and why you don't swamp beats me! You can't do *that* again. No man alive gone stay top of water today."

"Never mind that. I've *got* to get back. Where's that doctor?"

"What's the matter?" This was the woman. "Somebody get hurt? Bad?"

John turned to the kindliness in her voice.

"It's my wife. She's—she's going to have her baby. I've got to get the doctor to her, I tell you! What's his name? Where's he live?"

Mrs Oldstrom made a soft sucking sound of sympathy through her lips.

"It is not goot that you leave her alone," said she. "Yess-s, you should get back. You should not come away."

"But the doctor," insisted John. "She's not alone. There's Len——" The men in the room made no comment. They stood stolid, like so many graven images. They stared at him blankly, as though they did not understand. He turned back in despair to the woman.

"She will be all right." Mrs Oldstrom laid her hand on his arm. "It iss not so bad. I have had three."

"The *doctor*," cried John desperately. It was like struggling in a nightmare.

Mrs Oldstrom shook her head slowly.

"The doc ain't here," blurted out one of the men. "He's gone away."

"Gone away!" gasped John. For ten seconds he stood dazed by this new blow. "Well, where's he gone?" He recovered himself. He'd get him—wherever he was!

This time there were too many answers. As though a spell had been broken. Jimmy Waboose had fetched him, John made out. Two days ago. Something about Jimmy's squaw, or something. Up toward Tenakee, they thought. They were vague; but on one thing they agreed.

"He won't be starting back till this blows itself out." They were confident of that.

"Don't anybody know where Jimmy's place is?" persisted John in despair.

Nobody knew. John's face had turned grim again.

"Then you'll have to come," he told Mrs Oldstrom.

But Oldstrom himself intervened.

"She'll not," he negatived roughly. "There's no sense to it. You'll never get there. You won't get a mile the other side the point. Don't be one crazy fool. What's the goot of that—to anybody? And I got three kids," he added defensively.

John pleaded.

"With another man—I'll make it worth your while. I've got money."

"Money's no goot to a drowned man," retorted Oldstrom brutally, because his conscience stirred. He stared back at John with Scandinavian obstinacy.

The outside door had been opening from time to time to permit another spectator to slip in. The room was now jammed full. Over the intervening heads John could see that the newcomers included several more women. He appealed to them, but they looked blank and shrank back, like stupid cattle.

"But one of you *must!*" he implored in despair. "Don't you understand? It's life or death." He thrust aside the men to appeal to them directly. They looked frightened, but imperviously obstinate. "And you call yourselves women!" He gave it up in sudden angry contempt. "And it's life or death!"

One of the older men laid a hand on his arm.

"That's just it," said he soberly, "life or death. I know how you feel, lad, but can't you see it's no good? They want to help: we all want to help. But how does it help to go out and get drowned?"

"Nobody's going to get drowned," dissented John fiercely.

But they wagged their heads. They were sailors: they knew.

"You managed to get here because the Old Man had his hand under you," said one bluntly. "You can't get away with it twice. Don't be a fool. By tomorrow——"

"Tomorrow!" John caught him up bitterly. He looked them all over with a new chill dispassion. "Down where I come from we was raised different, I reckon," he drawled. He thrust them aside and made for the door.

"What you tank you gone do?" called Oldstrom after him. John turned.

"Go back where I belong." That was all John said, but the tone of his voice scorched and withered.

They muttered at each other. "The man's stark mad—can't blame him, but—just plain suicide, that's all—really ought not to allow him——"

John caught the last words.

"Try to stop me!" he said dangerously.

He turned back to the door and came face to face with a fourth, woman whom he had not seen before. Or rather, he had had an impression that there were four, but when he came to the point of making his appeal, there were three. Now she was back. She grinned at him.

"No guts, eh? I suspicioned it. So I got me a ready. Let's get going."

It took a second for John to recognize a change of fortune. In that flash he saw that the woman was bundled to the ears in wool: she was heavy and shapeless with the bulk of garments.

"Yes! I'm goin' wid ye," she assured. "But hold your horses!" She faced the other women. "Sure I know ye'd like me drownded, and now I'm going to oblige you. You're all good professin' Christians so I gave you first chance to save your dirty souls. But you're also a set of mealy-mouthed gutless bitches, so nat'rally you wouldn't. Thought I'd tell ye." She eyed them with apparent good humor.

Two of the women merely shifted uneasily. The third spoke up.

"Are you men going to stand by while this creature insults us!" she demanded.

The newcomer waited for ten seconds of the ensuing silence. She rolled her eyes toward the speaker.

"The *men* has all pulled out," she then remarked briefly. She seized John's arm. "Come on wid ye," said she. "If we're going to oblige by getting drownded, let's do it prompt."

"I'm not going to forget this," he babbled as they went out into the street. "I'll always——" He fired up. "I'll get you there!"

"Niver a doubt of it!" she said, as one soothes a child. She laughed a jolly laugh, then sobered. "But it 'll be you that 'll be doin' it, let me tell you that!" she warned. "I'm as much use on a boat as a cat at a prayer meetin'. I'm skeered of 'em, even the big ones. But you get me there and shovel me ashore, and maybe feed me a drink to remind me I'm still alive, and I'll do my best for your woman——" She stopped short. "Is that your boat?" she demanded sharply.

"She's small, but she's——" began John defensively.

"Your name Murdock?" the woman cut him short. "Christ!" she

breathed, "then it's Sally!" She seized his arm and hustled him down the ramp and almost hauled him bodily to the smooth deck of the ketch. She seemed to have surprising strength. For the moment she did not follow him, but turned with an elaborate air of surprise upon the men who had hesitatingly followed down the ramp.

"Here's your crew," she spoke over her shoulder to John, who was busy with halyards. "Every man jack just a-hopin' you're going to choose him!" John jerked his head around in sudden new hope that died at once at sight of the sullen faces.

"Look here, Murdock," spoke up one, "are you dead set on tackling this? Can't you listen to reason? We know these waters: we know what we're talking about." This was Jim Kearn, a seiner, an old-timer on the coast. He spoke with genuine feeling. It was the woman who answered.

"Go talk to yerself, then. We're goin'!" and then added with apparent irrelevance, "th' sweet little thing!"

She hoisted herself aboard by the backstay, clumsy in her bulk of garments.

"Do I help pull on that thing?" she inquired of John, as he laid hand on the jigger's halyard. "Tell me what you want. I know nothing of boats." She looked after him helplessly, unable to follow his quick movements. "I'm more of a hinder than a help, I see that."

"There's nothing you can do," John took a moment to say. "I can handle things." He stopped, considering. "You better go below," he decided. "It's safer." He said nothing by way of gratitude. He took that for granted; as she did. Later. Right now the job at hand. She nodded. No comment. No objection. No fuss. Fitted right into the situation. Thank God she was that sort. Well, he was about ready.

He whirled to the quick pat-pat of feet hitting the deck. He stopped, stiffened.

"What do *you* want!" he demanded harshly. He was in no mood for interference from this man.

"Well!" gasped the woman from the companionway. "Whoever in the round world would have expected *you!*"

"Or you, for that matter," retorted the newcomer coolly. "That makes a pair. One side!" He tossed a light pack past her down the companionway into the cabin. "Now down with you!" he commanded. She backed down the companionway.

"If I'm believin' my eyes," she said slowly, "I'm takin' back a lot of things."

"That's all right!" impatiently. Then softening, "I'm taking back a few myself." He snapped back toward John, "Haven't you a slicker? Put it on."

John did not move, nor shift his puzzled eyes from Ashley.

"Do you mean that you——"

"Of course; you can't make it alone." He moved restlessly.

"But why? I thought that——" persisted John.

Ashley threw his head back and faced John squarely. His eyes and his voice were steady, but a flush of blood crimsoned his face.

"I've owed you one for a long time," said he. "That machine business was a very dirty trick." He gave John no chance for reply. "For God's sake!" he cried, "let's get a move on and get out of here!"

He burst into activity, thrusting on John the slicker that the woman, without bidding, handed up from below; sliding shut the hatch and fastening it; coiling and lashing the mooring lines as they were cast off; trimming in the sheets as someone thrust the bow of the Tillicum out into the stream. The fishermen on the float, dubious, apprehensive, perhaps more than a little conscience stricken and shamed, gave a straggling shout of encouragement. They might as well not have existed as far as those on the ketch were concerned. Ashley braced himself in the cockpit. John settled himself to the tiller.

The Tillicum fairly flew to Klakan Point. The great gray waves pursued her, threatened her and then, at the last moment, lifted her. John, at the tiller, was able now to pay them no more than the necessary attention. He had proved to himself that he could handle them. But the other side of the point was going to be different! That was what was bothering him now. He'd had one taste of bucking wind and sea: and he had not forgotten how long it had taken to beat from the point to the floats and the hammering he had taken. "Don't believe I could have stuck it out another fifteen minutes," John acknowledged to himself. And that wasn't more than quarter the distance from the point back up the channel to the entrance. Four times as tough!—stick it out—Ashley—how about him?—at boats?—spell John off, maybe, at the helm. John looked dubious. Not much chance for more than one mistake! He looked toward Ashley, sitting braced in the cockpit, to see how he was taking it, and became aware that Ashley was doing a little scrutinizing himself. And that there was a sort of knowledged competence in his eye. Or so it looked to John. He had a sudden idea: to try him out—before rounding the point— now, while it was comparatively easy.

"Want to feel her out?" He raised his voice against wind and wave.

Ashley nodded and slid into place.

"Good idea," said he briefly. "Likely to be a two-man job when we begin to buck it."

He settled himself to the tiller, glanced aloft and, briefly, astern, gauging the pursuing seas.

"She handles mighty sweet," he commented presently and after that said nothing. John watched anxiously for a few moments, then relaxed. Handle a boat! he jeered at himself; why this fellow knew more about boats in a minute than you could ever even guess in a hundred years! For a while he forgot everything, just admiring the way the man did it. All John knew about it was to hold her on a beeline by main strength. "And believe me it takes it!" John was fervent in recollection. But Ashley hardly seemed to use any strength at all. Of course he must have—John could see his knuckles whiten at times. But only at times. Knows when to give her head, admired John. And catch her before she gets away from him: he could feel the Tillicum stiffen to obedience when the knuckles whitened. Like a high-strung horse—John understood when that parallel occurred to him—light hands!

An unreasoning confidence in the outcome of this adventure lifted his spirit. That very fact revealed to him a doubt that he had refused to acknowledge. He could afford to acknowledge it now. No more basis for it. All over but the shouting.

"You sure do that purty!" He had to release his exultation. He laughed. "Gosh, I'm no sailor!" he confessed humorously.

"Brought up on it," grunted Ashley. His face did not relax to John's boisterousness. Evidently he did not share fully John's satisfaction. "How she acts when she sticks her nose into it . . ." he added. He left the sentence suspended; but fifteen minutes later, after they had rounded the point, he completed his judgment. "We'll make it," he shouted to John, "unless something carries away!"

That was when John was almost beaten back again to doubt. They did not seem to be getting anywhere, and they were taking an awful beating. The waves had gone crazy. They leaped straight up and fell back—sometimes with a roar right across the deck, burying the ketch right up to the deadeyes. She staggered, but drained and gained way again. But more waves were ready to pounce. They came from everywhere, all directions at once, and clashed each other and rose in sharp pyramids. John had never seen anything like them.

"Tide rips," said Ashley. "We're getting on."

He jerked his head backward; and John, looking, saw that now indeed Klakan Point was falling astern. That was all right; but doggone it, how could any fabrication long hold together under such punishment!

"Out of 'em soon!" gasped Ashley, answering his unspoken thought. He did not seem to be disturbed. Must be all right. John felt a rush of something like real affection for Ashley. "I wouldn't have got to first base," he admitted to himself freely; "I wouldn't know what to *do* in a mess like this. I'd have just plain sunk—or had to go back." He wiped the sea water from his eyes and peered ahead. Hell of a long way across—his doubts returned—he's a damn sight huskier than he looks, but no man can stand this sort of thing forever. It's going to be up to me to take hold—— John sharpened his attention, trying to see just how Ashley did it. Couldn't get it—— Damn fool, expect to learn sailoring in one easy lesson! John sneered at himself savagely. Up to him, though.

"Want me to take her?" he made himself heard in a lull.

Ashley shook his head.

But after a while, abruptly, the seas changed. They were as high as ever, and the wind hurled their tops horizontally from crest to crest, but their confusion had fallen into orderly rank. The Tillicum steadied.

"You can spell me for a while now," said Ashley. John, with some misgivings, took the tiller. Whether it was because now he had a contrast of comparison with the tide rips, or because he had actually learned something from Ashley's expert handling, it seemed to him that he was doing better. The ketch felt to him docile, eager under his hand. He looked triumph at Ashley. But the latter shook his head.

"Oh, you're doing fine!" he reassured John's look of disappointment, "but we're getting nowhere." He saw he would have to explain.

"Tide and wind both against us," he shouted, "running together: that's why it seems good sailing. But we aren't getting ahead. We won't more than hold our own—till the tide changes. Then more hell. But we'll be getting along."

John did not quite see what Ashley meant until the tide did change. The wind was now blowing against the current, and as a consequence the waves reared steep, and their crests hollowed to a threatening overhang that needed but a touch to break with a roar. Now the deck was swept, not by the mere dash of spray or vertical slop, but again and again by solid green water.

"God!" sputtered Ashley, emerging from one such inundation, "she'd make a good submarine!" He had again taken over the helm. Both men were soaked to the skin: the slickers were now no more than a partial windbreak. Ashley's face was blue, and the muscles of his cheeks stood out as he clamped tight his jaw to keep his teeth from chattering. John looked at him anxiously.

"Better get below—little while—you'll perish," he managed to convey, between waves. But Ashley shook his head grimly. He would not trust John with the tiller. Secretly John very seriously distrusted himself. These curling, high and hesitating battering-rams of water were terrifying; even more terrifying than the tide rips. Nevertheless he was concerned about Ashley. The man looked to be on the edge of collapse.

He was trying to say something. John edged nearer.

"Nothing," disclaimed Ashley. "I was just saying that now we're really getting somewhere."

"*Getting* somewhere!" repeated John. As far as he could feel they had hardly been going ahead at all. Every time the ketch seemed to pick up any footing, a sea would instantly hit her on the nose and stop her dead.

"Take a look," said Ashley. He jerked his head astern. John was amazed to see the distance they had come. Klakan Point was way astern.

"Good tide—lifts us right along," said Ashley. "Just where's your hole?" He stretched his neck and peered ahead.

Why, there was the screen of the entrance! Almost aboard! They were almost there!

John moved over next to Ashley and directed him; and pretty soon they caught the comparative smooth, off the opening, of the inflowing tide. Ashley moved stiffly. Abruptly the life seemed to drain out of him. "You take her in," he mumbled, "you know your channels." He tried to get to his feet but could not control his body. John made to help him. "Watch your boat!" cried Ashley, aroused. He flexed his arms experimentally and stretched first one leg, then the other. "I'll be all right in a minute." He managed at last to draw himself to his feet by clinging to the backstay. He looked vaguely toward the gorge. The wind sucked through strongly. "No drifting and waiting today, thank God!" thought John. Ashley let go the backstay, nearly fell, recovered himself, staggered across the deck, slid back the hatch. "How you making it down there?"

"Foine, foine!" came back the woman's voice, "but I sure got some bumps!" A clatter told John that she was in the galley. Until this moment he'd forgotten all about the woman! Her head and shoulders appeared in the hatchway. "Anybody gets me in a boat again!" she informed the world at large. She looked about her curiously. "Are we there?"

"About half an hour yet," grated John between his teeth, because now he, too, was clamping down hard to keep from going to pieces.

"Sure, you look like a pair of drownded rats," said the woman compassionately. "Coffee comin' up. Where you keep it?"

"Top locker—above the stove." John's voice was shaking.

The woman withdrew. John concentrated on this terrible inner chill. If he ever started shivering! Where was Ashley? He'd disappeared. But John hadn't much left for anything but just holding onto himself and seeing that the Tillicum kept her course. Presently the woman was back with a coffeepot. He gulped the hot liquid gratefully. She stood over him while he drank. Time must have passed, for they were out of the gorge into the open. The sun helped. He began to revive.

"Where's Ashley?" was his first question. The man might have gone overboard—he might have——

"He's O.K.," the woman hastened to reassure him. "Below on the bunk. Dead to the world. All in. You look kind of all in your own self," she added. "Now if only I knew how to worruk a boat——"

"I'm all right," John cut this short impatiently. "We're pretty near there." He was all right. He knew when he was.

There was where the boom had been—there was the roof of the cabin. At the sight of it he came to himself with a snap. "God!" he half prayed, "what's happened!"

He got awkwardly to his feet, thrusting his knee against the tiller and peering anxiously ahead. There was Len moving down the trail: Len must have seen them coming in . . .

"My God!" muttered John. His mind struggled in helplessness against the inexorableness of space and time. Only a few hundred yards, only fifteen minutes—he tore at time savagely. He ripped off his slicker as though he intended to jump overboard.

"Now don't ye be frettin' yourself." The woman understood. "He don't walk like there's nothing wrong."

The tide was only half flood as yet. John dropped over the anchor, hauled the dinghy alongside. He did not bother about the sails—let 'em flap—he must get to Sally. The woman climbed in gingerly.

"It's sure a little boat for the likes of me," she muttered in dark distrust.

Len was at the cut bank. John shouted inquiry at him as soon as they were within hearing. Len made frantic pantomimes that John did not understand. The woman did.

"She's asleep." She stopped John from repeating his shout.

John dug frantically with his oars: he had to know more than that.

"Take it easy!" The woman was alarmed. "Ye'll have us in the chuck!" She clasped the gunwale on either side. John paid her no attention, but presently, when he had shortened the distance so he could make himself heard, he slowed down.

"Everything all right?" he demanded in a guarded voice. "Anything—anything happened?"

"Nothin'—yet," returned Len promptly. "Everything O.K. She's asleep right now." He squatted, reaching his hand to check the bow of the dinghy, but missing it completely because he was looking curiously at the woman. The dinghy hit the cut bank with a bump. Len did not mention his awkwardness. "Couldn't you get the doctor?"

"This lady——" John was scrambling ashore, regardless. Len clamped both hands on the gunwale to keep her from oversetting under the spurn of John's leap. What with the uncertain take-off and the stiffness of his muscles, he fell flat on his face, but immediately recovered and started toward the cabin without finishing his sentence. Len looked after him. "Go quiet: she's asleep, I tell ye!" he warned. He could not tell whether John had heard. He turned back to the woman.

"Climb out," he told her briefly. "Put your hand on my shoulder. You needn't pull it out by the roots!" he growled under her frantic grasp as the boat tipped and slid beneath her weight. With one strong heave he pulled the light structure up onto the bank. He rose to face her. "Well!" he said. "Why in hell did he fetch you? What's the matter with the doc?"

"The doctor's gone—up Tenakee way. And you'll wipe that look off'n your face, Two-Step Saunders, before I crack you one. I'm as good as any doctor at this business." She squared up to him belligerently, but at once deflated to concern. "How's she been?"

"I'm doggone glad you got here today," capitulated Len.

"Has she been bad?"

"Tough—in spells. I don't know nothin' about these things, but looks to me like——"

"Well, what you hanging around here for!" The woman started on the trail.

"I been skeered," confessed Len. "I couldn't see how John could possibly make it back before tomorrow——"

She had stopped and faced about on him so suddenly that he bumped into her.

"Let me tell you this, that nobody but him would have 'made it back,'" she minced the last three words sarcastically. "'Made it back,' is it! I'd like to get you out where we've been and bounce you around for a while so you'd know what you're talkin' about—before you drownded!"

She glared at him. But Len merely looked amused.

"Seemed sort of rough to ye, did it?" he baited her with deceptive mildness.

"You'll not be getting my goat, Len Saunders. Come on wid ye." She resumed her journey up the trail. Len followed, chuckling noiselessly to himself at the set of her square back. Len had had an anxious time: he was still anxious, but he could use a moment's diversion. However, he was to be disappointed. When she spoke again, presently, it was on the note of sober argument. "I do know that Oldstrom and Jim Kearn and every man jack of them tried to head him off. And when they couldn't do that, they laid down flat on any of them coming along. What good to anybody to commit suicide? That was their talk. And say what you want to, when it comes to sailoring those boys know their stuff," she admitted. "They wouldn't none of 'em come, and just betune you and me, I didn't blame 'em, even if I sorta *did* tell them they ought to be talkin' soprano. Whoosh! Do we have to climb that hill?"

"Up you go," said Len. "Whereabouts was ye when the tide turned?"

"How the hell would I know?" grunted the woman, who was beginning the steep ascent. "Ask Murdock—or the other wan." She jerked her head backward in the general direction of the Tillicum.

"Other one?" repeated Len. He looked back at the ketch. Len did not have to have things explained. "Why didn't you tell me? I'll go fetch him ashore. Who is it? Oldstrom?"

She stopped short and turned her feet carefully on the narrow trail to face him. In her eye was a glitter of anticipation so triumphant that Len almost dodged.

"You got a good strong heart, Two-Step Saunders?" she challenged. "You're goin' to need it," she continued when Len refused to come out of his shell. "It bowled me over," she admitted. "No, it wasn't Oldstrom," she paused, hoping for a question. Len did not oblige. "Ye'd never guess—not in a thousand years," she prodded. "Git your feet under ye—it's Ashley."

John checked when he reached the cabin and tiptoed cautiously across the veranda. He raised the latch, thrust the door open by inches and peered within. Sally was where he had left her, in a little huddled ball under the quilt on the bed before the fireplace. Her head was turned away. John hesitated.

"I'm not asleep, Len," said she. Her voice sounded tired. She turned her head slowly. "Oh, *John!*" and then again: "Oh, John!"

That was all she said, but for several seconds John could neither move nor make reply. It got a man, the way she said it, and the way she looked, so little and so white, and her eyes so big and dark and sort of—sort of—haunting like. He got all choked up and darn near caved in before he could get hold of himself. No way to act: brace up and be somebody . . .

He shut the door and crossed the room to her.

"How you feeling, honey?" he asked as he stooped to kiss her. Her cheeks were wet: she wasn't crying when he came in. "What's the matter? You all right?" in sudden anxiety. He tried to straighten up, the better to see her. She clung to him, would not let him go.

"Yes, yes, yes!" she assured him frantically. "Everything's all right—now that you're here." She held his head close and made little comfortable whimpers. "Don't mind me," she murmured presently, "it's just that I've had to hang on so——"

"I know, I know," murmured John soothingly.

"There!" said Sally. She unclasped her hands and gave John's shoulder a final pat. "Why!" she cried, "you're soaked through!" The discovery roused her, gave her strength. Her present situation was forgotten in her insistence that John must change, now, at once—you'll get your death——

"All right, all right!" She must not get excited like this. John kept looking toward the door. Where in hell—— Well, about time!

"The doctor couldn't——" he began and was swept to one side. The woman was on her knees beside the bed, and Sally's arms were around her, and the woman was crying, and so was Sally.

"Oh, Annabelle!" choked Sally.

CHAPTER XXXIV

THE BABY

THE WOMEN talked together in whispers. Across Annabelle's shoulder Sally caught sight of John.

"John, you *must* get those wet things off!" she implored. "Please, *please!*" She twisted restlessly out of the woman's arms in the force of her urgency. John shifted his feet, hesitating, looking from one to the other.

"Git along wid you," Annabelle put in her word impatiently, "don't you see how you fret her?"

"I was only waiting to find out—— What do you think?" appealed John to Annabelle. Annabelle arose to her feet.

"Now listen to me." She fixed John with the eye of authority. "Everything is O.K., and strictly accordin' to Hoyle. I'm tellin' ye; and I know. There's not wan thing you can do now, except stop fretting her and not come down sick. So you go rub yerself warm and crawl betune the blankets and get you some rest. Sure, you're drunk on yer feet wid sleep. And later, when we need ye, we want you fresh and strong."

"Please," begged Sally, "I'm just as comfy! Honestly!"

"You'll call me—promise?" John wavered.

"Sure, sure!" Annabelle faced him toward the bedroom door and

554

gave him a gentle shove in the back. She looked after him. "You've got you a man there," said she to Sally. She turned on Len so suddenly that he jumped. "Here, you," she ordered, "you go git him to bed. And then you come back; I'll be needin' ye." She sat down on the edge of the couch. "Now let's see, dearie," she began to consult with Sally. . . . "Well?" she spoke over her shoulder to Len when a little later the sound of the bedroom door evidenced his return.

"He just fell across the bed and was dead to the world," replied Len.

"Poor John!" breathed Sally.

"I t'ought so. And now go find out what that other galoot out there on the boat's been hollerin' about—— Gosh, he's found the fog horn!" as a hoarse blast came from the direction of the Tillicum.

"Sounds like he wants ashore," suggested Len.

"Well, go *git* him ashore! Do you need printed directions?"

"I just thought maybe you might be needing me here to——"

"To what?" she caught him up scornfully. "Scat!"

She moved about, examining the place, estimating its resources for the job in hand. Sally watched her. What a comfort! Just to let things drop: to leave it all to Annabelle! The whole room somehow seemed to brim over with cheer and confidence, so there was no space in it for anything else. She caught Annabelle's hand as she passed near.

"I'm so glad you came." She gave the hand a little squeeze and let it go. "It was heroic of you!"

"Well, I'm goin' to walk back!" snapped Annabelle; but her eyes misted. Len slipped through the door. "Oh, *you* back!" she sniffed disparagingly. "Well?"

"He didn't want ashore, says he can take care of himself on the boat," said Len. "What he was hollerin' for, he wanted me to come and git this." He held out a small old-fashioned valise. Annabelle opened it and peered inside.

"Now that's hittin' the ball!" she cried with satisfaction. "That feller's got brains as well as guts." She turned to Sally beaming. "I been kickin' myself for not thinking of it myself."

"What is it?" Sally wanted to know.

"The company's doctor's bag. Now we're set. Here, you," to Len, "where you think you're sneakin' off to?"

"I was just going outside. Git out of the way." Len stopped with evident reluctance.

"Well, you just stay put, right here inside. I'll tell you when you can go."

"What you want me for?" protested Len. He looked desperate. He even rolled an appealing eye toward Sally herself. "I don't know nothing about these things."

"Well, you know enough anyway to light lamps. It's gettin' dark." She kept silence while he hurried about this simple job, obviously to hasten his escape. "Now," she spoiled that plan, "you het me up some water—plenty of it—and warm some blankets. Don't think you're goin' to git away. I'm going to make a midwife of you, Len Saunders."

Sally laughed aloud. She could not help it, even though the pains were coming back again. Len's expression was so funny!

Annabelle turned toward her, pleased by the laugh. "Now that's good hearing——" she began and looked closely at Sally.

"Fly to it, you dawdling loafer! Get that hot water!" she snapped at Len; and then to Sally: "Easy, darlin'; Annabelle's here."

John yielded to the insistence of Sally and Len, and turned toward the bedroom. After that he remembered nothing clearly. He had instinct enough to hit the doorway instead of the wall; and he saw where the bed was. The next physical thing of which he was aware was the edge of the bedstead catching him at the knees. This threw him off balance. He toppled forward on his face. For a second or so the idea that he had promised something about wet clothes struggled for recognition, but he could not quite grasp it, so he heaved an enormous and tired sigh and let go all holds. . . .

But something was hindering, something persistent and nagging. He couldn't shake it off. Finally he had to arouse himself. The nagging thing proved to be Len. John cursed Len and told him to go away. But Len would not go: he wanted something. John tried to understand. Len wanted John's clothes. Len had clothes of his own; why should he want John's? Oh hell; it didn't matter. Just to get rid of him John made an enormous effort and staggered drunkenly to his feet. Somehow Len had the clothes—he was pulling the blankets up around John's shoulders. . . . Now at last John could let go . . . but not yet . . . something else . . . this time it was a thought of his own that held him . . .

"Be sure and call me when—if . . ." He got it out. "Promise!"

"Sure! sure! I promise!" That was Len's voice.

Now! John drew another deep and tired sigh and plunged into the depths of blackness. Down and down and down. The plunge slowed luxuriously. By and by he would stop, reach some point of suspension and rest there, cradled. . . .

But they wouldn't let him alone. Something was nagging at him again, trying to pry him loose, to drag him up. He tried to ignore it, to shut it away. He wanted to rest. He did not want to come to the surface again. But there he was, and the nagging was continuously beating at the thinning walls of sleep. He did not know what it was. Just something. Outside himself. Like people, whispering. Must be people whispering; for now he began to hear fragments of talk. They did not make sense. Arguing. Something about two cups of coffee. "Only two cups of coffee." No harm to let him sleep: no harm to wake him up. They droned back and forth. Then the name "Sally" came to him clearly, like a bell; and he was instantaneously awake.

"Sally," he repeated. "She all right? Do you want me?"

Len and the woman, Annabelle, were in the room, standing by his bed. And somebody else. Ashley. How did Ashley get ashore? Why were they all here in the room together? Why had they left Sally alone? Had Sally . . . ? Was Sally . . . ? The possibility choked John's throat, seized his heart as with an icy hand. Annabelle was looking at him and caught the horror in his eyes.

"Hootch! Quick!" and in the same breath to John: "Everything's O.K. *O.K.*, I tell ye!" She shook him by the shoulders, driving reassurance into him by sheer force of will. "That's better!" with satisfaction, as she saw the color returning to John's face. "Not now," she waved Len aside with the whisky, "not on an empty stummick. What he needs is food."

John passed the back of his hand across his eyes.

"Then what is it? Why'd you have to wake me up just when I'd got asleep?" He began to feel a little resentful. They were grinning at him, all three of them, like a lot of hyenas. That did not improve his temper. "You might let a man get a little rest!" he grumbled.

"How much rest you think you got to have, anyway?" This from Len.

"Huh?" said John. Something mocking in Len's tone had jarred him fully awake. "Say! What time is it, anyway?"

" 'Bout nine o'clock," said Len; "A.M.," he added.

Nine o'clock! Good lord! couldn't be! Why—why—John calculated—I must have been asleep nigh onto fifteen hours. Impossible. He looked from one to the other, incredulous. Must be, though—sun was out—ought to have noticed that. "I'll be damned," muttered John, profoundly astonished.

They seemed to find the situation amusing. Ashley leaned against the doorjamb, smiling. Annabelle was on a broad grin. John wouldn't have thought anything of that—it *was* sort of funny, his passing out that way. But Len had turned solemn; too dang solemn, John told himself. When Len looked that way he was generally fixing to put one over.

"We figgered you might want to eat," Len was explaining elaborately—and the drag of his drawl was further warning to John. "Some folks like to eat—at intervals. Of course they's some gits on all right without. Two cups of coffee wouldn't do *me* to Klakan and back—not in no storm—but then I wasn't raised rough." So that's what the talk was about "two cups of coffee," John's thoughts raced while he waited for what Len was driving at. No use trying to hustle the old coot: he'd learned that. Whatever was the joke he'd get it out when he got good and ready and not before. Yes, John was sufficiently dumb; but possibly there were excuses . . . "And anyway——" Len was resuming his leisurely unfoldment with relish; but the patience of his audience gave out.

"Aw, for God's sake, Two-Step!" Annabelle stopped that monkey business. "It's high time," she told John, "you took a look at the baby."

CHAPTER XXXV

THE WAVE COMES TO REST

HAVING THE BABY, Sally would confide—afterward—was nothing. Having John was the tough part. "I'm a husky woman," said Sally, "or it would have certainly weakened me down!" Actually she relished the episode, though just for a moment or two she was disappointed in the way things were going. After all, this was her first child, and it had been born in a log cabin in a remote wilderness, during a winter snowstorm, without benefit of medicine, and so forth, for as long as you cared to pile it on. Just as picturesque and romantic and commendable a pioneer show as her grandmother had put on giving birth to the first Jefferson, in a covered wagon crossing the plains. Nearly as good, anyhow. Sally was no sentimentalist, but she could hardly be blamed for building up a fanciful little scenario the least bit on the sentimental side— young wife, on her couch of weakness and pain, turning her face starry eyed toward the door through which the young husband— awake at last after his heroic ordeal—was stealing to her side, bending over her in awe and rapture of the miracle of parenthood.

It did not turn out that way at all. The young father burst into the room, partly and carelessly draped in a blanket—and apparently nothing else—his hair sticking out all ways and his eyes wild, trailed by the other three members of the household, trying in vain to shush him lest he overagitate Sally. They were not getting that idea over to him at all. John was too full of ideas of his own, and this particular one had not occurred to him. Primarily, he was vociferating at Sally, demanding first-hand assurance from headquarters that she was all right; and secondarily, he was trying to get across to the bed, but tripping over the blanket. The spectacle differed so completely from Sally's fancy drama of young parenthood that she stared round eyed in amazement for one incredulous moment and burst into laughter. She tried to stop, but it had got away from her. She was helpless. Only by a truly heroic effort did she check long enough to gasp reassurance.

"Of course I'm all right! *Certainly* I'm all right!" She steadied herself and wiped her eyes. "Well, *look* at me: don't I *look* all right? Aren't you going to kiss me?"

John leaned over gingerly and delivered a sort of long-range peck at her cheek, as though she were brittle—likely to go to pieces. Sally laughed again at this.

But John, irrationally, was suddenly overcome by a strange and inexplicable indignation, and an even more inexplicable insistence on knowing about things that did not in the least matter. Why didn't they call him: they promised to call him! They evidently had called Ashley! When did Ashley come ashore? How did he get ashore? Where had he slept? Where had Len slept—Sally was in his bed; where had Annabelle slept? He looked about him, and started afresh. Where's Chilkat——

As suddenly he realized his own absurdity. He stopped short. He'd never lost hold of himself like this, never before in all his life! Why! he was mighty nigh busting up, like a hysterical woman! He was thoroughly ashamed. He made no allowances for himself on account of his twenty-four hours without food, or on account of hardship, or anxiety, or on account of the long tension that had snapped back on him like a released rubber band. A man ought to be able to take it and still be a man! However, Sally understood. She was still laughing at him, but with tenderness.

"What—what time did it happen?" he asked in his normal manner.

"Glory be!" spoke up Annabelle, "he's actually remembered there's a baby!"

He turned toward Annabelle. He had utterly forgotten Annabelle, and also Len and Ashley, for that matter. Annabelle's eyes had the same look as Sally's. John suddenly felt tears. "Doggone! Brace up, you damn fool!" he apostrophized himself, "don't get mushy!" Sally was drawing a corner of blanket from a bundle at her side. John had not noticed the bundle. He leaned forward to look.

The sight was almost too much for John, on top of all the rest, and in his weakened condition. Annabelle ought to have warned him. He ought to have remembered—of course—it was a month or more too soon—premature baby—what could you expect? And Sally was looking at him with such pride—poor Sally, didn't she realize . . . ? He must say something, for Sally's sake . . .

He caught at a straw.

"Don't they ever outgrow it?" he blurted out before he thought.

Sally's eyes opened wide.

"Outgrow what?" challenged Annabelle flatly.

"Isn't it—don't it look a little—queer?" ventured John, but got no help, "but I suppose, being a month too soon . . ." He ran down. Annabelle snorted.

"Too soon!" she repeated. "On time, like a railroad train!" she demolished him. "Just couldn't count up to nine—and she a schoolma'am!"

"Come here, darling," Sally intervened. She held out her arms to the bewildered John. "Listen to me. He's a beautiful child. All newborn babies look like this. In a week you'll be proud——"

"I'm proud now," said John valiantly.

"Don't strain yourself." Annabelle was still indignant.

Len appeared behind her.

"Here's your pants," said he to John. "Better go put them on. Or if you like it the way you are, I'll go see if I can rustle you an eagle's feather for your hair."

John accepted the armful of clothing. He was feeling both let down and a little dazed.

"Get a move on you!" called Ashley from the kitchen. "Ham and hot cakes coming up!"

The words, somehow, cleared his mind, explained things. That was it: that's what he needed. Food! Suddenly he found himself unable to think of anything else.

Sally looked after him as he disappeared into the bedroom, carrying the armful of clothes. She snuggled down cozily in the blankets. She was very happy; and she chuckled a little at herself. This was so much better than that exploded sentimental drama. "Sacred parenthood!" she mocked herself. Chilkat, under the bed, thumped his tail.

"I *do* feel so much better!" cried Sally to Annabelle. "It's done me so much good to laugh!"

The storm had died during the night. Now the skies cleared and the chinook began to blow. By the second day much of the snow had gone from the lowlands, and black patches had begun to show on the slopes. The fragile silence of winter was shattered by the enormous voice of falling waters. The sides of the mountains were ribboned by them.

They moved Sally's bed so she could look out, across the inner flats, to her Protector of the Wilderness. At noon the air turned warm enough so they could open the windows. She breathed deep of the spring and crowed with the joy of it.

"I think I'm pretty smart!" she exulted. "I'm a month ahead of the game! Now we'll be ready to start north as soon as anybody!—in six weeks."

"Two months," amended Annabelle with authority.

They had distributed themselves very handily. Annabelle had moved into the room with the bed; Len had gone back to reopen his cabin; Ashley bunked aboard the Tillicum, which had been floated in on the high tide to her cut-bank moorings. John bunked down in Len's bedroom, on a mattress on the floor. Chilkat obstinately insisted his proper place was under Sally's bed; and, as

Sally backed him up, he made it stick. Everything was nice and comfortable and happy and sort of settled, as though it were going to stay that way indefinitely. But Ashley had responsibilities.

"I don't want to be a nuisance, and I'd like nothing better than to stay," he told John, on the morning of the third day, "but I ought to be getting back to Klakan. I'm expecting Mr Cole on the Portland's next trip north. You really don't need me any longer."

John was contrite. Dumb of him. Of course.

It was arranged. Len would sail Ashley across on next day's tide. Len assented, but a little doubtfully, his mind still on the U.S. marshal. Ashley laughed aloud when he learned the reason for Len's hesitancy.

"Doesn't sound like what I've heard of you, Saunders," said he, "or what I know of you, for that matter. I wouldn't suppose you'd scare for a fat man."

"It ain't the fat man," protested Len stoutly, "it's the tin star on his chest. When it's got 'U.S.' on it—not otherwise," he amended.

"Well, you needn't worry about this particular stuffed shirt," assured Ashley. He surveyed Len's doubt amusedly. "Besides," he added, "he isn't there any more. They took him off last winter."

"Why in hell didn't you say so!" cried Len, disgusted.

It seemed to John that Annabelle, too, would want to get back home. Neither Annabelle nor Sally thought anything at all of that suggestion.

"Don't you fret, dearie," Annabelle assured Sally. She turned on John. "If you think you're savin' a trip on me, you guess again," she told him. "You'll take me back 'special when I get ready. No use trying to get rid of me, young fellow!"

"Good lord! I don't want you to go!" cried John.

"All right then." Annabelle glared at him a moment as though in league with Sally against opposition. Apparently satisfied John was a pulp, she transferred her attention to Len. "Now you listen to me, you Two-Step. Don't you linger! You come on right back. Do your drinking and bragging later. You hear me?"

"Yes ma'am," said Len meekly.

Annabelle surveyed him for a further moment, then addressed herself to Ashley.

"I'm going to give you a list of what I want from the store and from my place. I got nothing here but what I stand in. You see it gets aboard. And you keep track of that lump and see he starts back prompt!"

"All right," laughed Ashley.

"I don't trust the old coot," added Annabelle superfluously.

She shooed them out of the house: she wanted Sally to rest. "And see you make no noise," warned Annabelle.

They tramped the short distance to Len's cabin. At once Ashley became enormously interested in the winter's fur take stored there. He ruffled back the cover hairs and parted the underlying fur to the roots, squinting down to the skin itself, rubbing the hairs between his fingers.

"Feller knows something about fur," Len confided aside to John. Ashley looked up.

"You've got an exceptionally fine lot here," said he. "Better than I've seen anywhere for a long time. You've got quite a bunch of money here." He hesitated. "How you figuring on marketing?" he asked finally.

John looked toward Len.

"Hadn't figured yet," confessed Len. "I've always dealt with Kelly. But Kelly's out."

Ashley uttered a short laugh. "So I understand." He hesitated again, glancing from one to the other. "I wish you'd let me handle these for you." He bit the words short, and a dull flush stained the olive of his cheek. "If you feel like trusting me, that is."

"Trust you! There's no man alive I'd quicker trust!" cried John. "I haven't said much, about the other day," he continued more soberly, "but that ain't because——"

"And I haven't said anything—about some other things," Ashley stopped him curtly. "And we're not going to. Fresh start." He stared ahead, waiting for Len or John, but as they did not immediately answer, he evidently took their silence for assent. "I'll get full value for you," he promised. "I'd hate to see you boys tangle up with these coast traders: they'd do you out of your eyeteeth." He raised an eyebrow at Len: Len grinned.

"I reckon Kelly got his share," he acknowledged.

"Well, if that's agreed, let's bale 'em up," said Ashley briskly.

They pressed the pelts into small bales and corded them and piled them outside. But before they undertook the carriage to the Tillicum they perched in a row at the veranda's edge to smoke their pipes. Len and Ashley gossiped idly. John had not much to say. Ashley leaned his back against one of the posts and let his eyes roam abroad.

"Certainly is a sweet valley," he observed. "Astonishing how few people know anything about it—even know it's here."

"You never been in here before?"

"Never," Ashley shook his head.

"I didn't know but what Nels Cole might have——"

Ashley laughed amusedly.

"Cole was in here three years ago, hunting. Johnny Mackamoose brought him in. He got so stuck on it that the minute he got out he sent over Peterson and a crew from the cannery and had that house built. Next spring, before the fishing season opened, he came over with one of the cannery tenders and a boatload of junk and spent about two weeks puttering around furnishing and fixing up. And that's the whole of it. He hasn't been back since."

"What?" John's attention was caught. "You mean to say he's never used the place at all?"

"That's right. Maybe he'll never see it again. He's made that way. He just can't like a place without building there. He's got a dozen or so shacks up and down the coast."

"Well, I'll be damned!" muttered John and relapsed into his brown study.

"I suppose that's how he come to stick a town up the side of a mountain," observed Len.

This aroused Ashley. "Shows how little you know," he told Len. "These little shacks are fooling, but when it comes to big things Nels Cole has a long head on him. Side of the mountain, yes: because there's no other place to put it." Plenty of flatter country than that—and islands—all over the place, objected Len. Not sitting squarely at the gateway into Alaska—catch 'em coming in and going out, countered Ashley.

"Good lord, Saunders," said he, "you're too much of an old-timer not to know that it's trade and permanent settlers makes a country, and not this gold business."

"I reckon the gold helps—when you dig it by the ton," observed Len.

"Hell!" For a moment Ashley appeared to abandon the argument in despair. He changed his mind. "Sure it helps," he answered Len. "It's good bait. It gets people into a country. Some of 'em stick. They're the ones who make the country. Not the gold diggers. Look at California."

"Just the same——" persisted Len.

"Just the same," Ashley caught him up with conviction, "you're going to see Klakan the biggest city in Alaska before you get through, even if it is on the side of a mountain; and you're going to see this part of the territory, round about—places like this valley here—populated and farming and——"

"You quoting Nels Cole, or have we started up a chamber of commerce since I was last in town?" interrupted Len dryly. " 'Buy now for the rise. Up the mountain,' " he declaimed. " 'I hear tell you can have your choice.' They's plenty of room right now."

Ashley checked with a laugh at himself.

"Quoting Mr Cole," he acknowledged. "But it's also how I feel myself. You wait. Klakan will still be building—up the mountain—when that Godforsaken north country has gone back to the kit foxes."

Though he had taken no part and looked miles away, John must have been following this chat.

"The country much different farther north?" he asked Ashley. "What's it like?" That it might be different had not occurred to John. Alaska was Alaska. But he had really not thought about it one way or another.

"Len can tell you better than I can. He's been all over the place. I've never been beyond Cape Spencer."

"They's some fine country beyond Cape Spencer," said Len defensively. "Nat'rally," he had to add, "farther north you git, the less timber and the more tundra. . . ."

Ashley did not press the point, but he looked faintly triumphant. He got to his feet.

"Let's get this fur down to the boat," he suggested. "Come on, Murdock!" as John did not stir.

"Oh! Yes!" John came to with a start.

They carried the bales of pelts along the trail to the Tillicum and bestowed them in the cabin. Then they perched on deck and filled their pipes for a rest. John spoke up suddenly out of a silence.

"There's an awful lot of salmon run into this place. And it's close to the cannery. Ain't you fellows overlooking a bet?"

"It does look that way," admitted Ashley. "You're right. There's a heavy run of fish. But you can't get them."

"How's that?"

"No good trap sites. Bottom too deep and too hard to drive piles. The company prospected the place years ago. Oh, of course, seining would catch fish—some—and probably seiners will get in here eventually. If so, we'll buy what they can bring us. But we're not in the seining business ourselves."

"That's the way I thought it was," said John. He flushed and looked embarrassed. "Look here," he blurted out finally, "I don't want to look like teaching my grandmother to suck eggs, and I don't know one thing about this business, but I got a sort of an idea. Probably ain't worth a damn, but——"

"Let's have it," Ashley helped him out; "you don't grudge a man a laugh, do you?"

"Come below and I'll show you," John yielded.

They sat at the table, and John produced a pencil and paper.

"It's like this," said he. "You see, I was working up high on the slope—hand-logging, you know—and so I could see down deep into the water pretty plain; and I noticed that the salmon comin' in,

through the entrance, followed pretty well along the shore line, and
they stayed pretty close to the surface. At least," he corrected himself, "an awful lot of them did: the bulk may have . . . ?" He
looked toward Ashley.

"No, that's right; that's how they do. That's how we pick trap
sites. But, as I told you, it's too deep and too hard to drive piles."

"Maybe wouldn't need to," said John. He drew the sheet of paper
to him. "I got to figgering—up there," he muttered in snatches, as
he sketched, "while I was working on the timber. Probably something haywire about it—but there you are."

He thrust toward Ashley the first crude design for a floating trap.
"I don't know as it would work," he disclaimed.

Ashley studied it with interest.

"Neither do I," he confessed, "but it looks as though it might, and
if it does—— Say, let me show this to Mr Cole, will you?"

"Sure Mike! Take it along. Hope it's some good to him. I owe
him some rent, anyway."

"He'll owe you a lot more than rent if this is as good as it looks,"
muttered Ashley, folding the paper. "And he'll see you get it," he
added.

They returned to the deck.

"Gosh!" observed Len, "warm as summer! Won't be long now
till things is popping!"

"Let's go see how's the family," said John abruptly. "Sally must
have waked up by now."

He stepped ashore. But then he stopped short and stood for some
moments frowning downward, apparently absorbed in digging with
his toe in the wet earth. Len and Ashley waited, for it was obvious
he was considering something.

"Come on back"—he had made up his mind—"I want to talk to
you fellows."

They stepped back aboard and once more perched on the deckhouse. For some time they consulted.

"All right." John at last brought the discussion to a close. "Now
let's go see Sally."

They mounted the trail to the cabin.

At the top of the rise they stopped short in surprise. There on the veranda sat Sally in one of the rocking chairs, all wrapped up in a quilt, smiling happily—and triumphantly—at them; and back of her, Annabelle, also triumphant.

The three men crowded about, uttering congratulations and pleasure. John looked a little anxious.

"It's perfectly all right," Annabelle assured him aside, "she never walked a step: I carried her out in my own two arms."

Relieved, John brushed them all aside.

"What are you doing? What are you going to do?"

Sally was startled by the abruptness of his movement.

John picked her up—chair, quilt and all—and held her at the level of his chest.

"Too much of a crowd." He was talking across her at the other three, half humorously, but his eye warned them. He stalked around the end of the cabin to its far side and set the chair down facing the meadow and the forest and the mountains. Sally raised her eyes to her old friend, the great mountain, and sent it a mental greeting.

"That's nice," she approved to John; "just us two again."

But immediately she perceived that John had something to say. She knew the symptoms.

"What is it?" she accused. "Confess!"

He hesitated, apparently casting about for the best expression.

"Break it gently," she teased.

"Listen," he blurted, "how'd it suit you if—that is, do you like it here—— Oh hell!" he gave it up. "Do you like it well enough to stay? To settle down, I mean. Listen, Sally," he forestalled a reply, "I've been talking to Ashley. He says Cole would sell this place cheap, if we want it. I know it looks kind of foolish first off, to grab at the first place we come to, before we've really looked around at all. But I've been talking to Len about that—and he knows the whole country inside out—and he says he don't know any place anywhere that's any better, or near as good, for that matter, as right here, for a man who's looking for a chance to better his lot and establish himself permanent while the country's new—and that's what we came up here for, after all, ain't it?" He looked up anxiously to Sally; but she made no comment. "Look at what we've got here," he urged. "We don't even have to clear land like you'd have to most places—or if you do get open land, there's generally no water. And here we've got a good five hundred acres all cleared for us; and there's worlds of water. And plenty of timber besides." The words tumbled out in a volubility wholly unlike John. Now he ran down.

"What are you arguing with me for?" asked Sally. "You've already decided, haven't you?"

"I wouldn't think of it for one holy minute if it didn't suit you," returned John stoutly.

She raised her eyes toward the great mountain across the way.

"I've loved it here from the first moment I laid eyes on it," said she simply. "It's as though I'd dreamed it. But I wanted you to be satisfied."

"Gosh, Sally!" He reached for her hand.

His relief of mind was profound, and for the moment it was sufficient. But Sally could not stand that. Her cheeks were pink with excitement. She stood it just as long as she could.

"I'm sorry." John was contrite. "I was figgering."

"Let me 'figger' too," pleaded Sally. "What are you figuring about?"

"Why," confessed John, "I wasn't really. I was just looking things all over again—in my mind." Suddenly he recalled something. "You remember, down in Seattle, that time we were hunting houses; and we'd looked that one all over from top to bottom and decided to take it; and then you insisted on going all over it again; and when I said we'd already been over every inch of it you told me that it was a *different* house now it was *ours*?"

"I remember," nodded Sally. She understood him now.

John leaned back against the post and filled his pipe and lighted it and sought her hand again. She snuggled happily down into the warmth of her quilt.

"Where shall we begin?" she asked. "I like our valley."

"You bet!" agreed John heartily. "Why, just think what we've got here, when you stop and size it up! If a man was to sit down and invent him a homestead he couldn't make up any better than we've got right here!"

"That's just what they did do," said Sally. He looked up at her in quick inquiry. "Your people—all your people from away back—your father and Marcus and Luke and the first John away over in Scotland—made up a dream and set out to look for it. And my people, too, I think."

"And didn't find it!" John took fire from her thought. "And here we are!" He looked about him. "Here we are!" he repeated. He drew a deep breath. "Do you remember, Sally," he said presently, "that day back in Seattle when we took a trip across the peninsula to the beach to see the ocean, and we walked down to the edge of the water, and we sort of joshed about how——"

"I remember every bit of it," she put in quickly. "I remember the very words you said—'I reckon this is about as far as the Murdocks can go'—that is what you said!"

"Well," chuckled John, "I sure spoke out of turn!"

He relinquished her hand and thrust his arms over his head in a long stretch.

"Soon as we can get a good truck garden going, we'll be fixed. Most people have to scrabble hard just to make out three squares a day and a place to sleep. Takes all their time: they never get a chance to get anywheres else. We've got that kind of a living just *handed* to us. We could Siwash it here comfortable the rest of our lives on the game and fish and clams and——" He waved his hand abroad, helpless to express himself.

"You wouldn't be satisfied with just that," said Sally.

"Just the same," John pursued his idea, "it sort of turns us loose—to do what we want—to make what we want—and take our own good time about it. Not like my dad, poor devil, at the Dalles. He had ideas. Of what could be done with that ranch—it was a good country. But he never got a chance. We had to eat." He knit his brow. "I reckon that might have been the way with the others, too. Our others, I mean. Sally, we're pretty lucky people!"

"I know *I* am," murmured Sally.

"So," went on John more briskly, "I reckon, first off, the thing to do is to start a truck garden. Fence off what we need in the bottom and break ground as soon as it drains from the snow. I'll have to fence, or the deer 'll eat us up. Those critters jump awful high. Take forever to split and haul enough rails to keep them out. But I got an idea on that. Want to hear it?"

"Of course."

"High poles and mesh wire!" cried John triumphantly. "Thought of it coming up from the boat. There's oodles of old mesh wire at the cannery—from last year's traps, you know. Good for nothing to them. They'd sell cheap. I bet they'd give it away. All I'd have to do is to cut poles and string it. What do you think of that?"

"Chickens!" cried Sally. "And flowers!" she added.

John looked dazed for an instant.

"Oh—sure! Why not! We can stick up as much or as little as we want, and anywhere we want. And take no time to speak of. That's the big point. We can get at *doing* things."

"What things?" asked Sally. "Let's plan!"

They sat there together and stared out across the meadow below. At first they saw it only with the physical eyes, as it was—an open space rimmed with forest, empty save for scattered groups of trees. But soon there was the truck garden, in the corner, just below. "Apples and pears—maybe peaches," spoke up John out of a pregnant silence. "It's only as far north here as Scotland—Ashley says so." And at once, by magic, there stood the orchard just beyond! "Berries?" contributed Sally after a time. John assented to the berries, but absently. He was engaged in selecting a site for the stables, close under the hill where there was good winter shelter . . .

"Stables!" echoed Sally when John presented her with that development.

"You don't expect to quit cultivating with a dinky little truck garden, do you? How you aiming to turn your soil? Spade it? And how you going to lug your poles and timbers and such? We're going to need one team of horses, at least. And"—John's eyes turned to inner vision again—"there's a lot of good feed—and there's the salt hay on the flats——"

"John!" Sally was laughing at him now. He joined her, a little shamefaced.

"Once a cow waddy, always a—— Anyway," he defended himself, "I bet a small dairy herd would make good by the time we could get around to it—when Klakan gets going." He stirred to a new enthusiasm, following out the thought. "Klakan's not so far off. If we get us a good boat with one of these new engines in it that runs with gasoline, it would be right next door. By golly! That's what we want next! I could build me a scow to tow, and we'd make a mighty good thing out of the fish!" He told Sally briefly of his idea as to floating traps. "Ashley thinks it will work. And of course there's the lumber. They'll be buying logs again."

"I thought you'd had enough of that."

"Oh, hand-logging, yes. But how about a donkey engine or two?" His mind was off again in new directions, racing like a dog after myriads of possibilities. Even Sally's vibrant eagerness could not keep up. Just for a moment she was overwhelmed.

"Sure, there's a lot of hard work in it," he agreed. "Why not? As long as we're getting somewhere, and it's fun. That's the main thing. We got all the time there is. Soon's it quits being fun, we'll take a vacation. Go look around."

"That's what I'm wondering." Sally was suddenly uneasy.

"What?"

"Whether after all your wandering about and adventure—— Len's going to be dreadfully disappointed." She had just thought of this.

"Len?"

"Going north—the Klondike," Sally reminded with a touch of impatience. "Now he'll have to go alone."

"Oh, Len doesn't want to go north," said John surprisingly, "he wants to stay here!"

"Well, I declare!" Sally threw out both hands in exasperation.

"You certainly have things settled among you! How long have you two been making your plans without consulting me, anyway?"

"About an hour," said John. "You were asleep. Struck me all of a sudden. Something Ashley said." He put his hand on her knee. "Tell you something, Sally," he confessed quaintly, "I didn't know it, but I've been getting restless to settle down somewhere." He considered for a moment. "Speaking of Len, reckon I better tell him I'll be taking Ashley over tomorrow, instead of him. Cole's coming up on the Portland," he explained. "I want to cinch this thing—and talk fish traps—and so on." He raised his voice to call. Immediately Len came around the corner of the veranda, as also Ashley and Annabelle. John laughed at the promptness of their appearance.

"Where's the dog?" he asked sardonically.

They did not answer this. Everybody knew where Chilkat was—under the bed. He had of his own volition taken on guardianship of the baby, and he believed in staying on the job.

"Well?" demanded Len.

"She says yes," said John.

Len broke into a broad grin. Sally's heart warmed. Len often crinkled his eyes; but she did not remember ever seeing his whole face break out like this in sheer delight. But it was Annabelle who supplied the action.

"Glory be!" She threw both hands over her head. She rushed forward and enveloped Sally in a great hug. "Whoosh!" She straightened up and beamed at them all. "And *that's* a load off me chest! I done all the mushing in my life *I* want to do!"

"Mushing?" repeated Sally.

Annabelle wheeled upon her, hands on hips.

"Did ye think for a minute I was going to let you traipse off by yerself?" she demanded belligerently. Her bristles smoothed. "I'm glad you've got *some* sense," she told John. She sat down beside Sally on the edge of the veranda and looked about her. "You picked you a good place; I just might think of settlin' here meself." She threw this out, as though at random. "I got as much right here as anybody. I'm getting dead sick of kickin' around."

Sally sat up straight.

"You mean—you mean to *stay?*" There was no mistaking her enthusiasm for this idea.

"I just might."

"Shucks," put in Len, "she's got it all picked out where she's aimin' to make me build her a shack! You couldn't drive her off with a company of skunks!"

"Well, I wasn't drove off by one," sniffed Annabelle, "skunk, I mean," she added, lest Len miss the point.

"You're making no mistake, Murdock." Ashley spoke up for the first time. "And you'll have plenty of neighbors in a few years. But you're getting first pick, and the best of it."

"Reminds me," said John, "I think I'll go over with you tomorrow, instead of Len. Cinch things. I'll want to see Cole."

"Good idea," approved Ashley. "You'll have no trouble with Cole. You're the sort of solid citizen he's looking for around here."

"Better be getting inside, honey," warned Annabelle, "it's beginning to get chilly."

"Just a minute," Sally begged. "John can bring me in. I've got something to tell him."

"What is it?" asked John when they were alone again. "What you got to tell me?"

"Only how happy I am, and how much I love you," said Sally.

She lifted her face. His lips touched hers. They were warm and alive. She closed her eyes, half opened them. "Pretty soon," she whispered as he drew away. John threw back his head and shoulders. He was now entirely happy. His woman was back with him again, by his side, ready to share all of life and dream and hope of future. By the time Jeff was grown enough—and the others—sure, there were going to be others!—they'd have something worth while to go on with. Hard work—as Sally had said—you bet, but with some *meaning* to it. He saw it, in his mind's eye, all completed.

"And a painted house." He spoke this aloud, voicing the peak and culmination of the frontiersman's ideal of civilization.

"Hush, listen!"

John listened. The faint clamoring was still far away, lost fitfully beneath the steady roar of falling waters, then heard again.

"Wild geese," John identified them presently.

"Yes! Remember that night? In Seattle?" Sally's voice was hushed. "When we heard them, down so near, over the roof?"

"I'm not forgetting," said John.

"Can you see them?"

John stepped from beneath the shelter of the veranda and shaded his eyes with his hand.

"Yeah, there they are. Gosh, they're flying high! Headin' north. Wonder how they know where is north." He continued to watch them. Sally could not see them, but she could follow their flight, not only by the sound of their exultance, but by the tilt of John's head as he traced them across the sky. Finally he turned around to look after them. He waved his hand.

"Good-by, boys—and good luck! You tolled us this far, but you ain't coaxing us any farther. We've lit!"